HUNTING HER BOX SET

EDEN SUMMERS

SAVIOR

1

PENNY

I burrow deeper under the covers, cocooned in luxurious silken sheets, nestled amongst extravagance.

I'm not ready to let go of sleep just yet. My mind still straddles the line of consciousness where the freedom of dreams overwhelms reality.

It's nice here.

Peaceful.

There's nothing but me and my imagination.

I fantasize about dragging my toes through the waves crashing against the shore in the distance. Raising my face to the sun. Swimming through crystal-clear water. I picture smiling faces beaming at me with gentle affection.

I visualize love.

"Good morning, my pretty Penny."

I freeze, my breath catching at the deep voice breeching my mental sanctuary.

The whiplash from dream to nightmare is harsh. Sickening. I panic, like always, then force myself to calm despite the lingering threat.

The owner of that voice is the devil.

He's the cause of my waking hell—a man without conscience or soul.

He's also the owner of this bed, and everything in it.

"It's time to get up." He tugs at the covers, dragging the material down to expose my face… shoulders… breasts.

I measure my breathing, not showing an ounce of emotion as he peers down at my naked body with a leering smile.

I'd prayed I wouldn't have to see him today. I'd begged, wished, and hoped he wouldn't return after he'd brutalized me last night, then left the house under the cover of darkness to undoubtedly destroy more lives.

I could've fled to my room with his disappearance. I should've escaped to my own bed instead of fearing a reprimand for leaving before I was dismissed.

But my prayers went unanswered.

They always do.

God can't help me here. Nobody can. I can't even help myself. Not against a heartless human trafficker such as the untouchable Luther Torian.

He scours my body with his gaze, trying to provoke me with the hunger in his eyes.

"Did you sleep well?" He drags the covers farther, along my stomach... pussy... thighs... all the way to my feet, exposing every inch of me in a deliberate incremental humiliation.

"Yes." I spare him the solitary syllable, giving the bare minimum of what he requires before I slide from the mattress, ignoring the lingering aches and pains born from his night of amusement.

"Did you dream of me?" he drawls.

I ignore the question and stare at the door, waiting for his freeing words of dismissal. He wants me to bite back—to snap—and I'm not going to give him the satisfaction.

Last night, he took what he needed. He devoured my aggressive fight along with my screams. Today, routine would suggest I'm meant to be allowed to rest.

"I said, did you dream of me?" He lashes out, grabs a fistful of my hair, and drags me toward him until I stumble into his tailored-suit covered chest.

My scalp screams in protest but I keep my lips pressed closed, my blood pounding through my veins as I clench my teeth and ignore the cloying need to scream for help.

His smile remains in place while his hold tightens. Always taunting. Always tormenting.

I blink slowly, remembering the one beautiful moment long ago when I responded to his devilry by spitting in his face. He'd balked. Stared. Snarled. His shock at my stupidity had been a reward, at least for a few brief seconds until reality set in and clenched fists rained down on me.

I used to lash out freely. I tried to deny him my humiliation whenever possible, yet he always claimed it more tightly in the aftermath.

Now I've come to realize I can manipulate him if my aggression is tactical. I only bite when I know it will work in my favor. I snap in the moments when I'm well aware he's going to violate me. I save all my fight for those moments *not* because his abuse still scares me after all these years, but because aggression is my only defense.

I scream and kick to excite him. To quicken his climax.

I bite and punch and thrash because my hostility is the only thing saving me from a far worse fate.

Now isn't one of those times, though. Not when he had me less than eight hours ago. Luther Torian is becoming an old man. I'm told he's already a grandfather. If I trigger any sort of a thrill the resulting perversion will take longer to conclude.

So I clench my teeth. Breathe deep. Force calm. And don't give him one fucking glimmer of what he wants.

"No." I hold my chin high. "I didn't dream of you."

His laugh lines deepen. "This is why you're my favorite, pretty Penny. You cling tight to your anger. It's invigorating."

He's right. I cling so tight.

Anger is all I have.

I hoard the emotion deep in my chest, using it as armor. I rarely show my fear anymore and never, ever weakness. I stopped giving him insight to those parts of me long ago, back when I figured out he detests fragility.

What he enjoys is the battle.

It's what he craves.

And as much as I hate to hand him his filthy perversions on a silver platter, it's far better to live under his roof than inside the haunted walls of the place where he houses the majority of his sex slaves.

Here, in his Greek Island mansion, I'm only forced to do unimaginable things once or twice a week.

If I was sent to live with his less fortunate captives, I'm led to believe I'd have to perform once or twice an hour. The beating and torture would be unending instead of intermittent.

Permanent, not cyclic.

He releases my hair and grips my chin, his fingers digging into skin. "Don't worry. One day I'll grow tired of you."

I swallow, the deep chill of fear increasing.

It's such a twisted, nauseating reality to want to be here. To fight to remain under this roof where I have clean sheets and a comfortable bed. I've made friendships in this gilded cage. I have relative freedom.

I'll do anything—*give* anything—to remain as far as possible from the revolving door of Luther's personal harem. And so far, my tactics have worked. I'm the longest-standing woman in residence, having seen innumerable victims —*sisters*—come and go during my time.

I can't lose my position.

I'll never survive if I'm forced to leave.

"Go." He shoves me backward, chin first. "Make yourself look pretty. We're going to have visitors soon."

I stumble, quickly righting myself, the voice of curiosity tingling at the tip of my tongue.

Visitors are never a good thing. New faces mean new perversions. Fresh instruments of torture.

"I'll make sure I'm at my best." I turn and walk for the door, my stride confident before I grab the handle and twist.

I should be relieved to have survived another night in his bed. But that emotion is never present. Not when I'm dead inside.

No, not dead.

Death would be a blessing. Pure nirvana.

Instead, I'm constantly plagued by life. Every breath is a punishment.

I step into the hall, my anger spiking when I see Robert standing in wait, his back against the wall, his mouth curved in a sickening grin.

"Afternoon." He licks his lips, his gaze riveted on my bare chest. "Did you have a good night?"

I maneuver around him, determined not to engage.

"It sounded like you were enjoying yourself." He pushes off the wall and follows after me, his bulky frame hovering close at my back, raising the hair on my neck. "You know your screams make me hard."

I keep walking, keep eating up the distance to my room.

"How does it feel knowing you'll soon be mine?" he taunts.

I stop, not just my steps, but my breathing.

"You heard right." There's humor in his voice. "Luther agreed to hand you over once he's finished with you. Isn't it a relief to find out you'll be saved from the whorehouse yet again?"

Everything kicks back in—my fractured heartbeats, my panicked speculation, and so much stifling anger. It takes all my strength not to let my emotions show.

Luther is a monster. Always has been. Always will be. But Robert's violations will be an even deeper layer of hell seeing as though I've been an untouchable temptation to him for so long.

I raise my chin. Square my shoulders. "I look forward to our time together." I don't wait for a reply. My numb feet carry me along the hall, his laughter haunting me as he leaves in the opposite direction.

When I reach the door to my shared bedroom, the slightest sense of relief warms my chest until quickened footsteps carry from the kitchen.

"Penny, wait." Tobias, Luther's son, runs along the hall, his tiny frame barreling toward me.

I force a smile. I force so much fake bravado for this boy that it physically pains me. "Hey, little man. What are you up to this morning?"

He beams up at me, not acknowledging my nudity or the myriad of new bruises and scratches now marking my skin.

The sight before him is normal. The brutality an everyday occurrence. This beautiful little boy, with his sleek black hair and his deep blue eyes, is immune to the horrors surrounding him.

"I finished the writing task you gave me."

"Already?" I ruffle his hair. "That was fast."

"I've been awake forever. Dad took me out last night to meet my brother and when we returned I couldn't sleep."

Unease slithers down my spine. "Your brother?"

"Half-brother," he corrects. "His name is Cole. He's big and scary-looking. He's really old, too. Even older than you. But Dad says we have a lot in common."

I fake a chuckle, the sound bubbling over the bile rising in my throat.

I knew Luther had an adult son. Some of the women I've met in here have told stories about him. The kind of Chinese whispers capable of making my skin crawl. They spoke of his reputation in Oregon. About him being a well-known criminal. A *murderer*. And also the apple of his father's eye.

I've just never known him to come to the Greek Islands. Not once in the lifetime I've been here.

"I'm not *really* old, Tobias." But I am *really* worried. Luther's son has to be the visitor. "And I'm sure your brother isn't either."

He shakes his head. "That's not what I want to talk to you about. I have to show you my assignment. It's really good."

My heart squeezes at his innocence. "You can show it to me later. Let me get dressed first."

His face falls. "Please?"

"Later." I ruffle his hair again. I have to speak to the other women and warn them of the approaching danger. "I promise."

He pouts and blinks those puppy-dog eyes at me. "Please. Please. *Please.*"

This time my chuckle isn't forced, only short-lived. "Later, gorgeous boy."

"Fine." His shoulders slump as he huffs and storms off in the direction he came.

I wait a pain-filled heartbeat, making sure he's out of sight before I rush into my room.

It's exactly how it is every day—three sets of bunk beds evenly spaced along the side wall. Five beds are perfectly made, with the lower bed in the middle bunk being the anomaly.

Lilly is still under the covers, curled in a ball, her gaze meeting mine. Those soul-shattered eyes are the only reason I don't blurt out the news about Luther's son.

This woman—this *girl*—is close to breaking under the pressure of our tortured existence.

She rarely leaves our small sanctuary, choosing to sleep away the nightmares as much as possible. There's no fight left in her. No life. It's only a matter of time before she slips through the revolving door.

"Morning, Lill." I continue to the closet, pull out a loose sundress, and slide it over my head, letting the thin cotton cover the bruises on my thighs and hips.

She watches me, her eyes dreary, her skin ashen. "Luther's son is coming."

I wince and walk toward her, climbing onto her bed to spoon under the covers. "Did you hear me talking to Tobias?"

"No," she whispers. "Chloe told me. It's all I can think about."

I relax a little, entirely selfish with relief at not having been the bearer of bad news. "How did she find out?"

"She overheard Robert and Chris talking." She sucks in a shaky breath. "It's a business meeting. She thinks he's going to help traffic more women."

I wrap my arm around her waist and hug her tight. "Lill, I need you to listen to me. I know you're scared, but you can't keep hiding in here. Luther loathes fragility. You have to find something to fight for. You can't give up, especially if his son is coming. You need to be strong."

"I can't." Her voice breaks. "I don't know how."

An ache forms under my sternum, the discomfort building.

She's going to be taken away. I've seen it happen too many times not to predict the separation.

"All I can think about is my family, which only makes me want to cry." She turns into me, her face pressing against my shoulder, her tears heating my skin. "I miss them, Penny. I just want to go home."

I hug her tighter and press my eyes closed, knowing exactly how hard it is to get out of the emotional minefield. "You need to forget your past. You can't think of anything before your time here. It doesn't exist. Not anymore."

A sob escapes her. "I don't know how you stay strong."

"There's no choice. We both know the alternative is worse."

If there was another option to combat my reality, I'd take it. But I've learned the ways of Luther's world. There's no escape. Only darker pits of despair if we don't comply.

I can't kill him. I wouldn't dare to try. Not when failure would turn this nightmare into something unimaginable.

Women have attempted before and the aftermath still haunts me.

One woman even came close to success. Cody. A victim barely in her twenties.

She'd been frail. Mindless. And didn't think of the consequences of stealing a visitor's gun before she aimed the barrel at Luther.

She also didn't anticipate the gun's safety lock or know how to switch it off after she failed to successfully pull the trigger.

Cody went from elation to annihilation in the space of heartbeats. But not through physical pain. At least not to start with. After Robert and Chris tackled her to the ground, Luther told them to fetch another one of the women from his personal harem—her closest confidant.

He'd then enlightened both women on how to turn off the gun's safety and held Cody's trembling hands steady as they found a new aim for the barrel.

He'd ripped out her heart with the pull of a trigger. He made her murder a woman she loved.

Then he tied her, face down, to the dining table, allowing anyone and everyone who walked into his home the chance to fulfil their perverted fantasies for days on end before he sent her through his revolving door.

"You haven't always been this way, have you?" Lilly whispers. "I've heard stories."

I stiffen, well aware of the tale she's referring to. The one where I foolishly thought my tactics were far better than anyone else's.

"It's been a long time since Luther has seen any weakness from me."

She pulls back to look at me with tear-soaked eyes. "But you—"

"Yes, I tried to kill myself. But that was out of strength, not instability."

It was how I planned to win this game.

A final *fuck you*.

All it took was a hair-dryer and a warm, soothing bath.

I don't even remember what it felt like. The electrocution. The death. One second, I was lying in the scented water. The next, I opened my eyes to Robert's angry face looming over me as he paused chest compressions while I lay on the chilling wet tiles of the bathroom floor.

"Did Luther go easier on you afterward?"

"No. It never gets easier. You need to remember that."

"Then how did you survive?" She punishes me with her sorrow. Kills me with her pained tone. "How could you…?"

I shrug. "Luther gave me no choice."

He kept me on a leash for weeks, dragging me everywhere he went. There was no reprieve from his horror. No respite from the constant onslaught of mental and physical torture. "But right now, you have a choice, Lill. You can either give him exactly what he wants or you'll be sent some place far worse than this."

Her lips tremble as her tears fall. "I'm not strong like you."

"You are. You have to be."

She sniffs and nuzzles back into my shoulder as heavy footfalls approach along the hall.

There's more than one set, the deep pound resembling a pack of men.

Robert, Luther, and Chris pass the open doorway, not glancing in our direction before they continue out of sight, the front door slamming shut moments later.

"They must be going to get Luther's son." I kiss her forehead and slide from the bed. "We need to get ready."

She doesn't budge. It's clear she doesn't have the strength to appease Luther's depraved fantasies, and my heart breaks at the imminent goodbye. She might last another week. Maybe a few days.

"Come on, Lill. Get dressed. Do your hair. It's better to fly under the radar than draw attention by being unprepared."

She sinks farther under the covers. "In a minute."

The ache in my chest grows arms, squeezing me from the inside, painfully compressing my ribs.

I can't let her weaken me. I can't soften for her.

I can't. I can't. *I can't.*

"Okay, beautiful girl." I swallow over the lump in my throat. "Come find me if you need me."

As much as I want to—as much as I've tried with other women—I can't save her.

I can't save any of them. I can only provide guidance to help lengthen their stay. And right now is one of those moments when leadership is key.

I stalk from the room, going in search of my friends—my sisters—finding Abi, Chloe, and Nina in the living room, each of them sitting on different armchairs.

"Morning," I offer in greeting.

They turn toward me, their eyes questioning. They won't ask how my night of horrors went. Not verbally, anyway. But I see the need for answers in their matching expressions of concern.

"Did you know Lilly is still in bed?" I ask.

Abi lowers her gaze to the floor.

"She didn't want to join us." Chloe slumps into her chair. "She's given up."

"And I don't know what else to do." Nina pushes to her feet and comes to my side, lightly wrapping an arm around my waist to snuggle into me. "Nothing I say seems to sink in."

"We're all wasting our breath." Abi continues to stare at the carpet. "She'll be gone soon. We're better off getting used to—"

"*Stop.*" I warn. "Don't talk like that. *Ever.* Do you hear me?"

They all react in their own defensive ways.

Nina nestles closer into me. Chloe weaves her arms around her waist, self-soothing. And Abi scowls, strengthening her resolve to distance herself from the emotional loss.

"We stick together. Always." I stare at Abi until she meets my gaze. "*Always.*"

She winces as Nina nods against my shoulder, the room filling with silence for a few beats before Abi sighs. "Did you hear about Luther's son?"

"Yes. And I think Luther left a few minutes ago to retrieve him, so we need to prepare."

"For what?" Chloe asks.

"Anything." I inch away from Nina so I can look her in the eye. "We all have to expect the unexpected. Sometimes visitors come and go without drama. But other times..." I let the sentence hang. They've already lived through enough torment to come to their own conclusions.

"What should we do?"

"Start tidying up. Make sure the house is clean. At least that way Luther won't have an excuse for additional punishment." It will also give my sisters something to occupy their minds.

"Fine." Abi huffs. "I'll vacuum."

"I'll dust." Chloe pushes from the sofa.

Nina's tired eyes turn my way. "I guess I'll clean the bathrooms."

"And once I get ready, I'll tidy the kitchen." I attempt to smile and hope I'm exuding calm instead of the nauseating anticipation twisting my stomach. "Don't worry. We'll be okay."

They don't respond to the placation as they leave the room. We all know a threat looms close. It's only a matter of the severity.

I try to follow my own strategy to keep myself occupied as the sand in my mental hourglass dwindles.

I grab a pair of shoes. I do my hair, finger-combing the long strands into a messy plait. The make-up I put on is understated and simple. I don't want to accentuate my features any more than necessary. Only enough for Luther to think I've made an effort.

I'm in the kitchen, wiping down the counter when the faintest sound of an approaching car brushes my ears.

"*They're here,*" Tobias calls from another room. "*My brother is here.*"

I stalk into the living room, finding Abi, Nina, and Chloe frantically scrambling to pack their cleaning supplies.

"Don't panic." I maneuver around the coffee table, then the sofa, and squeeze by Nina to get to the curtains and gently glide them an inch aside. "Take a few minutes to breathe."

I listen to my own advice and slow my inhales, expelling the air from my lungs gradually as Luther and Chris stride toward the house. But it's the men climbing from the parked car who steal my attention.

They're both tall, broad, with one man looking toward the house to reveal a face resembling Luther so closely it's clear he must be the son.

My hatred is instantaneous.

No introduction is necessary to determine he's the scum of the earth. Not when I've already heard enough whispers to know this confident man lazily strolling for the mansion doors is yet another monster.

"Go get Lilly." I glance over my shoulder and meet Nina's gaze. "Reassure her everything will be fine."

She nods and quickly leaves the room, Abi and Chloe following behind her while I release the curtain to fall back into place.

The front door opens in the distance. Tobias greets them with words I can't decipher before he rushes back down the hall in the opposite direction. Heavy footsteps approach, accompanied by murmurs from men without souls.

I toe off my shoes and creep across the room, listening, eavesdropping, and plaster myself to the wall beside the doorway. I hear disjointed conversation as they approach, none of which makes any sense. Then I spy a glimpse of Luther and Chris as they pass the living room and continue toward the back of the house.

Their guests walk by a few seconds later, and I stiffen at the malevolence ebbing from them. I can feel their malicious intent.

I wait for the footsteps to move farther along the hall before I attempt a peek around the doorway. The Luther lookalike is focused, eyes straight ahead, while his companion carries his menacing frame with confidence. He's strong, his suit-covered frame hiding what I assume is a lethal body beneath.

I need to see his face, though. To stare into those soulless eyes and determine what I'm up against. But it's too risky now. I won't bring unnecessary attention to myself by greeting these assholes before I'm summoned.

Below the radar is where I fly.

I silently inch back into the living room, prepared to remain in hiding until I can make an escape to find my sisters, when the face-less man glances over his shoulder.

I pause.

Freeze.

I hold my breath as his face comes into view. The deep scowl. The tight-pressed lips. The aura of a brutal man filled with darkness. And as his intense eyes narrow precisely on mine, his harsh attention fills me with dread.

2

PENNY

I HOLD HIS GAZE AS HIS BROWS PULL DEEPER, THE SLIGHT FLARE OF HIS NOSTRILS increasing my fear.

He's angered at the sight of me. Furious.

I fight all the instincts screaming at me to run and begin to breathe again when he turns away, continuing around the corner, the door to the outside entertaining area closing moments later.

"Oh, God." I collapse against the wall, sucking in gulps of air.

Each blink brings back a memory of hard eyes and an even harder scowl. Like every other man to walk through the front doors, Cole's companion didn't have an ounce of pity for my situation.

There was no surprise. No concern.

But there wasn't a taunting smirk either. His expression didn't hold the conniving prelude I've witnessed from the vilest of Luther's guests.

The patter of small feet rushes down the hall, forcing me to put my game face on right before Tobias runs into the room and skitters to a stop before me. His eyes are big as saucers, his inhales rampant.

"He's here... my brother." He waves a hand for me to hurry. "You need to come meet him."

"I'll be there in a minute."

"No." He shakes his head as Abi, Nina, and Chloe come to stand in the doorway behind him. "Dad wants to see you *now*."

"Toby, I said I'll be there in a minute. I just need to do something first." I have to claim a moment to gain my composure. I can't face a pack of wolves unless I'm in control.

He frowns, his annoyance beyond clear. "But Penny—"

"I need to put on my shoes. Is that okay?"

His stern expression remains in place, yet those innocent eyes lose their anger. He's torn. Nothing is more important than pleasing his father, but he hates upsetting me, too.

"Hurry." He turns on his heel to walk between Abi and Nina. "Don't take too long."

"I won't."

My sisters look at me, their expressions questioning.

"Play it safe," I whisper. "Nod and agree with everything they say. Don't retaliate to anything. Don't smile. Don't talk unless spoken to."

Abi and Nina nod.

"Did you see him?" Chloe asks. "What does he look like?"

"It doesn't matter. Be smart and you'll be okay."

"Hurry up," Tobias calls from down the hall.

I sigh. "You heard the little Nazi. Go. Get the introduction over and done with. I'll be out there soon."

They follow my instruction, leaving me alone to suck in deep lungfuls of air, the oxygen taking long moments to settle me into some semblance of control.

I tiptoe into the hall, clinging to my shoes as I measure a calm stride past the rooms with an armed guard. I run once I'm out of sight until I reach the other side of the house, closing in on the window closest to the outdoor dining setting.

The male voices are almost decipherable from here, the chitchat easily heard over the soft whir of the mist fan.

I want to know what they're here for. If their taste in perversion is more sinister than we're used to I need to prepare myself and everyone else, too.

I inch aside the curtain, chancing another peek.

Luther, Cole, and the man with the harsh stare all sit on the expensive furniture. I can't clearly see their faces, only the back of Luther's head and two stony profiles. But the heir to this lawless empire is still unmistakable.

Cole sits with the same confidence as his father—his shoulders strong, the tilt of his chin arrogantly high. The other man is more laid-back, his demeanor now entirely casual as he talks to Luther about the necessity for regular servicing of sex slaves.

His words chill my veins.

I was right. This man is heartless. Soulless.

"What the fuck do you think you're doing?" Chris growls.

I drop the curtain and swing around to face him entering the dining room. "I was checking to see how many guests we have." I straighten to my full height and pretend I'm not one wrong answer away from punishment. "I assume Luther wants me to organize refreshments."

He eyes me with predatory intent as his lips kick into a smirk. "You're right. He does." He strolls forward, skirting the dining table, not stopping until he's a foot away. "But that doesn't mean you weren't snooping." He reaches out, slowly gliding a hand around my waist, then farther to grab the flesh of my ass.

I tense, every muscle pulled taut through the degradation.

He won't hurt me, though. He wouldn't dare.

As far as he's concerned, I'm off-limits. Nobody gets to defile Luther's precious Penny. But that doesn't mean he can't play games and get me in trouble.

"What would Luther think if he found out you were spying?" he murmurs. "What do you think he would do to you?"

"I wasn't spying. I only wanted to know how many guests there are."

He inches closer, toe to toe, hip to hip, and grinds the hard length of his cock into me. "Are you sure?" He leans in, his mouth a breath away from my cheek. "I don't think I believe you, and I wouldn't be a valued employee if I didn't tell Luther what I caught you doing."

Anger heats my chest, his power sickening me. "Tell him whatever you like. Your threats mean nothing to me."

"Sure they do," he purrs. "Don't pretend you're not scared."

His toxicity invades me, curdling my emotions. I want to lash out. To tell him he's nothing but a leashed dog who jumps at his owner's command. Instead, I pull back and look him in the eye. "I was determining how many guests we have. And now that I'm aware, it's time for me to prepare refreshments."

He chuckles, the tone sinister. "Come on, pretty Penny. Admit your little heart is pounding at the thought of me fucking you."

"Luther would cut off your hands."

"You're right." He drops his hold and steps back with a non-committal shrug. "I guess I'm left to take out my frustration on poor Lilly. You realize she's still all alone in your room, right?"

Defeat hits me.

It's a hard punch to the stomach I can't take without lowering my head to hide my suffering.

I don't see Chris grin in response. I don't need to. I already know his mouth is spread wide, his eyes glistening with victory. His reaction is as predictable as the change in seasons.

I inch away, sliding between him and the dining table, then stalk from the room and into the kitchen. I ignore my turmoil as I put on my shoes, then pull a bottle of scotch from a cupboard. I suppress all the unwanted feelings threatening to overwhelm me while I grab liquor glasses and a serving tray.

What I can't do is pretend Chris won't make good on his promise.

He always does.

The only thing I can do is live with the guilt that I taunted him into taking his frustration out on my sister.

I grind my teeth and tighten my grip around the neck of the scotch bottle until my fingers ache in protest. I'm still there, strangling the liquor when the sound of the sliding door opens down the hall and the clap of numerous sets of heels approach.

Nina, Abi, and Chloe make their way into the kitchen, Tobias following them with tight-knit brows.

"Dad is looking for you," he snips. "He's gone to the bathroom, but he's not happy you've made them wait."

"I'm on my way." I pour a finger of scotch into each glass. "Abi, can you check on Lilly for me?" I give the woman a pointed look, then do the same with Chloe and Nina. "Chris was headed to our room and I want to make sure the two of them don't have another fight."

Abi's eyes narrow in understanding. "Sure." She nods and stalks from the kitchen, Chloe and Nina following.

I ignore Tobias as he continues to scowl in my periphery and grab the tray, my heart pounding beneath tightening ribs as I stalk for the hall leading to the sliding door. The glass is open an inch, letting me hear the soft murmur of Cole and his accomplice.

I can't make out the conversation, only the hushed tone.

There's nothing sinister in the voices. If anything, it's more tinged with conspiracy. Secretive and low.

I suck in a deep breath and square my shoulders as I use the toe of my shoe to slide the door wide. The tap of my heels is almost deafening against the tile. The beat of my heart is even louder.

The men stop talking on my approach, the descending silence thick and uncomfortable. Maybe I should've waited for Luther to finish in the bathroom. If these strangers don't know the rules—if they're unaware I'm not to be touched— I could be standing before a viper pit.

But it's too late to back out now.

I won't scamper away and trigger any sort of predatory chase.

Luther's son meets my gaze, his dark eyes scrutinizing. I quickly lower my focus, not wanting unnecessary attention as I place the tray on the coffee table and grasp two glasses of scotch. I hand the first to his associate, keeping my attention lowered to forgo another scorn-filled look.

I'm surprised when he grasps the offer gently, his large fingers smoothly wrapping around the rim of the glass. That doesn't mean I don't picture the same grip wrapping around a woman's neck, the effortless glide becoming tight. Squeezing. Choking.

How many times has he tortured the defenseless?

I back away and hold the second glass out to Cole. Just like the other man, his intent toward my offering is slow and calm. There's no rough grab or harsh snatch. He reaches out, preparing to take the scotch, then doesn't grasp the glass. His hand only hovers close without contact.

"Aren't you going to introduce yourself?" His tone holds the same arrogant authority as his father. The same superior self-worth I've come to despise.

I swallow over my hatred and chant a mental warning to remain civil.

"I'm Cole," he continues. "Luther's son."

I'm sure he knows I'm well aware of who he is and what he's capable of. This friendly introduction is merely a taunt.

I raise my gaze, answering him with a spiteful look. It's impossible to play nice, especially when I've conditioned myself to be vicious to all men.

"Have we met?" He rakes his gaze over me, from head to toe and back again. "I'm sure I've seen you before."

I don't know what he's angling for—familiarity? Kindness? Or worse, my vulnerability?

"You're mistaken." I shove the glass into his hand and backtrack. I'm ready to turn on my heel and flee inside when the glass door slides open and Luther ruins my chance of escape.

"Ahh, there she is." He strides toward me, sickening pride ebbing off him in waves before he wraps his arm around my waist, awakening my bruises as he drags me into his side. I flow with the movement, not giving him an opportunity to scold me.

"I see you've already met my pretty Penny." Luther tangles his fingers in my dress, reminding me my body is his to control. "I shouldn't have favorites, but it's no secret this woman has claimed all my attention."

"I can see why." Cole continues to eye me, the visual sweep a violation all on its own. "Is there a reason why I feel like we've already met?"

Luther pauses for a moment, glancing between me and his son. "I don't know. Maybe you've seen her on the television. Penny's not from Oregon. But the news of her disappearance may have crossed state lines."

"Penny?" the companion asks. "That's her name?"

Despite knowing I'm not to be touched by anyone but Luther, my unease is high over my status as the center of attention. My position is precarious. Even though these men might not have their way with me, it doesn't mean Luther can't demand I put on a deplorable performance.

It wouldn't be a first.

"Is something wrong?" Luther eyes Cole and grabs the remaining glass of scotch from the tray before taking a seat. "Have you two met before?"

"No." Cole's interest evaporates. "She must have a familiar face. That's all."

"I'm not sure about her face, but she has a truly unforgettable mouth." Luther laughs. "Don't you, baby girl?"

Humiliation burns holes in my chest as I smile and silently wish I had the power to slaughter them all. I picture myself grabbing Luther's glass, smashing it against the coffee table, and stabbing the jagged remains into his neck.

I could do it, too.

I could kill him. I *would* kill him. If only I wasn't scared of whatever new hell I'd be flung into when someone else claimed me as their possession.

I take a backward step, distancing myself from temptation.

"Where are you going?" He pats his lap. "Come here."

My stomach twists.

I need to check on Lilly. I need these men to find another focus.

But I also need to remember I have no choice.

I reluctantly sulk forward, taking note of the strangers who track my movements.

"Come on." Luther lashes out, grabbing my wrist to yank me down to him. "There's no need to be shy."

I stumble into his lap, my back ramrod as his calloused palm lands on my thigh to hold me in place. It's a familiar scene—my ass against his crotch, his hand a tormenting reminder against my skin, his audience held captive.

He drags the material of my dress higher and higher with the slide of his palm toward the apex of my thighs.

My skin shudders with an outbreak of goosebumps as I brace myself for violation. Soon I'll have to fight. To scream and kick and thrash because that's all part of the performance.

As the seconds tick by to my opening act, I focus along the oceanic horizon. I try to make the picturesque scenery soothe me. But the hard stare of Cole's companion from my periphery is a threat I can't ignore.

He's glowering at me, his nostrils flaring.

He wants me. I can see it in his eyes—the determination. The severity.

He barely blinks as he holds my gaze, not lowering his attention to the thigh Luther continues to expose.

Perhaps it's because his lust is threadbare. Is he dying for a taste or a touch?

"I don't mean to cock block," he drawls, "but is that food still on the way?"

I stiffen, confused.

"I'm starving." He turns his attention to Cole. "And you haven't even eaten today."

Luther's hand pauses on my thigh. The filthy sense of approaching doom dissipates. I'm just not sure if I'm receiving a reprieve or merely being toyed with.

"Yes. Food." Luther slaps my leg, the sting rushing through me as he shoves me from his lap. "We need to feed our guests."

I stagger to my feet, baffled. The gift of my degradation has never been rejected before. My humiliation has always been a coveted prize.

I'm so completely caught off guard I have to force myself to snap out of the bewilderment and hustle to the door to slip inside.

But I don't leave. I remain close to the glass, my heart in my throat as I listen to the disjointed conversation filtering through the barrier.

Their words are hard to hear over the rush of blood in my ears. There are references to a personal harem and I'm sure it's Cole's associate who announces he'd "part ways with a lot of money for just a taste."

So why did he reject the full dose of my humiliation?

I nudge the door wider, hoping for clearer insight, only to panic at the soft footfalls approaching from behind me. I swing around, praying I don't get caught snooping for a third time when Abigail creeps into the hall.

"What are you doing?" she whispers.

I wither in relief and place a hand to my chest, hoping to soothe my ragged heartbeats. "Nothing. Where's Lilly?"

"Chris got to her before we did."

"And?" My turmoil returns faster than it receded.

She cringes. "He messed around with her a little but got frustrated with her tears. She doesn't fight back anymore. She just lays there, playing dead. Now she won't stop sobbing. What should we do?"

We should make him pay. Humiliate and violate. I could spend days—weeks—torturing him before I stole his final breath. But wishes are for those with luck and we have none.

"Get her out of bed. Make her shower. Then force her to eat. Keep her busy the best you can," I explain. "If we occupy her mind we might be able to buy her more time."

She nods and focuses outside. "Are you going to tell me what they're talking about out there?"

"I don't think we need to worry about Luther's son." I reach behind me and close the door. "Their focus seems to be food, not play."

For the moment, at least.

"Are you sure?"

"For now." I walk by her, heading for the kitchen. "I need to prepare them something to eat. Take care of Lilly until I can get to her."

I don't look back. I'm too busy rebuilding my walls. Creating strength. Locking down emotion. I need to focus to make sure I'm ready for the imminent threats.

Abi sighs. "But—"

"Go," I grate. "Hurry up."

I stalk into the kitchen and pull open the fridge, struggling to juggle all the roles expected of me. I'm the savior and the victim. The leader and the servant. The nurturer and also so badly in need of nurturing.

And above all else, I'm a mess. Just like everyone else.

I grab an assortment of cheeses, along with grapes and pâté, placing them all on the counter when the sound of the sliding door brushes my ears again.

I keep my focus on the food in front of me, taking my time to place them on a serving platter as I wait for Luther to hurl abuse at me for being an unaccommodating host.

"Penny…"

I freeze at the unexpected voice, the tone far younger than Luther's.

I don't turn. I already know the low, husky cadence comes from the man with the stubbled jaw. The one who stopped the progression of a monster's hand along my thigh.

"My name is Luca," he murmurs. "I work for Cole."

The hairs on the back of my neck prickle. My limbs tingle with the need to protect myself. His tone may be laced with kindness, but I hear it for the deception it is.

"I know who you are," he whispers. "I know where you're from."

I stiffen as unwanted memories assail me, hitting like a slap across the face. I fight not to remember the long-forgotten place he speaks of—my childhood home. The friendly neighborhood I grew up in. The warmth. The love.

I place both hands on the counter, desperate for the smooth stability, and raise my attention to his. Up close I can make out the harsh hazel irises. They scrutinize me, trying to read my anxious thoughts.

"I know about your family." He flicks a cautionary glance toward the entryway on the opposite side of the kitchen, then returns his gaze to mine as he steps forward. "I can help yo—"

"I think you're confused." I force a smile. "Luther won't share me. So, whatever you're playing at, whatever stunt you're trying to pull, it won't work. I'm not to be touched."

His jaw tightens.

I've spoiled his plan. Or at least I've hit a sore spot. God only knows if this man is smart enough to listen to my caution.

He takes another step. "I don't want to touch you. That's not why I came in here."

"Then stay where you are." I back away. "Don't move another inch."

He doesn't listen. In fact, he grows taller in the diminishing space between us, his presence taking up more room as he creeps closer. "Penny…"

My name on his lips is sickening, the tone placating and authoritative at the same time. "I'm here to help you," he continues. "I can—"

"Stop," I growl. "Whatever you have planned, you'll get caught, then Luther will punish you. It doesn't matter who you think you are. You can't silence me. I'll scream."

His lips press tight. His nostrils flare. Pure frustration ebbs from him yet it's not enough. I need his defeat. I have to know he won't divert his sickening intent toward my sisters.

"I'll let you in on a secret," I whisper. "Luther may act like he's willing to share his harem, but believe me, he's far from generous. As soon as you lay a hand on any of us you'll be indebted to him and he always reclaims what he's owed."

"Luther doesn't scare me." His face softens. "And like I said, I have no desire to touch you."

I glare despite the likely retaliation I'll receive for my insolence. "So, you're one of those role-playing types?"

Each monster has a different strategy. A well-greased kink.

Some enjoy boasting their horrors. And others, like this man, prefer to play nice, luring victims with honey to later strike with sickening poison.

"Don't worry," I add. "Luther enjoys the same type of games. Sometimes he pretends he's had a hard day and wants someone to cuddle up against. But gentle cuddles always turn into vicious hands around a delicate throat. Or gouge marks along tender skin. He likes lulling victims into a false sense of security. I gather that's what you're doing now, right?"

His jaw ticks. "No."

"No?" I quirk a brow.

He holds my gaze, those hazel eyes softening back to their deceptive look of concern. "I want to help you."

"Help keep me in a sexual violation routine? Isn't that what you were discussing earlier?"

"Fuck," he mutters under his breath.

"Yeah," I drawl, despite the pulse building in my throat. This man is getting to me. The initial damage he caused by mentioning my home is eating away at my defenses to leave me vulnerable. "I heard. So stop wasting both our time. I need to get this food outside."

It's a mistake to admit how far I intruded upon Luther's privacy. The truth could come back to bite me. Hard. But the longer this man stares at me, his questionable intent putting me on edge, the more unsettled I become.

I want to believe the feigned sincerity in those eyes. I'd give anything to fall headfirst into his offer for help. If only it wasn't a sickening game.

"You need to trust me." He makes another cautionary glance toward both doorways, then approaches another step.

He's so close the gentle scent of his woodsy cologne burns a trail down my throat to scorch my lungs.

He leans in, his gaze never leaving mine as he murmurs, "I know your brother."

My heart stops, the harsh stab of déjà vu assailing me.

With effortless precision he attacks. Without physical connection. With barely audible words.

I have two brothers. Both of them the most caring, brilliant men in the world, and having this asshole use either one of them against me is despicable.

"Stop it." I keep backtracking, needing to maintain the distance between us. I can't let him push me into my past. I can't fall into that trap. "Leave me alone."

I stalk to the far cupboards and retrieve a packet of wafers. If I don't get outside with food Luther will punish me, and despite his heavy hand being less painful than the thoughts of my family, I won't open myself up to any more torture than I've already received in the last twenty-four hours.

"Listen to me." Luca's heavy footsteps approach, his presence closing in at my back, his hands clasping the counter on either side of my waist.

He traps me.

Cages me.

"I know you, Penny. I know how long you've been missing and that your brother never stopped looking for you until he thought he had evidence of your death."

His words whisper into my ears. The message is pure torture.

There are so many aspects to fixate on. Too many facets to assail me.

My brother stopped looking? *Which* brother? What evidence? Was it the tooth Luther extracted from my mouth without sedation? Or the fist-fulls of hair that have been ripped from my head over the unending months?

No.

It's all lies. All make-believe.

I don't have siblings. I don't have a past.

I suck in breath after breath, trying to ignore how he keeps goading me into a game I'm not equipped to handle. He's deliberately pushing my buttons. This man is merely violating me with mental manipulation instead of physical.

Fuck him.

Fuck. Him.

I swing around to face my tormentor, his body so close, those eyes holding mine. I glare, and glare, and glare some more, but all he does is stare right back. There's still no smirk. He's devoid of the toxicity that usually forewarns of an impending strike.

All he gives me is stony silence while he traps me in the cage of his arms.

"You've got the wrong woman." I raise my chin, strengthening my resolve. "I don't know who you're talking about, but it's not me."

I rebuild my mental walls, frantically attempting to make them stronger and stronger as he remains a brutal force in front of me.

I have no family.

No weaknesses.

No vulnerabilities.

There's only here and now. There's only Luther and this unending hell.

"I know you're scared." He gentles his voice, the delicate sweep of his breath brushing my lips. "But I know who you are. There's no mistaking it."

His softness is foreign. The look in his eyes is, too. Everything about him screams of sanctuary, but it's all a trick. A twisted, manipulative strategy.

"Stop it." I glance away. Each inhale is pained, the air filling my lungs carrying tiny thorns to pluck me from the inside out. "Leave me alone."

He's triggering my hope and there's nothing more dangerous to my stability. My hands shake from the internal battle of optimism and reality. I have to harden myself, to remember all the things I've endured and how the living nightmare never ends. There's no savior. No peace to come.

There're only beatings. And rape. And eventually, the peace of death.

"He lives in Portland," he continues to stoke my insanity, making my pulse spike. "I've been working with him."

"Stop." I squeeze my hands into fists, digging my nails into skin. He's filling my head, suffocating me with lies. I don't want to drown. Not from this. Not from longing.

It's too much.

My lungs squeeze.

My heart hurts.

"He's been dating—"

"*Stop*," I scream, my hand lashing out to slap across his cheek. "*Stop*."

My palm burns with the contact, the pain quickly sliding into my chest, restricting my air.

Oh, God.

He snaps ramrod straight, his eyes blinking in a daze.

Oh, God.

I hyperventilate through the mania, not realizing the stupidity of my mistake until the dark red of my attack seeps across the left side of his face.

Oh, God. Oh, God. Oh, God.

The damage I inflicted is blindingly obvious. It's a mark of defiance. Undeniable evidence of my rebellion.

"It's okay." He backs away. "Don't panic."

It's too late for that. I'm in full-blown hysteria, my breathing rampant as the glass door slides open down the hall and pounding steps approach.

"What's going on?" Luther's bellow echoes off the walls moments before he enters the room, Cole hot on his heels, both their rage clear to see.

Bile rises in my throat. My limbs tremble.

I huddle into the corner of the kitchen, clutching the counter on either side of me as Luca raises his hands in surrender.

He looks guilty, like he's the one who just threw away his life instead of me.

"Someone better start talking," Cole snarls. "My patience is growing fucking thin."

I can't speak. I can't think.

Luther will rain hell down on me for this. He'll take pleasure in the break of my bones.

"He didn't do anything." Tobias's timid voice carries from the doorway on the far side of the kitchen, his head poking around the frame from the hall.

My heart becomes a fragile butterfly, each violent beat threatening to break the thin membrane of my sanity and send me nose-diving.

He heard.

He heard, and he'll do absolutely anything to make his father proud. Even if it means stabbing me in the back.

"You saw what happened?" Luther asks.

"I was snooping." Tobias inches into the kitchen. "I know I shouldn't, but Penny sounded upset and I was worried."

"And?" Cole growls. "What happened?"

"Nothing. The man was being nice and Penny was…" Tobias glances at me, killing me with his guilt before he hangs his head.

I don't know what's worse: his conflict over betraying me or the inevitable possibilities if he tells the truth.

"What, son?" Luther approaches him, placing his evil hands on the boy's slight shoulders. "What was she doing?"

I silently beg Tobias to keep quiet. To lie. To betray his father even though I know he never will.

"She was being mean."

Pain slices through me, a soundless sob clogging my throat.

Luther grows an inch with his palpable fury. "You dare to make a guest of mine unwelcome?" He turns toward me, approaching with menacing steps.

I cower, turning my face away, wrapping my arms around my middle. I can't help the show of weakness. I'm fucking bathing in it, my fragility clear for everyone to see.

That man—that stranger—has fractured a resolve I'd built over years of torture. And he did it all with a few perfectly chosen words.

"I'm sorry," I plead. "I don't know what came over me."

"Fucking stupidity, that's what." Luther looms above me, fists clenched at his sides. "Do you need to go back to basic training? Or maybe I should send you to work with the majority of my women so you can understand how well you're treated here."

Horror consumes me.

"Please." I collapse onto my knees. "I didn't mean it. I apologize."

"It's my fault." Luca's voice breeches my nightmare. "I got carried away. I tried to make small talk and when I mentioned her past I think she took it as a taunt."

I hold my breath, the burn of building suffocation sliding through my veins. I don't understand his motive for taking the fall. Why would he? Why risk his safety for mine?

Luther grabs my chin, his rough grip forcing me to meet his gaze, his other hand raised in threat. "You need to be punished for your disobedience."

I know.

God, how I know.

And I'll accept his violations without protest over the hell of being sent away from here. He can hurt me as much as he likes as long as I don't have to step foot inside one of his brothels.

"Dad," Cole warns. "I'm growing tired of the adolescent distractions from these women. Can't we get the fuck out of here already?"

My heart stutters. Stops.

24

I don't want a delayed sentence. Giving Luther more time to think is dangerous. I need him to react on instinct, not with well-thought-out deviance.

When Luther doesn't respond, Cole huffs.

"Fine. We'll leave." He starts toward the doorway, murmuring something to Tobias along the way before he disappears down the hall.

I don't drag my gaze from my tormentor. I don't quit praying for him to strike. Not even when Luca's intense stare remains potent in my periphery.

I ignore the jagged seed of hope he planted under my skin. I fight to claw myself back to stability as I blink the heat from my eyes.

Maybe if I hadn't been here so long I could fall heavily into the fantasy of Luca being my savior. Back then I would've done anything, *given* anything for a warrior to haul me out of this nightmare.

But I've learned the hard way that there's no escape from this hell. And my reality is only cemented in place when Luca follows after Cole, leaving me alone with a little boy who betrayed me and a vicious man who I know is more disgusted in my show of weakness than my rebellion.

3

PENNY

Luther didn't hit me.

He did far worse. He left me kneeling on the cold tile, my thoughts in turmoil as he stormed from the kitchen.

I don't know where he went. Chloe informed me that Chris drove them from the house. Cole and Luca included. But even with the distance between us, it took hours to steady my rampant pulse.

"What are you going to do?" Lilly snuggles in bed behind me, returning the comfort I gave her earlier in the day, while the other women remain in their beds. "He's going to be horrible to you."

"I'll do what I've always done—be strong and fight back."

I spent the entire day, and well into the night, berating myself for falling victim to something I've built walls against since my first days in this living nightmare. I never should've taken Luca's bait. I'd thought I was immune to those types of taunts.

I'd thought my defenses held more strength.

"Where do you think they went?" Abigail asks from the bunk above. "They've been gone a long time."

"It's an event night." I clutch my pillow close to my chest and try to lessen my self-pity with thoughts of all the women currently being violated to make Luther money. "He won't be home until after midnight."

I still have a few hours.

I tucked Tobias in bed earlier and collapsed onto mine within minutes. Tomorrow will be challenging and I want to be at the top of my game. Not that sleep feels likely to bless me tonight.

"Are you ready to tell us what happened?" Chloe positions herself up on one elbow from the farthest bottom bunk. "What did that man do?"

I sigh.

I should tell them the error of my ways. Make it a learning experience. But the wound is still raw.

I'm humiliated by the few seconds of hope Luca awakened.

And frightened over how susceptible my family made me.

I have to work harder to forget them. I can no longer simply file their memories away in the back of my mind.

I need to eradicate every thought.

There were never any brothers who kept the sleazy teenage boys at bay. The tight-knit family didn't exist. There was no generous, nurturing mother.

It was all a punishing dream.

"We can talk about it in the morning," I murmur. "I'm too tired now."

"Tobias mentioned the man being nice to you." Abigail speaks softly. "Is that true?"

"Tomorrow, Abi."

"But what if he can help us?" Chloe asks. "If he was nice maybe he can—"

"He can't help us." I add steel to my tone. "Nobody can. The sooner you realize that, the easier each day will become."

The room falls silent.

I hate crushing their hopes. But it's a necessary evil. I'm being cruel to be kind.

"I'm sorry," I whisper. "I just don't want any of you to become optimistic. It's better to expect the worst. One day we'll get out of here, but it won't be because some dark prince came to rescue us. We'll be freed because we were smart and strategic. We don't rely on others. Least of all men who are associated with Luther."

They remain quiet, none of them accepting my apology because they're still holding out for a hero.

I lay there in the bitter void for hours, long after Lilly falls asleep snuggled against me and Nina lets out a soft purr of slumber.

Like I anticipated, it's well after midnight when the sound of a vehicle approaches outside.

Two car doors slam and moments later the thunderous footsteps of men ricochet off the walls. Lilly startles awake beside me. Chloe springs upward.

"Relax," I whisper. "They just got home. You can go back to sleep."

I wince through the placation because I'm not entirely certain everything is going to be okay.

Luther and his goons have been gone all day. He's had enough time to stew on my behavior. To scheme.

Those pounding footsteps could be a sign of his renewed aggression toward me. The forewarning to a brutal punishment.

The bright glow of the hall light flicks on, seeping into our room from the gap around the door.

There's murmured conversation, then Tobias's sweet voice saying, "But Baba, I want to go back to sleep."

"He woke Tobias," Lilly whispers. "Why would he do that?"

A rumble of chatter builds in the hall. A dark, aggressive reaction to the little boy's protest, which encourages my heart to beat faster.

I throw back the covers, crawl to the end of the mattress, then tiptoe my way to the door.

"What are you doing?" Nina peers down from the top bunk. "Get back in bed. If you're caught snooping…"

She doesn't finish her sentence. She doesn't need to. I already know the consequences and I don't quit my approach. I don't stop until my ear is placed to the doorframe and the now softened conversation becomes clear.

"We need to work together, son." It's Luther, his lowered tone filled with discipline. "This is important."

"Okay, Baba," Tobias replies. "But I'm tired."

The booming footsteps return. Approaching.

"Get back in bed," Abigail hisses.

I could.

I should.

But the thunder is too close. If Luther opens the bedroom door, I'll be caught scampering away.

I'd prefer to have him find me standing here—strong and sure—than see my weakness for a second time today.

Then the door is flung open and my heart squeezes.

I stiffen, facing the devil head on, his face partially shadowed, the light from the hall beaming down behind him.

He doesn't show surprise over my snooping. He doesn't express annoyance or delight either—just a stony mask of determination while Tobias stands like an exhausted angel by his side.

"You're coming with me." Luther lunges forward and grabs my wrist. "Chloe, you need to join us, too."

He doesn't wait for her to comply. He drags me into the hall, making me stumble as I cling tight to my refusal to show fear.

Gasps and whispers erupt from my bedroom as I'm taken from my sisters. I'm tugged toward the front of the house and into the living room with Tobias dragging his feet behind us.

Questions clog my throat. The need for answers is brutal. But I won't voice my weakness. I have to stay strong this time.

Chris stands at the far edge of one of the cream leather sofas, his expression tight, while one of the silent armed guards disappears through the doorway across the other side of the room, apparently satisfied Luther can handle the situation on his own.

It's safe to assume this is the start of my punishment, and the situation is made all the worse when Chloe inches into the room, her long dark hair loose around her shoulders, her skin pale.

Those sad eyes make me fragile. The tremble in her hands and lower lip are another battle I have to win in an effort to remain strong.

But the surprising thing is, both my tormentors aren't in their usual mocking, sadistic mood. Usually, I'm disciplined out of delight.

Tonight is different.

Luther and Chris appear frustrated, their hard eyes and tight features exuding anger.

The hairs on the back of my neck rise in foreboding. My fingers and toes tingle with anticipation of the unknown. This show of animosity can't be due to my outburst today. It can't. I've never seen these men so venomous toward me.

"Sit," Luther barks.

I comply, sinking into the cream leather, my hands in my lap, my fingers playing with the sheer material of my nightgown. Chloe takes her place on my left, her breathing shallow and ragged.

Luther moves to stand before us and indicates for Tobias to sit on the other side of Chloe. "You need to do something for me."

I hold my breath, unsure if he's talking to us as a collective or the boy on his own.

Having Tobias here must be another punishing strategy.

I knew this day would come—the moment when the child I helped raise would be used as a weapon against me. I'd known and still I hadn't been able to distance myself from caring for him.

"You made a mistake today," Luther growls at me. "A big one."

My pulse pounds everywhere. In my throat. My ears. My wrists. No place more painful than my chest.

"I'm sorry." The apology fumbles from my numb lips. "I lost myself. I promise I'll never do it again."

I promise to never, ever let hope blind me.

"I can make this right." I meet his gaze. "You know I can."

"Yes, I do." He inclines his head. "And you can start now."

I wait for him to lower his zipper and demand a vile act. Instead, he surprises me by reaching into his suit jacket to pull out two white tubes.

He hands one to Tobias and the other to me, the warm plastic smooth against my fingers.

"What's this, Baba?" Tobias asks.

I glance down at the instrument in my fingers, the cylindrical device resembling something akin to an EpiPen.

"Be very careful." Luther kneels in front of his son. "What you have in your hands is a device that can put someone to sleep."

Someone? Or me?

My thoughts rage into a tailspin.

I fight and claw not to show panic but I know Luther too well. I'm certain he's concocted an elaborate *Hunger Game*-type scenario where I'm pitted against a child I would never harm and a sister I adore.

Luther turns his focus to me. "Both of you need to do something really important. And there's no room for error."

"You want us to put someone to sleep?" I straighten my shoulders. "Who?"

"My son's associate." He pushes to his feet as I clench my fingers around the device, attempting to stop the shake of my hand. "I assume you'll enjoy the task seeing as though you felt inclined to attack him earlier."

Shock overwhelms me.

Shock and a whole lot of confusion.

"What about me, Baba?" Tobias's voice trembles. "What do I do?"

Luther pats the boy's head. "Your task is your brother."

My stomach bottoms out as Tobias gasps, his jaw slacking.

"Why?" I swallow over the drought taking over my throat. "And how do you expect woman and a child to overpower two full-grown men?"

"You don't need to overpower them. You only need to get close enough to stab that device."

"But Baba..." Tobias pleas. "I don't want—"

"You're not going to hurt your brother, son. You're only going to put him to sleep so we can bring him here." He crouches in front of the child again and places a hand on his knee. "His friends haven't been very nice to him. They're teaching Cole bad things about us. But once you put him to sleep, we will bring him back here and talk some sense into him."

It's a kidnapping. Of his own adult son. Facilitated by a fucking child.

"And what happens to Luca?" I stare at my tormentor, searching for answers.

He glares. "That's none of your concern. If I were you I'd take this opportunity as a godsend. You're not my most-favored possession at the moment."

Despite the fear coursing through my veins, I return his pointed look. I curl my lip and hope to remind him why I've always been his favorite.

I'm strong.

I'm a fighter.

The tactic works. His eyes soften. His tight lips twitch into a sly grin.

I raise my chin. "I'll do whatever needs to be done."

I know this task won't buy my forgiveness. The only way I can earn back my coveted position in this house is in the bedroom, under his body and beneath his fists. But I may be able to forego a far bigger penalty.

He smirks. "Good."

Tobias leans forward, peering around Chloe to look at me. To *really* look at me. He's scared. Panicked. He needs me to fight for him. To tell Luther this plan is destined to fail. And God, how I want to battle his demons for him even after he ripped my heart out.

But I can't.

Those sweet, innocent eyes tear me apart one slow blink at a time and all I can do is ignore him. I can't be his champion when my neck is on the chopping block.

I have to stay on the straight and narrow for a while. To obey with complete obedience. To lead my women by example and remind them that additional punishments are only handed out to those who don't play by the rules.

Even though it kills me, I can't win this battle for Tobias.

"What about me?" Chloe remains stock still at my side. "What will I do?"

Luther's lips incline lightly. Chris's do, too.

A skitter of foreboding descends along my spine, the discomfort prickling my skin.

"You, sweet Chloe," Luther purrs, "will be our guinea pig."

4

PENNY

THE GENTLE KISS OF SEA SPRAY BRUSHES MY CHEEKS AS THE BOAT BOUNDS ACROSS THE water's surface.

I hold Tobias at my side, helping him remain upright as we speed through the darkness before sunrise, our vessel quickly approaching an island in the distance.

I'm calm.

Focused.

I've been through a lot worse than stabbing a man with a sedative-filled syringe. And if I succeed, I'm sure I'll live through much more.

I listened with intent as Luther instructed Tobias on how to use the device. He'd told the boy how to hide the cylinder in his long shirtsleeve until the time was right. Then how to jam the tube against a body part, clothing-covered or not, and plunge the leaver with force.

I then watched as Tobias practiced on Chloe as she sobbed and begged him to stop.

Nobody acknowledged her pleas.

Not even me.

All I could do was hold her hand as Tobias jabbed the device against her thigh, then glanced at his father for praise.

I'd been shocked at the drug's quick effect. Panicked, too. The sudden crumple of Chloe's body made me question if something far more sinister had been injected into her system.

Something lethal.

But her pulse remained strong. Her breathing even.

Now, all I have to do is mimic the process, only on a man far bigger and stronger than I am.

There's no room for reluctance. I need to snatch the tube strategically placed in the waistband of my cream pants and strike without hesitation.

That is, if I can get close enough to my target.

"Penny?" Tobias glances up at me, his arms clinging around my hips. His hold tightens whenever we hit a bump in the water, yet the emotion peering up at me has nothing to do with the rough ride.

He's petrified.

Underneath the force calm, I am, too.

The new scenery should be a welcomed distraction from my regular confinement but I don't like being out here. Exposure coats my skin. I lose hold of even more of my strength in this great unknown.

As sickening as it is to admit to myself, I feel more at ease in my gilded cage. I know what to expect in my torture chamber. I'm entirely susceptible here.

"You've got nothing to worry about. You're going to be fine." I fake a smile even though it sickens me to lie to him. "It's all for the best, remember? Your dad is helping Cole. He's taking him away from the bad people."

Tobias's lips move in an indecipherable response. I can't hear him over the rush of ocean and the whirl of wind through my hair.

"It's okay." I crouch to his level and look him in the eye as Luther and Chris stand at the steering wheel a few yards away.

"No. That man was nice to you."

"That man?" I frown. "Your brother?"

"No, the other man. The one you were angry with. He's nice. He's Cole's friend. He's not bad… is he?"

Everything inside me clenches—stomach, throat, lungs.

There's still so much goodness left in this vulnerable child. I'm proud of him for being able to see past his father's lies to think for himself.

"He's not a nice man, Toby." I grab his hand and entwine our fingers. "He only acts that way."

I've had to remind myself of the same truth since the moment Luca approached me in the kitchen.

His intentions weren't kind. They were cruel. He knew exactly what to say to gain a reaction out of me. He's a skilled manipulator. An accomplished sadist.

"Everything will be fine." I squeeze those tiny fingers. "Your dad would never let anything happen to you."

His eyes remain riveted on mine, uncertainty staring back at me.

"I promise." My assurance is yet another lie.

I can't be sure of anything anymore. I'm not even certain this excursion isn't a trick. Or a test. All I know is that Luther will hand me over to his son as a peace offering and then try to facilitate a private moment for me to be alone with Luca.

"Tobias, you're going to make your father proud. He believes in you and so do I." I stand and turn my attention to the inky ocean, no longer able to watch his suffering. "We'll be okay."

We continue to bound over the water's surface, the tiniest glow of the upcoming sunrise barely visible against the boat's bright headlight.

A darkened pier comes into view on the island we approach, with another boat lying in wait. Slowly, a man is illuminated, his features unmistakable even from this distance.

Cole.

He's wearing a business suit, his tight expression a clear indicator of our lack of welcome.

His demeanor doesn't change when the boat's engine is cut and the vessel is tied in place alongside the pier. He just stands there, tension ebbing off him.

"What are you doing here?" He crosses his arms over his chest, his stylish jacket defining his muscled arms and shoulders.

"Morning, son." Luther walks to the side of the boat and holds out his hand for me to take. "We need to talk."

I remain quiet as I'm helped from the vessel, my bare feet dragging along the wooden pier.

I let their conversation wash through me. I acknowledge the aggressive chitchat and Luther's promise of not being armed. But my attention is focused on the darkness of the island, trying to find the target for my attack.

Luca isn't in sight.

He's not here to protect his boss. He's not the one patting down Luther or Chris—that task is left to Cole.

It isn't until the cold eyes of his son hit me that apprehension truly takes hold.

He's so much bigger than I am. And from memory, Luca was even larger in frame. Those meaty fists could knock me unconscious in seconds. Those hands could snap my neck in an instant.

"If you came to talk," Cole mutters, "why did you bring a woman and child as a shield?"

"A shield." Luther balks. "Do I need one against my own son? Because I brought her here as a peace offering. The woman is yours."

I'm shoved toward Cole, my footsteps fumbling.

"You're handing her over?" He scrutinizes me.

The weight of his appraisal is heavy. Cloying. The pinpoint focus makes me itch to brush my fingers over the hidden plastic tube to make sure it's not going to fall from my waistband.

I drag my gaze away to stop the nervousness from taking hold. I return my focus to the island. I work harder to find a man hiding in the scrub as Luther attempts to manipulate his son into inviting us up to the house, using Tobias's fatigue as an excuse.

They continue to argue under a tone of barely contained civility until finally Cole complies with a, "Fine. Go ahead."

He indicates for me to start walking. For *me* to lead us into battle.

I don't move.

Unease hits me like a freight train.

"Penny." Luther waves a hand, instructing me to hurry. "You first, my sweet."

My pulse catches at the endearment. *No*, it's a blatant warning.

I have no choice but to obey. I have to do this to regain my position of menial power. To reassert my strength.

Fuck.

I hold out a hand for Tobias, who walks forward to join me, then we both lead the way to the end of the pier and onto the island.

Murmured words carry from behind us, the subtle timbre letting me know everything remains faux civil as I make my way toward the light of the house up ahead.

Tobias keeps glancing over his shoulder, watching, waiting. I clutch his hand tighter, attempting to calm the tremble of his fingers. It's the only comfort I can provide. There's nothing else.

I can't gush soothing words. I'm unable to lie to him anymore. I can only attempt to give reassurance in the tightness of my hold as we continue along a winding gravel path, bringing us closer and closer to the large expanse of a mansion up ahead.

I take us into a house yard, my feet hitting cool cement tile placed around an immaculate pool.

"I'm scared," Tobias whispers. "I want to go home."

Me too.

"Be strong." I squeeze his sweaty palm tighter. "This will all be over soon."

I reach the glass door leading to the brightly lit living area and stop to wait for instruction.

"Go." Luther comes up behind me, shooing me forward. "Get inside."

"Wait," Cole barks. "You, the woman, and the kid can go inside, but your dog isn't welcome."

The demand twists my stomach.

I look at Chris—*the dog. Disdain crosses his* features as I wait for Luther to voice a reprimand that never comes.

I've never seen anyone disrespect this monster and get away with it. Not once. Not ever.

"Whatever you say," Luther complies.

It's an act. One I can't mimic.

"I guess I'll stay here then." Chris steps away. "Just so you can feel like more of a man for keeping me outside."

Cole claps him on the shoulder as he approaches the house. "If I were you, I wouldn't forget your best buddy ate lead yesterday because of me."

I suck in a breath as white noise assaults me.

Everything stops.

Every. Single. Thing.

Thoughts. Breath. Time.

I glance between the two men as they exchange muttered retorts my mind can't decipher. I'm stunned. Confused. And painfully hopeful.

Your best buddy ate lead.

Should I allow myself the luxury of believing the comment was made about Robert? That the vile, piece of shit might actually be hurt? Or better yet, dead?

He didn't return home with Chris and Luther.

They haven't made mention of him at all.

My stomach heats, the warmth spreading rapidly as Luther stalks toward me, his glare enough of a warning to get me to hustle my ass inside while Chris and Cole continue to swap barbs.

I don't allow hope free rein as I walk into the opulent house. I keep optimism's wings clipped as I take in the open living and kitchen area, the entire space immaculate apart from a few mugs on the dining table.

"Sit," Luther growls. "Here, beside me."

He claims the recliner and pats his hand on the armrest.

I do as instructed, sticking close to my nightmare, not only to be seen as an obedient slave, but to read his energy. I want nothing more than to confirm if the anger simmering below his surface is from the loss of his henchman.

Tobias settles away from us, perching on the opposite sofa, right where Luther foretold him to be—alone, ready for Cole to take a position beside him.

"Where's Luca?" I whisper. "What happens if he's not here?"

"He's here," Luther snarls. "Now quiet."

I snap my mouth shut as Cole enters the house, locking the door behind him and pulling across the sheer curtain. "The boy's no longer glued to your side?" he asks, his attention raking over the boy, then me, to rest on his father.

"We heard you're leaving." Luther shrugs. "I guess he wants to make the most of the moments you have together."

Leaving?

I scramble to understand what must have happened yesterday to cause their sudden departure. They were meant to be talking business. Discussing a partnership.

My outburst couldn't have caused the dissolution of their plans, could it? Surely my mindless rebellion didn't instigate an avalanche. If so, this stab-and-sedate attack won't absolve the mess I've made.

This punishment isn't enough.

Luther will want more from me. He'll want everything.

I clutch my hands in my lap, digging my nails into my palms in an attempt to lessen the instinct screaming at me to fight to the death.

It isn't until my target walks from the hall to take a few steps into the room, his chin high, his intense eyes finding mine, that the noise in my head lessens.

For the briefest second, hope flickers to life.

Painful, delusional hope.

I clench my teeth against the traitorous response as Luca glances away, disregarding me in an instant.

From bliss to devastation in seconds.

Stupidity to reality.

"What's going on?" He flicks his attention to Cole. There's no panic or apprehension. He's entirely mellow. At least on the surface.

"I'm not sure yet. But apparently, my father comes in peace," Cole drawls. "Is my little fox still sleeping?"

"She's back to the same tricks as she was on her first night here."

I sit straighter, trying to hear what isn't being said.

They're talking about a woman. Their own captive.

I hold in a snarl, my previous optimism entirely snuffed by disgust.

I knew I was right not to believe a word Luca said to me yesterday. I *knew* and yet the smallest part of me is still surprised to learn of his depravity.

They continue talking about her while anger coils itself around me, empowering me, making me greedy for my opportunity to strike. This man, with his laid-back air and unconcerned tone, couldn't give a shit about a woman held against her will.

He's just another monster, hiding his true colors behind a handsome face.

"Go check on her," Luther encourages Cole from my side. "By Amar's account, she took quite a beating yesterday. She probably shouldn't be left alone."

They beat her?

My fury increases, my train of thought pinpointing on my upcoming task. I read my opponent as they continue to talk. Luca stands tall, his attention sweeping the room, settling on Cole, Luther, Tobias, and finally me.

Those penetrating eyes narrow. His shoulders tense.

I mimic his posture, sitting a little straighter on the armrest. But I don't narrow my stare. Instead, I soften it.

I preempt Luther's promise to give me an opportunity to get within reach of this slimy devil. I act as if I'm not driven by retaliation. That I've learned my lesson from yesterday's outburst and I'm now a docile puppet who lives to please.

"I'm handing Penny over as a symbol of my apology." Luther's words break my focus. "Why don't you take her to one of the bedrooms and get her accustomed to a new way of life under my son's reign?"

Adrenaline kicks in as Luca glances at his boss with a raised brow. That disgusting tweak to his expression is a clear inquiry for permission. A filthy request to defile me.

"Go." Cole waves him away. "Enjoy yourself."

Luca doesn't move. He remains immobile, his expression still questioning.

"Go," Cole barks. "Teach her what she needs to know."

The taste of approaching revenge makes my heart happy despite its panicked beats. I'm going to make this asshole pay for his sins. I'll inject him with this sedative and hand him over to the devil to play with.

Then he can see what it's like to be a victim.

"Remember what will happen if you don't behave." Luther slaps me on the ass and I jolt from the impact. "Now make me proud."

"Of course." I let the words roll off my tongue as I maneuver around the coffee table and into open space to wait for Luca to join me.

He's the one who looks at me with skepticism this time, his hazel eyes wary for brief moments before he leads me into the hall.

The first step away from prying eyes isn't a relief. The solitude with this bulky predator is daunting but I'm determined. Focused. I'll earn my way back into Luther's good graces.

I won't fail.

"Take the last door on the right." He slows his approach, making me take the lead.

There's no excitement in his tone. I'm surprised he's not salivating at the opportunity to violate me. Usually, men get a sly swing in their step when they know their perverted fantasies are about to be fulfilled. They act differently. There's an edge to them.

But not this man. He isn't showing an ounce of enthusiasm.

His bliss is tightly bottled.

As we pass exquisite artwork hung along the walls and the long line of lights in the ceiling, he remains closed off. It isn't until I reach the door and push it wide that he dares to touch me, his arm brushing my shoulder as he reaches inside to flick on the light.

It takes all my restraint not to bristle. Externally, anyway. On the inside I'm coiled tight, my mind primed and ready for me to strike.

"I still don't want to touch you," he snarls. "Just thought you'd prefer to see."

I try to siphon as much information as possible from his actions. I attempt to hear the deceit in his tone, and still I get nothing.

I can't grasp his intent.

I know he has a motive. It's now common knowledge at least one other slave is here. But I continue to struggle with his faux kindness.

"Thank you," I whisper. "The light is appreciated."

I step inside, my spine tingling as I enter a room consumed with his scent. It reminds me of yesterday. Of his kind, lying eyes. Of his conniving deception.

When the door clicks shut behind me there's no stopping my heart climbing into my throat. I can't help thinking about the consequences of possible failure, not only from Luther, but this brutal man.

His hidden motives taunt me. The walls he's built to hide his true self leave me with no insight of what's to come if I don't succeed.

"What did he do to you?" Luca walks around me, coming to stand like a bulky statue in front of me.

"Excuse me?"

"After we left you behind like fucking cowards," he growls. "What did Luther do to you?"

I bristle, hating his renewed stance on this friendly facade. The building kindness is unsettling. "My punishment is being handed over to Luther's son. And to you."

His eyes narrow, then lower. His attention treks down my body, scouring every inch of me. And still I don't witness his sexual interest. This man has an uncanny way of hiding his desire.

"You don't seem scared." His gaze slowly returns to mine. "Does that mean you're open to trusting me?"

"Of course." My response slips out too fast, the hint of sarcasm not helping my cause. He needs to think I'm his to break. A toy. A puppet.

He sighs. "I'm not going to hurt you, Penny. You can stay as far away from me as you want, but we need to talk."

No. There's no room for chatter. I don't want him weaving his manipulation into my brain again.

"We're not here to talk." I shuffle closer, bridging the distance between us so there's only a breath of space. I look up at him through my lashes and try my best to appear meek. "You heard Luther. I'm a gift."

I'm not a viper coiled to attack. I'm an object. A slave.

Believe me, Satan.

He stiffens, his jaw twitching a fraction. His eyes narrow, the intensity of his stare making my heart skip a beat.

I wait for him to comply. To finally steal what's right in front of him.

"You're not a fucking gift," he snarls. "You're not a fucking slave. All that is over."

A twinge of yearning plucks at my heartstrings before I quickly shut it down.

"Whatever you say," I keep my voice meek, testing to see if he prefers weak and vulnerable to my usual strong and combative as I avert my gaze like a true submissive. "I'm yours to command. Just tell me what you need."

A growl emanates from his chest, the low rumble inspiring goosebumps along my exposed arms.

"What I need," he grates, "is for you to understand that I don't want to fucking touch you. Not now or in the future. I'm not Luther."

No, he's not.

I'm well aware he's an entirely new monster. One with different intricacies and fetishes.

"I understand." I keep my head lowered, the tube burning hot against my belly. "You're not like other men. You're special."

He scoffs. "No, I'm not. I'm just a guy who wants to fucking help you." He reaches into the back of his jeans and pulls out a cell. "Look."

He presses the screen a few times, then holds it up to me. My heart stops as he scrolls through images, picture upon picture of an innocent girl with a dazzling smile.

"This is you, right?"

It takes long seconds for me to shake my head, denying my past. The woman on the screen isn't me. Not anymore. I look nothing like her. The light left my eyes long ago. The natural exuberance no longer exists. What took its place is the polished beauty paid for by a wealthy sex trafficker. The perfectly waxed skin. The regularly manicured nails and tinted hair. With all these services dished out by people who ignored my plight for freedom.

"I know who you are," he continues. "I know your brother. Decker and I work together. Believe me, I won't do a fucking thing to hurt you. I'm here to help."

Decker.

My surname slices through me with the force of a steal blade.

Neither one of my brothers has ever taken our last name as a nickname. This man is making assumptions. Playing games.

He found my past online and is using the information to continue his trickery.

"You're confused," I whisper. "That's not me. I have no brother."

I focus on letting all emotion slip through me. I don't dwell on the aching memories. I shove everything from my mind, growing hollow... all except for the tiniest flicker of light beginning to creep its way through the darkness of my solitude.

What if he does know one of my brothers? What if he knows the woman I used to be?

I clear my throat, dislodging the instability trying to ooze its way back into me.

I'm not that woman on the screen anymore.

That life belonged to someone else.

There's no family waiting for me.

No love to welcome me home.

"What?" His brows pull tight, his confusion heavy. "Why are you denying it? This is obviously you." He taps the cell screen, scrolling through more triggers, weaving more manipulation.

I can't let him continue.

This has to stop.

"I'm sorry, but you're confused." I step into him and reach for his arm to lower the phone from view. "And besides, who I am doesn't matter when you're here to teach me the ropes."

I grip the softness of his T-shirt and maneuver my hands beneath the material to place my palms on his stomach. His muscles tense at my touch.

"Penny," he warns. "Stop."

My pulse increases. My chest tightens.

I wait for the usual revulsion to overwhelm me, but the nauseating protest doesn't appear.

For some reason, there's no humiliation. No sickening disgust.

Instead, there's apprehension. Thick and cloying concern.

He's not acting the way I've come to expect from Luther and his men.

He's not devouring this opportunity like a stereotypical predator.

"You don't want me?" I ask, sounding offended. "Aren't I as tempting as your little fox?"

The reminder of the other woman is for my benefit. I need to remember he's not innocent.

"You're a temptation, but not in the way you think." His tone is gentle as he steps back. "You don't need to do this."

He's wrong.

This is exactly what I need to do. I have to get closer. Distract him further. Add more confusion.

"I'm a gift." I grab his belt and begin to pull it from its confinement.

"Jesus Christ. *Stop.*" He pushes at my wrists. "Just fucking stop."

He's revolted by me and somehow this humiliation is far worse than what I'm used to.

I'm not good enough for him.

Or maybe I'm too used. Too abused. Too broken.

He has the opportunity to take anything he wants and he hungers for nothing. There's no perversion in his eyes. No deviance.

I don't know what to do. I need to be close. I can't strike from this distance. "Luca, I..."

Words fail me as my cheeks heat in shame.

Has my life sunken so low I now need to beg for violation? Is that where this hellish existence has led to?

"Please," I plea, my humiliation plunging marrow-deep.

"I don't want to fuck you," he snarls. "I want to *help* you."

"Then help me by letting me do my job. Let me make up for hitting you yesterday."

His nostrils flare. "As far as I'm concerned, I deserved your aggression. And I deserve far more for leaving you behind. But for now, you're going to wait in here while I go back out there to keep an eye on Luther."

No. Jesus Christ, *no.*

He can't distract Tobias from his mission. He can't stop me from succeeding, either.

Luca stalks around me, heading toward the door as undiluted fear sweeps through me.

"Wait." I pluck the hidden device from my waistband and tuck it into my palm, keeping the weapon out of view as I scramble to catch up.

He doesn't pause. He gets to the door and reaches for the handle.

This is it. I have to strike.

I run, raising my hand high, then launch myself at him.

5

LUCA

HER FRANTIC FOOTSTEPS APPROACH, HER SHADOW QUICKLY CLIMBING ACROSS THE door in front of me.

I wait until she closes in, her rampant breathing reaching my ears, before I spin around and grab the arm violently charging toward me.

She's got a weapon—some sort of plastic device—but I ignore it for now as I sidestep, forcing her to follow with a jolt of my wrist. She turns with my harsh movements, her lithe body malleable to my direction when I shove her toward the door.

A quick palm against the wood is all that saves her face from sudden impact as I twist her other arm behind her back.

She doesn't cry out. There's no plea for help or scream for salvation.

Instead, her breathing increases, her panic only shown in the short, sharp rasps for air.

"What the fuck?" I snarl in her ear as I focus on the cylindrical tube she clutches in a white-knuckled grip. "What the hell is this?"

She doesn't respond. There's no struggle or fight, only tightly coiled hostility.

"*What the fuck?*" I repeat, sliding my hold to her fingers to wrench the device from her grip.

"No," she begs. "Don't."

Her plea kills me, fucking strips me bare. I can't believe what I'm doing to such a fragile, vulnerable woman. If only it wasn't clear she was trying to take me down.

"Then start talking." I place my forearm against her back, loosely keeping her trapped as I inspect the weapon. "What is this?"

"Let me go and I'll tell you."

I snicker a scorn-filled laugh, attempting to gain answers through aggressive taunts so I don't have to take alternate measures. "Nice try. But no dice. Tell me what's going on before you get yourself in more trouble."

"Please." Her voice cracks. "You said you want to help me. So help me. Give it back. Let me walk out of here and pretend this never happened."

"No way in hell, shorty."

For starters, I'm not letting her go anywhere near Luther. Not again. Not after I made the mistake of following Cole's instruction to leave her kneeling on the kitchen floor yesterday. And I sure as shit won't be handing over the instrument she felt inclined to stab at my neck.

"Was this your idea or his?" I grip the crook of her arm and turn her to face me, her wide eyes blinking up at me in panic, her skin pale, those ruby lips parted. "Talk," I growl.

"Please don't say anything." Her delicate throat works over a heavy swallow. "It was my idea. Luther doesn't know. He isn't even aware I stole the syringe from him months ago. I just wanted to pay you back for taunting me yesterday."

"Pay me back how? What was the desired outcome? Is this lethal?"

"No." She shakes her head. "It's only a sedative. You would've fallen asleep instead of…" She glances away, her brows pinching.

"Instead of raping you?"

She nods, the movement gentle.

She's such a pretty little liar.

We both know I wasn't about to assault her. I was leaving the fucking room, for Christ's sake.

"Please, can I have it back?" She grates her teeth over her lower lip. "I promise I won't use it."

I hold in a scoff as I remain against her, so close I can hear the gentle rasp of her breath.

She's a contradiction—her body soft yet ready to strike, her dark eyes gentle even though trepidation lingers beneath.

"Please, Luca, it was a mistake." She grasps the top of the device, her fragile hand clasped over mine. "He'll kill me if he finds out. He'll probably kill me when he realizes it's missing from his stash. Let me take it so I can put it back."

I grin, the curve of my lips far from friendly. "But you're a gift, remember? There's no going back."

She should be fully aware there's no returning to Luther unless something else is at play.

"Tell me what's going on." I shove the device in my back pocket, not allowing her an inch of freedom. "*Now*, Penny."

A ragged exhale shudders from her lips. "You don't understand." She implores me with her frantic tone. "He'll kill me."

"He's not going to touch you."

"Yes, he will. And he'll hurt my friends, too. My sisters. You can't save me."

"Bullshit." I get in her face, eye to eye, almost nose to nose, making sure she's got a front row view to my sincerity. "I *will* save you."

There's no doubt in my mind. She won't leave this island a slave. Not while there's still air in my lungs.

Her gaze hardens, the deep brown turning punishingly dark. "And what about the little fox you've beaten? Will you save her, too?"

She tilts her chin, showing defiance. *Spite.*

She thinks she knows me, thinks she's got me all figured out.

"The beaten little fox isn't a prisoner." I back off, giving her animosity room to breathe. "She's on our side. *Your* side."

"Is that why you beat her?"

"I didn't," I grate. "Robert is responsible for hurting her, but he paid for that mistake with his life."

Her eyes flare.

For a second, the slightest glimmer of hope brightens her features, increasing her beauty, before it's quickly suffocated by suspicion.

"I don't believe you." She shuffles out from between me and the door. "Robert isn't dead."

"I think the bullet that took his life would disagree."

She blinks and blinks, her disbelief lingering. "She killed him?"

"No, Luther did."

"I don't understand." She screws up her nose. "Luther would never—"

"He had no choice. That asshole's death is the only reason Cole is still civil with his father. It's the price he had to pay for what his goon did to Anissa."

"Anissa?"

Fucking hell, I don't have the patience or the time for this. "The little fox," I snap. "Nobody hurts one of ours and gets away with it."

"Oh." Her mouth forms a pouty circle. "I..."

"What?"

She shakes her head. "I don't know... I... I want to trust you. Really, I do." She raises her focus to mine. "I'm just not sure how."

I don't buy it. She's still got tricks up her sleeve and I'm running out of time to figure them out.

"What if I gave you back your weapon?" I hedge. "Would you trust me then?"

Her tongue snakes out to quickly swipe her lower lip. It's devious. "You'd do that?"

I'm fucking tempted that's for sure.

It's those eyes. The strength. She undoes me with her determination despite the shattered pieces of her psyche I itch to place back together.

"Here." I reach into my pocket and pull out the cylindrical tube. "Take it. It's yours."

She inches back, her disbelief a sweet price to pay.

"It's okay." I nudge the device closer to her. "Take it."

Hesitation reclaims her features as she eyes the weapon, her attention moving from my hand, to my wrist, and farther along my arm.

Fucking subtle.

She's devising another plan to jab me. She practically has *Plan B* written on her forehead in neon.

"Thanks." She steps forward, cautious.

Those delicate fingers brush my skin as she claims her prize.

But the thing is, her touch is worth the upcoming battle. The graze of her fingertips is the softest friction. A hypnotic fucking spell. And when her attention returns to my face I can almost pretend she's peering back at me in sincerity.

Unfortunately, I know better in that regard, too.

She sinks her teeth into her lower lip, trying to play the timid yet thankful role. To get closer. To obtain the perfect vantage point to strike from. It's so fucking obvious it plays out in my head like a movie before she even makes a move.

"Really," she whispers. "Thank you."

I keep my jaw locked and pretend every one of my nerves isn't hyper-sensitive as I tell her, "Don't mention it."

My sincerity doesn't stop her from tightening her grip on the weapon, though. And the resulting twitch of my cock isn't my proudest moment.

Some sick part of me wants her to fight. Adrenaline floods my system at the thought of another reason to grab her.

"How do you plan on getting me out of here?" She creeps closer. "Just because Luther handed me over doesn't mean he'll allow my freedom. It's too big a risk."

"Let me worry about that." I remain still, on alert, patiently waiting.

I should warn her not to follow through with her attack. If I was the good guy I'm pretending to be, I'd tell her to think twice. But she's made it clear she has no desire to give me the truth. Not in words anyway. I'll figure her out from her actions.

"Okay." She nestles closer. "I trust you."

The jut of her hand is quick. Lightning fast. I almost don't catch it in time as she aims for my stomach.

"Too slow." I snatch her wrist before impact, pull her forward, and sweep out my leg to knock her feet out from beneath her. I push her off-balance, delight in her gasp, and keep clinging to her arm as she falls.

I guide her slightly, making sure she doesn't hit the carpet too hard. But then I'm all over her, pinning her body beneath mine and her hands above her head.

"I'm done playing games." I smother her with my weight. "This was never about payback, or getting the syringe to Luther."

She turns rigid, yet again refusing to call for help. It's clear she knows she's on her own. With no one to save her.

Well, she has me now. If only she'd fucking realize it.

"This is the last time I tell you—" I get in her face, her snarled lips a whisper from mine. "—I'm here to fucking save you. You hear me? You're free."

She bares her teeth. Glares. Thrashes.

Again, it's not my proudest fucking moment when my dick enjoys the extravaganza. I don't want to appreciate the way she writhes beneath me. God knows, Decker will kill me if he ever finds out.

"Stop fighting. Stop treating me like the fucking enemy." I keep her pinned. "That woman you think is here against her will is working with us." I shouldn't be telling her this. It's too dangerous. For her *and* me. "We're taking down Luther's operation. We won't stop until we succeed."

She lessens her fight for freedom.

"It's true," I continue. "The nightmare is over. You're going home. But I need you to tell me if this attack was you. You have to be honest and let me know what I'm up against."

She stares at me, those penetrating eyes scouring my face as if she's searching for the Holy Grail. She's starting to believe me. Finally, I'm getting through to her.

"Do you want me to call your brother? Is that it?" Slowly, I release her hands, keeping my attention on her weapon as I grab the cell from my jeans. "If I get him on the phone so you can speak to him, will you finally quit fighting?"

Her face pales, all the blood draining from her cheeks in an instant. "No." She shakes her head. "I told you, I don't have a brother."

Why the fuck does she keep saying that?

It's crystal clear she's Penny Decker—Sebastian's sister—the woman who was tempted away from the safety of her home by lies Luther fed her about a modelling career. If I've heard the story once, I've heard it a million times.

I know her. I've read the missing persons report. I spent all goddamn night scouring the internet, devouring everything I could find about her.

"Fine." I climb off her, snatching her weapon as I go. "Have it your way." I drop the cylinder to the carpet and crack it beneath my boot.

"*No.*" She scrambles onto all fours and lunges for my feet. "*Don't.*"

"It's done. Gone. Get over it." I press harder, twisting my ankle from side to side as the device fractures. "Now, I'm preparing to go out there, guns blazing, because I've got a feeling this attack wasn't your idea, but I need you to confirm it for me, okay? I need you to tell me, either way, was this you or him? Does Luther have anything else up his sleeve?"

She claws at my boot, thumping and tugging.

"Penny," I snarl. "I need information so I can protect you properly. So I can protect that fucking kid."

She slumps onto her haunches, her face crumpling with defeat.

"You or him?" I repeat.

More than her answer, I want her surrender. I want her to quit fighting and give in to me. To my protection.

"Penny," I warn.

Her head falls back, lulling on her shoulders. I stop breathing as her lips part, her silent acquiescence already the sweetest sound to my ears.

"Luca." Torian's voice punches through my anticipation, his call faint. "Luc."

Panic hits me, but it's the sudden flare of fear in her eyes that makes me freeze. She knows what's going on out there and it's scaring the hell out of her.

"Tell me." I grip her chin. "Tell me."

I should be running for my boss, gun in hand. Instead, I can't drag myself away from her. I tell myself it's only for one more second in the hopes she'll comply. Because information is key, right? I could gain an advantage over whatever the hell is going on out there if only she would give in to me.

"Luca," Torian roars.

Shit.

I shake off my obsession with her and rush for the door, grabbing my pistol from the back of my waistband.

"Luca..."

Her voice is heaven to my ears. If only it wasn't too little too late. I can't hang around any longer.

"Luc, wait."

Fuck.

I turn, finding her staring back at me, her forehead etched in pain.

"He's out to get you." There's remorse in her tone. In her eyes, too. "And I have no doubt he'll succeed."

6

PENNY

Luca dashes from the room, not acknowledging my pained admission with more than a narrowed stare.

He's going to get himself killed.

All of us could die in the melee.

Oh, God, *Tobias*.

I rush to my feet and scramble to follow him. As I enter the hall, I find Luca crouched before Tobias, a finger to his lips as he instructs Luther's son to remain quiet.

For a brief moment I'm struck with the kindness in his features. The gentle nurturing that seems one hundred percent pure. Then he looks at me, his gaze hardening as he pushes to his feet.

"*Go*," he mouths to Tobias. "*Hide.*"

The boy rushes toward me and I usher him into the room, mimicking Luca's warning to keep as quiet as possible with a finger to my mouth.

"What's going on?" I whisper.

"Dad told me to come get you. You need to go to him."

I nod. "I will. But first, you have to hide, okay?"

He opens his mouth to protest.

"Not now, Tobias. You need to listen. *Hide*. Get under the bed. Or in the closet. But don't come out, you hear me?"

"What's happening?" His voice breaks with a sob.

"I don't know. I have to go with Luca to find out."

"But you were meant to—"

I shake my head at him, cutting off his words. I'm well aware of what I was meant to do. I know I failed. "Did you do it? Did you sedate Cole?" I murmur.

He winces, his tiny shoulders curling in on themselves.

"Don't worry. You did great." I smile at him, my heart breaking at the thought of this possibly being our final goodbye.

Luther will kill me for failing.

Me, and the man I endangered.

"Now it's important you hide." I shoo him farther into the room and grab the door handle. "Don't come out until I get you."

I want to tell him I love him. There're so many things I need this little boy to know, but I close the barrier between us and force myself to remain strong as I turn to Luca.

He's in the middle of the hall, creeping toward the entry to the living room, his gun raised. He's about to start a war. And with Cole drugged, he'll surely get himself killed.

"Stop," I whisper. I run for him on the tips of my toes.

He doesn't listen, stepping into the light from the main room, his shoulders strong, his face stony as he points his barrel at a target I can't see.

"*Luther*," he yells. "Drop it."

I skitter to a stop beside him as gunfire rings out, the booming sound pummeling toward us.

Pop.

Pop.

I duck, my pathetic attempt to protect myself improved when Luca shoves me back into the sanctuary of the hall.

I stumble against the wall as he rushes into the living room, more *pop, pop, pops* raining down.

I'm too stunned to scream. I'm completely dazed, and it's not only because of the battle or the shouting voices. It's because Luca shoved me.

Protected me.

In the heat of the moment, when he was surrounded by danger, his first instinct was to push me out of harm's way.

He did as he promised.

He attempted to save me.

I remain immobile as voices brush my ears—the sound of Chris talking from outside, then Luther, and even a slurred response from Cole. Grunts and thumps carry from the main room. There are clear sounds of a struggle and all I can think about is the man who tried to help me. The one who is now eerily silent.

Luther's laugh is the only noise that penetrates my shock, the conniving tone filling me with dread.

"It's too late. I got him," he taunts. "Penny, check to make sure Luca's dead."

Oh, God.

I prop myself against the wall and beg my legs to strengthen beneath me. I can't stop shaking. I can't even breathe properly as I fumble my way to the hall entry and find Luther on the floor, leaning on his elbows, his face awash with smug satisfaction as his son sways on his feet, barely remaining upright.

Their expressions paint a horrid picture—Luther's victorious and egotistical, Cole's devastated and confused.

Guilt has me searching for the man who offered kindness. The one I find shielded behind the back of a sofa, his body lifeless, one cheek covered in blood.

A cry builds in my throat, demanding to be heard. I let the pressure assault me. Punish.

He was my only chance at freedom and I let him slip through my fingers. He was my savior and I treated him like a predator.

"Don't go near him." Cole fumbles over his words. "Get the fuck away."

I ignore him in my need to confirm Luca's death, not only to appease my tormentor, but for my own insight. I have to feel the void where there should be a heartbeat, to let the lack of life slice another scar into my tormented soul.

"Luther, I'm sorry." I inch into the room. "I'm so sorry. I tried to stab him with the sedative but he stopped me. He was too quick." The explanation fumbles from my lips. "I didn't know what to do. I thought maybe I could—"

"Just check him." Luther crawls to his feet.

I do as I'm told, starting toward Luca's prone body, following the crimson trail staining the ivory tiles. I scour every inch of him hoping for movement, my gaze trekking from the heavy boots, along his thighs, across his stomach, to his neck, chin, and mouth. My gaze finally comes to rest on the hazel eyes slowly blinking back at me.

He raises a shaky hand to his lips, requesting my silence.

I should tell Luther. I *need* to inform my owner of the threat, yet the words don't form. I'm incapable of announcing this man's vulnerability. Not after he tried to save me. Yet I have to say something.

"There's blood." My voice trembles. "It's coming from his head."

Luca crooks a finger, beckoning me forward.

My heart drops.

I don't want to go to him, yet I'm drawn. Pulled. My feet creep closer of their own accord, then I'm crouching, succumbing to his silent command.

"Penny," Luther growls. "What are you doing?"

"His pulse… I-I'm checking his pulse."

What I'm really doing is staring into the eyes of the man who has fractured me. The one who fills me with relief because he's still alive. But there's no justification for my celebration, not when I'm responsible for his injuries, and his upcoming death.

"*I'm sorry.*" I break our visual connection in an attempt to sever my guilt and focus on the lengthy gash along the side of his head, the oozing blood matting his hair. I'm about to reach out, to sweep the strands away to inspect his wound when Cole curses, the violent outburst from the other side of my hiding place enough to make me retreat.

"Get his weapon," Luther demands of me. "Then unlock the door and hand it to Chris."

"Don't do it," Cole snarls. "Don't fucking do it, Penny."

My heart sinks as I glance to my left and find Luca's gun on the tile a few feet away.

There's no choice. With Luther armed and Chris waiting outside, evil has already prevailed.

Gentle fingers brush my wrist, stealing my attention. My focus. I meet Luca's gaze. I see the struggle to fight etched in his features—the tight lips, the drawn brows.

"*Don't,*" he mouths, begging me with his eyes. "*Don't do it.*"

For once, I want to please him. A criminal. A *man.* I'd give anything to grant his wish. Instead, I paste on a regretful smile, hoping he understands the apology that comes with it.

I should've told him what was happening when we were alone in the bedroom. I should've let down my guard and believed his promises. Then this situation might have ended differently.

But the bad guys always win.

"She does what she's told," Luther seethes. "Otherwise she knows the consequences."

I straighten, hearing the threat loud and clear.

"What's to stop her shooting you?" Cole asks.

"She could try. But she'd be dead before she had time to aim. And then I'd kill all her friends just to spite her."

That's why I have no choice. *That's* why I have to take Luca's gun.

I reach for the weapon a few feet away, my fingers tingling as my palm slides over the blood-slicked exterior. It's a strange sensation—touching a gun for the first time. The slightest ebb of power flows through me as I grip the cold metal in both hands.

If only I could shoot Luther. If I had the experience and skills to risk everything on a quick draw, I would.

Luca's hand reclaims my wrist, the fingers trailing slowly over my skin. "*Give it here,*" he mouths.

I want to. I want nothing more than to let him continue to be the savior he promised to be. I just can't. I won't place my life in the hands of a stranger. Nor the lives of the women waiting for my return. Not when he's possible heartbeats away from death.

"*I'm sorry.*" My lips form the silent words as remorse slaughters me from the inside out. "I've got the gun," I announce to the room and stand.

I forget about the man at my feet. I shut out the guilt and shame.

"Keep it," Cole slurs. "Don't give it to Chris."

"Don't even think about it." Luther jabs his son in the shoulder with his gun as if sensing an act of retaliation. "You're predictable. Always have been."

"Too bad you've already admitted you won't kill me, old man."

I ignore their squabbling and focus on what has to be done. Everything fades away as my bare feet trek the cool tile toward the glass door covered by a sheer curtain. I can already see Chris standing in wait on the other side. I can feel his darkness. Can predict more bloodshed.

"Tell Penny not to give him the gun and we can talk this out." Cole's words are garbled. "That's what you want, right? To show me the error of my ways?"

I shut him out. I shut *everything* out.

There's only the wild beat of my pulse and hollowness. An empty void carves its existence into my soul, preparing me for death.

I don't stop my progression toward the door. I don't pause even though the only option I have makes my heart stutter.

Life doesn't flash before my eyes—it blinks slowly. Snapshots of memories I've longed to forget assail me. I see my parents. My brothers. My friends. Everything drifts into my mind until I reach the curtain and pull it aside.

"Tell her to stop. *Do it.*" Cole raises his voice. "Penny. Don't. Don't be stupid."

The argument continues behind me. I'm sure the sound of a scuffle or a fight brushes my ears, but all I see is Chris. The cold stare. The conniving smirk.

His crimes come back to haunt me as I tighten the gun in my grip, yet there's no uncertainty in his expression. There's no doubt in his mind I'll hand over the weapon like a good little slave.

His opinion of me is humiliating.

The condescension. The superiority.

I unflick the lock and yank the door wide, the sea breeze kissing my cheeks while his smirk increases.

He doesn't rush me. He only provokes with his confident leer, waiting for me to comply to yet another demand. Even with a weapon drawn in his direction he's entirely certain I won't shoot him. How could I when a lifetime of conditioning has ensured I'll obey?

"*No,*" Cole yells, the protest ringing in my ears.

I don't want to do this. I'm scared. Nauseous.

I raise the gun in both hands, slowly inching it toward my enemy, the aim creeping from his feet, along his legs, to his stomach.

The more dire my aim, the more Chris smirks.

"That's a good pretty Penny," he drawls, the taunt barely audible yet deeply unsettling.

Cole shouts another protest. There's another scuffle of feet. Then a warning from Luther.

A million rampant heartbeats pass and still the smirk beaming back at me doesn't falter. Not until I force myself to smile back, my lips slowly lifting in a mirrored taunt.

For a second, the most beautiful sight of trepidation blinks back at me. All it takes is a squeeze of the trigger to cement his fear in place.

Pop. Pop.

My arms shake with the blasts. My ears ring.

Chris jolts with both impacts, his eyes widening, his skin turning pale as a lake of red seeps from the holes in his shirt.

His descent is fluid, almost beautiful, as he falls backward, sailing through the air until his head hits the cement tile with a deafening crack.

Pride rushes through me as the gun slides from my fingers and a sob of achievement escapes my throat.

"I'll fucking kill you," Luther roars.

Yes, he will. That outcome was always blindingly obvious.

I close my eyes, raise my face to the dawning sun, and wait for piercing bullets to take my life.

"Get down," Cole yells. "*Hide.*"

I don't move. I crave the anticipated peace. I want the freedom of death.

"I've got her."

There's more scuffling. Footsteps patter behind me. But that voice. It wasn't Cole. Or Luther.

I spin. Luca charges toward me, his face stricken, the barrel of Luther's gun quickly trekking his movements.

I open my mouth, a scream of warning about to launch from my throat.

Pop. Pop.

Luca slams into me and we fall backward, hitting the floor with enough force to wind me.

Shouts rain. A frenzy of movement ensues. But all I can do is gasp for air as I'm dragged behind the kitchen island counter and propped against the cupboards.

"Are you okay?" He crouches before me, his blood-covered hands roaming my face, shoulders, arms. "Were you shot?"

I shake my head as I struggle for breath.

The side of his head drips with crimson, the rivulets descending from his hairline as he continues to search me, his gaze stopping at my cream pants now splattered with red.

"It's yours," I murmur. "I'm not hurt."

That penetrating gaze returns to mine, his intensity adding to the whir of adrenaline intoxicating my system.

"It's not my blood," I repeat. "I'm fine."

He nods, the movement laced with a wince, then pivots toward the danger, his back to me as he raises one leg of his jeans and retrieves a knife from a sheath attached to his ankle.

"It's over, Dad. Your new protege failed to inject me properly," Cole mumbles the words. "Your dog is dead. And you fucked up when you thought you took Luca out."

"You forget I'm the only one with a weapon, son."

I inch farther back into my hiding place, completely aware of Luther's power. He's got the gun. He isn't injured. He's in control.

"I'm sorry, motherfucker, but you're mistaken."

A woman's voice catches me off guard as she walks inside through the open glass doors.

She has to be the little fox.

She clutches a gun in her hands, her shoulders high and strong, her face hardened like a warrior's. "Lower the weapon, Luther. Hand it over and this may not have to end badly."

I need to help her. I have to stop hiding like a child and grab the gun I dropped. I can run. Sprint. Slide and snatch.

Luca glances over his shoulder at me and mouths, *"Get back."*

I shake my head and jut my chin in the direction of my weapon.

"Get back," he repeats, his arm reaching out to guide me into submission.

He ignores my plan—ignores me in general—as he creeps closer to the edge of our island hiding place and sneaks a peek around the cupboards.

"Don't shoot, Nis," Cole demands. "He won't kill me."

Luther won't kill him? Is he kidding?

I fumble onto my haunches, preparing to make a run for salvation as Luther drawls out a pithy insult. I either want to die in a rain of bullets or be completely freed. I won't sit by as the devil regains the upper hand so he can draw out my punishment for days.

Weeks.

Months.

I'm about to make a run for it when Luca lunges for me, his trunk of an arm tackling me around the waist to haul me back into him.

I fight his hold as he drags me between his legs, his thighs closing in around me, the knife clutched in his free hand.

"Quit it," he growls low in my ear, his voice barely audible over the threats and demands being continuously flung around the armed standoff. "Cole needs to finish this. It's his right. Otherwise I would've already done it myself."

I shake my head, denying his words and the voices screaming in my skull.

My instincts demand I take action.

"Don't be scared," he whispers. "Trust me."

I keep shaking my head, over and over, trying to drown out the mania.

I'm going to be tied to a table. I'll be brutalized by anyone and everyone who enters Luther's house.

"He's safe, Anissa," Luca speaks louder. "Give Cole your gun and let him finish this."

I struggle to focus on the conversation. Who's safe? Cole? Tobias?

Doesn't Luca realize nobody is free from harm when Luther is armed?

I wiggle, attempting to break free of his strong hold but Luca grips me tighter, hugging my back to his chest.

"I've got you," he murmurs. "Just drown it out. This will be over soon."

I try. I concentrate so hard on escaping to my mental sanctuary. I hide in silence, in darkness, and still the panic finds me.

Cole's slurred words brush the edge of my consciousness.

The woman's demands haunt me.

Then Luca speaks up. "I'm not hiding, asshole. I'm giving Cole space to finish this his way. And if he can't, I'm on standby with a knife in my hand, ready and willing to slit your throat."

There's so much vehemence in his tone. A wealth of determined conviction.

I want to believe him.

I can picture this man sinking his blade into my enemy's neck. But he won't. He can't.

Not when Luther always wins.

Evil. Always. Conquers.

Luca holds me tighter. I can't stop fighting and I'm not sure if it's because I want to escape his touch or I fear he'll soon be killed if I don't act.

It's too much.

It's all too much.

"Give him your gun." Luca waves at the woman. "Let him finish this."

No. *No.*

I rock harder, willing the madness away. Begging for my life to be over.

I can't go back. I won't.

The woman steps out of view and I sense a change in the air. The tension builds around us.

"Cole, I'm going to shoot," she announces. "I can't let him take another step."

Luther must be close. Almost within range of the island counter.

Luca loosens his hold and slides out from behind me, his weapon at the ready, his body crouching lower as if preparing for battle.

I need to fight.

I can't hide. I can't show weakness. But that's what my potential savior is asking of me—to remain vulnerable. To cower.

I slide back to the wall, bow my head and jam my fingers into my ears. It's all I can do to stop myself from running for that gun when everything inside me is screaming to *fight, fight, fight.*

I rock on my haunches like a child. I pretend it's only a matter of time before Luther is taken down, when in reality I know he's seconds away from killing this woman… then his adult son… followed by the man at my side… then me.

"Stop. *Luther. Stop,*" she yells. "Release the gun or I'll shoot."

I can still hear her. The panic. The fear.

I rock harder. Faster.

"Cole?" the woman pleads.

I can feel Luther behind me. It's as if he's right there, peering down, the whole world entirely still. Only me and him. Power pitted against instability.

Pop.

I jerk backward at the sudden blast, my ears ringing, my head filling with static.

Luca rushes to his feet and I frantically scramble to follow, both of us joining the woman who stands tall, and Cole who is hunched on the tile, as we stare at Luther laid flat on the floor.

Blood seeps from his mouth as he gurgles and splutters, the gun remaining tight in his grip.

My tormentor continues to breathe, his chest rising and falling while the barrel of his weapon slowly edges its way toward his son.

He's going to shoot. He's going to—

Pop.

Pop.

I jump with the explosions.

Pop.

Pop.

Anissa keeps shooting, over and over until the wild bursts of noise resemble hollow clicks and the man who stole my life stares blankly ahead. Not breathing. Not blinking.

Dead.

I always anticipated blinding happiness when I fantasized about this moment. I thought I'd want to laugh. To dance. To celebrate.

None of the jubilation hits me.

There's no bliss. Not even peace.

I'm still hollow.

Empty.

Until Tobias's sweet voice calls from the hall. "Baba? *Baba?*"

7

LUCA

I keep seeing her. The frantic rush across the room. The desperate way she scooped the kid into her arms and carried him into the hall.

I thought about nothing but Penny as Cole and I loaded the dead bodies onto Luther's boat. I escorted those fuckers out to sea while Cole tailed me in another vessel.

It wasn't hard to dispose of the evidence.

I weighed down the cadavers and threw them overboard, keeping watch until they sank from view. Then I gave Cole instructions on how to rig his father's boat to drive unaided, because my head throbbed so much I couldn't fucking do it myself.

Even now, as I clean my own blood off the living room wall, my brain protests every movement. It feels like I'm one sneeze away from an aneurism. Or a fucking stroke.

And still, Penny plagues my thoughts. She's been left alone for too long. Both her *and* the kid. The only reason I know they haven't attempted escape is because the sound of a sniffling child continues to echo down the hall.

"When are you going to speak to the boy?" I ask Cole.

He stops scrubbing the crimson splotches on the floor and leans back on his haunches. "I'm not sure. I thought it might be better to wait until his father's insides are cleaned off the tile."

I grate my teeth at his sarcasm. "The longer you leave it, the harder it will be."

"Then you go." He jerks his chin at me. "Play the hero. Go beat your chest and attempt to win over Decker's sister. See how far it gets you."

I ignore the derision and scrub harder, the pungent scent of bleach searing my nostrils.

This isn't about me 'playing the hero.'

She's been through hell, not only today, but for God knows how long. She's fragile. Temperamental. Volatile.

From the way she rocked behind the kitchen counter, I'd say she's one gentle gush of wind away from crumpling like a deck of cards.

It's in our best interest to keep an eye on her.

"Go on, Captain America," Cole drawls. "Save her from isolation."

Fuck it.

Fuck him.

He's been a major asshole since his father's murder, and I get it, the situation didn't end how he anticipated. He didn't take out the head of his family. A woman did. A Fed.

He made the mistake of sleeping with the enemy who swept the victory out from underneath him. But that's not my fault. I'd warned him about getting close to Anissa.

"Fine." I throw my cloth to the floor. "I will."

I stalk for the hall and follow the sound of a sniffing child all the way to my bedroom door. And there they are, huddled on the floor beneath the windowsill, Tobias snuggled in Penny's tight embrace.

As soon as I breach the threshold she stiffens, her panicked gaze meeting mine.

"It's okay." I creep inside the room. "I just wanted to see how you two are holding up."

The boy eyes me as if I'm his worst nightmare, his arms clutched around Penny's middle, his legs curled close to hers.

"We're dealing the best we can." She runs a hand through Tobias's hair, her mothering entirely natural.

"Can I get you anything? Food? Something to drink?"

Her gaze slowly treks me—from my face, all the way down to my hands. I do the same, taking in the blood splatter. Death stains every inch of me. My clothes. My skin. Some dried and cracking, other parts remaining liquified.

"I probably should've taken a quick look in the mirror before I came in."

She winces in agreement. "What's going on out there?"

I slowly inch to the bed and sit on the corner farthest from them, attempting a laidback demeanor. "We're just finishing the clean-up."

"What about the other woman? Is she still with you?"

"Anissa? No." I tread lightly in the hope Penny won't repeat information she never should've been privy to. "She's outside, clearing her head."

More accurately, I escorted her from the house because Cole couldn't stand to look at her. I'm sure she's down at the pier by now, impatiently waiting for a ticket out of here.

"I'd like to speak to her."

"Maybe later. For now, it's best if we all keep our distance It's been a long morning."

She falls quiet, her dark eyes filling with questions. "Can you at least tell me what happens next?"

"In terms of a detailed schedule, I have no idea." I shrug. "But you're not a prisoner, if that's what you're asking."

She sucks in a breath and straightens. "Good. Because I'd like to leave as soon as possible."

"Yeah, I get it. I'd be eager to get home, too. But it's going to take time. We're waiting on a jet—"

"No, I don't mean going home to the States. I'm talking about Luther's house. I need to get back there."

"What?" I push to my feet and she scrambles to do the same, panicked caution flooding her features.

"We need to leave." She drags Tobias to stand alongside her. "We have to get back to my sisters."

She straightens to her full height like a mighty warrior climbing from the pits of hell. But her invisible armor is flimsy at best. The bravado she exudes is fake. I can see under the facade to the frightened woman beneath.

I shake my head and mentally curse the resulting thud of my brain. "That's not an option."

"So I *am* a prisoner?" she rasps.

I massage my temples, attempting to alleviate the quickly building stroke. "If we're talking about being captive to your own stupidity, then yeah, I guess you're a prisoner. Because there's no way in hell you're leaving here until it's safe."

Her nostrils flare as I witness the little trust I'd gained flitter away with every spite-filled blink of her eyes.

"Look." I lower a hand from my temple, raising it, palm up, in peace. "It's not rational for you to be anywhere but here."

"It's not safe for my family if I stay." She starts for the door, Tobias tagging along at her side.

"Your family?" I stalk ahead and block their path. "I can assure you, they're fine. In fact, your brother is on his way here as we speak."

She stops, her eyes flaring, her gentle lips parted. Then the shock is hidden behind another firm squaring of her shoulders. "I don't have a brother."

Jesus Christ.

Not this shit again.

"Are you kidding me?"

"No, I'm not kidding you," she grates. "The only family I have are the women living in Luther's mansion, the ones who are fearing for my safety. The ones who are currently under more threat than I've ever been."

"They'll be okay. Cole will pull some strings and make sure they're taken care of."

"What strings?" Her question is flung like an accusation. "There are no strings when it comes to Luther's operation. The police won't help you. The locals won't either. Dead or not, Luther is still entirely in control, which means they're sitting ducks unless I can get to them."

The kid lets out a big sniffle, the sound shooting into my skull like another motherfucking bullet. I'm dying here. Slowly succumbing to the mental torment.

"I said we'd handle it." I return to massaging my temples. "You can trust me."

"I can trust you?" She frowns with incredulity. "The man who claims I'm not a prisoner, yet refuses to let me leave?"

Maybe if my brain wasn't currently being shoved through a grater I'd admire her tenacity, but this shit is getting old. For starters, Cole would never let her sail away from here with his half-brother. Not when she's not the kid's mother. She hasn't been missing long enough to carry the same blood as the child.

"I'm going to call your brother." I don't want to spoil the reunion. As far as Decker is concerned, his sister is dead. But I'm clutching at straws here. I don't know how else to get her to back down apart from pulling the cell from my jeans pocket. "You can speak to him for yourself. He can reassure you I'm trustworthy."

"No."

I dial his number anyway.

"I said *no*." Her expression turns frantic. Wide eyes. Pale skin. She's more scared now than when she was trying to jab me in the neck with a fucking syringe. "Turn it off."

I don't.

Instead, I switch the phone to speaker, the loud ring torture to my ears. "He thought he lost you a long time ago—"

"I said *turn it off*." She snatches for the device, attempting to claw it from my hand.

"What the fuck is wrong with you?" I hold the phone out of reach, the ringing continuing. "I thought you'd be excited to speak to family after all this time."

"I don't have a family." Her breathing becomes ragged. "Not back there. Not in the States. The only family I have is here."

She grabs at my arms, trying to get hold of the device, but the moment the call connects she freezes, her entire body turned to stone.

"This is me." Decker's voice fills the room. "Leave a message."

I bring the phone toward her as the answering service releases a high-pitched beep.

She doesn't speak. All she does is stare at the cell framed in my blood-stained hand.

"Are you going to say something?" I inch the phone closer.

She shakes her head, still staring.

Fucking hell.

I disconnect the call and place the device back in my jeans pocket.

"He's on his way." I lower my voice, trying like hell to comfort her as she wages a war behind those stricken eyes. "You're going to see him any minute now."

"No." She steps back, taking the kid with her. "I don't want to see him."

She's in shock. Fight or flight. Or any number of fucked up mental challenges associated with the shit storm she's been through. But she's on the home straight now. This is where her healing begins.

"It's okay." I reach for her, not sure what the fuck I'm doing. "You're safe."

"No." She slinks away from my touch, backtracking again and again. "*No*."

Fuck.

She's crumpling and that kid is about to go down with her if she doesn't pull up from the nose-dive.

"Penny, you're safe." I follow her, getting close to make sure she can hear, see, and feel my sincerity. "Robert, Chris, and Luther are gone. All the shit you've been through is over. And I swear on my own brother's life I'm going to get you home."

She shakes her head faster and faster, her breathing fractured as she stares right through me.

"I've got you." I reach out again, attempting to calm her with a touch. "It's going to be—"

"*No*." She scoots away. "I don't want to see him. I don't want to see any of them. I just want to leave."

I let her place space between us, taking it as a win that she's finally acknowledged her brother, no matter how minimal the admission.

"Penny…" Tobias tangles his fingers in her blouse, pulling the material down until he's close to popping a button. "I'm scared."

Her hyperventilating lessens.

Everything dilutes—the shaking of her head, the blink of fear-filled eyes. She reins in her crazy for the boy's sake.

"I'm sorry." She pivots to him, engulfing his shoulders in her arms to pull him tight against her. "There's no need to be scared. I'm just a little…"

"Overwhelmed?" I offer.

She winces and follows it up with a nod. "He's right. I'm overwhelmed."

"Is he still a bad man?" the kid mumbles, looking at me from his shielded position against her side. "Dad said he was telling Cole bad things."

Great. Fucking great.

I turn my attention to Penny and raise a brow. I'm not touching the kid's question with a ten-foot pole. One, because he sure as shit won't believe me. And two, because I have no idea what the fuck his scumbag father told him.

"We're going to be okay." She runs a hand through his hair, the placation timid at best. "Luca is trying to help us."

Trying?

My fucking ass I'm trying.

I conquered that bullshit when I risked my life to run through a spray of bullets and tackle her to safety.

We both know I mastered that motherfucker like a pro, but I don't have the focus or patience to point out the obvious.

"I'm going to leave you two alone." I hold tight for a few seconds, waiting for her to protest. Waiting for anything.

When she doesn't speak, I give up and back away. "I'll be in the living room. Call out if you need me."

Still, she doesn't react. All she does is continue to taunt my need to win her over.

I don't understand my obsession with earning her trust. But it's there, clawing its way under my skin.

It isn't until I reach the door that she breaks the silence.

"Luca." My name is gentle on her lips. "They don't have a lot of time."

"They?" I pause, not turning to face her.

There's a squeak of my mattress. She's on my fucking bed. "The women—my sisters. They aren't safe. Luther had plans to ensure we're never freed."

I remain in place, forcing myself not to imagine her sliding between my sheets. "How much time are we talkin' about?"

"I don't know."

"Okay." I nod, my back still facing her. "I'll take care of it."

God only knows how, but I will.

I leave them in the bedroom, my boots thudding down the hall, then into the living room where I find Cole still on his hands and knees on the bloodstained tiles.

"Have fun?" he asks.

"Yeah. A whole heap." I snatch my cloth from the floor and return to the gore plastered on the wall. "Just so you know, she's itching to get away from here. She says those women at your dad's house are under threat."

"I don't doubt it," he grates. "But we've got more important issues to deal with. Keira is already on the water. She'll be here any minute."

I pause my circular scrub. "Then I should also point out that Penny isn't doing cartwheels at the thought of seeing her brother, either."

He sits up straighter and cocks his ear toward the glass doors. "Well, that's too bad, because I can already hear their boat."

8

PENNY

I ENCOURAGE TOBIAS ONTO THE BED AND BEGIN TO PACE.

Luca had repeatedly referred to one of my brothers, never mentioning which of the two he was in contact with. Then he'd placed the call and the answering message had kicked in.

The familiar voice had collided with my skepticism, smashing it to smithereens.

Sebastian—the youngest of my two older siblings. The one who kept the high school bullies at bay. The playful jokester.

He has ties to Luca? He's on his way here?

"What's wrong?" Tobias pulls his knees to his chest and cuddles his legs. "What's happening?"

"Nothing." I stop mid-pace. "I'm just thinking."

"About Nina and Lilly?"

"Yes." I paste on a smile. "Abi and Chloe, too. We need to get back to them. It's really important."

He nods, not a moment of hesitation. "I don't want to stay here."

"Me either. And we won't. Not for long. But we might have to be a little sneaky to make sure we leave as soon as possible. Do you think you can handle that?"

"I'm always sneak—"

I hold up a hand, silencing him at the rumble of sound approaching the island. It's a boat. The grumble grows louder and louder.

My chest tightens. Arrhythmia takes over.

If that's Sebastian... if my brother is actually here...

A curdled mix of emotions strangle my insides—excitement, apprehension, impatience, fear.

I rush to the door and tilt my head to hear Luca and Cole's conversation. They're arguing about Anissa and when she should be sent home.

I hear the monotonous scrape of cleaning. The increased rumble from the boat. The building pound in my ears. Then the engine is cut and the fading gurgle makes me nauseous with indecision.

I itch to run for a brother that might be here to save me, yet I should hide from him, too.

I need him, and I have to stay away.

I can't fall victim to weakness now. Not when my battle is far from over. Those women in Luther's house are my top priority and succumbing to the allure of a savior won't help any of us.

A door whooshes open in the distance. An unfamiliar woman's voice rings out. And another. More men, too. But none I recognize.

I begin to sag with pained relief that my brother isn't here when a cocky voice enters the mix.

"I'm told I have some secret present waiting for me."

I suck in a ragged breath.

It's him.

Sebastian.

My blood surges. My heart pounds.

I'm torn. Broken in two. It's killing me not knowing if I should knock down my walls or build them higher. Keep battling or finally embrace vulnerability.

Every limb trembles with the need to surrender. I want, want, *want* my demons slain for me. It's all I yearn for. Yet I can't count on anyone. Not even a brother I previously would've entrusted with my life.

I back away from the door, letting longing slowly slip through my fingers.

"We need to get out of here, little guy." I paste on a smile and turn to Tobias still sitting on the bed. "Are you ready for an adventure?"

"Where are we going? Will we take Baba's boat back to Naxos?"

"Maybe. Do you know how to drive a boat?" I make the question light-hearted even though I seriously have no idea how we're going to get off this island. I'm not sure I'd even know how to drive a car anymore, let alone a boat.

He gives me a sheepish grin, the first pleasure-filled expression he's shown since this morning. "A little. Baba would let me steer the wheel sometimes."

"That's perfect."

It's entirely *not* perfect, but I'll figure it out.

If we can escape without being noticed maybe I can wave down a fisherman or some tourists. Someone has to be on the water nearby.

I help Tobias from the bed and lead him to the window. "We're going to climb out." I grip the frame, about to pull the window open when I notice the motion sensors attached to the glass.

Goddammit.

"What's wrong?" Tobias asks. "Do you need my help to lift it?"

My heart clenches at his sweetness. "No. It's okay. But maybe going out the window isn't the best idea."

I need to think.

Think. Think. Think.

My brain fails me, my concentration continuously returning to the mumbled words carrying from the living room.

"Penny?" Tobias grips my blouse. "I need to use the bathroom."

Shit.

"Can you hold on? Just for a little while?"

He winces. "I don't know."

"Where. The fuck. Is she?" My brother bellows from the living room.

He knows.

He's been told I'm alive.

I swing around, searching for another way of escape. I can't see him. Fragility already chips away at my bones.

"Penny?" Tobias tugs my blouse. "I'm scared."

I exhale a pained breath.

Think. Think. Think.

Pounding footsteps approach, the thunder echoing inside my chest, the noise adding to the thud of my pulse.

Then everything stops as if the world was carried away on the breeze.

There's no sound. No movement. Only the skitter of awareness at the back of my neck that tells me we're no longer alone.

"Penny?"

This time my name isn't spoken by Tobias.

It's *him*. The man I've fought not to think about for months on end.

I tremble. Everywhere.

It's hard to breathe as I turn and meet Sebastian's stare in the doorway.

Sweet relief floods my system, drowning me in happiness.

Weakness.

I raise my chin to the threat. Square my shoulders and force myself not to break.

"Penny?" he repeats, his forehead wrinkled in anguish.

He's older now, his bright eyes dull, his full smile non-existent. The man standing in the doorway has been hardened from the joyful young adult I remember.

I'm not sure I know this man and I'm certain he no longer knows me.

Tobias tugs my blouse again and whispers my name.

"It's okay, Toby." I clear the emotion from my throat but can't stop myself from guiding him to move behind me. "There's nothing to fear."

It's a lie.

I used to dream of this reunion. I'd picture how I would run to Sebastian once he'd saved me from this horror. I'd cry. He'd cry. Mom, Dad, and my older brother, Graham, would be there, too.

But those thoughts were merely fantasies when my captor made certain I would never be free.

I fear for my safety like never before. I'm scared this man will blind me to reality. That I'll get washed up in the reunion I've longed for and forget that Luther has a plan for me that won't end even though he's dead.

"Oh, God, I can't believe you're alive." Sebastian rushes forward.

I panic. Full-blown hysteria takes over.

"*Stop.*" I scramble backward, shielding Tobias behind me, one hand on his shoulder, the other stretched out in front of me in warning. "Stay where you are."

My brother freezes. "Penny, it's me." His voice is filled with rejection. And the way he looks at me. *God.* I can't take it.

I don't know how he got mixed up with Luca and Cole. I'm not sure I want to know. But I can't join him.

My sisters are still in danger. My *new family* need my help. And I won't be anything other than worthless if I let my brother take one step closer to my temperamental stability.

"I don't want to see you." I backtrack, inching closer to the window.

He jerks as if my words hit him like a physical blow.

I can't take the guilt. His sorrow strips layers from me—his judgment at who I've become slices deep.

"Please leave." I hold his stare, not softening the harshness of my expression. "Now."

His lips part. Shoulders slump. "I..."

Luca appears in the doorway, infusing me with relief.

"Get him out of here," I beg. "*Please.*"

"Don't panic." Luca edges into the room, stopping beside Sebastian. "You've got nothing to worry about."

I have *everything* to worry about—my brothers' safety, and that of my parents. I don't want any of them near me. Not now. Not ever.

"Make him leave." I creep closer and closer to the window.

"I will, I promise, but you need to tell me why."

I shake my head. I don't need to tell him anything. Not when my trust in him bounces like a rubber ball. One minute he's my savior, the next my captor.

"What the hell is going on?" Sebastian murmurs. "Why is she scared of me?"

The answer clogs my throat, the words filled with far too much depth and destruction for anyone to understand. Nobody here is capable of comprehending my fear over what I could do to him. What the dangers surrounding me will bring.

I just want to go back to pretending my family doesn't exist. My meager strength was far less brittle then.

Luca doesn't quit holding my gaze. He keeps the visual connection steady, not judging, not sympathizing. Just strong.

"Penny, Decker has put his life on the line for a long time all in an effort to find you."

I continue to back away, not wanting to hear the placations.

"He didn't willingly begin working with Cole," he continues. "It was all for you."

"You work for Cole?" I pin my brother with a stare, my insides begging for him to deny the betrayal. "You work for the family who took me?"

"It's not like that." He shakes his head. "It's complicated."

"We didn't know." A woman inches into the room. "We had no idea what was happening in Greece."

I cast my gaze over her, from the gleaming shoes, to the designer clothes, all the way up to her subtly perfect make-up. She's beautiful. But there's something about her that sets me on edge. A familiarity. "Who are you?"

"Keira." She gives a sad smile. "I'm Cole's sister. And I'm told this little guy is my half-brother." Her smile increases as she looks at Tobias. "It's an honor to meet you."

The hair on the back of my neck prickles.

The familiarity makes sense now. She's Luther's daughter. She even has the devil's eyes. His full lips, too.

"Get them out of here," I demand of Luca. "Or give me a way off this island. *Now.*"

Tobias trembles behind me, the tremors of his body sinking into mine.

"Penny." Luca's voice is smooth. "You're not a prisoner here. You can both move around freely—get something to eat, have a shower, get changed, sleep if you want. But it's not safe to leave."

"I can look after myself."

"Can you?" He raises a brow. "All on your own? Without the kid? Because there's no way in hell Torian will let you leave with his brother."

I don't react to the threat.

I knew Tobias would be their invisible shackle. Yet the delivery of the blow still leaves a gaping wound. "So he's the prisoner now?"

"No." Luca takes another step. "There are no prisoners. The kid is Torian's brother. He's family. You have no right to take him."

"I have every right. I'm the only parental figure he has left. I'm his teacher. His friend. His cook. His maid. I'm the one who tucks him in at night."

"Penny." Tobias clings tighter to me. "Please don't leave me." His heart-breaking kiddy sniffles return.

"You would take him from me after everything he's witnessed today? After all the stories he's been told?" I beg Luca with my eyes when I'd prefer to glare. Claw. Retaliate. "Can you imagine what he's thinking right now? Luther told him you were the enemy. He was forced to attack Cole. Now you want to take him from the only familiarity he has left?"

Toby's trembles increase, adding fuel to my argument.

"I'm not the enemy." The woman crouches. "Tobias, I would never do anything to hurt you. We're family."

Her words are gentle. The delivery soft. She's trying to win him over, bit by bit, second by second.

"You can attempt to brainwash him all you want," I snip. "Believe me, he's grown accustomed to the family trait, but he still can't stay here. He needs his medicine."

"What medicine?" Luca demands.

"He's diabetic." I squeeze Tobias's shoulder and hope to hell he realizes it's a sign for him to keep his mouth shut. "He needs regular injections. If I don't get him home soon he'll get sick. He could die."

Keira stands, her attention swaying from Sebastian to Luca and back again. "We need to tell Cole."

"Wait." Luca's eyes narrow on me. "The kid is diabetic?"

I swallow, suddenly unsettled with the thought of pinning more attention on Tobias.

"I assume there are risks associated with taking them back to Dad's house," Keira adds.

Dad.

God, the parental term when referencing Luther is abhorrent. He was never a father. Only a monster.

"The risks are monumental," Luca growls, his focus turning harsh. "They're not going back there."

I stand taller. "Do you plan on forcibly stopping me?"

"You bet I do."

"Luca," Sebastian warns. "Watch yourself."

My heart squeezes at the protection. Squeezes then flounders.

I remain locked tight in a visual battle with Luca, his scrutiny scathing as he attempts to stare me down.

"We need to talk," he tells me. "In private."

"Like hell you do." Sebastian steps closer. "I'm not leaving you alone with her."

Luca doesn't falter. He keeps his eyes narrowed on mine. "Now," he speaks to me.

I don't know what this is about. But I can see the determination in his expression. Whatever it is holds importance.

"Leave us," I murmur.

"That's not going to happen." Sebastian crosses his arms over his chest. "I'll never let you out of my sight again."

My heart protests the protection, wanting it and rejecting it at the same time.

"Get out." I raise my voice. "I don't want you here."

Pain seeps into his features, tainting everything it touches—his eyes, his lips.

"And take the kid," Luca adds.

"What?" I grasp Tobias's shoulders. *"No."*

"It's only for a few minutes. Keira can get him something to eat."

The woman nods. "I'll look after him."

I glare at her—the daughter to my rapist, the blood of my nightmares.

"Nothing is going to happen to him," Luca continues. "He's with family here."

"I don't like this," Sebastian growls. "I want to know what the hell is going on."

The room falls silent waiting for me to make the next move. I don't know what to do—succumb to my brother, give Luca what he wants, or forge ahead with my demand to leave.

Every option has pitfalls, but none more so than my lack of confidence to get off this island alone or my fear at dragging my brother into a mess he won't survive.

That leaves Luca.

"Let us talk in private." I glance away, wanting the surly man to know I'm not happily obliging to his request.

There's more silence, where I feel my brother's wince instead of seeing it. His disappointment ebbs through the room, dirtying my skin.

"If you need anything," he bites out, "you fucking yell, okay? Scream and I'll be back in here to kill this motherfucker before he can take another breath."

I don't show my appreciation. I can't. Letting my guard down and thanking him isn't something I can come back from. Instead, I turn to crouch before Tobias, yet again pasting on a dishonest smile.

"I don't want to go," he starts. "I want to stay with you."

"I know. But you're going to be fine." I pray I'm not lying to him. I beg the heavens to grant me this one favor. "It's only for a few minutes."

"You promise?"

"Of course I do. I'd never put you in harm's way. You know that." I grab his hands. "Go. Get some food. Take a look around."

"But—"

"It's time to listen, Tobias. This is important. Remember what I said about getting back home?"

He nods, his face pinched with understanding.

"Good." I squeeze his fingers. "We need to get the others. And to do that I have to talk to Luca."

He sinks his teeth into his lower lip as if fighting off the need to disobey.

"It's only a few minutes," I repeat. "Find me something to eat."

"Come on, kiddo." Sebastian's voice is filled with reluctance. "Neither one of us want to leave her, so let's do it together."

I ignore the ache in my heart and lean forward to whisper in Toby's ear. "Don't answer any questions. Don't tell them anything."

He wraps his arms around me, clinging tight as if we're about to be separated for months instead of moments. "I'll be smart."

"I know you will." I pull back and give him a quick kiss on the forehead. "Go."

He holds his head high as he walks toward the strangers, Keira reaching out a hand he refuses to take.

That little boy has a wealth of fortitude. With his upbringing, he had no choice. Violence has been an everyday occurrence. He was raised on a steady diet of brutality.

He hasn't even cried over his father's death—there have only been a million sniffles to hold the emotion at bay. He will break, though. Once he feels safe he'll temporarily slip into the child he's meant to be, letting the heartache free before he becomes the product of his emotionless father all over again.

"We'll be back soon." Sebastian starts for the door. "And we're not going far."

They leave together, each member of the trio taking turns in glancing over their shoulder with uncertainty before Luca closes the door behind them, trapping me in the room with him.

I try not to falter. To panic at the isolation with this formidable man.

"It's not a good idea to lie." He turns to face me, his eyes squinted in judgment. "So let's pretend it didn't happen."

"Excuse me?" I swallow over the building tension. This man is nothing in comparison to Luther, or even Chris or Robert. But he's devoid of innocence, too. There's something about him that niggles at my self-preservation.

"We both know that kid isn't diabetic."

I hold his stare, neither confirming nor denying his keen assessment.

"He hasn't had food or water for a damn long time," he drawls, "I'm sure he'd be showing symptoms by now."

Still I don't respond.

"But I get it." He approaches in a lazy stride. Cool. Confident. Blood still painted down one cheek. The gash on the side of his head still glistening. "You're scared. You're grasping at straws to get your friends to safety."

"My *family*," I correct.

He inclines his head with a wince. "Yes. Your family. Those women. I'd do whatever it takes, too. But lying isn't going to help you. If you lead Torian into a bloodbath based on bullshit you're not going to like how he retaliates."

I step back at the warning. "You're threatening me?"

"I'm protecting you," he snarls. "You won't get what you want if you base your plea on lies. I told you I would take care of it."

"Yes, you told me you'd take care of it, with no understanding of the situation you're facing or the looming deadline. If we're going to be telling each other the truth, the least you can do is admit you were fobbing me off."

"No, I wasn't. I was only attempting to clean up one fucking mess before I took on another." He pinches the bridge of his nose and squeezes his eyes shut.

For a moment, I'm struck by his show of vulnerability.

He's hurting.

I haven't seen weakness from a man since I was taken by Luther long ago. It's always been strong men with stronger fists. And yes, this man remains strong, but there's a sense of honesty about him, too.

"I made a promise," he grates. "I don't do that lightly."

"You've made many promises. Including setting me free."

His eyes open slightly, narrowed slits staring back at me. "You *are* free."

My yearning to believe him hasn't lessened. Neither has the determination not to trust him.

"I'll help those women," he continues. "Have faith I can get them out."

"You won't make it through the front gates without me."

"Then I'm happy for you to provide the necessary insight that helps us to get in another way."

"Us?" I ignore yet another refusal to let me leave and focus on obtaining more information about his plan.

"I'm not stupid enough to go on my own. Your brother will want to help, and Hunter is always looking for a bit of fun."

Fun? *Fun.*

"Wrong choice of words." He drops his hand from his nose and holds it up to me in placation. "I meant Hunter enjoys retribution. Especially against those who deserve a lot of it. Your tormentors will pay for what they've done."

"I don't care about revenge. All I want are my sis—"

There's a tentative knock at the door.

"Yeah?" Luca snaps.

The barrier to the rest of the world opens, Tobias's little face coming into view. He rushes toward me, keeping his distance from Luca as he passes to hold up a cookie.

"This is for you," he offers. "They said you need to eat."

"Thank you." I grasp the offering but can't stomach taking a bite, not with the lives of four people riding on my negotiating skills.

"Penny?" Tobias cringes and twists his legs together. "I really need to use the bathroom now."

Shit.

I glance at Luca in question.

"It's right in here, little buddy." He jerks his head at the ajar door across the other side of the room, then quickly squeezes his eyes shut again, wincing. "Walk through the robe to the door at the end."

Tobias peers up at me, waiting for approval.

"It's okay." I want to go with him, to lessen his fear, but I'm not finished with

Luca. Not by a long shot. "Freshen up while you're in there. Wash your face and hands."

He nods, keeping an eye on the stranger as he walks to the door before disappearing inside.

The conversation doesn't fall back into place once we're alone.

Luca's eyes remain partially squinted, his face pinched with discomfort.

Despite being uncertain about where to lay my trust, I don't like seeing him in pain.

"Do you need a doctor?"

"I'll be fine. It's nothing but a headache."

"It's not fine. Not when you expect me to entrust you with the lives of the people I love."

His nostrils flare. "You know what? The slightest bit of appreciation would go a long fucking way to ease the throb in my head. All I've done is try to help you and you keep spitting it back in my face."

I straighten, the tiniest fissure of regret breaking through my defenses.

He's right. I've shown very little thanks for what he's done. But that's because his promises of freedom don't feel real. The death of my captors seems like a dream.

Shock hasn't allowed for anything positive to sink in. Not relief or happiness.

Definitely not the appreciation he craves.

"I'm sorry," I whisper. "I'm not ungrateful. I'm just…"

"Forget it." He huffs out a sigh. "I've got a spare shirt if you want to get out of your stained clothes." His attention treks my body, the scrutiny far more subtle than what I'm used to. There's no desire. No threat. "Or Keira might have something you can borrow."

"I don't want anything from her." Not clothes. Not placations. "I'll make do with what I have."

"You can't go back to Naxos in bloodstained clothes."

I straighten. "Go back?"

"That's what you want, isn't it?" He raises a brow. "And apparently I can't get through the gates without you."

The appreciation he's been searching for finally hits me, the buzz filtering through my limbs. "Thank you."

"Don't thank me yet. Torian has to—"

"Penny." Tobias's frantic voice calls from the bathroom. "*Penny.*"

My heart drops, the cookie falling from my fingers.

I run, scrambling toward the plea for help, only to have Luca beat me to the door as he pulls a gun from the back of his waistband. I make it to the bathroom a step behind him to find Toby standing at the bathroom counter, looking at the side of his shirt.

His eyes bug at the sight of us, his focus turning to the gun, his mouth dropping open as if he's about to scream.

"What's wrong?" I push past Luca and place a hand on his arm to encourage him to lower the weapon. "What happened?"

Tobias shrinks into me.

"It's okay." I crouch before him and grab his waist, clinging tight to gain his attention. "Luca thought you were in trouble. He came racing in here to help. Tell me what's wrong."

"There's blood." He twists his shirt to show me the stain on the side of the material. "I think I'm hurt."

My pulse spikes.

I've been hit so many times during the height of an adrenaline rush that I know what it's like not to feel injuries until the intensity wears off.

If he's hurt and I didn't know... If he's dying and I didn't think to check him...

I stand, grabbing his shirt to yank it over his head, then mount a full-scale search of his body, frantically scanning him everywhere. Arms. Stomach. Back. Skull.

I can't find any cuts or marks. There's nothing. Only pure, delicate skin. But I keep searching, making him spin around one more time to triple check.

"I don't think he's injured." Luca approaches, his gun thankfully returned to the back of his jeans. "Even if he was, I'm sure he'd survive. You're a tough kid, aren't you, Tobias? Brave, too."

Toby straightens with the compliment, his tiny muscles moving under my touch. He nods, quick and sharp, the slightest sense of pride ebbing from him.

"Why don't you get him to take a shower or a bath?" Luca asks. "It might help. I can get him a clean T-shirt to wear afterward. Obviously it will swim on him, but it's better than walking around in stained clothes."

More pained beats pummel my chest. I don't like how his kindness affects me. The tiny fingers of comfort latch around my chest, threatening to squeeze me to death. It takes all my strength to ignore my doubt. For Toby's sake.

"What do you say?" I cup his cheek. "Do you think a relaxing bath will make you feel better? You've been awake for a long time and the water might help you wind down so you can rest for a few hours."

He stares at me with indecision, then shoots a nervous glance at the bulking man blocking the doorway.

"Don't worry, little guy. I'll leave." Luca steps back from the door and awkwardly bumps into the frame as he retreats.

I narrow my gaze, watching as he fumbles then sways on his feet before disappearing from view. Something is wrong with him. *Very* wrong.

"Toby, start getting undressed. I'll be back to run the water in a second." I follow after Luca, my stride long as I catch up to him in the bedroom. "Wait." I grab his arm when he doesn't stop and let go just as fast. My grip on his muscled bicep was a stark reminder of the threat he provides. Of his dangerous abilities.

He turns to look at me, and stumbles. His face is pale, a glimmer of sweat breaking across his brow.

Before I know it I'm latching onto him again, this time trying to keep him upright, the knitted muscle beneath my hands hard and unyielding.

"What's wrong?" I struggle to keep him standing. "Luca?"

He stares straight through me, his forehead creased. "Shit."

"I'll get help." I make for the door only to be stopped by rough hands gripping my upper arms. I freeze, my panic instantaneous.

I brace for violation. All the horrors Luther bestowed upon me lay out like a smorgasbord as I wait for Luca to make his choice.

"I'm fine. I just moved too quick." He releases me and fumbles forward to the bed, allowing me to breathe again.

I don't budge as he slumps onto the mattress, his head hanging, the wisps of his blood-matted hair falling to shroud his eyes.

Bile coats the back of my throat, the nausea coming thick and fast. I didn't realize how much faith I had in him until those hands gripped me tightly. There wasn't trust, but there must've been something else. Something to make me completely blindsided by his aggressive touch.

"I scared you." He massages the uninjured side of his head. "Fuck... I shouldn't have grabbed you."

I remain immobile while I pull myself together.

"Go check on the kid," he mutters. "I'll be out of here in a minute."

I should take his advice. I need distance to think.

It's his pain and the looming threat of losing the only person I may be able to rely on that makes me stay.

"You need to see a doctor," I murmur.

"I'll bounce back in a minute."

I don't believe him. Now I'm paying attention I can see his discomfort increase whenever he moves or speaks. It's only slight, yet always there, following everything he does.

He raises his head, looking up at me through thick lashes. Those eyes are dark, their depth punishing. But it's his dilated pupils that cause me concern.

I suck in a breath. "You've got a concussion."

"Yeah." He shrugs. "I've had worse."

The instinct to take him at his word is strong. I want to have faith in him. And I itch to reject the slight glimmer of trust at the same time.

"If you're not going to see a doctor, you should at least clean your wound."

"No. I'm—"

"A stubborn man who doesn't want to destroy his tough-guy status after surviving a bullet to the skull?"

He huffs out a chuckle. "My tough-guy status is the last thing I'm worried about." He speaks in a lazy drawl, yet the pointedness in his gaze insinuates I'm the focus of his current concern. That I'm all he's worried about. "Besides, I can't get a proper look at the side of my head. I don't even know what I'm up against."

Is he fishing for connection? For trust?

I suck my lower lip between my teeth, staring at him, trying to see the deception I'm sure he must have hidden. Men don't help women. They use. Hurt. Abuse.

Goddammit.

Why can't my life be easy for once? I don't want to keep questioning everything. Everyone. I just want nothingness.

No thoughts. No fear. No pain.

No struggle to get my sisters to safety.

"I can take a look. If that's what you want." I shuffle forward, tempting fate, testing this flimsy layer of protection he's shrouded me in. If this is all an act I'd prefer to know now, not later. Not once I've lost myself too far down the torturous path of trust.

He raises his chin, blinking up at me. Silent. Contemplative.

My heart flutters under his attention, my insides quavering. I'm scared, my fear tightly bottled. It's more than that, too. I tremble for reasons unknown.

The closer I get, the harder it is to think through the tormented sea swirling inside me. He's a trap. The temptation of his help lays in wait beneath the steel claws of his intentions.

I reach out, my approach tentative.

"Take care of the kid first." He tilts his head away. "He's waiting on you to run the bath."

I'm confused by his rejection, my arm hovering in the space between us, my fingers an inch from his hair.

"Go on. Look after Toby." He pushes from the bed, his hulking frame dwarfing me. "I'll find him a shirt to wear."

I retreat with uncertainty.

At least I understood the threat from Luther. I knew him so well I could anticipate his next move.

Luca is different. I can't foresee anything with him. Not his words or his actions. I can't even understand his claim to want to help me.

I backtrack, turning away from him to walk through the robe, then into the bathroom where Tobias is naked and standing in wait.

I ignore my confusion as I stalk to the bath and turn on the taps, making the water gush like a waterfall.

"Is he a nice man?" Tobias walks to my side. "Because I thought he was, then Dad said he wasn't. Now I don't know what to think because he still seems nice."

I kneel before the bath and swirl the water, buying myself time to answer.

I don't know what to say.

My heart wants to trust the man who protected us with vicious determination. It's my head that reminds me I've fallen victim to the lies of a predator once before.

"He seems genuine." I continue mixing the water. "Don't you think?"

He shrugs and steps into the bath. "I want to like him. But I heard some of the things he said to Dad before he..." There's another shrug, his sorrow building behind those innocent eyes.

I hate that he's hurting. And I detest that a monster's murder is the cause of his pain.

"Sweetheart, I know it's hard to think about your dad being gone. He was your family. But we're going to get through this. I'll make sure of it."

He sits in the building water and pulls his bended legs to his chest. "He hurt you."

I stiffen, unsure how to react. He's never mentioned the reality of my situation before. Not once.

"He hurt you, and Chloe, and the others all the time."

"Yes, he did," I whisper.

"Why?" His brows knit. "Why did he do that?"

Grief hits me. Grief at the life stolen from me, at the years I lost, at the scars I know will never heal, and how this little boy witnessed it all.

"Your father was..." My throat tightens.

"A bad man?" He blinks up at me. "I know he was. But I was scared, and I didn't know how to save you."

I want to sob. To let the tears roam free. If only my body knew how. "It wasn't your job to save me, gorgeous boy. It was a horrible situation and now we need to move on. I'm going to go back to the country I grew up in, and you're going to come with me. We're all going to be all right."

"Nina, Chloe, Abi, and Lilly, too?"

"Yep. All of us."

His lips curve in a smile, the happiness not reaching his eyes. "I'd like that. I want to get far away from here. Especially from Cole."

"Why Cole?" I reach around him to turn off the taps. "Did he hurt you?"

"No, but he will. He'll punish me for stabbing him. I didn't even do it right. It barely worked, but he was so mad."

"Oh no, sweetheart. I promise he won't hurt you." God, how I hope he won't. "He's a smart man. He knows you didn't want to cause trouble."

The brush of footfalls hits my ears as Luca edges into my periphery. He stands in the doorway, a towel and clothes scrunched in one hand, a bottle of alcohol and a tiny cardboard packet in the other. "Want me to come back later?"

"No. You can actually help set our minds at ease." I push to my feet and attempt to find a relatively clean spot on my blouse to dry the water from my hands. "I was just telling this beautiful boy that Cole wouldn't hold a grudge over what happened between them earlier. Do you agree?"

Luca walks toward us, shrinking the small space with his mountainous frame. "I definitely agree. Cole values family above all else. I'm sure he's just relieved you're safe."

Tobias takes in Luca's words with gradually building trust. "Do you really think so?"

"One hundred percent. You should've heard how excited he was to find out he had a kid brother. I'm sure once things settle down you two will become inseparable."

It's a placation, a kind one, and I can't help turning my back to Tobias to silently mouth, "*Thank you.*"

Luca inclines his head as he moves to the vanity, dumping the items in his hands onto the counter. "Toby, is it okay if I stay in here while you bathe? I'm hoping Penny won't mind cleaning me up a little bit."

"I don't mind." Tobias sinks into the bath to lay on his back, the water lapping at his cheeks. "As long as Penny doesn't."

The eyes of an inquisitive stranger stalk me from the reflection in the mirror.

"Are we still good?" he asks.

No, not at all.

Every time I look at him my pulse kicks up a notch. There's so much fear. So much torment.

There's something else, too. Something I refuse to believe is hope.

The mere thought of the weakness inspires anger. I won't let that conniving bitch spread her wings inside my chest.

I have to be tactical. Smart. And if that includes pretending I'm getting close to a stranger, then that's what I'll do.

I suck in a strengthening breath and indicate the counter with a lazy wave of my hand. "Rest back against the vanity and let me take a look at you."

9

LUCA

I DO AS INSTRUCTED, TURNING TO FACE HER, RESTING MY ASS AGAINST THE VANITY counter.

I ignore the hesitation in her voice. I shut down all the bullshit in my head telling me to keep my distance. Like an asshole, I pretend pushing her into trusting me isn't the wrong fucking thing to do.

She walks toward me, her steps hesitant.

"Before you get started—" I cross my feet at the ankles. Laid back. Calm. "—this isn't another attempt to get close so you can attack me, is it?"

"Maybe." She reaches my side and opens the vanity cupboards to my right. "Do you think the third time would be the charm?"

I smirk, appreciating her subtle humor. It's barely there, her expression remaining tight, but the derision is a starting point.

"I noticed you cleaned up the mess I made with that device you were carrying." There hadn't been any sign of the stabby stick I'd stomped into my carpet. "You kept it, didn't you?"

She closes the cupboards and stands tall before me, her silence a blatant answer.

"Does it still work?" I ask.

She holds my gaze, a million thoughts ticking behind those big brown eyes. "I'm not entirely sure."

Her truth is a gift. A fucking brilliant step in the right direction. "You won't need it for long. Once things settle, I can get you whatever weapon you want. I can make sure someone teaches you how to use them, too."

She licks her lower lip, the flick of her tongue fast, almost agitated. If I had to guess, I'd say she doesn't appreciate my attempt to build a bridge between us. My kindness scares her.

"That would be nice." She fobs me off with the half-hearted acknowledgement and moves to my other side. "Can you shuffle over please? I want to check the drawers."

I comply, sliding across the counter. "What are you looking for?"

"A cloth or something to help clean you up."

"You're not going to find anything in there. All the linen is in the hall cupboard." I lean forward, cringe against the pounding protest of my skull, and yank off my shirt. "Use this." I hand over the soiled material. "Douse it in alcohol and it should be fine. I'm going to have to burn it anyway."

She doesn't take the offering. Instead, she retreats a step, her attention riveted on my chest. There's nothing flattering about the way she looks at me. There's only trepidation. Undiluted panic.

Shit.

I didn't contemplate the underlying threat she'd see in my exposed skin. Not that I can think much of anything over the dizzying squeeze of my brain.

"That was a stupid move." I unfurl the crumpled shirt and prepare to pull it back over my head. "I'll go find something else to use."

"No." She reaches out, grasping the material, her fingers brushing mine. "I can do this."

She keeps her gaze averted from mine as she rinses the material in the sink, the pink tinge of blood seeping into the water. She doesn't seem to care about the possible diseases my blood could carry. Then again, she didn't seem to care when Luther was shooting at her either.

She wanted death.

Who knows if she still does?

"I can't imagine how hard it is for you to try and trust me. But there's no threat to you here." I murmur the oath softly, not wanting the kid to overhear our conversation. "We want to protect you. Not hurt you."

She shuts off the taps, wrings the water from my shirt, then lets the sodden weight fall to the sink. She stands there for silent moments, staring at herself in the mirror, her hands clutching the counter.

I want to know what she's thinking. To expose her demons and find a way to slaughter them.

"What's eating away at you?" I grab the wet material, and begin scrubbing my face, my neck, my throat, pretending I'm not ready to hang off her every word.

For a long time she doesn't answer. Instead, she raises her gaze to mine in the mirror, her fragility coming out to play as I feel her guard lower slightly.

"When I was growing up, I always thought horrible people were packaged accordingly." She keeps her voice soft. "I believed bad men were ugly, with easily distinguishable malice. I thought I'd always be able to pick the criminals with horrible intentions because they would look the part. But nothing could be further from the truth. Evil comes with many masks. Some of them more attractive than others."

"I agree." I start rubbing the damp shirt through my hair, the flakes of dried blood dusting the air. "You can't trust a pretty face."

She straightens her shoulders. "Kind words or smooth muscles, either."

She's talking about me. My muscles. My apparent malice.

"That's how Luther took me." She swallows, her tongue snaking out to moisten her lips. "I fell for a kind act and paid the price."

"And now you think I'm doing the same thing?" I keep scrubbing my hair, pretending her continued distrust doesn't get to me.

"I'm not trying to offend you. I just want you to understand my situation. I know you've risked a lot to help me. But until I'm in a place where I feel safe, I'm never going to trust you."

"Then why don't you tell me about this safe place so I can get you there?"

"I wish I could." She holds my gaze, her eyes devoid of hope. "I'm not sure it exists anymore. My nightmare will never be over."

"Of course it will. The memories will fade with time." I wince and grit my teeth as I hit a sore spot, the added pain ricocheting through my brain.

"Give it here." She holds out a hand for the shirt. "Let me do it."

I oblige, the invigorating boost of victory sliding through my veins. She rinses and wrings the material again, then sidesteps to stand in front of me, making sure to leave a generous amount of space between us. With her arm completely outstretched, she starts to wipe the damp shirt over my jaw, my cheek.

I can't take my eyes off her. Even if I could, I wouldn't want to. She's fucking beautiful. So beautiful I feel like a prick for understanding why someone would want to steal her. "You can come closer."

She doesn't pause her movements. Doesn't even acknowledge I spoke. But after a while she shuffles forward, inch by inch, gaining a better vantage point to clean my wound, her bare toes touching the front of my boots.

She comes close. A breath away. And with each progression the air thickens around us, the atmosphere gaining an edge of trepidation.

It feels like one wrong move will have the peace of this moment transformed into another attempt on my life, or worse, she'll retreat into the defensive, resentful woman who grates on my nerves.

"When I mentioned my nightmare never ending, I wasn't referring to the mental struggle I'm going to be up against. I was talking about Luther's men and how they'll make sure I disappear. They won't stop looking for me."

"They can't look when they're dead."

"And you're going to kill them all?"

"Damn straight."

She pauses, sighs, and shakes her head as she stares longingly over my shoulder. "Believe me, the bad guys always win."

"Well, lucky for you, I haven't been one of the good guys for a while."

She stiffens. Almost imperceptibly. The next dab of the shirt is a direct impact to my bullet wound.

"Fuck me, shorty." I jerk back at the stab of agony. "Can you try keeping the material out of my brain?"

"I-I'm sorry. I didn't mean—"

"Sure you did." I fake a smirk, trying to soften the fear I've reawakened in her. *Jesus.* She's more skittish than a wild animal. "You're trying to destroy my tough-guy status, remember?"

Her lips curve in a barely there smile. It's almost imperceptible. Entirely subtle. The brief glimpse of happiness reaches her eyes, transforming the cornered wild cat into a blindingly brilliant beauty of a woman. But as quickly as the vision hits, the carefree gorgeousness fades.

"You need stitches," she murmurs.

I stare at her, willing the beauty to return. I want to see that smile again. Bigger and brighter. Cemented in place.

My dick pulses with compounding need, the perverted reaction enough for me to right the approaching train wreck.

I clear my throat. "Yeah, I figured as much." I turn my head away to grab the tiny sewing kit I found in the utensils drawer of the kitchen. My idiotic libido is nothing more pain won't fix. "How are you with a needle and thread?"

"I guess that depends on how twitchy you'll be knowing I'm holding something sharp close to your skull." She takes the kit and opens it up to inspect the contents.

"I've got a pretty thick head. I don't think a sewing needle will penetrate."

Again, I get a brief glimpse of a smile, the curve of her mouth inspiring a more determined pulse from my dick.

Jesus fucking Christ.

Maybe I'm dealing with more than concussion. I must have brain damage. If not, Decker will soon ensure I do.

But not even the thought of being pummeled to a pulp can deter me from being consumed by her. She's mesmerizing. From the swell of her lips, to the gentle sweep of her waist, along with everything in between and surrounding.

She isn't merely beautiful. She's beauty itself.

"I need a chair to get a better vantage point." She raises to the tips of her toes. "I can't see properly from here."

I don't hesitate to kneel before her. I want her to know she's in charge. There's no threat from me.

For long seconds she peers down at me, as if understanding the underlying message in my submission. Her tension eases another notch. Her muscles lose their rigidity.

I win another square in this back and forth board game of ours.

"I'm not the best at this." She pulls a needle and thread from the tiny cardboard packet. "I've had to give stitches a time or two, but I'm not entirely sure what I'm meant to be doing."

"I trust you."

She pauses, the dark depths of her eyes seeming tortured by my admission.

"Just try your best. I can promise you, whatever the result, it will be ten times better than the hack job your brother would give me."

The mention of her brother snaps her out of the contemplation. Her discomfort returns tenfold.

She backtracks to the sink, cleans the sewing needle with the liquor, then returns to pour the liquid over my wound, bringing another slap of pain-induced clarity.

A wet path trails down my neck, my chest, my back. For all I know, I look like an oiled-up stripper on ladies' night. But I remain on my knees, keeping silent as she begins to tentatively stitch my wound.

"Tell me if you need me to stop."

"I'm good." I actually want her to quit being gentle and just slaughter the ever-loving fuck out of my skull. Her delicate fingers are only causing more issues. The soft brush of her touch is enough to make me twitch. "Does Tobias always float like that?"

She nods. "He could lay there for hours. And some days, he does. I think it's his form of meditation."

I lower my voice. "Does he know what happened?"

Her stitching ceases, her fingers paused on my scalp.

"He knows." She leans back to give me a pointed look. "I told him his father's death was an accident. That despite how confident and capable Luther was with a gun, it didn't matter when he stumbled around the edge of the sofa and fell." She shrugs. "He knows his father shot himself with his own gun."

I keep my mouth shut, not wanting to dissolve the cease-fire between us by telling her that story won't hold up for long. Once the shock wears off, the kid is going to realize there were too many gunshots for an accident. It was a fucking battlefield out there.

Then again, maybe that's her plan—to appease Tobias's concerns while he's here, but make him question Cole later.

"*What about Chris?*" I mouth.

Her face hardens. "He knows the truth about Chris, too."

I raise a brow, silently asking what truth she's referring to.

"I told him I killed Chris." She returns to her stitching, tugging the thread harder than necessary, not subtle at all in her request to cut the topic of conversation.

I don't push any further. We've come a long way in the last hour.

I've seen her hope and glimpsed the tiniest bit of her trust.

I won't fuck that up.

"I think I'm done." She leans in, inspecting her handiwork. "I just need to cut the thread."

I bow my head, giving her closer access. "Just use your teeth."

Her breathing hitches. It's only subtle. The barest hint of sound. And I can't help wishing I could hear it in a different context. From pleasure, not fear.

She hesitates long enough for the silence to become awkward. Uncomfortable. I lock every muscle, not wanting the barest twinge to spook her and still she doesn't move.

I'm about to straighten when she lunges toward me, the tension on the string pulled tight before a twang announces she's followed my order.

Her retreat is swift. The slide of her steps moving toward the vanity, the rush of water letting me know she's washing her hands.

I hide a smile from my lips as I drag myself to my feet, making sure to keep my distance as I turn to the mirror. "Thanks."

"You're welcome." She doesn't meet my gaze. Not once as she shuts off the taps and backs away.

Her visual disconnect doesn't stop me from staring at her though. I barely drag my gaze away as I take her place at the sink and cup water in my hands to splash over my face and head.

"You should probably try to keep it dry for a while." She wipes her hands on her stained pants, keeping her attention downcast. "I don't know a lot about infection, but I think moisture doesn't help."

"I'll make sure to do that." I will her to look at me. To trust me. I do it for so long it seems as though a day passes in the thickened silence until footsteps sound in the distance.

"*Luca*?" Cole calls from the bedroom. "Where are you?"

Penny's attention snaps to mine, her eyes flaring before she rushes to the tub.

Fuck.

"The bathroom." I grab the towel stashed beneath the numerous T-shirts I brought in for the kid and lob it at her. "Here. Dry him off with this."

She catches the plush material and spreads it wide as Tobias splashes to his feet.

"Don't panic." She smiles at the boy, the expression fake as she wraps him in the towel. "We're safe, remember?"

Her rigidity doesn't fade as Cole comes to stand in the doorway, Hunt and Decker flanking him from behind.

For a while, nobody speaks. None of them have to. Their visual accusation is loud enough.

The weight of everyone's focus shifts from Penny, to my fucking naked chest, the resulting glower from Decker harsh enough to cut stone.

"I'm told my brother is sick," Cole grates.

Penny lasers a frantic glance my way. Those dark eyes are filled with indecision. She's weighing her options. Wondering if she should trust me or keep forging ahead on her own.

"He isn't sick," I answer for her, holding her gaze. "There's nothing to worry about."

She stares at me, the questioning slowly fading from her features, transforming her look into something more threatening.

The building hardness in her expression is a warning. A blatant you-better-know-what-you're-fucking-doing. And with this, I do. Without a doubt I know she shouldn't fuck with Torian.

"Then why the hell was I told differently?" he asks.

"It was a miscommunication." I wipe the lingering moisture from my face with my forearm. "Tobias is fine."

"Fine?" Torian's eyes narrow. "I was told he was in urgent need of medical attention. Isn't that the story she gave my sister?"

"Like I said, it was a miscommunication." I pin him with a stare. With a silent warning I'm not going to budge. "But it doesn't change the fact her friends are stuck back at your dad's house. We need to get them out before someone is instructed to dispose of evidence."

"They're my family," Penny corrects. "Not just friends. They're my sisters."

"So I've heard." Cole scrutinizes her, the slow appraisal moving from head to toe. He's weighing his options, judging her concern and the worth of her sisters against the risk associated with rescuing them. "Keira is being rather pushy about sending us back to Naxos to get these women. What are your thoughts, Luca?"

Penny's focus snaps to me and in an instant she regresses from strong warrior to begging beauty. I could stand here for hours drowning in her silent pleas, the gentle sweep of her lashes, the subtle waver to her breathing.

"I need more details," I admit. "At the moment, I'm not entirely sure what we're up against, but I don't see why Hunt, Deck, and I can't go on a recovery mission. We could get information while we're there."

"I was thinking the same thing." Torian gives a subtle nod. "I'd be interested in any hard drives you could find. A prisoner would be even better."

"I'm sure that could be arranged." I grab a clean shirt from the counter and slowly drag it over my head, making sure not to bump the newest addition to my scar tally. "If Penny came with us it could save time."

"Fuck off." Decker pushes past Torian to get into the bathroom. "She's not going anywhere."

"Please." Penny ignores her brother and speaks to my boss. "I could get you whatever you want—files, computers, money—I can even show you where the safes are. Nobody else knows that place like I do. Not even the guards have been there as long as I have."

"Me too," the boy adds. "I know all Baba's passwords."

"Over my dead body," Decker snarls. "I won't allow it."

Penny hardens—her face, her posture, those damn eyes. "You're not my keeper." She returns her focus to Torian. "He's a stranger to me. He has no right to make decisions on my behalf."

Decker pulls back as if the verbal attack was physical. We're all quiet as a kaleidoscope of emotions barrage his features. First shock, then pain, and finally volatile fucking fury as he pins me with a glare. "You did this. I don't know how, but you're fucking responsible."

"I didn't do shit." The pound in my head increases, my vision darkening with the onslaught of raised voices. The gift of unconsciousness hovers close, but if I pass out Penny won't get what she wants. Nobody else is going to fight to get her friends back. "I'll make sure she's protected."

Decker snarls. "Like fuck—"

"Stop." Torian raises a hand in warning. "We're moving this conversation into the living room. Let the boy dress in privacy."

He stalks from the doorway.

Nobody follows.

Decker continues to glare at me. Penny remains on edge. And I'm pretty sure Hunt is only hanging around because he enjoys the dramatics.

"You heard him." I push from the vanity, willing my legs to keep holding my weight. "Start moving."

Decker sneers at me before storming from the room, Hunt shadowing.

I wait until their footsteps fade, for everything to dissolve into the distance, and turn to Penny. "You okay?"

She raises a brow. "Are *you*? Your skin has turned grey."

"We're not talking about me right now."

She nudges closer to Tobias and dries his hair with the corner of the towel. "I've been through worse than an argument with my brother."

That goes without saying. The thought of what she endured at the hands of Luther sits like a lead weight in my gut.

"I can look after myself." She keeps ruffling the kid's hair with the towel. "I just need you to convince them to take me when you go back to Naxos."

"I'll try." I'm not sure I want to make promises. I'm not even sure earning her trust is the right thing to do. "Why don't you freshen up while you're in here? I couldn't find any pants to fit you, but I brought in an extra shirt. And there's a lock on the door, if that helps."

I don't wait for a reply before leaving the enclosed space, my steps wonky as I enter the bedroom to come face-to-face with barely contained fury.

"I don't know what the fuck you've done to turn her against me," Decker seethes quietly, "but I swear on my life, you're going to pay."

"She's in shock. Give her space to sort herself out."

"And what about you? Are you giving her space? Because it doesn't fucking look like it. Seems to me, with that fucking stripper show, that you're trying to take advantage of her."

"I'm trying to show her I'm not a threat. She needs—"

"What she needs is her fucking family," he cuts me off. "Her *real* family. And you're building a wall between us."

My temples pound harder with his raised voice. "Look, Deck, earlier she was trying to stab me with a fucking sedative-filled syringe and refused to admit she even had a brother. Now she's willing to at least acknowledge you, and isn't trying to lay me on my ass. It's all forward momentum. So ease up and stop acting like another piece of shit who wants to control her."

His eyes flare. "I'm not trying to control her, you self-righteous son of a bitch. I'm trying to help her."

"So am I. I think it's clear whose tactics are working better."

He chuckles, the sound harsh. "You're getting on my last nerve, mother-fucker. I suggest you back off."

For anyone else, I probably would. I'd bow out, giving this pounding head of mine a breather from the bullshit. "I can't. Not when it comes to her."

His upper lip curls, exposing teeth. "So seduction is the game, is it? Your kink is damsels in distress."

I scoff and start for the hall. "I'm done with this."

"Fuckin' answer me." He rushes to block my path and shoves at my chest.

The resulting squeeze of my migraine is enough to make vomit clog the back of my throat. I breathe through the need to hurl and clench my fists. "Did she look like a fucking damsel to you?"

"She looks fucking broken." His nostrils flare, his chest rising and falling with heavy breaths. "She looks like a skeleton of the sister I used to know, and here you are pushing her back into hell."

"Get out of my way. I don't have the patience for your shit right now."

"*My* shit? *My fucking shit?*" He cracks his knuckles. "Then let me put you out of your misery."

The thought of him knocking me senseless is more comforting than it should be. Unconsciousness would be a blessing. Unfortunately, it's not an option. "You're going to hit a guy with a concussion?"

"No, I'm going to hit a guy who's pitching a fucking tent for my sister."

"Yeah." I nod, despite the resulting pound from the movement. "That's exactly what I'm doing. I was pitching a tent when I shoved her out of the line of fire and took a bullet to the head. And I sure as shit was pitching when I tackled her to the ground when Luther was trying to shoot her in the back. So many tents were pitched I could house a fuckin' army."

"You think sarcasm is going to get you out of this?" He steps closer. Right in my face. "I can see what you're up to."

"Then start swinging. One punch and I'll be out like a light."

"Perfect." He cocks a fist.

"For you maybe. But not for your sister and her friends. As it is, there's only three of us to take on however many assholes guard Luther's house." I throw my arms wide. "But it's your choice. Do you want instant gratification or do you actually want to help her?"

He jabs a finger at my chest. "Don't ever fucking question that I want what's best for her."

"I'm not questioning that. I'm saying you're letting your emotions get the better of you. She's fucking scared. I swear she doesn't know what she's doing apart from acting on instinct. And at the moment, the hope that comes with seeing you is obviously too much to take."

He pauses, blinking slowly as his wrinkled forehead loses some of the tension.

"Stop thinking about what *you* want and what *you* need, and let her run this show," I mutter. "Doesn't she deserve that much?"

His jaw continues to tick, but eventually he takes a step back, raking a hand through his hair. "I want to help her. I can't fucking stand being kept at arm's length after thinking I'd lost her."

"I get it. Anyone in their right mind would've expected your reunion to go down a lot fucking happier than this. But it didn't and there's nothing you can do about it. Give her space. And time. She'll come around. *Then* you can beat the shit out of me." I shrug. "Or at least you can try."

He gives a breathy chuckle, the sound vicious. "Yeah. I guess you're right. Delayed gratification will do just fine." He shoves me again, the whiplash jolting my head and blinding me for an instant.

I close my eyes as his heavy steps leave the room, the sound barely heard over the ringing in my ears. I'm in deep shit here. Any minute now and I could keel over, no punch necessary.

Fuck.

I sway with the building weight bearing down on me. I mentally battle to remain conscious.

"I'm sorry he's taking this out on you." Penny's whispered voice acts as a balm to my pain and a fucking trigger all at once.

I open my eyes. She stands in the doorway to the bathroom, Tobias at her side.

"I don't blame him." I squeeze the bridge of my nose and start for the hall. "You should get some rest while you can."

I don't pause for a reply, I stalk my ass out of there and into the living room, finding Keira, Hunt, Decker, and Torian seated around the dining table.

"Where's Sarah?" I drag out a chair opposite Penny's brother to keep an eye on the aggressive motherfucker.

"Escorting Anissa home." Torian drinks from a steaming mug. "They should be halfway to the jet by now."

"We're stranded? Again?" Jesus fucking Christ. We got into this mess because these assholes called our jet back to Portland. Now, we're stuck all over again. "Is that a good idea?"

"Another aircraft is on standby," he growls, making it obvious he doesn't appreciate my questioning. "We can fly out of here at a moment's notice. Now, tell us what's going on with her. What's she playing at?"

"She's not playing at anything. Her actions could be long-term PTSD. Or shock from today. Who the fuck knows? Only time will tell."

"Time isn't something we have a lot of. Especially not if you're suggesting taking her back to Naxos."

"Can we drop that line of thought right now?" Decker mutters. "She's not going back there."

"Protest all you like, but she's our greatest asset in helping to retrieve the other women, along with whatever information we can get our hands on. God knows the shit Luther was up to. This might be our only chance to find out."

Long moments of tension-filled silence pass. Nobody talks. Nobody moves. We all sit there, weighing our options or lack thereof. It's a case of saving the other women or letting them die, which, to me, means there's no option at all.

"Do you really think it's necessary to take her?" Keira asks. "Can't she just tell you everything she knows?"

"No, I think he's right." Torian leans back in his chair. "We've been to Luther's house once already. And I can't think how we'd get past the guarded gate without her. Those rifle-toting assholes won't let us in without permission. She could be our ticket inside."

"Fucking hell." Decker wipes a hand down his face. "There's gotta be another way."

"There might be. The question is—do we have enough time to figure it out?" I return to massaging my temples. Then the back of my neck. I do everything and anything to try and relieve the pressure in my skull. "Penny has already said Luther's men will start taking action if their boss doesn't make contact within a certain amount of time."

"How long is that?" Hunt asks.

"She doesn't know." I close my eyes, the lack of bright light helping to ease the pain in my head. "Our window for action might have already passed."

I relax into the darkness, my nausea receding. All I need is a few more minutes to pull my shit back together.

"What if it's a trap? She doesn't seem all that keen on sharing our company," Hunter adds. Maybe she wants to go back to the place where she feels comfortable. This could be a case of 'better the devil she knows.'"

"It's not."

My pulse spikes at the sound of her voice and I force myself not to react. I don't raise my head. I don't open my eyes either, not until Decker whispers a harsh curse under his breath.

I push upright and see her walking toward us dressed in one of the spare T-shirts I'd left in the bathroom. And no fucking pants.

The sight of her is pure fragility.

A gorgeous figure dwarfed by baggy material.

It's the strong set of her shoulders, the confident stride, and the high arc of her neck that make it clear she's not letting her guard down anytime soon.

"I don't want to go back to Naxos for any reason other than to get my sisters." She wraps her arms around her middle, the loose material hitching higher to reveal more of her perfect thighs. "And I promise I'm not setting a trap. As far as I know, nobody else was aware of Luther's motives for coming out here. His guards won't suspect foul play. At least not yet."

"How do you know?" Hunter grates. "I understand you've been stuck with him for a while, but you can't tell me you were by his side every minute of the day."

"Hunter," Keira warns. "Tread lightly."

"I am. I just can't comprehend the son of a bitch divulging information in front of one of his..." The sentence hangs and tense silence is the only thing left to fill the void.

"One of his sex slaves?" Penny finishes for him. "You can say it. A few words aren't going to break me."

Everyone winces, except me.

I see her strength. The determination. It's beyond admirable.

"And you're right," she continues. "He held his cards close to his chest. I rarely heard his plans for anything, except for the week when he punished me like a dog. I was leashed and dragged along by his side. He never let me out of his sight. I overheard every conversation he had for seven days. And none of them involved him sharing information with anyone other than Chris, Robert, and a few other people who I've never met before. His guards were always kept on a need-to-know basis."

Anger consumes me, the heat of rage inspiring a tick to form at the top of my right cheek.

Luther treated her like a dog. A fucking animal. And I can see from the ease with which she talks about it that it was far from her worst punishment.

I push from the table, breaking the silence and stealing the pity-filled glances away from Penny as I go in search of caffeine. "We can make a surprise attack."

"Maybe some of you could." Her gaze follows me. "That's still an option. But it's better to approach legitimately. Distract the guards with our arrival. We can pretend Luther wanted me taken back without him. That way any covert action is less likely to be noticed. It also gets a car inside the gates so we've got an easier escape."

"It also makes whoever is in that car a sitting duck," Hunt drawls. "It's too risky."

"No riskier than someone scaling the wall and getting stuck on the inside." She holds my gaze as if I'm the person she needs to convince. "They're trigger-happy. One glimpse of action and they'll shoot. They won't pause to ask questions."

"And neither will I." Decker shoves from the table, his chair scraping along the tile. "I also can't sit here and participate in planning something that will risk your life all over again. I'll help with whatever needs to be done, but I refuse to encourage any of this shit."

He stalks for the hall, Keira scooting from her chair to quickly follow after him.

Penny doesn't watch him leave. She keeps her gaze on me, her silent regret passing between us. I see her—the fragility beneath the strength, the love for her brother hidden behind her shields.

"Don't worry. He'll be fine." I pivot to the cupboards and pull out a tin filled with cookies. "You still haven't eaten."

"I'm not hungry."

"You're either lying, which I've already warned you about, or you're still in shock. And both would improve with a sugar fix." I place the tin on the counter, remove the lid. "It's non-negotiable, Penny." I slide the tin toward her, then do the same with a plate. "I need to be able to rely on you if we're taking you back to Naxos. That means a full stomach and maybe some caffeine, too."

She glances at Hunter and Torian, who have already returned to a conversation filled with strategy and weapons tactics.

"Don't worry about them." I tap the side of the tin. "Keep your eyes on the prize."

Her gaze softens, the tension slightly leaving her frame. "Thank you."

The appreciation is barely audible. It sinks into me though. Soul-deep.

"Don't mention it." I rifle through the drawers as she grabs something to eat, and pull out a pad and pen to place down beside her. "Once you're done I'm going to need you to sketch a map of what we're up against."

"I can do that." She holds a hand over her mouth as she chews. "I can also mark where the safes are and their pin codes."

"Perfect."

She keeps eating, leaving that delicate hand covering her lips. "But in return I need you to do one more thing for me."

And there it is—the foreboding, the ten steps back to my slight forward momentum. I can already tell I won't like her request. I'll hate it and want to comply in equal measure. "And what's that, shorty?"

"I need you to give me a gun."

10

PENNY

LUCA DIDN'T GIVE ME A GUN. HE DID, HOWEVER, LAUGH IN AN UNDERSTATED, totally endearing and equally demeaning way before declining my request with a subtle apology.

"You're too volatile at the moment," he'd said. "And it will ruin this tough-guy thing I've got going if a woman under my protection starts fighting her own battles."

He'd meant the latter as a joke.

I didn't find it funny.

But he, along with Hunter and Torian, listened in silence as I talked them through my rough sketch of the house and yard. I told them where I thought the guards might be—inside and out—and gave them my knowledge of the weapons they should be holding—a rifle and knife—along with my assumption of any training they may have had—limited to none.

I was treated like an integral part of the team. They asked innumerable questions, ran through strategies, and made me eat to increase my energy levels while we came up with different plans of action, each option having multiple contingencies.

By the time they were ready to make a move, night had fallen, and Tobias had claimed a few hours of awake time to become marginally settled in Keira's presence.

She was good with him. Too good. Which pissed me off. His naive kiddo brain took in every kind word she said like a sponge. He gobbled up her kindness and generosity as if it were edible gold. So now I like her even less.

Their incremental bond wasn't enough to make me feel comfortable leaving him on the island, but their connection appeased me to the point where I could step onto the boat knowing he was safer with Keira than he'd be back at home.

Then there's my brother, the man who no longer tries to meet my gaze. The one whose aura seeps with such deep sorrow as we race over the moonlit water I can't stop my breath from catching whenever I look his way.

"Are you warm enough?" Luca settles next to me on the boat's bench seat, his attention on the goosebumps along my arms.

"I'm good." The sea breeze makes my loose shirt billow at the hem, the sweep of mother nature's kiss the only comforting sensation out here in solitude. It's the beauty before the approaching storm, but I refuse to let the thought of what's to come send me into a spiral.

I need to stop thinking about the possibility of the guards not acting according to how I anticipate. Or that my sisters could already be dead. The unknowns try to haunt me like a conniving devil on my shoulder. I can't give in to the darkness. Not yet.

"You nervous?" Luca's voice is barely audible over the rush of water against the hull.

He makes me nervous.

Returning to the only home I've known for the last eighteen-plus months seems more natural in comparison. At least I can predict what will happen inside those walls. The suffocating fear of what comes next is almost a comfort because of its familiarity. It's what I'm used to. What I know.

With Luca, I'm in unchartered territory.

"I'm cautious," I admit. "I don't hold the same confidence you all have."

"You're our main priority. We're not going to let anything happen to you."

His protection attempts to seep into me, the wisps of kindness brushing over my extremities. I'd love for the effects to sink deeper. To penetrate. If only my self-preservation didn't see his ability to soften me as a threat.

"You all seem to know exactly what you're doing," I murmur. "How can you have confidence when you're going into a situation where you know you'll be outnumbered more than two to one?"

He grips the bench seat on either side of his thighs and ponders his answer for longer than necessary. He opens his mouth, only to close it, then glances away.

"You're faking the confidence, aren't you?" I try to read him. To see what he's attempting to hide. "This is all a huge risk."

"Of course it's a risk. Doesn't mean I'm not confident. I know what I'm doing."

"How? This situation can't be a common occurrence."

He pauses, his gaze gentle. "I've had training."

"Training? How can you train for—"

"I was a SEAL, Penny."

I pull back an inch, my surprise hitting me hard as he glances away. He seems embarrassed by his honorable past.

"I don't understand." I lean to the side, reclaiming his gaze. "Why did you—"

"It's not up for discussion."

Right… his past is a touchy subject. I guess I should be pleased we have something in common, but what he tries to hide only leaves me more unsettled.

"What about the others? I doubt my brother became a SEAL while I was here. What training does he have? Does he have experience with this type of thing? Is he used to killing people, too?"

His expression remains impassive, neither confirming nor denying. "What Decker does and doesn't have experience with is something you should discuss with him. I'm not getting between the two of you again."

My pulse increases as I picture Sebastian as a murderer. I see visions of him killing people. Fighting for his life. Gunning down strangers. The aggression doesn't fit what I know of the man from my past. It doesn't mesh at all.

"I want to know if he's going to be able to look after himself." The question grazes my throat, the hint of a plea layered in my tone. "He's different from the man I grew up with. He's a stranger now."

"Then get to know him." He jerks his chin at Sebastian, standing beside Hunter at the steering wheel. "I'm sure he'd appreciate you attempting to talk to him." He pushes to his feet, distancing me from necessary answers.

"Please." I reach out to stop his escape, my fingers an inch from contact before I retract at the last second. "Just tell me if he's capable of going through with this. Is he able to kill someone in cold blood?"

He glances down at my hand as my arm retreats, then slowly raises his gaze to mine. "He's capable."

Another part of me dies.

After everything I've been through, I wouldn't have thought it possible. But there it goes, the sinking feeling in my stomach expanding to take over my chest.

Despite our plan already being in motion, a part of me had hoped for Luca's uncertainty. That he didn't know if Sebastian was one of *them*. The bad guys. The brutal.

Not only did his words confirm it, his pity-filled gaze cements the walls of the hollowness carved out inside me.

Sebastian isn't Sebastian anymore.

"Hunter is more than capable, too," Luca adds. "So you've got nothing to worry about."

I scoff out a derisive laugh, hoping the effort will dislodge my vulnerability. "I wasn't overly concerned about him. The vibe he gives off is threatening enough."

A grin tweaks Luca's lips, the sly expression slightly endearing in the glow of the moon. "He may look scary, but he's got a soft side. If his woman asked him to put on a dress and perform a ballet recital, I'm pretty sure he'd comply without skipping a beat."

I raise my brows, not buying his bullshit. Not caring enough to voice it either. I'm already in mourning for my brother. I can't believe the gentle protector is gone. That he's now working for the enemy.

"You'll understand once you meet Sarah." Luca continues. "She's not the kind of woman you deny."

"Pretty?" I assume.

"Deadly." His humor fades. "Don't get me wrong—she's attractive, but she's the type of woman who could slit a throat with a smile on her face. It's like catnip to the big guy."

I bristle at the mental image of this woman. Lethal beauty. Black heart.

I'm out of my depth here. Surrounded by psychopaths. Then there's Luca, with his harsh promises and penetrating stare. Why does everyone else scare me, yet he's become some strange source of stability?

"You've got nothing to worry about, shorty." He takes a step back, preparing to walk away. "I'm not going to let anything happen to you."

And then there's that nickname. *Shorty.* The one word which is far preferable to the things I've been called during the last years. There's the slightest hint of an endearment to it. A lingering compliment of sorts.

But I'm not short. In comparison to him, maybe. Far from it, in relation to other women.

It's just one of the many thoughts plaguing me as I'm left alone for the rest of the ride into the Naxos port.

Even once we arrive, Hunter and Sebastian disembark without a glance in my direction. They know the drill as they each carry a duffel onto the pier, the bags stocked with guns, ammo, and communication devices.

It's Luca who attempts to help me from the boat, his arm outstretched, waiting for me to take his offering.

"I can't." I keep my expression blank in case anyone in the distance is paying us attention. "You're not allowed to touch me."

"Shit." He quits the gentlemanly gesture with a wince.

I don't think it's from the mistake though. It's his head. "You're still in pain."

"The bumpy ride wasn't exactly my best friend. But I'll be fine once we're on land." He glances around the quiet port. "Is there anything else I need to be reminded of?"

I don't answer. I'm too busy studying him—the wrinkles of pain, the skin tone lacking a healthy glow.

"Penny?" He raises a brow of impatience.

"I'm to be treated like Luther's girlfriend in public. Not a slave." I wave a hand to indicate my lack of clothing. "Like we discussed, you need to act like we've been out swimming all day. The police don't appreciate tourists nagging them to check on my welfare. So act normal. No degradation or punishments."

"Jesus Christ," he mutters. "I wasn't going to—"

"I'm just letting you know you're to act professional while I'm in the open. It's in front of Luther's guards or contacts where you'll need to treat me differently."

His jaw tightens. "I won't be treating you like shit regardless of our company."

"You will if you don't want to cause suspicion."

His lip curls, the faintest rumble emanating from his throat.

"What the fuck are you two doing?" Hunter yells from the pier. "Hurry up."

I keep my attention on Luca. On the beautiful intricacies of the disgust written all over his face. He feels sorry for me and I both appreciate and despise his reaction. He doesn't even know the half of what I've been through and yet he harbors pity.

"We're coming." I climb from the boat and wait for Luca to reach my side before we head toward land.

The march forward is accompanied by coded murmurs between the men surrounding me.

"Two at three o'clock," Sebastian says.

"One at ten," from Hunter.

"Three on the balcony at four," comes from the lethal man at my side.

Their constant chatter drills into my head, increasing my unease. I'm used to being surrounded by arrogant confidence, my captors well aware the only eyes daring to look at them would be from curious tourists or enviable deviants.

Now, everything is different.

I'm flanked by a protector. My safety is a priority. Yet I feel more vulnerable than ever. The slightest possibility of freedom has given me something to lose.

Everything to lose.

"So, in public you're treated like a girlfriend?" Luca shoots me a glance, his gaze falling to my feet. "But you weren't given shoes."

"We're on an island. A lack of shoes isn't out of the ordinary."

"How 'bout a lack of pants?" Hunter interrupts. "I don't know one hot-blooded guy who wouldn't pay you attention."

"Suspicion and attention are two different things. One requires police intervention, the other would increase Luther's ego. So, no, my lack of clothing isn't an issue. If anything, it's more acceptable than the full-length pants I wore out of here earlier."

"For the love of…" Sebastian runs a hand through his hair. "I wish I was the one to kill that motherfucker. He had all his bases covered, didn't he?"

They have no idea. I don't want them to either.

The more they learn, the deeper my shame will sink. I don't want them aware of the things I've done. The person I've become.

We reach land and walk through the parking lot to the street, the stabbing asphalt against the soles of my feet a welcome distraction as we approach a man standing beside a compact car, another vehicle parked directly behind it.

"You Luca?" the guy asks, his Greek accent heavy.

"Yeah. Are these our cars?" Luca doesn't leave my side, remaining mere inches away as the man lobs two sets of keys his way.

"Yes. Park them back here when you're done and drop the keys into the locked box over there." He points to a mailbox-type metal locker a few feet along the footpath, then returns his attention to our group. Specifically me, a grin appearing the longer his eyes linger. "I hope you enjoy your stay in Naxos."

He's recognized me. Who I am. *What* I am.

How could he not when I've been branded for years?

"She's a sexy little thing, isn't she?" Luca treats me exactly how he vowed not to moments earlier. "Feisty, too."

His descent into slimy arrogance is so flawless I shiver. The cocky tilt to his lips doesn't help.

"Luther's pretty Penny," the stranger drawls. "She's the stuff of folklore. Men around here would sell their wives just for a taste."

"Luther's not here," I grate through a fake smile. "Why not take the opportunity to indulge in your fantasies?"

The guy laughs. "There's that spite I've heard so much about. You trying to lure me to my death, whore?"

Whore.

The description shouldn't faze me after the years of repetition. I should be immune. Yet the degradation coats me in a layer of grime thicker than anything I've experienced now that I'm in the presence of saviors instead of monsters.

"One can only hope," I snarl.

The man continues to chuckle. "Maybe I will." He steps closer, his eyes raking a trail over my billowing T-shirt. "Maybe I'll teach you to keep that smart mouth closed."

"Please do." Luca steps closer to me. "Everyone keeps making it clear that I can't put hands on her, but they never said anything about scrawny assholes who don't know their place."

Again, he says it so smoothly. With calm and poise and a shocking amount of level-headed arrogance. And again, I shudder, this time in pleasure.

The man doesn't quit his laughter as he beams a bright smile. "I'm only playing." He backtracks, moving from the sidewalk to the desolate street. "I will leave you to enjoy your night."

He continues to a nearby car, his taunting gaze still on mine as he climbs inside and drives away.

All the while, my protectors remain quiet around me, the silence growing thick.

Sebastian scrubs a hand over his face, probably trying to wipe away the shame I've placed upon our family. Hunter is tense, his clenched fist clutching the duffel at his side. Then there's Luca, the man whose fierce attention burns the side of my face. He's staring at me. Judging me. He's seeing all the things I've done in an effort to keep air in my lungs. He's picturing the depravity. The sickening reality.

"He'll be dead by the end of the week," he murmurs. "I swear it on my life."

His vow catches me off guard. I thought I'd receive a reprimand for my spite. Or a warning not to draw additional attention. Instead, he gifts me with the promise of murder.

"Let's get the fuck out of here." Hunter dumps his duffel on the sidewalk, opens the zipper and pulls out the communication devices stashed inside, passing one to Luca and another to Sebastian. "Put them on in the car. We've got too many eyes on us here."

He refastens the bag and stands, handing over the heavy weight to my brother. "We'll give you a ten-minute head start. Let us know if you need more time."

Sebastian nods, then turns to me, a duffel weighed at each of his thighs, his gaze solemn. I don't want to read into his silence. I can already hear his thoughts.

He wants to say goodbye. Maybe even good luck.

I glance away, my nose tingling at the thought of the danger he's about to place himself in. The danger *I'm* placing him in because I refuse to leave this nightmare without my sisters.

"Look after her." He lugs the duffels to the closest car to place them on the passenger seat. "I'm holding you both responsible." He slams the door shut, then rounds the hood, not saying another word before he slumps into the vehicle and takes off.

I squeeze my eyes shut, unable to watch him drive away.

Ten minutes is going to be the only thing separating us. Six hundred measly seconds, while each heartbeat creates a cavern of space between us. Despite who he's become, I couldn't live with the thought of being the cause of his death.

My eyes burn behind the closed lids. I have enough guilt to contend with. I can't withstand anymore.

"He's going to be okay," Luca whispers. "This will all be over soon."

I hope so. I don't know how much more of this adrenaline high I can take. The arrhythmia won't stop. The tremble in my hands is incessant. And the pessimistic thoughts continue to multiply.

"Picture the end result." His gravel-rich voice brushes my ear. "Focus on what it's going to be like once we're out of here. If not, your thoughts can become your biggest enemy."

I comply, squeezing my eyes tighter until I see the smiling faces of my sisters as I help lead them to safety. I can't wait to tell them they're free. Or to fully drown in the sensation myself.

I'll apologize to Chloe and make sure she knows I'm sorry for remaining silent while Luther made her a guinea pig to the sedative trial. And I'll beg her forgiveness for whatever the guards took liberties to do to her limp body after Tobias and I were escorted from the mansion.

I keep picturing those moments as footsteps sound a few feet away, followed by a car door opening and closing.

"Come on." Rough fingers provide a feather of friction against my arm, the touch lasting the slightest second before withdrawing. "We need to get moving."

I blink him into focus, his comforting concern bearing down on me. There's something in those hazel eyes that undo me. They unravel my focus. Create havoc. I'm sure he knows, too, because he's the first to look away and start toward the remaining car.

"You're in the back," he offers over his shoulder as he makes his way to the driver's side and climbs in behind the wheel.

Hunter already rides shotgun.

I'm left on my own. Out in the open. With no cage or threatening figure by my side. It's a strange sensation. Welcoming and suffocating at the same time. I can breathe freely, the air seeming to carry twice as much oxygen.

Hunter lowers his window, his narrowed focus silently telling me to hurry up.

I'm not ready. Not yet. Just one more moment. One more breath before commonsense has to take over and I need to pretend I'm still a prisoner.

"I'm not an athlete," he mutters, "so run if you like. I'm not going to chase you. But if you want to help your friends I'm fucking ready to bust some skulls."

"I'm not running." I stalk to the car and slide in behind him. "I want those busted skulls more than you do."

"Then let's do this." Luca starts the ignition and drives lazily through the narrow streets, taking wrong turns and doubling back more than once on his way to Luther's house.

I lean forward as my panic ratchets up a notch. "Do you know where you're going?"

"It's all in the plan." He takes another wrong turn. "We're still buying Decker time to get set up, and I want to make sure we don't have a tail."

"Oh." I settle back into my seat, slightly appeased.

The confidence in Luther's men had always been something I despised. And somehow, the trait on a good guy has the opposite effect.

No, not a good guy. Just a different type of bad. I can't forget that.

"I'm headed in the right direction now, though, right?" He flicks me a glance in the rear-view. "Straight down this road, then take the next two lefts?"

I nod. "Yeah."

The closer we get, the more my pulse builds. My nausea increases at the thought of my sisters already being dead. Slaughtered. I've seen too much death already. Vacant eyes and lifeless bodies. Sisters who came and went from this world, the scars of their suffering the only thing left behind.

"You okay?" Luca asks. "What's wrong?"

My throat tightens, the bile climbing from my stomach. I can't escape the darkest depths of my memories. I'm battered with snapshots. Pummeled with remembered sounds. I know what those guards are capable of and if they've found out Luther was murdered—

"Penny?" Luca reaches into the back seat to jostle my leg. "What's going on?"

"Nothing." I fight the panic and swallow down the sickening taste building at the back of my throat. "I'm fine."

"Fine." Hunter scoffs. "Fuck I hate when women say that."

"It's not too late to back out." Luca returns both hands to the steering wheel, his scrutiny heavy from the rear-view mirror. "All you need to do is say the word."

"I'm ready." I force conviction into my tone. "And we're almost there, so quit worrying about me and focus. One wrong move and we're all dead."

Hunter chuckles. "That's one seriously messed up pep talk. I like your style."

The car slows as we reach the corner to Luther's street and Luca raises a finger to his ear, repositioning his comm piece. "Decker is ready. We're good to go."

I know what that means. My brother is already up there. At the house. Preparing to kill... or be killed.

"Is he okay?" I lean forward again. "Did he say anything else?"

"If there was something wrong we would've heard." Luca continues to stalk me from the mirror. "You need to relax. Sit back. Breathe."

"I'm breathing," I murmur.

He grins, the brightness entering his eyes a soothing blanket over my frazzled nerves. I don't know how he does it. He's harsh yet gentle. Domineering, aggressive, threatening, and so entirely reassuring at the same time.

It's unnatural.

No doubt an effect of my growing instability.

The car picks up speed as we round the bend and drive at a normal pace to Luther's property. The extravagant metal gates gleam in the moonlight, the door to my cage waiting for me to slip back where I belong.

"Game faces, people." Hunter's voice is barely audible. "It's time to dish out some karma."

I do as planned, sit tall, scowl in place, hands in my lap. I look straight ahead, not focusing any of my concern on the guard who approaches from the darkness, his rifle aimed at the car as Luca lowers his window.

This is it—the moment where any or all of us could be slaughtered because I made an incorrect assumption about the guards' knowledge.

"Hey, buddy," Luca greets. "How's things?"

"Back away." The middle-aged guy snarls, his accent heavy, the barrel of his weapon dropping to pin Luca in the chest. "This is private property."

"I know. I was here yesterday, remember?"

There's a pause, each beat of silence growing thicker.

"With Cole," he adds. "Luther's son."

I wait, hoping for the first sign of our success, when our failure will easily be announced with a gunshot. But there's no reaction. Not in understanding or threat. If the guard has any inkling Luther left here to attack Cole and Luca this gun-toting asshole isn't showing it.

"You shouldn't be here unannounced." He repositions the rifle at his hip. "What do you want?"

I let out a long breath and swallow to alleviate the desert in my mouth. The guard's question is the first sign of our possible success. He has no idea we're a threat. And yet the progress only adds more pressure to my insides.

"Luther requested some private family time with his boys. So he sent us here to enjoy ourselves. You know—" Luca gives a cocky chuckle. "—With the women."

The weight increases, the discomfort squeezing my stomach, shoulders, neck. I ignore how easily Luca plays his role, not wanting to drown in my thoughts of how he can keep effortlessly switching from protector to predator.

"No. I know nothing of this." The guard jabs his rifle toward the car. "Leave."

"Leave?" Hunt leans forward to meet the guy's line of sight. "Even when we've got one of Luther's girls with us?" He jerks a thumb toward me. "I'm pretty sure he'll be pissed if we sate our boredom with this one."

The guard leans down, his dark features peering into the window opposite mine, his narrowed eyes raising goosebumps on my skin. "Why is she with you?"

"We just fucking told you. Luther asked us to bring her back. He said he wanted uninterrupted family time and when the big guy gives an order, you obey, right?" Luca reaches into his jacket and pulls out a gun, pinching it between two fingers so it dangles without threat. "And he reminded us of the no-weapon rule, too." He hangs the pistol out the window. "If you don't believe me, call him. Just be aware he's going to be fuckin' pissed at the interruption."

The guard's attention flicks between me, the gun, then Luca, and back again. He's weighing up the bluff. "*Léne tin alítheia?*" He speaks my way, his question asking about my chauffeur's honesty.

"*Fysiká,*" I sneer. "Why else would I be here?"

His lip curls, his hatred unhidden as he steps forward and snatches the gun before jamming it into the waistband of his pants. "Give me your gun, too." He lowers the barrel of his rifle while he speaks to Hunter. "If you're caught with a weapon inside those walls you will be shot without warning."

Hunter complies, reaching across Luca to hand over his pistol.

We're being allowed inside.

The guard is letting Luca and Hunter fulfil their perversions, which means my sisters are still alive. No alarms have been sounded. The best-case scenario has been laid at our feet.

My heart pumps faster. Anticipation has my fingers twitching in my lap.

"*Échoume episképtes*," the guard grates into the communication device stashed into the sleeve of his suit jacket. "Luther's orders. Give them access to the *gynaíkes*." He returns his focus to the men in the front seat. "No more guns?"

"No more guns," Hunter answers. "Just the big pistol I'm packin' for the ladies."

I close my eyes, despising his casual reference to rape.

"Enjoy yourself."

That's the last I hear of the guard as the gates whir apart, allowing us entry.

I know what comes next. This part of the plan was set in stone. It's the only reason I open my eyes to seek out the guard returning to his position in the shadows.

"Look away, Penny," Luca demands.

I won't.

I pin my glare on the guard, his mimicked expression holding mine as a darkened figure creeps up behind him.

Our car moves forward, the sound of the engine and the opening gates enough to mask my brother's approach, but I stare harder at the guard, glare with more ferocity, hoping somehow to distract Satan's henchman from the sentence that approaches.

"Penny," Luca warns. "Look away."

My heart stops the moment Sebastian grabs the guard around the neck, pulling him backward and off-balance. There's a sheer second of surprised panic. A slash of a glinting knife. A brief struggle. Then death.

My brother kills the man right before me and yet it's done so easily, so effortlessly, it seems like fiction. A movie. There was no pause for contemplation or compassion.

"For fuck's sake, Penny, I told you to look the other way."

"Let her watch." Hunter comes to my defense. "I'm sure she's seen worse."

"Just because she's seen it before doesn't mean she has to see it now." Luca presses his foot harder on the accelerator. "And besides, she needs to fucking listen if we're going to get out of here alive."

"I'll listen." I continue to watch my brother as he drags the lifeless body toward a head-high bush. "But only when your instructions involve getting my friends to safety. Don't pretend you know what's best for me."

He growls, his anger a low vibration as we pass the gates. I chance a glance through the back window, trying to gain another glimpse of Sebastian.

"Eyes to the front," Luca commands. "Keep playing your role."

This time I obey, slumping into the seat as the car curves around the long drive to pull up in front of the overbearing mansion. I try not to let foreboding consume me, but that house has a soul. A dark one. It beckons to me, whispering promises of torture.

"Deck just took down another target." Hunter presses a hand to his hidden earpiece. "He seems to think these guys are easy prey."

I unfasten my belt to scoot forward. "Tell him not to become complacent. Some of them are brutal."

"Hear that, Deck? Your sister said not to get cocky." Hunter glances over his shoulder at me. "Would you normally be eager to get up close and personal like that? Or should you be keeping your distance?"

I can't help it. I'm anxious. Completely and utterly unsettled.

The engine is cut as I slide back. Seatbelts are unfastened. The men climb outside. Then Luca is at my door, pulling it wide to wait for me to join them.

I don't know how they do it—mask the adrenaline, play it cool.

I can't keep focus. I'm not the heartless automaton I thought I could be. I pictured myself coming here, entirely determined and lethal. Instead, I'm pretending not to desperately fight off paranoia as it slays me with a million possible pitfalls to our plan.

"Get moving, shorty." Luca keeps his expression impassive, not giving me a hint to his emotions. "We've got eyes on us from the front door."

I don't look. Don't nod.

"Ready?" His gaze bores into me, intense and filled with concern.

I give a subtle incline of my head and follow his lead toward the house. I stiffen when his gentle grip glides over the crook of my elbow, but it's too late to warn him of his mistake. Two guards exit the front of the mansion—Argus and Otis—both of them looking down at where Luca holds my arm.

"You shouldn't be touching her." Argus places the butt of his rifle on the ground, his pinched brows pulled tight.

"I know." Luca tugs me forward. "But she's a feisty little thing and I didn't want her attempting to run again."

"She tried to escape?"

"Tried. Failed. Got punished." Luca stops us before them and releases his gentle grip to run a taunting hand through my hair. "Didn't you, pretty Penny?"

I shudder.

His touch is kind... but those words... that name.

The provocation from his lips shakes me to my core.

I jerk my head away. "Merely keeping you on your toes, asshole."

He drops his hand from my hair to reclaim my arm. "You learned your lesson though, didn't you? And if you attempt that stupidity again, nothing will save you."

I suck in a breath at how real his threat sounds. How sickening. Then his finger gently strokes the inside of my arm, the delicate brush in contrast to his vicious words.

He's trying to comfort me. Attempting to ease his flawless act with a reaffirming touch.

I appreciate it. I appreciate *him*.

I don't want to. *God*, how I don't want to, but I do.

"So, let's get this party started." Hunter claps his hands together. "Point us in the direction of the women. I'm ready to see what all the fuss is about."

Otis starts for the mansion doors when a grunt of muted sound disturbs the night air from the yard. It's a noise of death that isn't entirely discreet.

Argus must hear it too because he stiffens, his focus shifting to the darkness over my shoulder. "What was that?" He raises his wrist, preparing to speak into his comms device.

Holy shit.

I break out in a cold sweat, certain our attack is about to be discovered.

"I heard it, too." Luca turns toward the yard, stepping closer to me, increasing the brush of his finger. "Want us to check it out?"

I stop breathing.

One wrong move…

One suspicious word…

One instruction into that communication device and my sisters are dead.

"No." Argus inches toward the driveway, his lips pressed to the mouthpiece in his palm. "Can we get—"

Luca lunges, landing a left hook to Argus's cheek, his other hand gripping the rifle. He yanks the weapon forward, sending the guard stumbling while Hunter lashes out at Otis, pummeling with one fist then the other.

I scramble backward, stepping out of the way as my protectors attack with brutal efficiency. The guards don't have a chance to retaliate. They drop. From knees, to palms, to stomachs.

It's such beautiful savagery.

That is, until the sound of gunfire erupts from inside and my brief sense of optimism vanishes in a punishing heartbeat.

11

LUCA

I SLAM THE GUARD DOWN ON THE CEMENT AS GUNFIRE EXPLODES INSIDE. THE SCREAMS of women follow.

Penny's friends are in trouble.

I shoot Hunt a glance, his ferocity meeting mine for a brief second before he lands a vicious kick to the guard laying before him, his boot making a direct jaw hit. Otis falls limp. Out like a light.

I'm not as kind. I drop to my knees, grab my blubbering enemy around the head, and break his neck with a swift jerk of my hands.

"Where is she?" Decker speaks into my earpiece. "Where's Penny?"

I scramble to my feet, snatch the rifle along the way to point it toward the sound of approaching steps.

It's Deck, his eyes filled with fury as he yanks two pistols from the back of his waistband. "Where the fuck is she?"

I drop the rifle, catch the weapon he lobs at me, then turn to find her. "She's…" I keep turning, not seeing her anywhere.

"Fuck. She must have slipped by me." Hunt snatches the second thrown pistol and makes for the mansion doors. "I'll get her."

"No." Decker rushes in front of him. "There's still one more guard outside. You take care of it. I'm going after my sister." He doesn't pause for confirmation as he shoves his way past Hunter to disappear inside.

"I'm going with him." I follow, stopping beside Hunt to hand over the car key. "Put Otis in the trunk. We'll need him later."

I maneuver inside the mansion, turning down the hall to the right as Decker runs in a crouch along the left.

I pass doorways, giving each room a cursory glance, my gun aimed and ready as I panic over finding Penny. She can't have gone far. She was right there. By my fucking side one minute and gone the next.

I don't stop my search until shouts carry from around the corner of the hall. I slow, quietening my steps as I lean close to the wall and chance a glance around the edge.

There's a guard a few yards away, his rifle pointed toward an open doorway, his aim low. "Get up, bitch."

Fuck. It could be Penny.

I shoot, blasting the motherfucker in the head to plaster his blood over a nearby painting, his limp body flopping to the floor.

More screams lash the air, the closest coming from that open doorway, the sound quickly smothered. There's the shout of men from another corner of the house. The thud of a struggle, too.

I creep toward the room, stepping over the dead guard, and chance a glance inside the darkened interior.

"Penny?" I blink to adjust to the lack of light and find three bunks. A dresser. A closet. But no warrior woman, only the faintest hint of movement from the far corner. "Shorty, is that you?"

I crouch slowly, the movement incremental, my gun still at the ready. "Are you in here?" I flatten onto my stomach, doing a visual sweep under the beds to find two wide eyes beaming back at me from under the farthest bunk.

It's another woman, her body shrouded in darkness.

I place down my weapon and tilt my hands skyward. "I'm here to help."

She doesn't move. Doesn't blink.

"My name's Luca. I was here the other day with Cole."

Still, no movement. No noise.

"Stay where you are, okay? I'll come back for you once it's safe." I reclaim my gun and brace to stand. "Have you seen Penny? Did she walk by?"

Her hesitation continues for long seconds before she finally nods. It's barely there. Almost unseen.

"Did she continue down the hall?"

This time her nod is more defined. Adamant.

"Okay. Good." I shove to my feet, thankful for the adrenaline faintly masking the pounding in my skull. Those gunshots messed with my head. The attack on the guard did, too.

I reclaim my position close to the wall and continue into unchartered territory, my vision not entirely at the top of its game. I have to blink to make things crystal, and that's a fucking worry all on its own.

"*Penny?*" I yell. "Where are you?"

A thunder of footsteps sound from the hall I just trekked. Not light. Not hers. As soon as the asshole comes around the corner, I shoot.

Pop. Pop.

He crumples. It's too fucking easy. And it's entirely fucking clear these guards aren't guards at all. They're puppets armed with the least tactical weapon on earth to be used indoors.

Their lack of skill doesn't make sense. Unless Luther truly was untouchable out here and these guards are for show.

"I've taken down two." I speak into the microphone hidden under my shirt. "But something doesn't feel right."

Someone grunts, the sound resembling a struggle.

More gunfire erupts, the noise carrying from outside.

"One more down." Hunt pants through my earpiece. "But Penny must've got her count wrong. I can still hear someone else out here."

Pop. Pop. Pop.

This time the shots ricochet from inside, the brain-piercing noise vibrating off the walls to tamper my ability to distinguish the location.

Women wail. A male shouts.

"Penny," someone cries. "*Penny.*"

I run, taking the first archway on my left to dart and weave through a dining room.

"Tadd, you don't want to do this."

It's her, the familiar voice carrying from nearby.

I don't stop. Don't even pause. I sprint toward the sound and skitter to a halt when I find her standing in an archway, her arms raised in surrender, light from inside the room bathing her in an ethereal glow.

"Penny, don't go in there." I keep running. Scrambling.

She ignores me to step out of view.

Pop. Pop.

I die at the sound of those shots. The accompanying screams are brutal. Gunfire takes over—from the other side of the house and outside. It's everywhere, the thunder pounding into my skull.

I push harder, sprinting into the unknown a few feet behind her, yelling a war cry in the hopes of stealing the attention of any threat toward her. As soon as I breach the room, shots rain down on me from an asshole with a rifle. I dive, the whistle of a bullet brushing my ear as I sail through the air, my gun steady.

I return fire—*pop, pop*—then hit the ground hard, the smooth tile helping me to slide behind the safety of a sofa.

For a second, I lie there, waiting for a lethal wound to announce itself, listening for movement of an enemy as blackness spots over my vision.

There's more screaming. More sobbing.

But no more fire.

The battle dies for a moment.

"Penny?" I struggle to raise to my elbows. "*Penny?*" I shove to my feet, cautious, and find the guard, barely in his twenties, dead on the floor.

Penny stands a few yards to his left, two more women close by her side, and another spread on the floor at her feet, her body and face shielded by the legs standing around her.

I edge my way toward them as I take in my surroundings—the floor-to-ceiling windows providing no protection from an outside threat, another archway at the far side of the room, and the extravagant furniture capable of hiding an enemy.

"It's okay." Penny collapses to her knees beside the prone figure, the other two women following suit from the opposite side of the motionless body. "You're going to be okay."

"Was she hit?" I back toward them, my gun and sight shifting between the open doorways. "Talk to me."

My answer comes in the form of slowly building sobs. First one woman, then another.

"In the stomach," Penny whispers. "She needs to get to a hospital."

Fuck.

There are no hospitals. Not for this type of situation.

"Hunt, Deck, I've found them. But I need you guys to give me an update." I reach Penny's side and peer down at the woman on the floor who's barely a woman at all, her face seeming more like an innocent child's.

"I've got one asshole playing hide-n-seek over here," Decker says. "But I think that's the last of them on my side of the house."

"One got away," Hunt adds. "He scaled the fucking wall."

"Did he see your fucking face?" I ask.

"Doubt it. The little bitch was running scared. I'm tempted to run after him."

"No. We've gotta get out of here, and I'm going to need help moving these women." Three of them at least. And the fourth who I left in the nearby bedroom. The fifth won't be going anywhere.

There's no saving her.

Blood seeps across the material of her silken nightwear, the building gurgle in her throat announcing the stream of liquid death about to spill from her lips.

Penny presses her hands to the woman's abdomen, placing pressure on the wound. "We're going to get you out of here, Chloe. We're free."

There's confidence in her voice.

Unwarranted, unwavering confidence.

"She's going to start choking." I indicate for the blonde to move to the left with a jut of my gun. "Get behind her and lift her shoulders."

Her trepidatious gaze darts between me and Penny before she finally scrambles to her knees to raise Chloe's head onto her lap. Not that her compliance matters. The injured woman coughs, the first burst of blood spluttering from her mouth.

"Hold on," Penny demands. "Keep fighting."

More blood bubbles across porcelain skin, the gagging and choking increasing.

The two other women sob. Cry. Hyperventilate.

But Penny doesn't lose her determination. She keeps pressing on Chloe's wound, her fingers drowning in blood as the spluttering loses its ferocity, the wide eyes of the dying girl growing dull.

"Chloe," Penny warns. "Stay with me."

There's nothing I can do, not one fucking thing, as Chloe's soul quickly slips from her body. She gurgles with the blood suffocating her, her shoulders twitching, once, twice. Then she's gone, her head slumping limp, the red stream of death still dripping from her innocent lips.

The other women wail, grasping at the deceased's hands and face.

They beg. They plead. They sob.

All Penny does is stiffen.

There are no tears or weakness. She doesn't show one ounce of vulnerability as she stares unblinking at her fallen sister.

The gunshot echoing from the other side of the house doesn't even make her jolt. It's the other women who scream and scramble to their feet to run for cover as heavy footfalls approach from the hall.

I step in front of Penny, shielding her, and aim my gun. A figure invades the doorway, tempting my trigger finger.

"It's me," Decker calls, withdrawing from view. "Don't shoot." He waits a heartbeat then re-enters as more thunderous steps carry toward us. "Hunter's behind me."

He takes in the sight before him with apprehension, his gaze sliding over the newest additions to our crew before settling on the corpse on the floor. "Is she dead?"

I nod. "Bullet to the gut."

Hunter storms into the room, his attention following the same path as Decker's. "We've gotta get out of here. The asshole who escaped could be calling backup."

"Did we get any intel?" Decker asks. "Have the safes been checked?"

"There's no time. I'm not willing to risk it." I start for Penny and jut my chin toward the two other women cowering on the floor. "Hunt, you help them. Deck, you get back outside and grab the duffels. We can't leave anything behind."

Decker eyes me, then Penny. He's about to make another comment about me getting between him and his sister, and I don't have the fucking patience.

"If I knew where you put the duffels I'd get them myself," I growl, "but I don't. So get your ass moving."

He glares, making me well aware I'll be paying for my actions later.

I don't fucking care. We need to move.

"Ladies, it's time to leave." Hunter starts toward them as Decker jogs from the room. "It's not safe here."

I don't wait to watch their reactions. I keep my focus on Penny, who remains at Chloe's side, her hands still pressed into the pool of blood on the woman's abdomen.

"Shorty…" I walk up behind her to crouch at her back. "We need to get moving."

She doesn't acknowledge me. Doesn't budge an inch as her attention remains riveted on the woman staring unblinking at the roof.

"Pen?" I brush her arm. "We need to go."

There's no sound. Nothing. She's emotionless. Catatonic.

"Come on." Hunter raises his voice. "You want to go home, don't you?"

"Home?" one of the women ask.

"Yes, home." Hunter claps his hands as if trying to gain the attention of school children. "We've gotta go."

The two women climb to their feet together, hand in hand.

"Penny?" the blonde asks.

She doesn't answer. Doesn't even flinch.

"It's okay. I've got her. We won't be far behind you." I turn my attention to Hunter. "I'm going to need to get her cleaned up. There's too much blood."

It's all over her hands. Her legs, too. She can't walk back through the Naxos port like this.

"Can you handle her on your own?"

"I'm good." I glide my grip around Penny's wrists and gently guide her away from Chloe. "There's another woman left hiding in one of the bedrooms. I'll get her to help. Just make sure you grab that fucker out of the trunk and put him into the backseat. If he's not awake, there's smelling salts in one of the duffels. And you're also going to need to get him to swallow some of the liquid E I've got stashed in there, too. We need to make him look like he's drunk, not a fucking prisoner, when we haul him to the boat."

He grins. "My pleasure." He turns for the door. "Come on, ladies. Let's get you home."

After a few moments of tear-stained contemplation, the women follow, leaving Penny behind with me.

I guess I should be thankful for their compliance. But I'm not. I'm fucking bitter they only spared a few seconds for Penny's concern when left with a stranger, after she put everything on the line to save them.

She fought for those women. She begged and threatened.

And they've walked away from her.

"Come on, shorty." I rub her wrists. "The worst is over."

She's still unmoving. Not even nudging out of her shock.

Fuck it.

I wrap an arm around her back and the other under her knees to lift her off the ground. She doesn't fight, barely gives a muted whimper as I carry her through the dining room, into the hall to the darkened bedroom with the three bunks.

"Are you still in here?" I place Penny on her feet. "It's safe to come out."

There's a rustle of movement as the woman crawls from under the bed. She's another wide-eyed innocent, her pain trapped behind generous beauty. "Penny?"

"Help me get her cleaned up. Can you get me some fresh clothes and a wet cloth?"

She nods, the movement jerky, before she hustles to the closet.

"You're going to be okay." I brush Penny's arms, trying to rub away the chill of shock as I lean in. Eye to eye. "You're strong. You can get through this."

She meets my gaze, sorrow thick in her dark irises.

"Here." The other woman returns with a thick layer of white material in her hands. "It's her favorite dress."

"Thanks." I take the offering, ignoring how inappropriate a frilly, feminine dress is at a moment like this, and fling the clothing over my shoulder.

"Let me help." The other woman moves closer, protectively nudging me out of the way as she makes easy work of Penny's oversized T-shirt, raising the hem from her thighs to expose pure nudity.

Holy. Shit.

Decker's sister is entirely naked under that shirt. No panties. No bra. Only smooth, perfect skin marred with sinister bruises along her hips and inner thighs. My gaze latches on to those marks—the sickening implications, the fucking brutality—as the other woman scrambles to cover Penny again, lifting the dress over her head.

"Wait." I halt her with a raise of my hand and quickly turn off the microphone around my neck. "Where's her underwear?"

She shakes her head. "We're not allowed." She doesn't pause as she helps guide Penny's head through the material.

"Wait," I repeat with barely leashed frustration. *Fuck.* I'm getting pummeled here. Visually. Verbally. The muttered conversation through my earpiece along with the approaching freight train of a migraine is making it hard to think. "She can't put on a fucking white dress when her hands are covered in blood. I'm going to need that cloth. *Now.*"

The woman retreats at my anger, her hands trembling.

"I'm not going to hurt her. Just get me that cloth. We need to get out of here."

She straightens her shoulders and nods, leaving me alone with the most heartbreakingly gorgeous woman I've ever laid eyes on.

"Penny…" *Fuck me.* I don't know what to say. I don't even know where to look as she stares at the floor.

"Chloe…" The name is whispered from her lips. "She's gone."

"I know." I shove my gun into my waistband, loosen the brain-numbing comm device in my ear so Hunt and Decker's voices stop punishing me, and reach for the nearest bed to tug off the coverings. "I'm sorry." I grab her wrist, needing to busy myself with something other than visual violation, and wipe the blood from her fingers. "You've been dealt a rough fucking hand, sweetheart. I can't imagine what you're going through."

I stroke her skin, over and over, sweeping away layer upon layer of death. "You're going to be okay." I keep my gaze trained on her arms as I utter the placation. In honesty, I have no idea if she'll physically make it through, let alone mentally. "Once we get you home, you're going to be fine."

She shudders out a breath, the warmth brushing my face.

I want nothing more than to wrap her in cotton wool. To shelter her. To slay every sick son of a bitch who dared to witness her suffering only to turn a blind eye.

"Lilly…" Penny blinks to awareness when the other woman re-enters the room, her trance of grief lessening the slightest fraction. "It's good to see you."

"It's good to see you, too." The other woman hands the cloth to me while her attention remains on Penny's arms. "Is that your blood? Are you hurt?"

"No. It's—"

Shit. "Lilly, I need you to go outside and find the others." She has to remain ignorant. I can't risk any more theatrical delays. "Tell them we're almost ready."

"But I want to stay with—"

"It's okay, Lil." Penny's voice is hollow. "Find the others. We won't be long."

I keep my attention on the cleanup as Lilly reluctantly backtracks from the room. I wipe Penny's wrists, her palms, in between her fingers.

"I can do that myself." She attempts to pull her hand away, but I cling tight, needing to remain tethered.

"I'm sure you could." I give a half-hearted grin. "But would you do as good a job as me?"

"Luca." My name is part plea, part exhausted warning. "I can do it."

"What did I say about listening, shorty?" I grab her other arm and begin the same ritual.

Soon, she'll be on her way out of this nightmare, and I'll be stuck thinking I didn't do enough to help her. That I left her in Luther's clutches when I shouldn't have. That I caused her more pain than necessary.

This is the least I can do. Mere swipes of a damp cloth over delicate skin. Bit by bit I clean away the blood, wishing I was cleaning away her suffering.

"I…" She lets out a long breath. "I think I blacked out in there. Or…" She sighs and shakes her head in confusion. "I don't know. I'm so tired."

"It's shock." I make quick work of her other arm, trying to remain gentle as her nudity taunts me. I can't stop myself from taking a glimpse. But it's not for pleasure. It's because of those fucking marks. "Those bruises…?" I can't finish my question. It's not the time or place to voice my angered curiosity when it's clear who marked her. "I'm sorry. I didn't mean to look."

"The exposure means nothing to me anymore," she whispers. "I lost ownership of my body long ago."

I clench my jaw. Tight.

Anger clogs my throat. Rage burns my veins.

I wipe the last of the blood from her hand, throw the cloth to the floor, and help drag the material from around her neck to cover her nudity. "Nobody owns you. Not Luther. Not his men."

"You don't understand." She busies herself righting the dress, her attention downcast. "You've got no idea."

"Then tell me."

She shakes her head.

"*Tell me.*"

She stiffens, her frantic gaze raising to mine. "Luther may be dead but his shackles still enslave me. There's no escaping what he did. He'll always own me."

"I fucking disagree."

"I wish I had your optimism. I guess it's true that ignorance is bliss."

Her argument is solid, but I refuse to fucking believe it. There's no way this woman can't bounce back. There's too much life left in her to give up now.

"We'll discuss this later." I grab her hand and lead her from the room, stepping over the dead guy in the hall. We reach the front door together, then as soon as Penny makes her way outside she stumbles forward to her friends. The other women are already crying, their sobs increasing tenfold as Penny engulfs them in a group hug.

"What the fuck took so long?" Decker storms toward me. "We need to figure out what we're doing."

"What do you mean?" I frown at Hunter as he approaches. "I thought the plan was to get straight back to the island."

"That was the original plan." He stops before me, one hand clutching his gun, the other raking through his hair. "But these women aren't stable. They haven't stopped crying to take a fucking breath. And you and I both know Torian won't be able to cope with that drama. He needs to focus to finish what you came here for. So it's best if we get them out of here now."

"I've already spoken to Torian," Decker adds, "and he agrees. He's going to make a call to the pilots and also find a way off this island via a private dock. It's less dangerous that way, seeing as though only one of us is going with them."

This is bullshit. Fucking bullshit. "You haven't thought this through. Penny can't leave."

Hunter raises a brow. "She can't? Or you don't want her to?"

I get in his face and smile. Laugh. I try to fake a disregard to his assumption even though it hits too close to home. "If you were smart, you'd remember the fight she put up just because she wanted to bring the kid on this little escapade. So if you try to send her to another country without him, you're going to have full-blown hysteria on your hands. *Contagious fucking hysteria.* Which means instead of four blubbering messes, you're going to have a group of inconsolable trouble."

"Then she can stay." Hunter shrugs. "From what I've seen she hasn't shed a tear anyway. It's the others who need to go."

"And who the fuck is going with them? They can't make that trip on their own."

"I guess that depends if Penny stays or goes. If she remains in Greece I assume lover boy—" he jerks his chin at me "—and big brother will want to keep hovering close. That leaves me to do the heavy lifting, because don't forget that asshole who got away could be planning any number of things."

I clench my teeth, biting back a reply to his "lover boy" comment that will only strengthen his derisive argument.

"It's the best option," Decker grates. "Hunt can go back and—"

He stops mid-sentence at the sound of crunching pebbles behind him. It's Penny, her fragile frame coming to stand a few feet away.

"I heard my name." She inches closer. "What's going on?"

Hunt clears his throat. Decker glances off in the distance while rubbing the back of his neck. Both of them act as if they didn't hear her question, making it fucking clear they expect me to be the bearer of temperamental news.

"Fuck you," I mutter under my breath, then walk to stand in front of her. "We're changing things up a little. It's for the best if we get your friends on a jet and send them home right away."

"What do you mean right away?"

"He means now. From here, to a boat, to the airport." Hunt speaks up. "You need to decide if you're staying or going."

Her eyes flare in shock, those dark depths cutting me down at the knees. "Without going back to the island to collect Tobias?"

"Yes." I nod. "Torian has already organized the jet."

Her lips part and her already pale skin turns ashen. "Then I'm staying. I won't leave Toby behind."

Decker winces. "You'd be safer—"

"I don't care what's safe. I'm not leaving without him. He's just a little boy."

"And what about your friends?" I ask. "You're happy for them to go without you."

"No, Luca, I'm not happy," she scolds. "But you've given me no choice."

A tense second of silence falls between us.

I don't want to do this to her. It's not fucking ideal. But those eyes hold me accountable. The glimmer of betrayal cuts me to the core.

"Okay, if that's settled, we need to make a move." Hunter starts for the other women. "Say your goodbyes."

"Jesus Christ," I mutter. "Have some fucking sympathy."

"Wait up." Decker follows after him. "I need to tell you where I hid the car."

They leave me alone with her pained judgment. Penny continues to stare back at me, her exhausted sorrow forever tattooing my mind.

"You're really doing this?" Her nose wrinkles as if she's trying to dislodge the tingle of building tears. "They're not strong enough to go without me."

"You don't need to mother them anymore." It's obvious Penny has been their rock. She was the one they turned to with questions of my sincerity. The three others took a step back at every opportunity when Penny rushed forward to save them. "Hunter can take care of it. He'll make sure they arrive in the States safely."

"They won't like that."

"Then convince them. Or go with them. It's your choice."

Penny's eyes remain hardened, but the severity loses its edge. She's exhausted. Bone-deep. "I can't leave Tobias with those people. Not when I know what they're capable of."

"Then, like Hunt said, say your goodbyes." I try my fucking hardest not to let her vulnerability wear me down. "You'll see them again soon enough."

She sighs, the breath of defeat punishingly brittle before she returns to her friends. She talks in a low murmur, her undecipherable words causing the women to erupt in more tears, their arms wrapping around her as they sob against her shoulders.

She clings to them, her fingers white-knuckled, but still she doesn't break. There're only strong eyes that hold mine as if begging for this new form of torture to stop.

She's been through murder, death, reunion, salvation, and now a farewell all in one day, and she hasn't shed a single tear. Not one. Any sane, full-grown man would have blubbered through the experience.

"Come on." I start for the car. "I need to get the fuck out of here."

12

PENNY

I walk on numb feet from the car to the start of the Naxos port, Luca at my side as he carries the duffels while Sebastian is up ahead, his arm wrapped around the guard who stumbles along at his side.

They gave him something. Ecstasy or speed maybe. I don't know. But the effects make the man appear drunk. He's swaying, not protesting as my brother slurs out a rendition of *"Fifty-Five Bottles of Beer on the Wall"* to increase the ruse that we're not taking one of Luther's men as a prisoner.

Yet all I see is Chloe.

I stagger along the pier, each blink punishing me with a snapshot of her suffering.

I climb into the boat as guilt consumes me, the fact I'm alive while she's dead is so bitterly unfair.

And when I take a seat on the cushioned bench and stare at Otis, who Sebastian shoves to the floor, all I want to do is make the guard pay.

I need his dried blood under my nails, not Chloe's.

I yearn to see the fear of death in his eyes, just like I had to witness in hers.

I crave the euphoria of hurting him, punishing him, torturing him. Because that's what they did to her.

To *all* of us.

His future suffering is what I focus on as my brother starts the boat and guides us from the port. But Otis doesn't suffer. He's not even scared. Whatever they gave him has plastered a delirious smile on his face, the expression pure evil.

I can't stand it.

Chloe is gone—left on the cold floor in a pool of her own blood, her soul forever trapped in that godforsaken house—and this man is blissed out.

It makes me sick.

I drag my gaze away and turn to the water, wishing the excruciatingly slow journey would pass faster. The minutes tick by like hours, the muted chuckle from the maniac on the floor a constant grate on my ears.

"You're dead, pretty Penny. They're going to eat you alive."

I ache at his words. Shiver. It isn't from fear, though. It's from suffocating anger. Every emotion bottled inside me has been increased tenfold—the grief, resentment, hatred, heartache and sorrow. I need to make it stop, I just don't know how.

"You're going to wish you never defied Luther," he slurs. "They're going to make you pay."

I close my eyes and pray for calm.

"You'll beg for death."

I swing around and lean toward him, inching closer, resting my elbows on my knees. "And who, exactly, is going to do all this to me?"

He beams a bright smile, his eyes lazily blinking. "Robert. You know Luther promised you to him. And the things he's going to do to you..." He laughs and flops onto his back, gyrating his hips to the night sky. "You will probably love it. Just like you loved everything Luther put you through."

I gasp. My throat constricts.

"You think I enjoyed what Luther did to me?" I can't keep the shock from my voice.

"You give him exactly what he wants because you love the dick. We all know. Luther does, too. He laughs about how pathetic you are."

He's serious. He truly believes I enjoyed the torture.

"That's why you stayed the longest. Luther loves that you love him."

"Well, Luther's dead." I burst to my feet, about to plant my foot into his ribs. "Robert, Chris, Tadd, Argus, and all the rest, too. And you're next."

"Hey." Luca starts toward me, cutting me off before I reach my target. "What's going on?"

"It's not true." I attempt to walk around him, to get to Otis, only to have the wall of muscle sidestep into my path. "He's wrong."

"Wrong about what?"

I shake my head, my cheeks heating. I can't repeat the conversation. I don't want anyone to even question what I did. How I survived. But my depraved strategy haunts me. I *did* give Luther what he wanted. I worked hard to make sure I was his favorite.

"Don't let him get to you." Luca steps closer, his hands reaching toward my arms.

I bat away his touch. "Don't let him get to me?" I keep repeating those words in my head, but can't quit the resentment that follows. Luca is asking for the impossible. Otis is already under my skin, his toxicity speeding through my veins.

"He's taunting me." My voice cracks. "He's practically laughing at me."

"That's the drugs. Things will change once we get him back to Torian."

I'm not appeased. Not in the slightest. Setting Otis on fire, one slow inch at a time, wouldn't give me enough satisfaction. "What will you do to him?"

"Whatever necessary to get information."

Information.

Shit.

"I-I was meant to help you find Luther's office. And the safes," I ramble, trying to drown out more regret. "I forgot."

"Don't worry. We'll get this fucker to talk. He'll give us a lead or two." He jerks his head toward the bench seat. "You should sit down and rest."

How can I sit when the scum of the earth thinks I enjoyed my punishments? How could I possibly rest with those accusations hanging over my head?

God. I feel so dirty. So worthless.

I turn away, dragging my feet to the back of the boat to stare across the inky black. It would be too easy to jump over the edge with one of those duffels tangled around my feet. I'd drown, the death not coming quickly or painlessly, but at least my suffering would soon be over.

There would be no more taunts of illusive freedom.

I'd finally escape this hellish existence.

"She's a fucking whore." Otis's voice raises over the purr of the boat. "A dead whore."

I close my eyes and wrap my arms around my middle, the weight of Luca and Sebastian's judgment on my shoulders.

I don't flinch at the thud that sounds moments later, or the cry of masculine pain.

"Ignore him, Penny," my brother demands. "Just fucking ignore him."

I try my best, but the alternate thoughts lying in wait are all about Chloe. About death and fear and failure.

By the time we reach Torian's island, I want to vomit. Bile teases the back of my throat. The only thing stopping me from falling to my knees is the knowledge I won't have the strength to get back up.

I remain in place as Otis is hauled to his feet and dragged onto the jetty. I don't follow when Luca calls out, "Are you coming?"

"In a minute." I need more time. Maybe a lifetime.

He nods, his focus already on retribution as he helps Sebastian drag the guard along the trail to the mansion, all three of them quickly disappearing from sight.

I stay there, alone in the silence, blanketed in darkness.

Is this what freedom feels like? Is it the tightness of pure isolation? The punishing weight of guilt? The acidic taste of failure?

Otis implied I remained in Luther's house because they thought I was a joke.

They laughed at my actions. They knew I was willing to sleep with my rapist, but they didn't spare a thought as to the reason why. Maybe nobody else will, either.

I dig my fingernails into my palms, pressing harder and deeper, attempting to lessen the emotional torment with something physical. When that doesn't help, I climb from the boat and use the sharp pebbles of the trail to punish me from my soles upward.

I walk with hard steps, increasing the pain. I stomp. I twist. I don't stop until the faint shriek of male torture leaves me motionless.

For a second, my excruciating thoughts cease, my suffering placed on pause.

My breath remains trapped in my lungs as I wait for more of that rewarding sound. My heart pounds with yearning. My palms sweat with impatience.

I have to hear that cry again. I want Otis to wail and scream and blubber. I need it to help ease my anguish.

I run for the house in search of the sweet comfort, sprinting around the pool to pull the glass door wide.

Keira waits in the kitchen, her eyes widening at the sight of me. "Are you okay?"

I ignore her in my trek for the hall.

"Wait." She hustles after me, cutting me off before I reach the archway. "What happened? Nobody has told me anything. Did your friends get to safety? I overheard Cole—"

"Three of my sisters are on their way home."

She huffs out a relieved breath. "I'm so glad to hear it."

"*Three*," I repeat. "When there were five of us. Not to mention all those who died previously at your father's command."

Her relaxation vanishes. "I'm so—"

"I wish I had a definitive number to give to you because I'm sure you guys have some sort of family death tally, but I gave up counting a few months after I arrived."

"Penny, I…"

"What?" I raise my brows. "You're sorry?"

"Yes. I'm sorry. For everything."

"Do you feel sorry when you're putting on your designer clothes? Or those expensive shoes? Because you know where your family's money came from, right?"

She pulls back, clearly offended.

"And are you sorry when you're sleeping with the man whose family you destroyed? Are you sorry when you're fucking my brother?"

"Penny." She raises her hands in placation. "I didn't do anything wrong. We didn't know what was happening here and as soon as we found out we took action."

"You found out three days ago?" I wave away my heavy sarcasm, not entirely sure why I'm trying to pick a fight. This woman means nothing to me. I don't care what she says or thinks. All I want from her is instructions on how to find Otis. I need directions to help stop the insanity beating down on me. "Do I turn left or right down the hall to find them?"

"Please don't blame me." Her face crumples. "I haven't gotten through this unscathed either. We're all suffering. Some more than others."

I should have *triggered* tattooed on my forehead for the number of buttons she simultaneously pressed. "Wow."

"Listen." She reaches for me, then thinks better for it, her hand falling to her side. "The perversions weren't contained to the Greek islands. They happened at home, too. And I was a victim."

It's my turn to pull back, my retreat made in confusion. "What sort of victim?"

"One like you. I was only a child when I lost my innocence to a man."

"Luther?" The name whispers from my lips.

"No. Not my father. But it was someone he knew was a monster and he allowed them access to me anyway."

My punishment increases. The anger I had for her moments before escapes in a vacuum. One minute, it's there. The next, it's gone, being replaced by more choking guilt.

Every time I think I've become accustomed to how shocking the crimes of men can be, the world teaches me differently. I'm repeatedly shown that there's no escaping the misery.

"What I was put through is nothing in comparison to what you've endured." She holds my gaze, now backing away from my scrutiny. "But I'm not clueless to your suffering. And I struggle every day knowing I could've put a stop to it sooner if I didn't think I was the only one. So I'm sorry." Her eyes begin to water as she sucks in a deep breath. "I'm sorry for my ignorance... I'm sorry for the actions of my father..." Her lips begin to tremble. "And I'm sorry for falling in love with your brother, but Sebastian is the one who saved me, and I'm sure he can do the same for you if only you'd let him."

Goosebumps skitter over my skin, every inch of me touched by her words.

I don't know what to say. I'm not strong enough to apologize to the daughter of my rapist, no matter the severity of her plight.

She gives me a sad smile through the awkward silence. "Would you like something to eat?" Keira doesn't wait for a response. She turns and walks for the kitchen, the muted sound of torture continuing to carry down the hall. "Tobias woke while you were gone. He asked about you."

Tobias.

Oh, God. For a moment, I'd completely forgotten about him, my thoughts entirely selfish. "Was he scared?"

"No. Mostly curious. He sat with me for a while. I made him hot cocoa and told him about his family in Portland. He seems like a good kid."

"He *is* a good kid." The muffled cries grow louder, the sweet promise of retribution plaguing me. "Did he go back to sleep?"

"He did. But I'm not sure how long he will stay that way with all the noise."

I cringe, knowing exactly how much that little boy can sleep through. His slumber could withstand the suffering of me and my sisters on a nightly basis. The current muffled cries are nothing in comparison.

"What is it?" she asks. "What are you thinking?"

"Nothing." I shake my head, but I'm unable to break free of the memories as I continue for the hall. Living nightmares blur my vision. The beatings. The restraints.

"Penny, wait."

I don't listen. I reach the hall and turn left into unmarked territory as her quickened footsteps give chase.

"You can't go in there." She rushes after me, stalking at my back as I pass door upon door, the wails building. "You don't want to see what they're doing."

I stop before the last door. The one that carries the blissful sounds. "Yes, I do." I want to see it. Remember it. Breathe it deep.

She squeezes in front of me, blocking my path. "I'm sorry. I can't let you in there."

"Are you sure?" I hold her gaze. "Because I thought we finally reached common ground."

"I'm trying to shield you from what's happening."

"And why is it that everyone seems to think they know what's best for me? First Luca, then Sebastian, now you. I've witnessed unimaginable things. Traumatic, disgusting things that will forever be stuck in my head. And yet you think I can't handle seeing a little torture? That I'm not owed the gift of his suffering?"

She doesn't answer. Doesn't move either.

"Get out of my way, Keira." I nudge closer. "Don't crack the fragile ground we stand on."

"God damn it." She steps to the side.

I push through the door to a soulless exercise room. It takes a few short seconds for another shout to tell me the men must be in the sauna in the far corner.

"Please be careful." Keira continues to follow. "They won't want to be disturbed."

"I don't care what they want." I yank open the wooden door to four sets of eyes turning my way. Cole sits on the wooden bench, leaned back, relaxed, while Sebastian and Luca loom over the bloodied man roped to a chair. Otis's eyes are now swollen and red with his naked chest marked with a hundred tiny cuts.

He's become unrecognizable in such a short space of time. So beautifully, brutally foreign.

"Can I help you?" Cole raises a brow.

Sebastian steps back from the man in the chair, his knuckles stained with blood. The tight pinch of his face speaks of shame. *My* shame. Otis must have told him something.

"What did he say?" I inch farther into the small space.

I get no response. Luca doesn't look at me. Sebastian turns away. It's only Torian who pays me attention.

"What did he say?" I ask him. "What did he tell you about me?"

"Does it matter? We're not here for a history lesson. We're only interested in shutting down my father's operation."

"Cole," Keira warns. "Don't be heartless."

He gives a tight smile. "Forgive me, sister. I assure you he hasn't said much."

Not much. But still something.

My heart clenches at the possibilities. I don't want them knowing. I can't stand the thought of them having access to the intimate details of my shame. It's too much. I can't breathe.

"He's only talking shit to waste time." Luca turns to face me, his eyes wild and animalistic. "He may have thought bad-mouthing you was a good idea. I taught him otherwise."

"What did he say?" I step closer. "What did he tell you?"

His mouth presses into a tight line, his jaw ticking as he wipes sweat from his brow with his forearm. "Nothing helpful."

"I told them you liked it, bitch," Otis sneers. "You fucking loved it. We all knew."

My eyes burn. My throat, too.

He told them. He repeated the lies from earlier.

"You should get out of here." Luca indicates the door with a wave of his hand. "Go on."

"It's not true." I shake my head, my hands trembling, my heart tapping out an erratic beat. "You can't believe him."

"Of course we don't fucking believe him." Luca steps into me, backing me toward the door. "We know it's not true."

The cringe on Sebastian's face says otherwise. His expression is the definition of judgment.

"I'm not leaving." I stand my ground, not retreating despite his approach. "Let me watch."

"No." Sebastian's denial is adamant. "Go back to Tobias. He shouldn't be left alone."

"He's asleep. And I have a right to be here." I speak to Luca. "Please."

He remains close. So close his warmth soothes the icy chill inside me.

"*Please*," I beg.

Tortured heartbeats pass until Otis begins to chuckle.

"See? She's a needy little bitch, isn't she?"

Luca turns, his fist connecting with the guard's stomach. Otis hunches, his laughter continuing as he gasps and coughs.

"She stays," Luca commands to no one in particular. "She has a right to watch him suffer."

My stomach twists at his support. Flips and tangles alongside the tumultuous mix of my emotions.

"Fine." Cole crosses his feet at the ankles. "But keep out of the way."

"But she likes to be in the thick of it," Otis slurs. "Don't you, pretty Penny? You're all about the thickness."

My fingers twitch, demanding action. I struggle not to let him affect me as I walk to the bench seat and sit rigid a foot away from Cole.

"Get out of here, china doll." Sebastian walks to the door, blocking Keira from moving inside. "You don't want to see this."

The woman hesitates, glancing at me before nodding. "I'll be in the kitchen. I'll let you know if Tobias wakes up."

The enclosed space remains quiet as she leaves, the dim lighting making the atmosphere all the more sinister.

I cling to the seat beneath me, my palms sweating.

"You've got an audience now," Luca snarls. "Be careful to watch your manners in front of the lady."

"She's no lady. That right there is a filthy whore."

Luca cocks his fist and lands another punishing blow, this time to the guy's face, the *thunk* of impact loud in the small room. "You're not all that bright, are you? I suggest you make this easier on yourself and start talking."

Otis spits a glob of blood in my direction, the remnants lingering on his lower lip. "I can tell you all you like about Luther's pretty Penny. That bitch took everything he gave her and never lost a bounce in her step. She even—"

Luca lands another blow, and another, and another, as if attempting to beat away my shame with vicious force.

"Shut him down." Sebastian clenches his fists. "Make him fucking stop or I will."

The guard snickers. "Is she a sore spot? Would it make you feel better if I told you she squealed like a pig—"

My brother shoves Luca aside and grabs Otis by the throat. "You piece of shit." His arms bulge with his exerted grip. "I'll fucking kill you."

"Either control yourself or get out." Cole shoves to his feet. "*Now*."

The air in the tight space becomes frenzied, adrenaline and rage making it harder to breathe. Sebastian keeps choking Otis, the constriction of blood making the guard's face swell.

"Let him go." Luca claps my brother on the chest. "Let him go, Deck. Let me do my job."

My brother doesn't stop. He keeps squeezing, tighter and tighter.

"Let him go, Sebastian." The instruction is mumbled from my numb lips. It's too soon for this asshole to die. He hasn't suffered enough.

My brother glances at me, his shame and sorrow bearing down on me again.

I've never hated someone's attention more. Not even predators. Or tormentors. The way my brother judges me makes my worthlessness unbearable. But he does as I ask, releasing his hold enough for Otis to gasp for breath, his coughs and splutters returning to raspy laughter.

"I'm done playing." Luca speaks to Cole. "How 'bout you?"

"Feel free to speed it up."

"No sweeter words were spoken," Luca mutters as he snatches some kind of tool from the floor—a small set of curved pruning shears. "Where are the other women, asshole? Where did Luther keep them?"

Otis smirks, exposing claret-stained teeth. "You'll never find them. Not alive."

"Have it your way." Luca walks around to the back of the chair and leans down.

I can't see what he's doing. It's the crunch, the almighty roar, the mass of splattering blood, and the lone finger that eventually falls to the floor that announces the new level of interrogation.

"I'll ask again." Luca returns to his standing position before Otis. "Where are they?"

The guard pants, his chest rising and falling as his attention turns to me. "Did you know I fucked your friends? I fucked *all* of them." He glares at me. "Luther may not have let us touch you, but we made up for it with the other bitches. They paid for your protection."

His words lash me like a whip, each injury deeper than the last.

I can't stand it. I can't sit here and take it anymore.

"Damn, Otis." Luca clucks his tongue as he returns to the back of the chair. "You're one slow motherfucker. I thought you would've learned not to mess with her by now."

There's another crunch. Another roar. Another drop of a finger to the ground.

It's not enough.

Not the tears in Otis's eyes. Not the drool blubbering from his mouth. He knows he's going to die and it's clear he won't share information no matter what's done to him. He will only continue to taunt me. To punish me.

"Chloe was the best," he slurs. "She had the tightest ass I've ever fucked."

I gasp as fury blinds me. I can't think through the need to strike. It's all I know as I push to my feet, snatch the shears from Luca's hand, and squeeze the blades together to sink the sharp depths into Otis's inner thigh.

"Burn in hell." I push the shears deeper.

He bucks, his roar ringing in my ears. There's so much noise. Shouts. Thoughts. Screams.

The past and present collide. Torture and freedom still battle in my mind.

I clutch those shears, staring Otis in the eye as strong hands wrap around my wrists and yank me backward. I can't hold on. My fingers slide from the grip, making the blades creep open while still imbedded inside flesh.

Then I'm swirled around and forced to face a brother who's ashamed of me. There's no hiding it. It's tattooed on his face.

"Let me go." I thrash. "*Let me go.*"

"Fuck, Penny." Luca becomes a comforting force at my back, ushering us to the door in shuffled steps. "You need to leave."

I plant my feet, determined to stay. I have to witness the continued suffering instead of feeling it on my own.

"Don't touch me." I fling my arms, trying to loosen Sebastian's unyielding grip. "Don't ever fucking touch me."

"Get her out of here," Cole demands. "*Now.*"

I wiggle. I thrash. I fight, fight, fight, but like always, I don't win.

"Let me take care of her." Luca speaks over my shoulder. "I've got this."

I drown in hysteria. Wanting and needing and suffocating.

Chloe is dead. Taylor, Anna, Emma, Ivy, Claire, Skylar, Naomi, and so many more, too.

They're all gone and I'm still here.

They're gone and I should be with them.

My legs give out beneath me as I continue to fight.

"I've got you," Luca murmurs over the madness. "It's going to be okay."

He's wrong.

So wrong, wrong, *wrong.*

I'm led from the sauna, stumbling and fumbling over my feet as a heavy hand encourages me to move faster from the low of my back.

"Keep moving." Luca guides me into the hall, then to the closest closed door. He swings it wide to drag me into the shadows.

He doesn't turn on the light. We're left in the dim hallway glow with nothing but the sound of my pounding pulse, labored breathing, and those haunting, tormenting thoughts.

"Talk to me." He begs. "What's going on in that head of yours?"

I wish I could answer, but I don't know. I don't know. *I don't know.*

I need him to make it stop—the voices, the guilt, the tightening noose.

"What the hell were you thinking, shorty?" He gets in front of me, those eyes still wild.

That I didn't want them knowing what I am. Who I am.

I don't want anyone to regret saving me. To question whether or not they wasted time or resources. And then I was thinking that maybe Otis was right. Maybe I'm a whore who asked for what I was given. That I deserved the grief of losing my friends because my lessened torture made theirs increase.

"Talk to me." He grabs my upper arms. "Let it out."

He's disappointed. Angered. And God, that feels horrible, too.

"I-I'm sorry." The words stammer over my trembling lips. "I'm sorry."

"Tell me what's going on. What's eating away at you?"

"I don't want to see him." I shake my head. I shake everywhere. "I don't want..."

"Who?" He gets closer, looking me right in the eye. "Otis?"

"Otis... Sebastian... Tobias..." I shudder, the tearless sobs congealing in my throat. "Oh, God, Toby... How am I going to tell him about Chloe? He's been through so much."

"Forget about telling him for now. We'll do it when the time is right. But you need to make me understand what's going on. I get that you wanted revenge with Otis. What I don't understand is the way you're treating your brother."

He'll never understand. And I don't know how to explain it. The words won't form.

"Do you think he betrayed you?" he asks. "Do you blame him for not finding you? Are you punishing him for being with Keira?"

Yes. Yes. *Yes.*

"It's all of that." I pull at my hair. "And none of it at the same time. I can't think. Nothing makes sense. But that look in his eye... He's judging me. He's ashamed."

"Penny, I—"

"Don't." I step away. "Don't placate me. Or belittle me. You'll never understand how he makes me weak." I wrap my arms around my waist. "Sebastian is a vulnerability I can't afford. Not when this will never be over."

"But it's already over. You're going home—"

"What home? There's nothing to return to." Hearing the truth out loud only increases my sorrow. "I can never be free. And I can't risk being around my family when I'll always have a target on my back. You should've just left me there to die."

13

LUCA

"This is the shock talking." I try to soothe her. "You're going to be okay."

Her suffering strips me fucking bare. I've never been sliced open by someone else's wounds before, but she does that to me. She carves. Hacks.

"You're either stupid or a liar." She retreats. "You don't know them. They're everywhere."

I follow after her. Step for step. "You didn't think I could free you from Luther, but I did. You thought I'd fail in rescuing your friends, but I did that, too. So why can't you believe me when I say you're going to be okay? I promise none of them will be left standing. I won't fucking fail."

"Then you'll die, too. Just like everyone else."

I don't know how to comfort her, but fuck, she needs comforting. And she needs to fucking realize her tormentors are all but dead. I won't let them step foot near her again.

No new scars will be inflicted over the old. There are only the lingering nightmares to face from here.

"I can't live like this, Luca." Her entire body is wracked with shudders. "I won't risk anyone else. The only person who is safe around me is Tobias because they won't touch him. Everyone else needs to stay away—Sebastian, my family. All of them. I don't want to see them ever again."

"That's not going to happen. Your family love you too much to leave you on your own."

"No. You don't understand."

"I do. I get it now." I step forward. "And what you're feeling makes sense. It's just unnecessary."

"No." She trembles. "*No.*"

"Come here." I reach out. My chest tightens, waiting for her to deny my offer of physical comfort yet the rejection never comes.

She remains immobile as I wrap my arms around her and draw her into my chest. I hold her tight as she remains rigid. I cling to her as if my hold can fix her broken pieces.

But even now she doesn't give in to weakness. There're no tears. No sobs. Just silence.

She keeps everything bottled, the powder-keg of her suffering lying under the surface, waiting to explode.

"It's going to be okay. I promise. We've all got your back," I whisper into her hair. "Trust me."

A shuffle of feet sounds near the door, making it clear someone is eavesdropping.

I expect to see Keira when a shadow passes the frame. Or maybe the kid. But when I tilt my gaze, it's Decker who stares back at me, his expression of utter devastation letting me know he overheard at least some of our conversation.

He lowers his attention from my face to my hold on his sister and with each passing second his suffering increases. "I need to speak to you."

Penny startles at his voice and shoves from my arms.

Yet again, I've taken two steps forward with her and ended up ten yards back.

"Give me a sec." I return my attention to Penny as she continues her retreat.

Those moments of comfort did diddly-dick to help her. She's still trembling, her face stricken and pale.

"Pen, I've gotta go and see what Decker wants. Will you be all right on your own for a minute?"

She doesn't respond, just keeps distancing herself from me. From help.

"Penny?" I walk after her. "Are you going to be—"

"*I'm fine.*" She raises a hand, warding off my approach. "I'm fine," she repeats softer. "I don't need you."

I'd love to say her words don't sting like a bitch, but they do. Again she's slicing me. Gashing.

"I'll be back." I stalk for the door, each step pained from the distance building between us, and enter the hall to be greeted by one temperamental motherfucker.

"How much did you hear?" I murmur under my breath.

"Enough."

"She needs help."

He scoffs. "I fucking know that. It's the person she's going to for the help that pisses me off."

"She thinks she's placing you in danger."

"I heard," he grates through clenched teeth.

"Well, did you also hear that she thinks you're judging her? That you're ashamed of what happened?"

His face transforms with fury. "Are you kidding?"

"No."

"Fucking hell." His voice echoes off the walls. "I'm not fucking judging her. I feel sorry for her. I *hurt* for her." He pounds at his chest. "But what good is that when she won't listen to me?"

I grab the sleeve of his shirt and drag him farther down the hall. "You need to sit her down and talk to her."

"I fucking wish I could, but I can't do it now." He jerks away from me. "She shortened our timeline with the guard. You need to get back in there."

"Shortened it how?"

"She stabbed him in the femoral. He's bleeding out."

Fuck. Fuck. *Fuck.*

"How much time do we have?" I start for the gym, striding out the distance.

"I don't know. I placed a tourniquet around his thigh, but it's not going to save him. We might only have minutes. An hour at most."

"How's Torian?"

"Pissed. He's sending her home."

Whiplash brings me to a stop, making Decker almost walk straight through me. "When?"

"As soon as the jet returns, she's got a one-way ticket to Portland." He shoves me forward. "Without the kid."

No, not without Tobias. That will fucking kill her.

I storm for the exercise room, needing to extinguish this fucking blaze before it builds. "Stay with her. Let me handle this."

"Me? What the hell am I going to do? She won't let me near her."

"Just watch her. Make sure she doesn't do anything stupid." I shove open the frosted glass door, make my way through the gym, and pull open the sauna.

Cole stands before the unconscious fucker in the chair, his hands bloodied.

"Is he still alive?" I ask.

"Does it matter? He's past regaining consciousness." Torian glares at me. "He's useless to me now."

I clamp my mouth shut, well aware that the look in his eyes is born from rage. There's no reasoning with him when he's like this. There's no hope in hell.

"As soon as the jet returns, she's gone," he seethes. "Not a second longer."

Fuck me, but I nod.

I agree because I want her away from all this.

I fucking comply because the sooner she's safe back in the States, the sooner she can heal. "Let her take the kid."

His lip curls as he straightens. "No. She gets no favors from me."

"The kid isn't a favor. It's a safety concern. Let him go with her."

"No," he snarls. "He stays with me."

"You're going to risk his life by keeping him here?"

"I'm not risking anything." He takes a threatening step toward me. "I protect my family. Always have. Always will. Reinforcements are on the way. Our asses will be covered soon enough."

"That's helpful, but—"

"We're done discussing this. I'm not negotiating for her. She's too much of a fucking complication. Her ass is leaving and that's final." He bumps by me to shove from the sauna, the quick nudge to my shoulder a burning poker to my brain.

Fuck.

I stumble into the gym after him, then stop to hang my head and massage my temples, hoping the movement will help me figure out where to go from here. How to fight for her.

"Is he dead?" Keira asks.

I glance up, finding her and Decker holding open the frosted door to the hall.

"He might as well be."

"What happens now?" Decker continues forward, looking to me for guidance I don't fucking have.

"She's leaving."

He winces. "With the kid?"

"No. But maybe it's for the best. For Tobias *and* her. She's not stable enough to be his main caregiver."

"Well, good luck telling her that." He crosses his arms over his chest. "She won't take it well."

"I'm not going to be the one to tell her."

His eyes flare. "You expect it to be me? Are you fucking kidding? Seconds ago you were hugging her, but I'm the one who has to deliver the bad news? She can't even stand the sight of me."

"She's going to have to get used to it. You both are. I'm not telling her, or taking her home. That's up to you now."

"Fuck me." He wipes a hand down his face.

"Unless you'd prefer if I was the one who escorted her." It's a joke. A lame one. But for a second my chest tightens at the thought of being her savior for a little longer. It's not a role I want, though. My sights are firmly focused on taking down Luther's operation one motherfucker at a time. I made Penny a promise and I intend to keep it.

"No way in hell." He turns to the door. "I'll take care of it."

I follow him with Keira close at my back.

We reach the open doorway to the bedroom, Penny's soft sniffles sounding from inside.

"Give me some fucking space," Decker grumbles, then disappears into the room, flicking on the light and closing the door in his wake.

There's a feminine murmur of protest from inside as Keira gently grabs my arm.

"Let them have some privacy." She attempts to tug me farther along the hall.

I don't move. "In a minute."

She blinks her pretty eyes at me, soundlessly begging me to follow.

"Not now, Keira. I said I'll follow in a minute."

"He needs time alone with her. Please don't make this harder for him." She pauses, waiting for a reply. "Please, Luca, don't interrupt them." She backtracks. "I'll be waiting for you in the living room."

I ignore her as she leaves, all my senses hyper-attuned to what's going on behind that door.

Yes, I know Decker is protective of his sister. But I am, too.

I'm not going to leave her at the mercy of a situation she doesn't want, even if she's going to have to face it sooner rather than later.

I lean against the wall beside the doorframe and listen for every word.

"Stay where you are," Penny demands. "Don't come near me."

Decker sighs. "I'm not going to hurt you. How do you not know that?"

She doesn't reply.

"You're going home," he continues. "I think Cole's waiting on his jet to return from this morning. Or maybe he's calling in one that's close by, but this is all over."

I picture her gorgeous face pale with surprise. Bright eyes. Shock-parted lips. Her panic would be a tragic sight I itch to see and the temptation to take a peek eats at me.

It's the painful reminder of the remaining news that keeps me in place.

"Did you hear me?" Decker asks. "Do you understand? You're going home. You'll be able to see Mom and Dad. And God, they're going to be so fucking happy."

Shit. I should've warned him not to mention their parents.

"I don't want to see them." Her protest is growled. "You can't make me."

"It will be good for you. They can help."

"Penny?" Tobias's voice carries down the hall, his sleepy face coming into view from a bedroom up ahead. "Where is she?"

I hold a finger to my lips as he approaches, lazily blinking away sleep as the shirt I gave him hangs from his shoulders like an oversized bag.

"She's in there," I whisper. "Talking with her brother."

"Can I see her?"

"In a minute."

"*No.*" Penny raises her voice from behind the wooden door. "You're not taking me away from him. Tobias stays with me."

The little boy's eyes widen. "They're talking about me." He lunges for the handle, determined to get inside. "*Penny?*"

For a second I consider grabbing him, using a hand around his mouth to smother his yell. It takes another split second to figure out how fucking stupid that would be. Not only because it would scare the shit out of the kid, but because there's no way Penny didn't already hear him.

"Tobias?"

The boy shoves open the door and rushes inside.

I don't follow. As much as it kills me, I remain there against the wall, giving them the privacy Keira requested.

"What's going on?" Tobias demands. "What's happening?"

"Nothing." I imagine Penny soothing him with a motherly cuddle. "My brother and I are just having a misunderstanding."

"It's not a misunderstanding, Penny. You're going home. After all this time you get to return to the people who love you the most."

"No," she yells, the pitch razoring through my head. "You're not taking me away from him. Tobias stays with me."

Silence stretches, and this time I have no trouble picturing the standoff inside that room. I can clearly see her defiance. The strong stance. The warrior expression.

"Penny, please," Decker begs. "Torian isn't going to let his brother go anywhere without him."

"Then he can return to the States with us. He can leave, too, because I won't go anywhere without Toby."

"Penny…"

"So help me God, Sebastian, if you separate us you're as good as dead to me."

Fuck.

I push from the wall and step into the open doorway. They all look at me. Three sets of eyes begging for my assistance.

"Talk to him," Penny demands. "Tell him I'm not leaving Toby."

I wish I could.

Right now, I'd give anything to make her panicked gaze soften. To relax the stiffness in a posture that must be almost crippled with exhaustion.

"It's not your brother's decision." I start toward her. "That lies with Torian, and he's not going to change his mind. Tobias needs to get to know his family. They will look after—"

"No." She shakes her head and clutches the boy's shoulders, dragging him to stand before her. *"No."*

"Let him get to know them. Let him spend more time alone with Keira and Cole now so you can see how comfortable he is before the jet arrives."

"No." Her eyes widen, growing frantic. "I won't leave without him."

"Penny, no amount of protesting will change Cole's mind. After what you pulled with the guard, you've stamped your own ticket home. It's your choice whether you willingly walk onto the jet, or if we need to take alternate measures to get you on there safely."

Her lips part on silent words and the pained betrayal she levels on me is fucking brutal. I've gone from being her rescuer to her tormentor in the space of a few heartbeats, and I've gotta admit, the punishment is more severe than the pound in my head.

I *want* to help her. I always have. But right now, I can't stop agreeing with Torian. She needs to get out of here. If not for safety reasons, then for her mental health. "Leaving without him will be a good thing. You can focus on yourself to start healing."

"Do *not* make decisions for me. You can't do this. You promised," she implores, clinging tighter to a boy who seems more frightened of her reaction than his future. "You said—"

"I promised to keep you safe. To protect you."

She backs herself into the wall, frantically dragging Tobias with her. "You said you wouldn't hurt me. *This* is you hurting me."

"Penny," I warn. "You're scaring the kid. I'm sure you realize the last thing you want to do is drive a wedge between him and the people who will now be taking over his care."

She swallows, her tongue frantically snaking out to swipe her lower lip. "I'm all he's got."

Somehow, deep down, I think she knows she's got the statement backward. *He's* all *she's* got. He's her hope. Her light. He's probably the only thing she has left to fight for, which makes this even harder.

"Penny, it's okay. I don't mind staying." Tobias peers up at her. "They were nice to me while you were gone. Keira told me lots of things about my family that I didn't know. I even have a niece who lives in Portland where Baba came from. But she's my age. Isn't that weird?"

The poor fucking kid is trying to console her and I'm sure she sees it.

Her wince says it all.

"She's also Luca's niece," he adds. "Luca and I share the same family."

Penny glances at me, her wince transforming to confusion before settling into more betrayal. She's judging me, disapproving of yet another connection to a crime-riddled syndicate. "You're family?"

I wish I could ignore my spike in annoyance but that fucker increases the pressure in my skull. "My brother married Torian's other sister, Layla."

She narrows her eyes. "Congratulations. Their relationship must be lucrative for you."

I don't respond, not with more than a mimicked squint.

I can be her punching bag if that's what she needs. Yeah, it fucking stings after everything I've done for her. But I get it. She's hurting.

"Tobias, why don't you let Penny have some space for a little while?" I reach out and beckon him forward. "She needs time to think."

"Penny?" The boy looks between me and the woman holding him hostage, searching for guidance from opposing sides. "What should I do?"

She drags her gaze to him, the tip of her nose turning red.

"It's okay." I keep my arm outstretched. "She's going to be right here. I just want you to get to know your family better before she leaves. It will be good for her to see you settle in."

Tobias continues ping-ponging his attention between us, raising the tension in the room. When he takes his first step away Penny's face falls, her arms wrapping around her middle as she squeezes her eyes shut.

"I'll take him." Decker reaches for the kid, placing a gentle hand on his shoulder. "Let's go see what Keira is up to."

Penny turns her back to me and faces the wall, her posture stiff as Tobias is led from the room. She doesn't cry. Or if she does, I don't hear it. There's no tremble in her shoulders. No more sniffling.

She remains strong. So fucking strong.

I don't break the silence and neither does she. I just watch her, wishing I knew how to make this easier.

"You promised," she mumbles. "You said you wouldn't hurt me, but you already have."

"This isn't me hurting you. Being sent home is a result of your actions, not mine. We needed that guard to talk and now he's useless."

"Useless?" She swings around to face me. "Why?"

"You hit an artery. He passed out from blood loss. And if he isn't already dead, he soon will be."

For a brief second, I expect her to crumple. To wither under the news. Instead, she squares her shoulders, emboldened by her increasing murder tally.

"We needed him for information. Now we're back to flying blind." I chance a step forward. "You can't blame Torian for being pissed."

"I can blame him for a whole lot of things."

I shrug. "And if it makes you feel better, go ahead. But you don't know the guy. He had no clue about his father's schemes. He didn't even know about Tobias. He might be a bit sketchy when it comes to the way he earns his money, but he's not like Luther."

"I find that hard to believe. Luther spoke to people in Portland all the time. Almost daily. They knew what was going on."

I nod. "I don't doubt that. Cole's old man packed up and left the States years ago, but he wouldn't have severed his connections. We knew he had lingering spies. His brother, Richard, was one of them."

She pulls back, the revolt minute but there all the same.

"You knew Richard?" I ask.

She clenches those arms tighter around her middle and glances away. "No, nobody can truly know someone so evil. But I've witnessed firsthand what he's capable of."

"What he *was* capable of."

Her focus returns to mine, her face slightly downcast as she stares at me through thick lashes. "Meaning?"

"Take relief in knowing he's dead. One by one, they're all going to get taken down. I won't stop until they're all gone. You can leave knowing I'm keeping my promise to end this."

She holds my stare, those dark eyes stirring up shit inside me that shouldn't be felt. Not for Decker's sister. Not for a broken, tormented beauty of a woman.

"I'm not leaving Tobias," she repeats, this time softer, without the theatrics. "I won't."

I nod, giving her a sad smile. "I wish you had a choice, shorty."

"Please, Luca." Her lips tremble. "I can't go without him."

More strikes lash my skin. Slicing deep. All I want to do is give her what she wants. Instead, I have to take solace in giving her what she needs. "You should freshen up. Take a shower and get some rest." I start for the door. "You've got another big day ahead of you."

14

PENNY

I SPEND A LONG TIME STANDING NEAR THE DOOR, LISTENING TO THE SOFT MURMUR OF friendly conversation between Tobias and Keira. She makes him laugh. Despite everything he's been through, he takes to her effortlessly.

And maybe that's what he needs—happiness. The freedom to breathe without restriction from a brutal father.

I guess he also needs the positivity and bright outlook that I've only ever been able to fake. I may smother him in cuddles and kisses, but my aura has always been filled with doom and gloom.

He yearns for something I can't provide. And who am I to keep it from him?

Nobody. That's who.

The more I remain in solitude, the more my drowning emotions shift, their slow retreat making it easier to think as the hollowness returns.

Everyone is better off without me. My sisters. Toby.

I've never been helpful to any of them. I was responsible for more women suffering because of Luther's obsession with me. Once Tobias finds out, he'll hate me. And so he should. Not only for the damage I inflicted, but because I can't bring myself to tell him about Chloe.

He'll have to find out from someone else. Someone foreign.

Keira, maybe.

I push from the wall and escape into the adjoining bathroom to take the shower Luca suggested. I hang my head under the spray. I try to let the water cleanse me, but there's no escaping the exhausting weight of my failures.

I never wanted to see myself as a victim. I'd always fought. Strategized. Manipulated. I stupidly had the misunderstanding that I was beating Luther somehow. That I was trapped playing his game, but I'd figured out a way to cheat him.

Turns out they knew what I was doing and punished those I love because of it.

And now I'm so goddamn broken I can't even cry to let the turmoil escape. My tears dried years ago, probably never to be seen again.

When the water turns my skin to wrinkles, I shut off the taps and dry myself, reclaiming the dress made from material that harbors a lifetime of unwanted memories. I've been choked in this dress. Gagged.

I have no energy anymore. No determination. I'm done.

There's nothing left to do but crawl into the crisp bed and pray for the peace of sleep that doesn't bless me for a long time. I doze briefly, my consciousness fading in and out until Tobias crawls onto the mattress in front of me to spoon against my chest.

"I'm sorry. I didn't mean to wake you." He nestles closer, not protesting when I wrap my arms around him.

"It's okay. I'm glad you did." I nuzzle my face into the back of his neck. "How was your time with Keira?"

"She's nice." He snuggles in tight, his warmth enveloping me. "We had more cookies and hot chocolate. And she told me how Sebastian always steals her favorite thin mints or hides them from her. I don't know what thin mints are but she said she'll buy me some when we get to her house."

"Her house?" My heart pangs, my entire body protesting his speedy connection to his half-sister.

"She lives in Portland." He yawns. "It's in Oregon. You know, where Baba was from? She says I can come live with her for a little while. Or with her sister and my niece. She said I get to choose. Where do you think we should stay?"

We.

He asks with such naive simplicity. As if I'll be with him, our futures entwined when I'm not sure they will even brush. "Why don't you decide?"

"Are you sure?" He pauses. "What's wrong? You seem sad."

I shake my head and refuse to sniff away the tingle in my nose. "I'm tired, that's all."

I'm sure if he was older he'd be able to see through the thinly veiled placation. My barely restrained resentment of Keira, too. He's slipping through my fingers so fast. I almost can't believe how easily he's taken to his new family, until I acknowledge the iron fist he's lived with since birth.

"I'm tired, too." He wiggles, bumping into me. "You can help me decide in the morning."

"I'm leaving soon, Tobias. You understand that, right?"

"Mmm." He nods into me. "You're going to America and I need to stay here with Keira and Cole. But it's only for a little while. Just like a sleepover."

I press my lips into his hair and close my eyes. "Yeah. Just like a sleepover."

There're moments of silence, the nothingness stretching into agonizing heart-beats. I want to cling to him. To squeeze so tight. But I refuse to let him see me suffer. He's already been through enough.

"You're not going to miss Baba, are you?" He turns toward me to stare through the darkness. "Not even a little bit?"

"No," I answer honestly. "I won't."

"I don't want to miss him either," he whispers. "But I do."

"Oh, sweetheart, it's okay to feel that way. You're allowed to miss him, and you're allowed to want to forget him, too. It's even okay to miss him one minute and want to forget him the next. There's no rules for grief."

"Grief?"

I give a half-hearted smile. "It's an adult word to describe the mix of feelings we have when someone dies."

"I don't like grief. It hurts."

"Yes, it does. But it gets easier with time." Or so I'm told.

"Keira lost her baba today, too. Do you think she knows he was a bad man?"

I exhale a heavy breath, not feeling comfortable answering anything where Keira is concerned. "I think she only found out recently. But maybe that's something the two of you can discuss. You can tell her what it was like to live with your father, just like she's telling you what it will be like to live with her in Portland."

He pulls back, pausing a moment. "I can tell her things? I wasn't sure I was allowed."

"Yes, you can tell her." It's time for me to give up my parental hold. Once I'm gone, I'm sure they'll never let me back into his life. I'll be a stranger. A fading memory.

"Do you think she's like him?"

My insides squeeze, my conscience preparing to wage war with my insecurities. "I think if she was like him you wouldn't feel comfortable around her. You're a smart boy, Toby. Listen to what your heart tells you."

"My heart tells me I'm going to miss you."

I struggle to breathe as I pull him into me, placing a punishing kiss to his forehead. "I'm going to miss you like crazy, little man."

"Keira said you would." He wraps an arm around my waist. "She also said you need to go home and be with your family. That they're the ones who will make all this better."

I don't appreciate her spinning those lies. I also don't appreciate her making this easier on him. That's meant to be my job. Yet I'm struggling to do it.

"That's right. Everything will be better once I'm home." I give him a quick squeeze, then drag my arm back to my side. "But now it's time for you to get some rest."

"Okay." He sighs, swiveling around so his back faces me again. "Good night."

"Good night, little man."

I stay there in the quiet while his breathing grows shallow. Peaceful. He doesn't twitch or cry out. For a long time, I wait for nightmares to plague him but when they never come I slide from the bed, too overtired to sleep.

I walk from the room and into the dimly lit hall. I don't hear chattering voices anymore. There's nothing. No sound.

I wonder if the guard is still in the sauna, his blood covering the floor, my crime readily available for anyone to see.

I question whether Torian will dispose of the evidence like he did with Chris. Will the body disappear? Will the scent of bleach fill the sauna the same way it does in the living room? Or will his body remain there, waiting to be found with my fingerprints on the shears?

I continue strolling through the house aimlessly. I reach the frosted door to the gym, then think better of returning to that nightmare. Instead, I turn to retrace my steps. I walk by a closed door with murmuring voices emanating from the other side—Keira and my brother. I keep going, keep passing rooms until I'm at the most familiar, standing in front of Luca's ajar door, the slight opening to the awaiting darkness taunting me to take a look.

I don't fight the desire. I'm done fighting all together.

I sneak inside to find him outstretched on the bed, the light from the hall casting him in a faint glow as one arm rests over his eyes. He's shirtless, his satin boxers the only thing covering a partial part of the landscape of dips and dives built of muscle and sinew.

I don't know why, but an invisible string pulls me forward. I can't stop the momentum.

Before—at the start—I hated him for the way he tempted my hope. Now I want to apologize for what I've put him through. He's done so much. Too much.

I continue my silent approach to the foot of his bed and watch him sleep, his inhales long and drawn, the exhales smooth and subtle.

I shouldn't be here. Shouldn't remain staring at him, the quiet minutes making him more familiar. But I'm caught up noticing the smaller details I hadn't noticed earlier. I see the stubble on his face, which is now longer than when we first met. He's more rugged. More ragged. Then there's his mouth, and those lips that appear far kinder when they're not pressed tight with disappointment.

"Can I help you?" he mumbles.

I gasp, my heart squeezing as I grasp at my chest. "I-I didn't mean to wake you."

He remains still, that muscled arm continuing to shield his face. "I haven't slept."

"Not at all?" I blurt. "You should've said something."

He lowers his arm, his dark eyes capturing mine. "I was waiting to see if you were going to try to kill me again. Then I began hoping you would because my head is fucking killing me."

I wince, wishing my gratitude over him saving me was enough to stop his pain. "I'll go." I backtrack. "I'm sorry for disturbing you."

"No. Stay." He places his hands behind his head, his brow pinching as he re-settles himself on the pillow. "What's on your mind?"

Nothing.

Everything.

I don't even know where to start.

"Can't sleep?" he asks.

"Not really." I lower my gaze to the bedframe and rest my fingers on the carved wood. "I think I'm too tired."

"Tell me what's worrying you." He sits higher, still wincing with the movement when he rests against the headboard.

He sounds sincere. So real. So caring.

I hate it and love it at the same time.

"What will happen to my sisters?" I divert the conversation away from me. "What will Hunter do with them once they land?"

"They'll be taken somewhere to regroup for a while. A safe house of sorts. That's where they'll be coached on what to say to their family and the authorities once they're ready to return home."

"But they definitely get to go home, right?"

"Of course."

"And what about me? Will I go through the same process?"

He shrugs. "Something similar, I assume. But that's up to Sebastian."

My pulse quickens. "Why him? Why does he get to decide?"

His lips part, his hesitation speaking volumes.

"Luca?"

"You weren't told he's the one taking you home?"

"No, I wasn't." I guess I should've expected it, yet here I am, surprised and beating away panic. "I could go on my own. I don't need him to take me."

"You'd leave an island where you were enslaved, with no protection, to board a jet with pilots you don't know, all because you don't want to be near your brother?"

"I told you why—"

"I know." He raises a dismissive hand. "I get it. But I'm not going to let you leave alone. It's not safe."

I wish he wasn't right. I wish so badly, because that flight will be hell.

"Have you allowed yourself to grieve yet?" he asks.

"I haven't stopped grieving since Luther stole my life."

He nods, the movement slight. "Want to talk about it?"

"No." Not the violations or the punishments.

"What about Chloe? Do you want to talk about her?" He stares at me, his comfort sinking into my heart. "How long did you know her?"

"Six months. Maybe a little more."

I remember the day she arrived, her face red and swollen, her cheek blackened with a hearty bruise. Some women took their time opening up to the other members of Luther's harem, but not Chloe. She fell into my arms at first sight and cried for hours.

"What will happen to her body?"

He sucks in a tired breath. "Honestly, I don't know."

"Please don't lie to me."

"I assure you, I have no idea." He rakes a hand through the unscathed side of his head, ruffling his hair. "I haven't discussed it with Torian. But if I had to take a guess, I'm confident you wouldn't be comforted by the answer."

I thought as much.

Her body will disappear just like Chris and Luther's. There won't be a funeral. Or a memorial for a woman who deserved so much more than the world gave her.

"I'm sorry," he murmurs. "I wish you weren't going through this."

I lower my gaze to the bed as I battle the effects of his sympathy. I haven't experienced kindness in a long time. Especially not from a man.

"Is there anything I can do?" he asks.

I could reiterate how much I want to stay. That separating me from Tobias is only going to make my life harder, but the quiet hours alone have made me realize that he'll be fine without me. It's better for him if he doesn't witness any of my upcoming meltdowns.

"I think you've done enough." I glance up at him through my lashes, our gazes brushing.

"I haven't done anything."

"Yes, you have. And I want to thank you for it all. I wish I could repay you."

"You can."

My heart stops, and for a brief moment I dive back into the heavy ocean of fear as I wait for him to request sexual favors.

"You can get help," he whispers. "Do whatever it takes to reclaim your life and be happy again."

A relieved breath escapes me. He keeps proving he's not like the others. But I return my attention to the covers, not wanting to lower myself to explain why his request is impossible. Can someone without worth find happiness? Is it even possible?

"You're important, Penny—you know that, right?" He pauses, the silence killing me softly. "Your life has meaning and value. People love you."

My eyes burn as he strips me layer by layer. Word by word.

"And if there's anything else you need from me, I'll give it to you," he continues. "Even if it means laying here in silence, pretending I'm asleep, while you try to figure me out."

"I don't need to figure you out. I'm leaving, remember?" I shoot him a glance.

"How could I forget?" He grins. "I'm devastated that I'm losing the one person who can keep me on my toes."

"Don't worry. Tobias will fill those shoes quick enough."

He chuckles, the sound husky and low. All his tenderness flows into me, the effect punishing. A raging flood after a lifetime of drought. "Is anything else worrying you?"

How does he know? How can he read me so easily? "You said one of the guards escaped. Doesn't that mean it's not safe here?"

"It's safe enough." He holds my gaze, his confidence reassuring. "We can hear anyone approach. And there are already mercenaries out on the water keeping watch. Soon, Torian will have this place locked tighter than Fort Knox. Then there's Hunter, too. He'll return as soon as he hands over your friends."

"Hands them over to who?"

"My brother."

I nod, slightly comforted by his answer. If his brother is even half the man Luca is, I'm almost convinced my sisters will be in good hands. "And what about you?"

"What about me?"

"Will you get help? Will you see a doctor? I don't think someone in your condition should even be sleeping unsupervised."

His lips kick. "Are you offering to keep watch, shorty?"

There's a beat of silence where I blink in shock at the unexpected flirtation.

"Fuck," he curses under his breath. "I didn't mean to…"

"It's okay." I shake my head, my cheeks heating.

"No. I'm fucking sorry," he grates. "I didn't mean anything by it."

"I know." I truly believe him, because why would a man like him flirt with a whore like me? It was clearly a mistake. "You don't need to explain."

A door opens directly across the hall and Cole steps out, his scrutinizing attention falling on me before coming to rest on Luca.

He raises a brow, drawing assumptions about my presence before he clears his throat. "The jet is here. It's time to leave."

I beat back the burst of apprehension and retreat from the end of the bed. "Am I allowed a few moments to see Tobias one last time? I won't wake him."

Cole gives a short nod, his face remaining tight.

"Thank you." I hate those words. I hate that I'm giving them to him. But they're necessary. He cleaned up one of my murder victims and I desperately need him to clean up the second.

I turn back to Luca. "Thank you again. For everything."

"Don't mention it."

I don't wait for the discomfort of this farewell to set in. Once I leave here, I won't think of my harsh protector again. I can't. People like Luca are only a temporary fantasy.

I hustle from his bedroom and make my way to Tobias, my heart squeezing at the sight of him resting peacefully in the single bed. I make sure not to get too close and remain hovering at the door, the brush of light footsteps approaching seconds later.

"Cole said you're leaving." Keira comes to stand beside me.

I nod, not dragging my attention from Toby.

"You're not waking him?" she queries.

"No." As selfish as it is, I'm going to leave without saying goodbye. He doesn't need to witness my theatrics. The poor kid has already been through enough without having to deal with whatever direction my unpredictable emotions decide to take.

"All he does is speak about you," she continues. "He said you're like a mother to him."

My eyes blaze, the promise of tears hovering close, yet so far.

"You can call him any time." She keeps her voice low. "You can video chat and email or text. Whatever you like."

"I don't have a phone."

"I'll make sure you get one. And if there's anything else, you only need to ask Sebastian. He'll get it for you."

With dirty money, no doubt, but I keep that thought to myself.

"Did Luca tell you how your brother came to be a part of our family?" She leans against the doorjamb, her body turned toward me.

"No, and I don't want to hear it. I'm not ready."

"I understand. But if you ever need someone to talk to, I'm always—"

"Keira." I turn to her. "I appreciate the offer, but I can whole-heartedly tell you I will never, *ever* seek out the daughter of my rapist as a comforting shoulder. I'm sure you can understand that, too."

She holds my gaze, her pained eyes punishing me. "Yes, I do."

"Thank you." I walk into the room to kneel before the bed. I place my hands on the edge of the mattress and my chin atop them to stare at Tobias.

"Is there anything I should know about him?" Keira inches toward me. "Any medical history or useful information?"

There's seven years worth of things she should know. All his demons. All the damage. But maybe those ghosts are better left buried until Tobias is ready for the outside world to know.

"He's allergic to grass," I whisper. "It's nothing serious. He'll break out in bumps all over his skin and he'll itch like crazy. Just make sure you put him in a bath and give him an antihistamine."

"Okay. I can do that."

"And he doesn't like carrots." My throat clogs as I recount memories of our time together. "At all. No matter what they're mixed with, he won't eat them."

She lets out a breath of a chuckle. "Stella's the same with corn."

"And don't listen to him if it gets to bedtime and he says he's not tired. He always is, and it's ten times harder to get him to sleep if you give in."

I can't remember how many nights he's talked me into staying awake an extra thirty minutes, only to throw an unruly tantrum when it finally came time to crawl into bed.

The kid has always been a master manipulator. At least where my heart was concerned. He knew he could talk me into anything if he tried hard enough. Usually, all it took was a bat of those innocent eyes and a pout of his kiddy lips.

"What time?" Keira asks.

"Excuse me?" I glance at her, confused by the question.

"What time should he go to bed?"

"Oh." I frown. "He'll be thrown out of whack because of the last two days. But usually he's in bed by eight-thirty. A little later on weekends if he promises to sleep in."

I turn back to him and reach out, sliding a lock of hair from his face. "I'm going to miss you, little man," I whisper, my throat tightening.

He whimpers, his eyes still closed when he says, "Penny?"

"Go back to sleep, sweetheart."

He nuzzles into his pillow and lets out a sigh. "Are you leaving?" His question comes so easily as he remains in sleep mode.

"Yes. I need to get to the airport."

He nods. "Keira says I can call you whenever I want."

"That's right. Whenever you like. No matter what time it is."

He nods again, his face remaining nestled against the pillow. He doesn't say another word. As far as I know, he's slipped back into sleep.

Again, so easily.

Without a care.

I lean in, place the lightest kiss to his cheek and begin to drag myself away, only to have him wrap an arm around my neck, holding me tight.

I smile through the heartache. I fucking die through it.

"I love you," he murmurs.

I close my eyes, pressing my forehead to his cheek. "I love you, too. I love you more than anything."

I remain against him for a tortured eternity, his hold slowly loosening, his breathing returning to the deep lull of slumber.

When he starts to let out the lightest rumble of a snore, I break away, gently guiding his arm to the mattress.

Each retreating step is done not only with reluctance, but with soul-tearing sadness. And when I turn to face Keira, she's not there, Luca having taken her place in the doorway.

He's dressed, in black jeans and a matching T-shirt, and with the growing stubble along his jaw, the mass of darkness makes his hazel eyes more intense.

"Are you ready?" he asks.

"Do I have a choice?

"Nope."

I sigh. "Then yes, I'm ready."

"Keira will take good care of him. She's always been great with kids. And I'll keep an eye on him, too."

"Thank you."

I follow him as he leads the way down the hall and into the living room. My brother is already there, leaned against the back of a sofa, a suitcase at his side, his gaze lowered. He doesn't look up as I approach. The only acknowledgement of my existence comes from the slight tightening of his shoulders. The lightest flinch.

"Well, I'll see you around, shorty." Luca gives my shoulder a quick squeeze, the touch lingering well after he drags his hand away. "Look after your—"

"I wouldn't say your farewells just yet." Torian pushes from his seat at the dining table to walk toward us. "You're the one taking her home."

There's an awkward pause. My stomach drops. Everyone glances at each other. Me to Luca. Luca to Sebastian. Sebastian to Cole.

"No, he's not." My brother straightens from the sofa. "I am."

"You were," Torian corrects. "But not anymore. It's Luca who has to leave."

15

LUCA

"No fucking way," Decker snarls. "I'm taking her back. Not him."

"There's been a change of plan." Torian pins me with a stare. "You need to return to Portland."

"Why?" Foreboding crawls up my spine. He's got that look in his eyes again. The one that announces he's made up his mind. "What happened?"

"You're hurt. It's not safe for anyone if you stay."

"Then give him some Advil and a fuckin' Band-Aid and he'll be fine." Decker clenches his fists at his sides, barely containing his anger. "Because she's not leaving with him."

"I'm not arguing over this. Luca is injured, so he's the one getting out of here."

"I'm not injured, Torian. I'm good." I might feel like I'm suffering the worst hangover of my existence, my eyes seemingly coated in a thin layer of gravel while my head continues to pound. But essentially, I'm good. "It's a fucking scratch."

"A scratch?" He approaches, his smile dark as he shoves my chest.

"*Fuck.*" I stumble backward, my skull clenching as if it's in a vise. "What the fuck was that for?"

Torian takes a swing, confusing the hell out of me.

I duck and lose my balance. I stumble, fumbling over my feet, my vision darkening as I land on my fucking ass. Hard.

"You're good?" Torian stands over me, looking down his nose at my fucked-up position on the floor. "Really? You can't even stay on your feet, which means you're far from good. You're a fucking liability."

"He's got a concussion." Penny rushes toward me, her eyes filled with concern as she offers a hand to help me stand. "Are you all right?"

"Don't." I bat away her offer and shove to my feet. "I'm not a fucking invalid. And I'm not going back with her." I shoot her a sideways glance of apology and feel like an absolute prick for the wince plastered across her face. "No offence, shorty, but my place is here. I earned the right to take down those assholes. I'm not leaving until it's done."

"You're injured," Torian repeats.

"Yeah, well, I'm no fucking doctor but putting me on a jet while concussed doesn't seem like a brilliant idea either."

"If you stay, you're a distraction and I've already got enough of those. So go home. Rest up. And if we're still here once you get back on your feet you can return."

"I can rest here," I snarl. "Decker's the one who wants to take her home."

"If Deck goes, it leaves Keira and Tobias without trustworthy protection. I may be paying those mercenaries by the truckload, but I need someone on the inside I can rely on."

Fuck him. Fuck this. "I was reliable last night. I led the entire fucking operation at your father's house."

"It wasn't my brother or sister's lives you were risking on that mission. And at the time, I was too caught up in my own head to realize how bad your injuries were."

"This is ridiculous." I scoff. "Why can't you get Keira to take her back?"

"I fucking agree," Decker snaps. "Let Keira do it."

"No, she stays to look after the kid." He walks away. "I'm not arguing over this. My mind is already made up. Safe travels."

I follow him, stalking two steps behind as we enter the secluded hall. "And what the fuck am I meant to do with her once we get to Portland? As it is, my brother can barely handle the responsibility of one woman, but you've lumped him with three fucking fragile victims. You expect him to take on a fourth?"

"No, I expect you to take care of it."

"Torian," I warn. "Stop fucking with me."

"I'm not fucking with you." He turns to face me. "And I'll never forget what you've done here. You've gone above and beyond for my family. It's a debt I hope to one day repay, which is why I'm starting right now by looking after you seeing as though you don't want to do it yourself."

"I'm fine." I launch my fist at the wall, my knuckles breaking plaster, pain shooting to my head. I need to stay here to make those fuckers pay. To make sure any other women are freed. To get Penny her revenge.

Torian raises a brow. "A few short days ago, you were bragging that your macho ex-SEAL ass could kick mine without effort. Now you're falling on that ass after I throw an air swing. So forgive me for relying on my own judgment to make this call." He claps me on the shoulder, hard. I'm sure it's in an effort to increase the pounding in my head. "Keep me updated. I'll see you in a while."

He continues down the hall, ending the conversation with a definitive slam of his door. *Again*, I'm sure it's just to trigger my migraine.

Fuck.

I slump against the wall.

I'd been apprehensive at the thought of entrusting someone else with Penny's safety. I'd even contemplated being the one to take her home. Now the reality is so fucking far from comforting it's almost scary.

I'm not the one who should be looking after her. Not after I slipped subtle flirtation into our conversation. And that isn't the worst of it. Those words hold no comparison to my thoughts. My fucking obsession.

She shouldn't be around me.

And I definitely shouldn't be entrusted with her.

I rest the back of my head against the wall, not moving when Decker enters the hall to storm toward me.

"Don't start," I warn. "I don't want to hear it."

"Too fucking bad." He stands in front of me, chest puffed, shoulders stiff. "Every time I take a breath you're getting closer and closer to my sister."

"Not by choice."

"I don't give a shit if it's by choice, or circumstance, or divine fucking intervention. If you so much as make her sniffle, I'll fucking destroy you."

I take his fury. Mainly because I don't have the mental capacity to retaliate, but also because I'd be equally bitter if the situation was reversed.

"Keep her safe. Keep her happy. Or I'll..." He pauses, his hostility ebbing as he diverts his focus blankly down the hall. "Just keep her fucking safe, okay?"

"I will," I vow, then hang my head, despising how this is really fucking happening. And after the bullshit I went through with Luther. The risks I took to take him down. The bullets I dodged. And the one I caught with my thick skull.

"I can go on my own," Penny's fortified voice carries from the entrance to the living room. "Nobody needs to escort me."

I don't answer her. Don't even look.

Neither does Decker. All he does is glare. At me. Like this is all my fucking fault.

"If someone can get me to the jet, I'll make it back by myself. It's no big deal."

"You're not going on your own." I push from the wall and sidestep her brother to continue toward her. "What's done is done. There's no changing Torian's mind."

"But you want to stay. And I don't need a bodyguard."

"It doesn't matter—"

"Yes, it does." She stands her ground, reclaiming her warrior status, not letting me pass into the living room. "I won't take this from you."

It's in those words that I realize my protests are truly pathetic.

The day Luther died she told me something that stuck with me. Something I despised.

She implied she was a possession. Explained that she was a gift.

It's now that I realize no truer words were ever spoken. She *is* a gift. And it should be considered an honor to accompany her home.

"You're not taking anything from me, shorty." I stare into those dark eyes and wish I didn't feel a thrum of connection. No, not a thrum—a fucking avalanche. "I'm being sent back because of my head and there's nothing I can do about that. My issue revolves around the promise I made to you. I told you I'd clean house with Luther's men, and I don't go back on my word."

"Will they still be taken down?"

"Yes," Sebastian answers for me. "Without a doubt."

She sucks in a breath and raises her chin. "Then you're not going back on your word. You're just letting someone else take care of it. Maybe that's for the best. Like Torian said, you need to rest."

"There's not going to be a lot of rest when I've got you to contend with." I wink at her, trying to ease the tension. "Somehow I think you're going to make it hard to keep you out of trouble."

She releases a rasp of a laugh, her smile slight as she lowers her gaze to the floor. Shy. Almost submissive.

Fuck, she's beautiful.

Breathtaking.

Tempting.

Trouble is definitely going to be on my radar. And there's no way her protection will ever take a back seat to my recovery.

But it's no longer Luther or his guards I have to keep her safe from.

The biggest threat to her right now is me.

Luca and Penny's story is continued in Luca.

HE DRAGGED me from hell and delivered me to salvation.

At least that's what I thought.

LUCA

1

PENNY

My heels tap along the floorboards as I make my way down the shadowed hall of my new temporary home.

It's nice here. Quiet.

I no longer need to constantly straddle fight or flight. There are no monsters knocking at the door. Only the haunting thoughts of my past to interrupt the peace.

I enter the living room, the warm lights illuminating the man waiting for me on the sofa.

Luca Hart.

He's my savior. My protector. An undefeatable force who rescued me from a life of sexual slavery.

His mouth kicks in a subtle grin, the coaxing tease of lips making me wish I could return the gesture with equal measure.

"You look nice." His gaze treks my body, from my face to my toes and all the way back again.

Normally, that sort of admiration would make me shudder, but the shiver wracking my body stems from something inquisitive. Something more aligned with anticipation.

He has a way of bleaching my past to make me feel clean, despite my mind's determination to do the opposite.

"Thank you." I lower my focus to take in the beautiful dress clinging to my waist, the shiny satin, the polished shoes. This isn't an outfit I'd usually enjoy wearing. In fact, it's something I would despise after the years being forced into exquisite attire by my puppet master, but Luca makes everything easier.

He pushes to his feet, all tall, broad and handsome, his black suit tailored to perfection. "Are you ready to leave?" He stops before me, his lingering gaze intense, yet somehow kind.

"Yes. I just need—"

A burst of noise assaults my ears. Glass rains to the floor from the French doors across the other side of the room.

Luca's smile vanishes. His body jolts in slow motion.

Everything slows—my mind, my movements, and my comprehension. What's happening?

"Luca?" I reach for him and that's when I see it—the blood. The approaching death.

A lake of deep crimson seeps out from beneath his jacket, the crisp white of his shirt transforming before my eyes.

Snapshots of a similar injury assail me.

Chloe was shot like this. *Exactly* like this. One minute, she was alive. The next, she was dead.

Please, *no*. Not again.

The world snaps back to match the hammering pace of my heart. "Tell me what to do."

Blood splutters from his lips as he stands immobile, his eyes blinking without focus.

Fear consumes me, pummeling me with sickening heartache. I grasp his arm, clutching tight, but he doesn't respond. "*Luca.*"

I don't know what to do. I'm lost. Helpless.

Those demons usually kept at bay rush back to attack me. They taunt me about losing my protector. They cackle about my approaching demise.

I'm nothing without him. I won't survive. I don't want to.

"Luca, *please.*"

He slips from my grip, falling to the tile, his head hitting with a reverberating thwack.

"Oh, God, *no.*" I collapse beside him, smothering his wound, trying to stem the blood even though it gushes through my fingers. "Don't leave me."

He stares at me. Gurgles. Chokes.

"No." I beg. "Don't do this. Stay with me."

"There's no use."

I freeze at the familiar voice coming from the other side of the room. The icy chill of horror slithers through my veins. I don't want to raise my eyes, but there he is, standing before the French doors.

Robert—the man I was promised to like an object, and now he's here to claim me.

But it can't be real.

He's meant to be dead.

I scamper to my feet, blood dripping from my fingers, bile rising up my throat. "No."

"Penny." He starts toward me, one slow step after another, his voice getting louder and louder. "Penny."

"No." I prepare to run toward him. To kill him with my bare hands for taking Luca from me. But my legs won't move. "You should've shot me," I scream. "Why didn't you shoot me?"

He smirks, chilling my veins. *"Penny."*

I startle and shoot upright in bed. I gasp for breath, as I cling to the soft sheets, my body coated in a sticky layer of sweat.

Every night, it's the same. One nightmare after another. One death that follows the next.

It's either my brother, Sebastian, my protector, Luca, my parents, or one of the many women I lost while living beneath the roof of a sex traffickers' mansion.

I've witnessed everyone I care about being taken from me. Always by the same man. The same ghost.

Yet, I'm never the one to die.

I know why, too.

It's because I don't fear death. If anything, I continue to crave it.

What frightens me is the loss of those I care about. That's the true taunt of the nightly demons. I'm constantly reminded I still have so much to lose. That this freedom is only a mirage.

I shudder out a shaky breath and wipe my hands down my face.

I hate this.

Every day starts with horror, and every night begins with dread. There's no escape.

I've been safe for days now, cocooned in the protection of Luca's inner suburban home in Portland.

I suck in a deep breath, forcing calm, and let it out slowly. Sunlight bathes the room, letting me know it's morning and I no longer need to battle for rest.

Because that's all I've been doing. Battling.

I fight to pretend I'm doing okay. I scramble to create some kind of normalcy in a world entirely unfamiliar to me. It's like I've been thrown into a melee of mental torment. My thoughts are my shackles now. This head of mine is a prison.

I never imagined freedom would be like this.

Painful.

Suffocating.

Now I know better.

I slide from the bed, drag my feet to the adjoining bathroom to take a shower, then dress and make my way through the house.

The hall is exactly like it was in my dream. Shadowed and empty. The living room is a carbon copy, too, those French doors tormenting me from my peripheral vision.

I attempt to distract myself by pulling pans from drawers and food from the fridge, like I have every morning since I've been in this sanctuary.

I cook. I eat. I clean.

And when Luca walks into the open living area, his hair mussed from sleep, his hazel eyes lazily blinking, I breathe a sigh of relief at the visual confirmation that my nightmare was nothing more than a cruel joke of my subconscious.

There's no suit this time. Only a black T-shirt and stone-washed jeans, the casual attire suiting him perfectly.

"Morning." He rakes a hand over his skull and winces when his fingers brush the slowly healing injury above his ear. He'd been shot while saving me, the bullet grazing his head, and there's not a moment when I'm not entirely aware of what he could've lost.

"Morning." I turn to the far wall of the kitchen and flick on the coffee machine. "I only finished cooking breakfast a little while ago. Your omelet should still be warm, but you might want to give it a few seconds in the microwave."

"I'm sure it's fine."

There's the slide of a plate behind me. The clink of cutlery. Then the low grumble of a man who appreciates a home-cooked meal. "This is good."

"I'm glad you like it." I pull two mugs from a head-high cupboard. "Strong coffee this morning?"

"Always."

I press buttons on the coffee machine, the tingle of his attention resting at the back of my neck as the sweet gurgle of liquid heaven fills the silence.

"What are your plans for today?" he asks.

I stiffen, hating this rerun conversation. "The same as yesterday, I guess."

"You should go out. Get some fresh air. We could even catch a movie."

I shake my head and pull the filled mugs from the machine. "Not today."

As much as it pains me to trap him here when he refuses to leave the house without me, I'm simply not ready to face the outside world. I don't want to be in the open, waiting to be found. Not by the police, my family, or Luther Torian's men. Right here is where I want to stay until I can figure out an alternative.

"You should leave, though." I turn and slide his mug toward him, seated at the opposite side of the island counter. "I can stay on my own."

He forks a mouthful of egg into his mouth, his reprimanding eyes holding mine as he chews. "No."

"You've shown me how safe the house is." The security system is state of the art. Video cameras. Door and window alarms.

"I'm not leaving you." His tone is final. *Lethal.* I wish I wasn't comforted by his stringent protection. "If you're adamant about staying, at least let me set up the phone so you can call your friends. You haven't spoken to them since Greece."

I disguise the pang of guilt with a fake smile. "Not today. They need more time to focus on getting their story straight so they can return home."

"Penny." My name is a warning. A barely growled admonishment as his jaw ticks. "One phone call—"

"Not today, Luca."

I hate his disappointment. It tears at me. But I'm not ready to speak to my sisters. I know it's hard for him to understand. Hell, it's hard for *me* to understand. This time last week, those women were my life. My everything. Along with Tobias—my captor's son. The little boy I helped raise.

It's clear, though, that I need to keep my distance. The only thing I can bring to their lives at the moment is negativity. And I won't risk my bad attitude rubbing off on them.

"Fine. Have it your way." He wipes the back of his hand over his mouth, brushing away any stray remains of his breakfast. "I guess staying home and chilling out is at the top of our agenda."

"Chilling out?" I scoff. "Do you even know how? You spend hours in your exercise room punishing your body as if you're preparing for Armageddon."

"Like you can talk. You flitter around the house all day, cooking, cleaning, doing laundry. It's like you're my fucking slav—" He stops mid-sentence, his chin hitching. "*Shit.*"

A slow burn creeps up my neck, my shame undoubtedly visible in the color of my skin. It's not the word that bothers me. I've been called a slave more times than anyone could count. What hurts is his reaction. His embarrassment. Over me.

He cringes. "I didn't mean—"

"Forget it." I fight harder to keep my smile in place. "You know it doesn't bother me."

He sighs and glides a rough hand over his forehead. "I need more fucking sleep."

"Yeah." I grab a cloth from the sink and begin wiping down the counter. "I agree. You go to bed too late."

He huffs out a faint chuckle. "Again, you're not the best point of reference. I'm pretty sure you get less sleep than I do."

I keep wiping, determined to remain busy as he continues to eye me like a bug under a microscope. He knows too much about me. Horrific details. Lies, too. He was told I enjoyed the torture Luther put me through. That I loved everything those monsters inflicted.

I hate him having that information. I hate even more that he might believe the slander.

"You're having nightmares, aren't you?" he asks.

"No." The denial slips out easily. "I'm getting a lot of sleep. I'm doing really well."

I don't want him wasting his time worrying about me. Not when I'm already a grade-A burden. He was never meant to bring me back to the States. He wanted to stay in the Greek Islands and help take down the sex trafficking operation.

Instead, he's here. Stuck with me, while doing his best not to show his resentment.

That's why I cook. Why I clean. Why I paste on a smile whenever he's around and pretend I'm climbing back on my feet.

I won't cause any more trouble than I already have.

"Sure you are." He forks another mouthful and scrutinizes me as he chews. I'm sure he sees through my fake facade, but until he calls me on it, I'll maintain this charade.

I'm content in his sanctuary even though the irony hasn't been lost on me.

I fought so hard to escape Luther's house only to mentally trap myself within another. I spent years trying to liberate myself from one man—now I'm racked with fear that the guy before me will cut me loose at any given moment.

It's a complete shift in situation. Yet the sense of being trapped is the same.

"Why are you looking at me like that?" I place down the cloth and reach for my coffee, attempting to shield my face. "I swear you keep scrutinizing me, hoping to find some hidden issue that isn't there."

"Penny, you know I—"

The doorbell rings, startling me. The jostle of my arms sends a splash of coffee over the lip of my mug.

"Don't panic." He places his fork on the counter. "I'm expecting someone."

My heart sinks, the painfully squeezing organ dropping to my stomach as I wipe up the liquid spill.

"Is it that woman again?" The question flies from my lips unbidden.

I shouldn't have asked. I've deliberately kept my curiosity to myself, not wanting to pry. Yet the lack of knowledge has plagued me.

"Yes." He glides off the stool and when I raise my gaze to his, those eyes have gentled, as if he's trying to soften a blow. "Do you want to meet her?"

"No."

She's come here every day for the past three days. They talk for hours, murmuring in low tones over unending cups of coffee. It's clear they're close. Or at least, they want to be. I'm certain my lingering company is the only thing keeping them apart.

That's one of the reasons I hide when she arrives. I haven't even met her, choosing instead to remain in my room, or in the secluded spot I've claimed on the back deck.

I've tried hard not to pry about the woman who keeps him company even though I get a sinking sensation whenever she arrives.

"I'll leave you in privacy." I keep clinging to my mug as I walk around the counter. "I'll be in the backyard."

I wish I could remain by his side. That I was whole enough to be a normal person, conversing and laughing whenever company arrived. Once, I even tried to imagine what it would be like to live here long-term. Like a wife. Just me and Luca. No outside world. No fears.

But those fantasies are for normal people. Unbroken women.

I'm nothing if not entirely damaged.

My only choice is to tread lightly and lessen the burden on a man who never wanted me here. I need to pretend I'm invisible and make sure I don't provoke any unwanted reactions.

Just like I did when I was a slave.

2

LUCA

THE DOORBELL RINGS AGAIN AS PENNY CREEPS ONTO THE BACK DECK, CLOSING THE door gently behind her.

"Fuck." I wipe a rough hand over the back of my neck, entirely out of my element. I don't know what I'm meant to do with her. I've given her space. I haven't pushed. But, goddamnit, all I've wanted to do is shove her into facing reality. She can't heal when she continues to ignore her past.

"*Luca*," Sarah shouts from the front yard. "Are you home?"

"I'm coming." I stalk down the hall and yank open the front door to find her scowling, a clump of filled shopping bags hanging from her hands.

"What the hell took so long?" She slams her haul at my chest, making me struggle to grasp the bags as she maneuvers around me to enter the house. "The least you could do is open the damn door when you're treating me like your little errand bitch."

I wrangle the straps of the bags into one hand and kick the door closed. "And the least you could do is have some fucking patience when it's barely nine o'clock."

I follow after her, but continue down the hall when she diverts to the open living area. I take the bags to my room, doing a quick search of the contents after I dump them on the bed. The self-help books I asked her to pick up are all there. The titles on trauma and PTSD wait for a time when Penny will be ready to read them. There're more clothes in there, too.

I keep buying shit in an attempt to help her... then can't bring myself to hand them over.

She's not ready for my input.

She has a process for dealing with her pain, and I have no right to mess with it.

I've gotta be patient—a fucking saint—while I watch her suffer.

I leave the bags in a pile on the mattress and return to Sarah in the kitchen, her hands already clasping a filled coffee mug.

My filled coffee mug.

"You know that's mine, right?" I stalk for the cupboards to retrieve another mug.

She shrugs. "Yeah, I know. But things always taste better when they're taken from someone you don't like."

Great. She's in one of *those* moods. The combative, poking, prodding type which does my head in.

"So, how is she today?" She cocks her hip against the counter. "Any change?"

"Nope." I play with the coffee machine, pressing buttons until it grumbles to life. "She's exactly the same, pretending life is peachy when clearly it isn't."

"Have you given her any of the things I've brought over? The clothes? The books?"

"I gave her the cell." I wait until my mug is filled, then walk around the island counter to reclaim my stool. "She didn't even bother to open the box. It's still sitting there. Untouched." I jerk my head toward the plastic-wrapped package on the dining table. "Every day I offer to set the phone up for her, but she doesn't want it. She has no interest in speaking to her friends. She says she's not ready. Which might be a good thing seeing as though I'm struggling to get in contact with Benji."

My brother was left in charge of taking care of the other women rescued from Luther's mansion. The three of them—Abi, Lilly and Nina—will remain with him until he's certain they've got their stories straight. Unfortunately, their freedom comes with a price. None of them can breathe a word about their time held captive.

"He's out of range." Sarah speaks through a slurp of my dregs. "Apparently, he's taken them to a cabin away from civilization."

"Says who?" I've been kept in the dark since returning to Portland—the isolation being partly my fault because I'm still pissed off at Torian for sending me home. But mainly because I want to keep Penny away from any unwanted external triggers.

"Layla. She said she spoke to her husband a few days ago and that he's trying not to pull his hair out. According to him, all the women do is cry."

Yeah, that sounds like my brother. Benji wasn't born with patience. Or common sense.

"Well, if you speak to her again, can you tell her I want him to call me? Even though Penny says she's not ready to talk, I want the information on hand in case she changes her mind."

"Sure. But have you actually asked her why she doesn't want to get in contact?" Sarah takes another gulp from her mug, then places it in the sink. "It could be something simple."

"I'm not pushing her." It's not my place even though I have to battle my instincts to do the opposite on the daily. "She speaks to the kid occasionally. Whenever he calls my phone, she picks up. But the conversations are brief. From what I've overheard, she stays on the line long enough to determine he's doing okay. Then she makes an excuse to end the chat. And she never asks to call him in return."

"She's distancing herself."

"No shit." I roll my eyes. "But from what? That woman is a fucking mystery to me. Is she distancing herself from the trauma? Or is it deeper than that? Is she trying to place space between those she loves because she still fears she's going to lose them?"

"Have you asked her?"

No. I try not to ask much of anything. "It's not my business."

She raises her brows, unimpressed. "I think you've earned the right to ask a few questions. Does she seem scared?"

"Yes, she's freaked, despite doing her best to act otherwise. She likes to paste on this fucking sweet smile and pretend she's fine." If only I couldn't see right through it. Her lips might lie, but those eyes never do. I see the pain she harbors.

"How do you know she's pretending? She might actually be healing. Maybe that smile is for real."

I pull my cell from the back pocket of my jeans and scroll to the app for the outside security cameras.

"Does this look like healing to you?" I swipe to the video feed of the backyard. She's sitting a few yards from one of the cameras, her face a picture of sorrow, her eyes dull as she stares blankly at the ground a few feet in front of her. "Look. She's fucking dead inside. She sits like that every minute she's not around me. Then as soon as I walk into view she switches to Mary freakin' Poppins."

Sarah leans into me, her attention on the screen. "Why is it that Torian's men have a thing with breaching the privacy of women? Does she know you're spying on her?"

"She *should*. I went through the house security with her when we first got here. But now she acts oblivious. I don't know if she forgot or if she's too numb to care. I don't even know if she remembers who you are because the vibe I got from her a few minutes ago felt..."

I'm not sure what it felt like. It was odd. Uncomfortable.

"Felt like what?" Sarah steps back, frowning at me.

"I don't know. It was like she thought she was intruding."

"On us?" Her voice holds a tone of incredulity. "As in, she thought we wanted privacy? Just the two of us."

"Yeah. Maybe."

She straightens, standing taller. "I hope you set her straight."

"I didn't get a chance. Someone kept ringing the fucking—"

"I come here for her, Luca. Not you." She scowls. "And for her to even assume—for *anyone* to assume…" She shudders. "You're so far from my type it isn't funny."

"You think I don't know that? *Jesus*. You're no dream boat yourself."

She gives a snake of a smile. "Hunter would disagree."

"Hunter's judgment is questionable. The guy's a walking, talking—"

"Choose your description wisely, my friend. I'd hate to have to hurt you."

"You mean to say you can hurt me more than this painful conversation?" I huff out a derisive laugh. "That would be quite a feat."

"You know I've got skills. But we're diverting off topic. What are you going to do about Penny?"

I slump against the counter, my forearms resting on the marble. "I don't know. I don't want to push her. Yet she lies through her teeth about how well she's coping. She just finished telling me she's sleeping well, and less than an hour ago I had to shout her name three times to wake her from whatever nightmare had her screaming the house down."

"She lies even though you woke her?"

"I don't think she knows I've been waking her. I don't enter her room. I yell from down the hall."

"Christ, Luca, you're such a pussy. Why don't you take charge? Demand change."

My hibernating anger awakens, the warmth in my veins heating. Sarah thinks I don't want to take charge? Like I don't fight every day against the instinct to take control and dictate how Penny should face her recovery?

I want more than anything to drag her out of the darkness. To shake some life into her. But she's so fucking temperamental. She hasn't grieved for those she's lost. She hasn't cried. Not even once. Which makes me fucking petrified I'll push only to break her beyond salvation.

"I'm done with this conversation." I slide from my stool. "It's time for you to leave."

"No, not today. I'm not going to let you block me from her anymore. Enough is enough. Forcing her to speak to me isn't going to kill her."

"You're not pushing her," I snarl.

"And you're not her keeper."

Like hell I'm not. Her keeper is *exactly* what I am.

Her savior.

Her protector.

Her whatever-the-hell-she-needs.

"Luca, you're meant to be watching her temporarily. To get her on her feet so she can return home."

"She doesn't want to go home," I grate through clenched teeth. "And if she wanted to speak to you she wouldn't have spent the last two days hiding in her room while you were here. Or fled to the back deck this morning. She's made it clear she doesn't want company."

"No, she's made it clear she wants to hide, and that's not how you recover from trauma."

"You're not a—"

"I'm done arguing." She starts for the French doors. "I'm going to let her know I've been coming here for her. *Nobody* else."

My pulse detonates, triggering the migraine I've held at bay all morning.

"Wait," I growl, stalking after her. "Stop." I'm about to grab her arm and yank her backward when she pauses and looks at me with a raised brow.

"What?"

"If you do anything to upset her, I'll..."

The grin is slow to curve her lips, taunting my threat. "You'll what?"

I grind my teeth harder, determined not to give her the fight she wants. "I promised myself I wouldn't push her. And so far, I've succeeded. I've let her do her own thing even though it kills me to watch her suffer. So don't you dare go out there and stir trouble."

"Me? Stir trouble?" She clasps a hand to her chest, her sarcastic look of offense taking a second to fade into something more serious. "Give me credit. I'm not a heartless bitch all the time."

"Says who?"

She scoffs. "I get it, okay? You care about her. You're protective. Even a little obsessive. Believe me, I don't want to do anything to poke that bear."

She doesn't understand. Doesn't get it.

I'm skating on thin ice here, barely managing my threadbare restraint when it comes to Penny. She's far more fragile than she was when I rescued her. Back in Greece she'd had fire in her belly. There'd been unending grit and determination, which I'd thought would see her through to a remarkable recovery.

That all changed the minute we stepped onto the private jet and began our return stateside.

The fight vanished. The determination and grit disappeared.

The woman who I was certain would grasp her newfound freedom with both hands turned into a quiet, timid ghost, too frightened to even leave the house.

"Don't worry, Luca." Sarah steps closer and claps me lightly on the cheek, taunting the pain in my head. "You know I have experience with trauma. I'm not going to do anything to make her life harder."

She reaches for the door and opens the barrier wide, the cool air sweeping inside. But she doesn't step onto the deck. She waits, letting me take the lead.

"Be civilized," I mutter under my breath as I walk around her, then farther along the length of the house to the place where Penny hides.

She's seated on one of my wooden chairs, her coffee mug cradled in both hands, a blanket tucked around the legs cuddled up at her side.

She pastes on that fake smile at the sight of me, the bright expression still not reaching her eyes. But when Sarah steps around to stand at my side, Penny stiffens, her face falling lax in a sudden show of apprehension.

"Penny, this is Sarah." I hike a thumb at the annoyance to my left. "She thought it was time you two finally met."

Sarah inches forward. "It's great to meet you. I've been coming over for the last few days in the hopes we could talk, but the big protective bear didn't want me near you until you were ready." She shrugs. "Today I pulled rank."

"Hi." Penny glances between us, apprehension, or maybe confusion, remaining heavy in her tight lips.

"You remember me talking about Sarah, right?" I walk closer to grab the seat beside her and pull it backward a few feet before sitting my ass down. "She's Hunter's fiancé."

A spark of understanding widens her eyes. "Oh. I vaguely remember... I just didn't realize..." She shakes her head, her brow pinched. "The last days in Greece are a blur."

"You spoke about me?" Sarah's voice is filled with unwarranted ego as she leans back against the deck railing. "I'm not sure if I want to know what was said."

Penny's cheeks blush. They actually fucking blush. All pink and sweet and shy. I wouldn't have picked her as a timid woman, but maybe that's who she really is beneath all the layers of damage.

"Okay, now I'm curious." Sarah chuckles. "What did he tell you?"

Penny glances from Sarah to me, then back again. "Nothing. They were a few brief words in the middle of madness. I can't really remember."

Yes, she can. I can see it in the way her gaze briefly flicks to mine. The unease. The concern.

"I told her the two of you have a lot in common." I lean back, faking relaxation in the hopes it will let her know there's nothing to worry about. "And that I thought you both might get along."

"What's with the rabid blush then?" Sarah asks.

I shoot her a glare, warning her to stop pushing. "I think that might stem from my off-the-cuff comment about you being the type to slit a throat with a smile on your face."

Her laughter returns. "Nice intro, Luca. Now her look of trepidation makes sense."

"No, it's not trepidation," Penny blurts. "I'm just..." She shrugs, shrinks into herself, then sighs. "I guess I'm still a little shell-shocked. It's been a whirlwind."

"That's understandable. As long as you know I'm here for you. Not *him*." Sarah whacks me on the chest. "I've been coming over with bags of gifts the big guy has demanded I buy for you. The least he could do is introduce us, right?"

Shit.

Sarah knows I've been holding back on giving those gifts. Why would she tell her about them? I don't think I'm even ready to hand them over. Not when some of the items are fucking idiotic.

"I was waiting for her to be ready," I mutter.

"You don't have to worry about me." Penny's expression fills with regret. "The last thing I want to do is be more of a burden."

"You're not a burden," Sarah cuts in. "You're part of the family. And we look after our own. Fiercely…well, maybe not as fiercely as Luca, but he's special, in a mentally unhinged kind of way."

Penny's lips lift. Her pleasure at my ridicule is slight, but beautiful.

So fucking beautiful.

"Tell me more about this unhingement," she says. "Us mentally challenged people need to stick together."

I know she's only trying to be a part of the conversation, and yeah, I chuckle to encourage more of her involvement. But Jesus, I hate her being down on herself. It makes me want to shake her even more.

"Well, that's my cue to leave." I grab the armrests, waiting for a protest from Penny to keep me in place. "If you're going to talk about me I'd prefer you do it behind my back."

Her eyes flash. Her lips part.

"Good. Go." Sarah shoos me with a wave of her hand. "It's time for some girl talk."

I remain poised to move, waiting, wordlessly demanding Penny to ask for help.

Just tell me to stay.

Ask me to protect you.

"Go on," Sarah demands. "Get going."

I pause for one more second. Two. But when Pen doesn't speak, I give up.

"You sure know how to make a guy feel special." I push from my seat and shoot a warning look at Sarah. "Be nice."

She snaps her teeth at me before stealing my chair. "Run along, soldier."

3

PENNY

LUCA WALKS AWAY, AND THE WHOLE TIME I WISH HE WASN'T LEAVING ME ALONE WITH her. I don't know this woman. I don't think I want to. There's a hardness in her eyes that unsettles me. A bitterness. And I'm unsure if it's aimed at me personally.

"Do you like it here?" she asks as soon as the French door closes behind him.

I continue to cradle the coffee mug in my hands and shift my focus to the backyard. It's simplistic. Fresh-cut lawn. A few shrubs. Two billowing trees. It's completely different to the perfectly manicured gardens of the hell I previously lived in, and for that I'm thankful.

"Yes." I appreciate being welcomed into Luca's home. But I hate being *here*. In my own skin. Cloaked in irrational emotion. Haunted by thoughts.

"You're not uncomfortable? You wouldn't prefer to be somewhere else?"

"No." The truth is, there is nowhere else. I have nowhere to go. Nowhere to belong.

"And what about Luca? Is he treating you well?"

I nod and begin to resent the manners instilled in me as a child that make it impossible to ignore her. I'm too tired for this conversation.

"Are you sure? He said yesterday that you've been cooking and cleaning. Is that out of obligation? Is he making you do those things?"

My narrowed gaze snaps to her. "No, of course not. He's been nothing but kind to me."

"So he hasn't implied you need to carry your weight? Or maybe return his hospitality with a sexual favor or two?"

I shove to my feet, the blanket falling from my waist to land on the wooden deck. "Not at all." My tone is harsh. Adamant. "He's been perfect." *Too* perfect. Especially for a man burdened by my presence.

"Okay. Good." She nods and indicates my chair with a wave of her hand. "Please sit. I meant no offense. I'm just doing my job."

"Your job?" It's her duty to question the man who saved me? The person who took a bullet to the head, risking his life to rescue a complete stranger? "And who gave you this job?"

She blinks back at me, those hard features softening. That's when the puzzle pieces fall into place with a deafening click. She's not here for me. She's here for my brother.

"Sebastian," I whisper. "This interrogation was requested by him."

"I was asked to keep an eye on you."

"Well, you can report back and let him know I'm fine. Luca has gone above and beyond to keep me happy."

Her lips tweak, her grin sly. "To be honest, I think that's what he's more worried about."

Again, it takes a second for comprehension to dawn, but when it does my cheeks heat at the innuendo. I glance away, my skin prickling.

"Please," she repeats. "Sit."

I don't want to. I'd love nothing more than to walk away. If only I wasn't certain it would cause a scene Luca would have to deal with.

"I had no doubt he would do right by you," she murmurs as I reluctantly slump into my seat. "He's a great guy. And from the sound of it, you already know that. But your brother is—"

"I don't want to talk about my brother." I still can't go there. Can't picture him remaining in the Greek islands, slaying my demons at the risk of his own safety. I need it all to be over. To fast forward through this chasm filled with worry for people I wish I didn't love.

"He cares about you."

I glance back at her in confusion. "Who does? My brother?"

"Yes, Decker," she clarifies. "But Luca, Hunter, Torian, and Keira, too. You're family, and we always take care of our own."

My insides scream at me to deny her. I'm not one of them. I don't want any association with my torturer's family.

I also want to make her well aware I can take care of myself. I had for years while in a situation far more dire than this. I've lived through the worst life has to give. Yet I can't honestly say I'm capable of anything anymore. I've lost the will to fight. I'm not sure how to find strength.

"So, what's the plan?" she asks. "When are you going to see your parents?"

I sigh. "Is this another question from my brother? Is there a list I need to get through so you'll leave me alone?"

"No. The interrogation is actually for your benefit. I assume you don't want to stay with Luca forever."

She assumes wrong. I have no desire to leave.

"You really do like staying here." She states as fact. As if she's finally beginning to understand the truth of my comfort. "If you're comfortable in your surroundings, why aren't you opening up to Luca? Let him in. Clearly you don't want to talk to me, and I get it—I'm an acquired taste. But you need to speak to someone. It isn't healthy to keep the past bottled."

How does she know I've kept it bottled? Unless Luca told her. Vented to her.

"Believe me," she continues. "You have to let it out before it eats you alive."

She has no idea.

There's no way anyone could understand what I've been through. Not a shrink. Not even the other women who accompanied me in Luther's cage. And definitely not this woman.

"Your thoughts are loud." She gives a brief smirk. "And yes, you're right. I have no concept of what you must have gone through. But I know about monumental loss. And utter helplessness. Not to mention the cloying anger and suffocating grief that come afterward." She holds my gaze, never letting go. "Those types of situations change you irrevocably, no matter how much you want to return to the person you once were. So ask Luca for help. Trust him. You never know—the guy might have something smart to say for once."

I huff out a laugh. If only the humor could stick around for longer than a heartbeat. "I'm sorry for your loss."

She inclines her head. "And I'm deeply sorry for yours. My point, though, is that you're going to get through this. Despite everything I endured at a young age, I found my calling. And I swear on the graves of those I love that you will find yours, too. You only need to be willing to work for it."

"I'm willing to work. I just..." I close my eyes and turn my head away.

I don't believe anything will change. How can I when I'm free—completely unshackled and unbound—yet I feel more trapped than ever before?

More helpless.

Hopeless.

Broken.

Something is wrong with me, and I'm scared I'll never be able to fix it.

"Your mind builds on what you feed it," she murmurs. "And you would have so much pity and fear that it's only natural to gorge on what you know. But that's not how you heal. You can't beat him until you turn the tables and take control."

Him.

Luther Torian.

The man who continues to torment my thoughts from beyond the grave.

"Your brother will hate me saying this," she adds, "but trust in Luca. He's a great guy. And from what I've seen and heard, he's willing to do anything for you."

"He's burdened to do everything for me," I correct, squeezing my eyes tighter. "He doesn't even want to be here."

"Really?"

When she doesn't elaborate, I look at her, finding her brows raised in question.

"Penny, do you really think a guy like that, all strong, determined, protective, and annoyingly stubborn would do anything he didn't want to do?" Her brows remain hiked. "He *wants* to be here. He *wants* to help you. Otherwise he would've hightailed it long ago, dumping your ass on my doorstep as he went."

"He's honorable. He wouldn't—"

"Make all the excuses you want. But like I said, if you feed yourself that negative bullshit, it's going to eat away at you. Use Luca while you've got him. What do you have to lose?"

His respect.

His sanctuary.

She gives me a pointed look. "What did I say about the negative shit? Your eyes seriously speak volumes. Maybe that's something you can work on, too." She winks at me and pushes from her seat. "Now, before I completely outstay my welcome, I'm going to leave. I'd like to come back tomorrow, though."

"For another highly motivational pep talk?" I ask. "Or to continue spying for my brother?"

She laughs. "Look at you letting down your guard to be a comedian. But just so you know, I'll totally be back for both. Now go find Luca and talk to him."

"About what?"

"Whatever comes to mind."

She walks for the door, leaving me to deal with the emotional whiplash as she disappears inside. One minute I'm content in my isolation, appreciating the distance Luca has given me—the next I'm thinking about where he is and if I should listen to her advice.

Since returning to the States, I've become increasingly indecisive. Almost constantly manic. Calm on the outside, a whole bunch of crazy on the inside.

In captivity, I'd only had the option to fight. Strategy was all that ran through my mind.

Now there's no need to battle physically, so my brain wants to make it a mental challenge.

I'm hammered with thoughts. Memories. Fears.

The voices in my head are a looped recording filled with panic and shame. And I can't quieten them. I've tried. They multiply no matter what I do. Despite how fortunate I am.

It's as if piranhas are constantly nipping at my ankles, eager for the taste of my suffering.

My mind doesn't want me to heal.

I sigh, entirely weary.

I want him to help. I want it more than anything. But talking to him means I'll become more of a burden. It will also wake him up to the reality that I'm not the person he saved in Greece. I'm not a fighter. Only a failure.

I still yearn to be rescued.

I swallow over the lump forming at the back of my throat and force myself to walk inside.

The house is peacefully quiet. Sarah must have left, allowing the comfort of normalcy to gently spread its wings around me.

It's back to being me and Luca. The way I like it.

If only there wasn't this new pressure slowly bearing down on me. The ability to recover seems entirely out of reach.

But what if she's right? What if he can help?

The sooner I get back on my feet, the sooner he can be unburdened from my annoyances.

My stomach churns as I make my way toward the rustle of paper down the hall. My nerves build when I realize he's in his room. In unchartered territory. Yet my feet move of their own volition, taking me to his threshold, the door slightly ajar.

He's near the huge bed, his back facing me as he rifles through a myriad of paper bags spread across the mattress. Some are crumpled and empty, the contents seeming to be the mass of material piled in front of him.

I take another step and the door hinges squeak in protest.

Shit.

Luca stiffens, his spine snapping ramrod. "Did Sarah leave?"

I wince. "Yeah."

"Did she go of her own free will or did you kick her out?" He turns to face me, a lock of hair falling over his forehead to tease his eye.

"I'd never kick someone out of your house."

"Why not? Don't be polite on my account. When it comes to her, you've got free rein as far as I'm concerned."

I know he's joking, attempting to make light of an awkward situation. Again, I'm appreciative. "Did you know she was coming around so she could report back to Sebastian?"

"I gathered as much. I don't blame him, either."

"But you speak to him, right? I've heard you talking on the phone."

He nods. "At least once a day. But it's no secret he doesn't trust me with your welfare. He's keeping tabs the best way he can."

I wince, wishing the way my brother kept tabs didn't add more of a burden. "Thank you, Luca."

"What for?"

"For having her over every day, knowing she was spying, yet keeping her on a leash. I know this can't be easy for you."

"Can't be easy? Are you kidding?" He waves me away and returns his attention to the mess on the bed. "You treat me like a king. All that cooking and cleaning. I haven't done laundry once since we got here."

"It's the least I can do."

He shoots a warning look over his shoulder. "Do we really have to have this conversation again? You know I don't want you lifting a finger."

"It keeps me busy." I bite my lip, hesitant to expose my vulnerabilities. "My hands and my mind."

"Well, I'll buy you a gaming console. You can button bash for a while instead of getting cleaner's elbow."

"No, thank you. I'm not a gamer." I take another step, the intoxicating earthy smell of his aftershave sinking into my lungs. It's everywhere. In every breath. "What are you doing?" I continue to the bed and focus on the mess covering the mattress.

"Tidying up crap I had lying around." He begins shoving things into bags, his movements agitated.

Something has changed. Something's made him uncomfortable.

"I've overstepped." My thoughts become words. "I'm sorry. I shouldn't have intruded on your private space."

"You haven't." He keeps shoving, shoving, shoving the items of clothing. "Give me a second and I'll have this all bagged up."

No, I've definitely triggered his annoyance. I can see it in the way his usually graceful moves have become jerky.

I retreat a step, preparing to leave.

"Penny, I'm serious. Don't go." He meets my gaze, his intense eyes holding mine. Demanding. "You've barely sought me out since we got here. Don't leave me now."

I don't want to. It seems like I've reached some sort of threshold by walking into his room. But... "Why does it feel like I've done something wrong?"

"You haven't. It's me." He waves a hand at the items scattered over the bed. "I'm the one making it feel weird in here."

"Why?"

He straightens, sucking in a frustrated breath. "I don't know."

"Are these things sentimental?" I lower my focus to the bags. "Do they belong to a girlfriend? Or an ex? Is that why—"

"No. I bought all this for you."

I tense.

Freeze.

The only movement I feel is the rampant beat of my heart.

The reminder of the gifts Sarah mentioned comes back to bite me. I do a frantic visual search of the items scattered in front of us, trying to understand where his discomfort could stem from.

"I blame the concussion." He snickers. "I went on a crazy bender, buying shit I thought you might need... or like... or whatever. I dunno. It was a stupid idea."

He grabs the two bags closest to him and walks around me to carry them to the corner of the room. "I'll get rid of them."

"Why?" It's my curiosity talking. My fear, too. *Always* my fear. I want to know what he thinks my needs look like. "What did you buy?"

"Nothing you're going to want. Like I said, it was stupid."

"Please let me look." I tentatively move forward, keeping my gaze on him as I grab the closest bag.

"It's not a big deal." He shrugs. "Just keep in mind I wasn't thinking straight."

The contents of the first bag make my cheeks heat—tampons, pads, a heat pack.

I wish I knew how to react, but emotion overwhelms me. There's appreciation, guilt, and shame. Always shame.

I reach for another bag and pull out the material contents to expose a casual, full-length dress, the pattern pretty with light pinks and shades of cream. Those emotions intensify. The exact same ones—appreciation, guilt, then shame.

My throat tightens as I reach for a third, finding more clothes. More dresses.

By the fourth and fifth bags dread begins to take over, the ickiness coating my skin.

"I told you it was stupid." He slumps onto the mattress near the head of the bed. "I'll give them to a local charity."

I want to tell him not to. That maybe one day these items will become useful. But that's a lie. "Luca, I wish..." The words clog in my throat.

"What is it?" He frowns, pushing to his feet to take a step toward me.

"No. Stop." I raise a hand, unable to handle closer proximity when my mental demons are overwhelming me. "I'm beyond thankful for you. And this." I swing out an arm to indicate the gifts. "But you're right. I can't use any of it."

He nods, pretending to understand.

He doesn't. How could he?

"The pads and tampons..." I rub my knuckles over my sternum in an attempt to ease the building pressure beneath. "I don't need them. Luther made sure of that."

He snaps rigid, his nostrils flaring. "Why? What did he—"

I shake my head, trying to stifle whatever he thinks that monster did to me. "He made sure there were no inconveniences—that's all. I have a birth control implant. It's temporary. I'll have to get it removed."

"I'll take you to a clinic. We can make an appointment for today."

I nod and smile the best I can. "Thank you. But I'm not ready."

Going to a doctor means touching. Poking. Prodding. An internal exam. And the outside world. It's too much.

"You tell me as soon as you're ready, shorty. You hear me?" His words are filled with venom. Fiercely protective. "Snap your fingers and I'll be all over it."

"I will. Thank you." I swallow. Nod some more. "Then there's the dresses... I can't wear them. Luther always forced us to—"

"I know." He cuts me off. "I remembered too late and I'm sorry. That's why I didn't want you seeing any of this. When we first arrived, I made the fucked-up assumption that you kept wearing the baggy clothes you ordered online because of a sizing issue. But it's deliberate, isn't it?"

My heart squeezes. My lungs and stomach, too. "Yes."

"See? I fucked up. I'm not the best woman whisperer, but I assume you already knew that."

I huff out a laugh at his charming self-deprecation. He's too good to be true, which scares me a little. I know who this man is. *What* he is—a criminal, a murderer. It's the heart of gold that sets him apart from the family he works for.

"You're doing just fine." I back away, hoping the distance will stop my chest from humming.

"You're walking out on me?" He glances at me from the corner of his eye, disappointment heavy in his voice. "Are we finished with this conversation already?"

"No." I keep walking until I reach the far side of the room, then lower myself to the carpet and sit facing him. "The opposite actually. I'm getting comfortable."

He juts his chin in subtle acknowledgement, but those eyes speak of relief. He's happy I'm stepping out of my comfort zone. He's pleased with me, and I both hate and love the sense of accomplishment it inspires. "I'm trying, Luca. I'll admit I'm not doing as well as I've led you to believe."

"Really?" His mouth lifts, subtle and sarcastic. "You haven't led me to believe you're doing well at all, shorty. I know you're struggling. You're not sleeping well either, are you?"

"No."

"Nightmares?"

I nod.

"I've woken you a few times," he admits. "I'm not sure if it helped though."

My throat restricts. My cheeks heat. "You've woken me?"

"Don't worry; I didn't disturb your privacy. All I did was call your name from my room, or the hall if you were determined not to wake up."

The heat increases, the fear disappearing as embarrassment takes hold. "But how did you know I was having nightmares?"

"You cry out. You've called my name a time or two, as well, which speaks volumes of the horrors you must be enduring." He shoots me a sly grin. "But all jokes aside, the first time I heard you I thought you needed my help. That something serious had happened. But once I reached your door, you were yelling for your brother, and then at Robert."

The humiliation increases, scarring me. I break our gaze, unable to look him in the eye when my burden on him continues to grow.

"If you're interested, there might be something in one of these bags to help you sleep better."

I shake my head. "I don't want to be sedated."

"No, not sedatives. After your first few restless nights, I did some googling. There's an air diffuser around here somewhere. It's got some type of oil that's meant to help. It's a lavender blend or something."

This is ridiculous. Seriously, ridiculous.

This man, with his cold calculation and criminal ties, is googling sleep aids and buying air diffusers. It's enough to make a delirious laugh bubble in my chest.

He narrows his gaze on me. "Did I say something funny?"

I stop fighting and let loose with an embarrassed chuckle. "You're this big, tough, aggressive bad guy. I never would've imagined the words 'lavender blend' coming from your mouth."

His grin stops my pulse.

So many men have grinned at me. Leered. Ogled. So many that I never thought I'd appreciate the beauty of a male's face again. I thought I'd always find their interest threatening. But when Luca smiles at me, the routine spike of apprehension fades into a strange sense of accomplishment.

"Laugh all you like," he drawls. "I'm only going to get more stir crazy the longer I'm stuck inside these four walls."

And there goes my happiness.

Poof. Gone.

"I know you're not ready to get out of here," he adds. "But how would you feel about writing a list of goals and attempting to take on one at a time?"

I glance down at my fingers tangled in my lap. I don't feel good at the prospect, not good at all, even though the uncharacteristic sweetness is appreciated.

I want to stay within my comfort bubble. Unhappy, unhealthy, yet cozy in the familiar surroundings. "Can we leave this for a few days?"

"I don't think we can. It's time to start moving forward." There's an edge of authority to his tone. "These goals can be small or big—you decide. And we only need to work toward achieving one a day."

"We?" I raise my gaze, my self-loathing growing at the determination in his expression.

"I'm in this for the long haul. We can do it together."

I return my attention to my hands and pick at the quick of my thumb. Truth is, I hate disappointing him. I have ever since the first day we met. And now a lifetime of events have passed between us. He rescued me, risked his life to save me. He deserves better than my resistance. I should be giving him my full compliance. If only it didn't feel like launching myself into a complete free fall.

"Which leads me to my hidden motivation." He pushes to his feet and walks toward me, towering above me with an outstretched hand. "I'm hoping the first task on your list might be to help me out."

"Help you out how?" I pause, not eager to place my hand in his. Part of my reluctance is due to my past. There's more than that, though. I don't fear him hurting me. My hesitation stems from something different. Something I can't pinpoint.

When I finally give in, sliding my palm against his, I hold my breath.

His warm, calloused fingers grip mine. Tight. Strong. He pulls me effortlessly to my feet, making me shiver.

"Don't look so scared." He drops his hold and takes a step back. "You stitched my head in Greece. I'm only hoping you'll work your magic to help take those suckers out."

4

LUCA

She follows me to the kitchen where I grab a notepad, pen, and a chair, then continue into the main bathroom. The blade, antiseptic, tweezers, and pile of tissues I attempted to use yesterday are still spread out on the counter as if waiting for the torture to begin.

Just like in Greece, when I hadn't been able to see the injury on the side of my head to stitch the wound, I now can't remove the cotton firmly embedded in my skin. And I've left it too long for the removal, not wanting to ask Sarah for help and also not feeling comfortable pushing Penny. But she's given me an inch. Maybe it's time to strive for a mile.

I place the chair down in front of the basin and meet her gaze through the room-length mirror. "Are you still happy to do this?"

"Of course." She nods. "Sit."

I take my place on the chair, sitting tall. I'm determined not to let her nearness get to me. Not under my skin or in my head. It feels like a lifetime since I opened my mouth in Greece and let the stupidity of flirtation burst out. But my attraction hasn't wavered. If anything, it's intensified.

Seeing her all helpless and meek taunts me into protecting her. And that baggy sweater and the loose sweatpants do nothing to temper my memory of her perfect thighs, slim waist, and perky tits.

She's a siren.

An intense trigger to my temptation.

She walks around me, moving to the injured side of my head, her eyes gentle as she takes in the healing wound. "It looks like you've been taking good care of it."

"Haven't taken much care at all. I attribute any awesomeness to the nurse who stitched me up. She did a remarkable job."

A smile teases her lips. "I appreciate the praise. I'm also thankful you don't have the ability to see the error of your words. The stitching resembles a hack job at best."

"I'm not a pretty boy. I don't care what it looks like as long as the risk of infection is gone."

She reaches out, her fingers lightly brushing through the shortened lengths of hair around the wound, inspiring goose bumps to blanket my arms. "Your skin has started to heal over the thread. It might feel uncomfortable when I pull it out."

I can smell her.

Actually, I can smell *me* on *her*, which is fucking worse. She must be using my shampoo. Even though I've placed five years' worth of flower-scented products in her bathroom.

"Do your worst." I swallow over the unwanted build of lust. "As long as you don't leave anything behind, I'm good."

She nods and grabs the blade and tweezers, dousing them in antiseptic, then returns to her position at my side. "Tell me if I'm hurting you."

She is.

The agonizing discomfort of her proximity is fucking killing me. The curiosity surrounding her use of my shampoo is a thorn in my side, too. Why does she want to smell like me?

She leans in, those fingers resting against my scalp as her breathing brushes my skin.

She's everywhere—in my lungs, in my head, forever in every room of this fucking house. And of course, my dick doesn't want to miss out on the admiration. It twinges to life as I clench my jaw, hard, determined to keep my libido in check.

Her first nick of the blade is tentative. So goddamn gentle and feather-light.

"Don't hold back, shorty. You're going to have to be more firm than that if you don't want to spend all day staring at my skull."

Her mouth kicks into a smile, but she doesn't change her tender style as she uses tweezers to gently pick at the cotton.

It's nice to see her smiling. *Really* smiling. Not the fake-ass, untruthful curve of lips she likes to placate me with.

I can't pull my attention from her as she works in silence, using the blade before tugging out a tiny strand of thread to place on the counter.

Bit by bit she removes the cotton, her breath a constant caress against my temple, her fingers an ongoing tease.

"Why don't we start making that list?" I wait until she leans back to look at me before I grab the notepad and pen from the counter. "What small steps could you take to help kickstart your recovery?"

She winces. Shrugs. "I don't know. Hasn't stepping out of my comfort zone to open up to you been a big enough achievement for today?"

"Definitely. But this is for tomorrow, and the day after. Just one at a time, Pen. That's all I'm askin'."

Her sigh is slight, barely audible as she leans in and tugs another piece of thread from my skull. "I don't know. I guess having the guts to call my sisters could be on the list. Or messaging my brother to tell him how I'm doing so Sarah doesn't have to keep spying."

I write both down in bullet points. "Anything else?"

She shakes her head. "I honestly don't feel capable of achieving anything else. Not even those things I just told you. Having a list is only going to add more pressure and increase the sense of failure."

She's not a failure. Not even close.

"What if I write some ideas down?" I ask.

"Write all you like, but you need to be aware your understanding of who I am and what I'm capable of is completely warped. This is going to be too hard."

No, it's not. And my perception isn't warped. If anything, I'm the only one who knows the real Penny and what she's truly able to achieve. I've seen her at her worst. This person beside me is merely a shadow of the remarkable woman waiting to break free. "Trust me."

There's another sigh. Another brush of painfully gentle fingers. "I do," she whispers. "It's the fear of disappointing you that makes this harder."

I don't know what part of her admission surprises me most—the trust I never thought I'd receive or the sweet way she wants to impress me. Both have an unwanted effect on my dick.

"You're not going to disappoint me." I scribble on the notepad, adding more tasks to the list. "We only need to focus on one goal a day. If you achieve it, that's great. If you don't, we can try something else."

She refocuses on her task, raising the blade to my wound, not acknowledging my words. She tugs at the stitches, placing more and more cotton on the counter.

I get that she hates being here—hates me pushing—but maybe Sarah is right. I can't watch her wallow. If this tactic doesn't work I'll try something else. And if that doesn't help, I'll find another way. I'm not giving up on her.

I keep writing as she tends to my head, the two of us working in comfortable silence until she gives a final tug to the embedded cotton, then leans real fucking close to inspect her handiwork. "You're doing a lot of writing."

"I've got a lot of ideas."

She sidesteps, the blade and tweezers dumped in the sink before she rests against the counter to stare at me. "Well, don't keep me waiting. What are these great ideas of yours?"

"You sure you're ready?" I ask. "This is going to change your life."

She crosses her arms over her chest, plumping her breasts beneath the heavy sweater. "You're well aware I'm not ready at all. So hurry up and get this over with."

I chuckle, appreciating her underlying spite a little too much. "Okay. Number one."

She straightens, as if preparing for torture.

"Watch a movie with me."

I didn't think it possible, but she stiffens further, her brows furrowing. "Watch a movie?"

"Yep. As simple as that. Sit your ass on the sofa and chill out to mindless television. It's better than the isolation of your room or the deck."

Those brows rise for long seconds before she says, "Okay. I can give it a try."

"Number two—teach me how you do laundry."

Her smile creeps back into the conversation, her brows knitting. "Laundry? Really?"

"Really. I've been a grown man who takes pride in washing his own shit for over ten years now, but my clothes have never smelled as good or felt as soft as they have since you've worked your magic."

She rolls her eyes. "It's called fabric softener, Luca."

"I don't have fabric softener."

"Yeah, you do. I found it in the back of one of your laundry cupboards. It's probably old enough to burn holes through your shirts, but obviously it's doing the trick."

"Obviously." I mimic her eye roll. "Number three—exercise."

She sucks in a subtle breath and I pause, waiting for the stereotypical female retaliation.

It's clear she doesn't need to lose weight. Her body is on point. What she requires is the shift in brain function.

"Right." Instead of a protest, she nods and breaks eye contact to focus on the tiled floor.

"Don't get huffy on me," I warn. "I'd never comment on your body in a negative way. Not only because it's fucking rude, but because you're stunning. With or without the small village supply of material covering you at any given time."

I wait for a smile that doesn't appear and mentally berate myself for not prefacing my suggestion. "Exercise lowers cortisol, which is a stress hormone, while helping to increase endorphins. In your case, working out is about mood and mental health—not anything to do with appearance."

"I get it." She nods. "You don't have to explain."

"Yeah, I do. I can already see you creeping back into that shell of yours and it's pissing me off."

Making her feel like shit has a reciprocal effect. The only bonus is my resulting limp dick.

"Sorry," she mutters. *Murmurs.*

Fuck.

I hold in the need to growl in frustration. "Number four—read a self-help book. Number five—meditate. Number six—go for a walk. Number seven—get plastered."

She doesn't respond, just keeps her attention on the floor.

"Penny?" We've come so far this morning. From no words to heavy conversation and even physical contact. I'd thought I was receiving the jackpot of recovery. Turns out it was only a slight detour. "You still don't like the idea of a list, do you?"

"No, it's not that." She pushes from the counter. "Your ideas are great. I actually like them."

"But?"

"No buts." She gives me a placating smile. "You make it sound too easy, that's all."

"I've got no misconceptions about how hard this is going to be. Despite whatever warped perceptions you think I have, I know you're trudging through hell at the moment." I push to stand, the notepad hanging idle in my grip. "This list is only an attempt to get you to live a little."

"I'm living, Luca."

"That's where you're wrong. And the sooner you realize, the easier this will be. You deserve more than this limbo. And I'm here to help. I'm not going anywhere. *You're* not going anywhere. We're stuck together for now. So share the load, because it's sure as shit harder for me to watch you struggle from the sidelines than it will be at your side."

Her eyes turn somber, the wrinkle stretching across her forehead burrowing deep.

"I'm only asking you to try. I have no other expectations." I hold out the notepad for her to take. "But, come on, Pen. Aren't you at least a little excited to try and get out of your funk?"

"It's not a fun—"

"You know what I mean." I don't want to give her struggle a toxic label, whether it's depression or PTSD. All that shit has negative connotations. "Aren't you the slightest bit interested in doing something different?"

She grabs the notepad and raises her other hand, cinching her thumb and pointer finger so they're a breath apart. "A little."

Good.

Fucking fantastic.

A little is all I need. For now. "What do you say if we keep the momentum going and cross an afternoon session of movie watching off the list?"

Her smile is subtle, the slightest curve of tempting lips as she lets out an exaggerated sigh. "What did you have in mind?"

5

LUCA

WE TICKED THE MOVIE OFF THE LIST WITHOUT A HITCH.

I don't care if she fell asleep before the dramatic climax to have a two-hour power nap. If anything, I count it as a victory that she felt comfortable enough to sleep in the same room. Her rest was peaceful, too.

No nightmares.

No murmured cries for help.

The next day we moved on to the laundry. And props to her for giving it her all as she talked down to me, slow and demeaning, with her instructions on how to unscrew the lid to the fabric softener and pour the contents into the allocated tube of the washing machine.

Day by day, hour by hour, she starts to open up. Gradually. The lessening of her fear is incremental. But it's there. That's all that matters.

"So, what do you have in store for me today, GI Joe?" She enters the doorway to my weights room, hands on hips, the baggy sleeves of her sweater scrunched at her elbows.

She's lighter today. Brighter. Her eyes have a healthy glow.

And even though her nightmares haven't disappeared, at least our new routine of a daily movie session has ensured she's getting a nap during the daylight hours. The time she now spends reading might be doing the trick to distract some of her negative thoughts, too.

"I want you to go for a basic run." I keep pushing out my muscle-up reps, dragging myself over the bar again and again.

"Basic run?" She steps into the room, moving toward the treadmill with trepidation. "Define basic."

"I want you to run a mile." I drop to the floor and shake out the burn in my arms. "Without stopping."

"That doesn't seem so bad. A mile isn't far."

"It is if you're not used to running. Hell, even a couple hundred yards can be difficult on the body if you haven't exercised in a while."

She climbs onto the machine and attaches the safety clip to her sweater as I approach the side of the conveyor.

She presses buttons, placing the starting pace high. Far too high for a beginner.

"You might want to dial it back a notch. You can work up to a fast pace over time. Today is about getting through the mile however possible. I don't care if you have to granny shuffle over the finish line."

"Granny shuffle? Where's all that faith you're supposed to have in me?"

"I've got faith. I just don't want you falling on that pretty face right out of the gate."

She huffs. "Fine. I'll start with a light jog." She presses buttons again, turning on the machine, the conveyor slowly sliding into gear. "Do you have any music?"

"Yeah." I return to the chin-up bar and grab my cell from the floor. "What's your preference?"

"I don't mind." She undoes her ponytail, her stride flawless as she refastens it higher and tighter. "Whatever you usually listen to will be fine."

I start my workout playlist, the intense beat of Slipknot's "Duality" filling the room.

I try to concentrate on my reps as she runs. I clasp the chin-up bar. Do another set of muscle-ups. But my attention keeps drifting to her. Her stride. Her ease.

She increases the pace, pushing harder, moving faster. I don't hear her panted breath over the music. Instead, I feel it. The heavy lift of her chest. The distinct purse of her mouth. Each step acts like a cattle prod to my libido.

"You're fit." I pull myself over the bar and pause, waiting for her response. "Why didn't you mention it when we were discussing the list?"

She presses the treadmill dashboard again, creeping the pace higher. "I didn't think you'd want to know the intricate details of how Luther liked his women in peak condition."

She's right. That information isn't welcomed. In fact, my anger spikes, the reminder of her captor spurring me to push out an additional two reps of pure frustration before falling to the floor.

I slump onto the bench press, watching her, *amazed* by her.

Tightness enters my chest and it has nothing to do with exercise and a whole hell of a lot to do with things I shouldn't be thinking about.

She decreases the pace for long enough to remove her sweater and throw it to the floor. Then she's back running again, her oversized T-shirt billowing at her hips. It's not enough to stop the display of her bouncing tits. Or to hide the hardness of her nipples pressing against the thin material.

It's times like this where I wish it had escaped my attention that she didn't have any underwear in yesterday's load of laundry. She has no visible panty line either. And maybe I'm daydreaming or living in a fucked-up fantasy, but I don't think she's been wearing underwear at all. Not now, and not since returning stateside.

Fuck me for being the prick who noticed.

I shove to my feet, needing an additional set of reps to drag my attention away from something that will get me killed. Something that's a fucking dick move to even think about.

She deserves better.

Decker trusted me with her protection. He didn't give me an all-access pass to ogle his sister.

I drag myself up and over the bar, punishing myself, pushing so fucking hard my arms scream in protest. And still I can't stop the imagery taking over my mind. Can't drag my fucking gaze away.

She's completely oblivious. She keeps running, surpassing the mile marker to plow straight ahead.

There's never been a more remarkable woman. More powerful. More inspirational.

I'm caught up admiring the perfection until I finally gain the restraint to drag my attention away. I stare out the window in front of her, wishing I had the power to give her a better life. To solve her problems.

I'm stuck in the daydream of making her smile... until my gaze catches on her reflection in the glass, those dark eyes staring back at me.

Shit.

I force myself not to look away and announce the wicked shit filling my head. And I try even harder not to readjust my cock. To put the fucker back in his place —into deep, dark confinement far away from her, all while she keeps staring, keeps undoing me.

"That's enough for today." I release the bar and drop to my feet. "You don't want to push yourself too hard when I'm going to make you come back tomorrow."

Fucking tomorrow—the necessary vicious routine that will help her, and slowly kill me.

"Yes, boss." She thumps a hand against the treadmill dashboard, making the conveyor stop. "Same time, same place?"

I ignore her sarcasm, too fixated on the nickname she gave me. If only she knew how bossy I could be. How demanding. How dominant.

A man like me isn't meant for a woman like her, no matter how incessant my attraction.

"Same time, same place."

The music cuts off mid song as my cell starts to ring. Torian's name is written across the bright screen while the device vibrates on the floor.

"Are you going to answer that?" She steps off the treadmill and raises the long length of her shirt to wipe the faint hint of moisture from her face, exposing sweat-slicked skin.

"Yeah." I snatch the cell and connect the call. "What's up?"

"How kind of you to finally answer your phone," he drawls. "Does that mean you've stopped holding a grudge over me sending you home?"

"Still holding tight, asshole. What do you want?"

He chuckles, the tone laced with aggression. "I thought you'd appreciate an update."

"I don't need one." I walk from the exercise room, leaving Penny alone, and continue down the hall to shut myself into my bedroom. "Decker calls me on the daily. He's kept me posted on your progress in Greece. Progress I deserved to be a part of."

"And from the progress reports I've received, it sounds like you're coping just fine in your cozy isolation," he counters. "I'm told the role of protector suits you. Maybe a little too well."

Fuck Sarah and her big mouth.

"What do you want, Torian? I've got shit to do."

A lengthy sigh travels down the line. "There are two things. First, I thought Penny would like to know your brother is returning the first of her friends home today."

I pause a beat. "Why are you telling me this? Why didn't Benji call me himself?"

"He's busy. And you told me he struggles to handle his wife, let alone look after three rescued women. He's also been out of range. But the process of returning them home has started, and I assume the information will be a relief to Decker's sister."

I agree. Doesn't mean I'm letting him off the hook for sending me home.

"Okay." I shrug. "I'll let her know. What's the second thing?"

The conversation gains another pause.

Another sigh.

"You're not going to appreciate this news."

I clench my fist, my impatience building. "So spit it out. It's not like you have an issue with pissing me off. If anything, I'm sure you enjoy it."

"It's to do with the kid and Keira."

The kid and Keira.

The kid—meaning Tobias. The son of Penny's captor, and the boy she helped raise. The kid she would claim as her own if she had the choice. And the child who is Torian's half-brother.

I cling tighter to the cell. "What about him?"

"He arrived in Portland a few days ago."

"A few days?" I grate, trying not to let anger consume me on Penny's behalf.

"Yes."

"And you kept it from us, why?"

"Because Tobias has come a long way since the death of his father. He's doing well. But every time he gets on the phone to Penny he loses momentum. She's dragging him down, and it's best if they keep their distance for a while."

I huff out a derisive laugh. "You're a fucking asshole."

"Am I?" he snaps. "Why? For protecting my brother?"

"For having no fucking concern for Penny."

"She's not my problem. She's yours." His usual sense of superiority enters his voice, the dictatorial aggression barely leashed. "I'm telling you out of courtesy and nothing else. It's up to you if you inform her of the situation."

"In that case, thank you," I drawl. "How fucking generous."

"Watch yourself. I've put up with your hostility for long enough. I've also let it slide when you don't answer my calls. But I assure you, my patience is growing thin. I'm doing what's best for everyone. Including Penny. Keeping her away from Tobias might be the push she needs to stop hiding with you when she has a family who would kill to know she's still alive."

"She's making progress," I snarl.

"Not fast enough."

I close my eyes and pinch the bridge of my nose. There's no negotiating with him. He's already made up his mind.

It doesn't matter that he's keeping Tobias from the essential pain of recovery. Finding a way to support and communicate with Penny is part of the process. Torian just wants to make this easier on himself. Less drama. Less theatrics. Less trouble.

I guess I've been doing the same thing. Not wanting to push Penny to leave the house or see a shrink all because I want to shield her from more trauma.

"Fine." I walk for my bedroom door and pull it wide. "Do whatever you think is best. It's too late to stop you anyway." The kid is already here. Probably within a few minutes' drive.

"You're not going to keep railing on me? I expected more of that aggressive, ex-SEAL defiance I've grown to despise."

My defiance has nothing to do with my previous life as a SEAL. If anything, it's the cornerstone that got my ass kicked out. Rebellion and misplaced loyalty have caused me to fall so fucking far from grace that all I seem to have done over the past few years is descend.

"I get it," I mutter. "You're trying to protect Tobias. And I'm going to do the same with Penny. I may have drawn the short straw this time, but I'll deal. I always do."

"It doesn't sound like you're dealing. If anything, I'm hearing a hint of defection. I hope you're not thinking of crossing the fence again."

There's a threat in his words. The most subtle reminder that I'm no longer one of the good guys, whether I like it or not.

"I'm dealing just fine. In fact, I'm even starting to think you were right to send me back," I lie. "I deserve a break. Consider me on vacation until further notice."

6

PENNY

I REMAIN IN THE EXERCISE ROOM, TINKERING WITH PIECES OF EQUIPMENT, TRYING TO teach myself how to use them while the barely heard mumble of Luca's voice carries from somewhere in the house.

Today's achieved goal has already started to take effect. I feel lighter. The burden of darkness doesn't hinder my vision like it has recently.

I don't know if it's the endorphins or the decrease in cortisol, but the sensation is comforting. Strengthening. The voices in my head have been quietened.

My feelings toward Luca are changing, too. I'm not sure where the subtle shift is leading. Yet I'm eager to get more of the enthusiasm I feel in his presence.

I'd even lost myself while staring at his reflection in the window. I'd been in awe of his power. Both daunted and inspired.

But then our gazes collided, his attention making me transfixed.

Usually male scrutiny chills me to the bone. And for a split second, it had. The routine fear made its presence known. It attacked, hard and fast. Then it flittered away, the withdrawal an exquisite dance as a hesitant curiosity took over.

I began to enjoy the way he watched me. The subtle hint of praise spurred me to run farther. Faster. I wanted more. Even craved it.

"Want me to show you how to use the machine?"

I spin around at the sound of his voice and pretend my heart isn't lodged in my throat. "No, thanks. It's a little out of my league."

"After that effortless run? I disagree." He walks toward me, his stride confident, his posture tight.

Everything about him intrigues me. Especially the secrets hidden behind those hazel eyes. It's the slight hum of attraction that catches me off guard.

I like the look of him. More than that. I like having him near.

After everything I've been through—after all the handsome men whose charming smiles turned into deviant smirks—I should remain as far away from him as possible. I'm sure it's imperative to my healing, despite my body attempting to make me feel otherwise.

"Sit." He juts his chin at the machine in front of me. "I'll walk you through it."

"Seriously, I don't—"

"Just do it." He comes up beside me, tall, broad. An effortless protective presence. "Sit your ass down."

My body obeys without mental consent.

"This is for upper arms," he continues.

I scoff. "I figured as much. I'm not completely ignorant."

He grins, the flash of perfect white teeth increasing the hum in my belly. He leans in, adjusts the weights stacked to my left, then pulls down the dangling bar hanging above my head.

"See how that feels." He hands over the bar. "Keep your core tight and do as many reps as you can."

He steps back to sit on another bench as I pull the weighted bar down below my chin, then raise it again. He doesn't watch me this time. He lowers his gaze to the floor and bends over, resting his elbows on his knees.

There's no comforting smile. No heated gaze. There's nothing. Only a flat line of lips against a blank expression that makes me think he's hiding something.

"Am I doing this right?" I continue to work the bar, my arms wobbling under the unfamiliar exertion.

"Yep." He nods, his gaze briefly raising only to catch on my chest. His face tightens. Hardens. Then he glances away, his jaw ticking.

I can't help following where he looked, my cheeks heating when I see my nipples beading through the thin layer of my shirt.

The bar slides from my grip. The weights clatter onto the stack.

Luca shoots upright, his attention flashing to me as he frowns. "You okay?"

I nod and slump my shoulders, feigning fatigue when what I'm really doing is loosening the material around my chest. "Sorry. I've never done arm weights. I didn't mean to let go of the bar."

I didn't mean to be sexually insensitive either.

It's just that I can't bring myself to wear underwear. Not bras or panties.

I'd dreamed of having those luxuries while I was a slave. I'd always thought I'd love the comforting feel of added layers of clothing after having the option taken away from me. But then I'd come here, and the dreams had come true, only to become another nightmare.

I'd hated the restriction. The suffocation. The itch of something foreign against my skin.

"Don't worry about it." He keeps his chin high, as if determined not to lower his vision. "We can try again tomorrow."

He holds out a hand and waits for me to stand. The offer is forced. There's something different about him. Something has changed since he reentered the room.

His eyes aren't as kind. His shoulders are too stiff. He's on edge, for reasons other than my appearance.

"Who was on the phone?" I ask.

Brief seconds pass as his hand falls to his side, the silence announcing where the shift in his emotion came from.

"Torian," he admits.

"What did he say?"

He sucks in a long breath, his muscled chest rising beneath his shirt.

"Luca, what's wrong?"

He winces. "I don't want to lie to you."

The admission is barely spoken, yet the words penetrate deep. "Tobias... Is he okay? Did something happen?"

"No. Nothing happened to him." He rakes a hand through his hair.

"What about my brother?"

"They're both fine."

I breathe a little easier. "But something's wrong... There's something you can't say..."

He holds my gaze, his expression hardening. "I don't want to keep shit from you. Problem is, wanting to protect you and also tell you the truth isn't possible."

I swallow as a skitter of unease ricochets down my neck. I want to know what he's hiding. I don't want to add to his burden either. "I trust you'll tell me anything I need to know when the time is right."

He huffs out a laugh and shakes his head. "You're not helping."

I hate seeing him struggle. It's strange. I never thought I'd consider or care about a man's feelings after what the opposite sex put me through. Yet here I am, wishing he wasn't battling whatever weight rests on his shoulders. "Luca, you always make the right decision where I'm concerned. I know you only want what's best for me."

"Jesus Christ." He drops back down to the bench, head hung, shoulders slumped. "Tobias is here in Portland."

My heart squeezes. *Tobias.* My beautiful boy.

"He's been here for a few days." He lifts his head to meet my gaze. "Torian thinks it's best if the two of you keep your distance."

That squeeze becomes a burn, incinerating me from the inside out.

There's pain. So much pain. But I knew this would happen. I predicted these people would snatch Tobias out of my life. I knew they would never want a constant reminder of their father's crimes around the child I spent years raising.

I knew...

Only the knowledge didn't prepare me for the consuming reality.

"I appreciate your honesty." I push to my feet and make for the door, needing to escape before my anger shows.

"Penny, wait." He follows. "It's only temporary."

Lies. All lies.

"Once you're back on your feet," he continues, "you two can catch up."

I keep walking, keep striding out the distance to the sanctuary of my room.

"Penny, stop," he demands.

I don't. I reach the bedroom and slam the door behind me.

"Jesus fucking Christ." He speaks through the barrier between us. "This *isn't* permanent. Every time you speak to Toby, he gets depressed. He's not coping with how you're acting, and who can blame him? In Greece, you were a force to be reckoned with. You led him and he looked up to you because of that. Now, whenever you talk to him, it's a two-minute, one-sided conversation. You can't expect him not to be affected by that."

Guilt slams into me. Hard.

He's right. I barely talk to Toby and our conversations are always short. I'm well aware of how toxic I am in this current state. I'd been getting better, though. With Luca's help, I've been improving. I just haven't spoken to Toby recently for him to hear the change. Doesn't stop me from being livid though.

Cole Torian has no right making decisions for Tobias. No right at all. He barely knows the boy.

"Penny?" There's a thump against the door and I picture Luca's heavy fist weighed against the wood. "Talk to me."

"There's nothing to talk about." I collapse onto the bed. "Maybe you're right. He's better off without me."

Another curse drifts from the hall, then he opens the door. "Don't go back to the place you were in a few days ago." His voice is harsh as he glares. "Not when we were finally starting to get a handle on this."

"There is no *we*, Luca. And there is definitely no 'handle on this.'"

"Like hell there isn't." His glare increases. "Quit the pity party. I promise this is temporary. I wouldn't stand for it otherwise."

I look away, my hands clenched into fists. Tobias deserves better. If only these decisions didn't make me feel completely worthless.

"Like I said," I mutter, "I appreciate your honesty."

He sighs and walks forward to crouch at my feet. The strength of his attention calls to me. His energy does, too. "Look at me, shorty."

I don't. I can't.

"Penny," he growls.

I close my eyes, letting the strength of defiance brush my senses before I finally surrender. Denying him is hopeless. I'm hurt and frustrated and mad as hell. Yet, I can't stand the thought of Luca feeling that way toward me. "What?"

"This *is* temporary. You'll see Tobias soon. I promise."

I've never wanted to trust him, but my heart always has. The pained organ finds comfort in his words.

"And there was more to the conversation with Torian," he adds. "It's good news this time. My brother is returning one of your friends to their family today."

"Who?" The question slips out with a shallow wave of relief. "When?"

He shrugs and pushes to his feet. "I don't know. But I can find out."

"No. It doesn't matter. I'm thankful regardless."

He gives a sad smile. "I thought you might be. Do you want me to call Benji so you can speak to them?"

I've yearned to speak to my sisters since we were separated in Greece. The only difference between Tobias and those women is that with them, I've had the strength to keep my distance, knowing I'd be a negative addition to their recovery. They are together. All three of them left the Greek Islands to return home. They had each other's support. They didn't need me hindering their bright future. "No."

"You don't have to use my phone. I can finally set up the new cell I gave you."

"No. It's better if I don't."

He closes his mouth, his lips pressing tighter the longer I remain firm until he says, "I disagree. I'll go get the phone."

"I said *no*." I slide from the bed. "Torian is right. I'm a negative influence. It's best if we don't speak."

"But they need you."

"They need the *old* me," I grate. "They need the maternal figure who kept them alive. The person who continuously battled for our survival. That's not me anymore."

"Yes, it is. You're—"

"No, Luca. Listen. I'm not that person. I can't help anyone. I can barely help myself."

His eyes harden, the flare of his nostrils feral. "You're not giving up because of him. I won't allow it. This phase is only a brief backward step. A slight hibernation period. It won't last."

"I'm not a goddamn bear."

"You sure?" He scowls. "Because you're acting like one."

It's my turn to grind my teeth and scowl. Fire ignites in my belly. Heat builds in my veins. The instinct to fight awakens in me after being dormant for so long, but I shut it down. I won't let Luther back into my life. He changed me, making me lash out at the first sign of fear. But I don't want to fight anymore. I don't want to be reminded of him every time I'm scared. Or angry. "I said, 'no.'"

"Fine." He turns and starts for the door. "Call them. Don't call them. I don't give a shit. But you're going to get your ass back into the exercise room. I've decided you're not finished for the day."

7

LUCA

I was surprised when she joined me in the exercise room. The continuous glare and tense muscles were predictable, though. I made her jog another two miles. Then demanded she sit her ass down on the sofa and continue our daily movie routine.

This time she didn't sleep. She kept giving me the silent treatment, her glare cemented in place.

I let it fly because I appreciated seeing her committed to something for once, even if that commitment was her annoyance with me.

I even anticipated the animosity seeping into the following day, but she woke this morning without bitchiness. In fact, she's acting as if nothing happened yesterday. She talked to me over breakfast, went for a run on the treadmill afterward, and has just joined me for a movie at our usual mid-afternoon screening time.

I know she's faking the sudden recovery. Ignoring and bottling all the hurt. But even being able to pretend she's not dying inside takes a level of strength beyond my comprehension. I bet she doesn't realize how incredible she is. How fucking remarkable.

If only she'd finally break down and face her past—completely—then maybe she might start to recover instead of merely providing herself with distractions.

"What movie are we watching today?" she asks from the outstretched recliner.

"We could try the second half of the superhero movie you checked out on two days ago."

I didn't continue watching without her. I changed the channel as soon as she fell asleep. Not that the viewing is anything more than a lullaby. She usually passes out like clockwork within thirty minutes.

Those moments have been the highlight of my existence. Her content face. Her relaxed, slightly parted lips. Her beauty.

Fuck.

I need to get out of this house. Hit the shooting range. Spar the fuck out of a worthy opponent.

But I won't leave her or bring anyone over here she's not comfortable with. I'm stuck in this tempting isolation. My blue balls are the size of gorilla nuts.

I turn on the movie and lie across the sofa, my attention on her from the corner of my eye—the long, dark hair splayed across the recliner as she rests her head back.

I don't focus on the screen as the actors do their thing, blowing up buildings and shooting up shit. I stare at her, fast becoming entranced by how fucking gorgeous she is as those lashes flutter closed.

It's such a sinking feeling of helplessness, watching someone battle an invisible enemy. If she had a physical wound, I could tend to it. I'd make sure any injuries were stitched to perfection. I'd be meticulous in applying new dressings. And when the site healed, I'd make sure she used the very best scar-lightening creams on her delicate skin.

I'd do anything.

Everything.

But she's not struggling with a physical injury. There are no men to hunt down or kill. Her fight is internal. Entirely out of reach.

All I can do is be patient. I've always been good at that.

Until now.

Until *her.*

The vibration of the cell in my back pocket breaks my trance.

I retrieve the device, the preview of a message from Sarah on the screen— *Open your front door, I've just pulled…*

Jesus. She's here.

The bitch had been smart enough to keep her distance after I spoke to Torian. That gossip grapevine is effective in these parts. Too bad she didn't have the smarts to stay away too.

I type back—*Fuck off. Penny is asleep.*

I don't want her here. I'm done letting her report back to Decker. If he wants answers about his sister, he can ask during the daily phone calls I have to endure. I'm not opening the damn door. She can crawl back into the hole she came from.

Instead, I lower the sound on the television, then switch off the movie when my cell vibrates again—*Turn on the news.*

The hairs on my arms rise.

I change the channel, flicking to news station after news station, trying to find something to trigger familiarity, but there's nothing. No reports of drama in the

Greek islands or issues back home surrounding Torian's questionable business dealings.

I'm clueless.

What am I searching for?—I send back.

Just open the goddamn door.

I push from the sofa, annoyed, tired, and so far over this shit with Sarah, Decker, and yes, Torian, that it takes a few seconds to recognize the woman's face that flashes on the screen.

The heavy weight of dread takes over.

It's one of Penny's friends. One of the women I helped rescue from the same sex-slave hellhole in Greece. The words beneath her picture state—*Up next: Missing woman dies by suicide.*

Holy shit.

I stare. At the woman. At Penny peacefully sleeping. At the stillness surrounding me that will soon erupt into sorrow.

The cell vibrates again—*Open the fucking door, Luca.*

Fuck.

I stalk from the room, measuring my footfalls so I don't wake the sleeping beauty, and reach the front of the house without taking a breath.

"What the fuck happened?" I ask as I pull the door wide.

Sarah stands there, her face somber. "I don't know. All I got was a call from Torian telling me to get my ass over here to help control the situation."

"I don't need your help controlling anything." I scrub a hand through my hair and try not to panic. "Why didn't he call me?"

"I guess he wanted you to have backup."

"What I need is information."

She shrugs. "I don't have a lot. Torian said Benji had been certain the woman was ready to return home. He'd prepped her the best he could. Made her realize talking about her time in Greece wasn't an option. And set her up with a backstory. Then he dropped her off a few blocks from where her parents live."

"Obviously, he fucked up somewhere," I growl.

"You can't know that. These women are unpredictable. How could they not be after that level of abuse?"

"Then he should've kept her long—"

"Luca?" Penny's voice carries from the living room. "Where are you?"

Jesus fucking Christ. I just need a second. One crystal clear thought. One hint of a plan so I don't make this harder for her.

"At the front of the house. I'll be with you in a minute." I pin Sarah with a scowl and begin closing the door. "I don't need backup. Not from you."

She steps forward, placing her foot at the threshold. "So how are you going to handle this?"

"That's not your concern."

"Luca." Her tone is derisive. Demeaning. "This won't go down well. She's going to lose it."

"No shit." But I've managed worse. A bullet to my head for starters. Not to mention the numerous times Penny has attempted to kill me. I talked her down from those ledges... well, I manhandled her from the cliff a time or two, but I still got the job done.

"So you can handle her tears? Her grief? Her heartbreak?" She raises her brows. "You can be a shoulder for her to cry on?"

"She doesn't cry. Never has."

"And you realize that's unhealthy, right? She needs to let it out."

Yeah, I realize. I realize too fucking much where Penny is concerned.

I pinch the bridge of my nose, squeezing tighter and tighter to stave off the building headache.

"*Luca?*" This time Penny's call is frantic, the tone etched in fear. "*Luca.*"

My heart drops to my gut. "*Fuck.* I left the television on the news."

"Goddamnit." Sarah lunges forward, shoving past me to jog down the hall as I rush to close and lock the door behind her.

The television volume increases as I run after her.

"*—Abigail Foster, a twenty-five-year-old who went missing four months ago,*" the reporter informs the viewers, "*miraculously returned to her family yesterday, only to take her life overnight.*"

I reach the entry to the living room and get hit in the chest at the sight of Penny standing before the recliner, a hand clasped over her mouth as she shakes her head.

The television cuts to a middle-aged woman cradled by the side of a stricken man. "Our baby had only just come home to us," the woman sobs. "Now she's gone." She buries her face in the man's shoulder. "*My baby is gone.*"

The vision returns to the newsroom, the anchor's emotionless face filling the screen. "*Initial reports state Abigail Foster's disappearance was due to a secret elopement. She only returned when the relationship dissolved.*"

"No," Penny seethes, no sorrow or tears in sight. "*No.*"

Sarah reaches for her. "I'm sorry for your loss."

My warrior pulls away, distancing herself from vulnerability. "What's going on?" She turns to me, blinking rapidly as those pleading eyes beg for information. "I don't understand."

"I'm sorry, shorty." I start for her, wishing I had more than useless condolences. "I don't know."

"This isn't happening." There's a wealth of conviction in her voice—so much pained adamance. "Abi wouldn't kill herself."

"I'm so fucking sorry." I don't know what else to say as I raise my hand to brush my fingers along her sweater-covered arm. "I wish there was something I could—"

"She didn't kill herself." She slaps my hand away. "She *wouldn't*. I know her, Luca. There's no way she'd take her own life."

Denial is a bitch. I know from experience.

"What you all went through in Greece was traumatic," Sarah murmurs. "It would affect each of you in different ways."

"Can't you hear me?" Penny snaps. "I *know* her. She would *never* do this."

"Penny." I reach for her again. "It's—"

"No." She shoves by me. "They're wrong."

The continued denial slices through me as she rushes for the hall, disappearing around the corner.

I should go after her. I should do *something*. But I'm still wading in indecision when her bedroom door slams moments later.

"That went well." Sarah turns off the television, the thick silence closing in on me. "What are you going to do now?"

I know what I want to do. It's the same damn thing I've itched to do since the moment we got here—to push her. To force her to face what's going on. To shove her toward tears instead of isolation. She has to stop hiding and finally start grieving.

"For starters, I'm going to call Benji and find out what the fuck he was thinking returning that woman to her family when clearly she was unstable."

"Don't blame Benji. This isn't his fault."

"It isn't?" I raise my brows. "You sure?"

She winces. "Luca, his job was to get them prepped for the questioning that would arise once they returned home. He only had to make sure they were aware of what would happen if they spilled any secrets."

"Well, maybe he made them too aware. Maybe he scared the fuck out of her to the point where she couldn't cope."

"Luca." My name is a warning. "You're too invested in this. It's just a job."

Like hell it is. I'm so far down the emotionally invested path with Penny that there's no going back.

"Thanks for your help, Sarah." I start for the hall, my tone demanding she follow. "But I've got it from here."

"I'm not going anywhere."

"Yes, you are. Get the fuck out."

"No, I'm staying until I know Penny is okay. Unless you plan on physically removing me, you need to get used to having me here."

I swing around, glaring.

I'd have no problem heaving her over my shoulder and dumping her on my front lawn. In fact, I'd appreciate the inevitable cat fight, my climbing blood pressure demanding an outlet. It's her rare expression of panicked concern that makes me pause.

She's worried. Not just for Decker's sake.

Fuck her and her perfectly managed manipulation. Even though I'm well aware she's potentially playing me, I'm struggling to turn away someone who cares for Penny. My battling warrior needs all the support she can get.

Even from a crazy-ass bitch like Sarah.

She holds my gaze, not moving, not backing down.

"At least make yourself useful and start the coffee machine." I continue to glare as I retrieve the cell from my pocket and walk onto the deck to call my brother.

My pulse pounds through my skull with every ring. Once. Twice. When the line connects I grind my teeth, waiting for the muttered greeting from the only member of my family I have left.

"What the fuck is going on?" I demand. "I'm here watching the news and wondering why the hell you didn't call?"

"Excuse me for having my fucking hands full. You've got no idea what it's like with these women."

"So it's true? The news reports have it right?" My nostrils flare as I strangle the deck railing with my free hand. "After days dealing with you, she finally returned home to kill herself?"

"How the hell would I know? I dropped her off and hightailed it out of there. I don't know what happened after that."

"How was she when you dumped her?"

"I didn't *dump* her. She was fine." Frustration tightens his tone. "She was hopeful. Maybe even fucking excited. The other women thought the same, too. Then this happened."

"This can't be completely left field. You had to have a clue."

"Don't judge me," he snaps. "She was *fine*. She was *happy*. She didn't dance a goddamn jig into the dining room every morning, but she was ready to go home. Don't blame me for what happened. This isn't my fault."

It never is.

"You should've called me before you took her back. You should've paid closer attention."

"Fuck you. I did the best I could. You don't know what I've been through. You've got—"

A burst of muted noise from inside steals my attention. A smothered thud. I swing around to the house, finding Sarah rushing for the hall.

"I've gotta go." I speak over Benji, then disconnect the call and run inside, sliding into the hall as Sarah grabs for the handle of Penny's door. "*Stop.*"

She stiffens, glancing over her shoulder to meet my gaze while crashing and banging thunders from inside the bedroom. "Let me go to her."

"No. Back off. Or go home."

"Listen to me." She speaks in a rush. "I have experience with this. I can empathize with her loss." She raises her hands in surrender. "Storming in there, flying by the seat of your pants, will only cause more damage."

Christ.

I don't know how to help. All I have is instinct and that adamant, demanding pulse is telling me to get my ass in there.

"Luca?" she begs. "Do you really want to risk hurting her more than she already is?"

I clench my fists. "You don't know that I will."

"You're a raging bull—face stark, hands clenched, shoulders stiff. You're going to scare her."

Fuck. I try to calm myself, attempting to relax my muscles and breathe deeper.

It's pointless.

I'm mindless over Penny. Mindlessly failing.

Another scream carries from inside the room, a heavy thud following.

"All I'm asking for is ten minutes." Sarah twists the door handle. "I can deal with this."

Maybe she can. Maybe it would've been better for her to manage the recovery from the very first day we returned from Greece. Maybe all I've done is fuck Penny's life even more.

But I can't bring myself to give Sarah permission to take over. All I can do is turn on my heels and stride back where I came from, my pride and a truckload of hostility clogging my fucking throat.

8

PENNY

I THROW THE BEDSIDE LAMP ACROSS THE ROOM, THE SHADE FRACTURING ON IMPACT, the base smashing before it falls to the carpet in fragments.

Abi's gone.

Dead.

It's all my fault.

I left her with a stranger.

I gave up when I should've been protecting her, and now her death doesn't even make sense. She didn't kill herself. She wouldn't.

If the news report featured Lilly maybe I could digest the information. Lil was always the weakest. The one unwilling to fight.

But not Abigail. She had fire in her soul. Determination in her belly. She wouldn't take her life when she'd just returned to her family.

I refuse to believe the lies, my pulse ramping higher the more my mind conjures memories of her parents on the television. Their tears. Their anguish.

I grab the bedside clock and haul it across the room, the weight thunking into the plaster to leave a dent.

The past returns to haunt me. Images of Abi pummel my mind. I can still feel her. Can still smell the sweet vanilla of her shampoo.

I yank out the top drawer of the nightstand and throw that, too, this time releasing a war cry as the projectile leaves my fingers.

The outside mania quietens the voices within. It soothes the rage. Momentarily.

I scream as I throw another drawer. And another.

"Penny?" The door opens, making me pause as Sarah cautiously glances inside. "Can I come in?"

"No," I pant, my chest heaving.

She ignores me, walking forward, her steps cautious as she closes the door behind her.

"Get out." I grab the last drawer in the nightstand and heft it at the wall, the hard *thwack* no longer bringing relief.

"Talk to me." She continues toward me, not stopping until she reaches the side of the bed. "Tell me what you're thinking."

I shake my head, stumbling backward to the window.

I want to tear my hair out. To scratch at my eyes. To claw at my skin. I want anything and everything to take away the violence inside me, the toxicity molding into my DNA.

"What hurts the most?" she asks.

That's the thing—I don't even know. Is this grief? I'm not hurt. I'm livid. The anger is marrow-deep. It accompanies every inhale. Every thought. It's in the past, the present, the future. I'm surrounded by punishment. The shadows creep closer with each heartbeat.

I let Abi down.

I didn't protect her.

I should've done more. For her. For all of them.

"Leave." I turn to the window, my sight focused on Luca's cream fence when my mind sees nothing but Abi. Her face blinks back at me. Her determination. Her strength.

It's all been extinguished.

Snuffed.

"When I lost my family. I couldn't pull myself together because too many emotions were attacking me at once." Sarah walks to the side wall and picks up the battered shell of the lamp. "The weight of it was brutal. And I was convinced nobody else would ever understand. How could they? How could anyone possibly know what it's like to have every loved one taken away? What I should've realized, though, was that I didn't need understanding. I only needed someone to listen."

"That's not what I need." I reach for the curtain, digging my nails into the thick material, tempted to pull the heavy weight from the looming rod.

I don't know what will help me right now, but it's not chitchat.

"I think you're wrong," she states, matter of fact. "I think you're scared of asking for help... scared of opening up to someone. I was like that, too. I didn't truly find my feet until I let Hunter in. He found me through the darkness."

I glare at her, disgusted. She may have been found, but that discovery led her to a life of crime. To a murderous fiancé.

"And I know you said your friend wouldn't kill herself," she continues. "But everyone handles trauma differently. We never truly know—"

"Stop." Her placations stoke the building flames inside me, the suffering increasing through my anger.

"Penny, you should—"

"*Stop*," I snap. "Your situation holds no comparison to mine. You don't know what I want. What I *need*. And you certainly have no fucking understanding of how well I knew Abi. She wasn't a friend. She was my sister. A *real* sister. Not like the crime-riddled family you joined to replace your own."

Her eyes flare. This formidable woman, with her steely determination and threatening demeanor, is taken aback by my words.

"Ouch. That was below the belt." She rubs her sternum as if I punched her. "But I'll allow it. I'm all for lashing out when I'm in pain, too."

I wince, hating myself. Hating her. Hating the whole damn world.

I don't want to lash out. I don't want to fight.

The reaction is beyond my control, the response engrained while living under the roof of a monster. Luther made me this way. Made me learn to attack at the first sign of fear. And I loathe myself for allowing the transformation.

I wasn't aggressive before him. I was gentle and kind once.

Now I'll forever be his slave.

"Oh, God." I suck in a breath, the shackles of my life sentence tightening. "I'm sorry." I swing around to the window. "I shouldn't have said that."

"Don't be. I didn't walk into a room where furniture was being thrown anticipating fluffy conversation and squishy boob hugs. You're entitled to your emotions. If you're angry, let it out. Same goes with the sadness. You can't bottle it up."

She's wrong. I *can* keep it bottled. Luther made it impossible not to learn the skill when he despised vulnerability. And besides, crying would be the end of me. I'd start and never stop.

"I'm a good listener," she adds. "Luca is, too."

I return my attention to the fence, staring mindlessly as I force myself to be calm. "Luca doesn't need to be burdened any more than he already is. I've destroyed enough of his life. And now his home."

"Pfft. The guy didn't have a life to begin with." The mattress squeaks as she makes herself comfortable. "Listen to me. At the moment, you're being pummeled. There's grief, confusion, and fear. There's loneliness, guilt, and long-ing. And that was before you even heard the news about Abi. Your only choice is to be overwhelmed. But you're going to need to quieten the mass of voices to be able to move on."

"You're wrong. I barely feel any of those things."

Hours ago, she would've been right. I was drowning in all those emotions. Not now though. What's happening in this moment isn't right.

It's different.

I'm different.

"Then what do you feel?"

I can't admit the truth. It's heartless, learning about the loss of a loved one only to feel anger in response. It's not natural. Not normal.

Luther's influence is seeping into me. It seems the more time I spend away from the nightmare of my past, the more I'm dragged back to it.

I'm changing, and not into someone I like.

"You're angry." She releases a breath of a chuckle. "I guess we're more alike than I thought, because that was my greatest struggle, too."

There's the slightest sense of appreciation in knowing my feelings aren't unique. Just not enough to bring comfort.

"Rage tortured me the most," she adds. "For weeks. Probably months. So I chased it down and figured out what it would take to silence the screams."

I glance over my shoulder, meeting her gaze. "How do you silence anger?"

"Revenge," she says simply. "I wanted retribution for what I'd lost. And what was taken from my family. That meant going after the man who destroyed us. I transformed my body into a weapon. I learned every type of combat and defense training you can think of. I did whatever it took to reach my goal."

I believe her. The physical lengths she went to are still evident at first glance. Her arms show defined muscle beneath the feminine facade. There are scars on her skin. There's hardness in her beautiful features.

"I killed those voices. And the man who murdered my family."

A flicker of respect sparks inside me.

I'm happy for her, but it doesn't mean I can do the same. Luther is already dead. Revenge isn't possible.

"I'll help wherever I can. Luca will, too. And there's no hurry. Don't even think about it today. But why don't you talk to the other women you lived with? They might be able to tell you about Abi's final days and help you understand what she was thinking."

I shake my head. Nothing could make me understand.

"If not for insight, do it for support. You can't keep battling on your own." There's another squeak of the bed. More footfalls. "Here."

I turn to her standing a few feet away, her finger tapping her cell screen.

"Talk to them." She passes over the device, a call to *Benji* written on the screen, the connecting tone humming through the loud speaker.

My hand shakes as I reluctantly take the offering. I don't want to speak to Nina and Lilly. Not yet. Not when my betrayal to them is raw. They'll blame me. They *should* blame me. I spent months protecting them only to leave when they needed me the most. Yet I can't bring myself to end the call, the anger inside me begging for salvation.

"Hey, Sare," a man greets. "This isn't a great time."

The voice is shockingly familiar, stunning me speechless. The tone is similar to Luca's. Deep and graveled.

"Sarah?" he asks.

"Benny, I'm here." She raises her voice from behind me. "Penny has the phone. Can you put one of the other women on the line? She needs to speak to them."

My heart pounds, the need to disconnect waging war with the necessity to be soothed.

"Yeah, okay," he mutters. "Give me a minute."

Silence rings in my ears, along with my heavy pulse, while I attempt to talk myself out of hanging up. This doesn't feel right. I just… can't.

Murmurs filter down the line. A scuffle of scraping sounds brush my awareness.

I push the phone toward Sarah. I can't do this.

"Penny?" The syllables are entirely brittle. Yearning and needy.

I close my eyes and stiffen against a surge of guilt.

"Penny?" she repeats, this time frantic.

"She's here," Sarah answers. "She's listening. I think she's finding it hard to speak."

I suck in a breath, dragging air deep into my lungs, praying for strength. All those emotions Sarah mentioned are right there—the guilt, the sorrow. They're banging on the walls of my anger, trying to get in.

"Oh, God, Penny," Nina sobs. "I don't know what happened. Abi was excited to go home. She wanted this so much. It doesn't make sense."

"So it's true?" I whisper. "She's dead."

I need to hear it, just once, from a reliable source. From someone I trust.

"Yes."

I open my eyes and blink away the sear of unshed tears. I can't cry. I won't.

"B-Benji took us there this morning," she stammers. "We watched from the end of the street as the police wheeled her covered body outside."

"She was happy." Lilly speaks softly in the distance. "She wanted to go home. Now I'm starting to think the home she referred to wasn't with her parents."

Bile churns in my stomach, threatening to join the party.

Heaven *was not* home for Abi. She would never mean that.

"Are you both safe?" My tongue protests against the words, making them sluggish.

"We're being looked after," Nina says. "Benji has given us everything we need. I'm just not sure where we go from here. We're in Eugene, in the neighboring suburb to Abi's parents, and were meant to be heading to my family in Gold Beach."

They're close. Within a two-hour car ride.

I could get to them. Help them. Protect them and make certain they're stable enough to be returned to real life.

I could… but I won't.

I'm not a leader anymore. My time as their protector is over.

I can't help anybody in my pathetic state.

"I'm scared," Nina admits. "What if Abi didn't realize how tough things were going to be until she reunited with her parents? What if the reality of returning became too much? The same thing could happen to me."

"It won't." I swallow over the dryness consuming my throat. "You're going to get back on your feet. Build a career. Be happy—"

"But *she* was happy, Penny. How does that disappear in the blink of an eye?"

"I don't know." I bite my lip. "We don't know what went on inside that house."

"What if this never ends?" Lilly sobs. "What if we're always going to suffer?"

Silence follows, and I know they're waiting for a familiar boost of positivity from me. Problem is, I have the same questions. I can't fake optimism for them anymore.

"Look, I've gotta go." I wrap my arm around my belly and squeeze tight. Speaking to them was a mistake. I can't help them. And they can't help me. Not anymore. All this conversation has done is bring more vulnerability. More agonizingly brutal suffering to everyone involved. "If you remember anything call Luca."

Sarah clears her throat. "Penny, you have your—"

I hold up a hand to silence her. I know what she's going to say—that I have my own phone. That they can contact me directly if all I'd do is let Luca set up the device he bought me.

I don't want that. I can't give my past twenty-four-seven access to me. And if I have the internet constantly within reach I'll succumb to my pained curiosity. I'll search for all the names of the sisters I've lost. I'll suffocate under the weight of the lives they left behind.

I'm not strong enough for that.

Despite all this anger, I'm nothing but goddamn weak.

"Goodbye," I whisper. "I love you."

"We love y—"

I disconnect, unable to listen, and hand the device to Sarah who looks at me with a mix of disapproval and pity.

"That wasn't really talking, now, was it?" She pockets the cell. "I told you, you need to let this out with someone. If not them, then Luca."

"And I've told you, he doesn't need more trouble from me. He's babysitting out of obligation. I'm only here because there was no alternative... Please, just leave me alone."

"He cares about you."

I shake my head, the movement taking too much effort. I'm not even going to argue.

A light tap sounds at the door, and the man of the moment pokes his head into the room, his intense eyes taking in the destruction of the room before settling on me. "Am I interrupting?"

"No. Come in." Sarah walks toward him. Both of them stop at the foot of the bed to stare at me. "Penny and I were just having a conversation about her coming to live with me for a while. I think it's for the best."

"What?" Luca stiffens.

I do the same, completely blindsided.

That was *not* what we discussed. Yet the denial remains caged in my tightening throat, waiting for his relief to show.

"You're no longer obligated to look after her," she continues. "It's my job now."

"Obligated?" His eyes harden. "She's never been a fucking obligation, Sarah. I chose to come back here. With her. If she goes, I go. I'm not leaving her fucking side. Not for a minute."

My emotions swirl, creating a washing machine of confusion and denial. I don't want to believe him. I *don't*. Yet I crave it, too. Oh, God, how I crave.

Sarah cringes. "Luca, we all know you got dumped with the babysitting job. Let me take over. I'm better equipped to look after a woman. We can have a girls' retreat at my place."

"Is that what you want?" His frantic gaze searches mine. "Do you want to leave?"

No. What I want is to make things easier on him. To stop being a nuisance. To take the burden off his shoulders.

"Penny?" He steps closer, his hand reaching out only to fall back to his side. "Do you want to stay with Sarah?"

What I want is to stop being this person that isn't me. To return to who I was before Luther and Greece and violation. I want peace. Normalcy. And more than anything, I want to be whole.

Sarah meets my gaze from over his shoulder, her lips tweaked in conniving satisfaction. "She's a hassle you don't need."

The truth hurts. But there's confusion, too.

Sarah is enjoying this, and I don't know why.

"Shut it," Luca growls, his eyes softening in my direction. "Tell me the truth, shorty. Do you want to get out of here?"

Sarah's smirk grows as she winks at me.

Winks. At. Me.

I struggle to understand the taunt. Then, like a light bulb, my awareness switches on to expose the meaning behind her tactics.

She's created this drama in an attempt to prove me wrong about the burden I've placed on his shoulders. She doesn't want to take me away. She wants me to feel at home.

"Penny?" Luca takes another step.

"I don't know." I swallow, wrapping my arms around my middle. "I don't know what I want."

The corners of his mouth lift in a sad smile. His head inclines the slightest inch in acknowledgement. Then he turns to Sarah, his height increasing as he straightens. "You did this. You messed with her fucking head. You made her question being here."

"Me?" She places a hand to her chest, her eyes wide with feigned offense. "Why would I do that?"

"Get the fuck out." He stalks for the bedroom door, jabbing a finger toward the hall. "And don't come back. I've had enough of your bullshit. Everyone knows I'll protect her with my life. I'm done trying to prove it."

Sarah remains in place, her attention on me, one brow raised as if to say, 'I told you so.'

I guess she did.

I knew Luca would be kind enough to deny wanting me to leave. I never imagined he'd be passionate about me staying. Or furious at anyone attempting to take me away.

"Are you sure this is what you want?" she drawls. "You don't have to stay under this psycho's roof."

"Get. The fuck. Out," he snarls. "*Now.*"

She rolls her eyes and gives another wink. "Okay. Okay. I'm leaving."

9

LUCA

I LEAD SARAH TO THE FRONT DOOR, WAITING UNTIL SHE'S GOT ONE FOOT OUTSIDE before I slam it on her ass, then lock the deadbolt while she mouths off.

I'm angry. Unjustifiably livid. And entirely fucking blindsided.

One minute, I thought she was helping. The next, she was attempting to steal Penny away.

I lean against the door, my head hung, a pulse ticking beneath my left eye.

Maybe if I hadn't interrupted when I did, Sarah would've been successful. It's not like she doesn't have a point about being better equipped to look after a woman. I don't know how to be the person Penny needs. But I'll be damned if I trust someone else to protect her.

There's no way in hell.

If she leaves, I'll follow.

I shove from the door, needing to get back to her. To stop her from questioning our sanctuary.

She's still standing near the window in her bedroom, her arms around her middle. Every muscle is pulled taut. Despite her stiffness, sorrow seeps from her. Her heartache escapes with every breath even though there are no tears.

She continues to trap her emotions inside. Caging them.

It's time to break them free.

"I'm sorry." I'm drawn to her side, my fingers itching to touch. "I know I keep sayin' that, but I've got nothing else."

She doesn't move. Doesn't react.

"You're going to get through this." I reach for her, stealing the physical connection I crave, my palm sweeping over her shoulder. "I'll get you all the help you need."

"Please don't." She flinches away. "I just want to be left alone."

No.

No more isolation. No more hiding from grief.

My limbs throb with the urge to grab her. Shake her.

She needs to let go. To cry. Not only for Abi, but the parts of her own life that died. Why can't she see that?

"Tell me what you're thinking," I calmly demand.

"That it's not true. That Abi didn't kill herself."

"How do you know?"

"I spoke to my sisters and they agree." She turns to me, her eyes filled with conviction. "They said she'd never do this. That she was excited to get back to her family."

"Okay. So maybe her death was an accident." I reach for her again, her violent shrug away stinging my pride. "But she's gone, shorty. That part you can't deny."

She winces. "Don't."

"I know you loved her. You two went through hell together. She was everything to you, which means there's no way you can get around grieving for her. No matter how hard you try."

She retreats a step. "You don't understand."

"You're right. I can't imagine how hard it is to lose her. You left Greece thinking the nightmare would end, only to have it follow." I inch closer as she backtracks. "And you're too scared to let down your guard to start healing. You're clinging to what you know—the sterility, the anger. You think you need to act the same way you did with Luther in an effort to protect yourself. To fight when you should crumple."

Her lips part as if in shock before a mask of annoyance settles into place. "Stop."

"I'm sorry, shorty, but I can't. It's time for this to sink in. For you to acknowledge what you went through. For you to break down the walls you've built out of fear. There's no peace in denial."

"There's no peace?" she asks. "What peace could I possibly obtain, Luca? What peace have I ever had?"

"Peace is on the other side of acceptance. You need to face what's happened."

"I said, 'stop.'" She makes for the door.

I follow, unable to let this go. "We're not running anymore. Maybe it was suicide. Maybe it was an accident. It doesn't change the fact she's gone."

"*Stop.*" She plants her feet and swings around to shove at my chest. "Stop it." Her eyes blink with unshed tears. "Just stop."

Her agony punches into me, my words injuring us both. But she's so close. The slightest crack forms in her defenses. "Luther's not here anymore. You don't have to keep fighting. Abi's dead, shorty. It's time to grieve."

The tears build, her dark eyes an endless pool of heartache bursting to break free. She shoves me again and again, harder and harder.

"She's not suffering anymore. She's free." I snatch her wrists. Tight. They tremor under my grasp.

Those eyes flare, her panic and fear slam into me.

But I can't let her go.

After all the days of sitting on my ass and letting her find her own way, it's clear I should've acted differently. She needs to be pushed to face reality. I feel it deep down in my bones. She can't move on until she acknowledges her past. Until she lets go of the hold Luther had on her.

"You're safe," I murmur. "He's not here anymore. He can't hurt you."

"Don't do this." She thrashes, attempting to break my hold. "*Let me go.*"

I pull her into my chest, releasing her wrists to wrap my arms around her back. "I'm not hurting you. I never will." I cage her against me as she bucks and pushes, doing her best to escape.

"*Stop*," she screams. Her loose hair whips my face. Her knee jabs me in the thigh.

She's a wild cat. Sharp movements. Feral ferocity.

I hope I'm not fucking this up.

No.

This is the right thing to do.

The *only* thing.

I hold tighter, increasing her struggle. "I've got you."

"*You're a monster*," she shrieks, wiggling one arm free. She thumps my chest. Slaps my face. Scratches my cheek.

"No, *he* was—*Luther.*" I take her fury, not letting her hatred penetrate. "*He* hurt you. *He* was the monster. I'd never raise a hand to you, Penny. I'd never do the things he did. You're safe now. I've got you."

She has to let it all out. Every ounce of the pain and suffering. I won't let her go through another day clinging to her abuse.

"Let me have your worst." I loosen my arms, allowing her space to whack harder into me.

"Let me go," she wails, raising her face, her mouth a breath from mine. So pretty. So tortured. "Get your fucking hands off me."

"No."

She strengthens her fight. Beating. Clawing. Bashing. "You fucking bastard." The first tear escapes, the glistening path trekking down her cheek like a break in the most arid drought. "I hate you."

"Hate me all you like. I'm not letting you go until you get this out of your system."

"I *can't* get it out of my system," she screams. "This is me. This is who I am."

"No, Pen, this is who you needed to be when you were around him. You needed to fight. You needed to attack and protect. You don't need to do that now. Not anymore."

"Let me go." She uses both forearms to push at my chest, her unyielding strength fucking admirable. "*Please*, let me go."

"I will, baby. I promise. Once you give in."

"I can't." More tears escape, both eyes drenched in sorrow. She's still fighting, still feral. But her aggression tapers. Her hits lose their ferocity. The clawing and scratching packs less of a sting as she begins to sob. "Please, Luca. I can't be weak. I can't be vulnerable."

My pulse spikes at her fragility, and there's no restraint that could stop me grabbing her chin to force her gaze to mine. "You could never be weak. You hear me? You're stronger than you know. But you need to let your guard down, shorty. It's time to let me help you."

She blinks back at me, one tear following the next, her eyes unfocused as if she's no longer listening.

If only it were that easy for me to switch off to her suffering.

I've been through combat. Killed more men than I can count. I've seen dead children and war zones that resemble nothing but blood and broken limbs. And through it all I detached, needing the sterility to work autonomously.

But not now.

Not with her.

She's stripped me bare. Made me the fucking weak one.

"Why?" she wails, the moisture trail on her cheek becoming the backdrop to a waterfall. "Why couldn't you leave me alone? You should've just left me in that house."

And there it is—her agonizing truth.

It's worse than I thought.

Deeper.

Darker.

This breathtakingly beautiful woman, with her warrior strength and harrowing selflessness, wishes she was back with Luther. Because there's comfort in routine, even in the worst of conditions.

"I should've died in Greece." She hiccups. "Those women should've killed me. They thought I protected them, but I caused them more pain. He punished them because of me. He made me untouchable and in return made me targets." She rambles. Cries. Blubbers. "It's all my fault. I hurt them. I'm responsible."

"No, sweetheart. That was him. All him." I tighten my hold as she crumples. "Don't you dare blame yourself."

"I should've died." She snatches at my shirt, her nails digging into the material. "Why didn't I die?"

I wish I had the answers. I'd give anything to snap my fingers and have this all be over—her suffering, her anguish. I'd trade places with her in a heartbeat.

God, how I wish I could. "Thank fuck you didn't. I don't know what I'd do without you."

Her knees weaken, her tears running rampant. She shakes with ragged breaths. Gasps. Fucking shudders as I hold her against me.

"I've got you." I rest my cheek on hers, murmuring in her ear. "I promise I've got you." I vow it on my life. No matter what happens, what she faces, I'll be there for her. "You can trust me."

Her suffering multiplies. Her legs give out. She collapses into me. Weary limbs and malleable flesh. The most perfect surrender.

I cling to her, keeping her against me as her tears soak my shirt.

"W-why would she do this?" she stammers. "Why would Abi give up?"

My heart breaks, a million sharp shards embedding into my ribs. "I don't know."

I haul her into my arms and step around the broken mess on the floor to take her to the bed, sit on the mattress and cradle her in my lap. There's never been a more satisfying feeling than having her settle into me, her head nestled against my shoulder, her fractured breathing teasing my skin.

"Luca?" Her voice is weary, the delicate murmur filling my chest.

"Yeah, sweetheart?"

She sighs, the heave of breath long and punishing. "I'm so tired."

"I know, shorty." Our heads rub as I nod. "I know."

"I just want it all to be over."

I stiffen. Her words are a hint to a clearly defined escape plan that follows where Abi led. And I get it. I understand the impatience to end the hardship. But understanding doesn't mean my throat doesn't tighten at the thought of her following through.

I feel for her. Not only possessive or protective. There's more. So much more that it's clear there's no going back. I've fallen for this woman, with her compiling scars. Her triggers innumerable. Her suffering lifelong.

I want her. I despise myself for even thinking it. But I want her with blinding need.

Mentally.

Emotionally.

Physically.

The instinct to heal her suffering with sex is overwhelming.

It takes all my restraint not to tilt my face into hers and kiss the misery from her lips. To turn her cries into moans. To increase her breathing for reasons of pleasure not more fucking pain.

For a woman who's been violated and tortured, the desire pumping through me is downright repulsive. And still I can't shut it out.

I want her beneath me. Our limbs intertwined. Our skin covered in sweat.

I need to taste every inch of her. To lick and bite and suck.

Fuck.

I grind my teeth through the building lust, my battle continuing for what feels like hours, the silence only breached by infrequent sniffles and the occasional hiccup.

Maybe she's right. Maybe I am a monster.

10

LUCA

I HELD HER FOR HOURS.

She spoke every now and then, giving brief whispers of insight into her past.

She told me more about Abi. Reflected on what she wished she would've done better during her time held prisoner. She even admitted it felt good to cry.

And later that night as I laid in bed, I'd been pleased with myself. Like a stupid fucking chump over my so-called achievement.

I'd thought pushing her into facing her grief was a great idea. I'd convinced myself she would heal afterward.

But days later, there's still no sign of improvement.

Instead, she no longer pretends to be happy. Those fake smiles that used to annoy me would be a breath of fresh fucking air in comparison to the overwhelming despair continuously plastered on her face.

Puffy red bags are now tattooed under her eyes. She barely eats. And those intermittent moments where she hid in her destruction-filled room have become one long stretch of isolation in between bouts of obsessive cleaning and cooking.

She continues to cry.

Fucking rivers.

Every morning.

I hear her in the shower, the gentle sobs echoing from the bathroom to punish me for what I've done.

I fucked up. I shouldn't have pushed.

I tried making amends with a flower delivery, disguising the offering as a tribute to her grief. In reality, it was a sign of guilt. I've asked, *no,* demanded she watch a movie with me. Exercise with me. Fucking talk to me.

All I get are tears.

From a drought to flash flooding, the deluge still in full flow as Sarah pushes by me at the front door, granting herself access to my house.

"Have you forgotten how to wait for an invitation?" I scowl, locking the deadbolt behind her.

"Have you forgotten how to be polite?" She leads us to the kitchen and makes herself a mug of coffee. "I came when you called. Usually, that requires a thank you."

"Thanks," I grate, not feeling appreciative in the slightest. I wanted her advice, not her company. But beggars can't be choosers.

"Before we do a deep dive on this," she purrs, "I think we should put it in writing that you pleaded for my superior knowledge like a little bitch." She settles into one of the stools at my kitchen counter, sipping from my favorite coffee mug with smug satisfaction.

"Don't start."

She grins. "So we're just going to ignore my superiority?"

I glare, thankful Penny is outside on the deck and not bearing witness to my castration.

"Okay. Fine." Sarah waves me away. "Tell me what's happened since you aggressively forced me from your house the other day."

I clench my molars, breathing deep until I'm no longer tempted to throw her back out the front door. "She hasn't stopped crying," I grate. "I thought forcing her to grieve would help. But this is just a different level of hell."

"It was necessary. You know that."

"Maybe. The question is—where the fuck do I go from here?"

"You need to tell her it's time to move on."

I scoff and slump back against the far counter. "Yeah, okay. No fucking problem. I'll just tell her to get over herself, will I?"

"Yes." She takes another superior sip of coffee. "Normal people have the luxury of grieving for months. Even years. But we're not normal. With our lifestyle, it's not safe to let down our guard for too long. She needs to be aware of that."

"Problem is, she didn't choose this lifestyle, Sarah. It was forced on her."

"It was forced on all of us," she drawls. "Nobody chooses to be here. That's just the way the cards fall. The sooner she gets used to it the better."

I don't want Penny to get used to it. I want her to be saved from it. Sheltered.

"You need to take charge." Sarah lowers her voice. "Push her."

"Pushing her is what led to this mess. Look what the fuck happened."

"You broke her down, soldier. It's time to build her back up."

I wipe a rough hand over my face, not wanting any of this. Not the breaking or the building. I'm not the man for that job. But she's right. I made Penny this way; I can't leave her now.

"I've tried talking to her," I mutter. "I've asked—"

"Don't talk. Don't ask." She screws up her face in disgust. "*Demand*. Assert your authority. Act like a SEAL, not a fucking pussy."

My anger bites, the teeth nipping at my insides. "It's not that easy."

"Why?" She takes another sip of coffee. "Because you like her?"

"Of course I like her. I wouldn't be going through this hell if I didn't."

"No. I mean you *really* like her. Lover boy Luca wants to make babies with Decker's sister."

I push from the counter, my teeth set in a snarl. "Don't joke about shit like that. Not after what she's been through."

"Calm your tits." She looks me up and down, seeming to find me lacking, which only increases my rage. "She's still a woman. And a beautiful one at that. Who knows? Fucking your sad ass might be the best thing for her."

"This was a mistake." I stalk forward and grab her mug. "It's time to leave."

She clings tight to the handle. "Don't steal my coffee, Luca. No man could survive that battle."

I itch to pull out the gun that lives in the back of my waistband. To threaten. To frighten. But I know the tactic won't work on Sarah.

Not today when she's an emotionless black hole.

"Fine. I'll stop, Okay?" She raises a hand in surrender. "Release the mug and nobody gets hurt."

"Bullshit. You don't know how to stop."

"You're right." She smirks. "How 'bout I promise to rein it in a little?"

"I'll still want to kill you."

The consuming frustration won't change until I fix this. I feel like a fucking caveman—all action and aggression. No mental comprehension.

I need fresh air. I need a release.

I need fucking guns and adrenaline and sex.

"Look, I meant what I said before." She tugs the mug from my grip and downs the contents. "You need to build her back up. Make her strong. Teach her how to defend herself. Scare her into action if you have to."

"Scare her? After everything she's already been through?" I grab my phone from the counter and scroll to the surveillance icon, making sure Penny is still seeking sanctuary in the deck chair. "You're a heartless bitch. You know that, right?"

She shrugs. "Put that title on a T-shirt and I'll wear it with pride, because realistically, having my opinion without emotional attachment works in her favor when you're too close to see what's really happening. You're enabling her. There's no way Decker would let his sister get away with this death by melancholy."

"I'm doing my best. He wanted me to treat her right. And I am. I even thought about buying her a goddamn puppy."

Her face turns deadpan. "Do *not* buy her a puppy, you fucking pussy."

"Stop calling me that," I snarl.

"Then stop acting like one. Seriously, who the hell are you, and what have you done with the badass I used to know? Where's the real Luca? Because this right here—" she waves a hand in my direction "—is a fucking pitiful replacement. You're pandering. To a woman. She's never going to be reunited with Tobias in this state. She's never going to be strong enough to return to her family. You need to push her again."

She slides from her stool and smoothes her leather jacket. "And just FYI. Torian came home yesterday, so you're—"

"Why the fuck am I still being kept in the dark?"

"Because I asked him to." She straightens to her full height. "You need all the space you can get. And as I was saying, you're running out of time to fix this. Hunt and Deck are still in Greece tying up loose ends, but they'll be back soon and what do you think will happen then? Decker won't continue letting you make choices for his sister when she's a goddamn mess. So buck up, asshole. Or prepare to stand aside."

I stiffen at the truth in her words. At the looming separation.

I won't let someone else take over Penny's care. Not even if it's her family. Especially when it's not what she wants.

"Handle it, Luca." Sarah grabs her keys and purse from the counter and makes for the hall. "And do *not* buy her a fucking puppy."

She walks herself out. I'm too busy wallowing in self-loathing to follow.

I hate that she's right.

Fucking detest it.

The thought of hurting Penny again makes me livid. But I need to make my move—before it's too late.

And, from the sight of Penny approaching the French doors in my periphery, now is as good a time as any.

"Did she leave?" She steps inside, cautiously looking around.

"Yeah. It's safe."

I receive a half-hearted smile in return, the gorgeousness quickly fading. "Why did she come over this time?"

I could lie. I could blame my upcoming actions on Sarah, too.

"Luca?" She approaches, her brows raised in question, her eyes bloodshot from recent tears. "What did she want?"

"To help."

"With what?" She continues to the fridge, turning her back to me as she grabs a bottle of juice.

"With you. She convinced me of something I didn't want to acknowledge."

Her movements slow while she pours a mouthful of OJ into a clean glass, drinks the contents, then returns the bottle to the fridge without a word.

I wait for her to ask for clarification. But she doesn't, instead placing her glass in the sink before walking toward the hall. She's already predicted what's coming. I swear she already knows.

"Penny," I warn. "Your time's up."

Her posture stiffens, her chin raising an inch in defiance. "Excuse me?" She doesn't turn to face me. Doesn't even glance over her shoulder.

"I said, 'your time is up.' You're not wallowing anymore."

There's no response. Nothing at all, before she continues walking.

"Goddamnit. Don't ignore me." I slam my palm down on the counter, the crack of noise making her jump. "I'm serious. We need to get back to your list."

"My list?" She turns, gradually, her brows pinched as she meets my gaze. "You think watching reruns of the *Fast and the Furious* is going to wipe away my suffering?"

I breathe in her pain, sucking it deep. "We'll create a new list. One that will teach you self-defense and weaponry. More rigorous exercise, too. You're going to start training."

"Exercise is your thing, not mine. I just want to be left alone."

"I've listened to you cry for days. I'm not doing it anymore. If you don't want to exercise, then we'll start on self-defense."

"No." She scowls. "You can't make me."

"I won't leave you defenseless, shorty. This world with the Torians isn't the same as the one you grew up in." I approach her, matching her scowl with my own. "You need to learn to protect yourself."

"I already know how. My time with Luther taught me that."

"Then show me."

Those deep eyes search mine, cautious, annoyed. "I don't need to prove myself to you."

"Then consider it a favor. I worry about you. This will help me sleep at night."

She scoffs. "You don't think, after all my time spent captive, that I didn't learn a thorough understanding of what I'm capable of when pitted against a man?"

I encroach, stopping when we're toe to toe, almost hip to hip. "Then. Show. Me."

Her expression loosens, her agitation changing to bone-weary sorrow. "Tomorrow."

"No. Now. Torian is already in Portland. Your brother will soon follow. If you want to stay here with me, you need to show you're improving, not going fucking backward."

Her lips part, her shock subtle before she shakes her head. "My sister just died. And *you* are the one who pushed me to grieve for her. To grieve for *everything*. Now you expect me to stop?"

"You can grieve all you like. But you need to be learning how to live in this world at the same time."

"Tomorrow," she repeats, swiveling on her heels to make for the hall.

I grab her. I fucking shouldn't, but my fingers latch on to her arm, the throb of connection sliding through me before I realize there's no going back. "Now, Pen."

Her breathing hitches, in fear or shock, I'm not sure. She focuses on where I hold her, where my palm grips the baggy sweater just above her arm, before her eyes finally meet mine. "Get your hand off me." The demand is barely audible, so fragile and weak it only increases my need for action.

I drop my hold and choose to walk into her instead. One foot after the other, intimidating her backward.

"Luca," she warns as she retreats, matching me step for step until she's flush against the wall, her head held high, her breaths increasing.

I know those quickened inhales aren't from lust. I fucking know it. Doesn't stop me feeling the heat in my veins, though.

The rise and fall of her chest. The soft, parted lips. The way those eyes hold mine.

She undoes me. Without words. Without actions. She fucking tears me apart. And there's nothing I can do about it.

"Try to fight me off." I loom over her, deliberately intimidating.

"I don't want to fight you."

"You need to learn. If you have a few tricks up your sleeve—"

"I'll what?" she interrupts. "I'll be able to fight off the next person who tries to abduct me? Is that what you think? Because self-defense won't help when I wasn't attacked, Luc. I was led. Luther talked me into leaving the States. The only thing you can do to help that is give me lessons on stupidity."

"He was a master manipulator. Everyone was fooled by him. Even his own son."

She sighs. "I don't have the energy for this."

"Then show me."

She leans back into the wall, defeat slumping her shoulders. "*Please.*" She reaches out, her fingers tangling in my shirt. "I'm just so tired, Luc."

I fucking love the way she says my name. The delicate cadence. The shortened familiarity. And that touch, the one that's entirely gentle, yet packs a goddamn punch.

My mouth dries, and I'm consumed by that feeling again—the one where passion and duty collide.

"We can do this tomorrow," she promises. "I'll work hard to have more energy then."

I ignore her and lean closer. "You need to place a jab just below the sternum—that's where there's minimal muscle to protect vital organs. Or aim for the crotch, eyes—even a stomp to the foot can help."

Her hands continue to tangle in my shirt, tugging, pulling, silently begging as her teeth dig into her lower lip.

I could drown in this version of her. The timidness. The exquisite feminine frailty.

I want to trap her further. Not just against a wall. But in my bed. Under my body. The attraction is so fucking potent it suffocates me.

Whenever I'm close to her like this, I become consumed by her.

"I don't want to do this," she murmurs. "I don't want to hurt you."

"You can't. You couldn't. Don't worry. I've got skills of my own."

She nods, yet those hands don't drop from my shirt. They burrow farther, her fingertips sinking beneath the material to brush my stomach.

Adrenaline rushes through me like a storm. My pulse goes manic. She affects everything. Every inch of me. From my drying mouth to my hardening dick. Then I start trippin', because the little sense I have knows that the timid swipe of tongue she lashes over her lower lip can't be reciprocated desire.

There's no way she can feel the same way I do.

No way her heart is pounding from lust like mine.

It's too soon. I fucking know it. But that rationale doesn't stop me from leaning closer to feel her breath brush my mouth in the most delicate tease.

Her teeth sink deeper into her lower lip. She bats those feminine lashes. Her hands splay, no longer fingertips against my stomach, but full palms, skin to skin.

I want to groan from need. To fucking moan against her mouth as her touch glides around my waist, then to my back.

After weeks wanting her, craving her, I can't fight anymore.

I'm done, and about to claim the luscious prize of her mouth when her arms swoop farther. She snatches the gun from my waistband, snaps it in front of me and jabs the barrel into my stomach. *Hard.*

I don't even have time to react before she raises a taunting brow at me.

"Are those skills good enough for you?" She jabs me again, the metal digging deep.

I should be pissed. Ashamed at the very least. She used my attraction against me like I was a sex-starved pervert. Yet here I am, still a slave to my pulsing dick.

"I can manipulate, too," she murmurs, her beautiful face so fucking close. "I'll never be able to physically defend myself against a man. I know that, Luca, because I've had a lifetime of failed experience. But I can distract and influence sometimes."

Distract and influence?

No. She tempted and seduced.

That damn woman has my cock tied in knots.

"Impressive, Pen. But that gun is loaded. The safety isn't on. One nudge of the trigger and I'm worm bait."

The reality should flatten my libido.

It fucking doesn't.

"Then maybe you should back off and take me at my word when I say I've got skills."

I force out a laugh. "Those so-called skills won't work on everyone." Just pussy-whipped chumps like me. "This manipulative display doesn't change anything. You still need to learn how to defend yourself."

"Do I need to pull the trigger to prove I'm defending myself just fine?"

I chuckle in an attempt to release some of the blinding aggression. God, I want her. Crave her. Fucking *need* her. "Don't kid yourself, shorty. I could get that gun out of your hand in seconds and have you flat on your back in a few more."

"You don't scare me."

"I'm not trying to. But if you don't lower that barrel I'll prove my point." *Christ,* how I want to prove that point. "So either shoot me or prepare for change, because I'm not backing down." I flash her a feral smile. "I'm done playing nice."

11

PENNY

I let him touch me.

I stand frozen before him, *continuing* to let him touch me.

It's a little daunting. Even somewhat intimidating. But I allow it because the physical contact brings an unfamiliar twist to my stomach. The sensation not loathsome in the slightest.

My pulse hammers, the beat erratic. And my breathing couldn't settle if my life depended on it.

He does something to me, something I don't understand. He has a way of wiping the past from my memory, temporarily covering my scars to transform me into an inexperienced teenager.

It isn't safe to feel like this.

I clear my throat, dislodging the uncomfortable tickle, and lick the dryness from my lips. "Please let me go." Sweat coats my palm, my grip on the gun slipping. "I need to use the bathroom."

He doesn't move. The only acknowledgement of my request is the flaring of his nostrils as his focus narrows on my mouth.

He's a wall of muscle. A large, protective wall I itch to melt into.

"You've got ten minutes." He steps back, giving me space that feels like abandonment. "Then you're getting your ass back here to train."

"Okay." I nod, my heart rampantly beating in my throat. I'll do anything, *say anything*, just to get more breathing room. "Ten minutes."

I start for the hall, only to have him block my path with a flawless sidestep. "Are you forgetting something?" He holds out a hand, palm up. "Gun. Now."

I return the weapon, my fingers accidentally dragging over his, the connection increasing the whirlpool of crazy sensations inside me. I literally scamper for the hall like a skittish dog, then continue to my room. I don't stop my escape until I've locked myself in the adjoining bathroom to stare at myself in the mirror. Panting. Gasping.

I barely recognize the woman reflected back at me.

She's frazzled. Mindless and wild.

For the first time since arriving in Portland, I acknowledge how much my appearance has changed. I was far prettier as a slave. All the visual benefits of the compulsory beauty treatments and hair-styling appointments have since faded. My lashes no longer hold the thick tint. The expensive makeup is no longer a daily requirement. And now I sort of wish they were, because I'm not looking my best for him.

For Luca.

It's ridiculous and pathetic. Downright insane, too. Yet I feel unworthy at the sight of my reflection.

There's no sense to my thoughts. None at all. There's even less sense surrounding the dampness between my thighs, my arousal seeping into the crotch of my sweatpants.

I don't like Luca *that* way. I can't.

I shouldn't like any man.

So why do I crave things I shouldn't be craving?

It's disgusting after everything I've been through. Especially when the fluttering sensations were triggered from a moment filled with menace and danger.

I'd had a gun to his stomach. I'd threatened to kill him. All the while, my hands itched to drag him closer. To pull him into me. Against me.

I'd yearned for his proximity. The closeness that always makes me feel sheltered.

"Goddamnit." I wince through the shame.

Luther did this to me. He's turned me into a mess.

He influences every second of my life, and it's got to stop. I refuse to continue being his slave. I hate myself for allowing him to shape me for this long. For not being able to sleep at night. For the inability to wear underwear. For the fear and the anger and the pain.

I cling tight to the vanity and fight the scream clawing up my throat. I *will not* let that man defeat me. I refuse. He may have won the game with Abi from beyond the grave but he won't regain a tighter hold on me.

"I won't fucking let you," I sneer into the mirror. "You're dead, you son of a bitch. *Fucking dead.* You can't control me now."

I storm from the bathroom, yanking my sweater over my head as I continue to the wardrobe. If Luca thinks self-defense lessons will help me, then so be it. I'll learn. It's not like I enjoy being this broken shred of a woman. I don't want to be useless.

I'm just not sure my shattered pieces can be recycled into something worthwhile.

I strip off my moist sweatpants without daring to look at them. That's when I pause, my hand poised near another oversized outfit when my gaze catches on the only set of figure-hugging yoga pants I mindlessly purchased with Luca's credit card when I first arrived.

I have a closet full of baggy items. But I no longer want to hide in those.

I want to be better. To be whole.

I'm not going to like this. I already hate it. Yet, I drag the stretchy pants from the shelf anyway and don't allow myself to acknowledge an ounce of discomfort as I yank them on.

I ignore the snug fit as the material clings tight to my thighs. And I don't take note of my figure after I drag a tank top from the shelf and pull it on. The inbuilt sports bra is the closest I've come to underwear in a long time.

Everything I wear is constricting. I try to make it embolden me, the taunting restriction working as a reminder of what I've been through. A conniving devil smothered over every inch of my body.

Then I turn on my goddamn heels and trek back to the living room, determined to find a piece of myself in whatever maddening defense lesson Luca has in mind.

If only the look in his eyes didn't lessen my wafer-thin enthusiasm.

I wish I could ignore this, too. The frowned shock at my appearance. The wrinkles of disapproval.

"Something wrong?" I ask over the lump in my throat.

"No. Nothing." His voice is gruff as he pushes the coffee table away from the sofa, creating space in the middle of the room. "Just surprised, that's all. It's been a while since you wore something that didn't resemble a sack."

I take a step back, my skin crawling with the need to hide.

"Get over here," he growls. "Let's get this done."

"If this is such a burden, why are we even doing it?"

"It's not a burden." The growl deepens. "It's—" He stops mid-sentence, his hand rubbing at the back of his neck.

"It's what, Luca?"

"Nothin'. Just get over here."

I bite my lip, not wanting to move, equally despising the warmth that has shifted from between my thighs to pool in my chest.

"*Now*, shorty."

"Okay, you don't need to bark at me." I walk forward, my heart fluttering wilder the closer I get, the furious beat only increasing when I stop a few feet away from him. "What do you want me to do?"

He doesn't meet my gaze as he repositions his stance on the rug, spreading his legs a few inches apart. "I'm going to teach you some basic moves first." He brushes his hands together, his biceps flexing beneath the cuffs of his T-shirt. "When someone's coming at you, you want to be assertive and as loud as possible. Obviously, aim for the groin if you can. That tends to drop a guy like a sack of shit. But if you can't, you can try a hammer punch." He clenches his fist and makes a predictable hammer movement. "Or your elbows. Or the heel of your palm. You want to use—"

"Look, I appreciate what you're trying to do, but I learned these basics in high school. I don't need to go through them again."

"Good." Finally, he meets my gaze. "Practice on me, then."

That rampant heartbeat falters. Stutters. "I don't wa—"

"You don't want to. You don't need to. I've heard it all before. Let's not have this argument again. Just because you think you don't need to learn doesn't mean you shouldn't practice. So throw a swing. Get out some of the built-up aggression you have toward me."

"I don't have built-up aggression toward you."

"The outline of the gun barrel in my stomach says otherwise." He beckons me closer with a jerk of his chin. "Come on. Let me have it."

I sigh and lunge forward, attempting to hit him with a gentle elbow.

"Seriously?" He bats me away. "That's all you've got? What happened to the woman who slapped me across the face in Greece? Or the one who attempted to stab me with a syringe?"

I flinch at the reminder.

Even when I didn't know Luca, I hated hurting him. There was always the slightest sense I was doing something wrong. Like I could see his kind soul through his aggressive and dark demeanor.

"And don't forget the tiger scratches you lashed my chest with the other day," he continues. "My cheek, too."

Oh, God.

My gaze snaps to his face, my hands instinctively reaching for the damage hidden beneath his growing stubble. It's an uncharacteristic move, my yearning for touch feeling shockingly natural. "Is that why you haven't shaved?"

He stiffens, his nostrils flaring. "I didn't think it was a good idea to advertise our fight."

"I'm sorry." My fingertips graze over the rough hair along his jaw, the prickle spreading under my skin. "I shouldn't have lashed out like that."

He doesn't respond, just stares back at me, expression tight, shoulders tighter.

"I didn't mean to hurt you." I trace the fading red line that stretches from his cheekbone to the side of his chin. "I wasn't myself."

"You didn't hurt me." He jerks away, rejecting me with the sudden retreat. "Now, let's get back to business. Throw a swing that would make Rousey proud."

"Rousey?"

"Forget it. Just take a swing. Don't be a wimp."

I launch at him, showing just how un-wimpy I can be. I swing and jab and elbow. One after the other, each move defended and dodged with effortlessness that is both enticing and incredibly annoying.

"Good." He nods in encouragement. "But like I said, be assertive. Don't let an attacker think you're meek."

I grunt with my next hammer punch. Yell with an elbow strike.

"Good… good… good…" He continues to placate me with fluid movements and profound skill. "That's the warrior I know."

I'm no warrior. I can barely keep up with my own punches, my energy almost fully drained.

I step back, panting, and slump over. "I've had enough of these moves. Can you teach me something involving blades or bullets?"

"We'll get to that. But can we kick it up a notch and try a choke hold?"

I remain hunched over, my blood chilling despite the sweat coating my skin.

Flashbacks steal my breath. My focus. Memories clench at my heart.

"Stand up," he instructs. "I'll run through the basics."

I can't straighten.

Here I was demanding more vicious attack strategies and I can't even handle the thought of his first suggestion.

"Come on." He claps me on the shoulder. "It won't take long."

"Just give me a minute." My voice cracks, the gravel coating my throat climbing higher and higher.

"You can rest after this."

"No." I look up at him, his hulking frame looming over me. "I don't think I'm ready."

He raises a brow. "You said the same thing about exercising. Yet it made you feel better, didn't it?"

I shake my head, unable to find the words to explain without increasing my pathetic state of mind.

This triggers vicious memories. Lingering nightmares.

"Don't shake that head at me, shorty." He waves me forward. "Get your ass moving."

My heart pounds beneath tightening ribs. My stomach churns. "Please go slow."

He frowns. "Of course. You'll be fine."

I inch forward, my body acting autonomously because I have no capacity to think. Only panic.

Luca raises his muscled arms, placing his hands delicately around my throat. The graze of calloused skin brings a wave of sickening remembrance. The pressure is barely felt. Featherlight. It steals my breath regardless.

"Are you okay?" His voice provides a temporary distraction, the sound giving me the opportunity to latch onto those deep hazel eyes.

I focus on him. On the familiar comfort. The picture of protection.

I don't want to disappoint him.

I can't let Luther win.

"Yes." Memories continue to haunt me from my mind's eye. The digging, scratching fingers. The choking fear.

I refuse to let panic take over. Each time I face my demons I get one step closer to my reunion with Tobias. If I can't do this for myself, I need to do it for him.

"Breathe through it." Luca's hold remains loose. Even kind. The gentle brush of the pad of his thumb is a coaxing reminder of the here and now. "Tell me how you'd get out of this."

His grip tightens almost imperceptibly. But the restriction increases my panic.

I breathe deeper. Shorter. My oxygen lessens as the flashbacks build in force.

A face so close to my own, twisted in sickening glee.

Pressure—so much pressure.

"Focus, Pen." He strokes his thumb faster. "How would you get out of this hold?"

I swallow and force myself to channel my emotions away from fear. "I don't know." I grab his wrists and attempt to push his arms away.

It's no use. He's too strong.

I raise my knee, my attack on his junk blocked with a swift slide of his thigh.

"That's a good start." He wiggles his arms. "You could put pressure on my wrists in the hopes of bringing me closer. The harder the better. Yank or pull my arms down."

I attempt to do as instructed, not achieving all that much when I'm pitted against a wall of muscle.

"Then what?" he asks.

"I don't know." I grow frustrated, the lingering panic mingling with helplessness. "You're too strong. There's no point."

"Stop sulking," he growls. "There's always a point. Hand-to-hand combat is difficult for everyone. The only winner is the guy whose buddy turns up with a gun. What I'm trying to teach you are ways to buy time. Or enough freedom to run. So go back to basics." He rubs his fingers along the sensitive part of my throat. "What are the best places to attack?"

I can't think. Can't concentrate between the memories and that delicately gentle brush of his thumb. "I don't know."

"Yes, you do. Focus. Don't let the fear take over."

I'm trying. Failing.

"Come on, Pen." He leans in, meeting my gaze at eye level. "You did good when you tried to launch an attack at my dick. But what would you do next? Eyes? Nose? Ears? Remember the basics. The throat is a good target, too, if you can get to it."

"Okay." I nod and go through the motions, gently thrusting and punching and swiping.

"Another option is where you grab my wrist with your left hand, then raise your right arm high and twist your hips toward me. This makes your shoulder act as a barrier, but you're also going to bring your raised arm down with a hard strike at the same time to break the hold against your throat."

I blink rapidly as I try to take in the instructions—raise arm, twist, hard strike.

I run through the steps in slow motion. Gently.

"Good." He nods. "That's real good. Now do it again, but this time properly. Pretend this is real."

His grip increases, the restriction on my throat becoming a living, breathing nightmare.

My pulse goes crazy. My sharp inhales sound like a freight train.

"You've got this, shorty."

I don't think I can.

I can't.

Visions blind me. There's Luther. Robert. Chris. Their hands. Their grip. Their unyielding strength. The black spots. The rush of blood to my head.

"Focus," Luca repeats, the soothing balm of his voice doing nothing to ease my mania.

"No." I yank his wrists, trying to break his hold. "Stop."

"It's okay. Just do it one more time with force."

Monstrous ghosts chuckle in my mind, loving my suffering. There's only the threat of rape. The ongoing torture of my pitiful existence.

"No," I repeat. *"Stop."*

He removes his hands, the liberation bringing relief, but not freedom. I still feel trapped in the past. The threat is right there, darkening my vision, making it impossible to get air.

I stumble backward, my throat drying to the point of torturous pain.

"Talk to me." He follows. "What's going on?"

I keep stumbling, keep retreating. There's not enough oxygen. I can't fill my lungs.

"Penny, are you having a panic attack?"

I spin around and stagger for the kitchen. *Water.*

This was all too soon. I'm not ready.

I'll never be ready.

I lunge for the faucet, cupping liquid so I can drink, drink, drink away the mindlessness.

"Tell me what's going on." His hand brushes my shoulder. "Jesus, just talk to me."

I hunch over the counter, sucking in breath after breath. I'm suffocating. About to pass out.

"He choked you." His words aren't a question. "He fucking choked you, and you didn't think to bring it up? Why?"

I sway, my head heavy, my legs weak.

"You should've told me." He grabs my arms, stabilizing me, tugging me toward him. Gently, he guides me to sit on the cool tile, the cabinets at my back. "Why didn't you tell me this was a trigger?"

I shake my head, still feeling the grip around my throat, still seeing Luther's face staring back at me with smug satisfaction. "Everything's a trigger."

"Then tell me everything."

"No." I squeeze my eyes closed. "That's not going to happen." Not only because I'd struggle reliving the intricate details of my imprisonment, but because Luca's demeanor changes whenever we talk about my past. His mood shifts. His posture changes. And even though his aggression isn't directed at me, I still don't appreciate being the cause of his negative energy.

"Did he do it more than once?" he asks.

"Luca..." I sigh to fill the void when words escape me. "Let it go."

"I wish I could," he grates. "How I fucking wish."

He shifts beside me, making me panic—is he finally leaving me, running from my multitude of problems? But when I open my eyes he's still there, his head pressed back against the cabinets, his expression filled with failure as he stares blankly ahead.

Weary silence consumes the few inches between us.

"I'm sorry I can't be the person you want me to be." It feels strange apologizing to him. A month ago, I didn't even know this man. Now he's my world. My recovery and survival. "I wish I was the warrior you think I am, but I'm not."

"I don't give a shit if you're a warrior. I just want to help." His words are growled. Brutal and guttural. "It fucking kills me to watch you go through this on your own. That you won't talk to me."

"Because I hate seeing you angry. Every time I mention him you change."

"Of course I change. Of course I get fucking angry." His eyes narrow. "Don't you understand how much I want to go back in time and kill Luther the way he deserved to be killed? You have no idea how I wish I could've found you sooner. How I'd give anything to have known you beforehand so you never had to suffer in the first place."

"Luca..."

"I'd do anything for you." He holds my gaze, intense and unwavering. "Anything."

The warmth he inspired earlier reignites, the flickering flame shedding light on the darkness within.

I swallow again, my mouth needing moisture.

My clothes become more restrictive. The sports bra tightens around my breasts.

I'm drawn to him. All the strength and protection.

I want to breathe it in, suck it deep. Fill my lungs, my heart, and my weary head.

"You're too good to me," I whisper. "Why?"

He huffs out a harsh laugh. "You've got a short memory. You're still on the floor after I pushed you into a panic attack."

I lean back against the cupboards and sigh. "It's not the only thing you've pushed me into. The good outweighs the bad."

"Like what?"

I shake my head, not wanting to delve into the details of why I had to change clothes. "It doesn't matter."

We fall quiet, nothing but our breathing to pepper the silence.

It's soothing.

Just Luca and I.

No expectations. No pressure.

I could stay here for hours.

"I'm proud of you." He places his hand over mine and gives a light squeeze. "We'll try this again tomorrow. Without the choke hold."

He makes a move to stand and I panic again.

"Don't go." I rush to grip his calloused fingers. "Stay with me a while."

I want the contact. Despite the anxiety and the flashbacks, I want his touch.

I *need* it.

"Okay." He settles back beside me, shoulder to shoulder, one leg stretched out, the other bent. "Are we talking or ignoring each other?"

It's my turn to chuckle. "Does it matter?" I shoot him a glance, getting caught up in eyes that smolder.

Why does he have to be so attractive? He's handsome and savage and beautifully lethal.

Those attributes scared me not so long ago. Attractive men were monsters. *All* men.

Now there's Luca. Visually appealing and soul awakening.

My heart beats harder as my curiosity piques. Will more closeness bring added comfort? Does this delicious ache inside me have the potential to assist my recovery?

"Would you let me try something?" I swallow. "I mean, in an attempt to see if it helps my recovery?"

He frowns. "Of course."

I nod against the surge of invigoration hollowing my stomach and rise onto my knees, turning to face him. I shuffle until my legs touch his thigh, his shoulders stiffening with the contact.

"Everything okay?" he asks. "You look scared."

I am.

No. I'm nervous.

I want to touch him. *Feel* him.

But those moments have always been tainted for me.

Touch has rarely been kind.

Not until Luca.

"I just…" I reach for him, my palm reclaiming its favored position against his stubbled cheek. "I…" I shake away my explanation when he stiffens further. "Do you want me to stop?"

"What are you doing, exactly, shorty?" His voice is low. Roughened.

"I don't know. Does that matter?"

"No." He offers the word simply, but his eyes are cautious. "Do whatever you need."

I have a feeling he'll regret the offer, because what I want to do is tentatively place my lips on his and see if panic overwhelms me.

I lean forward, holding his gaze, barely blinking.

Every part of me thrums. I can't hear through the static ringing in my ears. But I feel safe, protected, his strength luring me in.

I approach to within a few inches when his nostrils flare, the grind of his jaw rippling under my fingertips. He's uncomfortable and still I can't smother my curiosity.

I want to try this one thing for me. Not because I was pushed. Or frightened.

For *me*.

For healing.

"Penny." My name is a warning. "You don't want to do this."

"Yes, I do." I steal the space between us, brushing my mouth over his, the connection jolting through every inch of me despite the exquisite softness of his lips.

I awaken with sensation. With tingles and yearning and light.

Sexuality washes over me. But it's not degrading or demeaning like I predict. There's no fear or disgust.

Everything is slow and sweet, his kiss a gentle dance as a growl emanates from his chest.

He frees me, helping me spread my wings to soar while remaining immobile.

Warmth takes over. Building. The blaze burns hottest between my thighs.

I could cry from the relief.

I want to laugh and sob and sing.

Until he jerks away, breaking the heavenly connection with a scowl. "Shit. That shouldn't have happened."

I blink rapidly, entirely dazed. "I'm sor—"

"Don't you dare apologize." He shoves to his feet. "This wasn't your mistake; it was mine."

I wince. "I kissed you, not—"

"You were barely fucking coherent moments ago. You didn't know what you were doing. But I did." He shoves a hand through his hair, his scowl deepening. "I knew, and I didn't stop it."

He's wrong. I knew, too.

Heart, mind and soul, I knew.

"I took advantage." He backtracks, his hand falling to his side. "After every-thing you've been through, I still took fucking advantage."

"Luca, no." I scramble to my feet. "Please don't walk away from me."

"I'm not." He gives a sad smile. "But you were right. You need space. And time. I'm going to give you both."

12

PENNY

He's been true to his word.

He walked away without looking back and kept me at arm's length.

I'm not sure if it was another ploy, but the unspoken threat of being sent to live with Sebastian was enough encouragement to move my ass out of the pit of despair.

It's not that I don't love my brother. Not that I don't miss him. I'm just not ready to face my old life.

There's still overwhelming agony when I think of loving someone and being loved in return. For unending months, everything I cared about was not only stripped from me but tortured. Brutalized. Murdered.

One by one, my sisters were taken away through my entire stay in Greece. And even after my tormentor was killed, more women were stolen from me.

Chloe died. Abi, too.

It's far easier to keep my vulnerabilities at bay.

So instead of living in fear of being sent to stay with my brother, I focused on my health. Mental and physical. I didn't even dwell on the kiss.

At least not to begin with.

I put my mistake with Luca to the back of my mind and exercised. I ran and used the weight equipment.

I cleaned the destruction from my room and filled the wall dents, sanding them back to smooth perfection with supplies I found in his shed.

I unpacked the phone he gave me and watched online videos to learn more self-defense moves. I even used his credit card to order more clothes that wouldn't hang off me. I ordered extra underwear, too.

But each hour became lonelier with Luca's avoidance, and the memory of that kiss grew legs to run circles around every thought I had. Especially at night.

I started seeking him out after the first day—exercising at the same time he did, disturbing him when he stayed in his room to watch television.

It became obvious how my strength grew when I was around him. How my smile became easy and my heartbeats quickened.

He feels a change, too. I can see it in the tension coiling itself around him whenever he notices me. In the lingering eyes and three feet of space he keeps between us at all times.

Tonight is different though.

He stalked into the kitchen around dusk, dressed in charcoal jeans and a black shirt, his hair styled to cover his scar.

I place down the self-help book I'm reading, already on edge, as he pulls groceries from the fridge and starts to chop zucchini with heavy strokes of the blade.

I rise from the sofa, hating how he doesn't look at me as I approach to stop on the opposite side of the island counter. "You look nice."

"Thanks." He continues to chop, throwing onion and carrot into a wok. "I scrub up okay."

His appearance is far beyond okay. His demeanor, too.

He's solid strength and exuberant power.

"You're going out?" I hide the hint of unease in my voice. "Am I meant to be going with you?"

"No. I'm flying solo."

I knew this day would come. He couldn't trap himself in here with me forever. I just always envisaged he'd drag me along by his side.

"I know you don't want to leave the house," he continues. "So Hunt and Sarah are on their way over. They'll keep you company while I'm gone."

My stomach hollows. The painful stab of fear slices between my ribs, piercing my heart. The betrayal does, too. "Hunter's back?"

"And your brother. They flew in early this morning." Finally, he meets my gaze, the intensity in his features welcomed and unwanted at the same time. "Decker wants to see you tomorrow, if you're up for it."

I blink through the whiplash.

Everything is changing.

His gaze narrows. "Don't look so worried. You don't have to if you don't want to."

"No, it's not that. It's a shock to know I'll be here without you." *Without your security. Your comfort.*

"I won't be gone long." He chops more vegetables as the wok sizzles. "A few hours at most. And you'll be safe while I'm out."

I hate this. For all the hope the kiss gave me, I wish I could take it back because it's driving him further and further away.

"Is this for work?" I ask. "Now that Hunter and Sebastian are back, does it mean you'll be leaving the house more often?"

"No, not yet." He keeps chopping, those arm muscles working overtime. "I just need to get out of the house, shorty. That's all. I've got things I have to take care of."

He's running. From me.

He walks for the fridge and claims a packet of raw beef strips as the doorbell rings.

"Could you get that?" He glances at me over his shoulder. "It's Sarah."

My heart pangs.

I don't want her here.

I don't want Luca to leave me.

"Pen?" He closes the fridge door and returns to the island counter. "Can you get the door so I don't ruin your dinner?"

I nod, taking slow steps backward. "Sure."

I take off, my head reeling by the time I check the peephole and pull open the door.

"Howdy." Sarah walks inside without invitation.

"Yeah, what she said." Hunt juts his chin at me. "How's things?"

He doesn't wait for an answer as he follows her down the hall, leaving me to lock the door behind them.

I don't want this. *I don't.*

But I'm unsure how to get Luca to stay.

I creep back down the hall, stopping before the entry to the open living area to listen to the murmured conversation.

"Let her do her own thing," Luca says. "Don't crowd her. I won't be gone long."

"You only need two minutes, right?" Hunt asks.

"Very funny. I'll probably be out for a few hours. Three at the most."

"Are you sure this is the right thing to do?" It's Sarah this time, her voice filled with concern. "You don't want to think it over?"

"I'm not thinking about it anymore. This needs to be done."

Dread creeps into my stomach, growing with the blossoming silence.

I enter the room, all eyes turning to me as I pad my bare feet against the cold tile.

"Well, I'm going to make myself at home." Hunter places his keys and wallet on the kitchen counter, then heads for the sofa. "No chick flicks tonight."

"Is that so?" Sarah winks at me and follows after him. "I have a feeling you're going to be outnumbered, big guy."

I ignore them as I return to the island counter, noting the increased tension in Luca's posture as the television blares to life.

Something's wrong. Something that makes it hard for him to look at me.

"Is everything all right?" I keep my voice low, not wanting to be overheard. "I'm worried."

"Don't worry." He gives a half-hearted grin and shovels a scoop of stir-fry into a bowl. "Enjoy the time without me."

I thought I'd feared leaving the house, but the more the minutes tick by, the more I've come to realize that it isn't these four walls. It's Luca. *He's* the sanctuary. "Can't I come with you?"

He bristles, the kind expression vanishing. "Not this time."

"Why?"

He fills another bowl and another, placing them at the far edge of the counter. "Dinner's up," he announces to the room and sidesteps, grabbing forks from the cutlery drawer before handing one over. "There's things I need to do, and I can't have you with me."

"Because it's dangerous?"

He cringes. "No. It's..." He shoves a hand through his hair as Hunter and Sarah approach and grab their dinner. He doesn't speak again until they're resettled on the sofa. "It's just something I have to do on my own. You don't need to stress about it."

He isn't telling the truth.

I've had enough experience with liars to read them well.

When he stalks to the dining table it only proves my point. His gun is on display at the back of his jeans. I know it's always there. He's never without it. But that's to protect me, right? Does he really need a weapon if there's nothing to worry about?

He grabs a jacket from the back of one of the chairs, pulls it on and walks back toward me.

"Make life hell for them, okay?" He stops at my side, his body stiff as he leans in and places a peck at my temple.

The connection startles me.

After days with little communication and an invisible wall of space between us, the delicate kiss is out of place.

No, it's guilt in motion.

"If I'm late, don't wait up."

Without another word he's gone, striding away like a determined soldier about to slay his demons, the front door banging shut moments later.

I'm left hollow, staring at the filled bowl of food as my anxiety grows wings.

I don't know what I'd do if he got hurt. Or worse.

He's been my constant for weeks. My guiding force. My survival.

I can't live without him.

I *can't.*

The separation solidifies all the questions I've had toward my feelings for him. He may not have approved of our first kiss, but I certainly did.

It meant everything to me—hope, strength, new life.

I'm going to tell him, too. When he gets back—*if* he gets back—I'll let him know. I won't be daunted by my feelings anymore.

I'll do what he's always wanted. I'll open up. I'll talk and talk and talk until he's sick of hearing my voice.

"Everything okay, Pen?"

Sarah's question pulls me from my thoughts. She and Hunter are staring at me from the sofa, their movie paused.

"Come over here and have dinner with us." She waves her fork at me. "It's actually really good. Who knew that dirt bag could cook?"

"Thanks, but I'm not hungry."

"What's wrong? What happened?" She kneels on the sofa. "Pen? What's going on?"

"Will he be okay?" I let my fears blurt out. "Is he going to be safe?"

Hunter frowns. "Who? Luca?"

"Yes."

"That dumbass will be fine." He forks food into his mouth. "Even if he's not, an STD or two ain't gonna kill him."

"Don't." Sarah smacks him on the chest, glaring. "That's not what she was talking about."

No, it wasn't. My thoughts weren't on STDs at all.

My mind was nowhere near sex.

"He's joking," she placates me. "You don't need to worry about Luca at all. He'll be home before you know it."

She gives another warning glance to Hunter, the two of them clearly exchanging a silent communication about me. About Luca.

"I don't understand." I steady myself against the counter, my stomach hollowing. "What is he doing exactly?"

"Work," Sarah offers. "Torian needed him to throw his weight around with a local thug. It's nothing major."

"But he told me he wasn't working."

She pauses, seeming lost for words.

"I don't know what the big deal is." Hunter shovels more food into his mouth. "He's going out to get laid. And I'd bet good money he'll only need two minutes. Five if I'm being generous."

The information hits like a backhand, causing a rush of blood to my cheeks. "He has a girlfriend?"

"No." Sarah shakes her head rapidly, as if the fast tempo can wave away my heartache. "He doesn't know the woman. It's just sex. Nothing more."

Nothing more.

I keep repeating those words in my mind, praying they dislodge the sense of betrayal.

"Oh, okay." I paste on a smile and pretend I don't care. That I'm not being torn apart.

I swallow over the tightness strangling my throat. The same throat his gentle hands stroked only days before with comforting reverence.

He's going out to have sex. To be with another woman.

I don't want to picture him that way, I don't, yet the mental images play on a loop.

I imagine his naked body. His perfect muscles. His expression of rapture. I see him giving pleasure to a beautiful woman, one far prettier than I could ever be.

I hear it.

I feel it.

My insides revolt. Twisting. Turning.

I'm going to be sick.

"You okay?" Sarah pushes to her feet. "Do you want to talk?"

"No." I wave her away and start toward the hall. "It's fine. Really. It's none of my business. I'm just going to read for a while."

I measure my pace, one foot after the other, forcing myself not to run for the sanctuary of my room.

The thought of Luca's strong hands on another woman guts me in ways I never imagined. It's not due to disgust over an act that previously sickened me. It's not my damaged past making me nauseous.

Strange as it is, the thought of sex doesn't haunt me. That role is now exclusive to jealousy.

I picture him grinding, thrusting, her head kicked back as she cries out for pleasure I've never felt.

I close myself into my private bathroom, tears pricking my eyes.

I can't stay here. I can't face him once he returns.

Not after that kiss. Not when the burden I've placed upon him was far greater than I ever imagined.

As soon as Hunter returned stateside, Luca left. All this time, he's wanted freedom.

For sex.

Did he conveniently forget I was a whore?

That my purpose was pleasure?

He should've just asked for me to earn my protection. God knows, the only skills I have are when I'm on my back.

I wash my face, the cold chill sweeping away the weakness.

I knew I was a burden to him. I *knew*. And still, he adamantly denied it.

Lied.

My pulse hammers with anger. With the need to fight. But the person I want to battle with isn't here.

I return to my room, slide on a pair of sneakers, scoop my hair into a high pony, and tiptoe back into the open living area. Hunter and Sarah are still watching the movie, the sound loud enough to drown out my approach to the kitchen.

"I should check on her." Sarah pauses the television.

"Why?" Hunter snatches the remote and presses play. "A woman like that isn't going to be cut up over a guy getting laid. I'm sure the last thing she wants to think about is sex."

A woman like that.

A damaged, sexually abused woman.

He's right. Someone like me shouldn't be gutted at the thought of their protector seeking solace with someone else. My thoughts are just another vicious layer of damage.

"She likes him," Sarah replies. "If you would've seen them together over the last week, you'd agree with me. She's smitten. And he can't get away fast enough."

Oh, God.

I clench my stomach as I reach the island counter, holding in a sob.

I'm a joke. A fucking punchline.

All this time I never knew.

I slide my hand over the marble, my palm covering Hunter's keychain and the attached car fob.

I have to face my fear of the outside world and escape this fake environment. I'll take his car. Drive far, far away. Then… I don't know.

I'll think of something. All I know is that I can't stay here.

I drag the treasure toward me, the slightest clink announcing my robbery.

I pause, but it's too late.

The movie stops and Hunter glances over his shoulder. "What are you doing?"

I freeze. Panic. After a lifetime spent lying to protect myself, I'm at a loss for words.

"Penny?" Sarah asks.

I inch my hand behind my hip and shrug. "I thought I felt hungry. But now that food is in front of me I've changed my mind again." I give a chuckle that sounds too brittle. "I might take a shower and have an early night instead."

I slowly retrace my steps toward the hall, not meeting their gazes even though their combined focus burns holes through me.

"Penny," Hunter grates. "Show me your hands."

I flinch, my body's involuntary reaction a glaring red flag as I move closer and closer to the hall.

"Show me your hands," he repeats, his hulking frame rising from the sofa.

My heart lodges in my throat.

"Penny," he warns.

I run.

I don't stop when I hear him curse. I push faster, only pausing to fling open the front door before scampering outside. I sprint across the icy lawn to the huge black suburban parked in the driveway, clicking the buttons on the fob until the indicators flash bright into the fading daylight.

Freedom is within reach. Frightening, isolating freedom.

I yank open the car door as Hunter explodes from the house, Sarah following behind.

"Don't even think about it," he yells.

He's right. The time for thinking is over.

I climb into the tank of a car, tug the door shut, and lock it as both of them barrel toward me.

There's so much panic. I can't think straight through my pounding pulse, my shaking limbs.

It's been years since I sat behind the wheel. Everything is foreign. The push start. My foot on the pedal. I don't even bother to figure out how to move the seat forward in an effort to help me drive properly. There's no time.

I press the button ignition. The engine rumbles to life. Hunt reaches my door, tugging at the handle, banging on the window.

"Open up," he warns. "Get out of my goddamn car."

"Penny, please," Sarah tries to soothe me. "We can talk."

There's no turning back now. Not when Hunter's expression bleeds with anger—fierce eyes and snarled teeth.

I shift the car into reverse and press my foot on the accelerator. The car launches, the movement far more vicious than I anticipated.

I squeal, clutching the wheel tight as the vehicle bounces onto the road.

Both of them run after me, Hunter reaching the passenger side to pound on the window with a closed fist, his eyes promising retaliation.

I should be scared. I've seen that look before. I've had it bear down on me from men who left scars that will never heal. But the fear doesn't breach the betrayal spurring my pulse harder. What Hunter could do to me is nothing in comparison to what Luca has already done.

That pain is far greater. Ten times deeper.

"I'm sorry." I shift into drive and press my foot down, screeching the tires as the car propels forward.

I ignore the thunder of Hunter's fist against the side of the car. I push back the internal voice telling me to stop. I drown out the fear of the outside world that barrels down on me and drive, and drive, and drive, passing unfamiliar streets and houses.

Each mile spurs my pulse higher, makes my thoughts more punishing.

I need to get out of here.

Out of Portland.

Out of Oregon.

All I need now is money… and I know just how to get it.

13

LUCA

"Do you use the dating app often?" The blonde seated before me leans forward, her tits plumped, her ruby lips set in a coy curve.

"No. Never." I look away, focusing on anything but her cleavage as the waitress places our drinks on the table—mine a beer, hers some colorful cocktail covered in fruit.

"You're not much of a talker, are you?" Her knee brushes mine under the table. Once. Twice.

I don't enjoy the connection.

"Not usually." I swipe at my beer and throw back a gulp. "Small talk isn't my thing."

"We don't have to talk. Why don't we skip dinner and get out of here?"

I take another mouthful. Continue to avert my gaze.

I should be jumping at the chance to get laid. That's why I'm here. I can't keep walking around the house drowning in lust, my dick constantly at attention.

Penny worked her way so far under my skin I can't catch a fucking breath through my need to have her.

Banging out the obsession with another woman is the only option. Yet, here I am, sitting before a sure thing, stalling for reasons unknown.

"Okay. I guess we're staying." The woman sips from her straw. "Why don't you tell me about yourself?"

"You first." I hate this. Not just the small talk—the fucking pathetic hesitation.

I should take this woman to the restrooms. Fuck Penny from my system in a filthy bathroom stall. Then get home.

I should.

I just can't bring myself to do it. Not yet. I need to wait until the hum of liquor dulls the doubt.

"Tell me where you work." I throw back another gulp and force myself to meet her gaze. "What do you do for a living, Rebecca?"

"Rachel," she corrects.

Shit.

I'm screwing this up. She'll cut and run soon, and I'll be left to head home and jerk off in the shower every five fucking minutes just to dull the edge while my obsession sleeps in a nearby room.

"Sorry." I raise my beer and glance over my shoulder, wordlessly letting the waitress know I need another drink. "Tell me, Rachel. What do you do for work?"

She's a stunner. Light blue eyes. Short, pixie hair. Blinding smile.

She's bright and chipper. The opposite of my current obsession, which is why I swiped right. There can't be anything to remind me of where I want to be.

"There's nothing super exciting to tell." She sits taller, her knee continuing to rub mine. "I'm a medical receptionist at a clinic a few blocks from here. It isn't a career as such, but it pays the bills. What about you?"

I think about the possible answers I could give. All the crime and destruction. The blood and death. It's a temporary distraction for two point five seconds before my mind scampers back to Penny.

I never should've left her. Not when we hadn't discussed the situation first. She could be scared without me. Fucking petrified. But I'd been desperate. Thoughts of that kiss lash brutal blows at my restraint. I've been beside myself. Itching to get out of my own skin, all because of my need to have her.

"You look like a security guard." The woman fills the silence. "I can see the outline of your muscles through your shirt."

Christ.

I can't even deal with the flirtation. How the hell will I react to her naked?

This was meant to be a hookup. A quick fuck. But I'm the one who couldn't bring myself to meet at a hotel, instead suggesting a dinner date. As if being with someone behind Penny's back was more excusable if I bought the woman a meal first.

Still feels like cheating.

How can it not when she's been everything to me for weeks?

I want her. I'm obsessed with her.

But that ship is never going to sail.

Never. Going to. Sail.

I need to remember that. Fucking tattoo it on my wrist.

I snatch at the beer the waitress places before me and knock it back in one long pull before slamming it down. "Let's get out of here?"

The blonde's face lights up. "Perfect."

I stand, grab my wallet from my jacket pocket, and throw a few bills to the table. Once I get my rocks off I'll be fine. A new fucking man.

The isolation has been killing me. Messing with my head. I'd be bat shit over any woman I'd been trapped with for that long. Anyone would.

And lord knows it doesn't help that Penny is so easy to be around. Or that she's admirably strong. Or so fucking gorgeous.

Being stuck in that house was a ticking time bomb, the impending explosion even more catastrophic after Decker returned home.

Nothing good could come from succumbing to my libido.

Penny doesn't need the confusion. And I don't need to be riddled with bullets by her brother.

Fucking Rebecca is a win–win.

It just feels like a loss, that's all.

I trudge from the bar and head for my car parked out the front. The tap of heels behind me is far from a turn-on. Doesn't matter though. I'm still haunted by the residual hard-on I've been carrying for weeks.

There ain't nothin' going to break my cock's enthusiasm.

"Slow down, honey," the woman purrs. "I can't walk that fast."

I pause a few feet from my vehicle as my cell vibrates from my jacket pocket like a sign to abort this mission. I pull out the device and stare at Hunt's name on the screen.

I shouldn't answer. He's the type to call just for the sake of interrupting a fuck session. I wouldn't be surprised if his sole purpose was to laugh at my expense.

But Penny...

If something is wrong I can't ignore it.

"I need to take this." I glance at my soon-to-be bed buddy and take a few steps away. "I won't be long."

"Sure thing."

I connect the call, turning my back to her as I bark, "What?"

"We've got a problem," Hunt mutters. "A big one."

I keep walking, making sure I'm out of hearing distance. "What sort of problem?"

"Your bitch stole my Chevy."

"Very funny." I remotely unlock my car, letting the woman climb in. "What do you want, Hunt?"

"I'm serious. She snatched my keys from the kitchen counter and took off in my fucking car. I don't know where she is."

I hold my breath, waiting for the punchline. There's gotta be a fucking punchline, because if there isn't—

"Luca?" he snaps. "Are you listening to me?"

"You better be fucking joking." I clench my cell. "Either way, I'm going to kick your ass for—"

"I'm not goddamn joking, you stupid son of a bitch. She lost her shit and took off. You need to get back here. *Now.*"

The line disconnects; my mental function, too.

It takes seconds for me to snap out of the shock, then I'm running for my car, skirting the hood to fling open the driver's door.

"You need to get out." I slide into my seat and start the ignition. "Now."

"Excuse me?" The blonde stares at me, unmoving. "What's going on?"

"You need to get the fuck out of my car," I snarl. "*Now.*"

She balks, her face growing pale as I rev the engine.

"*Now,*" I roar.

She scrambles, frantically unfastening her belt to climb out and slam the door shut. "You're a dick." She speaks into the closed passenger window. "I hope you—"

I shift into gear, pulling the fuck out of there.

Buildings and traffic blur as I drive.

I cut corners, overtake on busy streets, and swerve in and out of traffic. I don't dare to think about what could be happening to Penny until I speed into my driveway, slam on the brakes and launch from the car.

"*What the fuck?*" I storm toward Hunter and Sarah on the front lawn, the moon's glow illuminating Sarah's concern and Hunt's livid anger. "What did you do?"

"I didn't do shit. She was fine." He squares his shoulders as I approach. "One minute she's in her room, the next the fucking klepto is stealing my keys."

"Who else have you called? Which way did she go? Have you checked your car's GPS?" I bark questions at him, my palms sweating.

He raises a brow, his look condescending. "You think I'd have any sort of tracking device on my Chevy with the shit I do on the daily?"

"*Fuck.*" I pace. "Then what have you done? Who have you spoken to?"

"I rang Deck. He's freaked. Torian said he'd make some calls. Both are on their way here so you should probably hide. Her brother is going to kill you."

"Me?" I glare. "I looked after her flawlessly for weeks. Then she spent two seconds with you and decided to run."

"It wasn't us she was running from." Sarah speaks up. "It was you."

"What the fuck does that mean? What the hell did I do?"

"Who gives a shit?" Hunter asks. "She took my car. My ninety fucking thousand-dollar car."

I stop pacing and lunge for him, grabbing the front of his shirt. "She's missing, and all you care about is your fucking car?"

He bares his teeth, his eyes narrowed. "That car is fully customed, asshole."

"Your face is going to be fully customed soon, motherfucker." I shove at his chest and back away before I kill him. "Which way did she go?"

"Why don't you give her a few minutes?" Sarah follows after me. "She might calm down and come home on her own."

"Calm down from what?"

She cringes. "She was asking questions about where you were. Hunter told her the truth."

"The truth?" After weeks with minimal headaches, my brain pounds with an energetic migraine. "*What* did he tell her?"

"That you went out to get laid."

Her answer hits me like a sucker punch.

Penny knows. She knows, and she ran.

"Forgive me for not being aware it was a huge fucking secret." Hunter gives me the bird. "A little insight would've gone a long way."

I'm going to kill him. Slowly. Painfully.

"Decker's here." Sarah jerks her chin toward the road as a car pulls into the curb.

In seconds, Penny's brother is running toward us. "Where is she?"

"I don't know, but I'm going to start searching." I make for the driveway, unwilling to stand here with my dick in my hand. "Don't go anywhere." I shove a finger in Hunter's direction. "Call me as soon as you hear anything."

"How come I get stuck here?"

"Because you've got no fucking ride, you piece of shit."

I climb into my car, gun the engine, and start circling blocks. One after another, after another.

Apart from making the decision to run, Penny's a smart woman. She wouldn't have gone far. I'm pinning my hopes on her remaining close to familiar territory.

But the more blocks I circle, the more I panic.

She could be anywhere. Without a phone. Without money. Without a fucking safe haven.

"Fuck." I smash my palms against the wheel. "Fuck. Fuck. *Fuck.*"

This is my fault.

If I hadn't let her kiss me… If I'd been able to keep my fucking dick in line…

"Where the hell are you, Penny?"

I drive faster, scanning darkened sidewalks and house yards.

If something happens to her I'll never forgive myself.

Never. Fucking. Forgive.

My phone rings. This time, it's Decker.

"What?" I answer.

"I just got a call from Torian. He thinks he found her."

"Where? Is she okay?"

"I don't know. Just get back to the house. He said he'd meet us here."

14

PENNY

I'M LOST.

I don't know what side of the city I'm on. I have no clue which direction leads home.

Home.

God.

That's not what Luca's house is. Not anymore. Not when visions of what he's currently doing assault my mind with every blink.

I should never have relied on him in the first place.

Now I've lost Abi and Chloe. Tobias is no longer in my care. And my protector is gone, choosing to share his body with a stranger.

I'm stupid not to have figured it out earlier. I'd been floating in a dream-like state as we'd kissed, my lips gently pressed to his, while he drew back in revulsion.

He couldn't get away fast enough.

I pull over and shift the car into park on a quiet industrial road, barely able to see through the blur in my vision.

I'm not going to cry again. Those days of tears didn't help anyway.

Grief still weighs me down. My past hasn't changed.

But the pain from Luca intensifies.

I'd wanted him to like me. I'd carelessly thought he had. That his protection was more than a job. That he wasn't like the other men who were only interested in sex.

Boy, was I wrong.

"*Goddammit.*" I pound my fist against my thigh and scream. The piercing sound fills my ears. My head. I keep belting my heart out until there's no voice left to give. Until my lungs are dry and my throat is hoarse.

Then I slump into the leather seat, and become illuminated by the bright lights of a car pulling up behind me.

Shit.

They found me. Already. I haven't even successfully left the city, let alone the state.

Seems I can't do anything right.

I sit up straight, tilt away the rear-view mirror and its blinding reflection, and wait for retaliation. In my peripheral vision, I see a figure approaching the side of the car. A masculine frame that's big and bulky.

I square my shoulders against the threat. I won't let him daunt me. If I want to see Tobias again, I need to get over my outburst and become smarter than the unpredictable person I've been.

When a shadow creeps over the side of my face I drag in a breath and wait for Hunter's demand to get out of his car. Or a growled order from Luca.

I don't get either.

There's only an ominous *tap, tap, tap* against the glass.

If they expect me to apologize they've got another thing coming. I don't care if I stole a car.

I jerk my head toward the window, glaring, only to be met with shadowed eyes staring back at me from beneath a thick ski mask. The *tap, tap, tap* repeats, the noise coming from the barrel of a gun against the glass.

Oh, God.

All the air escapes my lungs on a heave.

Everything stops.

Time.

Movement.

My heart.

I plant my foot on the accelerator, the car roaring to life without movement.

Oh, shit.

I fight to put the gearstick in drive as a mighty *boom* thunders beside me. A circle of splintered glass appears on my window, the integrity still intact.

Holy fuck. He's shooting at me. At bulletproof glass.

I shove the gearstick into place and slam my foot harder, my hands shaking as the wheels spin. I escape in what feels like slow motion, the *tink, tink, tinks* of sound against the car frame continuous until the back of the vehicle jostles, a tire seeming to take a bullet.

"Please, please, please let me get out of here."

I keep my head low and speed through the night. I turn left. Turn right. Turn left. I become more lost in the labyrinth of streets until I finally reach a busy road and get stuck in traffic, heading God knows where, fleeing God knows who.

I wind down my window, unable to see through the bullet impacts, and hyperventilate.

I never should've left the house.

I never should've left Luca. Now all I can think about is returning to him, to his protection, but I don't know how.

I have no phone. And the arduous jostle from the back of the vehicle is getting worse.

If I pull over the shooter could find me. If I don't stop I have no clue what will happen to the car.

A siren squeals behind me. Blue and red illuminate the interior. *The police.*

For a second, there's relief. Sweet, overwhelming relief.

Then reality hits like a nightmare.

I don't have a license or identification. As far as the authorities are concerned, I'm dead. A ghost. And I want to stay that way.

"Oh, my goddamn shit, please help me get out of this." My pulse pounds everywhere—throat, wrists, temples. I break out in a cold sweat, my fear of yet another imprisonment making it impossible to breathe.

I don't want to go back to a cage. I can't attempt a high-speed escape, either. Not on three functioning tires. I wouldn't even know how with four solid treads and a record-breaking sports car.

I reluctantly pull over, the police car mimicking my movements, a male officer lazily climbing from his vehicle.

I can imagine what he's seeing—the flat tire, the dents left from bullets.

"Evenin', ma'am." He stops next to my window, one hand calmly resting at his side, the other placed on his holster. "Do you know why I pulled you over?"

I squint against the brightness of his flashlight, unable to speak.

"Ma'am, did you hear me? I asked if you knew why I pulled you over."

I swipe at my nose to dislodge the building tingle and shake my head. "No, sir."

"Do you realize you only have three tires?" He leans forward to glance inside the car, his gaze trekking over the passenger seat to the floor.

"I-I-I—" I shake my head frantically and puff out an exhale. "I-I'm sorry. I knew I had a problem. I just thought I could make it to a gas station."

"Driving on the rim is going to cause some pretty major damage. You know that, right?"

I keep shaking my head. "I'm not good with cars."

"I gathered." He raises his hand from the holstered gun, holding his palm out to me. "License and registration please."

Bile creeps up my throat, the burning acid bringing tears to my eyes. "That's a funny story." I chuckle, the sound far from humorous. "I had an argument with the person I was staying with and took off without grabbing my purse. I-I don't even have my cell."

I try to think. To come up with a story capable of getting me out of this.

"Do you know Cole Torian?" I ask.

The question is risky. It announces a link to crime and gives this officer more ammunition to interrogate me. But Luther had all the Greek police in his pocket. If Cole works like his father, maybe this man can help me. Then I can finally get back to Luca.

"He's, umm…" I swallow at his narrowing eyes. "A well-known business-man. I just thought if you knew him, you could call him for me."

His hand falls back to his holstered gun. "Ma'am, I'm going to need you to climb out of the vehicle."

"No, *please*, no."

Think. Think. Think.

"Officer, I'm not safe here." I scramble, mentally clawing at the walls of my mind for a way out, each ticking second making his fingers grip tighter on his weapon. "A man was shooting at me." I lean toward my window and poke my head outside to find the fresh dents in the side of the car. "Can you see those marks? Those weren't there fifteen minutes ago. They're from bullets. The damaged tire is, too."

He's not convinced, his steps creeping farther and farther away. "You're telling me this car is bulletproof?"

I don't know. I don't know. *God, I don't know.*

"*Please*, listen to me." I sink back into my seat and start raising my window.

"*Stop*," he barks. "Get out of the vehicle."

"*Please*, just look." I nudge the window an inch higher, the circles of shattered glass now visible in the middle of the thick tint. "Those marks are from bullets."

His brow furrows, the slightest sense of contemplation breaking across his face.

I need to come up with something to bring this home. Something convincing. Something he can't ignore.

"Sir." I lower the window again. "I'm in danger. I've been placed in witness protection. That's why I don't have any identification. But they found me." The lies effortlessly slide from my lips, the instincts I'd honed in Greece finally awak-ening. "I need to speak to Anissa Fox of the FBI. *Please*. As you can see from the car, my life is at risk. They could come back any second."

He snaps rigid, his attention stalking our surroundings. "What's your name?"

"Penny."

"Surname?"

"Please, officer, if you could just get in contact with Agent Fox she'll know who I am." She has to. She's my only hope. "*Please*. I'm begging you. Just try and get in contact with her. She'll know what to do."

But what if she doesn't?

The only connection I have with the Fed was a brief introduction in Greece. She was there when I was rescued. Yet, I never understood her involvement with Cole in the first place. They told me she was helping to take Luther down, only she hasn't sought me out once since my return to the States. There was no investigation. No welfare check. I don't even know if she lives in Portland.

"Stay in the vehicle." The officer backtracks toward the patrol car. "Don't move. I'll return soon."

I do as instructed, remaining still, barely even blinking as time passes and the contents of my stomach threaten to make an escape.

I sit there forever. The minutes accumulate into a mass of hysteria.

I never should've left the safety of the house and run off like a jealous teenager.

Under Luther's rule, I'd been entirely stringent with my emotions. Now I'm reckless. A complete danger to myself. And others.

It isn't until another car pulls in behind the cop that I pause my silent prayers for salvation.

The woman who opens the driver's door isn't entirely distinguishable through the glare of the patrol car's headlights. She's dressed in a pantsuit, sophisticated and empowered, but thankfully recognizable as the woman I briefly met in Greece.

She greets the officer at his car with a handshake. They chat in lowered voices, glancing toward me every few seconds.

I itch to run to her. To plead my case before anyone else is dragged into this mess. But within moments, the officer is climbing back into his patrol car and the confident woman is striding my way.

"Penny?" Her brows are furrowed, her eyes full of concern as she spares me a glance, then takes in the damage to the car. "What happened?"

"Can you help me?" I ask in a rush. "I need to get out of here."

"Are you hurt?" She leans closer.

"No. I'm fine. But whoever shot at me could be watching. They could be anywhere."

"It's okay. I won't let anything happen to you." She placates me with a raised hand. "Did you know who it was? Did you see them?"

"They were right next to my window. Closer than you are." A sleek black Porsche pulls in front of us as I speak. "But whoever it was wore a ski mask."

My throat tightens at the unfamiliar vehicle. This could be the shooter. The only thing keeping me in place is the agent's unflinching confidence. "Who's that?"

She sighs, stepping closer as she watches the newest addition arrive to this mess. "Cole. The officer called him."

The door to the shiny car opens. The formidable man climbs out and casually walks toward us. Dark suit, dark hair, dark eyes, and an even darker soul buried somewhere beneath. He fills me with dread, the resemblance to his father hitting me hard.

"Anissa." He purrs the greeting, his mouth holding the faintest taunt of a grin. "Nice to see you."

"Cut the crap, Cole. She's scared. I need to take her in for questioning. It's time this was handled by the book."

His expression tightens. "No. You're done here." He jerks a hand at the patrol car, signaling for the officer to leave. "Pretend this never happened."

She scoffs. "This isn't Greece. I'm no longer your toy. And I sure as hell won't go on my merry way when someone is shooting up Portland."

Cole's gaze snaps to mine. "You were shot at?" He doesn't wait for my response as his attention skates over the car, then back to Anissa. "Get out of here," he orders. "We can catch up to discuss this some other time. Preferably over dinner."

"I'm not having dinner with you," she growls. "And I'm not leaving until I'm assured she's going to be safe."

He smiles, the show of teeth more of a snarl. "Then I assure you she will be just fine. If she hadn't stolen a hitman's car none of this would've happened. You and I both know the target on Hunter's back can sometimes outrank mine."

A hitman's car.

Oh, shit, a *fucking hitman's car.*

I hang my head and close my eyes. Of all the things that could've slipped my attention, Hunter's notorious criminal reputation shouldn't have been one of them.

The pair continue to bark, one barb after another, the conversation brushing past my ears without sinking past my self-loathing.

I just want to go home.

Not to my parents or my brother, but to the only place I've felt safe in a long time.

I want to be with Luca, even though I'm forcing myself to hate him at the same time.

"Please, Agent Fox." The plea is murmured from my parched mouth. "Just let me go." I open my eyes to meet her gaze. "I can't stay out here."

She frowns at me with concern and confusion. "Are you sure?"

I nod. "Positive."

She sucks in a deep breath and straightens her shoulders. "This can't happen again, Cole. I swear to God I won't keep covering for you."

He chuckles. "Sure you will."

"I'm fucking serious, you smug prick." She reaches into her suit jacket, pulls out a business card and hands it to me. "Call me if you need me. Anytime. Day or night. I'll be happy to help."

I take the offering, brushing my finger over the embossed lettering before placing it in my pocket. "Thank you."

"What about me?" Cole drawls. "Can I call you anytime, day or night?"

She rolls her eyes, not bothering to reply as she starts for her car.

"Come on, Nis. Where's the love?"

"Fuck you, Cole," she yells in the distance.

He laughs, creeping closer to Hunter's car, his attention on her for long seconds until his arm comes to rest on the window ledge.

When his eyes turn to mine the humor is no longer there. No smile. No friendly familiarity. "It's good to see you again, Penny. Although, it would've been appreciated if this were under better circumstances." There's a lingering threat in his tone. An ice-cold sterility that leaves me chilled. "Did you see who shot at you?"

I shake my head and stare out the windshield, no longer able to meet his gaze. This is why I didn't want to leave the house. Because of people like him and feelings like this.

"Maybe next time you'll make a smarter choice about which car you steal."

"There won't be a next time," I whisper.

"Good. Now tell me where were you running to?" His attention raises the hair on my neck, my skin breaking out in goose bumps.

"Anywhere. I just needed to get away."

"From Luca?"

The question stings. The answer punishes me even more. Both leave me speechless.

"I heard he went out tonight," he continues. "Were Hunter and Sarah's arrival the issue or Luca's departure?"

"It doesn't matter." I turn to him, scowling, letting him know this is the end of the discussion. "Can we leave now?"

"Whatever you say." He opens the door and holds out an open palm. "Give me the keys."

I hand them over. "Will the car be okay?"

"Hunter can take care of it." He yanks the door wider. "Let's go."

He leads the way to the Porsche, sliding into the low seat while I hustle fast to get into the safety of the new vehicle.

He pulls from the curb in silence, the murmur of his radio too low to stifle my apprehension as he drives. I know I can handle any punishment he might dish out. Luther was a far more menacing man. But I no longer have the determination I did when I was a slave. The will to fight doesn't embolden me.

"In between now and Luca's house, you need to explain." He shoots me a glance. "I suggest you start soon."

"There's nothing to say. I felt like taking a drive, so I did."

"I don't appreciate secrets." His threatening tone grates on my nerves, annoying the hell out of me as the adrenaline flushes from my system to leave me drained.

"Me either. And I guess Luca feels the same." I give him a faux smile. "That's why he told me you already brought Tobias to Portland and how you plan to keep him from me."

He doesn't react, not physically. There's not even a twinge of guilt in his features. He doesn't care that he's hiding that little boy. "Yes, he returned to live with my sister."

I despise the ease with which he torments me, the same way his father always did. "How is he?"

"Good. Resilient. You'll be able to see him once I know you're stable."

I huff out a laugh and turn my attention to the bright Portland skyline. "Stable? What does that even mean?"

"It means when you're functioning like a normal person and not running away for no reason."

"I had reasons."

"Then tell them to me. I didn't get you out of Greece for the hell of it. I want you to live a good life, Penny."

Lies. All lies.

I don't know the real reason he arranged my rescue, but it certainly wasn't out of kindness.

"This will be the last time I ask," he snarls. "Why did I get a call from Hunter telling me you'd run away?"

I press my lips tight, keeping the truth from him just like he's keeping Tobias from me. But my frustration builds, demanding to be heard. "Because Luca left me to have sex with a stranger."

The awkward silence returns. The seconds tick by in agonizing lethargy. I don't know if he thinks I'm naive or childish. I'm not even sure if he's annoyed I caused this mess over something so trivial. All he does is continue to drive, the side of his mouth curving upward in a condescending smirk.

"Do you enjoy my suffering?" I whisper. "If so, it only confirms you're exactly like your father."

His fingers squeak against the leather as they tighten on the wheel, his knuckles turning white. "I'm nothing like my father. And it's not your suffering I enjoy. It's the karma."

"Whose karma?"

"Your brother's." He glances at me. "For a long while, the thought of Decker with my sister was a very sore spot for me. It still is most days."

"I don't understand."

He huffs out a laugh and returns his attention to the road. "All the resentment I harbored toward my sister's feelings for your brother, all that rage and animosity, is now something he will have to deal with between you and Luca."

"It's not like that. Luca doesn't have feelings for me."

That huff of laughter returns, intensified. "I assure you he has enough to get himself in trouble."

"I disagree. And I think I'd know better, seeing as though I've lived with him for weeks."

But I hadn't known. It was Sarah who'd pointed out Luca's desperation to get away from me.

He shrugs. "Maybe you're right."

He doesn't say another word. There are no placations for my dying heart or offers of support.

I turn away, staring out the window as we pass things I recognize from my escape—the corner store, the house with the red mailbox, then finally, the pretty pink roses from the garden beside Luca's.

My stomach falls as Cole pulls into the drive behind another bulky SUV, our headlights swinging past a grimacing woman and three men standing on the front lawn, none of them happy to see us.

Sarah and Sebastian are the only ones whose expressions hold the slightest tinge of relief.

Hunter is plain mad.

And when my gaze reaches Luca I have to raise my chin and suck in a breath to steal myself against the fury bearing back at me.

"If you don't want to stay here I can make other arrangements," Cole murmurs. "Returning to Portland with Luca was your choice, but you can change your mind at any time and stay with your brother."

"And if I don't like either option?"

"They're all you've got for now."

I should get away. From here. From Luca. But anger at my protector is a better option than the vulnerability I'd face with my brother.

"Can I think about it?"

He kills the ignition. "Take all the time you need."

I steal myself for what's to come and open my door, only to be stopped by a punishing grip capturing my arm.

"There's one more thing." Cole's eyes harden as I glance at him over my shoulder. "I've made sure you're financially taken care of while under Luca's roof. I'm certain you know you can have anything you need if you ask. So if you steal from me again, we're going to have problems. Do you hear me?"

I fight the instinct to lash out, fervently holding myself in check because I don't want to risk Tobias being stripped from me forever. "I told you it won't happen again."

I won't steal a car.

I won't even steal time from Luca.

He inclines his head and releases my wrist. "Then good luck. By the expression on Luca's face you're going to need it."

I shudder and open my door to slide out, keeping my gaze averted from the wall of tumultuous male emotion in front of me. I don't look toward the men on the lawn as I walk around the hood. I don't even chance a sideward glance as I pass.

I head straight for the front of the house, my head high, my shoulders straight.

"You're seriously going to walk by me without so much as a fucking explanation?" Luca demands.

I ignore him, refusing to stop and chat when the heat in my eyes is overwhelming. I won't let him see me cry. Not again. Not over this.

I keep walking, thankful the house is unlocked as I slip inside. But he's hot on my heels, snatching the door as I let it go, slamming the heavy wood closed behind us. "Don't walk away from me."

"Why?" I quicken my stride down the hall. "You did it to me first."

"Jesus Christ." He follows me into my darkened bedroom. "I almost had a fucking stroke worrying about you. The least you can do is explain."

"Leave me alone."

"I know you're angry." His tone softens, slaughtering me with pity. "But, fuck me drunk, Pen, what the hell were you thinking?"

I was thinking he had feelings for me. That I was more than a job.

I turn to him, facing his hostility head-on. With him in front of me, a stranger's kisses lingering on his lips, my humiliation digs deeper, clawing at my mind. "I'm sorry I ruined your night. But I'm safe now; you can get back to what you were doing. Or *who* you were doing."

His eyes flare, shock and wrath beaming back at me. "You think I give a shit about who I was with? You think that's why I'm mad?"

"Yeah, I do." I return his glare. Fury to fury. Madness to mindlessness.

I cared for him so much. Without knowing, without understanding, he'd become my world. And now I don't know how to breathe in the vacuum.

"I think you're pissed because I stole a car. *Wrecked* that car. But more importantly, because I disturbed you on your date." I'm making a fool of myself. I can feel it. The heat in my cheeks is a glaring indication. I'm just thankful the faint glow from the living room is the only illumination through the shadowed surroundings.

He scoffs. "I don't even know where to start with that load of ignorant bullshit."

"Start by telling the truth. Start by acknowledging how worthless you made me feel."

"Excuse me?" His brows pinch in a lethal frown. "*I* made you feel worthless?"

"Yes. Why wouldn't I feel that way when you left to have sex with a stranger when you already have a professional fucking whore living under your roof?" My voice raises with every vehement word.

"What *the fuck* did you just say?"

My cheeks flame hotter, the shame scarring me.

He stalks forward. "Don't you ever talk about yourself that way again."

"Why not?" I stand my ground, trembling in fury. "Fucking is the only job I've had. It's all I've ever been good at. The only thing I've known. Yet, for some reason, I'm not enough for you."

"Stop it," he warns.

"You know it's true. I don't know why you can't admit it. I can do your cooking and cleaning. You can even waste your time watching stupid movies with me, but I'm not good enough to fuck."

"I said, 'stop it,'" he snarls. "I'm not joking."

"You did this," I accuse. "You're the reason I ran, because apparently you can't get away from me fast enough."

I throw Sarah's words at him, hoping he'll finally admit the truth. Or at least stop being angry at me.

The opposite happens.

His jaw tenses. His hands clench. He keeps stalking forward, towering over me until I'm forced to backtrack into the wall.

God, I wish I was scared of him. Even just a little bit. But the intense emotion taking over me is something different. Something starved for attention.

It's hatred.

I hate how much I feel for him.

Hate that he doesn't feel it back.

"You're right. I couldn't get away from you fast enough." He looms over me as I press into the cold plaster, foot to foot, almost nose to nose. "Because you're in my fucking head, Penny. You're under my goddamn skin. I can't help you when I'm like this."

Every inch of me thrums, wanting to attack and succumb in equal measure. "I'm sorry I'm such a burden." I grind my teeth. "But I've been saying that from the start."

"Stop." He growls the word, so close to me. So painfully, agonizingly close his breath brushes my mouth. "You drive me fucking crazy."

He stares at me, the intensity climbing into my chest. Every part of me reacts. My heart. My pulse. Everything except my mind which goes blank.

I'm dumbstruck over what to do, caught speechless under the heavy weight of yearning.

I want too much from this man. His guidance. His attention. I want it all.

"Mindless," he murmurs as he swoops forward, smashing his lips against mine.

I gasp into the kiss, my palms instinctively pushing his chest, my nails digging deep to stop the attack. But as fast as my panic arrives, it flees, allowing a crazy clarity to sink in.

My pushing turns to grabbing. My digging fingers cling. I scramble to find a stronghold to withstand the madness, yet all that remains is warmth and frightening exhilaration.

He punishes me with his mouth, his hands clutching my hips.

I've been forced to kiss before. But I've never kissed like this. Never when my body demanded more connection than the force could provide.

I should hate this. Instead, it feels like home. I revel in his warmth. I succumb to the hard press of his chest against mine and the determined lashing of his tongue.

Then, as forcefully as his kiss arrived, it vanishes.

He retreats. One step after another. Again.

Revulsion consumes him just like it did the last time. I can see it.

I slump back against the wall, my fingers raising to my lips as if the touch will soften the burn. "Did you do that to shut me up?" I ask, breathless.

"For the love of sanity, Penny. You've got no idea what's going on here." He rakes his hands through his hair. "Don't you get it? *This* is why I left."

He stalks back toward me, body tense.

I shrink into the wall, a little nervous. A little scared. But it's not of him. *Never* of Luca. I'm frightened of how much I want him.

"This is exactly why I had to get out of here. Because you're still petrified of me." He shoves his hands against the wall at either side of my head, caging me, the rapid rise and fall of his chest animalistic. "Because all I can think about is wanting you more than my next breath, yet you scamper away from me."

"I don't scamper—"

"Yeah, you do. And you should, because what I want to do to you is far from good, Penny. I want to fuck you within an inch of your life. If I had my way I'd shatter all your progress by taking what I want. What I *need*. So don't for a goddamn second think I want you out of here, because having you near me is all I've wanted from the moment I laid eyes on you."

I suck in a sharp breath. Unblinking. Unmoving.

He chuckles. Grins. Neither are kind. "See? Now do you understand?"

No, I don't. It doesn't make sense.

"You're lying," I whisper.

"No, I lie every time I keep distance between us. All I want is your body on mine. I lie when you go to bed at night and I pretend I don't want you sleeping beside me. I lie every goddamn day pretending I'm not obsessed with you because I know I'm not good enough, gentle enough, fucking calm enough."

He creates a whirlwind of emotion inside me. A tornado I'm stuck in the middle of. "You're not making sense."

He grinds his teeth, his shoulders bunching. "I ran because I can't quit noticing how incredible you are. You might be oblivious to your gorgeousness, but believe me, I'm not. I've had a front-row seat to the recovery of the most beautiful woman I've ever met. I get tortured on the daily by her strength. By her fucking unshakable determination to get up every time she's knocked down. And as fucking perverted as it feels after what you've been through, my dick takes notice, too."

I lean further against the wall, attempting to distance myself from my confusion.

"So forgive me," he snarls, "if I thought it was best to try and take the edge off with a stranger because it's crystal clear I can't have you."

I can't reply. I can't even shake my head. All I can do is swallow over the heat licking my throat.

He holds my gaze for long moments, those eyes narrowed with spite.

I want to pour my heart out to him. To tell him how I feel. But I don't understand it myself.

I don't want sex. The thought of it scares me. But I want him.

I crave his protection. His praise. I want to have him close to me.

He shoves from the wall and turns to stalk away, each step creating a painful chasm between us.

"Please, Luca." I shudder out a breath. "Don't walk away from me again."

He stops, his shoulders slumping. "It's not like I want to. Believe me, it's my only choice."

"Why? Because I'm damaged?"

He tilts his head to look at me. "No, shorty. Because I'm falling in love with you. Because despite how fucking stupid that is—how inappropriate and unreasonable—I love every fucking thing about you. And that shit isn't healthy for either of us."

I pull back, my head hitting the wall, my gasp audible. He doesn't love me. He couldn't. And I'm not sure I want him to anyway.

Love means loss.

It gives power to my invisible enemies, and makes me weak.

But the invigoration... it's euphoric. Tear-inspiring happiness tightens my throat, threatening to suffocate me.

"Finally, you understand." He turns his attention back to the hall and starts walking. "Now you'll know why I'm keeping my distance."

"*No.* Stop" I push away from the wall, my demand adamant. "What if I feel the same way?"

He doesn't speak. Doesn't move.

"What if, Luca?"

I don't know how I feel. I don't know much of anything anymore. But what I do know is that he's my rock. He's the shore to my crashing waves. The steadying ground beneath my tumultuous storm.

"Will you answer me?" Slowly, I approach, each step increasing my exhilaration and vulnerability. "What if I feel the same way about you?" I walk around him to meet those shadowed eyes. My heart hammers in my throat as he remains silent, his mouth set in a straight line. "Please answer me."

"Don't do this, shorty." The plea is barely audible. "The last thing you need to deal with right now is cleaning up the mess once your brother kills me."

A loud knock sounds at the door, the banging thunderous.

"On cue," he drawls. "See? Deck already has a sixth sense for these things."

I reach for Luc, my fingers brushing his in a brief swipe before I lose confidence and drop my arm back to my side. "Sebastian will stay out of this."

"No, he won't. And he shouldn't." He waves a hand between us. "This is never going to happen. It can't."

I whisper out a scoff. "How poetic—the man who rescued me from someone who gave me a lifetime of something I didn't want is denying me the only thing I crave."

"You don't crave me, Pen—"

"Don't tell me what I crave." I step closer and he stiffens. "You have no idea how I feel for you. How I've always felt for you. I never knew it myself until you walked out on me."

"I didn't walk out."

"You did. You left me." This time, I don't falter when I reach for his hand. I grab it tight, entwining our fingers. "With a psychopath and his doting sidekick."

There's a flash of a smirk that quickly fades. "Pen..."

"I need you, Luc." I tug him, attempting to drag him closer. He doesn't budge. "Are you going to make me beg?"

His nostrils flare as I keep tug, tug, tugging.

Finally, he stumbles forward, his foot sliding between mine, and we're chest to chest, hip to hip. A growl rumbles in his throat as those gorgeous lips reclaim my mouth, this time in a kiss that's slow. Controlled. As if he's worried I'll break.

I don't.

I awaken.

I luxuriate in him, shedding another tormented layer of my past while in his arms. He helps me escape my mental anguish with gentle swipes of tongue and a possessive hand at my hip. He makes everything right. Yet, I can't stop hearing the taunting devil on my shoulder. I'm tormented with his treacherous, haunting words.

This bliss won't last.

15

LUCA

Another hammering of the front door reverberates down the hall.

Fuck.

I pull back to stare down at her, fucking besotted as I cup her face. "If we don't stop, our next milestone will be my funeral."

She nods. "Okay. We stop."

The front door opens, the approaching footfalls siphoning my buzz.

"Shit. He's coming. Stay in here." I make for the hall, finding Torian sauntering toward me.

"Don't have a coronary," he drawls. "I ordered the others to go home. I thought you two could use the time alone." He keeps walking, bypassing Penny's bedroom.

"Right…" I give her a brief placating smile as I close the door and follow him. "That doesn't explain why you're still here."

"We need to talk." He turns into the living room, walks straight for the coffee machine, and starts to make himself a mug. "Could you have picked a more complicated conquest?"

"She's *not* a conquest." I keep my distance for his safety's sake, and rest my ass against the end of the nearby dining table.

"Fine. Fuck buddy. Piece of ass. Whatever you want to call it." He grabs his filled mug and takes a sip.

"It's been a long day, Torian. Don't push me."

He smirks. Slow and demeaning. "I seem to remember you telling me not to stick my dick in dangerous places not too long ago, but I'll save you the reciprocated speech because there are more important things to discuss." He starts toward me, taking the seat at the opposite end of the table. "I didn't inform the others about the shooter yet. I wanted to get answers first."

"What shooter?"

"She didn't tell you? What were you two doing in there if not discussing the harrowing ordeal she just faced?"

"Cut the shit." I grab the chair before me in a death grip. "What shooter?"

"It's best to get the news from her. I barely know the details. What I do know is that she got pulled over by a local traffic cop, mentioned my name in an attempt to get help, and when the officer didn't take the bait, she asked to speak to Agent Anissa Fox of the FBI."

Shit.

I knew back in Greece that telling Penny about Anissa's identity was a bad idea, but I hadn't been able to stop myself.

"How did she know Anissa was a Fed, Luca?" The question is level, no rage, no menace despite both lurking in his gaze.

"I told her. I had no choice. She wouldn't trust me when we were trying to gain the upper hand with Luther. She thought Anissa was a slave, and that we were involved in the trafficking."

He takes another mouthful of coffee, those predator eyes scrutinizing me from over the rim of his mug. "You didn't think to discuss it with me first?"

"I didn't have time. I was in the middle of being attacked with a syringe, and if memory serves, so were you."

"That may be the case, but you've caused complications. I know I don't have to mention how important it is for a man in my position not to be associated with the Feds."

"Maybe you should've thought about that before you stuck your dick in one."

He slams his mug down on the table, the contents splashing over the rim. "Don't fuck with me on this. Anissa is not to be discussed, not even mentioned. Wipe the name from Penny's mind or I'll do it myself."

I grind my teeth. I can't push him too far. This is my life now. He's my general. My family. "I'll make sure she understands."

"Make sure you do," he snarls. "Now there's one more thing we need to discuss before you drag her ass out here. I told you to take care of her financially, yet she still stole from me. Why?"

I scoff. "What could she have possibly stolen?"

"Money. I've got a contact at the bank who's been keeping an eye on my father's accounts. He told me a stack of cash has been withdrawn."

"And you're pointing the finger at Penny? What about your dad's informants? Or your sisters? How do you know they didn't take the money?"

"Because I called them. Neither know how to access the accounts. I also mentioned the issue to Penny, and she didn't deny it."

I straighten, not believing his story. "So she confirmed it?"

"Not exactly. I'm well aware she's not in her right mind at the moment. That's why I need you to discuss it with her. Find out where she keeps the keycard and destroy it."

"It's fucking impossible. She came home from Greece empty-handed."

"Her hands might have been empty, but did you do a cavity search? Or did you save that until you got home?" He winks.

"Fuck you." My nostrils flare as I grip the chair tight enough to make my fingers ache. "I'm not sleeping with her. And I'd bet good money she isn't responsible for touching your father's accounts."

He shrugs. "I'll have proof in the form of security pictures soon enough. I suggest you speak to her before then. Now get her out here; I've got other things to do before the night is over."

I pause a second, unsure if I should be placing Penny in front of his barely leashed mood.

"I'll be civil," he drawls, as if reading my mind. "Just get her out here."

"You better be." I call over my shoulder. "Penny, can you come out here?" I wait for a response that doesn't come. "*Penny?*"

"For your sake, I hope she didn't steal my car this time."

"Very funny." I start for the hall only to be stopped by her walking into the living area.

"You wanted me?" she asks.

Without doubt.

Always.

"Take a seat," Torian instructs. "I need to get details on what happened tonight while they're still clear in your mind."

She glances between the two of us as she approaches, wary yet confident. She takes the seat to my right, sitting tall, her hands placed on the table. "I can't tell you much."

I fling out my chair and sit beside her. "What happened?"

"I drove—"

"Where?" Torian interrupts.

"I don't know. I was just driving, trying to get out of Portland. But I had to pull over."

"Why?" I ask.

She shoots me a pained glance, then returns her attention to Torian. "I wasn't in the best state of mind. So I parked on the side of the road in some sort of industrial area. Not long after, a car came up behind me. I thought it was Luc or Hunter. And because I was still angry, I didn't even look as the man approached. I just waited for someone to order me out from behind the wheel."

"You're sure it was a man?" Torian leans back in his chair, still calm, still unconcerned.

"Yes. The frame was too big for a woman. He came right up to my door and tapped the barrel of a gun against the glass."

Jesus.

Why the fuck didn't she mention this earlier?

"Then what?" I reach for her hand and squeeze her fingers.

"I planted my foot. I tried to get out of there straight away, but the car wasn't in gear. So I panicked, and scrambled for the gearstick. That's when he fired at the glass. By the time I got out of there he'd shot at me four or five times. Twice against the window, a few against the side panels, and at least one in the tire."

I wipe my free hand over my mouth, holding in the string of fear-filled aggression. My migraine pulses between my temples. She never should've been in that situation. I never should've forced her to run.

"Then what happened?" Torian asks.

"I kept driving, even when I lost the tire." Her words accelerate, tumbling faster from those gorgeous lips. "I don't know where I went, but the patrol car eventually caught up with me and pulled me over. I didn't know what to do. I'm not even meant to be alive as far as the government are concerned, so when the officer demanded my ID, I asked if he knew Cole Torian, and when he didn't react I made up a story about being in witness protection."

She looks entirely fragile as she relays the story. Fragile yet solid. Vulnerable and strong. Such contrasting facets that make her all the more mesmerizing.

"You mentioned Anissa, too," Torian grates.

"I had no choice. I didn't want to be arrested."

"It's okay. It's over now." I entwine our fingers, trying to offer more support. "Can you tell us anything else about the shooter? What did he look like? What did he say?"

"He didn't say anything. Just tapped the gun against the window." She shudders, her fingers trembling in mine. "He wore a thick, black ski mask. His entire face was covered, and his eyes were shadowed with the headlights beaming behind him. I couldn't even tell you what color they were because all I wanted to do was get out of there."

"Did you get any details on his car?"

"No." She shakes her head. "I didn't see anything. I'd tilted the rear-view mirror away to stop the glare from his headlights. I have absolutely no information at all. Nothing."

I meet Torian's gaze. "What do you want to do?"

He pushes from his chair. "I'll put out some feelers. We'll find who's responsible. Do you have any requests once I catch the culprit?"

"Yeah. Let me deal with them."

Penny stiffens, but I'm thankful she doesn't deny my revenge. Nothing will stop me from slaughtering the person who tried to take her life.

"I can do that." Torian looms over the table, jutting his chin at our entwined hands. "You might want to keep that under wraps. I don't feel like disposing of another dead body in the near future."

Penny's hand slips out from beneath mine, the retreat frantic, as I glare at Torian. "Thanks for the tip."

He smirks. "I'm nothing if not helpful." He starts for the hall. "If you remember anything, I want to hear it."

I stand and turn to Penny as she rises to her feet. "I'm going to walk him out. Why don't you take a shower?"

She nods, her eyes darting from me to Torian who stalks away. "Have I caused a huge mess?"

"It's okay. There's nothing to worry about." I kiss her quick. Hard. "I won't be long."

I leave her standing there, lengthening my stride to catch up to Torian as he opens the front door and turns to face me.

"Do you know what you're doing with her?" he asks.

"No," I answer honestly. "I've got no fucking clue. The only thing I'm certain of is that I don't want Decker finding out until she's ready."

"Well, he won't hear it from me, but you realize it's written all over your face, right? He's going to take one look at you two together and know straight away. He probably already does, with the way you chased her into the house."

"I've got time. I'd only finished telling him I hadn't laid a hand on her when you pulled into the drive. The way she brutally ignored me when she got out of the car helped, too."

"Seemed like a lovers' tiff to me. But what do I know?" He steps outside, glancing at me over his shoulder. "I've got a hundred dollars that says he figures it out next time he sees you, and that he attempts to take your life with your own gun."

"Thanks for the vote of confidence."

"I didn't say he'd succeed." He keeps walking. "Enjoy the rest of your night. It might be the last you have."

Asshole.

I shut the door, locking it behind him, then make my way back toward Penny's room.

She's in the shower, the water loud through the pipes.

I decide to do the same, turning off the lights and checking the doors, before I shut myself into the bathroom to wash away the events of the day.

I need to scrub off the layers of lust she painted over me, the depth of her touch that makes it hard to concentrate on what's important. All I can think about is that kiss... the way I pinned her against the wall... how she'd only just come home from being fucking shot at.

She would've been filled with adrenaline. Fucking crazed.

Now there's a homicidal shooter on the run and I'm standing here with my dick in my hand.

I'm such an asshole.

I hope she's already gone to bed by the time I wrench off the taps. I don't want to see her again. Not when I know that the second I do, everything will come flooding back—the hunger, the need, the cloying obsession with wanting her to be protected.

But I'm walking from the adjoining bathroom, a towel around my waist, ruffling the water from my hair with my hand when I notice her in the doorway to my bedroom.

Just like I predicted, I'm hit with a tidal wave of shit I shouldn't be thinking, shouldn't be feeling. It doesn't help that she's wearing nothing but an oversized T-shirt, the material hanging loose at mid-thigh, her hair damp over one shoulder.

"How was your shower?" I start for my bedside table and pull open the top drawer to grab a fresh pair of boxers.

"Good." She watches me, her attention never straying as she leans against the doorframe.

"Are you calling it a night? I'm ready to crash like you wouldn't believe."

"I actually hoped to finish our conversation from earlier."

Shit. "It can't wait until morning?" I tug the boxers on underneath my towel. "What else did you want to discuss?"

I don't like her in here. In my room. In such close proximity to my bed. She's too seductive and doesn't even realize it.

"I still have questions." She moves from the doorway, approaching me. "Is that okay?"

I close the drawer harder than necessary. "What sort of questions?"

"I want to know if you slept with her."

I straighten, my muscles tight as I untangle the towel from my waist. "No. I didn't have sex with her."

"Did you kiss her?"

My chest tightens, hating these questions, hating even more that her expression is pained while asking them. "No, Pen. I didn't touch her."

She sucks in a breath, standing taller. "Would you have gone through with it if I hadn't run away?"

This time, my answer doesn't come as quick. I don't want to lie to her. I don't want to hurt her either. Neither option is favorable. "I don't know."

She winces and glances away, focusing across the other side of the room.

"I needed to," I continue. "Didn't mean I wanted to."

"Why?" The question is uttered softly. She's so fragile and fucking innocent. "Why did you need to?"

"You know why, shorty."

"No, I don't." She turns back to me, her brow furrowed. "Is it because you think you're capable of forcing me? Raping me? Is that why you have to let off steam with someone else?"

"What? *No.*"

Fuck.

I drop the towel and cross the room to stand in front of her. "I'm fucking scared of manipulating you without even being aware of it. Hell, I've already done it twice."

"How? You've never manipulated me."

"I did when you kissed me the first time. You were in the middle of a panic attack. It was my job to hold you in check and I fucking failed. I did it again tonight. You would've been flying high on adrenaline when you got home. What happened in your bedroom was a mistake."

"Don't say that." She winces. "Don't even think it, because it makes me sound weak."

"You telling me you're strong, shorty?" I inch closer, unable to refrain from placing a hand on her waist. "Haven't we been having this argument for weeks?"

Her chin hikes up, her eyes narrowing. "I'm strong in some things, smart ass. And you're one of them. Everything else is static."

I chuckle, unsure whether I should be humbled or panicked.

"You make me feel alive, Luca." She places a hand on my chest, nestling her body closer. "I want to feel that way more often."

Panic was the right option. Pure panic.

"I'm glad you feel that way." I step back, well aware any brush of her against my hardening dick will be a bad idea. "But space is a good thing, too. Some pretty crazy shit happened tonight. You need time to let it sink in. You should get to bed and rest on it."

She raises a brow. "Which side?"

"Which side of what?"

"Your bed. Which side am I sleeping on?"

Oh, no.

Oh, *hell no.*

"Tap the fucking brakes, shorty, and back up the truck. You're not sleeping in here."

"But I went through some pretty crazy shit tonight," she mocks me. "I don't want to sleep on my own."

"You're hilarious." I walk for the door, hoping she'll follow. "Come on, get your ass to bed."

She looks at me in defeat. "Luc, please. I want to stay here."

The way she says my name. The sorrow. The plea. When she wraps her arms around her middle in a blatant show of vulnerability I'm entirely done for.

Doesn't she know this is what I've battled all along? That this is where I've wanted her from the first day we met?

In my room.

In my bed.

"It's not a good idea." I strangle the door handle. "Your room is a better option for now."

"I know. But this is what I want. I need it, Luc."

Fuck. I scrub a hand down my face. "You need what, exactly?"

"To be near you. To sleep knowing I'm protected. I'm sick of the nightmares."

She hits me right where it hurts. One sucker punch after another.

"Please," she repeats. "Just for one night to see what it's like."

Once will never be enough. There'll be no going back after those flood gates open. Surely she knows that.

I huff out a growl. "Pick the side you want."

"Thank you." She walks around the bed, moving away from the door. "Is this side okay?"

None of this is okay, and there's not a damn thing I can do about it. I can't bring myself to deny her, though. Or myself. This intimacy is a train wreck waiting to happen.

"Yeah, fine. But you might want to move the gun out from beneath the pillow and stick it under mine."

She doesn't show an ounce of shock as she does as instructed, grabbing the weapon tentatively to slide it across the mattress.

I wait until she's settled, her cheek on my pillow, her long hair spread out behind her before I turn off the light.

I'm not going to get a wink of sleep. Not with her scent on my sheets, her inhales caressing my ears. The hours until sunrise are going to be hell.

I climb into bed in darkness, sticking to the far side of the king-size mattress. There are still two feet of space between us and I'm acutely aware of each millimeter as she sucks in a deep breath and sighs.

"Night, shorty."

"Night."

I stare into inky blackness, completely wired.

I spend my time forcing myself to figure out how we're going to nail the guy who shot at her when we've got no description to go on. I think about the leverage tonight will give me over helping her step out of her comfort zone tomorrow. But I also struggle not to think about this all ending soon.

One way or another, this closeness won't last long.

For her, this is a phase of recovery. She wants me for my protection. Everything else is curiosity. Once Decker finds out, he'll put a stop to it.

Maybe that's what I need, too—for him to find out so at least someone has the balls to end this mess.

"Luc?"

"Yeah?" I mutter.

"Can you move closer? Just so I know you're near."

Jesus. Fuck. "I swear you were sent from the devil to test me." I scoot toward her, each inch made with weighty reluctance.

"No. It's you who were sent from the heavens to get me through my trauma, and this is something I need help with."

To hell with her logic.

I'm the last person who should be considered heaven sent.

If only she knew the things I've done. The people I've killed. And the ones I wanted to slaughter before they got away.

I stop a few inches from her, resting on my side to watch her darkened silhouette, the warmth from her body seeping into the sheets and surrounding me. But we don't touch. I make sure of that. I keep an invisible barrier between us, a firm boundary that she proceeds to shatter to pieces when she shuffles closer, nestling into my chest.

"Relax," she whispers. "I'm not going to hurt you."

If only she knew the pounding ache her proximity provides. I hurt everywhere. My legs. My arms. And no place throbs more than my dick. "Get some sleep."

She releases a weary sigh, resting her face into my chest. "I'm trying."

I feel for her. I always do.

I wish I could clean away her troubles and make her life effortless. Yet it seems staying here has only caused more problems.

I could've lost her tonight, and that fucking scares me. She could've been taken in by the cops. Or murdered. My selfishness almost cost this beautiful woman her life, and I'll never forgive myself.

The guilt is brutal, the pound building in my veins. My thoughts try to convince me she's already gone despite her body being close to mine.

Slowly, I wrap my arm around her waist, just to hold her. To make sure she's still whole. Still real.

I don't know how I'll let go of her in the morning. I'll have to pry my fingers from her soft skin.

"Luc?" Her voice is barely audible.

"Yeah, Pen. What's wrong?"

"I need you to touch me."

I close my eyes and press my lips to her temple. "I am touching you."

She sucks in a breath, her exhale ragged. "No. I need you to touch me the way you were going to touch that other woman."

16

PENNY

He doesn't move. Doesn't speak.

He remains rigid beside me, not breathing.

I pull back to stare into the darkened shadows of his face. "Luca, I need to know that part of me isn't broken. That I'm still a woman."

"Trust me, you're the most exquisite fucking woman there is."

He doesn't understand. I don't expect him to. But this is something I want to know. I *have* to know. I need to determine if the tingles he awakens in me are merely surface deep.

"Please." I place my hand on his chest. "Help me with this."

"I don't think I can be that man, Pen. I'm not a good guy."

The rejection stings. *Really* stings.

"Okay." I turn onto my back. I'm not going to force him into intimacy he doesn't want. Manipulating my way into his bed is bad enough.

"You know I want you." His voice is bleak through the darkness.

Yeah, I know. He wants me, just not the damage that comes with the package. He wants recovered Penny. Mentally stable Penny. "I said it's okay. Don't worry about it."

I lay in silence, my despair growing teeth.

He doesn't shift. I'm not sure if he's fallen asleep or if he's waiting for me to retreat to my own bed. I have no idea what he's thinking at all. I guess it's better that way.

"Why me?" he grates. "Why trust me with something this valuable?"

"What do you mean?"

"Intimacy. It's…" He doesn't continue, not in words, but his hand slides beneath the covers, his fingers raking over the top of my shirt to rest on my stomach.

"The only currency intimacy has with me is pain," I admit. "I've never known anything different. That's why I asked. I was hoping to wipe the slate clean of the bad memories."

"What about before?" His fingertips circle delicate details over my covered abdomen. "There had to be good memories then."

"There was nothing before. No steady boyfriend. No casual hookups. There's only my experience with Luther."

His hand pauses, his shock almost palpable through the seconds of thick silence. "You're a virgin?"

"I'm far from a virgin, Luc. But before Greece, no, I hadn't been with—"

"Greece doesn't count," he growls. "That wasn't sex. That was *nothing* like sex."

Maybe I shouldn't have asked. Maybe he's not the right person despite my body screaming otherwise.

"It doesn't matter. I don't want to talk about it anymore."

He returns to his circle work on my stomach. The gentle sweep of his fingertips is contained to a small space, yet the vibrations filter much farther. I feel the tingles all the way through my chest. Down my legs.

It's nice. Welcomed.

It's exactly what I asked for, just in diluted detail.

He traces my belly button. Swirls intricate patterns along my covered waist. The path he travels grows over long minutes of bliss. No words. No bad memories. Just kindness and what I hope is adoration in the delicate sweep of his touch.

I crave more. So much more I squeeze my legs to soothe the unfamiliar pressure.

My pulse pounds in my ears. In my throat.

I shouldn't want this. But I do.

I want to gorge on the kindness. To never, ever leave this moment.

The swirl of fingertips descends in minute increments, from my abdomen, to my hip, my thigh, then the hem of the T-shirt. When skin meets skin, I suck in a breath, the heated contact far more potent in its perfection.

"Too much?" he asks.

"No. Not at all."

He skims his hand under the shirt, hiking the material gradually as he ascends. There's nothing demeaning about it. Nothing threatening or brutal. It's pure gentleness, the only abrasion coming from the brief scrapes of the calluses on his palm.

My heart hammers the farther he travels along my thigh. The sensations are entirely new. Slow and soft and sweet.

"You're in control," he murmurs. "Tell me to stop whenever you need."

I nod into the darkness, incapable of words.

"Penny, you have to answer me. I won't keep going unless I know you're comfortable."

"I'm comfortable," I pant. "I know how to tell you to stop."

"Good." His touch skims to my inner thigh, the sensitive skin bursting into a valley of goose bumps.

It's remarkable. All the tingles. The burn where his attention doesn't even touch.

The approach to my core is painfully lethargic. He takes his time, learning every inch of me, creeping forward one minute, only to double back. Circling. Grazing. Branding.

By the time he reaches the juncture where leg meets groin I'm a mess of rampant breathing, my throat dry, my core pulsing.

I contemplate telling him to stop.

Ending this now—happy and blissed—is far better than the uncertainty that awaits. I can't get through this without acknowledging my trauma. Can I? Being like this with him can't be that easy. I have to break down soon. It's inevitable. I'm merely waiting for the switch to be flicked.

"Luc…"

"Hmm?" He guides my legs apart with slight pressure, exposing my vulnerabilities.

He doesn't say a word. Doesn't move his body closer to mine. He only continues to circle and swirl. Tease and tempt.

It's nothing like my past.

A completely foreign experience. Strikingly, agonizingly different.

"Nothing." I shake my head and clutch the sheets as he circles my pussy, the lightest glide of two fingertips moving around and around my outer edges.

This is far beyond what I wanted.

It's more passion. More kindness.

I envisaged sterility. Fear. Sorrow.

Yet here I am, tempted to beg for more, my hands itching to clutch him to my chest as his inhales labor.

Tension builds inside me. Sweet, needy tension.

I don't know how to sate the pulse becoming an adamant force deep down in my core. It makes me mindless, all the tingles and bliss.

He continues the circles, gliding closer and closer until he's brushing my pussy lips.

I shudder, anticipation trapping the breath in my lungs.

I don't know what comes next, but I want it. I *need it.*

"Luca?"

"Yeah?" His voice is breathy. Graveled.

"Don't stop."

He groans, his digits parting my folds to slide through slickness. My back arches. My breasts tingle. One finger enters me. Gradually. Agonizingly slowly.

I pant, wanting more as I close my eyes.

But bliss doesn't greet me in the mental darkness. Luther does. His conniving face stares back at me, smirking.

I scramble backward, the claws of panic snatching at me.

"What is it?" Luca asks. "What happened?"

"Turn on the lamp." I scoot to the head of the bed as the light flicks on, my arms around my legs, my knees near my chest. I gasp for breath.

The man who comes into view washes away the fear. He holds the memories at bay with the concern in his expression. The silent promise of protection.

"I took it too far." He covers my legs with the sheet.

"No, not at all. I was loving everything until I closed my eyes."

He winces. "It's okay. There's no rush."

There is to me.

There's now a finish line I want to pass. A victory over past demons I have to claim.

I reach for him, my fingers tentatively gliding over his chest. He sucks in a breath at the connection. Tenses.

"I'm wound tight, shorty."

"Me, too. But I don't want you to stop." I sink back onto the bed, turning onto my side to roll into him. "I need you to keep going." I can't quit here or I may never return.

"Why don't we save this for another day? We're not—"

"Please, Luc."

His nostrils flare, his frustration clear in the heavy exhale. "Whatever you want."

I've seen enough men consumed with lust to recognize the sight before me. He's pained with need. And his restraint is a monumental gift I've never received before.

Men don't hesitate to take from me. They steal and torment and punish.

But not Luc.

This time he guides my thigh to rest on top of his, propping my legs apart. He looks down at me, pussy splayed, wetness dripping.

"Fuck you're beautiful, Pen. So fucking beautiful."

I wilt for him, completely slump into a puddle of adoration. "Please kiss me."

I drag my hand around his neck and pull him close. He groans as our mouths meet, the vibration sinking into my chest.

I lose myself in him. Sucking. Licking. Biting. But most of all, learning. I notice the way he growls when I sink my teeth into his lower lip. I pay attention to the way he deepens the kiss if I inch back.

We smother each other, the passion climbing higher and higher with each sweep of our tongues until his fingers sneak back between my thighs.

I didn't think I could become needier than I was before. I never would've thought desire could be this painful. Or that bliss could be entirely consuming, like the way it is when his fingers slide back inside me.

I dig my nails into his neck. Cling. Claw.

"Oh, God." I gasp.

He resumes his slow torment. His digits glide into my pussy, stroking, then retreating completely. Back and forth. Over and over, delving deeper with each pass.

His breathing increases as he continues to kiss me, scraping me with his stubble.

This man may think he's falling in love with me, but my feelings are certain.

I adore him. Treasure him. *Love* him.

He put his future on the line. His *life*. All for me.

My gratitude will never die.

He slides his fingers farther inside, deeper and deeper, the heel of his palm placing pressure on my clit.

I need more.

So much more.

I grate into him, following his rhythm with my hips. I kiss his shoulder, his jaw, his cheek.

He stiffens further, his chest and arms becoming stone. Still he doesn't take from me. He gives and gives and gives. Not protesting when I dig my nails into his skin. Not backing away when I bite his neck.

"How did I get so lucky?" he growls into my ear. "What the hell did I do to deserve you?"

His adoration triggers something inside me. It breaks open the hardened fear and sets my demons free.

I latch onto his wrist between my thighs, rocking harder, faster, until my world splinters away from the destruction and pain and realigns with peace.

I realign with *him*.

I come undone, my core spasming. Pounding jolts of pleasure blindside me.

My breath is stolen with another kiss. My thoughts, too.

"Keep going, shorty." He speaks against my lips. "Don't fucking stop."

I don't want to. I could stay like this forever.

Thrumming.

Throbbing.

I cling to him, rock, rock, rocking, until the waves of bliss recede and all I'm left with are peppered kisses, depleted energy, and an overwhelming sense of exhilaration.

Wow.

"You're incredible." He holds my gaze as I collapse onto the mattress. "How are you feeling?"

"Breathless," I pant. "Overwhelmed... Happy."

"Good." He places a peck on my temple. "Because I need to leave you for a minute."

I don't want him to go. Not now. Or ever. But I don't protest as he slides from the bed, giving me an unrestricted view of all the scars peppered across his back like confetti.

"I won't be long." He walks to the bathroom door on the far side of the room, latching the lock behind him.

My euphoria rapidly recedes.

I'm almost lonely now.

The shower turns on, and the rapid rush of water falters, then rhythmically sloshes. He's pleasuring himself.

Without me.

I turn cold. Should I have offered him relief? Or maybe he ran so fast because he didn't want the offer at all. Maybe he didn't want to be with someone who could be harboring a wealth of STDs, because no matter how paranoid Luther was about the cleanliness of the women he raped, it doesn't mean I'm not dirty.

Luca hadn't wanted to touch me to begin with. Had barely bridged the space between us before I asked him to turn on the lamp.

"Stop it," I snarl to myself and slide from the bed, unwilling to let the negativity burrow further. Not tonight. Not after what just happened.

I make my way to the bathroom down the hall, distracting myself by using the facilities and freshening up.

I even tidy the vanity cupboards in an attempt to keep the taunting thoughts at bay, but it doesn't help. I question myself, wondering if I moved too fast. If the intimate moment should've been more difficult. If I'm a fraud for not being shattered by a man touching me.

Should I have hated the experience?

Why was it easy for him to bring me pleasure after so much pain?

The thoughts pound through my mind, gaining force, stealing away what bliss I had and replacing it with a cage of mental torture.

A tightening, restricting cell.

Breathing becomes harder, my lungs unable to be filled.

The light thud of approaching footfalls soothes me. Luca is here. Outside the bathroom door. I can feel him as if he's on the other side of the wood, waiting for me to come out.

"You're not okay, are you?" he murmurs through the barrier between us.

His insight draws a sob from my throat. "I'm confused. That's all."

The door creeps open, and I'm forced to step to the side as his stern face of concern bears down on me, authoritative and strong.

"Talk to me," he demands in a gruff growl.

"I don't know what to say."

"Say whatever's in your head. Did I hurt you? Are you scared of me? Did I push you too far?"

"No. It's none of that."

"Then why are you upset?"

"I'm not. I promise. I'm just overwhelmed. Both happy and… I can't explain."

"Self-sabotaging?"

I open my mouth to protest, but pause instead. "What do you mean?"

"I don't know. I just thought that either way, this exploration had to end badly. Either you hated it and felt accordingly. Or you didn't, but your mind and body are so used to feeling like shit that you don't know how to react any other way."

I cock my head, blinking as I hold his gaze.

Maybe that's it.

Maybe that's exactly it.

I want to be happy. The euphoria and bliss were everything in the heat of the moment, then as soon as thoughts had the time to fester, they turned the light to dark. "How did you know?"

He gives a sad smile. "'Cause I'm brilliant."

"No, really. How did you know?"

"Trauma has a lot of shitty bonus prizes that tend to bite you on the ass when you least expect it."

"You know from experience." It's not a question. I can see it in his eyes.

"I know enough. But none of that matters now. Let's get you back to bed."

I want to pry, to learn the parts of him he keeps hidden. I want to know everything there is about this man. "Will you tell me about your experience?"

"Sure. If you stick around long enough." He winks and takes my hand, leading me to the hall. "For now, though, you need to get some rest."

17

LUCA

She settles into her side of the mattress, her silhouette unmoving beside me.

Even in the shadows she's becoming easier to read.

Back in Greece, she hid everything—her thoughts, emotions, reactions. Now it's as if she's a written text, understood and deciphered from the slightest cadence change to her breathing.

"Get over here." I reach for her, dragging her into the middle of the bed.

She lets out a gasp of shock, but there's no protest. She comes willingly, draping her arm over my chest. Maybe her escape attempt was a blessing in disguise. Or it could've been, if she hadn't almost died.

We wouldn't be here otherwise.

She wouldn't be mine.

In my room.

In my arms.

But she's quiet. Too quiet. That isn't a good sign.

"What's on your mind, Pen."

"You're tired," she whispers. "There's all the time in the world to talk tomorrow."

"I don't need sleep. And apparently, neither do you. So spit it out."

She chuckles, subtle and breathy.

It's so fucking good to hear that sound from her. The comfort after all the pain.

"It's nothing." She rakes a finger over my pec, her touch pausing on scars. "I was only thinking that I don't know a whole lot about you."

"You're thinking that *now*? Isn't it a little late to be having cold feet?" I add humor to my tone to hide my apprehension.

I'm all in with this thing between us. Balls to the wall. Heart on my fucking sleeve.

I don't want her second-guessing anything. Let alone me.

"No. It's nothing like that. I was just thinking about all the things I know…"

"And wondering about all the things you don't?"

"Yeah." She nods. "I barely know anything, apart from the way you make me feel and how you like your coffee."

"So ask."

"Okay…" She shuffles beside me, raising on to her elbow. "Where are you from? And how did you end up here? You told me in Greece you used to be a SEAL, but never explained why you aren't anymore. I also want to know more about your brother. And your parents—"

"That's quite a list." I stop her there. Deliberately. "We'll be up until sunrise at this rate."

I don't see her smile. I feel it. There's something in the air that warms with her happiness.

This Penny isn't like the warrior I rescued from a predator. Her edges are softer. She's more woman. Less wild, caged animal.

"I've barely even started." She chuckles again. "How long have you lived here? When was your last relationship? How did you end up working for Torian?"

"My brother." I tread carefully, wanting to get this over with before she nose-dives any further into unwanted territory. "I was on a mission overseas when I found out Benji had gotten tied up with the most notorious crime family in Oregon. I dropped everything in the hopes I could pull him out before it was too late."

"But ended up working for them instead? Did they force you? Threaten you?"

"No." Despite her probably wanting a different answer, I tell her, "I'm here by choice."

"You gave up being a SEAL to work for Cole Torian?"

"Not exactly. I gave up for the love of my brother. It was a case of leaving my post too often to maintain my role. And the last time was in the middle of an op. But Benji needed me, and he's all I've got. I'd do anything for him. So I acted against instructions not to abandon my post. Even ignored my superior's threats to have me court marshalled."

There's a beat of silence where her hand freezes on my chest. "Weren't you worried?"

"I was more worried for my brother."

There's another pause, then, "Did they go through with their threat to court martial?"

"You bet your ass they did. I was dishonorably discharged."

The only stability I'd ever had in my life was gone. I'd been left with nothing. Nothing but Benji in a fucked-up situation.

"That's a heavy price to pay for being the older sibling."

"I'm not older. My big brother has a few years on me. Doesn't change anything though. It's how it's always been. He gets in trouble, and I try my best to drag him out of it." I place my hands under my head, feigning calm. "Isn't that what family are for?"

"I don't know. It's been a long time since I've had one. I barely remember what it's like anymore." She sucks in a deep breath and sighs. "How about your scars? Are they from your time as a SEAL or from working with Cole?"

I force myself not to flinch as she makes a direct hit on a shitty subject. "That's a long story best saved for another day."

"You don't want to share it with me?"

I don't want to share it with anyone.

Not now. Not ever.

"Does it have something to do with the trauma you mentioned before?" She looms over me. "I'm not pressuring you to spill secrets… I just thought if we had something in common…"

"It's not a conversation I want to have, Pen."

There's a slight tweak to her muscles. A flinch that consumes me with guilt.

"I'm sorry." She rests back onto the bed, stealing away her touch. "I won't ask again."

No, I bet she won't. She's too considerate for that.

I'll just be left to feel like shit for denying her.

"I'm getting tired." She rolls away from me to wrestle with her pillow. "Good night, Luc. Thanks for everything."

Fuck me.

Fuck me for pretending all my ducks are in a row when clearly they're not.

Fuck me for forcing her to face her past when I barely attempt to face my own. It's not fair. If only I knew how to function any other way.

"Night, Pen." I reach for her, gently running my fingers through her hair in silent apology. "Wake me if you need me."

"I will."

I lie there for hours, staring at her black outline as she sleeps. I don't know when I pass out, but it feels like seconds before I startle to consciousness, blinking rapidly at the sun beaming around the edge of the curtains.

I groan and reach for the bedside table to grab my cell, but it isn't there. I drag myself to the edge of the mattress to scour the floor, still coming up empty.

Shit.

I'm going to have to get up and search for it. There's no rest for the wicked when I need to find the asshole who shot at Penny.

Despite wanting to lie beside her forever, I can't today.

I slide from bed, swiping my gun from beneath the pillow, and wipe my free hand over the back of my neck, getting caught up in the sight before me.

She's peaceful, her gentle face relaxed, her beautiful lips parted.

The loud bang from the front door steals it all.

She startles, launching upright as the pounding continues.

"Luca, open the goddamn door."

Torian.

Fucking, Torian. That's what woke me.

"Don't panic." I stalk for the dresser, pulling out a pair of sweatpants and a shirt. "I can't find my phone. He'd be having a stroke because he couldn't get hold of me. Go back to sleep."

She reclines onto her elbows. "Are you sure?"

"Positive." I tug my pants on and shove the gun into the back of my waistband. "Everything's fine."

At least I hope so. For all I know, Decker could also be waiting at my door ready to take a dick swab. Or a vital organ.

"Sleep." I make for the hall. "I'll wake you when I've made breakfast."

I close the door behind me and stride for the front of the house as the knocking continues. A quick check through the peephole confirms Torian is alone, suit-clad and frowning as he attempts to bang my house down.

"What the fuck?" I pull the door wide.

He scrutinizes me with a raised brow as I tug the shirt over my head. "By the look of the claw marks on your neck, I'd say you had a fun night. I hope it was consensual."

"Fuck you."

He laughs and steps forward, nudging past me to enter the house.

"By all means," I grate. "Make yourself at home."

"You didn't give me much choice. I've been calling for an hour." He leads me back into the living area to take a seat at my dining table where my silenced phone lies in wait, the notification light blinking. "Did you just wake up?"

"Yeah. I was completely out of it." I scrub a hand over my face. "I'm tired as fuck."

"I bet." There's the slightest hint of judgment in his tone, but he doesn't put words to it. He doesn't need to.

"What do you want, Torian? What's so urgent that you couldn't wait until I found my phone?"

He sits back in the chair and shoots a glance to the kitchen. "If I were you, I'd start the coffee machine. You're gonna need it."

"Fine." It's a demand to make him a mug, but I don't give a shit because I *do* need it, likely more than he does. "Are you going to tell me what's going on? Or do I need to play barista first?"

"I'll wait."

"Suit yourself."

He doesn't speak again until I've got two mugs in hand and have taken my seat on the opposite side of the table. "What's got your asshole in a bunch this morning?"

He grabs the mug, takes a mouthful, then meets my gaze. "I told you last night that she stole from me."

Jesus Christ.

"Not this shit again. I haven't discussed it with her." I didn't bring it up because it wasn't the time. It'll never be the time. "I'll pay whatever she owes. Just leave her the fuck alone. She's gone through enough."

"She doesn't owe a dime." He places down the mug and grabs his cell from his suit jacket, pressing buttons before he slides it in front of me.

A pixelated black and white photo spreads across the screen. A stocky guy stands before an ATM, the majority of his head shrouded by his hoodie, sunglasses, and heavy beard.

"I was wrong." He taps the picture. "It was this guy."

"And who the hell is he?"

He shrugs. "No clue. But it's someone close enough to my father to have been trusted with a keycard."

"Someone old school or do you think we have new blood in town?" The niggle of apprehension raises the hair on the back of my neck. Luther always had allies here, even after he fled the country. The last thing we need is unfamiliar men stirring up trouble when nobody knows the kingpin is dead.

"Either is possible. The access to a keycard might be how he paid his local associates. My concern is that a threat from Greece slipped through our fingers and came here to cause trouble, because I've never seen this man before."

"He's unfamiliar to me, too." My apprehension increases. "But you're not here for me, are you? You want Penny to take a look."

"Yeah. I do."

I wipe a hand over my mouth, biting back the need to deny him. "She's sleeping. She needs her rest."

More than that, she deserves a few days of peace to get her head straight after last night. From both the fear and the bliss.

"I'm not waiting." He narrows his eyes. "Either you get her or I will."

I grind my teeth. Fist my mug. It takes every ounce of restraint to take another sip without choking on anger.

If I didn't have the slightest sense of concern over the piece of shit in the photo, I'd fight harder to have her left alone. But instinct tells me this isn't the time to make a stand.

"Give me a few minutes." I walk for my bedroom and ease the door open.

"You're back already?" She stretches, lazily blinking up at me.

"Sorry, shorty. I didn't want to wake you again, but Torian wants to see you."

She sits upright, then scoots from the bed. "Why?"

"It's nothing exciting. Just get dressed and meet us in the living room." I don't wait for more questions. I trek back down the hall, stopping at the main bathroom to wash my face in cold water. By the time I'm heading toward the living room, she's right behind me, dressed in jeans and a loose sweater as she pulls her hair into a high pony.

"Morning, Cole." She follows me to the table and takes a seat while I stand beside her.

"Morning." He gives a fake smile. "I don't know if Luca already told you, but this isn't a social visit."

"Okay." She frowns. "What's going on?"

"Last night, I accused you of stealing. I was wrong."

I remain coiled tight, listening to the admission that is far from the apology she deserves.

"It was a man." He taps his cell again, lighting up the screen with the picture on it. "I'm wondering if you recognize him."

"Me?" She glances at me in confusion before settling her attention back on Torian. "Why would I recognize him?"

"No reason. Just covering all my bases." He pushes his phone toward her, letting her frame it in both hands. "The image quality isn't the best."

She stares at the screen, not seeming to show any sign of recognition. At least not until I notice the tremble in her fingers and the lighter shade to her cheeks.

"Pen?" I slide into the seat beside her. "Do you know who it is?"

"Is this a joke?" She looks at me, her face ashen. "Please tell me this is some sick—"

"You recognize him?" Torian asks.

"When was this taken?" Her eyes scream with panic.

"Yesterday afternoon."

I reach for her, but she drops the phone to the table and pushes from her chair, distancing herself as she stands. "Where?"

"At a gas station ATM," Torian answers.

"Where?" She repeats. "*What* gas station? *Which* ATM?"

"The one on the corner of Boulevard and Cheshire. It's a ten-minute drive from here."

A heaved breath shudders from her lips. Followed by another and another, her shoulders trembling with the exhales.

"Penny?" I slowly rise to my feet, not wanting to spook her further. "What's going on?"

"You lied to me," she whispers. "You told me he was dead."

"Who's dead?" Torian's chair scrapes as he stands.

"*Robert*," she yells. "That man in the photo is *Robert*."

"No, shorty." My refusal is adamant as I reach for her. "You're mistaken. It's not him."

"The image is blurry at best." Torian speaks over me. "The guy's face is mostly covered."

She shoves me away, regaining space. "You think I wouldn't recognize a man who tormented me for years? I'd know him anywhere. And yet he was *here*. In *Portland*. A mere ten-minute drive away."

"No…" I reach for her again and she revolts.

"You promised." She backtracks. "You promised he was dead. You promised I was safe."

"You *are*." I follow her. "I would've bet my goddamn life he was dead."

"Instead, you bet mine." She places more space between us, one step after another. "You staked *my* life, Luca."

"I'd never do that."

I don't get it.

I don't fucking understand.

"Pen, calm down," I beg. "You didn't sleep well last night. Why don't you take another look at the photo—"

"I didn't sleep well?" Her eyes plead with me. "You don't believe me?"

I hold up my hands in placation. "I'm just trying to understand what the fuck is happening."

Trying.

Struggling.

I'd been in that room in Greece. I watched as Luther drew his gun and vowed to handle Robert. But we had to leave.

Anissa had been hurt. Scared. In danger.

I heard the gunshot. That blast rang in my fucking ears.

"I need to leave." Penny scrutinizes her surroundings, glancing around the room as if threatened by the furniture, scanning the yard as she retreats step after step toward the hall.

"You're safe," I vow.

"How can you say that? You have no idea what you're up against. You don't even trust me. You think I'm crazy."

"I *do* trust you."

"Then listen to me." The tremble in her hands increases as she glances between me and Cole. "*Please*, Luca, you need to believe me."

"Okay." I keep my arms raised. "I believe you. I promise I believe you. Just stop walking away from me. You don't get to run again."

"I don't know what else to do. I can't stay here. He'll come after me. He won't stop."

"Neither will I. You hear me?" I bridge the space between us and pull her against my chest. I stare at Torian over her shoulder, noting the skepticism heavy in his features. "I won't let anyone near you."

"You don't understand what he's like. He won't give up."

I squeeze her tighter, only to have her scamper from my hold.

A gasp breaches her lips. Her eyes flare. "Last night… oh, my God. That was him."

"Okay, that's enough," Torian warns. "You need to stop jumping to conclusions. Even if by some stretch of the imagination Robert is alive, he'd know Portland isn't a smart place for him to hide."

"He'd never hide." She pulls back. "He'd be here for payback. He's here for *me*. I want a gun, Luca. You need to get me a gun."

I nod. "We'll discuss it later. Right now, we have to make a move. Go pack your things. We're getting out of here."

She doesn't wait for any further instruction. She rushes for the hall, her fear-filled expression haunting me even once she's out of view.

"You don't buy this crazed bullshit, do you?" Torian holds my gaze, his eyes narrowed. "After everything that happened, you still think it's possible that asshole is alive?"

I'm trying to piece together the possibilities. We'd heard the gunshot, but we'd left the room. We didn't physically see Robert dead.

"Did you hear his body hit the floor?" I ask.

"What?"

"Back in Greece. We left the room just as the gunshot was fired." I pace, raking my hands through my hair. "But did you hear his body hit the ground? There would've been a hard clap of his fucking head against the tile. We should've—"

"You're saying you think she's right?" He scoffs.

"What I'm saying is that I can't remember hearing Robert's fucking body hit the floor."

"We had other things on our mind," he grates. "Jesus Christ, Luca. You're thinking with your dick."

No, I'm not thinking at all. I'm panicking. "What if she's right? Are you willing to risk your family? Are you willing to risk Anissa? Because if that prick is still breathing, I'm sure he's going to want revenge for what we did over there."

And he's not the type of psychopath to draw out the torture.

18

PENNY

I clean out my wardrobe, packing my belongings into paper shopping bags while Luca remains in the living room with Cole.

I overhear parts of their aggressive argument.

They mention Anissa. My sisters. And Tobias.

My sweet, sweet Tobias.

I fall to my knees. Helpless.

That little boy is entirely vulnerable. But Robert would never hurt him. Not physically. They were like uncle and nephew. It's the mental threat he poses that I can't ignore.

Robert wouldn't stand for Tobias being taken care of by the people who arranged Luther's murder. And my sisters…oh, God.

Bile climbs up my throat.

Abi.

I knew she would never kill herself. I knew, and Luca didn't believe me. None of them wanted to believe me.

I clutch a hand to the base of my neck and bow my head, begging the contents of my stomach to retreat.

Robert killed Abi. He tried to kill me. Who knows what he will attempt next.

"Pen?" Luca enters the doorway and falls to his knees before me. "Are you okay?"

"I need to get out of here."

He nods. "We're leaving right now."

"Where?"

"Torian's house." He hits me with sad eyes. "Don't worry. It's a gated property with heavy surveillance. He's already called in a security team to man the perimeter."

I don't think surveillance will matter. Or security. Nothing will stop Robert getting what he wants. Nothing but death.

"I want that gun, Luca. I need to be able to protect myself."

His brows pinch. It's the slightest cringe of a response.

"Luca?" I sit back on my haunches. "You said you could get me a gun. You promised in Greece."

"You're not going to need it. The house will be protected."

"You're denying me?"

"No." He grabs my hands, tangling our fingers. "I'm telling you it's not necessary. We're taking this seriously, Pen. We're going to cover all our bases, which starts with moving everyone to Torian's house. That includes his sisters, our brothers, Hunter, Sarah, Stella and Tobias. It's not a good idea to have you carrying a gun around those kids."

"Tobias is going to be there? I'm going to see him?"

"Yes. We'll all be living under the same roof for a while, which means it's not smart to have guns in the hands of someone untrained."

"Then train me," I beg. "Nobody will protect Tobias like I will. I'd give my life—"

"And I'd give mine." He speaks over me. "For him. *And* you."

I sit back on my haunches, sliding my hands from his. "But I won't make mistakes."

He pulls away and I steel myself against his pained expression, not letting the guilt sink in.

This morning, I'd woken with a smile. I'd been a different woman. Hope had flown through me. I'd been wholeheartedly adamant my life had turned a corner.

Now that's all gone.

Everything is—the security, the glimpse of positivity.

"I didn't mean that. I just…" I wince.

"I get that you're mad. You have every right to be. But you'll see once we get there that you don't need to protect yourself or anyone else." He rises to his feet and grabs my bags from the bed. "Grab whatever else you need and meet me in the garage. We're leaving as soon as Hunt and Deck get here to escort us."

He strides from the room without a backward glance, the slightest slump to his shoulders the only evidence I kicked him where it hurts.

I didn't want to upset him. That wasn't my intent. It's the insanity building inside me that demands to be heard. There are too many thoughts. Overwhelming questions. A punishing outlook.

I push to my feet, snatch the last of my toiletries from the bathroom, and yank on a comfy pair of Sketchers before following him. I run into Cole in the hall, the two of us walking in tense silence until we reach the garage where Luca shows me to the back of his Suburban.

"You're going to have to lay low." He opens the door and waves a hand for me to get inside. "I don't have all the bells and whistles Hunt's car has. So you need to spread yourself out along the back seat and stay out of view."

"What does that mean?" I climb into the vehicle and swivel to face him.

"It means my car isn't bulletproof." He closes me inside and returns to his conversation with Cole, the two of them murmuring in low tones before Luca skirts the hood to get in the driver's side. "It's time to get down, Pen." He opens the garage with a remote, the mechanical burr slow and ominous.

"What about you?" I meet his gaze in the rear-view and appreciate the lack of deserved hostility. "What's the point of worrying about me when it's just as likely you'll get shot?"

"Nobody is getting shot. It's only a precaution." He makes the Suburban grumble to life and reverses into the bright sunlight. "Now, Pen."

I hesitate, glancing through the side window to see Cole follow us down the drive on foot, the garage door closing in front of us. "Are you sure you're safe?"

"We've practically got a presidential escort. Hunter's going to be in front, with your brother and Torian in the cars behind. We're literally sandwiched between trigger-happy assholes. They won't let anything happen to us."

I look through the back window, confirming the cars are ready and waiting.

They're taking this seriously. Even if they don't believe me, they're at least taking precautions. "Can you let me know if you see anything?"

"I'm not going to see anything. Just lay down and enjoy the ride."

I sigh and stretch along the seat, resting my head on my bent arm as Luca reverses the car onto the street.

We don't talk. I'm left to fidget in silence, nothing but crunching asphalt and traffic in the distance to keep me company for miles.

I try not to let my thoughts wander. I seriously work hard to concentrate because I know the darkness of instability waits in the wings.

All the nightmarish thoughts are there. Hovering. Impatient for their time to strike.

"How much farther?" I raise my head to peek out the side window.

"Stay down. It's only a few more blocks." He turns on the radio, the gentle hum of an unfamiliar song doing nothing to soothe me. "You'll get to see Tobias soon."

I wait for excitement to flood me.

Instead, nervous apprehension weighs heavy in my belly. I love that boy, but I don't know what he's been told over the past weeks. About me. About the deaths of Chloe or Abi. Or if he'll be informed of Robert's presence in Portland.

Our reunion will either be shrouded in secrets or tears. Neither option is comforting.

"Only one more block." Luca makes a turn, then another, still without a care in the world. "We're here."

The car jolts as if we've risen onto a driveway and I cautiously sit as we pass through gates attached to a large brick wall.

The setting is reminiscent of my hell in Greece. It's just another set of gates and walls to lock me inside.

"You'll like it here." Somehow, Luca soothes my thoughts. "It's massive, with enough room for you to hide from anyone you don't want to speak to."

He drives the car around the front of a two-story mansion, the manicured gardens perfectly symmetrical with their trimmed hedges and rose bushes. The neighbors' homes are equally overbearing and ostentatious from the other side of that looming brick wall.

"This is the safest place for you to be right now." He cuts the engine and meets my gaze in the rear-view. "But, if at any time you don't feel comfortable, tell me and I'll fix it."

"Fix it how? You'd get me out of here?"

"I'd figure something out." He opens his door, slides free, then helps me from the car. All the while he cautiously scrutinizes the yard, as if he's taking in every swaying branch and rustling leaf.

We're alone. No other cars. No people in sight.

"I thought you said Sebastian was following us." I beat back panic at our conspicuous position. The boundary walls are large, but the neighbors' houses' are far bigger. What if we're being watched? An itch of unease skates along my arms. "Where are Cole and Hunter?"

"Decker and Hunt kept driving once we reached the gates. They need to help escort everyone here. And Torian went to park around back in the garage. He'll let us in through the front door in a minute."

I nod, only slightly appeased.

My arms break out in goose bumps beneath my sweater. All my hairs stand on end. It's as if I'm in the sights of a well-trained assassin and any sudden movement will end my life.

"You can wait at the front door." Luca jerks his chin toward the house. "I'll get our stuff."

I don't listen. Instead I follow him to the trunk and help to carry my paper bags while he hauls a heavy duffle. It's instinctive to remain by his side, and I suppose it shouldn't be. Not when walls are crashing down around me. I need to find a way to make it on my own. Without reliance.

By the time we reach the front double doors, Cole is there to let us inside.

He leads us down a wide hall, the white tiles immaculate, the walls filled with artwork. It's too similar to Luther's Grecian home. My prison. This place is another picture-perfect house, haunted by criminal activity.

"Separate rooms?" Cole stops before a closed door. "Or together?"

"Separate," I murmur, as Luca says, "Together."

Cole raises a brow. "I'll leave you two to come to a decision. Make yourselves at home. But once everyone arrives we need to have a meeting. Don't keep me waiting." He continues down the long hall, back straight, stride confident, and opens another door to disappear inside.

Luca doesn't speak. He stands there, staring where Cole had once been, his jaw tense, his hand wrapped tight around the duffle strap.

"Separate rooms would be better." I break the silence.

"You're sick of sleeping with me already?" He makes for the door in front of me, flings it wide and stalks inside.

"That's not it." I remain in the hall, unwilling to follow. "You said my brother will be here. I don't want him seeing us together."

"Fuck your brother," he grates from inside the room. "I'll tell him I'm sleeping on the floor. I'm not letting you out of my sight."

I cling to my bags, the paper crinkling under my tightening grip. "No, it's best if I stay somewhere else."

He dumps his duffle at the foot of the bed and returns to the doorway, his shoulders stiff. "I get it; you're angry at me. You don't trust me anymore. But distancing yourself isn't going to help."

"*You're* the one who doesn't trust *me*, Luc. You don't believe me."

He steps closer, not stopping until his face is inches from mine. "No, I don't *want* to believe you. There's a difference."

"It sounds the same to me."

"Well, it's not. I believe that you think Robert is still alive. And that he was the shooter last night. But I don't *want* to believe it because that means I fucked up. Not just a little bit, but a whole damn lot. Believing you're right means I risked your life and I'm not sure I can handle that."

"How do you think I feel? You made me believe in fairy tales. You convinced me I was safe. Now I don't know what's real and what isn't. I need to step back and protect myself. *On my own.*"

He reaches for my bags, drags both from my arms to steal them inside. "Everything between us is real." He speaks over his shoulder. "So whatever you need to figure out, you can do it in here."

I sigh and trudge after him, stopping at the threshold. "You can't blame me for questioning my safety, Luc."

He dumps my bags on top of a dark wood dresser, then turns to me. "But you're not just questioning your safety. You're questioning me. You're questioning all the things I've done to protect you. All the time we've spent together. All the things that happened over the past weeks. I'm only asking for you to give me a chance to redeem myself."

I slump against the doorjamb and cross my arms over my chest. "You don't need to redeem anything. I just need space."

"I call bullshit. Last night you pleaded to get in my bed. Now you're pushing me away because I fucked up."

"No, I'm pushing you away because you made it clear last night that you won't let me intrude upon your past despite how much you demand of mine. If anyone has been pushing it was you."

My lips snap shut as his shoulders straighten.

I didn't need to say that. My insecurities are meaningless in comparison to the situation with Robert. Yet I feel better for getting it off my chest. One of the millions of voices in my head has been heard.

"Is that what this is about?" He frowns. "My past isn't a topic either one of us want to discuss."

"I understand, but it doesn't stop me questioning the secrecy. Maybe this is more of that self-sabotage you spoke about." I shrug. "I don't know. All I can say is that I feel isolated from the truth right now. And I'm not sure how to get on top of that when the one person I thought I could trust can be physically near me, yet mentally keep me at arm's length."

19

LUCA

"GET IN HERE," I DEMAND.

Her throat works over a heavy swallow. Her chin hikes the slightest bit in defense.

She's uncomfortable. Unsettled.

We're fuckin' twinsies.

"No." She pushes from the doorjamb and stands tall. "I'll find another room."

"Do I need to carry you over my shoulder?" I start toward her, thankful she scoots inside before I slam the door shut. "So me spilling my past will stop you feeling isolated?"

"That's not what I'm saying… I just—" She throws her hands up in the air. "I don't know. I don't know anything anymore. One minute I'm in your house, in your bed, and I begin to feel happy and optimistic and whole. I started imagining a future that wasn't a waking nightmare. And now we're here and all those daydreams are gone, leaving me to question everything."

She wants my secrets.

My truth.

I guess I owe her that much.

"They're cigarette burns," I admit, each word slicing open old wounds. "The marks all over my body aren't from shrapnel. They're not battle scars. Each and every spot of mutilated skin is from the burned end of a cheap roll of tobacco."

Her face falls. Her lips part.

She stares at me for long moments, thoughts running rampant in those eyes, but no questions come out.

"How's that for un-isolating truth?" I drawl.

She shakes her head, her forehead wrinkled in a wince. "Do I want to know who caused them?"

"Probably not. But I'll tell you anyway." I back away from her, moving to the bed to slump onto the mattress. "The lighter, more frequent ones are from my father. Because he liked to constantly remind me he was an asshole. Those few that are deeper came from my mom. She wasn't as carefree about leaving abusive evidence behind, but when she did, she tended not to hold back."

Pity takes over her beautiful face. Such sickening, unwanted pity.

I can't look at her when she stares at me like that.

I don't want sympathy. I don't even want acknowledgement.

"Obviously, they weren't the best parents," I say through clenched teeth. "But my scars are nothing in comparison to my brother's. He bore the brunt of their abuse."

"That's why you're always helping him?"

"I help him because he helped me for years. He made sure he was the main target whenever my folks went on a rage bender. He kept me alive through childhood and has far more scars to prove it. Mental and physical."

He grew accustomed to fucking up for the sake of saving me. It was his routine for so long the habit followed into adulthood.

"How long did the abuse last?" She approaches, stopping within arm's reach.

"Benji was willing to risk living on the streets for as long as I can remember. He only hung around because I was too much of a chicken shit to leave. But as soon as my seventeenth birthday arrived, I forged my parents' signature and signed up for the Navy. I was out of there and never looked back."

"And Benji? What did he do?"

"Whatever he could to survive. He got a job. Rented a shitty apartment and kept his head above water with the money I sent him each payday." I meet the sickening pity still heavy in her gaze. "Is that enough insight? Do you feel better now?"

"Please don't ask me that." She wraps her arms around her middle. "If I would've known what you were hiding I never would've made demands."

"I didn't tell you, Pen, because I haven't told anyone. Not child services when they came to check on us. Not the few friends I had as a kid. Not a single soul since I left that fucking house and never looked back." I shove from the bed and bridge the distance between us, untangling those arms to place them on my waist. "Nobody knows. I don't even think Benji told his wife."

"I feel horrible." She speaks into my chest. "I never should've said anything."

"It doesn't matter. I'm sure you would've found out soon enough. I can't keep shit from you."

She sinks into me, her cheek to my shoulder, her warm breath on my neck. "Where are your parents now?"

"Don't know. Don't care. As far as I'm concerned, my childhood never existed."

"But from your childhood you became a protector. You became a SEAL—"

"I became a SEAL because it felt good to create havoc for the right reasons. To be someone who was the best of the best instead of a cowering little kid who made his brother take his beatings. They were the first family I ever had."

"And then you lost them…"

"I did." I shrug. "But I gained a new one here. These guys have my back, even though they act like pricks most of the time. This job wasn't a hard transition, even though I never would've guessed it beforehand."

"But you went from doing good to bad."

"Did I?" I pull back to look down at her. "I saved you, after all. Doesn't that make me a little bit good?"

She winces. "Yes. Of course it does. I didn't mean…"

"Killing heartless criminal assholes isn't something I feel guilty about. Sometimes people deserve more than a jail cell. I don't lose sleep thinking about the bodies I've buried."

She stares up at me for long moments of contemplation. No agreement. No response.

"Does knowing more about me make you feel any better, shorty?"

She swallows and swipes her tongue over her lower lip, the sight fucking tempting. "I'd be lying if I said no."

"You sure I didn't scare you?"

Her lips pull in a half-hearted smile. "Again, I'd be lying if I said no."

"Okay, I'll make sure to leave the closet open for you to dig through my skeletons. But I think it's too early to chat about the work I do for Cole. I can see you're uncomfortable with it."

Her chuckle is breathy. "Yeah, maybe."

"Okay." I grab her chin, grazing my fingers over her soft skin. "I'll do whatever you want. You only need to ask."

I press my mouth to hers, eating up her faint whimper as she settles against my chest. The connection is soft. Slow. Exactly the opposite of what the blood rushing through my veins demands.

"How are you feeling about last night?" I ask against her lips. "No regrets?"

"None." She deepens the kiss. "Only more curiosity."

I keep the laughter buried in my chest. The agonizing, punishing laughter. This woman is going to get me killed.

"I think it really helped me," she continues between nuzzling pecks.

It didn't help me one iota.

I'm fucking dying to have her. Dying trying to keep my restraint in check.

She sighs. "Will you—"

The slam of a door cuts her question short and drags us apart. The patter of light rushed footsteps lets me know this moment isn't going to last any longer. The kiddie giggle only confirms it. The unmistakable squeal from my niece sends my dick into hibernation.

292

"I think the mini stampede means Tobias is here." I drag my hands off her. "You should go say hello."

She glances to the closed door, her lips parting.

"What are you waiting for?" I walk to my duffle, busying myself with pulling out a change of clothes. It's not my business to intrude on her special moment, no matter how much I wish it was. We're not at that stage yet. Maybe we will be one day. Who the fuck knows? But I'm not going to crowd her. "Go on. Enjoy the reunion."

"Thank you."

I don't look back at the sound of her fleeting footsteps. I get dressed, pulling on old jeans and a shirt loose enough to hide the gun buried in my waistband.

I try not to focus on all the fucked-up scenarios potentially waiting for us, but it's hard not to imagine the worst when the hits keep coming.

If Penny's right and Robert is still alive, it's not merely his revenge we need to worry about.

His ability to blow Torian's secrets sky-high is more than a huge fucking dilemma.

None of us will be safe, now or in the future, if news of Luther's arranged murder becomes public knowledge. And if that information is paired with the inside info that Torian was working with Anissa—a Fed—our deaths won't come easily.

In this world, snitches get more than stitches. They get a one-way ticket to unending torture to set a blatant example for anyone else who might want to do the same.

Men will die.

Women, too. Maybe the kids.

I doubt anyone will be spared.

Things would be different if Anissa was dirty. Turning a cop, a Fed, or a government official is worthy of a five-star bonus. But that woman wants to remain clean, meaning we're all as good as fucked if Robert is kicking and decides to expose the truth.

So my days could be numbered, and if that's the case, there's no place I'd rather spend them than by Penny's side, my hands in her hair, my mouth against hers.

I walk from the room toward the noise and find the living area filled with familiar faces—Hunter, Sarah, Torian, Decker, Keira, Layla, and my niece, Stella. All of them watch as Penny kneels on the plush rug in the center of the room, hugging the heck out of Tobias.

Her smile is amazing. Far more brilliant than anything I've encouraged.

Shit. That little fucker makes me jealous.

Her entire face is alight. From her skin to her eyes. Even those lips.

"Long time no see." Hunt comes up beside me, nudging my shoulder with his. "Was she okay after we left last night?"

Torian walks past, snickering, his smirk enough of an answer before he continues to the sofa.

"She was fine," I grate. "*Everything* was fine."

"Everything *except* my car," Hunt clarifies. "But just so you know, Decker ambushed me earlier. He wanted to know why Penny ran yesterday."

I face him, trying to read his expression. "And?"

"And you owe me. I told him I must've made her feel uncomfortable, so she took off. He's buying it for now."

The goodwill doesn't make a lick of sense. Unless Sarah put him up to it. Even then, kindness isn't their style. "Thanks."

He grins. "I'm not looking for kind words, bucko. Like I said, you owe me."

"Great. That's just what I need." I turn back to the room, my glare fading as my niece catches my eye.

"Uncle Luca." Stella runs toward me, her hair bouncing around her shoulders. "I missed you."

I crouch and open my arms, hauling her into a tight hug. "Hey, sweetheart. How are you? I hear you've been looking after Tobias."

She smiles. Nods. "Uh-huh. He's fun. Really smart, too. Mom says he might be starting school with me next week."

"Is that so?" I release her to ruffle her tangled hair. "I'm not sure that's the best idea. How will your teachers handle two Torian brats in the one place?"

"I'm not a brat." She giggles. "Not all the time."

"I think your father would disagree."

"Daddy thinks I'm an angel." She plants a playful punch on my thigh and skips away.

"If that's the case," Hunt mutters, "then her dad is a fuckin' idiot. That girl is the devil."

I chuckle under my breath. He's not wrong. On both counts. "You try telling Benji that."

I return my attention to the reunion. Tobias is enthusiastic with rapid arm movements as he describes the park near Stella's house, then proceeds to recount the names and descriptions of all the friends he's made.

Penny takes it all in. She's parental affection personified. Kind eyes. Energetic nods.

"I've got so much to tell you," Toby rambles. "Oh, I almost forgot." He leans forward, whispering something in her ear.

Her surge of tension is almost unnoticeable. The stiffening of her spine is minute. But I see it. I see everything.

She glances over her shoulder to me, the brief expression of panic quickly hidden under a fake curve of lips. She leans forward, returning a secret message to the boy's ear, then pushes to her feet, rubbing his arms in affection. "Don't fret. There's nothing to worry about."

He nods, his bubbly nature returning as he stares up at her. "What about you?

What have you done while you've been here? Have you seen much of Portland? Did you know I'm going to school next week?" He jolts, as if hit with another truckload of questions. "What about the others? Why aren't they here? I want to show Chloe a picture I drew."

She doesn't flinch. Doesn't even falter. Not until she opens her mouth. "They're um…"

"Hey kiddos…" Stella's mom, Layla, interrupts. "Why don't the two of you pick where you want to sleep before the adults steal the best rooms?"

"That's a great idea." Keira waves them toward the hall. "I'll help."

"*Yes*." Stella dashes around her aunt. "Toby, I'll race you."

"No fair. You got a head start." Tobias runs from Penny's side without a backward glance, the two little brats leaving in a whirlwind of excitement.

"I'll keep them occupied as long as I can." Keira gives Penny a sad smile and continues for the hall. "But you might want to come up with a plan. He's been asking about the other women for days now."

Penny hitches her chin at the news.

I want to go to her. To pick her up and make all the shit fade away. And I would… if her brother wasn't in the kitchen watching her like a hawk. Watching *me*, too.

Despite Hunt covering my tracks, I swear Decker is waiting for the opportunity to hang me from the closest shower railing.

"Does Tobias need to be told?" Sarah asks. "Don't you think it's best to keep them in the dark? At least for now?"

"We can talk about it later." Torian stalks to the fridge. "Help yourself to whatever food or drinks you need. It's time to have a meeting while the kids are occupied."

There are nods of agreement, shuffles of feet, food grabbed, and coffee made.

Penny remains in the center of the room, those arms wrapped tight around her middle, desperately trying to self-soothe when I could do a far better job. I can't stand idle anymore. I can't watch her struggle.

I start toward her, seeing her brother take notice from the corner of my eye.

He watches, unmoving as I go to her, stopping a foot away to offer wordless comfort.

Her plea for support is equally silent, the furrow of her brow deepening, her nose scrunching.

"What do you need?" I keep my voice low, almost unheard.

She cringes and bows her head. "You… I just need you."

I don't hesitate.

Fuck her brother.

Fuck what's right.

I step into her, pulling her into my arms, hugging her close to my chest. She doesn't return the embrace—merely stands there. Broken. Battered. Her cheek nestling into my neck.

"I fucking knew it," Decker snarls. "You son of a bitch."

I shoot him a warning glare as Penny remains defeated in my arms.

He's furious, his narrowed eyes promising retribution as he sneers, "Is everyone else watching this shit?" He swings around to take in Hunt and Sarah's lack of reaction.

"I'm seeing it." Sarah takes a bite from an apple, a mug of coffee in her other hand. "I just don't give a shit. Luca's been helping—"

"Get your fucking hands off her." Decker skirts the kitchen counter, coming toward us. "Do it before I do it for you."

"Take a walk, Deck." Hunter strolls forward, blocking his path.

"I'm not walking anywhere."

"Like fuck you aren't," Torian demands. "Walk now or you'll be on your own until you cool down."

Decker curls his hands into fists, his face turning red. "That shit better be platonic," he seethes. "Otherwise you're dead."

"Walk," Torian growls.

"Fuck you." Decker storms from the room, spewing a mouthful of colorful language. The verbal barrage doesn't stop for long moments, the creative threats making Hunt chuckle.

"Has he been watching too much TV?" he asks. "He's overly dramatic."

Torian moves to the fridge and pulls the door wide. "Just wait until he finds out they're sleeping together. You're going to want popcorn for that show."

"Ignore them," I whisper in Penny's ear. "This is how they get their kicks."

A door slams in the distance and laughter murmurs through the room.

They all think this is a joke—Pen's situation, Decker's outrage. Maybe I would too if I was on the other side of the fence. But each quip hits her harder. I feel it in the tension coiling through her.

Hunter glances over his shoulder to us. "If this is the way he reacts to you guys hugging, you might want to rest with one eye open. My man might slit your throat in your sleep."

"We're not fucking," I snap. "Y'all are as bad as he is."

"Those scratches don't lie, buddy. Just wait until he notices them. He's going to snap your spine like a twig."

Penny stiffens, her arms finally weaving around my waist in a protective hug.

"They're just having fun," I whisper. "Don't worry about it."

"Yeah, Pen, don't worry." Sarah chuckles through the placation. "We'll protect Luca. We won't let him get too much of a beating."

Vibrations echo from under my feet, the muted *pop, pop, pops* carrying in perfect rhythm.

"What's that noise?" Penny looks up at me in concern.

"There's a shooting range in the basement. Your brother is letting off steam."

"Or perfecting his aim." Hunt grabs a cookie from the jar on the kitchen counter, shoving it into his mouth to chew with an exaggerated smile. "My guess is the latter."

"That's real funny, asshole." I rub Penny's back, trying to loosen her rigidity. "Seriously, don't worry about your brother. I'll speak to him after he cools down."

Keira reenters the room. "Guys, I don't know how much time we have. Layla will keep the kids occupied as long as she can. But who knows how long the nanny will take to get here on short notice?"

"Okay. Everyone, hurry up." Torian leads the way to the hall at the other end of the living area. "My office. Now."

I give Pen a final squeeze, then step back. "You've gotta be hungry; you didn't eat breakfast." I grab her hand and lead her to the kitchen. "Food? Coffee? Both?"

"A piece of fruit will be enough. My stomach isn't playing nice."

I grab an apple and raise a brow in question.

She nods. "Thanks."

I lob the Granny Smith at her and pour myself a mug of caffeine. Sarah and Hunt help themselves to the fridge. Within minutes we're all in Torian's office, Keira sitting in the middle of an elegant sofa, Sarah and Hunt leaned against opposite armrests, while Penny and I remain standing, side by side.

"So, what's this about one of Luther's men being here in Portland?" Hunt asks. "I thought we took out those fuckers in Greece."

"I thought we did, too." Torian takes a seat behind the large wooden desk, and turns his Mac screen to face us. "Penny, on the other hand, thinks this is Robert. One of my father's nearest and dearest."

The bank ATM image is on display, the poor picture quality magnified with the larger size.

"Looks like a big blur to me." Sarah leans forward, squinting. "How can you be sure?"

"I'm not." Torian swings the screen back to face him. "We're playing it safe. But whoever it is stole from us."

"It's Robert," Penny murmurs. "There's no question."

Everyone looks at her, their expressions differing from mild skepticism to Hunt, who rolls his eyes with blatant disregard.

"How do you want us to go about finding this asshole?" I ask. "It's in our best interests to keep this shit quiet and smoke him out as soon as possible."

Torian nods. "It needs to be fast and unnoticed. So far there have been no whispers about him being in town, which means it's either not him, or he hasn't made his presence known to any of my father's men."

"It's him," Penny repeats. "I swear to God, it's him."

"It's okay." I take a mouthful of coffee and close in behind her, rubbing my free hand along her arm. "Why don't you go spend some time with Tobias while we figure this out?"

"So you can question my sanity without me here?" She swings around to face me, her eyes pleading. "You still don't believe me. You think I'm crazy."

"I believe you." It's the truth. "I trust your judgment."

"Nobody thinks you're crazy," Sarah adds. "We just need to be sure of what we're up against."

"Speak for yourself," Hunt mutters. "She stole my car. If that doesn't scream batshit I don't know what does."

I glare at him. "I'm done with the jokes. If Robert's here, we all need to watch our backs."

"He *is* here." Penny faces Torian. "And my sisters need to be taken care of, too. Who's looking out for them?"

"Benji should already be on his way back. Once he arrives, I'll get him to arrange security."

"He's coming here?" I disguise my annoyance with another mouthful of coffee. "Does that mean all the women are with their families? Why the hell haven't I been updated on this?"

"He's taking the last one home today."

"I can get started on the security arrangements," Keira offers. "That way the other women will be taken care of sooner than later."

Torian shakes his head. "It can wait. We've got more important things to focus on."

"More important things?" Penny seethes. "More important than their lives?"

I dump my mug on a nearby bookshelf and return to my position behind her, placing both hands on her waist. "That's not what he meant."

"Then what did he mean?" She shrugs away from my touch.

"Penny," I warn.

She can't make waves in here.

At my home it's different. She can rail on me all she likes without consequence. But here, Torian will use her anger against her. He'll make her regret the outburst.

"No, let her speak." He leans back in his chair. "If she wants to criticize how I've saved her and her friends, by all means, let her continue."

She doesn't reply. Not immediately. She stands tall against his taunt, the tension seeping from her tight shoulders. "I'm sorry if I seem ungrateful." She enunciates the words slowly. "I have nothing but appreciation for what you've done."

She pauses, the silence growing uncomfortable.

"But?" he drawls.

"But one of my sisters was murdered moments after leaving Benji's care. And it's now clear Robert took her life. So I'm struggling to comprehend why a man of your means wouldn't rush to provide the necessary security to stop the bloodshed happening again."

He narrows his eyes on mine. "Who was murdered?"

"Abi." Penny steps forward, demanding his attention. "I don't care what was reported. She never would've killed herself. It had to be Robert. Or someone working with him."

Sharp glances dart through the room. Sarah to Hunter. Keira to her brother. All of them returning to Penny, silently questioning her theory.

"Abi didn't kill herself?" Torian repeats. "She was murdered?"

"Yes." Penny nods. "Without a doubt."

"And Robert is responsible?" There's an edge to his tone, an aggressive, barely leashed skepticism.

She keeps nodding. "He has to be."

"Right... So let me get this straight, because I'm starting to see a pattern." He pushes to his feet and rounds the desk to lean his ass against the front edge. "The police and news outlets reported Abi's death as a suicide. But you claim otherwise because...?"

"Because I know her."

"Of course." He inclines his head and crosses his arms over his chest. "And even though Luca and I assured you Robert is dead, you also think that's a lie due to a grainy, undistinguishable image?"

"Don't be an ass," I snarl. "Give her the benefit of the doubt."

"I need to get the facts straight. Here I was thinking I was dealing with a one-off situation where she truly believed Robert was alive. But this is just panic gone wild, isn't it?"

"*No.*" Penny balks. "It's not. That photo is Robert. I know it is."

"And Abi was murdered, despite the police having labeled it an open-and-shut case?"

"Cole, stop messing with her," Keira pleads. "Let it go."

"Unfortunately, I can't. Because now she's got me thinking." He pushes from the desk, slowly stalking toward her. "Do you know how many people were aware of her location? How many were trusted with the knowledge of her return?"

She keeps her shoulders rigid, not backing down. "I don't know."

"One," he growls. "I kept everything under wraps for this exact reason. Nobody was updated on where her parents lived. Nobody knew what town or suburb. Not even me. There was only one person who knew those whereabouts. Only one person who could be held responsible for what happened if what you're claiming is true."

Shit.

That one person is Benji.

"Back off." I move in front of Penny, blocking her from the man now livid from her accusations. "She's still mourning the loss. It's only natural to question what happened."

"What she's questioning is my family. *Your* brother."

"She didn't kill herself." Penny raises her voice. "I *know* she didn't."

Fuck.

I turn to face her. "You need to stop. This isn't the time or place, okay?"

"Then when?" she pleads. "When's the time and place for me to get answers? When can I be heard?" Mindlessness enters her tone and her eyes. "You don't even believe me. I can see it on your face."

She's losing her shit.

Derailing.

"Get out of here." I jerk my head toward the hall. "Go take a warm shower. Calm down. Breathe."

"I'm not leaving." She stands her ground. "Not until I have answers."

And those answers will only come from scrutinizing my brother. By throwing him under the fucking bus.

"Penny, I understand what you're going through, but you've gotta chill the fuck out." I lightly grab the crook of her arm and start for the door. "Come on, I'll run you a bath."

"No."

I tighten my grip as she attempts to break my hold.

"Please, Luca."

I ignore her pleas as I tug her across the room. I'm almost prepared to haul her over my shoulder when I reach the threshold to the sound of thunderous footfalls barreling down the hall.

Decker greets us on the other side of the doorway.

He takes one look at me, his sister, then my grip on her arm and turns livid. "Get your fucking hands off her."

He doesn't wait for my compliance. He launches. Fist first.

20

PENNY

Luca releases my arm, ducks, but doesn't miss the impact. My brother's fist pounds into the side of his face, the crack of flesh on flesh sickening.

He's knocked sideways, his head hitting the wall with a heavy thwack.

He falls to the tile at the same time the apple rolls from my numb hand. I'm too stunned to move. The office erupts. Hunter and Sarah barrel past me. Keira curses.

I don't know what to do.

Luca is on the floor, glaring at my brother, and I'm unsure whose side I should be on.

"What the absolute fuck, Decker?" Hunter shoves Sebastian down the hall, out of view.

"Why the hell did you do that?" Sarah yells.

I remain silent. Keira does the same behind me, her wordless judgment scratching at the back of my neck.

"This is just one of the many reasons people don't run their mouth around here." Cole's tone is glib. "Making false statements only leads to trouble."

I glance over my shoulder, meeting his soulless eyes.

"Opinions have no place here. Only facts." He returns to his desk chair, seeming unfazed by Luca on the floor or the snarled aggression coming from Sebastian. "It's in your best interest to remember that."

He doesn't scare me. He's nothing in comparison to his father. What concerns me is his connection to Luca. They're family. Just like Benji, who I'm beginning to believe is a far more sinister man.

I drag myself to the hall, ignoring the underlying threat as Hunter shoves my brother again, over and over, pushing him farther away.

"Are you okay?" Sarah holds out a hand to Luca, his cheek dark pink and swelling, blood dripping from his nose.

"Fucking perfect." He ignores her offering and shoves to his feet, using the wall as leverage.

He doesn't look at me. Doesn't even acknowledge my existence as he leans against the plaster to massage his temples.

"How much does it hurt?" I reach for him, not sure what else to do, my fingers grazing his shoulder. I've seen that look on his face before—when he had a concussion, and migraines for days.

"It's nothing." He scoffs. "That asshole can't punch for shit."

My remorse builds, morphing and expanding, as his expression tightens with obvious agony.

I want to help him. To fix what I caused. But I also can't bring myself to apologize for attempting to clear up the misconceptions surrounding Abi's death. They need to know.

Everyone needs to know.

She deserves the truth.

"That punch is only a taste of what I'm going to do to you," Sebastian yells. "You're a fucking piece of shit, Luca."

"Shut your trap." Hunt pushes him again. "The shit you just pulled was a low blow."

"The shit *he's* pulling with my sister is lower. I can't believe you all stood there and watched him manhandle her."

Hunter gives a harder shove, pushing my brother into the living room. The barrage of abuse doesn't end once they're out of view. Sebastian keeps yelling. Keeps threatening.

The only thing that changes is the awkwardness settling around me. I stand before Sarah, her judgmental gaze fixed on me as Luca works his jaw from side to side.

"Can I get you anything?" I ask. "Ice maybe?"

"I'll get some Advil." Sarah turns on her heel and strides after her fiancé.

The air around me thickens. The weight of obligation to my sisters wages war with my remorse. These people don't understand me.

They don't see things the way I do.

They'll never realize the intuition that comes from living around evil men and constant tragedy. Either that, or they simply don't care about Abi. They don't want to hear about her at all.

"You can stop staring at me. I'm fine." Luca pushes from the wall and staggers toward our bedroom.

I follow like a chastised puppy, walking a few steps behind until I pass the threshold where he stands in wait.

He closes the door behind us, the sound of the clasping lock a definitive, isolating click.

"Is that necessary?" I whisper.

"You didn't have to follow me in here." He continues to the bed, his feet dragging as he turns to sit on the mattress.

"I'm sorry he hit you."

"I don't give a shit about that," he mutters under his breath. "What I want to understand is why you're throwing my brother under the bus."

"That's not what I'm doing. I only wanted everyone to know Abi didn't kill herself. I want someone else to care; is that too much to ask?"

"What have I ever done to give you the impression I don't fucking care?" he asks. "I care, Penny. About you. About Abi. About Tobias and your whole fucking posse. But there's a way to have your voice heard and this isn't it."

The disappointment in his eyes is a staggering punishment. I hate it so much.

"I won't apologize for what I said, Luc. I have all the evidence I need."

His gaze narrows. "So you're telling me you think my brother is responsible? You think Benji played a part?"

My throat tightens. "I don't know."

"Are you serious?" He jerks back. "You're trying to pin Abi's death on my brother?"

"No, I'm pinning it on *Robert*. I didn't consider anything about your brother until Cole brought him up."

"And still you continued with the accusations. You realize speculation like this can get Benji killed, right? The mere possibility of betrayal could be enough for Torian to end his life."

I close my mouth. Swallow.

"Answer me." He keeps his voice low. "Explain what the hell is going on in that mind of yours."

"I don't know." I shake my head.

There's too much noise. Too many voices. Some of them tell me I'm right—Abi didn't kill herself. Robert is responsible. Others suffocate me, laying blame at my feet, telling me I'm wrong, wrong, wrong. "I can't explain how I feel. All I know is that I'm certain Robert killed her."

There's more. So much more, but I don't know how to tell him.

"You don't get it. If Robert killed her, it means Benji is involved. Or he fucked up." He shoves his hands into his hair. "You heard Torian. Nobody else knew where she was. Not one single person had any idea where those women were."

"It's not his fault if Robert followed them."

"From where? The airport? After they were hurried onto a private jet from Greece?" He shakes his head and winces with the movement. "You think Luther preempted his own death, arranged for a jet, and had Robert waiting here in Portland?"

"Maybe Abi called someone. She could've told anyone she was going home."

"Benji wouldn't have risked it. There's no way he would've let that information get out."

"Then I don't know." I throw my arms up at my sides. "Maybe someone found them. Maybe some random person suspected something when they went for food, or gas, or whatever. Maybe Luther had a database of all the women he stole."

I'm clutching at straws. Scrambling.

Luca grins, the tweak of lips unkind. "You think Luther had a database? You seriously think he documented his crimes for someone to find?"

"No," I admit. "He was too paranoid, but—"

"*You're* too paranoid," he counters. "You're losing your shit, Pen. You need to pull yourself together."

"And you're complacent and dismissive. There are things you don't know, Luca. Things I haven't told you."

His eyes narrow. "What things?"

I don't want to say. Not now. Not after his heartfelt admission earlier.

"Penny?" He shoves from the bed. "What things?"

I lick my lips to ease the painful dryness. "I don't want to cause more trouble between us." I need to keep this to myself. Even Tobias knew not to announce his suspicions until he whispered them in my ear.

"There's no trouble between us, shorty. That's not what this is."

"Then what is it?"

"A learning curve." He eats up the distance between us, the tight pull of his brows announcing the pain continuing to pummel him. "No matter what happens, I'm still protecting you with my life. Nothing changes that. There's not one damn thing you could tell me to cause trouble."

"I could test that theory." I could... but I don't want to.

"Let me prove myself to you."

I shake my head, unable to voice my deeper suspicions.

"Come on, Pen. You know you can trust me."

I stare at him. At the conviction. The plea for understanding.

The problem is, I believe him. I believe everything he says yet he can't give me the same in return. "I recognize his voice, Luc."

"Whose?" He scrutinizes me.

My heart thunders, each beat rampant. "Benji's." I swallow again, unable to get enough moisture as Luca frowns at me. "I heard him on the phone the day Abi died. At first, I thought he sounded familiar because his tone is a lot like yours. But that's not it. I didn't realize until Tobias said something that his voice was familiar because I'd heard him speaking to Luther."

"What did Tobias say?"

"That the voice of Layla's husband sounded like one of the men his baba spoke to all the time. That he hadn't met your brother yet, but was worried he was a bad man."

He stiffens, his shoulders snapping rigid. "What conversations did you hear? What was discussed?"

"I can't remember." I wrap my arms around my waist. "Tobias didn't say, either. And I admit, I didn't sense a bad vibe when I first heard him in Portland, but now things are getting messed up and I don't know what to think."

Incrementally, his tension lessens. The rigidity fades as he cups my cheeks. "Do you hear what you're saying? You have no basis for these accusations. Your head is filled with stress from trauma."

I pull away. "No. That's not it."

His arms fall to his sides. "*Yes*, it is. Of course they spoke on the phone. Luther was his father-in-law. They were family. Benji is the parent to that asshole's only granddaughter. It's only natural you and Toby recognize his voice."

My breathing falters. "I knew that."

I knew, yet it slipped my mind. I knew, and still it didn't make me back away from speculation.

"You're grasping at straws, shorty. And the worst part is that you don't realize the trouble rumors like this can cause."

"No." I'm not being irrational. This can't be paranoia. "I never heard Luther talking to Layla or Keira. Only Benji."

"Luther was a man's man. He had little time for the females in his family. Ask Torian's sisters and they'll tell you the same thing. Their father never cared to speak to them."

I continue to shake my head. "That might explain the voice recognition, but it doesn't change Abi's death."

Luca gives a sad smile. A placating, condescending curve of lips. "I get that you don't want to believe she killed herself, even despite what she went through. But accusing people without plausible reason will only cause more bloodshed. I need you to trust me. I need you to understand that just like you know your sisters, I know my brother better than I know myself. He wouldn't be involved in this. Not after what we lived through growing up. You have to start telling your-self Abi's death was an accident."

"No."

"Someone has to be wrong, Pen. It's either me, Abi's parents, the police, and the medics. Or you, on your own, without proof."

The approach of footsteps carries from the hall and Luca turns away, knitting his hands behind his head as a light tap sounds against the wood.

"I've got the Advil," Sarah says. "Want me to leave it at the door?"

"Yeah." Luca begins to pace. "Thanks."

There's the rattle of a pill bottle, retreating footsteps, then silence.

Pained, punishing silence.

I don't like us being on different wavelengths. I hate the emotional distance resembling a chasm between us.

"I know you think I'm crazy." I clear the restriction from my throat. "Believe me, I'm sure I'd think the same if we switched places. But I can't change the way I feel. It's an instinct I refuse to ignore."

He sucks in a breath, letting it out slowly. "Then I'll talk to him. I'll get the answers you need to put your mind to rest." His hands fall to his sides. "But in return, I need you to promise you won't blurt shit out in front of Torian again. Words aren't just words here. They're ammunition. Next time you've got something eating at you, I need you to tell me privately, okay? Nobody else."

"Okay." I grab his hand and entwine our fingers, yearning for the warm connection that comes when we touch. Even though he's annoyed with me, the strength I gain from his presence is unmistakable. He's like a shot of stability. "I'm sorry, Luc."

"Don't be." His thumb rubs in circles around my palm. "I just have to know these things. I can't fix what I don't know."

More footsteps trek down the hall.

Another knock sounds.

"Time's up, fuckers." Hunter's voice carries from the other side of the door. "Big brother is about to go postal if you two don't show your faces."

"We'll be out in a minute." Luca slowly tugs me forward, making me stumble into him. Within a bated breath his lips are on mine, the exquisite softness feeling like an apology.

"It's best if you don't come with me," he murmurs against my mouth. "Spend the time with Toby. Try to relax."

I attempt to retreat, hurt by the exclusion.

"Don't pull away from me." He tightens his grip on my hand. "Let me fight this battle for you."

"There's more than one."

"I can handle them." He growls, oh, so protective and dominant. It's hard not to believe him. "I know exactly what you want."

"I bet you don't." I tangle my hands in his shirt.

What I want is more of this. The clear-headedness that only comes when we're body to body. Chest to chest. Everything else fades when he's close. The guilt. The pain. The sorrow. He wouldn't have a clue of my desperation for more.

He chuckles. "Believe me. I know exactly what you want, and it's fucking hard to walk away."

He deepens the kiss, the vibrating rumble in his chest sinking into me.

I cling to him. His fingers. His shirt.

When we're like this the rest of the world doesn't matter.

There's no looming threat. No potential danger.

There's only me and him. Only protection and safety.

"We'll finish this another day." He diverts his mouth to my jaw. My neck.

I whimper as his lips brush the sensitive column of my throat. So soft. So sweet.

Then all too soon, he steps back.

That expression of pain still wrinkles his forehead. The swelling on his cheek has darkened.

I sweep my fingers along the damage and hold his gaze to gauge his reaction. "Does your head hurt as much as it did in Greece?"

"It's just a headache. I'll get over it."

"Would you tell me if it was more?"

He smirks. "Would you overreact and panic?"

Probably.

Definitely.

He scoffs out another chuckle. "I promise I'll tell you if there's something to worry about."

I nod, inching in to steal one last kiss. One last taste of clarity. I don't want to let him go. I need a few more strengthening seconds.

"It's okay, shorty. I'm not going far. You call and I'll come running."

"I'll call and you'll come stumbling."

"Either way, I'll still be there." He sweeps his mouth over mine. Once. Twice. "I'll find Robert and figure out what happened with Abi."

The reminder siphons my warmth. "And what if your brother—"

"Forget my brother." This time there's a warning in his tone. "Nothing is going to come between us. Not while I'm still breathing."

He makes for the door, each step of distance filling me with isolation. The loneliness only increases when he walks from view. There's the rattle of a pill bottle, muttered conversation in the distance, then the click of a closing door from another room.

I'm left an outsider, forced to follow on silent footsteps to stop outside the now closed office as the meeting continues without me.

I rest against the wall and listen to my brother bark threats at Luca. One argument follows the next, strategy seeming to come in second place to the aggression born from my existence.

Luca fights for me. For my sisters. He makes demands about their protection, offers to pay for their security, and finally convinces Cole to contact Benji after the meeting to obtain Nina and Lilly's whereabouts.

It doesn't seem enough though.

Nothing does.

I want them here. Yet, that will never happen.

They've only kept me around because of Sebastian. I have a plausible reason for being in Portland, while my sisters are loose threads to tie Cole to his father's crimes.

But I could prepare them. Warn them.

My pulse increases at the thought of reaching out. Then my confidence waivers.

I'd destroy any sense of happiness they had with the news. I'd steal their optimism for the future all because of an instinct. A hunch.

I slide to the floor, my legs bent before me, my elbows resting on my knees.

Do I have the right to ruin their freedom without proof? Because what if Luca is right? What if my thoughts are paranoia? If I'm losing my mind, I'll take Lilly and Nina down with me.

Padded footsteps from the living area break my focus. I glance to my side and see Layla approach.

"Hi," she whispers.

"Hi." Apprehension skitters along my arms. I know this lady least of all and yet she's been the one looking after Tobias. "Am I breaking the rules by being here?"

"Not at all. Have they said anything interesting?" She moves closer to the office, cocking her head.

"I'm not really listening…" I lie. "I just didn't want to stay in the bedroom and wasn't sure where else to go."

"That's okay." She smiles, kind and genuine. "If Cole was concerned about you snooping, I'd know about it. He also wouldn't hold a meeting in a place where you could overhear. So don't worry, because I'm not." She holds out a hand for me to shake. "I'm Layla, by the way. Stella's mom."

I glance at the offering, unsure if I can take her hand. We both know she's not just Stella's mom.

"Yes, I'm also Cole's sister and Luther's eldest daughter." Her arm falls to her side. "I'm sorry for everything you've been through."

I cringe and rest my head back against the wall, still unsure how to take apologies when they come from the blood of my tormentor. "You're also Benji's wife—am I right?"

She nods. "And Luca's sister-in-law. I wear many hats."

I drag my attention to the office door, wishing Luc was here with me. I could do with some of his strengthening stability. "I haven't met your husband yet. Is he anything like his brother?"

I'm fishing, hoping to catch a trail that leads to confirmation of my suspicions. One clue to wipe away my insanity would be enough.

"He's a good man. And an even better father." She leans against the plaster beside me, looming close. "I can't count how many times he's put his life on the line for me and my family."

I wince. This isn't the information I want.

"I miss him," she continues. "Even more now that the stakes are rising. But he always has to be in the thick of everything, trying to save the world."

"He sounds a lot like Luc." I lower my head, hiding my remorse. She's making me question myself even more.

"He is. But don't get me wrong—he has his days."

"What does that mean?" I shoot her a glance.

"He's great, but in the end he's still a man." She shrugs. "Sometimes he leaves the toilet seat up or doesn't listen to a word I say. Or he'll tell Stella she can have ice cream when I've already told her she can't. Nobody is perfect. What's important is that we're good together, which says a lot when we're usually in each other's pockets, at home and with the family business."

"The family business… I haven't been told what that involves exactly."

She falls quiet, the seconds stretching until she releases a sigh. "It's complicated. I want you to know it's nothing like what my father was doing, though, if that's what you're asking."

I feign indifference. "No, it wasn't. I was only curious. Luca hasn't said much about his brother. He hasn't heard from him either. I think he's worried."

"Nobody has heard much from Benji lately. Not even me. Apart from being in and out of phone range, he's needed space." She crosses the hall to look at me head-on. "He hasn't told me as much, but I think he holds himself responsible for what happened to you and the other women. He feels guilty for not figuring out what my father was up to. I do, too."

I wince with renewed remorse. Her husband sounds honorable, despite how relative that term can be in this world. If only I could quit questioning Abi's death. "I'm sure it's a heavy burden to bear."

"Sorry." She cringes. "I don't mean to be insensitive if that's how it came across."

"Not at all." I offer a half-hearted smile. "I appreciate you trying to make conversation."

"I've been trying to figure out how to approach you for hours." She lets out a whisper of a chuckle. "This situation isn't easy."

I nod, no longer capable of words. Every kindness she utters makes me question my theory about Abi's suicide. I don't want to lose faith in my sister. I refuse. The Torian family are still my enemy.

"Why don't you come cook with me and the kids?" Layla waves for me to get up. "I've been left in charge of making lunch, and it may not be edible if I don't get an extra set of hands to keep Stella and Tobias under control. I still have no idea when the nanny will show up."

My heart stutters. Not only at the kind offer, but the carefree image of Toby she inspires. I want to see that side of him again. I yearn to be involved. "You wouldn't mind?"

"Not at all. It will give me an opportunity to get to know you."

Yes. And it will give me the ability to shed my weakness and dig deeper on her husband.

21

LUCA

I'm relegated to a private room at the back of the house with my MacBook, given a burner phone, and told to substantiate Penny's claims.

It's my job to prove Robert is alive.

I'm also left to establish whether Abi's death was murder or suicide, and I don't know which conclusion is preferred when I can't get hold of my fucking brother.

Penny has gotten into my head. Those instinctive feelings of hers are wearing me down. She's making me question everything—Robert's execution, the protection I've provided, and worst of all, Benji.

I haven't doubted him before.

His sanity, maybe. His loyalty? Never.

I can't quit scrutinizing Robert's actions as I scour hours of video surveillance. I fast forward and rewind unending vision from the gas station, trying to get a better view of the man who stole the money. Or his fucking car. I watch different angles of the same timespan over and over, attempting to catch a glimpse of familiarity until my headache builds into a migraine. And still, all I think about is my brother.

Something isn't right. Benji isn't usually distant. He keeps me updated to the point of annoyance. Yet today, alone, he's already left ten of my calls unanswered and hasn't responded to a single text.

He's gotta be in trouble. *Big* trouble. And I'm having a fucking painful time digesting the possibilities.

It isn't until mid-afternoon that I'm disturbed from the isolated hell of my thoughts by a light rap on the door. But the prospect of company isn't welcomed.

For the first time in weeks, I'm not excited at the possibility of seeing Penny. Not when I don't have answers.

"Come in." I remain on the spare bed, my back against the headboard, the Mac on my thighs.

There's a rattle of cutlery, then the door creeps open.

It's not Penny who stands on the other side. It's Tobias, his tiny frame leaning over to lift a wooden tray of food off the floor, his shoulders taut as he marches inside.

"Do you need help, little man?" I slide my Mac to the mattress.

"No. I can do this." He keeps his gaze firmly affixed to the rattling glass of juice and the plate of sandwiches, his footsteps cautious until he reaches the bed to dump it at my feet. "It's a late lunch."

"I can see that." I smirk. "Thanks. Did you make it yourself?"

"I helped." He steps back, crossing his kiddie arms over his tiny chest. "Layla did most of it."

"Well, thank her for me, okay?"

He keeps his gaze downcast. "Yeah… okay."

This isn't the running, giggling kid from this morning. The boy standing in front of me is defensive, with his shoulders pulled back and his brows pinched.

"Is everything all right, Toby?"

His gaze snaps to mine, his eyes set in an exaggerated glare. "Everything's fine."

"You sure? You seem agitated."

He huffs. "I'm just fine."

I raise my brows and incline my head. "Okay. How about the others? Are they all fine, too?"

His lip curls.

This kid, who's apparently fine, looks like a fight dog about to attack.

"They're fine, too," he grates.

Yeah. Right.

"How 'bout you?" He glares at the swollen side of my face, despising my injury. "Are you *fine*?"

"I got sucker punched."

He puffs out his chest, as if pleased. "I know."

"Decker and I got into a bit of an argument."

"I know that, too."

"You saw?"

"No, I *heard*. Decker punched you because you were hurting Penny."

I push from the bed and the kid scampers backward, his arms falling to his sides, his aggressive expression transforming to fear.

I raise my hands in peace. "Calm down, little guy. I would never hurt you. Or her."

"You already did. That's why Decker hit you." He stands taller, his face filled with defiance as fear enters his eyes. "You're just like my father."

"*No*. I'm not. I'm nothing like that piece of shit."

"You lie," he snarls. "You brought her somewhere she doesn't want to be to make her do things she doesn't want to do. Just like him."

I jerk back, blindsided. Is that what he thinks happened? Is that his justification for us being here? "That's not what this is, Toby. This isn't like Greece."

"It's *exactly* like Greece. She's scared and you hurt her. She doesn't want to be here and you're forcing her."

"It's not like that." I keep my hands raised. "I'm trying to protect her. She's here so we can keep her safe."

"Safe from what? I thought we were here for family time."

Fuck. He's got me there.

"Luca?" He tilts his chin as if victorious. "They told me we were here so I could get to know everyone." His words drip with saccharin sarcasm.

He knows.

He probably always knew.

I shouldn't have expected anything less from the son of a sex trafficker.

I sit back on the bed and exhale a heavy breath. "What do you want to know, little man?"

He stares at me, his head still high. He takes his time, giving himself long moments to ponder whatever is going on in that brain of his before he asks, "Why did you hurt her?"

I guess I should be thankful that through all this—after the death of his father and being dragged from his home—his top priority is Penny.

"She was getting in trouble with Torian. I needed to get her out of his office before he snapped."

"Cole wouldn't hurt her."

"You're right; he wouldn't," I lie. "But he was angry, and sometimes when people are angry they say mean things they can't take back. All I wanted to do was get her out of there. So I grabbed her arm to lead her from the room. And yes, I know I shouldn't have touched her, but I thought I was doing the right thing."

He frowns. "You grabbed her arm?"

"Yeah."

The frown deepens. "Then Decker hit you?"

I nod, the movement throwing lighter fluid on the smoldering flames of my headache. "He doesn't like me very much right now."

"Because you grabbed her arm?"

"That, and other things. Mainly because he's worried about Penny, and I'm the perfect outlet for his concern."

He falls quiet again, his gaze fixed on me for long moments. "Why are we really here? In this house?"

It's my turn to take a mental breather. Kids aren't my thing. "Why do you think we're here?" I act like a fucking shrink, buying myself time.

"I know it's because something is wrong. Stella said she never stays at her uncle's house unless bad things are happening."

Great. Two snooping kids. Just what I need.

"That's something you should ask Cole. I've given out my quota of information."

"No. Please." His annoyance vanishes, a pity party taking its place. Big blue eyes blink up at me, begging. "Is it about Robert?"

I fight not to flinch at his direct hit. Where the hell is this kid getting information from? He's a miniature fucking spy master. "Why would you ask about him? What do you know?"

He doesn't answer—just keeps blinking those puppy-dog eyes.

"Tobias? What the hell do you know?"

He shakes his head. "Nothing. I just heard..."

"You seem to hear a lot."

He straightens. "Baba taught me how to listen."

"He taught you how to snoop," I correct, and he nods. "Tell me what you heard."

"It's nothing, I swear. His name has been mentioned a few times. That's all. I guessed he's the reason we're here... I'm right, aren't I?"

I contemplate my options. This kid could be useful. He could also be a huge pain in the ass if he rats on me. "I don't know." The paper copy of the bank surveillance image burns a hole in my pocket. If anyone could confirm the man in the photo is Robert, it's Toby, but I don't want to get my brains blown out for involving a minor.

"Yeah, you do," he snaps. "You know. You just don't want to tell me."

"Because you don't need to worry about things like this. We're taking care of it."

"*Tell me.*" He turns savage. Fisted hands. Red face. A true fucking Torian. "Is Robert here? Has he come back for her?"

I attempt to ignore the icy chill shuddering through me, but it hits hard. The assumption that Robert would be back for Penny... The instinctive response...

"We don't know." I retrieve the paper from my pocket and unfold the image for him to see. "Do you know who this is?"

Recognition sparks in his eyes.

"Who is it, Tobias?"

"It's him." He stares, transfixed or maybe frightened. "It's Robert. He grows his beard like that sometimes." He points to the blurred mouth of the man in the photo. "See the patch of missing hair right below his lip? It's from a scar. It always made him look stupid."

I don't know whether to be relieved or livid at the confirmation that the fucker is here. On one hand, I'll have the opportunity to kill him like he deserves. On the other, the news will only spike Penny's fear.

"Thanks. I appreciate the help." I refold the paper and shove it back into my pocket. "Can you do me a favor and keep this between me and you for now? I don't want Pen getting upset."

"She doesn't know?"

"I don't think she's one hundred percent certain, which is allowing her to sleep at night. If she knows for sure—"

"She'll be scared," he cuts me off. "He did horrible things to her. He hurt—"

"I know." I clench my teeth against the knowledge. "And I want to save her from the fear for as long as possible. That's why I asked."

He pauses a long while as he swallows. "Will you find him?"

"Yes." I fucking vow it.

"Will you hurt him?"

This time I'm not as quick to reply. Like Luther, Robert meant something to this boy. He was raised to look up to his father's right-hand man.

"Luca, will you hurt him?"

"Yes." I keep my teeth clenched. "I'll fucking hurt him. Because of what he did to Penny and all the other women. I'll kill him for what he's done."

Heartbeats of silence follow where I question giving him more details. He doesn't move. Doesn't speak. I bet he's one breath away from squealing like a pig when he gives a succinct nod.

"I won't tell… if you don't tell on me."

I frown. "What would I tell on you for?"

His attention turns to the tray of food. "I don't think lunch is very nice today."

I follow his gaze, narrowing my attention to the tiny pieces of fluff and hair sticking out from the side of one of the sandwiches.

He backtracks. "Maybe you shouldn't eat it." He shrugs and continues his retreat to the door. "And I don't think the orange juice is any good either."

I hold in a laugh and lean forward, looking into the glass to find tiny white bubbles in the sea of orange.

The little shit corrupted my lunch and spat in my OJ. "I guess I'll hold out for dinner."

He nods and turns for the door.

"Hold up, Toby. I'm not finished with you yet."

He freezes, like a criminal caught in the act.

"Penny mentioned you recognized Benji's voice." I lean back against the bedhead. Calm. Casual. "Have you been able to remember any conversations you might have overheard?"

He glances over his shoulder at me, fear clear in his eyes. "She told you?"

"She trusts me, and you can, too. I want to make sure you both feel safe here."

He swivels slowly, returning to face me. "But he's your brother."

"He is." I incline my head. "Does that worry you?"

"Baba always said a man should never turn his back on family."

Luther may have said it. Didn't mean that fucker lived by it. He continuously threw his children under the bus. "I agree with the sentiment, but that doesn't mean family don't get punished for doing the wrong thing. If you think Benji is involved in something he shouldn't be, I need to know, okay? And I need you to tell me first so I can protect everyone. You and Penny most of all."

His eyes narrow, almost imperceptibly.

Fuck. I pushed too far.

He shakes his head. "I don't remember anything."

And I don't believe him. Not when his discomfort is increasing.

"That's okay." I give a half-hearted smile. "I just want you to know I'll protect you no matter what happens. I've got your back."

He nods, but there's no belief. He's entirely untrusting.

"Okay, kiddo. You can go play. If you find Penny can you tell her I'd like to see her?"

"She's not allowed. Torian said she has to leave you to work in peace."

"Right." Now Tobias' visit makes more sense. "That sounds like something he would say. Can you give her a message for me instead?"

He nods.

"Tell her I miss her, and that I'm working as fast as I can to get back to her."

It's sappy as fuck, but it's for the kid's benefit. I'll earn his trust through Penny, no matter the cost.

He smiles, nods again, and dashes for the hall, leaving the door open to allow the mumble of distant chatter to enter the room.

I wait a while, attempting to decipher the garbled conversation as I picture Penny out there, surrounded by people she doubts. Her discomfort encourages me to get back on the phone in search of answers. My paranoia over Benji keeps me working for hours without so much as a snack break.

I reach out to people who know people, who know more people. I try to get my hands on Abi's preliminary coroner's report, along with more surveillance images from the businesses surrounding the gas station.

I dial my brother's number over and over again, leaving innumerable messages, sending additional texts.

The more he ignores me, the more my gut protests.

I'm almost convinced he's fucked up again. That he's dragging me into a mess bigger than ever before.

I thought he'd settled down after becoming a husband. A father. He made me believe this new life with a crime-riddled family had been the right decision. That these circumstances weren't the best, but at least *he* was.

I've seen it with my own eyes. I've noticed the positive change.

He rarely drinks anymore. He has a purpose.

Problem is, all the positive changes don't mean dick if he's stuck in old habits.

If anything, Benji's good fortune could be more reason for him to fuck up. He doesn't know how to be happy. It's a foreign concept. Self-sabotage may be the only routine he knows.

I fucking stew on those thoughts as I work. All I get in return for my hard hours are a few snapshots of a green sedan I think Robert was in. No plates. No make or model. And then there's the vague promise that the coroner's report might come through if my contact at the hospital can pull a few strings.

I don't drag my ass from the bedroom until after sundown when my stomach can't take the lack of food any longer.

Penny's the first to see me walk into the living area. She pushes up from the sofa, relief brightening her expression as she walks up to me, her hand reaching for mine. "Any luck?"

There's a wealth of hope in her eyes. So much fucking dependence, too.

I've let her down. All I have is confirmation of Robert's existence from a kid she'd resent me for involving. "I'm still working on it. Has anyone heard news on Benji? I thought he'd be back by now."

"No." She sinks into my chest, her face nuzzling my neck as if she was born to mold against me. "Nobody has told me anything."

At least Tobias didn't spill his guts. That's a bonus.

"Luca," she whispers against my throat, "What happens if I recognize him?"

I fight against the need to tense. "Recognize him from where?"

"Greece. Or from here."

Icy dread slithers through me. She means from being a rapist. From being part of the sex-trafficking operation.

"What if he was one of the men who helped lure me away?" she asks.

My brain regains its agonizing throb. The *thump, thump, thump* of my pulse is incessant against my temples. "Is that what you've been thinking about all day?"

"Not all day." She pulls back to meet my gaze. "It's just that Layla spoke highly of him. As a father and a husband. But I can't stop questioning him. I keep thinking—what if? And then it gets worse because I start thinking I'm going to lose you, too."

"I'm not going anywhere. I love my brother, Pen. I'd do anything for him. But if he's capable of doing the things you're talking about then he's not the brother I know. He's not my blood at all."

Hollowness gnaws at me. Not because I'm lying. Because it's the God's honest truth.

I'd disown him for that betrayal.

Fucking kill him.

The other guys return to the house for dinner soon after. The mass of people scatter around the living room, some at the dining table, the kids on stools at the kitchen counter, while a young female nanny keeps watch. Hunt and Sarah are on the sofa. Penny remains by my side while Decker glares at me from his standing position in front of the sink.

That fucker wants to hit me again. Or worse. *Definitely* worse.

"Has anyone heard from Benji?" I shove a wedge of pizza in my mouth and pretend I'm not fully invested in the answer.

"Not today." Layla sips from a wine glass. "He probably didn't charge his cell again."

"He's got sketchy reception," Torian offers around a mouth full of food. "I'm sure he'll be here soon."

The two hours that pass prove him wrong.

I help clean up after dinner and watch the nanny wrangle the kids to bathe, then later, put them to bed. The whole time my patience keeps levelling up. I'm left to dig through surveillance recordings on the sofa while Hunt and Decker head out to talk to more people, and Torian retires to his office. Penny doesn't leave my side, the twitch of her fingers becoming more fidgety as she pretends to watch whatever movie plays on the big-screen TV.

"Why don't you have a shower and get some rest?" I take a break from staring at the computer screen and run my hand through her hair. "I'll wake you when he gets here."

"I wouldn't be able to sleep anyway."

She still thinks a monster is going to walk through the door in the form of my brother. The more time that passes makes me believe it, too.

One by one, Sarah, Layla, and Keira retire to bed, leaving the two of us alone in the silent house.

I keep failing to get in contact with Benji and start praying he was in a minor car accident, for his sake, because unless he's physically incapable of dialing my number, I'll break his face for not returning my calls.

It's past eleven when Torian walks back into the living room, his cell in his hand, his hair mussed as if he's dragged his hands through it a million times. "He's here." He jerks his chin toward the front of the house. "I just let him through the gate."

Penny straightens from her leaned position against my shoulder, her eyes blinking away exhaustion.

"About fucking time." I close my Mac and place it beside me on the sofa. "Where was he driving from, Mexico?"

"Ask him yourself. I already told you I don't know where he's been." Torian continues to stare at his phone as he stalks away. "But give him my regards. Some business has come up that I'm going to have to deal with. I'll be in my office if anyone needs me."

Penny pushes to her feet in a flourish, her tired face turning pale.

"It's going to be okay." I reach for her, pulling her between my legs. "You trust me, right?"

She doesn't respond. Doesn't even act as if I've spoken.

"Penny?" I shove from the sofa to stand against her, dragging my hand over her hip. "You trust me." This time it's a statement. She *does* trust me. We both know it. I just need her to remember. "Whatever happens, I'll take care of you."

Her breathing labors. Her fingers fidget at her sides. When the front door opens and footsteps approach, she turns rigid under my touch.

"Breathe," I whisper. "Just breathe."

She nods, her attention on the entry to the hall behind me.

I don't turn to watch my brother walk in. I keep my eagle eyes on her. Scrutinizing. If she knows him, I want to see it for myself. I need to catch the first sign of panic so I can react accordingly.

"Hey, Luc," Benji greets. "Long time no see."

Her stiffness doesn't dissipate. She doesn't flinch as he approaches, neither confirming nor denying her fears.

She gives me nothing to go on. No hints. No leads.

Fuck.

"Hey yourself, big brother." I give her a reassuring smile and turn to the man who's a little shorter and leaner than me, despite his older age. "I've been calling."

"No shit." He continues toward me, dumping his suitcase at my feet before grabbing me in a bear hug. "I thought you'd get the hint I wasn't in the mood to talk."

"And I thought you'd get the hint it was important. You should've answered."

"Well, I'm here now." He retreats, his attention shifting to Penny as his arms fall to his sides. "You must be the woman I've heard so much about. You're Decker's sister, right?"

"Penny." I reach for her, dragging her into my side to place a protective arm around her waist. There's still no change in her expression. No clues. "Shorty, this is my brother, Benji."

She doesn't move. Doesn't speak. The only change in her appearance is the slight raise to her chin.

I can't tell what she's thinking. Not when she's back in warrior mode. Everything is tightly bottled, her thoughts barricaded from view.

"The others told me about you," Benji continues. "You sound like quite a woman."

"Your wife told me all about you, too." Penny clears her throat, adding strength to her tone. "But I already recognized your voice."

The hairs on the back of my neck raise. Every nerve is on edge.

"I've heard you before." Her tone is level, no hint of emotion. "Many times."

Benji's brows tighten as he shoots me a look. "What's she talkin' about?"

Now *that's* an expression I can work with. He's defensive.

"She overheard conversations between you and Luther while she was in Greece." I rub my thumb along her side in a vain offer of support. "Turns out you spoke to your father-in-law more often than most."

He nods. "Yeah. He was always dialing my number. What did you overhear?"

She stands taller, taking a few seconds before she says, "I don't remember specifics. Not yet, anyway."

"Lucky you." Benji huffs out a laugh. "I remember vividly. How does that saying go? You can pick your wife, but you can't choose your in-laws."

"Yeah, it's something like that." I slide my hand from Penny's waist and grab her hand instead. I need a sign to point me in the right direction when it comes to her emotions. I've got no fucking idea if I should be relaxing or preparing for war.

"Did you ever travel to Greece?" she asks.

"No." He scoffs. "*Fuck* no. I was smart enough to keep my distance. Luther only used me to keep tabs on his daughters. Apart from that, he kept contact to a minimum."

"But you two spoke a lot," she counters. "I remember—"

"You remember what?" Benji's tone thickens with warning. "Is this an inter-rogation? Because if it is, I'm too fucking tired to deal right now." He grabs his suitcase handle, the veins at his temples pulsing.

"It's not an interrogation." I raise a hand in placation. "Let's just chill and bench this conversation until tomorrow."

"Fuck tomorrow and fuck this conversation." He glares at me. "I don't need to put up with this shit."

"I didn't mean to sound accusatory." Penny backtracks, moving out of reach. "I just…"

There's a pause of awkward-as-fuck silence while Benji holds my gaze, his eyes remaining narrowed for long seconds before he huffs out a breath.

"Forget it. Times are tough," he mutters. "We're all dealing with shit we don't need. And by the look of the swelling on Luca's face, he's handling more than most." His shoulders loosen slightly while he clings to the suitcase. "Did you get in a fight?"

"Decker took a cheap shot."

He huffs a laugh. "What about my girls? How are they? It feels like forever since I've seen them."

"Both are good. They went to bed a while ago." I hike a thumb to the far hall. "They're down that way somewhere. I don't know which room."

"Speaking of bed…" Penny gives a fake smile. "I'll leave you two to talk in private."

"You don't need to go." I grab her wrist before she can walk away and she gasps on impact. "Are you okay?"

She chuckles. Again, it's fake. "I'm fine. You surprised me, that's all."

"You sure?" I lean in to whisper in her ear, "You're not thinking of running, are you?"

"No. I learned my lesson last time."

I keep watching her, looking for a tell as I release her wrist. "I'll follow you soon."

She inclines her head and places a kiss on my cheek. "Good night."

"Night." I keep quiet as she pads to the hall, all the while wishing I was alongside her. I want to know what she's thinking. What she's feeling. Specifically about my brother.

"So, tell me why you didn't return my calls, Benj." It's time to drop the shit. Like he said, we're both too tired for this. "You've been ghosting me for weeks."

"I've been ghosting everyone for weeks. If you're not aware, I've been stuck looking after crazy-ass women, twenty-four-seven. You've got no idea how fucked up they are. Lucid one minute. Psychotic the next. It was PMS on acid. I'm surprised only one of them took the easy way out."

"Don't joke about that," I grate. "Don't *ever* joke about Abi in front of me again."

He laughs off my aggression. "Chill, Luc. I'm just saying they're messed up. That's all."

"You also told me they were doing good."

"Jesus Christ, that was a relative term. What's gotten into you? And not that I should have to mention it, but *you* judging *me* for the way I handle those women is fucking rich when you've got your hands all over one of the damaged."

One of the damaged?

I step back, because if I don't, I'll launch right through him, my headache be damned. "Did you really just say that?" I clench my fists, tighter and tighter, trying to squeeze away the need to strike.

"Are you kidding?" He focuses on my hands and scoffs. "You're going to hit me?"

I want to. What I wouldn't give to lay him flat for running his mouth. "Tell me why you were dodging my calls," I snarl. "Tell me what the fuck is going on with you."

He steps closer, getting in my face. "I already did. I had a lot of shit going on. Excuse me for not wanting my judgmental brother breathing down my neck after that woman decided to slash her wrists on my watch."

"Bullshit." He's lying. I don't know why. But that feeling Penny was talking about has taken over my gut. It's in my fucking head, poking, poking, poking me to dig deeper.

"Don't look at me that way," he seethes. "I bet you haven't spared a thought as to what I'm going through. Have you wondered what it's like knowing your innocent daughter has spent hours alone with a rapist? A fucking pedophile? Do you have any idea what it's like to try to console a wife whose father is a monster? To have to contemplate telling your daughter why all the photos of her grandfather are being removed from the house? Have you got any idea, Luc?"

No, I don't.

But cluelessness doesn't stop my anger toward his newfound attitude.

"You're only proving my point." I release my fists and spread my fingers, forcing myself out of the aggressive stance. "You always lay your problems on the line with me. Why have I been kept in the dark?"

"Maybe I quit wanting you to fight my battles. It's about time I grew up."

"You grew up earlier than any kid I know. You had to. We both did."

"Don't start that shit. Not everything is about our childhood."

"Isn't it?" I lean against the side of the sofa, feigning calm despite my throbbing pulse. "That's why we're here, isn't it? Why you chose to drag us down this path instead of a normal life."

He scoffs out a hate-filled laugh. "I never asked you to follow, Luc. It was your decision to be here." He retreats, dragging his suitcase toward the far hall. "Thanks for the warm welcome, though. It's always good to know you've got my back."

22

LUCA

I don't bother going to bed. There's no point.

I'm too invested in trying to work out Benji's role in all this.

I sit on the sofa armrest and stare at my reflection in the wall of glass leading outside. I go over everything, from the moment I thought Robert died till now. I try to figure out what Benji could be involved in, and when I don't come up with anything easily digestible I go in search of Torian's liquor cupboard and help myself to a bottle of scotch.

The alcohol goes down too easily. One mouthful after another, the burn helping to smother the panic as time ticks by.

"You're still awake?" Torian strides into the room, his suit jacket discarded, his tie loosened. "It's late."

"Yeah." I take a gulp of liquor and close my eyes with the swallow. The buzz has already hit me. My head swims in the small amount of alcohol.

He grabs a glass from the kitchen and continues toward me. "Do you plan on sharing?"

I pour him a generous finger and return my attention to my reflection, not wanting a distraction from my thoughts.

"Did you come up with any new information tonight?" he asks. "Any images? Leads? Answers?"

I clench my teeth, hating the reminder. "No. I've only got the few blurred side images of the suspected car."

"But you still believe Penny is right about Robert?"

"Yes. Now more than ever."

He studies me. "Why?"

Because your tiny half-brother backed her up.

"Call it intuition." I keep staring at my reflection, keep wishing for a better outlook to appear. I can't *not* believe her. I won't let my faith in her be anything other than one hundred percent.

"Well, you made the right decision," he mutters.

My gaze snaps to his, my brain taking a few seconds to catch up. "Meaning?"

"Meaning, there's been another incident."

I push from the armrest, the liquor sloshing in my glass. "What kind of incident?"

"With one of the rescued women. There was a break and enter. Masked men. Ski masks. Guns. They took nothing but shot the place up pretty good."

I keep my responses to myself. The guilt. The intense anger.

Penny predicted this. She fucking knew it.

"Didn't you have men on her? You said you were going to arrange security."

"I said I would get in contact with Benji to get their location. But he didn't answer my calls."

Fucking Benji.

"Nobody died," he continues. "Not yet, anyway. But time will tell. Apparently, the woman took a few bullets and lost a lot of blood. She's currently in ICU."

"*Jesus fucking Christ.*" I throw back the remainder of the scotch and pace.

I can't ask the questions hammering into me. I can't speculate. Because if Torian is anything like me, he'll turn the spotlight of blame firmly on my brother.

"Robert must have worked over one of my assets," he says around a gulp of liquor. "Maybe someone at the airport put a tracker on Ben's car. Or accessed bank records to get location receipts."

It's a long shot. Too fucking long for Torian to be aiming at.

"You think so?" I plant my feet and scrub a hand over my mouth, my neck.

"No." He narrows his eyes on me, waiting, tormenting. "I don't know how he's finding them." He shrugs, losing the hint of suspicion. "But the resources of my father and his men no longer surprise me. The one thing I *do* know is that we need to shut this down, and quick."

I keep rubbing my neck, attempting to relieve the tension building at the base of my skull. "What about those women? When are you going to start protecting them?"

"It's done. Benji gave me the details when he called for me to open the gate. Men are on their way now."

On their way to where?

I want to know those details. I need to find out if Benji took so long to get here because he was one of the shooters. "You don't want me to go for a drive and bring them back to Portland?"

"No. I don't want them any closer than they already are. I need to remain distanced from my father's mistakes. For now, they're safe." He places his empty glass on the coffee table. "You should get some rest. Tomorrow is going to be a big day."

I nod, not turning from my tormented reflection in the glass as he walks from the room.

My headache returns full force. My stomach wants to revolt.

I need answers, goddamnit.

I have to know if Benji is involved. If he has anything to do with Abi's death or this afternoon's shooting.

I have to fucking know.

The longer I stand here without a clue, without fucking grounding, the more I picture my brother doing stupid, unforgivable shit.

"Jesus fucking Christ." I snarl. "*Jesus. Fucking. Christ.*"

I cock my fist, needing to punch something. Anything.

I need answers. Not in the morning. Not when Benji's ready.

Fucking now.

I slam my glass down on the coffee table and stalk for the far hall. I open door after door, finding Tobias sleeping, then spare room after spare room before hitting the jackpot.

I don't have to see my brother through the darkness to know he's here. The familiar stuttered snore says it all and Layla's quiet breaths are an unwelcomed accompaniment, as I pad forward to stop beside the bed.

He's barely visible. There's only the red glow from the bedside clock to give the faint perception of where he is. But it's him. I know this man almost better than I know myself. At least, I thought I did.

The pound of my chest increases as I watch him sleep. He's saved my life a million times. He's all I've ever had. And now he could be everything that brings me undone.

He's unsettled while he rests.

Twitchy.

Something's playing on his mind, and I'm certain it could get us both killed.

He grunts. Groans. Snores some more. The restlessness adds fuel to my paranoia, ratchets my pulse, and feeds the pain in my temples.

All my adult life I've attempted to make up for needing his protection as a child. I've tried to repay him for the beatings he took on my behalf. I gave up income and a career and grounding.

But if he's helping Robert... If he's assisting in the murder of innocent women...

I pull the gun from the back of my jeans, my hand trembling as I guide the barrel to rest against the side of his throat.

He's guilty. Of what I'm not sure. But he's guilty of something.

I press the barrel harder, digging it into his neck.

His breathing shudders.

Chokes.

He stiffens. His eyes open.

"It's me," I growl, keeping my voice low. "It's time to start talking."

"Jesus," he hisses. "Are you insane? You'll wake—"

"If your snoring didn't wake her, this won't either. So, start talking, otherwise Torian is going to get involved, and I have the distinct impression you're not going to want that to happen."

He falls quiet, confirming my suspicions, fucking nailing them to the wall.

"Did you kill her?" I squeeze the gun in my sweating palm. "Did you kill Abi?"

"No," he snarls.

It's fucking bullshit.

"What about the woman attacked today? Were you involved?"

"What woman? What fucking attack?"

I scoff a breathy laugh. "Don't play dumb. I swear to God, it's only out of loyalty and your marriage to his sister that Torian isn't all over your ass right now. He'll see through the blinders soon enough."

"Get that fucking gun away from me, Luca."

I dig the barrel harder. "*Then fucking talk.*"

There's a rustle of bedsheets. A squeak of mattress springs. A murmured, "Daddy?"

My stomach dives.

Stella is in here. In the bed. Near the pointed gun of a man influenced by alcohol.

"It's okay, baby," Benji whispers. "Go back to sleep."

I lower to my knees, sinking into the darkness as my gun remains in place.

For long moments, there's no movement. No noise. Then the slightest whimper of sleep breaches the air, the sound feminine and young.

"Get out of here," he seethes. "We'll talk in the morning."

"No. We do this now."

"Jesus, Luc." There's a tremble in his voice. "I didn't hurt those women."

I don't believe him. I fucking don't.

God knows I want to. I'd give anything to build a life here with Penny. To settle down and find some sort of normal. But every time I gain footing, he pulls the rug out from beneath me. "You've got two seconds to start—"

"I'm cheating on her," he whispers.

I snap rigid, mindlessly blinking for long moments. I don't understand. What he confessed doesn't make sense. "What did you say?"

"I'm cheating on Layla. There's another woman. *That's* what I've been keeping from you. *That's* why I've been distant."

No.

He wouldn't be that stupid.

He *couldn't.*

Cheating on Torian's sister is a death sentence. He knows that. Hell, everyone in a hundred-mile radius is well aware without anyone needing to write the fucking memo.

"I didn't plan for it to happen," he continues. "It was meant to be a one-time thing. I was a wreck with this goddamn Luther mess. I just needed an outlet."

I fall on my ass, the news hitting hard.

If this gets out Stella will lose her father. Layla will bury a husband. I'll have no family left.

I shake my head and lower the gun, unable to hold it steady. "Who? Where? How long?" I can't stop the questions.

"It doesn't matter. It won't change anything."

I hang my head, my legs bent before me, the darkness consuming everything. Inside and out. "If Torian finds out—"

"I know."

"If anyone finds—"

"*I know*," he grates. "And I'll fix it. I just need you to buy me some time."

"Me? How could you be so fucking stupid?"

He doesn't answer. He doesn't have to.

If the past is any indication, he's already consumed with guilt. He always is. But it never stops him causing more destruction. The remorse doesn't starve his need to self-sabotage.

I push to my feet and shove my gun into the back of my waistband before I'm tempted to do something I'll regret. "I swear to God, Benji. Find a way to keep this quiet or I'll kill you myself."

23

PENNY

I STARE AT THE DARKENED CEILING, UNABLE TO SLEEP.

I don't know where Luca is or how long he'll be gone. The only thing I'm certain of is the discomfort of not having him near.

I'm nothing without him. All my happiness and comfort is woven with each of his breaths. And when he's close, I'm okay with that dependence.

It's far better than keeping the company of hopelessness.

I try to picture what a future between us would look like. I shut my eyes, imagining normalcy and routine. What I wouldn't give for those things.

It isn't until sleep brushes me with gentle strokes that the bedroom door squeaks. Open, then closed. I tense, instinctively assuming a threat draws near. But my frantic heartbeat quickly fades at the measured footsteps making their way to the bathroom, the door clicking shut before the light flicks on to cast a slight glow over the room.

My stomach warms as the shower starts. The thought of Luca relaxed beneath the water makes me smile.

I slide from bed, needing to be closer to him, my oversized T-shirt billowing at my thighs as I pad to the bathroom. I shouldn't disturb his privacy. He'd never do the same with mine. But I can't help testing the door handle, and when I find it unlocked, I have no restraint to remain distanced.

I blink rapidly against the bright light and enter the room to lean against the vanity.

His head is bowed under the shower spray, his hair shrouding his eyes as his arms stretch to the wall before him as if it takes all his strength to hold himself upright.

He's not the picture of relaxation I envisaged. He seems defeated. Exhausted.

I don't think he even knows I'm here as he remains immobile, the rivulets of water coursing over the rugged lines of his shoulders and the angry scars along his back.

He's gorgeous.

Physically. Mentally. Probably spiritually, too, if I'd taken the time to learn more about him instead of being stuck in my own head.

I never could've imagined looking at a male's naked body without feeling anything but fear. Yet that icy chill doesn't brush my senses. Instead, warmth increases, and it's not from the steam filling the small space around us.

"What are you doing in here, shorty?" He keeps his hands on the tile, his head dropping lower.

"I couldn't sleep." I don't let my gaze dip below waist-height, not willing to face that challenge just yet. "I wanted to see you."

His tension doesn't lessen as he shuts off the taps and opens the shower door, the faintest wrinkle settled between his brows. He grabs a towel from the rail and gently scrubs the water from his hair, unfazed by his nudity while he wipes himself dry and tucks the plush material around his waist.

"Does your head still hurt?" I ask.

"Yeah." He steps onto the bathmat, his chest peppered with water droplets. "Turns out your brother can pack a punch after all."

"Do you need to see a doctor?"

He walks toward me, frowning. "Stop worrying about me. I'll sleep it off."

I can't. I am worried.

His pain seems deeper than normal. And the distinct scent of alcohol on his breath only heightens my concern.

"Where have you been?" I push from the vanity and raise a hand, sliding a palm over his cheek, stroking his prickly stubble with my thumb.

He tilts his face into my touch. "You trying to keep tabs on me already?"

"No. I—"

"It doesn't matter where I was, shorty. I'm here now."

I ignore the twinge of rejection.

He doesn't want me clued in, and I have to be okay with that.

I won't demand his secrets again. For once, it seems my savior needs saving and I want to take that role. "You're exhausted. It's my turn to look after you."

His grin is subtle. Half-hearted, yet so unbelievably handsome.

I inch closer, placing my lips to his, facing another fear as I taste the liquor on his tongue.

He groans into the connection, his hands tangling into the shirt at my hips before he pulls back. "I should sleep in another room."

"Why?" My hand falls to my side.

"I can't do this tonight, Pen."

My heart tears. Fractures. "Do what? Be around me?"

He cringes. "The world is fucking crumbling, and I can't think clearly. I've got no restraint. I shouldn't have started drinking."

"You're not a monster, Luca. You don't need restraint."

"No. You—"

"*No.*" I counter, more adamant. "This shouldn't be one-sided. You can't be the strong one all the time. I need you to need me. I need you to want me."

He closes his eyes and rests his head against mine. "I've always fucking wanted you."

I feel those words, the agonizing admission sinking into my marrow. I can't stop myself from sliding my hands around his waist to pull him farther into me. Body to body. Hip to hip.

I freeze as the hard length of his shaft presses against my pubic bone. I clasp my lips tight, holding the gasp inside my throat.

I shouldn't be shocked… but I am.

I shouldn't be scared… yet there's some of that, too.

"It kills me every time you tense at my touch," he murmurs. "That's why I don't like doing it. I fucking hate hurting you."

"It's muscle memory. Or habit." I slide my hands over his chest to his face. "It won't last forever."

"Maybe not, but I'd prefer to give you space until it's gone." He attempts to pull away again, but I hold tight, clamping his jaw in my hands.

"You need to stop seeing intimacy as my biggest hurdle when being like this is my greatest reward. This isn't comparable to what I went through with Luther. What he did was vicious and cruel. But this…" I shake my head, frantically searching for the words to explain. "This is hope and optimism. It's kindness and consideration. It bears no resemblance to my nightmares."

"I get it—"

"No, let me finish." I implore him with my eyes. "Trying new things might bring up bad memories, but *you* don't. *You* wipe it all away. You're my prize, Luca. Please let me enjoy it."

He huffs out a laugh, the sound lacking happiness.

"You don't believe me?" I grab his hands and guide them to my hips. "Why is it so hard for you to understand that with each touch, each kiss, you help to make me feel normal?"

"Because you'll never be normal, shorty. *Never.* You're too remarkable to be mainstream."

My heart clenches. Hard. Tight. Punishing.

He keeps strengthening me. Over and over. Constantly making me a little more emboldened with every roughly grated compliment.

"Have I told you how happy I am that you found me?" I run my arms around his neck and brush my mouth over his.

A rumble emanates from his throat, his fingertips tightening on my hips. He kisses me. Gentle. Soulful.

But all too soon he breaks the spell, pulling away to rest his forehead against mine. "There's something you should know."

I lean back, seeing the emotion in his eyes differently than I had before. I was wrong. It isn't exhaustion. It's sorrow.

My heart clogs my throat. "Something else has happened, hasn't it?"

He nods. "Torian told me—"

"Wait." I place a finger to his lips. "Are Tobias and Sebastian safe?"

He winces. "Yeah, they are, but—"

"No. Don't say it," I beg. "Whatever it is, don't tell me. Not tonight. Don't steal me away from being here with you." I hold his gaze as I swallow over the lump in my throat. "Please just let me have this moment."

He remains rigid, his muscles locked tight.

"*Please.*" I shuffle closer, not sure how else to convince him not to ruin this.

I know I'm being selfish. I can't help it.

I'm needy when it comes to Luca.

I long for his compliments and even his desire. I want everything he has to give and I won't stand for those moments being marred by inevitable hardships. For once, darkness can wait until tomorrow.

"Please, Luca." I tug him forward by the edge of his towel.

He releases an agonizing groan, his restraint increasing my pulse.

That's the part of him I enjoy the most—his discipline.

He's much more of a man than I've ever experienced. So much so that I find myself lowering, about to fall to my knees to perform an act I've never willingly given before.

"What the fuck?" His hands lash out, one grabbing my upper arm to keep me from sinking farther, the other grasping my chin.

"I want to do this for you." It's the truth. I'm curious. And maybe a little sadistic, too. Or even self-sabotaging, waiting for him to disappoint me. But at least I'm doing this of my own free will. It's *my* choice. Nobody else's.

"Like hell." His nostrils flare as he glares. "Get off your fucking knees. *Now.*"

His vehemence shocks me, his grip unflinching until I rise to stand before him.

"You will never kneel before a man ever again." His breathing increases, his chest rapidly rising and falling. "Do you hear me?"

I open my mouth, but words fail me.

"Never," he growls. "From now on, Pen, you take your fucking place on a pedestal. There's no servitude. No fucking selflessness."

"But what if I want—"

"Then you find another fucking way. Do you understand? As long as I live, no man will ever look down on you like that again."

He renders me speechless and grabs my hips, lifting me to sit on the vanity.

I'm stripped bare of response as he falls to his knees before me, his rough hands sliding along my thighs to grip the side of my ass still covered in the bulking T-shirt.

"What are you doing?" I can't stop the stupid question escaping my lips. I blame it on the adrenaline rushing through me. The complete madness filling me with power. He elevates me to some sort of godly status, the reversal of our positions making my belly flip and tumble.

I've always been the servant. The slave.

Now I'm his master, growing more empowered by the leashed hunger in his eyes.

"Tell me you want this." He gently parts my legs, slowly inching forward, placing one gentle kiss after another along the flaming-hot skin of my inner thighs. "Or tell me to stop."

I can't imagine wanting anything else. For a moment, I'm so caught up in needing to be closer that I wonder if this was what it was like for Luther all along.

Did he crave me this way?

Was his desire for me as uncontrollable as mine for Luca?

Did his heart pound and throat tighten? Did his palms sweat and limbs shake? Is that why he stole me—because he was compelled?

"Don't go back there," Luca murmurs against my skin. "Stay with me."

I lick my lips, trying to wipe away the dryness. "I'm trying."

"What's stopping you?" He pauses the gentle kisses and pulls back an inch.

"Oh, God. I'm beginning to second guess if this is natural. Maybe there's something wrong with me."

His eyes narrow. "Whatever you feel is natural. If you want to keep going. If you want to stop. Even if you change your mind every five seconds. It's all normal."

He's right. It's natural. I guess I asked the wrong question. "What I meant is, is this healthy? Do I want you like this because I'm sick?"

He doesn't speak for long moments, the silence making my pulse beat faster. Is he about to give evidence to my growing instability?

Those lips press back against my inner thigh, his gaze remaining locked on mine as he says, "I wondered the same thing after what happened last night. But you said it yourself—this is nothing like what you experienced. It's the exact opposite. And after everything you've been through, I can't think of anything that's healthier, or that shows more strength, or trust, or more commitment to healing, than a woman wanting to gain pleasure from a man who adores her."

An ache builds behind my sternum. There's so much pain.

Good pain.

Restorative pain.

I drag in a breath, filling my lungs to capacity. "I love you, Luc."

His eyes flare, shock bleeding across his features before he bows his head into my legs, not saying a word.

"Luca?" The agony builds. "I'm sorry, I…"

"Don't be sorry." He raises his face again, staring back at me with ferocity. "You know I love you, too, shorty. I'd fucking kill for you."

"You already have."

He inclines his head. "And I'd do it again. Every single day for the rest of my fucking life. Without pause or doubt."

I burn—eyes, throat, heart. The heat overwhelms me, leaving beautifully wistful memories to soothe my scars.

"Now spread those thighs," he demands. "I want to make you feel good."

24

LUCA

The scent of her drugs me.

The heat of her consumes me.

But those eyes... those fucking eyes enslave me, leaving me powerless.

Everything inside me screams to dive farther between her legs, to lunge forward and take what's readily offered. Instead, I battle temptation, moving agonizingly slowly, my stubble grazing her inner thighs.

Each inch of devoured space intoxicates me more. Makes me burn. Pushes my restraint further.

All I want is to sate my need. But more importantly, I want to feed hers.

I stop a breath away from her pussy and close my eyes against the allure.

My mouth waters at her scent—sweet soap and heavy arousal. I can already taste her; the juices make my tongue swell in anticipation.

But still, I don't take.

I withstand the temptation. Teasing myself. Testing.

I need to know the mindlessness she inspires can be tamed because I won't hurt her. Not like this. Not ever. If I did, I'd—

"Luca," she begs. "I can't take the anticipation any longer." She shudders with an inhale. "I feel like there's a constant stream of electricity coursing through me... I'm trembling."

"Tell me what you need."

She whimpers. "I have no clue. This is new to me. But I trust you to know what you're doing."

I've got no fucking idea. Not with her. Not with someone I'm petrified of hurting.

Yet the compulsion to provide and protect latches its claws deep. I won't leave her wanting.

I nestle farther between her legs, placing my mouth right before her core.

Her breath catches with every inhale. Her tongue snakes out to nervously swipe her lower lip.

She's so fucking beautiful.

There's never been a prettier sight.

"Don't keep anything from me," I demand. "Not your fear or your pain. At the first sign of hesitation, you make sure you tell me to stop."

"I will."

I bridge the space to her pussy, my hands digging into her thighs. I never quit watching her as I take my first taste, the slick heat of her arousal coating my tongue.

She gasps. Jolts.

Her surprise fucking moves me. Soul deep.

I lick again and again, slow strokes, tender touches, until those jolts lessen and she settles into the sensation, her hands finding my hair.

At first, she's hesitant. Gentle touches. Gliding fingers.

But I need more. I want her to share this obsession. This compulsion.

I delve deeper. Lashing her pussy with longer swipes and teasing flicks against her clit.

The jolts return with each new movement, and it takes too fucking long to realize it must be because the sensations are foreign. She's never had this. Never had a man pay homage to her perfection.

The insight makes me work harder to please her.

I suck her clit, earning a throaty moan and a tightening of those gorgeous thighs around my head.

My dick pulses with need. From base to tip. Balls included.

I fucking throb for her, the urgency making me mindless. The torture of my headache is the saving grace stopping me from blowing my load in the towel.

I yank her closer to me, holding her on the edge of the vanity, her heels coming to rest against my back as one of her hands grips the counter. It's the perfect view, the landscape before me filled with smooth waist and perky tits covered under the thin layer of her shirt.

She doesn't quit watching as I devour her, nuzzling against her pubic bone, lashing her with harder strokes.

Her teeth dig into her bottom lip, her brows furrow, and that breathing, *fuck*, her breathing is so short and sharp I ache to claim her mouth.

"Come up here," she pants. "I want you."

No. I'm not fucking her.

The last thing she deserves is some pussy-starved, threadbare man rutting into her.

"Please, Luca."

I hold tighter to her thighs, lapping, sucking.

She whimpers. Wiggles. *"Please."*

I don't listen. I keep devouring, every last drop of arousal sliding down the back of my throat.

"Luca, stop," she begs.

I freeze, instantly, and lean back on my haunches. "You okay?"

She nods, straightens, then reaches forward to grab my jaw, guiding me to stand with such exquisite confidence. "Drop the towel."

"Penny, we're not—"

"Please, Luc, just drop the towel."

I growl. "We're not having sex."

"I didn't ask for sex." She blinks up at me, all innocent and meek. "I only want to see you."

I'll give her anything she asks for when she looks at me that way. My towel. My sanity. My life. I tug at the material around my waist and release it to fall to the floor. But she doesn't take what she requested. It's the same as when I was in the shower; her gaze doesn't lower.

"What is it?" My dick remains hard, not bothered by her lack of attention. "What's wrong?"

She stares at my chest, her breathing remaining heavy. "I'm nervous. I've never seen a man naked without feeling threatened."

I tense. "And do you feel threatened now?"

"No."

"Then look at me."

Her brow furrows, those dark eyes wincing.

"Shorty, just because I'm hard doesn't mean I'll ever take something that isn't offered. You never need to feel vulnerable around me."

The wince deepens, her struggle intensifying. "I know."

"Then look."

She nods, her brows pinched as she lowers her gaze from my chest, to my gut, slowly descending all the way to the apex of my thighs.

I've never been self-conscious a day in my fucking life. Not about my body or my dick. But she makes me doubt my worth. I'm not good enough for her— never have been—and that's more apparent than ever as her innocent eyes survey my junk.

For long moments she remains quiet, her attention taking me in. "I never thought I'd find that part of a man tempting." She swallows. "It's funny how you always have a way of surprising me."

I don't know if it's pride, arrogance, or fucking relief filling my chest. Maybe it's a mix of all three that make me stand taller.

She returns her gaze to mine, raises her hand to lick her palm, then grasps my dick without a word.

I hiss with the brutally tempting restriction, the pleasure engulfing me. "*Jesus.*"

"You'll never hurt me," she states as fact.

I nod. "I'll never hurt you."

She strokes my length, the smooth slide of skin gliding up and down my shaft.

I grind my teeth against the thrill... the consuming need for release... She feels so fucking good. "Can I touch you?"

She drags her teeth over her lower lip, still stroking, still tormenting. "Always."

I slam my mouth against hers, shoving a hand into her hair.

I rock my hips with her strokes, hungry for more as I lower my free hand between her thighs to penetrate her dripping pussy with two fingers. Her core clamps around me, soaking my palm as she grinds into the touch, her grip lethally tightening around my cock.

"Jesus. Fuck." I kiss her harder, faster, eating up her moans and needy whimpers.

I can't get enough. Not in taste or touch or sound. The pain in my head lessens, the agony meaningless when pitted against her perfection.

I want more. So much fucking more that I become mindless with need.

I twist my fingers inside her, flick her clit with my thumb. The pace of her stroke quickens, her attention remaining at the sensitive head of my shaft.

"Penny," I growl into her mouth. "I'm close."

She bites my lip. Bats those sultry lashes. Grinds harder.

I can't hold back.

I fucking come, my seed pulsing from me in waves to lash her thigh as I groan my pleasure. Over and over, the rivulets of milky liquid mark her skin.

I buck. I growl. I kiss.

And when I'm finally done, I fall to my knees, spread her legs, and this time, I fucking dive for her pussy.

I lick and lap and suck. I flick and graze and bite.

I add my finger to the mix, penetrating her slit and teasing her ass until those bated breaths become panted entreaties.

When we're like this it's hard to remember where she's come from. It's almost impossible to contemplate what she's been through.

Penny isn't damaged when she's lost in pleasure. There's no sadness or scarring. There's nothing but beautiful vibrancy, and I'm so fucking greedy for more.

Her fingers return to my hair, this time tearing, tugging, making my dick twitch all over again.

"Luca." She pulls harder. "*Luca.*"

She rips the shit out of my scalp and I grin as her walls spasm around my fingers.

I keep sucking. Keep licking.

I don't stop as she trembles around me, crying my name while she comes.

It isn't until her fingers lose their grip and she quits quivering that I pull back, falling onto my ass to stare up at her with pride.

I'm entirely spent. Physically. Emotionally.

She siphoned me of strength, but something else has taken its place. Something committed and lifelong.

This woman is everything. My priority. My goal. My future.

I don't want to be without her. Not for a week, or a day, or a minute.

She's mine. And not in the way she's used to. There will be no unwilling possession, because I'm equally hers for as long as she'll have me.

"Let's get you washed up." I push to my feet and grab her hand, helping her from the vanity to lead her to the shower.

She's quiet beside me as I turn on the water, and I hope that means she's peacefully content. I could watch her like this forever—her face flushed, eyes bright as she stares blindly ahead.

I smirk. "Need help taking off your shirt?"

The corners of her mouth rise with the hint of a smile. "No, I can do it on my own."

She reaches for the hem, and I do the same, my fingers brushing hers. We drag the material above her stomach, over her shoulders.

I'm hard again by the time I drop the shirt to the tile. Any man would be.

She's breathtaking. Mouthwatering.

I can't stop dragging my gaze over her, the lush curves of her hips, the smooth stomach, the perfect breasts. But the pièce de résistance is my seed sliding down her thigh.

"Like what you see?" she drawls.

"Without a doubt."

She lets out a breathy chuckle, the sound heaven to my ears.

I want this more often. The laughter and smiles. The subtle happiness that increases her beauty tenfold.

I lead her into the shower and close the door behind us. She moves under the water first and tugs me along with her, her arms raised between our chests, her head resting on my shoulder.

We stand in silence.

In contentment.

I kiss her forehead. Her cheek.

I can't stop pressing my lips to her delicate skin, tasting the salt, drowning in the warmth while she remains snuggled into me.

"You're quiet." I place my mouth on her temple and force my libido to tap the brakes.

"I'm happy."

I return my lips to her forehead, holding them there for long moments. "You sure?"

Despite being on cloud nine, I know this can't be easy for her.

"I think so. It's hard to explain."

I hold her tighter. "Try."

She's quiet for a while as she peppers slow kisses against my neck. "My stomach is giddy. It's all fluttery and warm." Her arms snake down to her sides, then wrap around my waist. "Good sensations have been foreign to me for so long that there's a sense of guilt that comes with them. Or maybe it's not guilt. Maybe it's the fear of this all being taken away."

"It won't get taken."

She sucks in a long breath and releases it slowly. "You can't know for certain. Nobody can predict what will happen tomorrow. Or the next day. Or the day after that. So there's this giddy, tingling part of me that I love, then there's this nagging, opposing side that chooses to be a constant reminder of how quickly life can change for the worse."

I get it.

I know she doesn't think I do, but I lived my entire early childhood in that zone. Every time I caught my parents laughing or smiling, the childish optimism in me would think they'd finally figured out how to be happy without causing pain.

It never stuck though.

And I can't oppose her way of thinking when I still have bad news to tell her. I'm worried I'll lose her trust and break her heart with the information of another attack. Then if she finds out I involved Tobias... *fuck.*

Maybe she's right. Maybe this will all be taken away, but she'll be the one doing the taking.

I tighten my hold on her, my migraine returning with the fear. "I'll always protect you. I promise I'll never stop."

"I know." She pulls back to look up at me with heart melting eyes. "But who will protect you?"

25

PENNY

I WAKE TO THE SOUND OF THE NEIGHBOR'S DOG BARKING INCESSANTLY, THE SLIGHT glow seeping around the curtains announcing early morning.

The house is quiet. No voices. No kiddie giggles.

There are only me and the memories of last night to make me smile. I roll onto my side and stare at the man sleeping peacefully next to me. I'd fallen into slumber with his arms wrapped around my middle, his chest warm against my back.

I can't remember succumbing to pleasant dreams so easily.

There'd been no fear. No panic.

Only a building sense of hope with the protective embrace.

My love for him is scary. I think it's always been there, in the security and trust, but now it's also in the flutter of my stomach and the tightness of my throat whenever I look at him.

It carries through every inch of my body.

A rhythmic *pop, pop, pop* startles me, the familiar muted gunfire stealing a bite of my happiness. I slump back into the mattress. Sebastian must have headed straight for the shooting range as soon as he woke up.

I hate that he despises the man I adore. It makes me sick thinking of his anger.

I want to fix it.

Fix *them*.

If I'm going to reclaim my life, I need them both. No aggression. No threats. Just support and guidance.

I may have very little control over anything else right now, but I can make Sebastian listen to me. All I need is to be strong enough to face him, and I think Luca has already ensured I am.

I slowly inch from the bed and tiptoe to the dresser to pull on the pants and oversized sweater I left there the night before.

"Where are you going?" Luca grumbles, his face plastered into the pillow.

"I can't sleep with that dog barking. I'm going to get coffee."

He groans. "Do you want me to come with you?"

My heart swells as I bridge the space between us to place a kiss on his unmarred cheek. "Thank you. But I'm okay."

He grabs my hand and squeezes. "I'll be up soon."

"Don't. You need the rest." I reluctantly walk for the hall to head toward the continued gunfire at the other end of the house.

I drag my bare feet past the empty living area, then farther along the far hall, not stopping until I reach the door where the muted pops escape from.

I grab the handle, the gentle vibrations from the other side making my hand tremble, my pulse stutter. I want to back out already but I don't. I inch open a door, finding soundproofing on the walls and an ominous staircase leading down into fluorescent light.

More pops assail my ears, these ones harsh and biting. I quickly scoot inside, not wanting to wake anyone else, and clasp the door shut behind me.

It's cooler down here, the polished cement freezing my toes. I will myself to descend. One step after another. One punishing heartbeat after the next until I'm at the bottom landing, staring at a bulking man who isn't my brother.

Hunter wields the gun, his cannon arms pointing toward the far end of the long, expansive basement.

He stands before a professional shooting station, protective headphones covering his ears. It's not a downscaled DIY set down here. It's like I've seen in movies as a kid. Three individual stations. Paper targets hanging from the roof.

Another *pop* sounds, the blast ricocheting off the walls to make me flinch and gasp. He glances over his shoulder, his weapon lowering as his narrowed eyes pin me in place.

"Sorry." I wince. "I thought you were Sebastian."

He glares, then returns his attention to the target, raising his gun. He hates me. And why wouldn't he? He had a nice set of wheels before I got my hands on them.

"I'm also sorry about your car," I add. "I didn't plan for that to happen."

He lowers the headphones. "When you fly by the seat of your pants, you don't hold back, do you?" His tone is gruff, making it hard for me to tell if he's angry or attempting to make light of the situation.

"Is it fixable?"

He shrugs. "It's just a car."

"I know, but I'm sure it was expensive."

"It's just a car," he growls the statement with such venom I grip the staircase banister in preparation to flee.

"It's just a car. It's just a car. It's just a fucking car." He lazily circles his finger in the air with each repetition. "Sarah told me to keep repeating the mantra in the hopes it will stop me from putting a bullet in your head."

All the air leaves my lungs on a heave.

"Calm down." He rolls his eyes. "I'm joking."

"Right..." I force out a laugh. "Hilarious."

He turns his back to me, raising his headphones, then his gun to take aim at the target. "If you're going to stay down here, you need to get yourself a set of ear plugs."

I don't move, not sure if the muttered request is an invitation to stay or a demand to leave.

"The door or the plugs, Penny." He jerks his head toward the wall behind me, the mass of shelves displaying a myriad of equipment. "Hurry up. I've got bullets to waste."

I nod and hustle to the shelves to grab a set of plugs, shoving them into my ears as another set of *pop, pop, pops* erupt. This time, the sound reverberates through my chest, the vibration rattling my bones. It brings a slight buzz to my system. A building awakening. It's the power. The threat. I want it for myself.

I walk toward him, stopping a foot behind to watch as he aims and fires, the paper target dancing with the direct hit in the head.

Pop, pop, pop.

In a flurry of finesse he releases the magazine, loads another, then takes aim.

Pop, pop, pop.

Pop, pop, pop.

He's brilliantly lethal. Mesmerizingly intimidating.

When he stops firing, I raise my voice. "Would you teach me?"

"Teach you what?" He pauses, arms still straight in aim. "To shoot?"

"Yeah. I've never done it before."

"Where's Luca? I'm not the sort of teacher you want."

"He's asleep. And I don't think the noise is something he's going to want to be around for a while after he received another hit to the head."

He shoots me a scowl. "Then what about your brother or Sarah? Even Keira would be a better option."

"Nobody is awake." I shrug, feigning indifference while my pulse hammers, waiting for him to lose patience with me. "And we're both already here..."

Just like I want to fix the rift between Luca and Sebastian, I also need to mend the damage I've caused with Hunter. The less enemies I have, the stronger I'll be.

"Fine." He pins me with that scowl. "You're going to have to move closer."

I inch toward him, my pulse ramping higher as I stand beside his bulky frame.

"Here." He grabs my wrist and smacks the gun in my hand, the casing warm from his hold. "You're going to want to—"

A throat clears behind us and I swing around to see Sebastian, his eyes wary, chin high as he stands at the foot of the stairs. "Am I interrupting?"

"Fuck no." Hunter snatches the weapon from my grip. "I was praying for a savior." He maneuvers around me, all strength and thumping footsteps as he yanks off his earphones and throws them at my brother. "Godspeed."

I'm left stunned silent as Hunter storms up the stairs, slamming the door behind him.

For moments, Sebastian and I just stare at each other. Sister to brother. Victim to criminal.

I think this is the first time we've been alone since Luther stole me. *Truly* alone. Without weighty emotion or people hovering close. And now that we're here, I'm not sure what to say.

"I didn't mean to interrupt." He shifts his focus over my shoulder, no longer meeting my gaze. "Was he teaching you how to shoot?"

I nod, finding it hard to come up with a response when he looks entirely defeated. I'm the one who broke him. Me and my feelings for Luca. "But he wasn't overly enthusiastic about talking to me, let alone handing over his gun. He told me he wouldn't be a good teacher."

Sebastian huffs out a laugh. "I don't know why. He would've killed more people than you went to school with."

My mouth falls open. I hadn't been oblivious to Hunter being a murderer, but those numbers aren't what I'd pictured.

"It was a joke," he drawls. "I'm sure the number hasn't reached triple digits."

It's my turn to breathe out an awkward laugh. "You all have really inappropriate humor."

"It comes with the work environment."

The criminal environment, I mentally correct. The death and destruction.

Silence returns. The awkwardness, too.

"Want me to leave you alone?" he asks.

I want to say yes. It still hurts to see him. To remember our childhood and the familiar bond we had. The yearning for the past is excruciating. But I have to think about him. And Luca. I have to concentrate on the future. "No. I actually came down here looking for you."

"Is that right?" He raises a brow, the slightest hint of hope entering his eyes.

"I thought it was time we talked."

He straightens, broadening his shoulders. "What do you want to talk about?"

I swallow over the adamant pulse in my throat and drag in a steadying breath. "I wanted to apologize for the way I've treated you, am treating you, and will probably continue to treat you."

"Okay..." He winces. "So this hatred of me is a lifelong commitment?"

"No, it's not. And I don't hate you, I just..." My chest tightens, painfully squeezing. "I'm trying to protect myself the only way I know how."

"And you think you need protection from me?"

"Not *from you*, no. I need protection from the possibility of losing you. Everything else has been taken from me, Sebastian. Too many sisters in Greece were murdered. And anyone who defies Luther always disappears... Maybe if you weren't a part of this—" I wave a hand to encompass the room. The house. Everything. "—my return would be different. But it feels like loss has followed me here."

"I'm not going anywhere." He starts toward me. "No way in hell would I leave you."

"I know it wouldn't be by choice. But your job... And Robert." I wrap my arms around my waist, trying to hold in the building hollowness. "You didn't choose a vocation that's overly generous when it comes to lifespan."

"Robert can go fuck himself." He stops before me, his face pinched. "He's one man attempting to start a war with an army. He doesn't have a hope in hell of surviving. And yes, I admit working for Torian has its downfalls, but I'm more of a tech guy. I hide behind a computer most of the time. I'm not on the frontlines like Hunt or *Luca*," he snarls the name, adding to my emptiness.

"He's a good man." I let my eyes do the pleading. "I wouldn't be here right now, standing before you, if it weren't for him. And it's not just because he physically saved me in Greece. It's so much more than that. He rescued me mentally, too. Emotionally. He's the reason I'm whole, Seb. It's all him."

He presses his lips tight, his nostrils flaring.

"Why is it so hard for you to understand?" I ask.

"It's not hard to understand," he grates. "It's hard to digest. He shouldn't be touching you."

"Well, rest assured he feels the same way. But I like him touching me. After everything I've been through, he brings me comfort. Can't you see how monumental that is?"

"No, it only reeks of manipulation to me."

"You don't think I know all about manipulation? I spent a lifetime in hell getting to know every single facet of deceit. And it's not what Luca is doing."

Sebastian's jaw ticks. He doesn't believe me. There's no faith.

I squeeze my arms tighter around myself, creating courage. "I love him. More than myself. More than air. More than life. He's become the reason I get up in the morning. He's my hope for the future. And the balm to my past. I know you don't want to hear it, but right now, he's everything to me. He's the reason I breathe."

"And what happens when he's not? Where does it leave you mentally and fucking emotionally when he walks out?"

A sharp dagger stabs through my heart, piercing skin and bone. "Hopefully by then I'll be strong enough to stand on my own two feet." I drop my hands to my sides. "He's not obligated to a lifelong commitment, and he never should be. But while he's inspiring happiness, I want to cling to him. Surely I deserve that much, don't I?"

He cringes. "This isn't about what you deserve. It's about—"

"I know exactly what you think it's about. What I need you to comprehend is that I would've ended my life many times over if it wasn't for him. He's the only reason I stand before you. The *only reason*, Sebastian. I know that's hard for you to hear. It's even harder for me to admit. But it's the truth. And I think he deserves your gratitude for that. At the very least, you should stop threatening him."

His mouth snaps shut again, his jaw ticking.

"Please, Seb."

He looks away.

"*Please.*"

"I'll work on it," he growls and turns for the stairs.

Before I know what I'm doing, I reach for him, my fingers tentative against his wrist.

He stops. Stiffens.

My heart is a frantic butterfly in my throat as I walk to stand before him, not pausing for contemplation before I sink into his chest.

He stiffens further, every muscle cinched tight. He remains statuesque while I tremble, fighting hard against the burn in my eyes.

The contact is awkward. No warmth. No comfort.

He doesn't say a word.

I'm about to pull away in heartbreak when he releases a deep breath and drags me harder into his chest. His body relaxes into mine as his arms encircle my back, his mouth softly pressing against my forehead in a brotherly kiss.

The heat in my eyes increases, the threat of tears so close before I desperately blink them away. "Please forgive him."

He sighs. "I'll try."

"I need you to do more than that," I whisper. "I need this feud between you two to be over."

"How 'bout I start by not killing him and see where that leads?"

I huff out a laugh. "You all seriously have a warped sense of humor."

"Yeah... I was totally joking," he drawls.

I nudge him in the ribs and step back "Promise me you'll play nice."

"Fine." His arms drop to his sides. "I promise."

It feels strange to be having a conversation with my brother again. To argue and beg like I did as a child. It brings an overwhelming sense of home and the brief taste makes me want more. "Thank you."

He gives a sad smile. "All bets are off if he makes you cry, though. You know that, right?"

"Yeah, I know." I start for the stairs, Sebastian following close behind.

I hold the door open to the hall and we walk in comfortable silence toward the voices coming from the living area. Everyone is there—Hunter and Sarah at the dining table, Cole and Keira in the kitchen cooking, Layla, Benji, the nanny, and the kids on the sofa in front of the television. It's Luca who steals my attention, his hip cocked against the island counter, his stance casual even though I can read the tension in his eyes as he glances between me and my brother.

"It's about time you two got up here." Cole pulls plates from a cupboard. "Breakfast is almost ready."

"Perfect timing." Sebastian squeezes my shoulder and strides ahead, taking the furthest route from Luca as possible.

They eye each other, the evil stares not amounting to anything other than tension.

I guess the lack of verbal threat is a starting point.

Luca pushes from the counter, flicking me a glance as he stalks for the glass doors leading outside. I follow, my toes protesting the bitter chill while I breathe in the icy morning air.

"Morning." I don't stop until I'm in front of him, my bare feet brushing his boots as I lean into his chest.

"Morning, shorty." He engulfs me in a lazy hug, the familiar scent of his aftershave soothing me.

"I gather from the damp hair and fresh clothes that you didn't fall back asleep."

He stares across the courtyard, the towering mansion next door looming right beside the brick fence as the neighbor's dog continues to bark. "I got out of bed as soon as you left the room. I wanted to make sure I was close by if you needed me."

A grateful smile curves my lips. "I always need you."

He tightens his hold around me for a brief moment, then sighs. "Is everything okay between you and Decker?"

"It's better than it was."

"I'm glad to hear it." He strokes my hair. "How about the poison? Is that sinking in yet?"

"Poison?" I pull back, taking in his faint smirk.

"Has Sebastian turned you against me?" He appears calm on the surface, but I see the underlying fear in the tight set of his jaw. He's joking on the outside. On the inside he's worried.

"No, and he never will. You're stuck with me."

The smirk fades as he returns his attention to the neighboring building. "There's something I need to tell you."

I square my shoulders, preparing for the worst. "Is this what you wanted to tell me last night?"

He nods. "It's not good news, Pen."

I already gathered as much when he brought it up yesterday. I just hadn't been willing to face it. And if the news hadn't been about Tobias and Sebastian, that only left my sisters. "He killed one of them, didn't he? Robert found Lilly or Nina."

His chin hitches almost imperceptibly. It's all the answer I need for a wave of grief to take hold. I steel myself against the onslaught, straightening my shoulders in anticipation.

"Not dead, shorty. But Nina is hurt pretty bad. She's in hospital."

Relief doesn't come. It's as if the sorrow is merely placed on the back burner, waiting for the follow-through. "Will she make it?"

"I hope so. They're not sure at this point. The only good news is that Torian now believes you."

Again, my relief is non-existent. I'm left to drown in guilt. I should never have let them leave Greece without me. We should've stayed together.

"This isn't your fault," he murmurs. "I should've made sure they were protected. And when I found out, instead of telling you, I focused on getting my rocks off."

"No, you didn't. I knew. I may not have had the specifics, but I knew." I graze my fingers over his jaw. "We both needed the distraction."

He scoffs. "That doesn't stop me from feeling like a prick."

The glass door slides open. The dog bursts into more aggressive barking as I glance over my shoulder to see Keira poking her head outside. "Sorry to interrupt but breakfast is ready and Cole wants us all together to talk about what's happening."

Luca jerks his chin in acknowledgement. "We'll be there in a minute."

She smiles and sneaks back inside, closing the door behind her.

"I'm going to have to get out of here today." He drags me into his chest, his arms locking around me. "I can't sit on my ass while that fucker is out there."

I nod, already feeling the distance that will come between us. The exposure. The fear.

"Will you be okay without me?" he asks.

"No. But I'll manage, as long as you promise to stay safe."

"I can do that."

There's little conviction in his tone. There's definitely not assurance. I tilt my head to meet his gaze and stare into those harshly intense eyes, wordlessly begging for a more confident affirmation.

"I need you to return to me," I whisper. "You have no idea how much I need it."

His lips lift in a half-hearted smile. "Yeah, I do, shorty. Because I feel the same way."

26

PENNY

WE SIT AT THE TWO REMAINING SEATS AT THE DINING TABLE. BENJI IS SLOUCHED IN the chair to Luca's left, his wife at his side. Sebastian is strung tight at my right beside Keira, while Sarah and Hunt sit across the table from us as Cole claims the head chair.

The kids are no longer around, their laughter and occasional shouts carrying from a far corner of the house.

"Penny, I've got something for you." Sarah slides what looks like a black leather wrist cuff across the table, a shiny metal design on the front. "I thought it might be a nice start to your arsenal."

"My arsenal?" I reach for the offering, running a lone finger over the metal.

"What is it?" Luca asks.

"A blade," Hunter mutters. "I bought it for her a while back, but apparently my gifts aren't appreciated."

Sarah grins, saccharine sweet. "I appreciated it on merit. What I didn't approve of was the hidden GPS tracker you told me nothing about." She holds my gaze with a cautionary stare. "Just a word of warning, these guys tend to trample over privacy and personal boundaries. Make sure you remember that if Luca ever buys you jewelry."

"It's the thought that counts, right?" Cole smirks. "It's the little things we do to keep you protected."

Sarah ignores him, keeping her attention on me. "The metal part is a retractable blade. I can teach you a few tricks with it later if you're interested."

"I'd love that." I place the cuff on my wrist, then turn my arm to clip it in place as the rest of the table eat their breakfast. "I'd appreciate anything you're willing to show me."

"Are you two finished now?" Cole asks around a bite of bacon. "We've got a lot to discuss."

He isn't lying.

He spends the next half hour relaying a mass of information that steals my appetite.

He explains how Nina was attacked by masked men in her parents' home, taking two bullets—one in the chest, the other in her thigh.

Luca squeezes my leg as I'm told of her precarious situation in ICU. I think I'm supposed to be appeased, or even thankful, when Cole tells me men have now been assigned to keep an eye on her, along with Lilly, but I'm not placated in the slightest.

"We're nailing this fucker to the wall as soon as possible." Cole turns his gaze on me, his dark stare narrowing.

With one look, I understand why he's feared by grown men. There's no soul behind those eyes. No warmth. Or fear.

"I assure you those women are taken care of." He enunciates the words slowly, the bitter grate to his tone making the reassurance more of a threat. "The men assigned to their protection are ex-military. They know what they're doing."

He goes on to vaguely mention the informants, authorities, and members of his outer circles who are currently searching the state for the man of the hour and his unknown sidekick. Luca adds details of a green sedan. Hunter stops eating to mention a potential lead who left a voicemail in the early hours of the morning, while my brother remains quiet, holding Keira's hand on the top of the table for all to see.

Then the rules start.

The kids won't be attending school. Us women aren't allowed to leave the house without an escort. And everybody is to advise Cole of their whereabouts at all times.

"I know I'm stretching the limits of our task list, but can we add the death of your neighbor's dog to our daily chores?" Hunter asks. "That fucker kept me up all night."

"It wasn't just the dog." Sarah's attention turns to Luca. "Don't forget about the people fucking in the bathroom beside ours."

My cheeks flame. Red-hot. And I try to ignore the way Sebastian's fingers clench tighter around Keira's.

"I've said it before, and I'll say it again," Luca snarls. "We're not fucking."

"Yeah, whatever." Hunter waves him away, his focus on Cole. "Can we kill that dog or not?"

"Talk to the old lady who lives there." Cole pushes from the table, taking his dirty plate with him. "But make sure you're prepared before you knock on her door. She's a typical Italian mother. You won't leave her house with an empty stomach."

"Speaking of mothers." Keira turns pained eyes to my brother. "We need to cancel tonight. It isn't safe."

Sebastian inclines his head. "I'll make the call."

"Cancel what?" Cole continues to the kitchen, placing his plate in the sink before he returns. "What isn't safe?"

"It's nothing." My brother sits taller. "We'll postpone."

"Postpone what?" Cole pins his focus on Keira. "If Robert is stopping you from your usual plans, I want to know what they are."

Sebastian scoffs. "You just confined the women to the house. How is that any different?"

"It's okay." Keira remains calm. "We were going out for dinner, that's all."

"With who?"

"It doesn't matter."

Cole smirks, the expression becoming unkind. *"Who?"*

"My parents," Sebastian snaps, pushing from his chair.

Luca's hand presses harder into my thigh, offering adamant support.

"They're here?" My voice is high-pitched with apprehension. "In Portland?"

"This had nothing to do with you, Pen. We made plans weeks ago for Keira to meet them. They weren't going to come anywhere near you. And we sure as hell weren't going to mention anything that's happened." Sebastian shoves his chair back into place. "It was just meant to be dinner and drinks. A laid-back welcome to the family."

I tense, keeping all the threatening panic low in my belly. The thought of Mom and Dad being near is overwhelming. They're in the same state as I am. The very same city.

"You're not cancelling." Cole returns to his position at the head of the table. "We don't hide."

"Despite all of us having to relocate to your mega mansion?" Sebastian bites out a vicious laugh. "I'm pretty sure this is the definition of hiding."

"This is *protection*. It's fucking *strategy*."

"Call it whatever you want. But I'm not dragging my parents into the line of fire. Not for you. Not for fucking anybody."

Cole raises his brows. "Not even your sister?"

"Torian," Luca warns.

"No." I swallow to ease the dryness taking over my throat. "This has nothing to do with me. I don't want them dragged—"

"You're not cancelling." Cole pulls his cell from inside his suit jacket and frowns as he taps the screen. "This is the perfect opportunity to draw Robert from the shadows. We'll make it a joint family event. We'll invite everyone. I'll even host at the restaurant and pick up the tab."

"No." I slide my chair back only to be stopped from making a dramatic outburst by Luca's hand grasping mine. He demands my attention with the squeeze of my fingers, his determined eyes attempting to assure me.

"It's okay," he soothes. "We need to talk this out."

"I don't think it requires much talking." Keira glares. "It's heartless to bring more people into this."

Cole slaps his cell down on the table. "How do you not understand that they're already fucking involved? *Anyone* Penny cares for is a target. Maybe not right now, but certainly in the future if this drags on. What the hell do you think is going to happen when Robert can't get his hands on her?" He stares at me. "He's been successful in finding your friends. How long do you think it will take for him to start coming after us? He already shot at you once."

"We don't know it was him." Hunter stabs a hand through his hair. "It still could've been someone looking for me."

"Bullshit. You don't believe that. He came after Penny, and soon he'll come after us all. And not just everyone at this table, but Decker's parents, and our fucking kids. We need to think about Stella and Tobias."

"I'm not risking them," Sebastian seethes.

"There is no risk. We'll have the neighborhood surrounded. I'll place guards on the door. We'll have men scanning the surveillance recordings and on street corners and rooftops for blocks. He won't get near the party. We only need him to get close enough for someone to take him out."

"Right..." Sarah glances around everyone at the table. "And you can arrange all that before tonight?"

"Watch me."

I shake my head, my stomach twisting in knots. I can't let him do this. I can't.

"How do you even know he's nearby?" Hunt asks. "You said he was responsible for the attack yesterday. He's probably still driving around the countryside with his dick in his hand."

"Because of this." Cole unlocks his cell and slides it across the table. "He took more money from Luther's bank account this morning."

"You couldn't have led with that information?" Luca snatches the phone and shows me the email.

"Look at the time stamp, asshole. I only just got the notification."

"Fuck." Sebastian slumps back into his chair, his elbows on the table, his head in his hands. "You're asking us to use our parents as bait."

"No, I'm asking you to have dinner with them in a controlled environment," Cole corrects. "After the last shooting, the restaurant windows are bulletproof. I'll ensure the security is second to none. They'll be safe."

I keep shaking my head, but Sebastian doesn't react.

He's caving.

How is he caving?

"No." Blood surges in my veins, fueling me. "I won't let you." The weight of everyone's attention presses on my shoulders, my chest. It's hard to breathe. "Please, Luca." I turn to face him, my knees brushing his thigh. "Don't let him do this."

"He doesn't have a choice." Cole reaches out a hand, wordlessly requesting his phone. "This needs to happen."

"Not necessarily. If we find him today there won't be any risk tonight." Luca shoves to his feet and stares down at my brother. "What time are you meeting your parents for dinner?"

There's a beat of hope-filled silence before Sebastian raises his head to glance over his shoulder. "Seven. Why? What are you thinking?"

Luca focuses on his watch. "I'm thinking we've got twelve hours to find this fucker. And I don't plan on wasting a single minute. So let's get our asses moving."

27

LUCA

I STALK BACK TO OUR ROOM, PENNY HUSTLING TO KEEP UP AT MY SIDE DESPITE knowing she's going to be stuck here all day. I head straight for the duffels in the corner, pulling my Mac from the bag as she escapes to the bathroom and turns on the shower.

I'm still hunched on the floor when someone else enters the doorway behind me.

I don't need to look to see who it is. His resentment already thickens the air.

"If you're going to kill me, make it quick. Otherwise I've got shit to do." I push to my feet and start for the bed as the shower door grates from the adjoining room. I dump my ass on the mattress and open my computer, scrolling to my home-surveillance software. I looked over a million hours of recordings yesterday, but none of them were mine.

"If I kill you, I promise it won't be quick." Decker leans against the doorframe, wishing the life from my lungs with his narrowed stare. "What are you doing?"

"Checking my security feed from the other night. If it was Robert who shot at Penny I might have recorded his car. And if I've got his car, I might have his plates, which means we've got something to track."

He pushes from the doorframe and moves to the end of the bed, continuing to glare down at me as I play the feed from the night Penny ran.

I watch in double time as Hunter's car pulls into the drive, another vehicle following moments later. I hit pause, rewind, and watch it again.

It's that green fucking sedan with what looks to be a blurred hooded man behind the wheel.

I hit rewind again. Pause. "You got a pen?"

"No," Decker grates.

"I need to figure out these plates." I look up at him from my lowered vision. "You want to help your sister, don't you?"

"I'd do anything for my sister. *You*, on the other hand—"

"Quit the bullshit. Either take down the details or fuck off."

He remains in place, pulling his cell from the back pocket of his jeans. "Well, what the fuck are the details, you perverted fuck?"

I grind my molars as I skip the video back and forth, trying to get a clear view. I relay letters and numbers through clenched teeth, and hope they're the right ones, before pressing play on the video.

I scrutinize every aspect of the pixelated car. The busted headlight. The dents and scratches. Every detail counts.

"Jesus Christ." I hit the slow-motion button and watch the replay of Hunter and Sarah walking across the lawn to the front of the house. "Jesus fucking Christ."

"What is it?" Decker moves to my side, staring down at my Mac. The car creeps onto screen at the same time as Hunt knocks on my front door.

"They were right there. *Right fucking there.* All they needed to do was look over their shoulder and none of this would've happened."

"If you want to see it that way, you could also say this never would've happened if you didn't cozy up with my sister and take her back to your house in the first fucking place."

I ignore the throb reigniting in my head.

I count to ten.

Breathe.

I do whatever calming voodoo I can muster to keep my ass on the bed instead of launching my knuckles into Decker's face.

"Does it show him following Penny after she left?" he mutters.

I keep every muscle clenched while the video continues.

My fingers twitch as I watch the desolate street, not a single vehicle passing before Penny runs from the house. She's frantic, and I have to fight a wince at the pain in her features. The pain *I* caused.

She scrambles into the black Suburban in my drive and doesn't stop when Hunter and Sarah come rushing after her.

The seconds after she speeds away make me furious. As my friends reach for their phones and pace my front lawn, the green sedan drives by, following less than a minute behind. He must have circled the block and been watching the house.

"He was *right there.*" I jab a finger at the screen. "If Hunt was paying attent—"

"It's not Hunt's fault."

I scoff. "No, it's mine, right?" I shove from the bed, my brain screaming in protest at the sudden movement. "This is all on me."

"I didn't say that." Decker relaxes, settling into calm superiority. "But it sounds like you think so."

Fuck him.

Not only for the judgment and the threats. Fuck him for nailing exactly how I feel.

It's my fault for not realizing Robert had found her. It's my fucking fault for not confirming he was dead in the first place.

I should've been all over this. I should've fucking known.

"Do you really blame yourself?" He shakes his head and scoffs. "Do you seriously think you could've stopped this from happening?"

Without a doubt, if I'd been on the top of my game. If my focus had been aligned.

But instead of protecting Penny I endangered her. Became distracted by her. And even now, with one of her friends dead and another injured, I don't think I can regret falling for her.

"You couldn't have seen this coming. Torian told me Robert was dead. That *all* Luther's men were taken care of. Get your head out of your ass and realize you're no better than anyone else. You couldn't have predicted this. You're just as helpless as the rest of us."

"It was my job."

"Yeah, well, it was my job to find her in the first place. She's *my* sister. So quit the pity party."

Is that it? Is all this macho hostility because I found her instead of him?

"And while you're at it," he snarls, "quit fucking her, too."

"Don't push me, Decker." I grind my teeth to the point of pain. "I've told you I'm *not* fucking her."

He scoffs and looks away, his jaw ticking.

The need to fight this out is reciprocated. There's only one reason we aren't, and she's a few feet away, behind that bathroom door.

"Look." I huff. "I care about her. And whether you approve or not, I'm going to keep protecting her."

"With your dick?"

"Enough," I warn. "We don't have time for this."

He straightens, his vicious eyes meeting mine. "Fine. But we also don't have time for you bitching about how you let her down. So powder your fucking vagina and make up for your mistakes."

My ears keep deceiving me. Through the threats, his demands sound similar to thinly veiled approval.

I breathe out a laugh. "She got to you this morning, didn't she? Whatever she told you in the basement has you second-guessing putting a bullet between my eyes."

"Hardly. I'm still trigger-happy, motherfucker. Keep pushing me and you'll see how close I am."

354

There's little intimidation in his tone. Penny must've dug deep under his skin, and a whole heap of pride accompanies that knowledge.

She's healing.

Slowly, but surely.

The water cuts off in the shower, then the screen door clatters open.

"She's going to be out here in a minute." I clap my Mac shut and sidestep Decker to grab my wallet and car fob from the bedside table.

"Where are we going?"

I pause. "We?"

There's a beat of silence as I turn to face him.

"Yeah, *we*. The two of us are all she's got. And I'm not going to put my family in harm's way because of my hatred for you. I want to find this fucker, and it needs to be before tonight."

The bathroom door opens and Penny pads into the room, her loose hair damp around her shoulders, her skin flushed, her T-shirt and jeans still incredibly baggy. As soon as she notices I've got company, she stops, her eyes growing wide. She glances between me and her brother. "What's going on?"

"Nothing." I walk for the duffle to dump my Mac inside. "Deck and I are getting out of here."

Her gaze turns frantic. "The two of you?"

"It's all good, Pen." Decker jerks his chin at her. "We're setting our differences aside. For now."

She pins me with a stare. "Is he serious?"

"Quit eying me like that. You heard the guy; we've become best buddies." I wink at her. "But we need to make a move. We've got a lot to do."

She continues with the visual tennis match as she slowly nods. "Okay. What should I do? I need to help."

"Nothing," Decker answers for me. "Relax. Read a book. There isn't anything you can do."

The moron has no idea she's incapable of relaxation. She needs a distraction.

"You said you remember Luther talking to Benji." I walk to her, gliding my hands over her upper arms. "It would help if you started recalling anyone else he might have spoken to. I need names and specifics. Come up with as many details as you can. No matter how big or small." I run my fingers over her chin and lean in for a kiss. "Robert's working with someone, and the more information we have, the easier it will be to find him."

She nods into me. "I can do that."

Decker mutters something under his breath and trudges to the hall.

I take a second to breathe her in. To remain close before I have to leave. I kiss her again, deeper, and my dick appreciates the proximity.

"I like this." I skim a hand down her arm to the leather cuff firmly affixed to her wrist. "It looks good on you."

"It's the only weapon I have, which means I'll never take it off. All I need now is to learn how to use it."

I lean back, already regretting the distance I'm about to place between us. "I'll teach you as soon as I can, okay? And I'm sure Sarah would be happy to show you a trick or two."

"Okay."

I step away, retreating toward the door. "I'll have my phone on me all day. Do you still have the cell I bought you?"

Her eyes widen. "I didn't bring it."

"It's no big deal. I'll be back as soon as I can. But if you want me for any reason, just ask one of the others for a phone. They've all got my number."

She bites into her bottom lip, her teeth digging deep. "Please stay safe."

I smirk. "Always."

She attempts a smile. "I mean it. I need you to come back. And I need you to look after him." She glances toward the hall and lowers her voice. "Please don't let anything happen to Sebastian."

"I will." I cross a finger over my heart. "I promise."

I just hope I'm capable of fulfilling the vow.

28

PENNY

I STARTED ON THE LIST AS SOON AS THEY LEFT. IT TOOK A WHILE, MY UNWANTED memories unwilling to come forward after I've spent weeks attempting to suppress them.

When I'd finished, Keira texted the information to Luca.

She didn't seem surprised by the names I came up with. Nothing triggered her interest—at least not from what I could tell. Her disregard only made me strive to focus harder on my past in the hopes of coming up with something pivotal.

Even after she sent the message, I relived my time in Greece like a rolodex, flicking over one memory to the next, trying to recall the details of Luther's conversations only to gain tiny snippets that seemed inconsequential. There was too much static to think clearly. Too much debilitating anger that blocked the finer details of the past.

By mid-morning, I was frantic with the need for a distraction without Luca by my side.

There were no updates on his progress as I watched Tobias and Stella play with the nanny. I surrounded myself in their laughter because each passing hour made my apprehension grow.

The other women spent their time making calls and dinner plans. I overheard Layla cancelling reservations people had already booked at Cole's restaurant, while Keira contacted extended family to invite them to the special occasion.

None of the men came home for lunch.

Neither Luca nor Sebastian interrupted the afternoon "Female Empowerment" session Sarah made me attend in the basement.

I both appreciated and cursed every minute that ticked by as I held a gun in my hands and learned how to aim and shoot. And although I adore the leather cuff strapped to my wrist, I much would've preferred Luca to be here giving me good news instead of having Sarah instruct me on how to slice someone's carotid with lethal efficiency.

"They're going to find him," were the only soothing words offered to me from Layla while us four women sat outside in the afternoon sun, the neighborhood now sickly quiet without the barking dog.

It wasn't until later in the day when the sun began to set and Keira excused herself from another chat session around mugs of tea in the kitchen that my confidence in Luca's promises faded.

She didn't give an excuse for leaving my side, but it was clear she needed to get ready for the evening with my parents. They all did. Which meant I was left to sit on the sofa by myself, drowning in fear.

I hadn't let myself believe Luca and Sebastian would return empty-handed.

But they have. I can feel it.

When the front door opens not long after and heavy steps down the hall bring Luca into view, the sight of him only confirms my despair.

Even though he stands tall, head high, shoulders straight, his expression speaks of failure. Those usually intense eyes now beg for forgiveness.

I swallow over the tightening in my throat and look away, my hands clutching the sofa beside my thighs.

"We tried everything," he says in greeting as he walks my way. "We looked everywhere. Spoke to everyone. We fucking interrogated and threatened and threw our weight around, but nobody knows a damn thing."

He stops before me, his red and swollen knuckles clenched at my eye level.

I fight against the need to blame him. To yell and scream even though it's not his fault.

"Where's Sebastian?" I keep my gaze lowered. "Did he come home with you?"

"Yeah. He's getting ready."

A sharp stab enters my heart, penetrating deep. "So, that's it? There's nothing more that can be done? I just have to sit back while my parents are used as bait?"

"They're safe. Nobody is going to get to them. Torian has men set up everywhere. There's not an inch of space in a three-block radius that won't be watched."

Yet again, I'm defenseless against the demands of powerful men.

Everything is always out of my control.

"Your list helped." He strokes a hand through my hair. "Just not enough to find anything concrete."

I jerk my head away and push from the sofa. Antsy. Angry.

"I tried, Pen," he murmurs. "I fucking tried."

I know. That's what makes this worse.

I don't want him to exude defeat and wordlessly beg for forgiveness. It only increases my suffering.

"I'm hoping he's left Portland," he continues. "We've got so many eyes on this city, someone would've had information if he was still here."

I nod, but there's no belief to accompany the gesture. I'm well aware Robert is in control inside his perfect hiding place.

He's preparing.

Scheming.

And I refuse to let him win.

"So, what now?" I suck in a deep breath, forcing strength. "What am I supposed to do?"

"We wait it out. If someone catches sight of him tonight, then Hunt and Sarah will handle it. If not, we try again tomorrow."

"Right… We wait…" I scoff at the ridiculousness. My parents are lambs at the mercy of hungry wolves, and I'm expected to kick back and watch television as if their lives aren't on the line.

"There are things I hate about this, too, Pen. I want to be the one to find him —to fucking slaughter him. I don't want to be stuck here all night either."

"Then don't. I'm not stopping you."

His eyes narrow. "I get that you're angry. But don't pull this shit with me. You know you're my priority."

I can't help it. My rage grows and my helplessness along with it.

"Come here." He grabs my wrist and tugs me into him, wrapping his arms around my back. "This will all be over soon. And your parents won't even know they were a part of it."

"I hope you're right."

Slowly, his confidence seeps into me, strengthening my resolve. When he releases me, I'm no longer clinging to anger.

"I need to take a shower. Come with me."

"Not this time." I slump onto the sofa. "I need to clear my head."

"You sure?"

"Positive." I want space. Even if only for a few minutes.

"Okay." He reaches for the television remote on the coffee table and hands it to me. "I won't be long. Find a movie to watch, and I'll order dinner once I come back."

I nod.

"You know I'm proud of you, right?" He gives a sad smile. "You're taking this like a warrior."

"It doesn't feel that way. I'm so angry I could kill someone."

He chuckles, soft and low, then leans in to place a quick kiss on my forehead. "Aren't we all?" He retreats, heading toward the hall. "I'll be back soon."

I scoot farther back on the sofa and stare into space.

While he's gone, the others return to the mansion to prepare for the party. Chatter echoes through the halls. The kids' laughter carries from different rooms. Doors slam, and hinges squeak with the flurry of movement.

Then one by one, they leave while Luca and I eat Chinese out of cardboard boxes and pretend this might not be the worst night of my rescued life.

The only people left behind are us, the children, and the nanny, the sudden quiet of the once bustling house leaving me numb.

It doesn't take long for anger to return. Then jealousy.

Everyone else is meeting my parents.

My mother.

My father.

And I'm here, watching as the nanny herds Tobias and Stella down the hall to shower and dress for bed.

"I'm not sure if you want to hear this, but Torian sent me a text." Luca tilts his cell screen my way from his position beside me on the sofa.

I've doubled the security on the house. If you go somewhere, take a tail with you.

"Why would we go somewhere?" I ask. "Do you plan on leaving?"

"Not at all." He gives a subtle shake of his head, his expression turning sympathetic. "But it's not too late if you want to see your parents."

"No." My answer is immediate.

I'm not ready.

Maybe soon. But not now.

"I don't mean face-to-face." He pockets his cell. "We could drive by the restaurant. You should be able to see them without leaving the car."

I open my mouth to repeat my protest, only the words don't come. Yearning clogs my throat instead. It's a painful, agonizing hunger for closure.

I'd kill to see them. Even if just a glimpse.

The thought of my mother's smile… the remembered sound of my father's laugh…

The slightest glimmer would mean the world to me.

"What about Robert?"

He shrugs. "Like Torian said, we wouldn't leave without protection. I'd make sure we were covered."

I swallow over the anticipation tingling like wildfire in my stomach. The pounding of my pulse becomes thunderous.

I want this.

With every pain-filled heartbeat, I really, truly want this.

"Okay." I nod. "But only if you think it's safe."

He gives a half-hearted grin. "Let's get you in the car."

I scoot from the sofa. "Hold up. Let me get changed first. Can you tell the nanny?"

He inclines his head and then I run for the hall, yanking off my baggy sweater to throw it to the bed.

I pull on jeans, a comfy suede jacket, and a pair of Sketchers before meeting Luca at the front door.

"I've arranged the escort." He releases the deadlock and pulls the door wide. "One of the guards from the gate will lead the way to the restaurant."

"Good." I follow Luca to his Suburban, my hands shaking by the time we reach the doors and climb inside.

"You should lie down." He winces in apology. "We don't know who's watching."

"Not this time, please. I'll stay on alert. I promise."

He sighs and starts the engine, not answering my plea.

We drive from the property in silence, following a silver sedan slowly through the streets.

"You look nice..." Luca keeps his attention on the road. "For someone who has no intention of leaving the car."

My cheeks heat, stupidity warming my face. "It's silly, I know." He doesn't answer, the quiet compelling me to fill the silent void. "Even though they're not going to see me, I want to look presentable."

"It makes sense." He grabs my hand and entwines our fingers. "But you don't need to explain."

I ignore the world gliding by around us and focus on him—the one who continues to devote his life to making mine better. But the increasing happiness doesn't detract from the rampant beat of my heart as we drive closer to my parents.

My palms grow slick with sweat. My throat dries.

"You're going to be fine," he murmurs. "It'll do you good to see them."

I know.

I really do.

It's the gravity of the situation. The vulnerability I've always feared.

"When you finally do stand face-to-face with them, what will you say?"

I balk at his question. "I don't know. I have no idea."

His lips curve in a thoughtful smile. "You're going to cry like a baby."

I know that, too. My tears well just thinking about it.

"It's going to be beautiful, Pen." He shoots me a glance. "Seeing you happy. Smiling. Even through the tears. It's going to be so fucking beautiful."

I'm lost for words. For thoughts.

His care for me is unlike anything I've experienced. Even from my adoring parents.

I love him. God, how I love him.

"What?" He scrunches his nose before returning his focus to the road. "What's that funny look for?"

"Nothing." I swallow and turn to face the windshield, unwilling to let emotion get the better of me.

"We're almost there."

My breath catches as the silver sedan's brake lights flash. I dig my teeth into my lower lip. Sit straighter. Scan the sidewalk.

"See those men on the corner?" Luca jerks his head at the two casually dressed guys leaning against a brick wall, their attention on their cell screens. "They work for us." He tilts his chin to the other side of the road. "Those three, too."

I trek my attention to the small group chatting out the front of a bar.

"There are men all over the streets. In parked cars. Inside buildings. On top of roofs. All armed and ready at a moment's notice."

I nod, no longer concerned about cover when my pulse feels capable of instigating a heart attack. I can sense my parents nearby. It's as if their hum fills the air; my belly, too.

The sedan pulls into a parking space on the side of the road up ahead, allowing Luca to overtake and glide into the next available spot. I scan my surroundings, looking along the shopfronts to my left.

"Over here." Luca focuses out his window. "That's Torian's restaurant right there."

I scoot forward in my seat, transfixed by the bright glow coming from the wall of glass. The interior of the building is filled with a mass of mingling people, all of them standing and drinking from champagne flutes and pints.

I search the guests, my nervousness building with each unfamiliar face.

"I can't see them." I scoot farther along the seat, my ass hovering on the edge. "I can't even see Sebastian."

"He's in there somewhere." He points a lazy finger from the steering wheel. "There's Hunt and Sarah."

I nod, not caring about those two. Or Benji. Or any of the Torian family. I need to see my parents. After allowing hope to build, I'm now frantic to lay eyes on my mom and dad.

"Want me to drive past?"

"Yes." I nod. "Please."

He pulls onto the street, the creep of the car slow as we approach the restaurant with the front door guarded by two hulking men, another situated at the far end of the building.

I scour the crowd of smiling faces in a frenzy, my attention moving from one person, to the next, to the next. "Where are they?" My stomach churns. Nausea takes over. "I still can't see them."

"Do you want to take a closer look?"

"From where?"

Luca glances at me, his apprehension visible as he frowns. "I can take you around back and sneak you in through the kitchen."

"No." Although I appreciate the suggestion, disappointment overwhelms me. "It's too risky."

"We'll take our time." He continues driving down the street, past the restaurant, and turns at the corner.

"It's okay." I peer over my shoulder, confirming the silver sedan is following us before I sink into my seat. "It wasn't meant to happen tonight."

He turns again, taking a side street behind the back of the buildings. We pass small staff parking lots until Luca pulls into one filled with vehicles, Torian's Porsche parked closest to the few steps leading into the restaurant.

"What are you doing?" I ask.

He stops the Suburban in the last available parking space and cuts the engine. "We're going to sit here for a while, in case you change your mind."

"I—" I cut my sentence short, already second-guessing myself.

If only I could see them. Just a glimpse.

Time passes as my indecision intensifies, the clawing temptation making it difficult to think while Luca watches me. Each minute spent under his gaze is a million heartbeats filled with anxiety and hesitation.

I'm not ready to speak to them… I can't face their questions and tears… I'm not prepared to explain my past…

But I'd give anything to see them.

Anything.

"Are you sure I won't be seen?" I release my belt. "How will this work?"

"I'll go in before you. Then you can follow when the coast is clear."

He's out of the car and opening my door before I can move. He leads me through the parking lot, my breath frosting the air.

The night is still. Behind us there's nothing but silence while up ahead is street noise and the sound of people laughing and chatting.

I pause. "Maybe we should go back to the car."

"I won't let them see you."

I sneak a glimpse over my shoulder, the hair at the back of my neck standing on end. The silver sedan is waiting in the shadows on the side street. The darkened face of the man sitting inside stares straight at me.

"He's keeping an eye on anybody that approaches. And he's not the only one."

I nod, only slightly appeased, and continue after him, one slow step after another until Luca is reaching for the back door, pulling it open with a squeak to poke his head inside.

He blocks my view of the interior for pained heartbeats before he sidesteps and allows me entry into a bustling stainless-steel kitchen.

"Come on." He holds out a hand and drags me inside.

The new noises are overwhelming. The sizzle of hot plates. The clink of saucepans. There are barked orders from a man wearing a chef's uniform as he scans the four workers situated at different cooking stations.

None of them pay us attention as Luca leads me across the room, this time stopping at a swinging door with a circular peephole.

"Here." He peers through the opening. "They're over the far right of the room. Talking to your brother."

My insides squeeze.

Heart. Chest. Stomach.

I can't move.

After years of trying to forget the love and support of my parents due to the weakness it brought, I struggle to take the final step.

"Pen?" Luca tugs on my hand. "Come on."

I stare into those eyes, the noise increasing, my pulse deafening.

He lessens the panic. There's the strong hold of his hand, the unfaltering focus, the confident tilt of his chin. Everything about him makes me want to be bold.

I can do this.

After everything I've been through, I can do this one simple thing.

I inch forward, stealing my hand from his to place my palms against the door for grounding. At first, the view is the same as outside. People are everywhere, the faces unrecognizable.

Then I spy Sebastian in his suit with Keira wearing a floral flowing dress and cream jacket nestled close at his side.

I hold my breath as my gaze drifts over the people in front of him. The shorter height. The greying hair.

My eyes blaze as I stare at the back of my parents' heads.

That's all there is through the crowd. Their familiar hairstyles. The recognizable frames.

But it's them.

My heart.

My home.

Overwhelming gratitude consumes me. I stare at them for a lifetime, the noise disappearing, the outside world evaporating.

"You're smiling." There's pride in Luca's voice. "Really smiling."

I sniff through my tingling nose. "It may only be the back of their heads, but I'm currently seeing the most beautiful picture right now."

"Yeah." He pauses. "Me, too."

The emotions intensify and I tremble with thanks as I turn my attention to Luca, ensnared in his pride-filled eyes.

"Go on." He jerks his chin at the peephole. "Keep lookin'. I'm going to steal something to eat and stop distracting you." He winks and walks away, aiming for the kitchen staff preparing hors d'oeuvres.

"Thank you." It takes a moment for me to drag my gaze back to the party. I watch. Listen. Pretend I'm part of the festivities.

I let the laughter from the people inside the restaurant sink into me, the happiness, the calm, and attempt to read Sebastian's lips as he continues to talk to our parents.

I don't move as waitstaff walk in and out of the kitchen, the whoosh of the door beside me bringing clearer insight to nearby conversations. I hear names and punchlines. Drink orders and compliments.

Then horror.

Every ounce of my joy evaporates when a male voice asks, "Hey, Dodge, how have you been?"

That's all it takes. One question. One name.

Dodge.

Ice enters my veins. My breathing labors.

I can't see who the speaker is. I can't even determine who they're talking to, but that name brings crystal clarity.

My memory hadn't triggered this morning when I wrote that list, but it does now.

Dodge was a man who supplied Luther with information. A spy of sorts. A traitor to Cole.

I inch back from my peephole and try to get my memories to cycle while attempting to hear the respondent at the same time.

I fail at both.

I remember thinking Dodge was a snake. A slimy, manipulative piece of shit, but I can't pinpoint specific references, only the repeated farewells Luther often spoke.

Keep digging for me, Dodge.

Don't let me down, Dodge.

"What's going on?" Luca comes up behind me, hovering close. "Did they see you?"

I shake my head, still trying to tear pieces of information from a brain that refuses to release them. I need proof. It took too long for me to be believed about Robert.

"Pen?" Luca grabs my shoulders and turns me to face him. "Talk to me."

I try to find answers in his eyes. Still, nothing comes. There are only repeated farewells and snide compliments.

You're invaluable, Dodge.

Luther rarely gave out compliments. Not to his sons, or his right-hand men. It was only to those he manipulated to further his goals. Only to pawns caught in his web.

And now one of those conniving puppets is in the same room as my parents. Within threatening distance of those I love.

"I recognize a name from someone in there." I watch Luca's expression, searching for support. "A name of someone who previously conspired against Cole."

Luca stands taller, shooting a glance out the peephole before returning his attention to me.

He transforms before my eyes. From calm and in control to a strung-tight, laser-focused soldier in a heartbeat.

"Tell me the name," he demands.

29

LUCA

"Dodge," she whispers. "The person's nickname is Dodge."

I hold myself in check, not reacting as my stomach bottoms. But she notices the freefall, her attention narrowing in concern.

"This is bad, isn't it?" she asks in a rush. "Do you think he's here for me? Or my parents? Could he be working with Robert?"

"No. It's okay." I rub her arms and paste on a fucking painful smile. "I've had my suspicions, that's all. And I know how close he is to Torian."

How unbelievably, fucking close.

Breaths escape her lips in panted panic. "What about my parents?"

"They'll be fine. Nobody is stupid enough to risk anything tonight. But I need you to do something for me, okay?" I guide her away from the door, my hand on the low of her back as I lead her to the storeroom. "Wait in here for a while. Just until I handle this."

She plants her feet, her frantic gaze searching my face. "Handle it? What does that mean?" She leans closer, whispering, "Are you going to kill someone? Please, Luca, I want to get my parents out of—"

"They're fine." I open the storeroom, flick on the light, and place pressure on her back to encourage her inside. "I'm only asking for ten minutes. Don't leave this room."

I don't wait for a protest. I shut her inside, the sight of her fear-filled expression haunting me as I stalk for the dining room, past the swinging doors, and into the crowd of guests.

I pass Torian's relatives, friends, and trusted informants as my fury builds. I stalk by women whose husbands have worked with the crime family for years while a tick forms under my right eye. Then I stop before Dodge and look that motherfucker in the eye, knowing on instinct Penny is right about him. Knowing that whoever referenced his nickname tonight is one of the few old-school elders who stood by Luther's side from the beginning of his crime-riddled reign, because they're the only people who have ever called my brother by that name.

The sight of him infuriates me. Fucking sickens me.

I ignore the older man flanking his side, and grab the front of Benji's shirt, bringing an abrupt halt to their conversation.

"Outside," I snarl. "*Now.*"

His eyes flare wide. A flash of fear and guilt hits him before quickly being smothered under anger. "What the—"

I yank his shirt, making him stumble, then release him to storm for the kitchen, not stopping until after I've shoved open the back door and jumped down the stairs to the loose asphalt.

He's slow to follow, descending to ground level with stiff hesitance. "Luca, whatever it is—"

"Save it." I launch my fist at his face, my knuckles colliding with bone.

He jolts backward, stumbling, but I hold him on his feet with an unyielding grip around his throat. "You fucking snitch." I keep my voice low, too fucking aware of the watchful eyes lurking in the shadows. I shove him, over and over until he's up against the brick wall. "You were working with Luther."

He doesn't fight me. Doesn't even protest my grip as his face turns red. All he does is hold my gaze, wordlessly spewing guilt in my direction.

"You fucking piece of shit." I drag him forward and slam him back again. "You stupid, fucking piece of shit. How could you be so reckless?"

"You weren't here when Luther was around."

All the air leaves my lungs on a heave. Despite how things were adding up— even though evidence was mounting—I still hadn't believed.

Not entirely.

Not until now.

I release his throat and stumble backward.

He's dead.

Benji is as good as buried. No trial. No second chances.

"Jesus goddamn Christ." I shove my hands into my hair, pulling at the strands to try to make the mania stop.

"You've got no idea what it was like." He straightens from the wall. "You wouldn't understand."

I can't deal. Can't even fucking fathom his level of stupidity.

Problem is, if I don't take this to Torian, I'll be dead alongside Benji. And if I rat out my own blood, the admission probably wouldn't absolve me anyway.

There's no way out of the mess he's created. There's no possible way I can fix this shit.

"Why?" My question is barely audible. "Why the fuck would you even…" I can't finish the sentence through the bile thickening at the back of my throat.

"How did this all start? You had to have known what he was doing. There's no way you weren't aware of those women."

His shoulders slump, and he throws his hands up at his sides. "He—"

The back door to the restaurant opens, quickly dragging my attention to Layla whose mouth gapes at the sight of us.

"What's going on?" She slams the door shut and scrambles down the stairs.

"Get out of here, Layla." I glare at her. "This is a private matter."

"No," she pleads. "It's not. He's my husband. This includes me, too."

I scoff. "You've got no idea—"

"Yes, I do." She rushes in front of Benji, acting like a shield to my rage. "I know exactly what this is about. *Please,* Luca. We've been waiting for the news to get out for years. We never thought our actions would cause this much trouble."

Our actions

I'm blindsided. *Again.* Completely and utterly dumb-fucked.

"It was my idea for Benji to tell you there was another woman," she pleads. "I'd hoped it would stop you from digging further. We just needed a little more time. Once Robert was taken care of this all would've blown over."

"Blown over?" I seethe. "How the fuck do you think this would've blown over? Your husband was ratting on your brother."

"Layla," Benji warns. "Let me deal with this." He grabs her arms, attempting to drive her away. "Go back inside."

"I can't." Tears form in her eyes. "This is because of me. *I* started this."

"Layla," Benji snaps. "*Get back inside.*"

She reaches for me as she's pushed to the side. "Luca, please let me explain."

My nostrils flare. My fucking head threatens to explode.

I don't want to hear from her.

The only explanation I need will come from Benji. But that asshole isn't as open to being a Chatty Cathy like his wife.

"I was a horrible person when I first met your brother," she says in a rush. "I was materialistic and petty. Like everyone in my family, I craved money, but I wanted some for myself. Some that was my own. *Our* own," she clarifies.

"I wanted to have financial security because Dad kept telling me Cole would never succeed in taking over the business, and the thought of being poor scared the hell out of me. I was the one who put pressure on Ben to do something about it. Something above and beyond the work he did for my brother." She blinks those long lashes at me, her tears building. "When Dad offered to pay us to keep tabs on Cole, I didn't think it would be a big deal. It was only a father wanting to be updated on his son. At least, that's how it started."

"Layla," Benji grates. "That's enough."

"Shut the fuck up." I clench my fist, preparing to silence him. "At least she has the balls to talk."

"Fuck you. I can talk fine on my own." He tugs down his shirt, righting the crinkles as he speaks under his breath. "It was only meant to be brief updates on business dealings. I'd be financially compensated if I kept Luther in the loop. That's all. We thought we were setting Stella up for the rest of her life in case things went south under Torian's leadership. But before we knew it, the demands got bigger and the threats started. It went from being harmless information to phone taps and spy software."

Fuck. "Phone taps and spy software?"

Layla hangs her head, but Benji lacks the same remorse. He holds my gaze, unblinking.

"He was like a father to me," he mutters. "A *proper* father. He saved me. *Guided* me. He gave me the chance to have a family, for once in my life. To have money and power and pride. I was a fucking man, no longer needing you and your white knight routine to save me from myself."

I scoff. "Well, there's no fucking white knight to save you now, is there? Nothing can help you this time."

"You don't need to." Layla lunges forward, reaching for me, her fingers gripping my jacket as those eyes continue to beg. "Cole doesn't need to know."

I huff out a laugh. "And I guess Penny doesn't deserve to find out either? She doesn't get to learn how Abi really died."

Neither one of them speak. Both remain silent while I compound their crimes.

"That's how your scheme got fucked up, right? Robert got involved? You gave him information," I sneer at my brother, all vicious teeth and seething hatred. "Tell me you gave him insight on Penny. Tell me and I'll end this now."

He doesn't answer, and I don't pause in my response. I nudge Layla out of the way with my shoulder and swing a fist, my knuckle pounding into Benji's gut.

He hunches, coughing, spitting.

Layla wails, her ragged breaths pathetic when coupled with her corruption.

I lean close to my brother's ear as he clasps his hands on his knees, trying to catch his breath. "Tell me."

"Fuck you," he chokes. "I didn't tell him jack shit about her."

"You're a liar." I see red. I *feel* it. There's only heat and rage and mindlessness as I raise my fist again.

"Stop, Luca," Layla cries. "Please. He didn't give any information to Robert. It wasn't him. *I* did it. *I* told Robert where they were."

My brother pauses his recovery, the shock on his raising face seeming genuine as he looks at his wife. "No, you didn't." He shakes his head. "You wouldn't."

"I didn't have a choice. He threatened to tell Cole everything. And you kept refusing to give him information. You thought you could handle it on your own. You were going to get yourself killed."

"She's lying." Benji looks at me. "She had no idea where I was. Nobody did. But it's true about that fucker threatening us. He's going to tell everyone. That's why I was late yesterday. I was trying to find him and fix this myself."

I glance between them, having no clue which one is bluffing. "I swear to God, if I don't get the full story, without contradictory bullshit, I'm going to lose my shit."

"I already told you." Layla's tear-soaked eyes plead with me. "I had Benji's location on my phone. I always do."

"Like hell," he spits. "I was using a burner."

"Yes, but you had your main cell with you. In your bag or the car. I don't know where exactly, but it was with you, Benji. I'm not lying." The first tear escapes as her lips tremble. "I did this. I'm responsible for that woman's death. And for the attack yesterday. It's my fault."

I stare at her. At the beautiful face that hid those sinister actions.

"Why didn't you tell me?" Benji collapses against the wall. "Why the fuck—"

"Because you wouldn't have given him what he wanted. You were more likely to come clean to Cole," she sobs. "I had no choice. I did it to protect Stella."

"You did it to protect yourself," I snap. "To protect your perfect fucking life in your perfect fucking house—"

Benji straightens, shoving from the wall to pull Layla into his side. "What's it matter? The damage is done now. We need to move on. We can bury this."

"Bury it?" My head fucking throbs. "And then what? Wait for Robert to come after Penny?"

He scoffs. "You barely know her."

I gnash my teeth to the point of pain. Clench my fists until my knuckles burn. I could kill him. Right now. In this moment. I could retrieve the gun from my waistband and shoot him for his blatant disregard for her life.

"This is my *family*, Luc. My daughter."

"If you tell her, it's one more loose end," Layla pleads. "If Cole finds out, he won't hold me accountable. He'll blame everything on Benji. He won't care that it was my fault."

"That's because your husband is a grown-ass man who never should've done this in the first place. Now tell me what else you told that son of a bitch."

The back door swings open and Hunt and Sarah step outside, their curiosity switching between the three of us.

"What are you doing here?" Hunt directs at me. "Aren't you meant to be at Torian's with the klepto?"

I ignore the taunt as they continue down the stairs, the door banging shut behind them.

"Who died?" Sarah asks.

"Nobody," I sneer. "I'm just trying to have a conversation with my brother."

"Must be a serious conversation." She plasters her hands on her hips, all smug and superior. "I'm sensing a wealth of hostility."

The door squeaks opens again, and I curse under my breath at the added audience. It isn't until I glance up to see who it is that my world drops.

Penny.

Her gaze treks over me, from my clenched fists and intimidating stance to the stupid asshole in front of me who bears the brunt of my anger.

It takes a brief second for her expression to change. From curiosity to horror, the color draining from her features.

"It was him," she whispers, still holding the door as if unsure whether to flee back inside. "It was your brother."

Benji's gaze bores into the side of my face as her eyes beg for answers.

I don't know what to say. I don't know how to fix this.

My brother has dragged us into a mess I can't even comprehend, and all I want to do is get her out of it.

"Shorty, I need you to go back inside for a few more..."

My words drift off as Torian comes up behind her, still wearing the mask of hospitable exuberance he always radiates at these functions. He shows no shock at the gathering. No surprise at all at his sister's tears.

"Why did the party move to the parking lot?" He reaches over Penny's shoulder, opening the door wide to get out.

Decker follows a few steps behind. "What the hell are you doing here, Pen?"

Nobody speaks. Nobody moves.

"Don't look at me." Hunt raises his hands. "Sarah and I came out here to fuck."

Torian stops at my side. "Do I need to ask again? Why is my sister upset?

"It's been a long week, Cole." Layla sniffs. "I'm overemotional. That's all."

I fight the need to glare at her as Penny cautiously descends the stairs. Her approach is slow, but her head is high, her shoulders straight. She's preparing for battle.

I start toward her, needing—more than anything—to get her out of here. "We came for a drive to see if we could catch a glimpse of Penny's parents. We're leaving now."

"You're not going anywhere until I have answers," Torian's tone is calm as he lashes out to grab my arm in a white-knuckle grip. "Tell me why my sister is crying."

My pulse detonates.

His hand on me is enough to push my rage beyond my control.

My lip curls with the restriction. The hair on the back of my neck rises.

"Just drop it." Layla wipes her nose with the side of her hand. "I had a fight with my husband. That's all. It's none of your business."

Torian ignores her, and my brother, too. Instead, he pins me with his narrowed stare, wordlessly siphoning the truth.

"Get your fucking hand off me." I yank my arm from his hold and reach into my pocket, retrieving my car fob. "Sarah, I need you to take Penny back to the house. I don't want her parents seeing her before she's—"

"No." Penny shakes her head. "I'm not going anywhere."

I walk to her, not stopping until we're toe to toe. Chest to chest. I wrap my arms around her and pull her so damn close my mouth is a breath from her ear as I whisper, "I need you to do this for me. Trust me."

She stiffens and draws back until those frantic eyes meet mine.

A myriad of thoughts dance in those dark depths. There are questions. Accusations. Fears. I can hear them all, the volume deafening.

"I'll follow soon." I mark the lie with a quick kiss.

God only knows if I'm going to get out of this to see her again. And from her gasped exhale, I think she knows it, too.

"I don't have all fucking night," Torian seethes. "We have guests to return to. Get her the hell out of here, Sarah."

Penny's eyes widen as she shakes her head. "Please, Luca."

"*Go.* Everything will be okay." It's another lie. After weeks of priding myself on telling her the truth, I'm now tainting this thing we have between us. "Make sure the car on the side street follows you."

"I'll take care of it." Sarah comes up behind her, wrapping an arm around her shoulders to lead her away.

Penny's first step is fumbled, her feet stumbling before she sucks in a deep breath and continues on her own. Everything in her expression speaks of sorrow, the pain marrow deep, but I remain quiet, stiff, my focus returning to the group as the two women climb into my car and slam the doors.

"Someone better start talking," Torian warns. "I want to know what the fuck is going on."

"Color me curious, too," Hunt drawls. "The suspense is killing me."

Benji keeps his mouth shut as Sarah drives from the parking lot, the purr of the second car starting moments later.

It's Layla who crumples as she turns to face her brother. "It was a misunderstanding. I thought he was cheating on me."

Jesus.

Fuck.

Not this bullshit again.

I fight a telling reaction. I force myself not to close my eyes at the compounding lies. I use all my strength to hold back a sneer. But the weight of Decker's gaze bores into me from the top of the steps. He's reading me, his narrowed stare demanding the truth.

"I've set her straight." Benji wraps an arm around his wife's waist. "She was paranoid with me being away too long."

"Is that right?" Torian straightens to his full height, all regal and superior. "Why do I have a feeling you're lying?"

"I swear on my life, I'm not cheating on her." Benji holds up a hand in surrender. "I never would."

I mentally scoff. His life isn't worth dick. Cheating or not.

"Layla," Torian warns. "Tell me the truth."

"I am." Her throat works over a heavy swallow, her guilt clear for everyone to see. "He's not cheating."

"Shit. This is serious." Hunt inches closer. "What's going on? And why wasn't I involved?"

"Stay out of this," I warn. "The last thing this night needs is your commentary."

"Touchy much?"

"Quit the shit." Torian raises his voice. "You realize this neighborhood is being watched, right? I told you all I'd have men everywhere. Did you think about that when you were having your domestic argument out in the open air?"

He's bluffing.

"Do you want to know the updates texted to me while I was inside trying to entertain our guests?" he continues. "Want me to show you?"

They're lies.

We kept our voices down. The guard in the silver sedan would've only seen the fight. Nobody would've heard us. But *fuck.* I wouldn't stake my life on it.

Everyone falls silent as I struggle to come up with a plan. I need to get Benji out of here. We only need a head start.

"You look tense, Luc." Torian's tone is threatening. "Want me to take a guess at why?"

"I fucked up." Benji speaks before I get the chance. "Luca's not involved."

"Shut your mouth," I warn.

"It's true." He straightens, raising his chin. "I need to take responsibility."

"I said, shut the fuck up, Ben." I glare at him.

"Please, Benji." Layla grabs his wrist. "We'll talk about this at home."

"No, you'll talk about it here." Torian steps closer to my brother. "*Now.*"

"He stole money," I mutter. "He stole money from *me* and I'm pissed. That's all this is—a family matter. It's nobody else's business."

"No, fuck that." Benji holds Torian's stare. "I betrayed you. I went behind your back and—"

Before the sentence is finished, Cole pulls a gun from his waistband and places the barrel to my brother's forehead.

I don't move, not an inch, as Layla screams, the piercing shriek slicing through my throbbing skull.

"Keep talking," Torian sneers.

"I was a rat for your father."

"*No.*" Layla falls to her knees, her manic sobs increasing. "It was *me.* I did this. *I* made this mess."

Torian's aim doesn't waiver from Benji's head as I take in my potential opponents—Hunter with his chest puffed out, his fingers twitching at his sides, and Decker whose face is emotionless, not a hint of anger.

"I need everyone to calm down." I step closer to Benji only to have Hunter's attention snap to me.

"Back off." He points a finger at me in warning. "Stay out of this."

"I can't." I shake my head. "He's my brother—"

"He's going to be your dead brother if he doesn't start talking a lot faster." Torian jabs the gun barrel into Benji. "Spill it all, you son of a bitch."

"It was *me*." Layla tugs on his trousers. "*I* caused this. I begged him to do it. Dad made me believe—"

"Don't worry. I already assumed Luther convinced you I was worthless," Torian snarls. "You had no faith in me."

"It was a long time ago." She slowly drags herself to her feet, tentatively reaching for the gun, only to be shoved away.

"Get inside. I'll deal with you later."

"Cole, *please listen*."

"So help me God, Layla, if you don't walk back into that restaurant and pretend this never happened, I will make you regret bringing a daughter into this world."

She gasps, her tear-streaked face losing color. "What does that—"

"*Now*."

"Do what he says." Benji jerks his chin at her. "Go."

"No." She shakes her head, frenzied. "This was *my* fault. *My* decision. I did this, Cole. Not him."

"Either get inside or watch your husband die."

Fuck.

I reach for my gun, prepared to aim at Torian, when Hunter makes the same move. I turn my attention to him instead, both of us staring down the barrel of the other.

"Fucking hell." Decker jumps down the stairs. "Why don't we all take a breath and get the story straight before we start turning on each other?"

Torian ignores him. "On your knees," he demands of Benji.

"I said, get the story straight first." Decker pulls out his gun, placing it to the back of Torian's head.

Holy fucking shit. It's a Mexican standoff.

No winners. All losers.

Layla stumbles backward, shaking, sobbing, her hand raising to cover her mouth.

"What the hell are you doing, Deck?" Hunt snaps. "Lower your fucking gun."

"I can't." He shrugs. "Cole's protecting his family, and I'm protecting mine."

"How the fuck do you figure that?"

"If Benji dies, Luca could be next by association. And unfortunately, my sister has caught feelings for that asshole, which means he's as good as family to me. I can't stand by and let this happen. Not until the full story is heard."

30

PENNY

I STARE INTO THE DISTANCE, MY BODY HEAVY AS I STRUGGLE NOT TO THROW UP.

I know what I saw back there.

Luca had been blindsided. By his brother.

I feel it in my gut; Benji is Dodge. I just can't bring myself to believe it. That truth would have major consequences and I don't want to contemplate any of them.

"Want to talk about it?" Sarah gives me a sympathetic look from behind the wheel as we turn and head down a street I'm unfamiliar with.

"No." I glance over my shoulder, checking to make sure the silver sedan is behind us.

"Don't worry; he's following. He won't leave us." Sarah gives another one of those pitying looks. "I'm just taking a more populated route home instead of the fastest."

I nod and settle into my seat, not seeing anything but the scene back in the parking lot as we pass block after block.

I can't get Luca's stricken face out of my head. The anger. The agony. I want to be there with him. By his side. Learning the truth.

"Your parents are nice," Sarah murmurs. "Quiet, but doting. They seemed to have had a great time driving around the country in their RV."

I don't answer. Not only because the inane chitchat is life-draining, but because I can't add thoughts of my parents to the washing machine of turmoil building inside me.

I want her to take me to Luca. I need to know what's going on.

I'm about to ask her to turn around when a car horn blares behind us, the flashing lights of high beams illuminating the interior.

I rise in my seat, blinded by the car behind us as a white truck speeds past on the wrong side of the road. I panic, bracing for an attack when it turns down the next street, practically on two tires.

"It's okay." Sarah gives me a half-hearted smile. "Just another asshole who doesn't know how to drive."

No, it's an omen. A stark sign I'm heading in the wrong direction.

"I have to go back." I clear my throat as we approach an intersection, still able to hear the screeching truck in the distance. "I need to talk to Luca."

"Take my phone." She grabs her cell from her jeans pocket and hands it over. "Call him."

"I don't want to call him. I need to see him."

She ignores me, pulling to a stop at a red light. The longer she remains silent, the more I hear the taunting sounds of that truck, the squeak of rubber, the rev of the engine.

The noise adds to my urgency, pushing me to hurry up and get to Luca. "Please, Sarah. Turn us around."

The light changes to green and she accelerates.

"*Sarah*, I want—"

Tires shriek.

A horn blasts behind us.

We reach the middle of the juncture, my focus moving from Sarah to the beaming lights barreling toward us from her side window. "*Sarah*," I scream. "*The truck.*"

I brace for impact, my hands white-knuckling the seat. But it's not enough to stop the force slamming through me.

My airbag deploys, knocking the oxygen from my lungs, belting me in the face.

Darkness steals my vision. I gasp for breath and blink rapidly, attempting to dislodge the inky black as my ears ring.

"Sarah?" I blindly reach for her. "Are you okay?"

She groans as my sight shifts from dark, to grey, to an almost decipherable blur.

I hear things. A rapid mass of noise. The hiss of something mechanical. A car door slams in the distance. Screams. Then gunfire—rapid, bone-chilling gunfire.

I scramble to undo my belt around the inflated airbag. "Sarah, wake up. You need to wake up."

The shots ring louder. From different directions, the closest approaching.

My hands shake in my search for the goddamn buckle, my fingers trembling as I finally release the clasp.

"Sarah." I reach for her again, this time seeing the crimson blood staining the airbag beside where her forehead rests. "*Sarah.*"

Everything quietens. The outside world becomes still as my heartbeat intensifies.

She's hurt. Bad. The color once brightening her face is gone.

"Please, Sarah."

She groans again, filling me with rampant hope.

The familiar tap against my window that steals it away.

I stop breathing.

Swallow.

Tap, tap, tap.

I remain frozen, caught between the need to scream and hide. Fight and surrender.

I know who's at my door. I know without doubt before I turn and come eye-to-eye with Robert, his face now clean-shaven, his hair in a buzz cut as his gleaming smile bears down on me.

The instinct to flee is overwhelming; the necessity wails inside my skull. It takes all my will to shut it down.

What takes its place is a maniacal huff of laughter. I knew I'd never escape. Not from him. Not from the nightmares in Greece.

I could scramble into the back of the car and run from the other side, but he'd catch me.

I could yell for help, yet all I'd achieve is a bigger tally to the dead bodies lying on the ground outside.

The bad guys always win. Always.

He quirks a brow in question and shifts the aim of his gun from me to Sarah.

"*No.*" I push open my door. "Stop."

He smirks and lunges for me, pulling me from the Suburban by my hair. I struggle not to cry out from the pain and scramble to find my footing while he pats me down with an aggressive hand, his gun still trained on Sarah.

"She's dead," I lie.

"Then shooting her isn't going to matter, is it?"

"No, Robert, please." I clasp my palms in prayer. "I'll go with you. I'll go willingly. Just leave her alone."

He smiles, a true, genuine smile that may have had the potential to be handsome if he wasn't a monster. "You missed me, didn't you?"

I press my lips tight against the need to defy him, to spit in his face and wipe the smug satisfaction from his expression.

"Don't worry." He winks. "It'll be just you and me before you know it."

"Let her go," a man yells in the distance.

Oh, God.

"*No,*" I scream as Robert swings me around, not pausing a beat before he shoots in the direction of the demand, hitting a man in the chest.

The shock on the stranger's face, along with the sickening jolt of his body, shoves me straight into the horror of my past. All of it comes rushing back—the helplessness, the torture. It suffocates me. It's impossible to breathe.

"*You piece of shit.*" I lash out, smacking and punching as his grip tightens in my hair. *"You fucking monster."*

"There's my pretty Penny," he taunts. "It's good to see you've still got fight left in you, because all Abi did was cry like a little bitch."

I scream, pummeling his chest, scratching at his face until he reefs me along beside him, storming for the silver sedan behind us, the hood and windshield peppered with bullets.

People scramble to safety in the distance. Some frantically talk on their cells. Others flee the scene.

There are so many witnesses. So many potential casualties to my demise.

"Quit fighting." Robert tugs me harder, making me stumble. "It's time to get out of here."

I don't stop punching at him as he drags me toward the car and over the driver's dead body lying on the asphalt, a gaping head wound sending bile rocketing up my throat.

I gag. Choke.

Robert doesn't care. He continues to yank me along at his side before reaching into the driver's side of the vehicle to pop the trunk.

Oh, God, no.

I increase my struggle, clawing and scratching like an animal. Hitting. Kicking.

People call out from their hiding places, pointlessly threatening him to stop.

"The police are on the way."

"I've got a gun. Let her go or I'll shoot."

They won't take him down. And the police won't get here in time.

I'm going to die at the hands of a rapist. Just like I knew I always would.

"Get in." He releases my hair when we reach the back of the car, and pulls the trunk open. "Hurry up. I don't want to have to damage that pretty face any more than it already is."

The sight before me makes me wither. I stare down at my new prison, the dirty carpeted interior seeming more of a sanctuary since it will be away from his touch. But it's only the start. The deceptive prelude.

"Come on, pretty Penny." He leans close, his breath making me shudder as he whispers, "It's my turn to have you now. Didn't I tell you you'd be mine?"

Yes, he did. And I'd believed him.

With everything inside me I knew it was true.

It was Luca who made me forget. He temporarily distracted me from my future. From my fate.

"Get in." Robert shoves me with force. "Protesting won't save you, but it will permanently destroy your beautiful face."

"Fuck you." I stand my ground.

"Have it your way." He lunges for my legs, hauling me off the ground to topple me into the trunk.

Metal collides with my hip, sending shooting pain around my waist, and I cry out as my head hits the dirty interior. Neither impact stops me from scrambling to my hands and knees.

"Don't even try it." Robert pulls his gun on me and I freeze. "That's a good girl." He looms over me with a leering smile. "You wouldn't believe how easy it was to get to you. How fucking simple when I had someone on the inside. And I can't wait to tell you my plans for the future, but for now, enjoy the ride." He shoots me a wink and reaches to close the trunk.

I quickly duck, missing another impact to the head as he locks me inside the darkened space.

As soon as his footsteps recede, I scramble to get a textural hold on my surroundings, panic overwhelming me.

I slide my palms over everything, searching for an end in the carpet to pull upward in the hopes of finding something beneath. But I can't lift the floor when my weight already rests on top of it. I can't even slide my fingers into the cavity below to search for a jack or any sort of tool.

A door slams. The engine growls to life.

I fight tears as the car moves forward, the pace increasing. Sirens wail in the distance and I set my gliding hands in search of the tail lights. I rip at the upholstery, tugging and tugging until my fingers scream in protest.

The more I rip and yank, the faster the car accelerates, sliding me around the trunk with each of Robert's sharp turns.

I begin to pray for a vehicle collision. That this psychotic asshole will wrap us around a pole, because death by his hands would be better than a life under his fists, but then the red illumination of the tail lights seeps through, the glimpse of light in the darkness giving me hope.

I squeeze my fist into the opening. Tug at the wires. Thump at the warm metal at the back of the light. I thump and thump and thump as I'm thrown around the small space like a doll. I swear I'm about to break through, and that the anticipation has increased the static in my ear to drown out the sirens. Until I realize I can still hear the rumble of tires against gravel. The low hum of the radio.

Oh, God.

The wail of cop cars trails in the distance. Robert must have lost them.

I'm on my own.

I fight back panic as the vehicle turns and turns again, then slows... stops... The grumble of a garage door grates from right outside my spacious coffin.

Wherever we are is still in Portland. Maybe even suburbia. But far from the police that previously gave me hope. Now there's only resignation as I slide back into the woman I once was. The victim. The slave.

From hell to salvation and back again. All in the blink of an eye.

I'd been so happy this morning. Despite the trials and tribulations, I'd breathed freely, yet I took it for granted for too long. I hadn't embraced the gift of reclaimed life. I'd refused to grasp it in both hands.

Maybe that's why this has happened.

Maybe my lack of gratitude has brought me full circle.

I shouldn't have held back in telling Luca how I felt. He deserved to know he was everything to me. Not just a savior or a protector. He was my hope. My future. My life.

The trunk opens and Robert greets me with his smirk still firmly in place.

"We're here, milady." He reclaims my hair, making me scramble as he drags me out of the car to my feet.

I don't let a hint of fear escape. Not one glimmer of sadness or anger.

I lock everything inside, taking on the painful build of adrenaline.

He wants me to be scared of him, so I won't.

He wants me to feel helpless, so I refuse.

"Where are we?" I take in everything within the limited restriction of my view as he continues to grasp my hair.

The three-car garage is empty apart from the vehicle he stole. It's pristine, too —the floors polished, the storage shelves in perfect order. Either the owner of this house has OCD, or they have cleaning staff.

"This is a temporary pitstop." He drags me toward a door across the far side of the room. "I've got a few things to take care of before we can return home."

Home.

The word chokes through me.

"You can't be serious." I stumble as he tugs me harder, opening the door with a harsh kick. "Greece will be the first place they look for me."

"They?" He laughs. "There won't be anyone left behind to look." His hand pinches tighter as he drags me down a darkened hall, the inside of the house smelling like death. It's putrid, the vile scent bringing a gag-inducing taste to my mouth.

"You'll get used to it." He yanks me harder, past art on the walls, beneath high ceilings, along plush carpet.

I attempt to cover my nose and mouth as I stumble, only to have my arm fall to my side at the sight of a woman lying face down on the carpet.

"Watch out for the old girl. She's resting." Robert keeps pulling me. "Her dog is, too."

Up ahead, a large Golden Retriever blocks the path, its limbs stiff.

I can't hold the bile in any longer. I retch, the meagre contents of my stomach falling a few feet from the dead bodies.

"You need to toughen up, pretty Penny. You never used to be this weak."

He gives my hair one long, hard yank then shoves me away as he flicks on a light, exposing a gleaming white foyer with a staircase bordering both walls. The picture-perfect scene brings a whiplashed contrast from the darkened death and destruction.

"Go on." He jerks the barrel of his gun at me. "Get upstairs."

I can't move. Can't think.

Back in Greece, Robert was a monster. He tortured my sisters, raped them, and tormented me. But he was leashed. Luther held him in check.

Now he's a free agent. Willing and capable to cause unimaginable horror. And I don't know how to effectively fight against it.

"Don't worry about Mavis, my love." He jabs me in the shoulder blade with the gun. "You wouldn't have liked the old bitch."

All the air shudders from my lungs.

I know where I am. With heartbreaking dread, I know exactly who the elderly woman is.

"You just figured it out, didn't you?" He snickers. "Surprise. I've been watching you." He jabs the gun again, this time into my stomach, making me grunt. "Now you're going to watch me."

I backtrack, heading toward the staircase. "Watch you do what?"

"Kill everyone who betrayed Luther."

Blinding panic overcomes me as I walk without thought. I'm too focused on trying to force myself to think, but nothing comes.

I can't run. Can't hide.

I need to fight. I just don't know how.

We reach the top of the staircase and he shoves me left into a darkened bedroom with the moonlight spilling through the open curtains.

"Take a look at the view," he taunts. "It's spectacular."

I don't move. I don't want to see.

"*Look*," he demands, digging the gun into the back of my skull.

He won't kill me, not yet. But I comply regardless, not wanting the little strength I have left to be beaten from my body.

I approach the window to stare down at Cole's yard.

Even though I anticipated the sight, the reality stabs through my chest like jagged glass.

The illuminated empty living room is right there. The place where I spoke to Luca outside this morning is in clear view.

Robert approaches, settling in behind me, his arm wrapping around my waist. "I watched you with another man," he growls in my ear. "I saw him place his hands on something that's mine. Do you understand how that made me feel?"

I close my eyes and force myself to remember that moment. The bliss. The warmth.

Luca is always the light in the darkness. The protection in the face of my fears. I can't forget the strength he's given me.

"I got a front row seat to the way you looked at him," he snarls. "That's why it's important you watch what comes next."

"You won't kill him," I whisper. "He's smarter than you."

"Really? You don't think I've taken the time to prepared to take down your SEAL? I killed Abi and got away with it. You should've seen her, all meek and vulnerable in her childhood bed. With her parents close by, she didn't dare to raise her voice to me. It was all tears and whispered pleas as I slit her wrists. She made it so fucking easy to creep out of there unnoticed. I would've done the same with Nina, but I needed a little more excitement. I decided to shoot that bitch instead."

I sink my teeth into my lower lip, battling the need to release the screaming voices inside my head. To kick. To attack. I bite until I taste blood and bile. I clench my fists until I've gained enough control to turn in his grip and face him.

"But you failed." I hold his gaze, his nose bare inches from mine. "You didn't kill Nina and now she's more protected than ever."

His eyes narrow. "Bullshit."

I smile through the hatred. "Luther would be disappointed in you."

There's a second of hesitation. A small bite of stillness before he lashes out, grabbing my throat in a choking grip.

I grasp at his wrist, attempting to break the hold as I struggle for air. I can't remember what to do. There's no memory of what Luca taught me before I'm shoved backward into the window.

"Don't worry, Pen. I'll fix my mistake. I might even make you join in."

I gasp for breath as footsteps creep down the hall, alerting me to another threat. I tilt my head, trying to get a gauge on this second enemy that lurks in the darkness.

"That's right. I'm not alone." He grins. "And I have the best leverage to take down everyone responsible for ruining my life."

"You're wrong. I'm not a big enough draw card to pull anyone into a trap."

"I agree. You're worthless." He bridges the space between us, pulling me close to kiss my jaw, my cheek, making my skin crawl. "That's why I made sure I had something far greater than a whore to make them fall to their knees."

"Like what?"

"You'll find out." There's confidence in his gaze, a gleaming assurance capable of sending a shiver down my spine. "For now, let's get you down to the kitchen."

He clasps a hand around my wrist, his grip directly above the leather cuff I'd completely forgotten.

I release a sob at my failure.

After everything Luca taught me, I couldn't break from a choke hold, and didn't even remember my weapon. Nothing has changed. I'm just as careless and ignorant as when I was first taken.

The only difference is that I now refuse to give up. I won't let him win when he plans to hurt Luca.

I'd give my life for the man who saved me.

My soul.

"Come on." He tugs me toward the door. "I have a fresh length of rope that's going to look perfect against your skin."

31

LUCA

Torian keeps his weapon trained between Benji's eyes. "I can stay like this for however long necessary. We all know as soon as one of the guards watching this block stumbles upon the asshole with a gun to my head, they'll take you out."

He's right. I've been lucky so far but that luck will soon run out. "He's my brother. He's yours, too."

"He's no brother of mine."

Benji raises his hands in surrender. "There's no excuse for what I've done. But let me explain. Let me tell you why."

"I know why. *Money*. For fucking pieces of paper, you greedy shit."

"Torian, I've had enough. I'm done here." Hunter lowers his weapon and walks to Benji's side. "We can't do this. Not out in the open. We have to move this somewhere else."

Torian doesn't budge.

"I'm serious," Hunter growls. "You're angry. And for good reason. But whatever's going on in that head of yours can't happen in a public place. You also need to give him a fair hearing. If Layla—"

"Leave her out of this," he snaps.

Layla lets out another sob. "I'll never forgive you, Cole."

"You'll never forgive me?" he roars. "Are you kidding?"

She flinches, then hikes her chin and straightens her shoulders. "Stella will never forgive you. Keira will never forgive you." She adds strength to her tone. "Luca and Hunter and Decker *will never forgive you.*"

He doesn't respond. He just stands there. Weapon pointed. Finger on the trigger.

"I'm lowering my gun, too." Decker points his barrel to the sky as it descends. "We can discuss this with civility. Stella deserves that much."

Still, there's no movement from Torian. Not a flinch or loosening of his posture.

I keep my aim on the back of his head, the weight of this situation becoming heavier through the quiet.

I'll never get away with killing him. I wouldn't want to anyway.

One bullet would steal everything I have.

I built a life with these assholes. I found a semblance of home.

"I'm lowering my weapon." I stare at Benji, hoping these aren't our last moments together. "We're going to do this the right way."

Torian scoffs. "You trust I won't kill your brother, then shoot you, too?"

No, I don't. This could be suicide. But I have to put faith in everything we've been through. I have to trust I've earned enough of his respect to grant Benji a hearing.

"We're family. And families fuck up sometimes." I lower my gun, my heart pounding at the vulnerability as I place it back in my waistband. "You can't expect any of us to be perfect."

Torian swings around, removing the threat from my brother to place the barrel against my chest. "I can expect whatever the fuck I want."

I hold his gaze, glare for glare. "You're a smart man, but you're not thinking straight. Don't let a knee-jerk reaction destroy your family."

His lip curls, his weapon digging further into me.

"I risked my life for you in Greece," I add. "And I'd do it again. You know me. You know Benji. He fucked up; that's all."

Torian breathes out a laugh. "This is just a fuck-up?"

"He'll pay a price. A heavy one, I'm sure. But you can't kill Stella's father. You can't kill your own brother."

He steps close, snarling. "I ensured the death of my own father. This piece of shit will mean nothing in comparison."

I don't bite. Not when he's begging for me to engage.

He wants a fight, and I won't give it to him.

"Come on." Hunt steps close. "Go back inside. We'll take care of this later."

Torian smiles, slow and brutal. "We're not done here." He places his gun inside his suit jacket. "As soon as the party is over I'm dealing with this." He levels Hunter with a stare. "Keep an eye on Benji." He doesn't wait for a response before stalking for the stairs, pulling the door wide to disappear inside.

There's a collective sigh of relief. A sniffle from Layla. A curse from Decker.

"Well, that's definitely not what I expected when I set out to fuck my fiancée in the parking lot," Hunt drawls.

I ignore him, bridging the distance to my brother to grab his arm and drag him out of earshot of the others. "What's your plan? Are you going to run?"

"I'm not a coward," he snips. "And I won't leave my daughter."

I keep my mouth shut, unwilling to point out the alternative might mean dying as a traitor.

"This is my mess, Luc. I'll fix it for once." He walks to Layla, grabbing her hand as he calls over his shoulder, "Maybe it's time for you to focus on your own issues."

He's talking about Penny. And she's far from a fucking issue. But he's right about me needing to focus on her. I jog toward them as they start for the steps, blocking their path.

"What did you tell him about Penny?" I sneer under my breath. "Does he know about the party?"

She lowers her gaze, her guilt clear.

"Is she in danger? Did you risk her fucking life?"

"No," she pleads. "I made sure the event was safe. I told him everything would be heavily guarded, and said he wouldn't get within three blocks of the restaurant. Along with the extra security at Cole's front gate. He knows he can't do anything tonight."

"Either that or he knows what to fucking prepare for."

"Leave her alone." Benji walks into me, shouldering me out of the way. "Torian will deal with this. It's not your job."

I clench my teeth as they walk inside, and pull out my phone to dial Sarah's number.

"What are you doing?" Hunt attempts to snatch the device. "Put the cell down and tell us what the fuck is going on. Was Layla talking about Robert? Has she been running her mouth to him?"

"Give me a minute." I turn my back to him. "I need to make sure Penny got home." I listen to the ringtone, each unanswered trill poking my pulse back into agitated territory. When she doesn't answer, I try again.

"Who you callin'?"

"Sarah. And she's ignoring me." I start for the cars, only to remember she took my fucking Suburban. "I need some wheels." I swing around to face the two enforcers now staring at me with raised brows.

"What the fuck is going on?" Hunt demands.

"Nothing." I huff out the congealed air thickening in my lungs. "Can I borrow a car or not?"

"Don't look at me, fucker," he grates. "She trashed mine, remember? And besides, we have to talk about what the hell just happened first."

"Not now. I need to get to Penny." I switch my attention to Decker. "How about yours?"

He eyes me for long moments, his narrowed focus judgmental as he reaches into his pocket, then lobs his key fob at me. "I'm coming with you."

"Why?" I catch the offering and start backward toward his truck. "Your parents are still inside."

"I don't like the look on your face. You seem to know a lot more about what's going on than I do, and I have a feeling Penny's involved."

"All I know is that Sarah isn't answering her phone. They should be settled at Torian's by now."

Deck flicks a glance to Hunt. "Call her."

I keep trekking backward, unwilling to wait as the big guy huffs and pulls out his cell to dial.

I'm beside Decker's truck when Hunter lowers the phone. "She's not answering me either. I bet she's already in the shower."

"Tell Torian I think something is wrong." I yank the driver's door open. "And get in contact with the lookouts. Make sure nothing is on the radar."

Decker races toward the passenger side of the car. He's barely in his seat when I gun the engine and slam my foot down, sending us screaming backward out of the parking space before shoving into drive.

"Keep trying to call her." I clench the steering wheel as I increase my speed through the streets, taking the back roads, cutting corners and flying through amber lights.

"Jesus Christ." Decker grabs the side of his seat in one hand and the rail above his head with the other. "I'm sure they're okay. Sarah's smart."

Props from the glorified tech guy don't mean much when pitted against the sinking feeling in my stomach. I never should've let Penny out of my sight. I never should've brought her to the restaurant in the first place. It was her curiosity—her fucking hope—that made the risk seem insignificant.

"Is she still wearing that wrist cuff?" Deck reclaims his phone.

"Yeah, why?"

"I'll check the GPS. Saves you wrapping us around a pole if they're at Torian's."

I lean over, briefly focusing on his device. "You've got access to the tracker?"

"Who do you think installed it? Hunt doesn't know dick about tech." He falls quiet for a moment, pressing buttons repeatedly until he flashes the screen my way. "See? There's nothing to worry about. They're at the house."

I squint at the red dot in the middle of a map, the tiny writing indicating Torian's street.

"Now maybe think about laying off the gas," he drawls. "I don't appreciate you setting a time trial while I'm in the car."

I ease off the accelerator and relax into my seat, but the twist doesn't leave my gut. If anything, it intensifies.

"Like Hunt said, Sarah's probably taking a shower."

"Yeah. Maybe." I don't buy it. The raised hair on the back of my neck tells me otherwise. But paranoia isn't uncommon when I think about Penny. "Once we get to the house, you should drive back to the party to keep an eye on your folks. Robert's still out there somewhere."

He nods, remaining focused on his cell as I turn onto Torian's street.

"How are they anyway?"

He ignores me, raising the device closer to his face.

"Deck? I asked about your parents."

"Slow down." He sits straighter and shoots a glance out his window. "I need to check something."

"What is it?" I ease off the gas. "What's going on?"

"The GPS isn't syncing." He glides his finger over the screen. "Now that we're closer, it's saying she's next door."

"Why wouldn't it be syncing? How accurate is this thing?"

"Accurate. It's previously pinpointed Sarah to within a few feet. It shouldn't be out by an entire house." He keeps pressing buttons. "But even if it's up to date, it's no big deal, right?" His voice is edgy. "She's only next door. Maybe they went to speak to the old lady about the barking dog."

Like hell they would. Neither one of those women are stupid enough to be walking around the streets at night. Not even to the neighbor's house.

"Hold up." He raises a hand as we reach the ostentatious white, double-story building beside Torian's, with its open front yard, billowing trees and thick bushes. "Should we check it out?"

I stop before the driveway, placing the car in park. "Call Sarah again."

He complies, the muted ringing uninterrupted until voicemail cuts in.

"Would Penny have taken the cuff off?" He shoots me a panicked glance. "Then, I dunno, thrown it over the fence or something?"

I wipe a hand over my mouth, not buying that story either. "I'm hoping your app is a piece of shit."

"It's not. I've been tracking a long list of people with this for months."

I cut the ignition to climb outside. I stare at the darkened house, the only illumination coming from the window in the very middle of the lower level, the light seeping through the sheer curtains from a distant room.

For a house earlier consumed with high-decibel dog barking, it's now eerily quiet. The canine doesn't even yap when Decker follows me outside and slams his door shut.

"Something doesn't feel right." I rest my arms against the top of the car. "We need to keep moving."

"Wait a minute." He takes a step toward the gutter. "There's someone in the upstairs window. Third from the right."

I trek my gaze to where he's looking and squint at the darkened curtain.

After what I just went through with Benji, I'm hoping it's another dose of paranoia that has me imagining a gun barrel pointing in our direction. I blink to dislodge the mirage, only it doesn't budge. Instead a red dot appears, the glaring gun laser gliding toward Decker.

"*Get down.*" I jump onto the hood, and dive over the car to tackle him to the ground. We land in a heap, my shoulder colliding with asphalt. "*Move. Move.*

Move." I grab his jacket, dragging him to his feet. "Find cover." I run for the bushes, hunched over, and pull my weapon from the back of my pants.

Decker follows a heartbeat behind, but the gunfire I anticipate doesn't rain down. There's nothing. Only panted breathing and the fucking chirp of crickets.

"Tell me I wasn't the only one to see that." I peek through branches, my gaze levelled at the window that no longer has any sign of life.

"You weren't."

"Then we're in some heavy shit." I keep low and creep closer to the house. "Message Hunt. Tell him to get his ass here asap."

"Do you think Penny's in there?"

I can't talk about her. One nudge of that trigger and fear will take over my decision making instead of logic. I hunch, running as close to the ground as possible toward a nearby hedge.

Decker remains in my shadow, pulling out his phone and tapping at the screen. "Are you going to answer me? What the fuck are we doing?"

"You wanted to stop. So we stopped." I glare. "Now, I need to know what the fuck is going on."

"You think she's in there." It's a statement this time, one laced with panic.

"What I think is that a gun laser was pointed directly at your skull. So either the old lady living here quit taking her meds, or someone else is in there attempting to start a war."

"Fuck." He pockets his cell, palms his Glock, and checks the magazine. "What do you want me to do?"

"Keep quiet and follow me." I scramble from one bush to the next, moving toward the farthest corner of the front yard.

The chances of gaining any advantage are dick to none. They know we're here. I can only attempt to find the fuse box and shut off the power, which might leave our enemy scrambling long enough for us to get inside unnoticed.

"I hope you're good with dogs." I run for the head-high sandstone wall blocking us from the back of the house and scale it with a few well-placed footholds.

My boots hit the ground and I tense, waiting for the scramble of canine feet that never eventuate.

The only change to the night is the brighter glow coming from around the rear of the house more than fifty yards ahead.

Decker lands beside me with a heavy thud. "Where's that fucking dog?"

"No idea. But I'm not hanging around to find out."

I haul ass along the side fence, noting the lack of ground-level windows along this part of the house. Only small rectangles for the basement and large squares on the upper level. Or there's the too obvious option of the side door.

"We'll make our way in through the basement." I jerk my chin toward the first small window. "That way we can start clearing rooms from top to bottom."

"But?"

"I don't see any screens or sliding partitions to be able to dislodge. If we break glass we're going to be heard."

"What about the door?" He inches closer. "I've got a bump key. I could get it open in seconds."

"They'll expect it. We need an edge." I scan every inch of the side of the building and yard. "I can't see any cameras; can you?"

There's nothing. Not even the fuse box.

"I can't see shit," he mutters.

"Then we're going in without cutting the power." I run for the house, keeping a low profile as I make my way to one of the lower windows. I fall to my knees and skim my fingers over the glass edges, looking for a weak point, shoving it with the heel of my palm, thumping it with my elbow.

"Let me try the door." Decker backtracks.

"Leave the fucking door—"

A scream carries from inside, the guttural cry filled with fear.

My heart stops. My fucking world tilts.

"That's Penny." Decker sprints for the door. "To hell with being stealth."

I shove from the cement, scrambling to stop him from doing something stupid. But he's already pulled a key from his pocket to jam in the lock by the time I reach his side, his jacket swept off to wrap around it. With a few quick taps of the butt of his gun, he jiggles the handle, then twists.

"Like I said, it's easy as shit." He shoves his arms back into the jacket.

"Keep your mouth shut." I nudge him out of the way, staying low, my weapon ready as I creep inside.

It's shadowed in this part of the house.

Quiet.

There's no fucking sound apart from the barely audible squeak as Decker closes the door.

I visually sweep the laundry, making sure each dark corner doesn't hold a threat before I continue to the open doorway.

Footsteps tread lightly from another room.

"I know you're close," a familiar voice taunts from nearby. "I can hear you."

"Luca?" This time it's Penny, her call stabbing through me as I remain quiet. *"There's only two of them,"* she screams. *"They're not—"*

Her words are cut short with a wail.

Decker makes to rush past me. I'm forced to block his path, shoving him backward before holding a silencing finger to my mouth. "Think," I warn under my breath. "Don't react."

I'm fighting with every fucking breath to run for her myself.

I can barely think through the instinct to get to her as fast as possible. But that shit isn't smart. We need to do this right. I'd knock Decker out before I'd ever risk him endangering her further.

I inch toward the doorway, and glance along the hall. To the left there's nothing but shadow. To the right there's a soft glow coming from the far end of the house.

She's down there, and if there's only two of them, that could make for easy work.

It's getting from here to there without being noticed that's the problem.

I indicate with a finger motion that we're moving forward and take the first silenced steps into the hall. Decker stays on my ass, his exhales breathing down my fucking neck.

A twinge of sound carries behind us. A footstep, then a snicker.

I swing around, about to take aim when something rolls along the floor toward us, the cylindrical device looking like a grenade in the low light.

"*Move.*" I lunge for the closest door, grabbing Decker by the shoulder, to launch us both into the room. We fall, but it's not onto carpet—it's down a fucking staircase.

My head hits a sharp corner directly against my healing bullet wound.

Fuck.

I tumble, flipping through the air like a son of a bitch.

The pain and vertigo are nothing in comparison to the burst of blinding light and the accompanying thunderous sound exploding in my ears.

A fucking flash-bang.

The noise is deafening. The resulting shriek inside my skull is torture.

I land in a heap at the foot of the stairs as Decker fumbles beside me.

I can't see.

Can't think.

Can't stand.

I'm on my hands and knees, my stomach revolting with nausea, my nose wet with an accompanying scent of blood, my brain squeezed in a life-threatening vise.

There's nothing but static and agony as I fail numerous attempts to get onto my feet only to land on my ass when something hard presses into my skull through the darkness.

"Long time, no see, Luca," Robert greets. "Now, tell me, which one of you wants to die first?"

32

PENNY

I scream, rattling the chair I'm bound to, yanking my arms against the rope knotted behind me.

The blast had rocked the house, the loud boom hitting me in the chest while a bright burst of light exploded down the hall. I'd initially thought it was an attack strategy from Luca, but Robert's henchman standing guard at the door to the kitchen didn't show any shock at the eruption.

In fact, he's smiling, pleased with himself.

I scream again, longer and louder, using the noise to disguise the grind of my cuff blade against the rope.

"Shut up and quit struggling," he shouts. "Or I'll hit you again."

I ignore him, letting out another throat-piercing shriek as I pull and tug and slash.

"Nobody's coming to save you now, bitch. We came prepared." He points his gun toward me, shooting another glance down the hall. "Things are about to get wild."

He's young. Probably my age. Mid-twenties, with a thirst for blood if the excitement in his eyes is any indication.

"You expect me to listen to you?" I spit. "You're nothing. Nobody." I saw at the ropes, making my hand cramp from exertion, until the restriction at my wrist begins to loosen. I push harder, cut faster, then scream again, this time in pain when the blade slices through skin.

The warmth of blood trickles over my palm as the asshole storms toward me to slap a meaty palm across my cheek. "Shut. The fuck. Up."

My head flings to the side, the impact blazing across my face, reawakening the throbbing injuries from earlier. The violent jerk of my shoulders frees my right wrist, the blade still tightly clutched in my palm.

I gasp. Not in pain.

It's energy. *Electricity.*

I snatch for the ends of the rope, making sure they don't fall to the floor and expose my partial freedom as I return my attention to my tormentor. "Fuck you, you weak piece of shit."

He smirks, levelling his gun on my chest. "Fuck me?"

Air congeals in my lungs, the pressure building. I can already anticipate the impact of the bullet. It's right there, demanding me to keep my mouth shut.

The need to distract him pushes me to take the risk. I refuse to let Luca jeopardize his life to save me again.

"You won't shoot. You *can't,*" I correct. "If you kill me, Robert will do the same to you."

"I'm getting to a point where I'm willing to find out." He leans closer, getting in my face. "So either shut your fucking mouth or I'm putting a bullet in your head."

I drop the rope. Swing my free arm. Aim the blade for his throat.

The metal nicks skin, the contact barely penetrating before he lashes out, pushing me away to send me toppling backward in the chair. I hit the tile hard, the blade escaping my grasp, my left arm painfully restricted behind me.

I scramble with my free hand for my weapon, fumbling it between my stretched fingers as I tug to loosen my trapped wrist. I raise the blade in defense, but I'm not under attack. Robert's thug backtracks, a hand clamped over his throat while his other trembles with the pointed gun.

He stares at me in shock, lips parted, eyes wide as blood seeps between the fingers on his neck, the drops of crimson falling one by one onto his white shirt.

I roll from the chair, my wrist still trapped in rope, and frantically saw at the binding. My heart hammers. My breathing stutters. He's going to shoot me.

"You're losing a lot of blood." I tug and tug at the chair. "You need to get to a hospital."

"Sh-shut up." He releases his throat to inspect his hand, sending a deluge of gore down his neck.

I gasp. It's bad. That small nick must have hit his carotid because the amount of liquid is extensive. That motherfucker is going to die. Fast.

I huff out a breath, the thrill of victory giving me a vibrating sense of hope.

"Fuck you." He jabs the gun in my direction as I keep sawing. "You stupid c-cunt." He stumbles into the kitchen counter, the weapon tumbling from his hand, his legs collapsing beneath him.

I tug at my bindings, the final length of rope loosening enough for me to yank my arm free. I'm on my feet in an instant and running for his gun. I fall to my knees and slide, snatching the barrel. But he doesn't fight back. He spreads out on the floor, blinking sightlessly at me, his mouth moving without words.

Holy shit. He's done for, the pool of blood building around him.

I point the barrel at his head, my finger twitching against the trigger.

"B-bitch," he chokes, his grip uncurling around his throat. "F-fuck you."

I watch the life seep from him as I sheath my blade in the cuff. I wait precious moments, making sure he doesn't experience a resurgence of energy before I make for the hall, ignoring the putrid smell to stop at an open door leading into darkness.

Grunts and groans carry from inside. Indecipherable muttered words, too.

"Shed some fucking light, Greg," Robert snaps. "I can't see dick down here."

I freeze, caught like a deer in headlights.

"Ahh, so it's not Greg," he muses. "Is that you, my pretty Penny?"

He's in control, the excitement in his voice fueling my fear.

"I think you're going to want to see this," Robert drawls. "The switch is right near the door."

"Penny, run."

Sebastian? He's here?

My knees weaken.

"*Now*, Penny," Robert snarls. "Before I lose patience."

There's a groan of pain, then another growled demand to, "Just run."

My vision blurs under the burn of tears. My heart squeezes. "Luca, are you here?"

"*Run.*" He answers me, the word grated in agony. "Get out of here, shorty."

I can't.

I won't.

Oh, God.

He never left me to fend for myself. I would rather die than turn my back on him and the gun trembling in my hand could change everything. I could kill Robert. I could save Luca.

My limbs shake as I reach inside, sliding my hand along the wall to flick on the light. I quickly slip back out of view, careful to remain hidden as I glimpse down at the staircase illuminated before me and a vacant corner of the room below.

I can't see them. Not any of them.

There's only the sense of horror lurking close.

"Come join us," Robert coos. "You already know you're safe. It's your loved ones who may not last the night."

I plaster myself against the wall, unsure what to do.

I don't have a phone. And I can't risk leaving them, even momentarily, to search for help.

I steel myself against what I'm about to see and descend the stairs, the gun raised.

The room comes into view gradually.

I notice Sebastian first, his tense frame facing me. Then there's Robert a few feet behind, a weapon held in both hands, with another down the front of his pants. He has one barrel trained on the back of Sebastian's head, the other arm pointed farther away.

"What did he do to you?" my brother snarls. "What the fuck did he do?"

"Don't worry." Adrenaline has masked my pain. "I'm okay."

I take another step, my heart lodging in my throat at the sight of Luca on his knees a yard behind, his face pale, his eyes filling with regret.

"Get out of here, Pen." He can barely keep his head up. "I need you to run."

"Drop the gun." Robert advances on my brother.

"No." I aim it at my enemy's head, the weapon shaking in my fragile grip.

"You can't kill me, baby. I've told you before I've got the sweetest fucking leverage known to man. You're gonna want to know what it is before you pull the trigger."

"Then tell me."

He laughs. "In time. Now don't make me count. I'm growing impatient." He cocks a brow, waiting one tense second, then another. "Fine, have it your way." He lowers the barrel, aiming at Sebastian's thigh, then pulls the trigger.

The gunshot blasts the air, ripping a scream from my throat.

Sebastian roars, falling to the floor and curling onto his side, desperately clutching at his right thigh. Luca falls, too, clasping his head, his face burying into the carpet.

I choke on a sob, the sight of their suffering far more punishing than any horror Luther ever inflicted.

"Penny, get the hell out of here. *Now*." Sebastian struggles to get back up. "Run."

"Fucking *run*." Luca lashes out, the futile swipe of his arm knocking him off balance.

"Or you could drop the gun." Robert smirks. "You already know you're not going anywhere."

He's right.

My heart is in this room.

Slowly, I place the weapon on the step at my feet, my eyes blazing.

"Good girl. Now come down here and join us."

"Don't do it." Luca pushes onto his hands and knees. "Please, Penny."

I don't think I've heard his desperation before.

He's scared, and I can't stand his fear. It rips me apart in the most agonizing torture.

"It's okay." I suck in a breath, blink away the threat of tears, and descend the stairs. "Robert doesn't want to kill me."

"Don't." Sebastian battles to get to his feet, hissing and wincing as he grabs at his injured leg. His black suit pants cling around the bullet wound, the blood seeping onto his boot, then the floor. "Get out of here."

No. This is my domain. I know this monster better than they do. Neither of them stand a chance without me, and I refuse to live in a world without them. So we're in this together.

Live or die.

"She was never going to leave," Robert taunts. "She can't walk away from those in need. She wants to be the savior, but like always, she's the cause of the bloodshed. She was responsible for the death of hundreds of women through my pure frustration. Weren't you, my sweet?"

I fight against the penetrating words, refusing to let them sink in as I reach the bottom of the stairs.

"If you would've stopped manipulating Luther and become like every other slave, many lives would've been saved," he continues. "But you had to be better than everyone, didn't you?"

"They still would've been used and discarded," I whisper. "The only difference is that I would've joined them."

I return my attention to Luca, a knife twisting in my gut at the sight of his ashen skin. He's hurting, badly, but I can't see an injury. "What did he do to you?"

"Forget about me." He sits back on his haunches. "Save yourself."

"It's time to hurry this along, pretty Penny. We don't have all night." Robert inches closer, his guns trained on the back of Luca and Sebastian's heads. "We're going to play a game. One where you get to choose which one of them lives and which one dies."

More sobs clog my throat, the building sorrow tattooing my heart. "You'll kill them both no matter what I do."

"I promise I won't. You know why?"

I shake my head.

He smirks. "Because watching you live with the guilt for the rest of your life will be fucking bliss."

This time the torment escapes, the agony parting my lips. I sob, believing him. He's sick enough to follow through.

"Decide," he taunts. "The brother or the lover."

My lips tremble. Everything does. I can barely think over the shuddering rack of my body.

"It's okay, shorty." Luca hunches over, his hands on his knees, his forgiving eyes on mine. "You know the right choice. You need him more than me."

"Don't pull that bullshit," Sebastian mutters.

"How honorable." Robert jams his gun into the back of Luca's head. "Make your choice or I'll do it for you."

"Wait. *Stop*," I beg. "I'll decide. Just give me a minute."

I need more time. I can't do this.

"Don't leave me hanging," he growls. "Fucking tell me."

I glance from my brother to Luca, knowing there's only one choice.

It hurts. Oh, God, how it hurts but there's no other way.

Someone has to die.

"Penny," Robert growls.

My pulse becomes a staccato, the thunder pounding in my ears. "I choose…" I can't say it. Can't get the words out.

He snickers, loving every moment of my struggle.

"*Run, Penny,*" Luca roars. "Just fucking *run.*"

I raise my chin, strengthened by the reminder of his salvation. He's always been my shield. My lifeline.

No matter how much this hurts, I'm indebted to return the favor.

I turn my attention to Sebastian, hoping he understands my heartache—the gut-wrenching agony—as I cement my choice. He smiles at me in return. A pained, yet comforting smile forever etched in my mind.

Then I divert my gaze to the monster, swallowing over the agonizing dryness of my throat as I start toward him. "I choose me."

33

LUCA

My heart drops as she breaks into a run.

I can barely hold my head up, even struggle to see, but she's clear before me, her determination obvious as she sprints to take her own life.

I pivot on my toes, swaying with the movement and lunge, diving for Robert's legs. Gunfire pummels my ears, the double shots striking fear in my veins as I take the motherfucker to the ground.

Penny screams. It's all I hear, the high pitch, the terror.

I climb on top of my blurred opponent, swinging my fists at the darkening obscurity of his body, sometimes connecting with hardened flesh, other times with empty air.

More screams ring out. Pain lashes at my face. My head fills with pandemonium. The only notable thought I'm capable of holding revolves around Penny's safety as knuckles punch into my cheek, my jaw.

She can't be taken. Can't die.

Not by him.

Decker yells something about a gun, but I struggle to make out the words. I don't care anymore. Not about my life or my pain. Nothing matters except Penny's safety as I search blindly for this fucker's throat, latching on with both hands to squeeze with all my strength.

The impacts to my face increase. My consciousness fades.

I close my eyes against the vertigo.

Clutch harder.

Pray.

I roar with the effort of staying alive, fingers clawing at my skin, Robert bucking beneath me.

"I said, I've got a fucking gun," Decker yells.

I don't let go.

One more burst of gunfire and I'm as good as dead anyway. My brain can't take anymore. I keep squeezing, harder and harder, until the punches lose their strength and the bucking stops. It's then that I open my eyes, the double vision making it hard to distinguish if the fight-less asshole beneath me is dead or bluffing.

I squint. Lean forward. Blink and blink.

He wheezes, still dragging in breath.

I'm about to swing a heavy punch at his face when Penny dives to her knees beside me, shouting a war cry as she stabs a blade into his throat. She doesn't pause after one attempt. She repeats the severity over and over, continuing to yell her lungs out with every puncture of skin.

I slide off of him, falling onto my ass like a pile of garbage.

Despite the horror, the clarity of her is a fucking sight to behold.

She's fierce.

Strong.

So fucking beautiful.

My head continues to swim as I struggle to my feet, my body swaying. I attempt to right the sudden lurch of movement, stumbling backward, but it's no use. I'm completely fucked, unable to stand straight.

"Luca?" Decker's voice calls over the static. "Luc?"

I blink and blink, getting obscure snapshots of him grabbing Penny's arm to drag her away from mindless destruction.

He'll protect her.

He'll do what's right.

I bump into something. A desk. A box. I don't fucking know, but it sends shit scattering around my feet.

"Luca?" Her voice is pained as she turns to me.

I want to be strong for her, but there's no fucking strength anymore. I can barely keep my head up as I plant my feet, willing my sea legs away.

She rushes forward, those dark eyes taking over my vision. "You need to get to a hospital." She cups my cheeks, the warmth of gentle hands slowing the world's spin just a little.

"We don't do hospitals." I kiss her forehead. "You be strong, okay? Don't take shit from anyone."

"Why are you telling me this?" Her face turns stark, the brief glimpses of clarity cutting me to my core.

"Take care of yourself."

"Stop it." She increases the pressure of her palms. "Look at me."

I'm trying. But everything is heavy. My head. My hands. My feet.

"Focus," she pleads. "Look at me."

Decker comes up beside her, his frame no more than a sickening blur. "How bad is your head?"

I huff out a laugh, my sardonic humor only making the sway worse. "It's nothin'." My words are slurred, my tongue thick.

"Come on." Decker limps close, sliding an arm around my back. "We'll get you to the car."

He's got no hope. Even without a bullet in his leg he wouldn't be able to budge me. And it sure as shit doesn't help when my face starts diving for the floor.

It's a smooth glide, like I'm flying in slow motion, gentle and welcoming against the snatch of Decker's hands as he fails to hold on to me.

Penny's cry fills my ears and I want to tell her it's okay. I want to tell her so many things. But my face hits the floor and my world ends.

34

PENNY

I stare at Luca on the hospital gurney, his bulky body dwarfing the bedframe. He's still. Almost lifeless. And after hours spent sitting here in silence I can't bear the sight, yet I refuse to look away.

His face is battered. The bruise from my brother mars his cheek and the fight with Robert is evident from the swelling and scratches everywhere else.

But the internal injuries make my stomach churn in fear.

"He'll wake soon." A woman speaks from behind me. "I promise."

I glance over my shoulder at the nurse standing in the doorway and wish I had her optimism. I want Luca to recover more than anything. I want him to wake without complications.

I need him to still be mine even though he's been battling a bleed on the brain, probably since Greece, the severity of his injury having the ability to alter his decision-making.

"He's a tough cookie," she continues. "How long ago did you say he sustained the initial impact to his head?"

I hesitate, unsure what I told her earlier. "A few weeks, I guess."

When Sebastian dropped us off outside the ER, he told me to keep my mouth shut. And I have, to an extent. As far as the hospital staff are concerned, we had a car accident. The only complication came when their scans outlined evidence of a brain injury sustained prior to tonight.

"As far as subdural hematomas go, his is relatively minor."

"But the doctor said it could have caused personality changes, right? His decisions over the past few weeks might not have been his own."

She shrugs. "It's possible. Why? Had he been acting irrational or unlike himself?"

That's the thing—I don't know.

I'd barely spent a few moments with him before he risked his life to gain the initial head injury. Everything we shared after could've been a side effect.

"I'm not sure." I wrap my arms around my middle, holding myself tight. "Maybe."

She steps into the room, her eyes kind as they trek over me. "And how are you feeling? I'd still like to take a look at your injuries whenever you're willing."

"I'm fine." I drag my jacket sleeves farther down my hands, not wanting her prying eyes to notice the blood or rope burns. "The impact with the airbag was the worst of it."

"Those can be a bitch." She smiles, the building silence uncomfortable for long moments before she inches back toward the hall. "Please trust me when I say there's no need to worry about him. He's a lucky man."

"She doesn't know the half of it." The graveled murmur from the bed stops my heart.

I keep staring at the nurse, as those words repeat in my ears. I don't drag my attention from her until she glances at the bed, her smile widening.

"I think your man is awake." She grins at me then turns her attention to Luca. "I'm going to quickly page the doctor. You've got two minutes of privacy before I come back to check your vitals."

I nod, my vision blurring.

I'm not going to cry.

I am not going to cry.

The nurse walks away, leaving me to rein in the rampant beat of my heart and the building shake in my fingers.

"You're not talking to me anymore, shorty?" he whispers.

That voice. *Oh, God,* that voice.

I drag my gaze from the door and meet the gorgeous eyes of the man laid out before me. With one glance he warms me. Makes me whole.

But he's still pale. Entirely fragile beneath the muscle-man persona.

"They didn't know when you'd wake up…" I grab his hand. "I wasn't sure if you would."

"Pessimism?" He grins. "From you? No way."

I squeeze his fingers, both loving and hating his sarcasm. "It wasn't pessimism. It was fear. I could barely breathe through the thought of losing you."

"I'm not going anywhere."

My heart pounds. Squeezes. Wrenches so tight. "Do you promise?"

"You know I'm a sucker for giving you anything you want."

Yes, I know.

But his face sobers and for a moment there's only silence and contemplation before he says, "I can't remember everything. You need to bring me up to speed. What happened? What's going on?"

"I don't know." My lips lift in an apologetic smile. "I wish I had answers, but

I haven't heard from anyone. When you collapsed, Sebastian wouldn't let me call an ambulance. Instead, we dragged you into his truck and drove you here. I haven't seen or heard from anyone since. Not my brother. Or Cole. There's been no police to question what happened either."

He sits, wincing as he repositions himself against the pillows. "What did you tell hospital staff?"

"Not much." I reach for my chair, dragging it closer to the bed, not once releasing his hand. "I told them we had a car accident."

"Good." He nods. Cringes. Groans. "My head is fucking killing me."

"You've got a bleed on the brain. They think you've had it since Greece."

He raises a brow. "That would explain the headaches."

"It could explain a lot of things."

"Meaning?" He frowns. "What's wrong? You look upset."

I *am* upset. So damn upset at the thought of our future uncertainty. "The doctor asked if you've been acting differently because it's common an injury like yours could cause a change in behavior."

"And?" His brows pull tighter. "You're going to have to dumb it down. I'm still not catching on to what's worrying you."

"We barely spoke before you hit your head in Greece. Now we're…" I wave a lazy hand between us. "I don't know. I just thought maybe this thing with us is the change in behavior they were referring to."

He grins, the curve of lips announcing a complete lack of seriousness. "You think the way I feel about you is due to brain damage?"

"Please don't joke. It's not unlikely—"

"Pen, if being with you is a side effect, then I give you permission to give me a love tap to the head every once in a while to keep the momentum going. I'll even buy you your own bat." He drags my fingers to his lips for a quick kiss. "I'll take an ass whoopin' every week if that's what it takes."

"That's not funny, Luca. I'm seriously scared."

He breathes out a chuckle. "You should be more scared about being stuck with me. 'Cause I ain't letting you go."

My chest burns under the weight of his promise, the heat increasing when his expression turns serious.

"You're everything, Pen. You always have been. What I feel for you isn't fake."

"I'm not saying it's fake…"

He squeezes my hand. "I know what you're saying, and it's not true. I fell hard for you the first moment we met. I was done for before I even hit my head."

I smile. Nod. It's all I can do against the build of hope. "I'm glad you feel that way."

"What else is bothering you?" His fingers retreat from my grip to delicately sweep over mine. Back and forth. Over and under. Gently coaxing. "Is there something I don't know?"

"Not really. I'm just unsure of what's happening with everyone else. Sebastian was shot. Sarah was hurt, too. And I keep expecting the police to walk in here and demand answers." I lower my voice. "I killed a man, Luca. I watched him bleed out."

"Don't think about it. The cops aren't coming. Your brother didn't call an ambulance because he planned to go back to the house and clean up. We'll hear from someone once all the loose ends are tied."

"But it's been hours. And he was—"

"I'm sure he's fine. And tidying loose ends takes time. All hands would be on deck to sweep that shit under the rug."

I'm not convinced, but I try to believe him. I need to stop listening to the fear that shackled me for so long and learn to trust in him wholeheartedly.

Robert is dead.

Luca is alive.

My family is safe.

It's time to be free.

Except... "What about your brother?" I hold his gaze, hating the cringe he gives me. "He was working with Robert."

"Torian will deal with Benji."

"What does that mean?"

He shrugs. "I honestly don't know. But no matter what happens, I'll make sure you're safe."

"*We're* safe," I correct. "There's no me without you."

He huffs out a half-hearted chuckle. "And vice versa, shorty. I don't want to be here without you."

I bow my head into our hands, shielding my face due to the building tears. His fingers find my hair, his touch drifting through the strands.

"I love you, Pen," he whispers. "When I found out Robert had you, I..."

"He's gone." I add strength to my voice as I return my gaze to his. "You saved me again."

"Like hell I did. I don't remember much, but I can still see you running for him. Don't ever do something like that again."

I would. I'd do it now if I had to.

This world needs Luca. The good guy disguised as a villain.

"Your face is bruised." His fingers stop their delicate caress, his eyes narrowing slightly. "Did he hurt you? Before I got to you, did he—"

"No. I'm good. Robert rammed his truck into Sarah's car. The worst of my injuries are from the deployed airbag."

I don't want to concern him with the intricate details of my battle scars. None of that matters now.

He sinks farther into the pillows, his shoulders losing their tension. "Then tell me what I need to do to make you happy. I want to see that gorgeous smile."

My stomach does a swooping roll, tumbling and turning. This man is everything. All my hope. All my security.

He's my way home. I have to finally let go and allow him to guide me there.

"I am happy." I smile from deep in my heart, with all of the optimism I can muster. "You make me unbelievably happy."

He doesn't respond. Not in words. Just with the lazy grin that fills me with unending warmth.

"Sorry to interrupt." The nurse walks into the room, skirting the bed to stop before the heart monitors on the other side. "It's time to check the patient. And you—" She gives me a one-second glance. "—have a visitor."

"Me?"

She nods and turns her attention to the door.

I do the same, finding my brother standing there, face solemn, legs stiff.

"Oh, God, Sebastian." I shove from my chair and rush to him, gently engulfing him in a hug.

He tenses, taking two seconds to relax into the embrace before returning the gesture. "Hey, Pen. I'm glad to see you, too."

"Are you okay?" I inch away to look at him. "Have you seen Sarah?"

He eyes the nurse with suspicion. "She's recovering. It takes a lot to knock the wind out of her sails."

I step back, understanding his hint for subtlety.

"How's he doing?" He jerks his chin toward the bed. "Did they give him the lobotomy I hoped for?"

"Very funny," Luca growls.

The nurse chuckles. Sebastian gives a faint smirk. But something's not right. I see more than weary exhaustion in his features.

"How's your leg?"

"Flesh wound. It'll heal."

"Then there's something else. What's wrong?"

He shrugs. "Nothin'. I just, ahh…" He rubs the back of his neck. "I thought with your enforcer laid flat you might want some additional support."

I nod. "Thank you. I'm glad you're here."

He cringes, meeting my gaze. "Pen, I wasn't talking about me."

"Then what do you mean?" I lower my voice. "What's going on?"

He pauses, the silence growing tense. My heart beats double time, drawing out the quiet. It isn't until his nose crinkles in apology that I understand. Without words or action, I know exactly what he's done before he says, "Mom and Dad are waiting at the entrance to the ward."

I hold my breath against the arrhythmia.

"Jesus Christ, Decker," Luca snarls. "Are you a fucking idiot? You can't dump this on—"

"It's all right." I shoot him a forced smile. "I'm okay."

I am.

Really.

I can handle this. I can face my parents.

I'll walk right up to them and say hello. We'll hug… and cry… and…

Oh, God. I can't do this. I can't see them without losing myself. Without releasing my thin grip on stability.

"Sir, you need to rest," the nurse demands. "Sir, please."

I blink out of my panic to see Luca flinging back the covers in an attempt to climb from the bed.

"Stop," I beg. *"Please.* I can do this."

It's a lie.

I can't do this. I don't know how.

"I'm coming with you," he growls.

"No. I should do this on my own."

It's another lie.

I need him. I'll *always* need him.

But there's no escaping this reunion. And I owe it to my parents to have it take place in relative privacy.

"Trust me." I give him a genuine smile. "It's time."

His hand clutches tight to the bedsheet, the intensity in his features never wavering. "You sure?"

I nod.

"I love you," he vows. "And I'm right here if you need me."

The swooping roll of my insides returns. "I love you, too. With everything I am, I love you."

Sebastian clears his throat, the sound awkward as he rubs my arm. "You don't have to do this now. As far as Mom and Dad are concerned, they're here because I needed to see someone about this pulled muscle in my thigh." He winks. "They're not expecting you. They still don't know."

The chance of escape brings relief. Temporary, misguided relief.

I can't put this off forever.

"I'm doing this." I nod to convince myself. "Take me to them."

My pulse beats erratically in my throat, the rhythm and severity increasing as Sebastian leads me from the room and into the hall.

The ward is quiet, the early morning hour making my surroundings desolate.

"Do they know what happened last night?" I ask.

"No. Once I left the party, Keira took them to their hotel. They're just as clueless as they've ever been. But your car accident is starting to hit the news. I caught sight of a sketchy video on the television an hour ago."

My legs grow heavy with each step, the building throb in my veins becoming too much.

Then I see him—my dad.

He stands on the other side of the open ward doors, his attention focused on something out of view, the glow of the sunrise highlighting his face.

My feet stop of their own accord. I can't move any farther.

"It's okay," Sebastian whispers. "It's all going to be okay."

It doesn't feel that way. My body is in overdrive, my thoughts and fears colliding into a mass of hysteria.

I'm about to turn and hide when my dad looks our way. His face brightens at the sight of his son, then completely falls when he sees me.

He stares in horror. Wide eyes. Gaping mouth.

"What is it?" my mother asks, her arm reaching into view. "What's wrong?"

He doesn't answer. He's frozen.

Sebastian continues without me, walking to our father's side while my mother stands.

I want to run.

To them. *Away* from them. But I can't move.

I blink the blur from my vision as my mom turns to face me, her hand immediately raising to cover her mouth.

All I feel is panic and pain.

All I see is heartache and loss.

"Penny?" My mother glances from me, to my father, to my brother, and back again, her confusion unwavering.

"Pen, is that you?" my dad asks.

I tremble. Arms. Legs. Heart.

The eight feet of distance between us is so close, yet unbelievably far. No matter what I do, I can't get my feet to move, my voice to speak.

"It's her." Sebastian starts toward me. "It's really her."

My chest restricts. My heart and lungs are ripped from me.

My mother takes a step, a sob breaching her lips. "Penny…" She runs, the pace hobbled, her face stricken. "My baby girl."

I break, my tears rushing free, the heated trails searing my cheeks as air heaves from my lungs.

I'm engulfed in restricting arms, my mother's love circling me even tighter. I close my eyes against the emotional onslaught, sucking in breath after hiccupped breath, not wanting the love to weaken me, and not being able to deny it at the same time.

"I don't understand." My dad's voice approaches. "How did this happen?"

More arms engulf me. The scent of my father's aftershave sinks deep into my lungs.

There are sobs and laughter and sniffles.

Hugs and questions and comfort. So much soul-shaking comfort.

I let it wash over me. Consume me.

I sway with the waves of emotion, taking in all the sensations of home as I squeeze my eyes tighter in an attempt to stem the unending blubbering.

"Everything is going to be all right, baby girl," my mother soothes. "Everything is going to be just fine."

After years spent denying my suffering, I give in.

I succumb to the pain. I let my grief break free.

I cry until the tears clean away the heartache, all my memories purged from the deepest, darkest depths of my soul. And when my sobs finally subside, I begin to breathe again, knowing I'm finally ready to start healing.

35

LUCA

I SCOWL AS THE NURSE FLASHES A LIGHT IN MY EYES.

"You don't need to look at me like that." She lowers the mini flashlight and grabs my hand. "I get that you're not happy being here. I'm just doing my job, and apparently, looking after you is a top priority, so grip my hand and show me how macho you are."

I clench her fingers, my scowl remaining in place. "Who says I'm a top priority?"

"My supervisor. I was told to make sure Mr. John Doe was taken care of and that he receives everything he asks for." She holds my gaze, raising a brow.

I chuckle. "Feel free to call me John."

"How kind of you." She drops my hand and grabs the other. "Want to tell me what happened to your head, John?"

"I have no idea."

She rolls her eyes and steps away, removing a blood pressure cuff from the monitoring equipment near the head of the bed.

While she's wrenching my arm into submission, I cock my ear toward the door, trying to catch a hint of Penny's voice.

This shit with Robert might be over, but the battles she has to face are only just beginning. And I want to be by her side for every single one of them.

"Your blood pressure is a little high."

"No shit." My girl is in the hall, facing one of the most monumental moments of her life, and I'm laid flat, unable to help her. "Give me some aspirin and a ticket out of here. I'll be fine."

"With all due respect, *John*, you've got a subdural hematoma. Which means you're not leaving anytime soon. You need to be under observation to ensure the bleeding doesn't increase."

I revert back to glaring, not appreciating her calm superiority as Decker limps into the room. He moves to stand against the far wall, watching silently as the nurse takes my temperature like I'm a five-year-old with the flu.

He doesn't talk. Doesn't change his masked expression of exhaustion. He doesn't give one hint as to what's going on with Penny or why he's left her out there on her own.

"What the fuck are you doing?" I growl.

He answers by cocking a lazy brow.

It's the nurse who stiffens and meets my gaze. "Do you need me to leave?"

"Is that an option?"

She sighs. "Like I said, I was told to give you everything you asked for, which includes privacy if it's requested."

"It's requested," Decker murmurs.

"Definitely requested," I grate.

She huffs out a breath and places the thermometer back into the stand near the head of the bed. "I'll give you five minutes. Then I have to come back and finish my obs." She makes for the door, giving a quick glance at me over her shoulder before leaving the room.

Still, Decker doesn't speak. He remains against the wall, exhaustion heavy in his slumped shoulders, expression indecipherable.

"Where is she?" I ask. "*How* is she?"

"In the hall. And you'd be a better judge of how she's feeling than I would. All I know is that her tears don't fill me with giddy optimism."

"Tears were inevitable."

"Yeah, I know. I just don't appreciate seeing her like that after everything she's been through." He leans forward to massage his thigh with a wince. "Do you two have plans?"

What the fuck sort of question is that? "Plans for what? Today? This week? The next ten years?"

His expression doesn't change. He just eyes me with disinterest. "All of the above."

I sit, readjusting myself against the pillows, and eye my clothes on the bedside table. I need to get out of here. "That's her decision."

"Don't dodge the question. I'm asking if you plan to stick around. Is this thing between you two temporary or long-haul?"

"I'm not dodging anything. I have every intention of staying by her side. Thick and thin. Good times and bad."

Still, there's no reaction. No protective brotherly response. No encouragement or threat. He either lost a lot of blood from that bullet or something is going on. Something that will require me getting my ass out of here, consequences be damned.

I tug out my cannula and grab my clothes from the side table. "Do you have more questions?" I slide from the bed, my vision darkening with the movement. "Or are you just going to stand there and admire me all day?"

He pushes from the wall and shuffles forward, stopping to grab the wooden board at the foot of the bed with both hands.

I jerk on my jeans, impatiently waiting for whatever brotherly threat he has up his sleeve. "You preparing to hit me again? Is that it?"

"No, I'm done with that. You've proven yourself."

I yank up my zipper and clasp the button. "Well, fan-fucking-tastic. Sounds like all my dreams have come true." I tug off the gown and throw it to the bed. "All I've ever wanted is to prove myself to you."

He scowls.

That's all he does. There's no snarky retaliation. No threat of violence.

I'm prepping him to fight and he's giving me nothing. Something is seriously wrong. "What the hell is going on? Where is she?"

"Penny's fine. She's in the hall. I thought I'd give her a few seconds alone with our parents."

"And my brother?" I clench my jaw, tight, hoping like hell I'm not about to be given a death notice.

He shrugs. "He's still alive. For now."

"Then what the fuck is this really about?" I grab my shirt from the mattress and tug it on. "I know you're not in here to welcome me to the family."

"You're right. I'm not." His voice is low as he narrows his eyes on me. "I'm trying to determine how fucked up your head is."

I pause in the middle of straightening my shirt. "Why? Because you think I can't look after your sister?"

"No. Because there's shit that needs to be done, and I'm not sure you're capable."

"What shit?" The question comes with hesitance. "Robert's dead, right? My memory is foggy, but I could've sworn—"

"He's dead." His face hardens as he glances toward the door, then returns his attention to me. "Problem is, he wasn't jerkin' our chain when he said he had leverage."

Adrenaline floods my system, the panic overriding the dull throb in my head to bring some semblance of clarity. "What leverage?"

He sucks in a breath and straightens. "He took the kids." His face turns pained, the fear and desperation finally seeping through. "He kidnapped Tobias and Stella, and we've got no fucking idea where they are."

***

I hope you enjoyed Luca. Are you ready for the final instalment in the Hunting Her series?

I FELL FOR THE ENEMY. A man whose actions resembled the devil so closely it was sickening. But I learned from my mistakes.

At least I thought I had. Until I'm tempted back into his life with a case I can't refuse. Cole Torian needs my help. And I'm unable to deny him.

Click here for Cole (Hunting Her #6)

For more information on this series, join the Eden Summers' Newsletter or join the fun-filled Facebook Reader Group.

You can also receive new release notifications from BookBub.

Turn the page for a preview of Cole.

COLE

1

ANISSA

My shrink stares at me over the top of her reading glasses. "I think we need to dive deeper on this. You seem to be fixated on finding a reason for your feelings, and that's okay. My concern, though, is that you're focusing on something that doesn't fit."

"It does fit," I grate through clenched teeth.

She doesn't understand.

I can't blame her. Since our sessions started I've given half-truths and misguided information in a vain attempt to keep the complexity of my time with Cole *conniving* Torian to myself. But it doesn't stop me from needing answers.

"Anissa, I know this is hard, and we're going to work through it together. I just need you to understand that what you feel for this man isn't Stockholm syndrome—"

"That's bullshit."

She clears her throat and straightens in her chair. "Okay. Let me explain again and make things more clear. Stockholm syndrome is a condition where hostages develop a psychological alliance with their captors—"

"Which I did. I also felt sympathy for his cause, and negative feelings toward police and authorities, which is literally the textbook definition, is it not?"

"Somewhat. The problem is, you're leaving out the fact that, even though you were taken against your will, you never truly feared this man."

"Well, maybe when I initially made that admission I was wrong. Maybe deep down I did feel threatened."

She quirks a brow and scribbles on her notepad. "So you believe he was going to kill you if you didn't follow his commands?"

I glare, hating how my insides squeeze in denial.

Cole was never going to kill me. I know that with every breath I take. Yet it doesn't mean I'm willing to give up on this diagnosis.

"You also said Stockholm could occur when the abuser opens up and shows kindness through the trauma. *He* did that. He told me things nobody else knew. And the isolation, too." I push to my feet and pace her light grey rug. "You mentioned Stockholm happens when you're isolated with your abuser. You don't get more isolated than an island in the middle of nowhere."

Now, *that* part I'm still not sure she believes.

I wouldn't be surprised if she thinks I'm making this whole thing up.

"True." She scribbles another note. "However, you would've needed to feel like there was no escape. And from what you've told me, you actually declined the offer to leave. He gave you the option and you decided to stay. Isn't that right?"

Fuck.

"But couldn't that have been a symptom of Stockholm itself?" I ask. "If I was already affected by it, and had these uncharacteristic feelings, of course I was going to stay."

She leans forward in her chair, her pen poised an inch from the notepad teetering on her knee. "Why is this diagnosis so important to you? What will the label achieve?"

I pause, my feet planting an arm's length from the shrink's trusty sofa.

My pulse quickens. My fingers twitch at my sides.

I need the label because it would excuse my feelings. It would explain my obsession and justify why I can't get a bloodthirsty criminal out of my head. Plastering the Stockholm sticker on my chest would help me understand why his world held a semblance of comfort and why my life now feels hollow. It should also dissolve the guilt I feel for my actions. My father would be so ashamed of me.

"Anissa?" She gives a placating smile. "Why do you need this?"

Because it would condone my stupidity. It would absolve me of all these insane thoughts about a man unworthy of my attention.

"It doesn't matter." I grab my purse from the sofa and start for the door. "We're done here."

"Wait. Our session isn't over." She stands, placing her pad and pen on the desk behind her. "We need to work through this."

No, what I need is a diagnosis she won't give.

What I *need* is something to help me understand why I can hate Cole with every breath, yet still tingle with warmth whenever I remember our time together.

Every memory is filtered through a haze of attraction.

Every moment—even those when he drugged, bound, and threatened me—are all relived with a sickening gravitational pull toward admiration. Or worse, lust.

It doesn't make sense.

It's not who I am.

"Thanks for your time." I yank her door open and stalk toward the receptionist, holding out my bank card to pay before continuing my thunderous steps outside into the cool late afternoon air.

I can't keep doing this.

I have to quit thinking of him. Thinking of *us*. Thinking there's some stupid connection between me and a psychotic murderer when those reflections tear my ethics and principles to shreds.

He manipulated me.

Groomed me.

Just like his father did with all those stolen women he turned into sex slaves.

Cole instigated a mind game I couldn't resist. And he won.

End of story.

I continue onto the footpath, thankful for the long walk home because, apart from alcohol, a casual stroll is the one thing capable of stabilizing my pulse.

If only I could find the peace I crave.

Insomnia would be a blessing right now. Instead I pass out nightly, the dreams of Cole luminous and palpable.

"Hey, Fox, wait up."

I freeze at the sound of Anthony Easton's voice behind me, my mindlessness temporarily interrupted. My fellow FBI agent has been the only stability through this entire ordeal. He's the one who convinced me not to go back to work until I'm ready, and I haven't.

He's the lighthouse in the storm. The steady shore.

And despite having limited knowledge of what happened between me and Cole, he's intuitive enough to make sure he bad-mouths that motherfucker constantly, making me despise my inappropriate thoughts like a mentally stable person should.

But Easton also increases my self-loathing. Being around him, with his kindness and generosity, is a constant reminder that I crave the wrong things. He's been my rock, yet I still fixate on poison-filled kisses from a predator.

I turn to find him strolling toward me, his suit crisp, his jawline covered in thick stubble, and those gentle eyes filled with concern.

"What are you still doing here?" I paste on a smile. "I told you I could walk home."

"I know. But after dropping you off, I had nothing better to do, so I thought I'd wait around and give you a ride." His gaze narrows. "You finished early, though. Is everything all right?"

"Everything's fine. Apart from me and my shrink having a difference of opinion." I force out a laugh. "I don't think we'll be seeing each other again."

His expression softens, the kindness transforming to pity. "Is that a good idea? You need someone to talk to. It's been weeks since you last ran into Torian and you're still struggling to cope."

No, not weeks.

He has no clue I had an unscheduled reunion with my satanic libido builder last night. On the side of the road. With a police officer present.

Penny, Decker's sister, had needed help. The recently released sex slave had stolen a hitman's car and wasn't prepared to be targeted for the drive-by shooting that followed.

But that deluge of information is a rabbit hole I refuse to crawl into with Easton.

"It's okay." I continue along the sidewalk, determined to make my way home. "I'll figure it out."

"No, wait." He rushes after me, his strong grip latching onto my wrist. "You're not alone in this. Let me help."

I stare down at the fingers gently embedded in my woolen sweater. I want to feel relief at his touch. Warmth. Affection. I wish something other than the need to compare would overwhelm me whenever he paid me attention, but that's what it always amounts to.

I'm constantly pitting him against Cole and he never wins.

He's not fierce enough. Strong enough. Possessive enough.

"You've already helped a whole heap." I clasp my hand over his and squeeze. "And I'm thankful. But I'm going to be okay. I promise."

He keeps scrutinizing me, his brows furrowing. "He really messed with you, didn't he? Whatever happened between the two of you is far bigger than you've let on." He takes another step, bringing us a foot apart, face-to-face. "I don't know why you're protecting him."

"I'm not." Keeping my lips shut has nothing to do with Cole's safety and everything to do with averting humiliation.

And shame.

I regret everything that happened between me and the manipulative mastermind. If I could, I'd return to the day of Cole's uncle's funeral and catch myself before the temptation to taunt him became too much.

Instead of flaunting my authority, I would've kept to my job, helping my team arrest his father. I shouldn't have become sidetracked by the gorgeous man with the sinister soul.

My stomach flips, protesting the thought.

Goddamnit.

I can never win. It's as if Cole's games never stopped, only became internalized. Now my thoughts wage war against my feelings. My morals battle for supremacy over my yearning.

I'm a fucking nut job in need of sedation—I'm just too stubborn to down the bitter pill.

"Why don't we have dinner tonight?" I stand taller, determined to get a hold of myself. "My treat. We can watch a movie and have a few drinks..."

My insides do that flippy, uncomfortable thing again, warning me against a bad decision. Or maybe hating the possibility of being cut off from a long-standing addiction.

"In your apartment?" he asks. "Again? You don't want to go out and grab a bite from a restaurant this time?"

Like a date? A proper, kiss-you-at-the-end-of-the-night situation?

My brain fumbles for an answer, my hand dropping from his as my internal battle intensifies. I should do this. I *need* to do this.

Stockholm syndrome be damned.

Heated memories forsaken.

Instead, I wince, my fucking weakness claiming victory as I fail to vocalize an affirmation. "Let me think on it." My pulse increases, the pull of want and need dragging me in two different directions.

He's handsome. So goddamn handsome, with his sky-blue eyes and slick blond hair.

But he's not what I hunger for. He's buttered toast pitted against the extravagance of fine dining.

Poisoned fine dining.

"Come on." He jerks his head toward his car and backtracks. "I'll convince you while I give you a ride home. I can be persuasive when I want to be."

2

ANISSA

EASTON DIDN'T CHANGE MY MIND. HE DID, HOWEVER, ORDER THE PIZZA AND PICK the movie.

He was also the one who made the decision to sit side-by-side on my sofa, putting me on edge with his proximity.

Actually, that could've been my fault.

After genuine conversation and a few laughs at the dinner table, liquid courage had me plopping my ass on the three-seater with him soon following to sit beside me. I'd thought it would be nice to see what happened.

Would he make a move?

Would I like it?

I should've kept with tradition and maintained my distance by claiming the recliner. Now his arm is spread behind my neck, his body so close I can smell his woodsy aftershave, and I can't handle the apprehension that smothers me.

He crosses his legs, his attention remaining on the television. "You're tense."

No shit.

We've worked together for too long, our relationship kept strictly professional since the moment we met, and this, right here, feels like a huge leap into high school awkwardness.

He gently massages his fingers against my shoulder. It heightens my sensitive nerves.

"I, umm… I'm still thinking about my shrink. I should find a new one." I clear my throat, my heart demanding I scoot away but I grin and bear the discomfort. "You're right about needing someone to talk to."

This is Easton.

Straightlaced, by-the-book Anthony Easton.

If he knew half the things I'm guilty of he wouldn't be rubbing me like this. In fact, I'm certain he'd be disgusted. Those kind eyes would turn feral, stripping layer upon layer of my already flimsy pride.

"Want me to ask around and get some recommendations?" He turns to me, his knee brushing my thigh. "I think one of my high-school buddies sees someone on Billow Street."

I clear my throat again, the tickle at the back of my tongue becoming more persistent. "Thanks. But I'd prefer to find someone on my own. I don't want to rush into it."

"Sure. That makes sense."

We fall silent, my attention returning to the television where actors speak words I don't bother listening to as the air turns into pockets of fragile glass around us.

I don't want to budge an inch from fear of destabilizing the atmosphere. I really don't.

Then again, maybe I should.

Maybe I need to beat back this arduous twist of my insides and take a leap of faith.

I should kiss him. Bite the bullet. Dive straight in, getting the experiment over and done with. Because so far, it's working. I haven't thought about Cole in hours. I've been successfully distracted. Until right this second, when his face stares back at me with each blink.

Easton chuckles.

I stiffen. *Can he read my mind?*

I'd almost believe he's capable if his eyes weren't glued to the television. He must be laughing at the movie.

The coaxing massage against my shoulder grows more adamant, awakening tiredness in my weary bones.

I can do this. I *should* do this.

A peck on the lips isn't the end of the world. And my loco, bat-shit-crazy status gives me a neon-sign excuse if I fail this crash test.

It's a win-win.

So why does kissing someone other than Cole seem like a shitty consolation prize? The bushfire flames of attraction are nowhere in sight. Lust isn't anywhere on my radar.

I clear my throat again, pissed off at the relentless tickle, and turn to face my friend.

He remains lazily focused on the screen, but I know he's aware of my train of thought. His understanding is subtle in the slight lift of his chin, the gentle detour of his hand to the back of my neck.

His fingertips graze my skin, up and down, inspiring goose bumps. It might not be the ungodly heat that engulfed me whenever Cole—

No.

No.

I'm not going there.

This is about Easton. Moving onward and upward. Reclaiming my moral high ground instead of slumming it in the streets.

I suck in a deep breath and regroup, relaxing my muscles one at a time—jaw, shoulders, stomach. I force myself to focus on the handsome man before me with his warm tan and gelled hair.

Finally, my throat tightens with anticipation. My mouth dries. I lick my lips to ease the discomfort and steel myself against what I'm about to instigate.

I'm going to do this. One kiss. One test.

"Are you sure you're okay?" He turns his face to mine, his gaze gentle. "You seem different tonight."

"Yeah…" I nod. "I'm super."

Super?

Fuck me. Who the hell is this ditsy airhead and where did the Bureau bitch rush off to?

I'm not flighty or meek.

I've made fearless criminals cry with subtle threats and intimidation. At least, I used to. Now those moments seem like a lifetime ago.

"Super?" He quirks a brow. "Maybe you should lay off the—"

My cell buzzes from my jeans pocket, the vibration sinking into my pelvis. For a moment, it feels like a sign. I'm just not sure what kind—affirmation or a blinding veto.

The vibration doesn't stop. The *buzz, buzz, buzz* adds to the awkwardness.

He grins. "Are you going to answer that?"

"Should I?" I pause.

He raises a brow and shrugs, the heat returning to his eyes.

It's daunting. The chemistry is all off.

"Just give me a sec." I pull out my phone, suddenly appreciating the disturbance, only to have my pulse stop at the name on the screen.

The Devil.

My heart shoots to my throat, choking me.

All those flames I'd yearned for with Easton—all the thrill and chemistry —engulf me.

"Who is it?" he murmurs.

I reject the call and shove the cell into my pocket. "Nobody."

Nobody I'm going to continue fixating on.

Nobody I can succumb to.

I settle back into the sofa, my pulse taking long moments to find its normal rhythm while I stare blankly at the television.

Did I just conjure a phone call to get out of moving on? Or did Cole perfectly time the interruption at the very moment I was trying to expunge him from my life, like a freaky coincidence?

No, not a coincidence. A succinctly scheduled intrusion.

Has that fucker bugged my apartment?

I shove to my feet, my eagle eyes frantically scanning my furnishings. If there's a camera in here, I'll run him down in my car and reverse a couple of times. I'll shoot and dismember and mutilate.

"What is it?" Easton sits forward. "Who was it?"

"Nothing... Nobody." I rush for the television cabinet and run my fingers over the back of the screen, then the nearby lamp, and the curtains.

My cell vibrates again, the ongoing buzz announcing another call.

I snatch for the device, *The Devil* taunting me again.

"What's going on?" Easton pushes from the sofa, his gentle steps approaching. "It's him, isn't it?"

The wildfire continues to overwhelm me in scorching flames. Head to foot. Organs to nerves.

Even with the threat of Cole yet again breaching my privacy, my body awakens at the mere thought of him being in my home. Touching my things. Paying me attention.

Not Stockholm syndrome, my ass.

If this doesn't scream certifiable, what does?

"Anissa?" Easton stops at my side as the call ends. "Why is he calling you?"

I keep my gaze locked on the cell, asking myself the same question.

I didn't speak much to Cole last night. I couldn't. We weren't alone. There were only a few barbed words to fill the silence before I left Penny in his capable hands. But there'd been unfinished business between us. There has been since Greece—I've just refused to let him close enough to carry on the madness.

One hurdle at a time, please, Satan.

"It's probably nothing." I guide a stray strand of hair behind my ear and nod to myself. "He probably wants to give me an update on what happened last night."

"What do you mean, last night?" Easton's voice thickens with tension. "What happened?"

I sidestep, moving around him to walk to the kitchen. "There was an incident with a mutual contact. I got to the scene before he did."

"You got to the scene?" He enunciates the words slowly. "You saw him? Is that why you're an emotional wreck today?"

"I'm not a wreck." I trudge to the fridge, pull open the door, and grab another beer. "I'm tired. That's all."

"Don't lie to me. You're showing the same crazy upheaval from a few weeks ago. And yet again, he's the cause." He stalks toward me, holding out a hand. "Give me the cell and I'll block his number."

"No." My denial is too fast. Too defensive. I can't help it. "I can handle this on my own."

"Like hell you can. You're not sleeping. Not exercising. Not working. Pretty soon the Bureau is going to write you off completely, then you won't have a job to return to. All for what?" He scans me with pained eyes. "What did he do to you, Nis?"

Oh, God. That nickname is foul on his lips.

An abomination.

Cole was the first person to ever call me Nis, Nissa, and even Nissie. I'd been his little fox, too. Yet the same endearment from a friend sounds sacrilegious.

"You know what he did," I lie. "He humiliated me. He made me his alibi when his father escaped custody."

"The time for bullshitting is over. We both know there's more to it than that. You disappeared for days. You fell off the face of the fucking planet and returned a different person."

I did.

Cole changed me.

"I—"

My cell vibrates again, this time short and sharp with a text.

The Devil: We need to speak. Now.

I grimace, wanting to comply with every breath and loath to do it at the same time.

"I'm turning it off." I press the power button and hold up the device for Easton to see. "I'm ignoring him." I turn away, placing the cell on the counter, my stomach resting against the cool laminate as a jittery discomfort eats away at me.

I want those phone calls. I crave more texts. Everything inside me screams for Cole's attention but I have to deny myself.

I grab my beer, twist off the cap, and down half the contents before gasping for air.

"Why won't you talk to me?" Easton comes up behind me. "What are you afraid of?"

"I'm not afraid." I take another gulp, eager for more liquid to douse Cole's flames while the hair on the back of my neck rises.

"Did he hurt you?"

Yes. "No."

"Did he scare you?"

Yes. "No."

"Are you searching for retribution?"

I sigh, unsure of my answer.

I want so many things from Cole—answers being my most prominent wish. It kills me to have no understanding of how I went from hating a man to willingly sleeping with him within the space of days.

I became lost in a murderer. And it wasn't as if he hid his venom behind that wickedly handsome face of his. He took every opportunity to show me the demon living within. He exposed me to his deepest, darkest depths, and still, I became entranced.

Fucking Stockholm.

"I can help you." Easton closes in behind me, his hands sliding over my shoulders, his fingers massaging softly. "We can take him down together."

I flinch. Tense.

Taking down Cole had been the driving force that pulled me into this mess in the first place. I'd wanted nothing more than to see him behind bars. Now all I can think of is seeing him between silk sheets.

"No." I place my beer on the counter and turn to face him, his large frame looming over me, his hands falling to his sides. "I just want to forget. Okay?" I force a smile, pretending it's all sunshine and optimism in this fucked up head of mine. "I'm going to take this last week off work and really pull myself together. Once I get back into my old routine I'll be fine."

"Is it this place?" He raises a brow, not backing out of my personal space. "Do you feel safe staying here on your own?"

I know where he's going with this, just like I've known what all the lingering stares and constant touches mean. He wants to stay. To spend the night. Again.

"I'm fine. Really." I reclaim my beer and slide out from in front of him, leading the way to the sofa. "And I appreciate everything you're trying to do, but I don't need saving."

I slump back onto my seat, ignoring his approach as he comes to take up the vacant space at my side. I increase the volume on the television, hopefully giving a glaring indication I'm finished with this conversation, and attempt to relax.

One muscle at a time.

One breath.

We don't talk for long moments. I use the lull to think long and hard about my situation.

Cole is my enemy. A manipulative predator who successfully brainwashed me into psychosis.

Easton is my partner. A protective, caring friend, who hasn't grown tired of my constant PMS-on-steroids personality.

He's safe.

He's trustworthy.

He's…not Cole.

And that's a good thing. It *has to be* a good thing.

Any forward momentum with him will drag me further away from where I shouldn't dwell.

I lean over, placing my bottle on the coffee table and settle back into the sofa. When his arm maneuvers from his side to wrap around my shoulders, I fight the need to move away and instead snuggle closer.

I rest my head into him. I breathe in the aftershave that's remarkably different from—

No. I'm not thinking about the devil anymore. Or the way he smelled. Or tasted. I have to cast every disillusioned thought from my brain.

I pull back slightly and turn to my friend, my heart hammering as our gazes collide. It's an all-or-nothing moment. Sink or swim. Fight or flight.

My insides squeeze. My pulse stutters.

I lick my lips and his attention narrows on my mouth.

I'm torn in a million different directions, the static of confusion blaring in my ears.

I shut it all down—the thoughts, the sensations, the warnings—and lean in, placing my lips on his.

3

ANISSA

HE SITS FROZEN FOR A SPLIT SECOND, THE CONNECTION STALE AND LIFELESS. I'M about to pull away in rabid humiliation when his mouth slowly moves beneath mine, the kiss tender. He wraps his arm tighter around me but still excessively gentle, as if I'll break.

It's all so slow and calm and…weak.

There's no passion. No possession.

Christ. What am I thinking?

This is a first kiss. It's not meant to be a porn audition. I'd just hoped for more.

I *need* what I previously had.

Ferocity.

Obsession.

I keep our mouths fused as I straddle his waist and cup his cheeks. I've never had a brother, but I'm starting to think this is what it might feel like to make out with one. The more I try to add kindling to the stack, the more my emotions assemble road blocks to all my nerve endings.

There's no fire. No flame. Not even a spark.

I try harder, sliding my tongue between his lips.

Everything is gentle. Soft. Deflated.

Until a knock at the door has his hands snapping to my hips as if in protection.

It's a brief moment of aggressive force, the hold inspiring my heartbeat to rampen.

I pull back, curious, yet thankful for the interruption. Then confusion takes hold.

I don't have any friends. Not apart from the man I'm straddling. And even if I did, I would've trained them well enough to know I'm not the type to want visitors after ten o'clock at night.

"That was…" Easton clears his throat. "Unexpected."

Had I imagined his attraction? Please, for the love of all things holy, don't make his flirtation another part of my vastly increasing mental delusions. "Unexpected?"

The knock sounds again, this time a booming thud.

Not only do I not have any friends who would attempt to beat down my door, I don't have any neighbors who aren't equally as reclusive as I am. And my landlord wouldn't dare to bother me at this hour.

Easton's face turns grim, his eyes narrowing. "It's him, isn't it? He's here."

"No." I should pretend I don't know who he's talking about. That my whole life doesn't currently revolve around one *him*. "He wouldn't be able to get into my building."

He scoffs. "Do you really think—"

The knock sounds again, louder and louder.

"Open the door, Nis, I know you're in there."

Oh, fuckety fuck.

I scramble off Easton's lap. He glides to his feet, far more elegantly than my baby-giraffe fumble.

"Why is he here?" He stretches out a hand to help stabilize me, but I move out of reach, unable to stomach more contact.

"I don't know." I keep my voice low. At least, I try. It's hard to know what's loud with the pulse booming in my ears.

The tingles I'd been hoping for with that kiss flood me. Everywhere. No place more potent than my chest.

My heart.

"I'll handle it." Easton sidesteps me, starting for the door.

"No." I snatch at his wrist, yanking him to a stop. "Hold on a goddamn minute. I'm not a damsel in distress. This is my apartment and my guest… or intruder… or whatever the hell you want to call him." I straighten my shoulders, those tingles turning into tremors at the thought of coming face-to-face with my mysterious syndrome creator. "I can handle Cole." I point a finger at his chest. "You be quiet."

His chin hikes in offense.

"I'm sorry. I didn't mean to snap. I just…" I sigh. I hate this new normal. The confusion and lack of confidence. I want to go back to feeling alive again. And not just in the moments that involve Cole.

The thunderous knock at the door gets louder, probably waking my neighbors.

"I'm *coming*." Fucking hell, that man is an impatient ass. "Stop banging."

I wince at Easton in apology and stalk for the door, yanking it open enough for Cole to see me and nothing else.

I'm poised to yell at him. To rail and curse, but the sight of arrogance personified standing suave and sophisticated in my hall is enough to steal my voice. The dark and devilish hair. The predatory blue eyes. The perfectly chiseled jaw.

"Nice to see you again, little fox."

My blood surges, the anger and animosity colliding. The unwanted attraction, too.

I glare. "What the hell are you doing here?"

His mouth kicks in a cocky grin. It's so subtle. The finest tweak of gorgeous lips. It's enough to make me gush with intolerable amounts of desire.

Fuck him.

Seriously, fuck him and his hypnotic appeal. I don't know what it is about this man that flicks all my switches, but once I figure it out, I'm shutting down that fuse box.

"I tried calling you. And I know you got at least the first of my texts." He shrugs. "Then I'm assuming you turned your phone off."

I scoot closer, holding the door handle behind me as I lower my voice. "If you've bugged my apartment, I swear to God—"

"I haven't bugged your apartment." He smirks. "Come on, Nis, what do you take me for? Would a man like me really corrupt your privacy like that?"

He corrupts *everything*. Every heartbeat. Every thought.

"You can't do this," I hiss. "You can't just come here and—"

He steps forward, bridging the space between us, making me snap ramrod straight.

I won't backtrack. I can't.

I'm not going to let him win.

"I just want to talk." He stares down at me, those devilish, ocean eyes focused on my mouth.

I swallow, already feeling his lips against mine. The buzz I'd wanted with Easton is right here, without a touch, without movement. The lust is suffocating.

"Let me in." He reaches for the door.

"*No.* You can say whatever you need right here."

His smirk increases, mirth dancing in his eyes as he leans a little closer. "It's not fit for public consumption. We need privacy."

Just the thought of being alone with him, in a confined space, is enough to make my nipples tingle. Harden.

I swallow over the desert taking hold in my throat and stand my ground. "Leave."

Another snicker brushes my ears as he takes one more step, walking into me as he pushes the door wide open.

Shit.

I want to grab him. To stop his momentum.

But touch isn't an option.

If I snatch for him I'm not sure I'll ever let go.

He strides past me as I tense, waiting for the eruption of male testosterone that never eventuates. Easton isn't in sight. He's not in the kitchen or the tiny living area. He's gone. There's only me and Cole, and the realization that my bedroom door is now slightly ajar.

"I'm serious," I warn. "You can't be in here."

What if he mentions Greece? What if he talks about our affair? Or what I did to his father?

My fucking life will never be the same if Easton overhears.

"Having a party?" Cole stops a few feet away, his attention scanning over the mess—the beer bottles, the empty pizza box, the television with its action-packed movie. He turns to face me, one brow raised. "It looks like I interrupted a good time."

"Every day is a party when I don't have to deal with you."

He beams a player smile. White, perfect teeth. Dark, devilish eyes. He knows he's under my skin, and he fucking loves it.

Asshole.

He licks his lower lip and lazily strolls toward me. "Admit you miss me."

My eyes flare. "What's to miss? You're nothing but a pain in my ass."

He chuckles, not stopping his approach, not even once he reaches my hyper-sensitive personal space. I'm forced to retreat. One step. Two. Until my butt hits the door, knocking it shut.

"That's not how I remember our time together." He closes in, caging me with his presence like the most powerful predator.

I'm rendered speechless, my pulse sky-rocketing, my limbs trembling.

How can he control me like this? How can he snatch my common sense and leave me defenseless?

"Something is different about you?" He scrutinizes me. "You're flushed."

"And I bet you think you're responsible."

"No." His gaze hardens. "Your cheeks were already pink when you answered the door. Why?"

I should admit the truth. I need to end this crazy thing we have going on and simply tell him I was with Easton. But the words refuse to make themselves heard over the rush of intoxicating warmth.

"What do you need to tell me?" I swallow, squaring my shoulders. "Hurry up and spit it out so I can go to bed."

That vulturous gaze studies me for long moments before he relaxes into his normal sense of superiority. "You need to lay low for a while. At least a few days. Don't leave your apartment. Don't even cross the street for coffee."

Each demand makes me balk. Not only due to the underlying threat, but because he arrogantly thinks I'll comply.

"I'll have men watching the building," he continues. "However, it's best if—"

"Whoa." I hold up a hand. "For starters, you will *not* have your men watch me. And second, I know how to take care of myself. I'm a goddamn FBI agent, Cole."

"How could I forget?" His expression tightens.

"What's this about?" I hike my chin, matching him stare for stare. "Why do you want me to hide?"

"You don't need the details. Just lay low. It's only for a few days."

"You can't barge in here and demand I put my life on hold for no reason." I scowl. "Who do you think you are?"

I'm gifted with another one of those subtle, taunting snickers. He inches closer, getting in my face, the heat of his breath brushing my lips. "You know exactly who I am."

My pulse detonates. My inhales transform into teeny, tiny gasps.

I want him. *God*, how I want to bite and claw this man out of my system, right on my carpeted floor. Our clothes strewn. Our bodies covered in sweat.

What I wouldn't give to feel his heavy chest pressed down on mine. His lips on my flesh. His cock—

Fuck.

"Why?" I snap, my attention flicking to my bedroom door in guilt before trekking straight back to the wall of dominance before me.

He sighs, his superiority fading under the weight of something heavier. "I need you to trust me."

Trust? Something seriously sinister must be happening if he's asking for such a prize.

"Tell me." My fingers itch to reach out. To physically demand answers and sate my need to touch him.

His jaw ticks, an internal battle coming into view behind those eyes. "Robert might still be alive."

All the air leaves my lungs on a heave.

Robert.

The same Robert who humiliated me. Beat me. Threatened to kill me.

I've worked hard to suppress the memories of that monster. I did everything in my power to pretend those moments didn't exist. Now they all come rushing back in a wealth of icy goose bumps.

"How do you know?" I keep my voice low.

"There was money taken from one of my father's bank accounts. The security image isn't clear, but Decker's sister insists it's him."

I blink and blink, trying to beat back my shock. "Where?"

He winces. It's slight, the minute narrowing of his brows, yet it's enough to make my stomach bottom.

"Where, Cole?"

"Here," he grates. "In Portland."

Frigid fingers of panic grip my throat. "For how long? When did he arrive?"

"I don't know. Could be weeks—"

"And you're only telling me now?" My voice rises. "How could you—"

"I only just received the smallest hint of confirmation." His lips curl in a snarl as he gets in my face. "And you're the first fucking person I've told. I've got a house full of people waiting to find out, and I came here. I came to *you*. I'd never let..." His words trail, and I can't help but bow my head, needing to break the potency of his stare in an attempt to make sense of what's happening.

Robert was meant to be murdered for what he did to me. I heard him beg for his life. The gunshot had blasted my ears.

I'd been the reason for his supposed death.

And if he remains alive, I'd be one of his biggest targets.

"Hey." Cole grips my chin, raising my face until I'm staring back at him. "I'll protect you."

Goddamnit.

The last thing I need right now is protection from an unwanted infatuation.

My lips part as I try to think of something strong and affirming to say. But the squeak of my bedroom door steals the words away.

Cole stiffens, his attention snapping across the room, his fingers tightening on my chin. We both stare at Easton standing in the doorway, his hair mussed, his muscled body on full display as he stands in nothing but his underwear, his shirt hanging loose in his hand.

He's playing the role of awoken lover, and I can't fathom his audacity.

"What the fuck are you doing here?" He scowls at Cole and yanks the shirt over his head.

I'm frozen in a nightmare. Unable to do anything except watch the carnage from behind slowly blinking eyes.

Cole lets out a barely audible growl, his fingers sliding from my chin to leave me hollow. "I could ask you the same thing." His gaze cuts back to mine. "But I won't."

He glares at me. Glares so hard and vicious I'm made to feel worthless under his attention.

He's jealous.

Hurt.

His pain lashes through me like a lethal injection.

"I guess I didn't need to warn you. You've already got all the protection you need." He reaches behind me to pull open the door. "Excuse my interruption. It won't happen again."

No. He can't leave. Not like this.

I want to scream at him to stop. To listen. To understand.

Instead, I let him walk from my apartment, the latch clicking shut seconds later as I remain rooted in place. Stunned.

"What the hell was that all about?" Easton approaches, his sleepy facade disappearing. "What were you two talking about?"

I slow my breathing, taking one long drag of air after another in the hopes more oxygen will decrease my mania.

"Nis? What the—"

"Stop." I warn. "Don't call me that."

"Jesus Christ. I'm sorry, *Anissa*. But you've gotta understand how fucking mind-blown I am at seeing him all over you. I think I deserve some answers."

I puff out a breath. Numb. Cold. Alone.

So goddamn alone.

The wildfire flames have been snuffed. All that's left in Cole's wake are dying embers.

"No." I cross my arms over my chest. "It's time for you to explain why the hell you came out here acting like we'd just slept together."

4

ANISSA

Easton retreats into the room and returns moments later carrying his jeans. "Would you have preferred if I pulled my gun?"

"I would've preferred if you'd let me handle it, like I asked." I grate the words through clenched teeth. "You've only made things worse."

He pulls on his pants, yanking them hard up his thighs. "I was trying—"

"No. Forget it." I raise a hand for him to stop. "I don't want to hear it."

His intent was clear. He deliberately acted like a scorned lover to start some sort of macho pissing contest.

"Please leave." I cross my arms over my chest and stare at the empty beer bottles on the coffee table, unable to keep looking at him.

"Are you serious?" He starts toward me. "What else was I going to do? I could—"

I backtrack, remaining out of reach. "Please just leave."

He plants his feet… sighs… waits.

"Now, Easton. I'm not going to change my mind."

"This is ridiculous." He strides for the kitchen, swiping his keys and wallet from the counter. "I'm sorry, okay? *Christ*. I'm the one who was blindsided. Doesn't that count for something?"

He's not the only one who didn't see this coming. Not only Cole's appearance, but the resurrection of Robert. The thought of that heinous man still walking the earth has my stomach tied in knots.

"I'll call you tomorrow." Easton starts for the door. "Then we're going to sit down and talk about what the hell is going on."

I don't respond. I wait until he leaves, then make my way to the window to peer at the street below. I remain in place until his sedan pulls from the curb.

Then I stand there even longer, hoping Cole's Porsche will follow so he knows I haven't let anyone spend the night in my apartment.

But that black sports car doesn't pass. Nobody does. The city street remains desolate until I drag my weary ass to bed.

The next morning, I didn't hide. I ignored Cole's demands, strapped my gun around my waist in a Velcro holster, pulled on a sweater and active pants, then went for a run.

I jogged block after block, appreciating the thrill of being watched. I knew, no matter how angry the devil was, that he wouldn't stop his men from stalking me. *Protecting* me.

And if Robert was around, I wanted to drag him out. Lure him in.

But he didn't show his face. Not during the long morning, or in the afternoon when I made sure I'd ditched my invisible tail with some grade-A driving skills to turn the tables and shadow Cole.

I parked down his street, watching cars pass in and out of his property gates. Last night, he mentioned having a house full of people and that much is evident from the constant back and forth of vehicles. The property is guarded, too. A security team stalks the perimeter. Contractors. I don't recognize the men through my binoculars.

I remain there until night falls, and one by one, a long line of cars leave through the gates. Security in front, then Hunter and Sarah, Benji and Layla, Decker and Keira, and finally Cole, followed by more security.

I follow, trailing in the distance to the Torian family restaurant. I circle the block after all five vehicles head toward the back of the building, and find a parking space within view of the floor-to-ceiling glass out the front.

Staff inside work in a synchronized frenzy, polishing cutlery in an open-plan area previously filled with tables and chairs.

I watch for a long time as guests arrive, the number of people growing by the hour until the entire restaurant is full of mingling criminals drinking alcohol and eating canapés.

Nobody is hiding from Robert. If anything, they're being blatant with their lack of fear.

Especially Cole, who constantly parades the room, suave and sophisticated in his tailored suit, his hair styled, his smile sly yet welcoming. He makes some of the women blush through mere conversation, and I'm sure if I were in there I'd hear their flirtatious giggles.

It seems two can play the jealous game.

Bitterness eats away at me as I sit in silence, nothing but damaging thoughts to keep me company.

Decker, my previous informant turned criminal, talks to an older couple with Cole's sister, Keira, close at his side. Hunter and Sara mingle. Benji and Layla speak with relatives of the Torian empire.

Everyone is in attendance except for Penny and Luca—the other man who was complicit in my abduction to Greece. I can't find them as I skim the crowd slower through my binoculars, concerned for the welfare of the woman once held as a sex slave under the same roof as Robert.

She must be petrified.

I'm seated on the edge of my seat, leaning forward, eager for a better view, when a light rap at my driver's-side window scares the ever-loving crap out of me.

I reach for my gun, yank it from the Velcro as I drop my binoculars to find Easton peering down at me.

"Shit," I mutter under my breath.

He glowers as he rounds the hood to the passenger side, waiting impatiently until I unlock the car.

"Want to know how long I spent driving around trying to find you?" He drops into the seat beside me, slamming the door behind him.

"Not really." I shove my weapon back in place and stare out the window, unable to withstand his visual criticism.

"Don't worry; it didn't take long. This is the first place I looked. And surprise, surprise, you're here."

"Please don't start this again. You've got no idea what's going on."

"Then tell me." He turns to face me. "Fucking clue me in so I understand why you're risking your career and your fucking life by hanging around this asshole."

I clench my teeth, forcing myself not to respond.

"Jesus Christ, Fox." He scoffs. "I don't understand you anymore."

That makes two of us.

I can't figure out where I went wrong. I shouldn't have set my sights on taking Cole down—that much is clear. But when did my need for justice become smothered by my obsession for the man himself?

"I wish I could explain…"

"No, you don't," he grates. "If you wanted me to know, I'd know. But instead, you choose to keep me in the dark and I have no idea why. Especially when I'm one of the only people who has never judged you."

"You're judging me now."

He falls silent, allowing an uncomfortable awkwardness to settle between us.

I wouldn't even have a clue where to start if I did tell him all the wrong turns I've taken to get to this point. I'd have to admit I'm no longer worthy of holding an FBI badge. I'd be forced to confess the feelings I'd had for a manipulative murderer.

The feelings I *still* have.

"Easton…" I sigh, unable to continue. There are no words to explain this mess.

"At least talk to me about that kiss." His gaze bores into the side of my head. "Was it a mistake or did it mean something?"

My stomach flips. Not in a good way.

I don't want to make things worse between us. I can't lose the only person who has been kind enough to see through my flaws and not hold me accountable for my father's mistakes.

"I don't know." It's such a weak, pathetic response. The old me would spit in the face of the woman I've become, but I can't explain something I don't understand.

I can't illustrate how I hoped the kiss would mean something and how, even after the fact, I'm still not sure if it did.

"Did you sleep with him?" He huffs out a derisive breath of a chuckle. "I don't even know why I'm asking. He set you up. He fucking played you. But I can't shake the sex vibes I'm getting between you two."

"He had information on my father." It's not a lie. It's barely a glimpse of the truth, but still, not a lie. Just enough of a fact to hopefully push him away from exposing the worst of my decisions where Cole is concerned.

"What information?"

"It doesn't matter."

"Of course it fucking matters. What did he tell you? And why didn't you fill me in sooner?"

"Because it's nobody's business." Easton knows how I feel about my father's disappearance. It's the easiest escape from this conversation. "The Bureau labeled my father a turncoat. Anyone he worked with has already drawn their own damning conclusions, and I'm not going to waste my energy proving them wrong. I want to move on with my life."

"I'm not asking for them. You used to trust me. What changed?"

I wince, hating how he thinks this is about him. "Nothing changed. I still trust you. You know you're all I've got." I meet his gaze, my wince remaining in apology. "I just didn't want to reopen old wounds."

He reaches out, his palm sliding over my wrist, back and forth. "I'm sorry."

I tense, not appreciating the contact. "Forget it. Can we pretend this conversation never happened?"

"I can…" His hand stops its gentle movement. "But what about the kiss? Do I forget that, too?"

To hell with that kiss.

And to hell with the man who drove me to commit the insanity in the first place.

"Don't worry, Fox." His touch retreats. "I'll put it to the back of my mind. Temporarily. But sometime soon, I'm gonna want to figure out where that affection came from and if there's any hope for a repeat."

I nod, cringing on the inside. I owe him an explanation. Stupidity and shame be damned.

"What are you doing here anyway?" He shifts his attention to the restaurant. "What's with the underworld festivities?"

"I don't know." I follow his line of sight, my gaze immediately seeking Cole only to come up empty. I can't spy him among the crowd. I can no longer see Hunter or Sarah either. In fact, Decker, Benji, and Layla are all gone, too.

I sit taller, scanning the guests once more.

"Is Cole even in there?" Easton asks.

"He was. They all were. I can't find any of them now." I reach for my binoculars.

"Are they up to something?"

"Aren't they always? We both know they live to hatch new schemes. That's not going to change anytime soon." I itch to get out of the car. My skin literally crawls with the inability to find my target. "I'm going to take a closer look."

I unfasten my belt and open my door, only to have Easton grab my wrist again.

"There. Look." He jerks his head at the restaurant. "He just came in from the kitchen."

I narrow my focus. Cole returns to the party. Benji and Layla follow a few minutes behind. Then Hunter.

They all seem different now. Cole is tense, the player smile no longer plastered on his face. Instead, he scowls, his lips pressed tight. And his posture denotes a sharp stick has been shoved up his usually impenetrable ass.

I still can't find Decker.

Something must have happened.

I want to believe the change in Cole has something to do with Robert's capture. But I know him well enough to determine the shift in his demeanor isn't from good news.

He's on edge. His glances pointed.

He's been spooked, which forces me to feel the same.

"It looks like a typical night in their shady lives if you ask me." Easton speaks softly. "And even if they were up to something you know you're not the person to be handling this. Why don't you let me take over?"

"I'll leave soon."

He laughs. "You're lying to me now?"

"No. I'm tired." Emotionally and physically. Cole has that effect on me. "I'll go home in a few minutes. I promise."

"Is that a hint that you want me to leave?"

I don't answer, letting him form his own conclusion.

"Okay, Fox. I'm outta here. But only if you promise to call me when you get home." He opens his door and waits.

"I'll be fine."

"Just fucking call me, okay? I'm not going to sleep until you do."

He's such a nice guy. A protective, caring, thoughtful man. Why can't my libido be turned on by those attributes instead of predatory darkness?

"Fox?"

"Okay. I'll call." I shoo him away with a wave of my hand. "Get out of here."

He gives me a final look of concern, then closes the door to walk down the street behind me and turn the corner.

For each second of the next twenty minutes, I sit in hope of Cole doing something to give me an excuse to barge into the restaurant. I pray he'll cause a scene or break the law so I have a valid reason to strut my ass in there and face him.

In the same seconds, I fight to drag myself away. To place necessary distance between us so I don't fall deeper into obsession.

I hate what he's done to me.

I absolutely loathe how he took a hammer to my morals and made it impossible to piece them all together again.

I was an honorable FBI agent once. Now, I'm nothing. At least I won't be when everyone finds out how I assisted in criminal activity. No, not just assisted. Participated. *Instigated.*

I start the car and pull from the curb, driving past the restaurant. For a second, I think Cole's gaze meets mine. That there's a tiny spark of recognition in his eyes. But then it's gone, another passing car stealing my attention before I'm forced to focus on the road.

I have to stop doing this. *Why* am I doing this?

Stock-holm syn-drome.

Police sirens wail in the distance as I start toward home. Red and blue lights flash up ahead. I slow behind banked traffic and lower my window, peering outside in a vain attempt to understand what's happening. I can't see anything but cars. There are only frantic shouts for help from unseen people.

I pull over and get out, jogging along the sidewalk. I pass one parked vehicle after another, a crowd building up ahead, as an officer stands on the other side of crime scene tape, staring them down.

"I need you all to take a step back," he growls. "Better yet, go home. Have some respect."

Respect?

The crash comes into sight as I pass the next parked vehicle.

It seems like a truck plowed into a Suburban in the middle of the intersection.

A *familiar* Suburban.

The plates are Luca's.

I run harder, approaching the group of people with their phones at the ready. I shoulder my way to the front, my pulse pausing at the two dead bodies on the road. One up ahead to the left. Another splayed yards away to the right. The crime scene is so fresh the victims haven't had a chance to be covered.

"What the hell happened?" I ask.

The lady nestled against my shoulder casts me a sideways glance. "There was a shooting. This one guy gunned down both men and kidnapped a woman. Even placed her in the trunk of the dead man's car and took off. The only person left behind is the lady currently being interviewed by police."

She points to the Suburban where two officers are nestled close at the open passenger door.

I don't pause for contemplation. I grab the crime scene tape and duck beneath it, running for Luca's car.

"*Hey,*" the policeman yells. "*Stop.*"

"I'm family," I call over my shoulder and keep running, needing to see the survivor, having to confirm who was taken.

Shattered glass blankets the asphalt as I approach Luca's beat up car. The smell of gasoline permeates the air. I close in on the officers at the passenger door and hear the shorter blond guy talking calmly to whoever is caged in front of him.

"I already told you," a woman snaps. "I have no idea what happened."

I know that voice.

It's Hunter's fiancé.

"Sarah?" I skitter to a stop as the policemen turn to face me.

"Ma'am, this is a crime scene." The taller officer stares down his nose at me, his hand moving to his holstered gun. "You need to get back behind the tape."

"I'm her friend."

I'm not even stretching the truth. It's a blatant lie.

The closest I've come to being friendly with Sarah is the silence we shared on opposite ends of a private jet when she escorted me home from Greece.

I lean in, seeing her slumped in the passenger seat, her nose bloodied, one cheek bruised. She straightens at the sight of me, her eyes alighting with strategy as she cradles her ribs.

"Yeah, a friend." She nods. "She's here to take me home."

"She's not taking you anywhere until we're finished talking," the shorter officer warns. "Two people died and another was taken. This is clearly gang-related, yet you're claiming you've got no idea what happened."

"Can't you see she needs medical attention?" My blood boils. "Where are the paramedics?"

"She refused medical help," the taller man snips. "Now, get behind the barrier tape before we're forced to escort you."

Sarah shuffles forward in the seat, wincing as she attempts to climb from the vehicle. "I'm going with her. I've already told you all I know." She jumps to her feet, whimpering on impact. "She can take me to the hospital." Sarah jerks her chin at me. "She's got more authority here than you, anyway."

I cringe, knowing what's coming next as the cops straighten to their full height.

"More authority?" they ask in unison.

"She's a Fed." Sarah hobbles toward me. "She can give me a ride."

"This isn't a Federal case," the shorter officer warns. "You've got no jurisdiction here."

I muster bravado that I seriously lack the energy to maintain. "Not yet it isn't.

But one phone call and it could be. So do the right thing and let me take this woman to a hospital. You can ask your questions later."

"I don't even have her name." Short guy frowns. "I need details."

"Jane." Sarah reaches my side and leans into me. "Jane Doe...erty. Jane Doherty."

Goddamnit.

She's not even striving for subtlety.

"I'm going to need to see your badge." The taller man demands of me. "And I'll be noting this in our report."

Fuck.

I do as he asks, snatching my ID from my pocket to flip open my credentials.

I'm going to get in so much shit for this—the involvement in a police matter. Escorting a victim/witness from the scene under false pretenses. And, no doubt, the disappearance of said victim/witness when they later search for her.

Sarah won't go to a hospital. They'll never find her again. Not once Cole gets involved.

"Is there anything else you need from me, Officer?" I keep showing my badge as he takes note of my details.

"No. Get her to the emergency room. We'll check in with her once we're finished here."

"Great." I keep the sarcasm from my tone and start for my car while Sarah hobbles at my side. Once we're out of listening range, the wail of more sirens approaching in the distance, I shoot her a glance. "What the hell happened?"

"Don't know. Can't remember." Her words are sharp. Pointy.

"Right." I stop in the middle of the street, the peanut gallery on the footpath watching our every move. "Maybe I should leave you with the cops then."

She glares, the expression made all the more fierce by the bruising and swelling taking over the bridge of her nose. "I need a goddamn phone. Can I borrow yours?"

"No problem, just as soon as you tell me what happened."

She scoffs, then winces. "You're going to be that bitch? Really?"

"I'm trying to help you. At the expense of my career, I might add, seeing as though you just threw me under the bus."

"Don't pretend you don't have your own agenda." She shuffles ahead, moving away from me.

"An agenda? What agenda could I possibly have right now? I got you out of there and all I want in return is to know if Robert was involved. For my own fucking safety."

She shoots me a skeptical glance, the faintest hint of surprise flashing in her gaze.

"Yes, I know he's still alive." I follow after her. "Cole came to see me last night. I need to know if this was Robert's doing."

"I can't remember." She shrugs. "And I would've kept telling the cops the same thing."

"Okay. Fine." I walk faster, outpacing her. "Find your own way home. God forbid you take my help."

A string of muttered curses brush my ears as I place a few feet of space between us

"It's not like you're more gracious than I am," she snarls. "You were just as thankful for my help when I brought you back from Greece."

I scoff, not stopping my stride until I reach the police tape and duck underneath. "There's a big difference."

"Of course there is," she calls from behind me. "Because I'm in a shitload of pain... and I'm fucking scared. Okay?"

My heart squeezes. Twists.

I keep hold of the tape. Not moving.

I've learned a lot about Sarah through my investigations. About her massive loss. Her orphan status. I don't blame her for falling in with the wrong crowd when she had nobody else in her life. And for her to be scared after everything she's been through would surely mean a woman like me should be petrified.

I wait for her to catch up before I meet her gaze. "Why are you scared?"

Her face hardens. "I don't know, Miss Priss. Maybe because someone plowed their truck into my face, then sprayed bullets like confetti." One hand fidgets at her side. "I really need a phone. Can't you let me make one call?"

"Who was the shooter?"

"Don't know."

Again with the short and sharp response.

She's hiding something.

"It was Robert, wasn't it?" I scope our surroundings, taking in the potential witnesses. "He did this. He tried to kill you."

Any number of nearby people could probably confirm my suspicions. I could simply start asking them. I know what Robert looks like. I'll never forget his features.

"I honestly don't know," she repeats. "I blacked out. I didn't see him. Now can you please give me your goddamn cell?"

"Fine." I reach into my pocket, seeing three missed calls from Easton on the screen before I hand it over. "Make sure you choose your words wisely. That's a work phone."

I continue to my car, giving her privacy as I attempt to figure out how the hell I'm going to explain this to the officers on scene. To Easton. To my boss.

This will act as another nail in my career coffin.

The long list of grievances the Bureau has against me is currently superficial. They align me with the bad name of my father. They despise me for being Cole's alibi when his father escaped custody. But this...

My actions here go against protocol. I'm helping a criminal flee a crime scene.

What the hell am I doing?

I bypass a traffic cop now directing the banked up vehicles away from the area, and slump against the hood of my car, watching Sarah.

She's frantic in her conversation, sheer panic etched across her face.

I want to help her despite our differences, even without the connection to Robert.

It has to be another side effect of Stockholm.

The rev of an engine draws my attention to the back of the waiting line of cars. The deep vibration transforms into a screech of wheels, then a streak of black as a familiar Porsche accelerates along the parking lane to stop behind me.

Cole climbs out, stalking forward, cell in his hand, scowl set in stone. The closer he gets the deeper his brows pinch, until he's glaring at me.

"Thank Christ." Sarah jogs toward us, her arm tight around her ribs. "I tried calling Hunter but he must be on the phone. And Luca isn't answering. Where is everyone?"

"My house. Or on the way there. What the fuck happened? Where's Penny?"

Penny?

Sarah doesn't speak, but the fear in her eyes says it all as she stares at Cole.

"She's meant to be here?" I ask. "She was in the car with you?"

They ignore me, Cole's face tightening, his shoulders stiff.

"Robert has her?" I push from the car, demanding their attention.

"I was out of it," Sarah pleads with Cole. "I don't know if she ran or if she was taken?"

My stomach free falls.

"She was taken," I confirm. "Witnesses watched a man put a woman in the trunk of a car before he sped off. I need you both to tell me everything you know." I step closer, right up to Cole. "What information do you have on him?"

"The time for shared knowledge is over," he states in a flat tone. Emotionless. Detached. "That was your choice."

"Don't be an asshole. If Penny's in trouble—"

"Penny is none of your concern."

"Cole," I warn. "Listen—"

"No, *you* listen. You made your choice. Now deal with it." He glares at Sarah. "Get in the car."

He stalks to the passenger side of the Porsche, and I follow as he opens the door and helps her inside.

I'm poised to plead my case when he turns on me, his eyes filled with animosity as he says, "Keep your mouth shut. Breathe one word of this and you're going to have a problem on your hands."

"You're threatening me?" My hackles rise, the hair on my neck tingling in response. "What are you going to do, Cole? Kidnap me again?"

He smiles, the curve of lips different than anything I've witnessed from him before. There's no flirtation or superiority. It's pure hostility. One hundred percent venom. "No, Anissa. Our days jetting across the globe are over. You won't be treated that kindly again."

Like so many times before, I'm assaulted with the wrong emotional response.

I should be shocked at the audacity of him calling my abduction a kindness. I should be pissed that I'm being treated like the bad guy. I should even be so entirely fearful for Penny's life that his menace doesn't matter.

Instead, I'm left empty at what he called me—Anissa.

My full name.

Without abbreviation or flirtation.

What the fuck is wrong with me?

5

COLE

I walk past Anissa, skirting the hood of my car to slide into the driver's seat.

I've never had to clutch tighter to my threadbare restraint than I do right now.

Tonight has been a fucking nightmare.

The party at my restaurant was meant to draw Robert from the shadows. I had an extensive team of hired men scattered throughout the neighborhood to catch that fucker. But what I hadn't expected was the revelation that Benji, my own brother-in-law, has been working with him.

It doesn't matter that I know my sister was the driving force behind the betrayal. Benji made the decision to follow Layla's lead. *He* was the one in my inner circle, playing me like a fool. And *he* will be the one who pays the heavy price.

I'd already been on edge, not only due to the threat of Robert, but because Anissa had gone against my directives to stay hidden, choosing instead to flitter around the fucking city all damn morning before outsmarting the men I had following her.

Nobody had been able to find her until she turned up out the front of the restaurant. Right where I didn't want her to be.

I shouldn't give a shit. Not one iota.

After watching Easton walk from her bedroom last night, it should be easy to forget her. Instead, all I want to do is spend my days destroying his life, and making her watch.

I'll show her how pathetic he is. I'll make him wish he'd never laid eyes on her, let alone his filthy hands.

But seeing her here *now*, after the bullshit of the last twelve hours, only makes my blood boil.

I fight the instinct to gun the engine, escaping in a screech of tires, and pull from the curb slowly, pretending she has no effect on me as she stands on the footpath, her eyes pained.

"Tell me everything," I demand of Sarah. "Don't leave out any details."

"I seriously don't know what to tell you. One minute I was driving; the next, Penny was yelling. I caught sight of the truck plowing toward us for a split second, then I blacked out on impact. I didn't see the driver. And Penny was gone when I gained consciousness."

"What did the police say?"

"They think it's gang-related. The security guard you had tailing us is dead, and I overheard them talking about the murder of an innocent bystander who tried to help Penny. This has to have been Robert."

Fuck.

Luca is going to lose his shit.

And Robert... that fucking prick will make Penny regret her freedom.

"I have no idea what's going on between you two." Sarah fastens her belt. "And I know she's a Fed. But Agent Fox was really only trying to help."

I ignore her, pressing the button on my steering wheel to activate my cell. "Call Hunt."

The car speakers come alive with the ringtone as I inch toward the banked traffic. I blare my horn until the long line parts enough for me to cut through and head in the opposite direction.

"We've got a situation," Hunt growls in greeting. "And I can't find Sarah. She's not answering her fucking phone."

"I'm here," she speaks up, repositioning herself in her seat with a wince. "I'm okay. But Penny's gone."

He releases a long breath. "Thank fuck you're okay. I've been calling—"

"I tried calling you, too. I left a message." She sits taller. "Listen, we were hit by a truck. I got knocked out, but when I came to she was gone."

"Are you okay?" he asks.

"I'm fine. But Penny isn't."

"She's here. Well, she was. Decker just drove her and Luca to the hospital."

"What happened?" I press my foot harder, speeding along the street.

"I've got no idea. I can't figure out the mess. Even the guards at your gate are clueless. All I've got is a damn war zone in your neighbor's house with nobody here to tell the tale."

"And Benji," I snarl the name. "Where is he?"

"He's with me, helping start the clean-up. I told him to call Keira and Layla. They're going to spend the night in a hotel, but they want the kids out of your house asap."

"I'll get them. I'm on my way now. Find out what hotel they're at and text it to me."

"Will do. And Cole..." There's a pause. "Our problem has been taken care of."

Our problem—*Robert*.

Sarah glances at me, her bruised face relaxing.

"Entirely?" I turn the nearest corner, easing my foot off the gas.

"Yeah. Entirely. It's only a matter of getting him off the grid."

I shoot Sarah a grin as she exhales in relief. "Good work."

I disconnect the call, my night finally seeming to change for the better. At least momentarily. I still need to make an example of Benji. There's no way around it.

I've given too many free passes for betrayal lately. I can't do it again.

I'll punish him in a way that ensures everyone knows I'm not to be fucked with. And I'll make sure Layla knows she's to blame.

I pull onto my street, my attention narrowing on Decker's car parked in front of my neighbor's house, Benji's car positioned directly opposite.

I slow, a skitter of foreboding crawling down my neck at the sight of Mavis' house illuminating the early morning darkness. I hope the old girl survived whatever went on in there. Then again, it might be better if she didn't. She'd never feel safe again. Not all alone in that big house.

"What do you think happened?" Sarah asks.

"I don't know. We'll get the details soon enough." I grind my teeth through the mental onslaught of possibilities. That fucker came too close. Way too fucking close. "Once I grab the kids and drop them off to my sisters, I'll call the doc and make sure you're checked over."

"I'm fine. It's a few bruises. That's all."

"You're seeing the doctor. It's not up for discussion." I continue driving to my front gates, opening the thick metal barrier with a click of a remote, and stop beside the waiting guard.

He keeps a hand over his side piece as I lower my window, his gaze stalking our surroundings while he leans down to eye level.

"What happened?" I growl.

"Your guess is as good as mine. We heard an explosion. Our guys on the perimeter thought there were gunshots, too. Silenced, though. But nothing crossed the fence. No bullets. No threat. Nothing."

"You didn't send someone next door to check it out?"

"No, sir. It was our job to maintain the safety of *your* property and the residents inside. My men did their boundary checks every ten to fifteen minutes as scheduled. Then kept a closer eye on your neighbor after the disturbance. But we never left our post."

I don't know whether to be proud or infuriated.

"Make sure nobody disturbs my men." I tilt my chin toward Mavis' house. "I don't want anything coming within a foot of the front yard. No cops. No visitors. Not even a fucking squirrel. You hear me?"

"I hear you." He straightens, retreating from the Porsche. "I'll let you know if we have any issues."

I raise my window and drive through the gates, continuing around the back of the house, passing two more armed guards in the shadows before parking in the garage.

Sarah doesn't say a word. She stares straight ahead even after I kill the engine.

"What's on your mind?" I unfasten my belt and release the steering wheel.

"He took her," she whispers. "Robert took Penny."

"Yeah, he did. But he's dead now."

"And what about her?" She shoots me a glance. "What happened between the time she left me and the moment that rapist died? What did he do to her?"

"Whatever happened couldn't be worse than the life she had in Greece." It's a pathetic comparison. But it's the truth. "She survived living with my father. She can survive this, too."

"I was meant to be looking after her." Her voice wavers. "It was my job to keep her safe."

"It was also the job of the guard you had following you. We should all be thankful your fate, along with Penny's, wasn't the same as his."

She shifts her focus back out the windshield to the darkened garage. "That's not comforting."

"Well, it should be." I shove from the car, waiting as she slowly unfastens her belt, her movements more stiff than earlier. "Stay here. I'll organize the kids."

"No." She opens her door, cautiously climbing out. "I'll get Tobias. You can handle Stella. That little girl is the devil when woken from her beauty sleep."

She isn't wrong. My niece—although, the most beautiful princess I've laid eyes on—can be Satan when the mood strikes. It's an unfortunate trait she gained from her mother.

I lead the way into the house, along the darkened hall, the light from the kitchen the only glow to highlight the closed bedrooms. I pass the nanny's door to gently ease open Stella's, then creep inside, walking from memory because the room is too dark to see shit.

I don't stop until my shins hit the unforgiving hardness of the side of the bed. *Fuck.*

I kneel with a snarl, placing my hands on the mattress. "Stella, sweetheart. You need to get up."

There's no response. Not even a shift in the silence around me.

"Stella?" I reach out, swiping my palm over the bed. My fingers glide over vacant sheets. "Sweetheart?"

I can't hear her breathing.

I can't hear a damn thing.

"*Stella?*" I scramble for the door. Flick on the light. Expose a completely empty room.

There's no sign of my niece.

"*Sarah.*" I storm for the hall, into Tobias' doorway, and flick on the light. She stands before another empty bed, the fear in her features mimicking the sensation pummeling my chest.

"Are they having some sort of camp-out in another room?" She rushes toward me. "Could they have heard the explosion and gotten scared? Maybe they're with the nanny."

I send out a silent prayer. I mentally beg the fucking heavens for her to be right as I run down the hall, swinging the nanny's door wide.

"Tanya." I flick on the light and everything drains from me—thought, comprehension, knowledge.

The girl, barely in her mid-twenties, lays strewn on the carpet, face-up, a hypodermic syringe hanging from her arm. Vomit is pooled on the floor near her mouth. Urine permeates the air. And those eyes. Those vacant, unblinking eyes.

"Oh, Christ." Sarah shoves past me and falls to her knees beside the woman to place a gentle hand to her cheek. "She's stone cold."

6

COLE

I search the house, scouring every room, calling Tobias and Stella's names with every breath.

I hope they're in hiding. That they heard someone messing with Tanya and made the smart decision to flee.

"They're not here." Sarah catches up to me in the kitchen, her face pale as she holds up a dirty cloth. "But I found this under Stella's bed."

"What is it?" I approach.

"It's doused in chemicals. My guess is chloroform. Someone took them."

I run a hand down my face, attempting to compartmentalize this goddamn situation. "That means they're not dead. Whoever did this wouldn't go to the effort of sedating them if they were going to kill them."

She cringes. "Maybe. But chloroform isn't a great sign either. It's highly toxic. Inhaling too much could easily kill a child."

The hits keep coming, one after another, the horror compiling.

Anyone accountable won't survive. They won't want to after I start reaping my revenge.

"What do you want me to do?" she asks. "I can go get Layla and Keira if you want. It's better to tell them face-to-face."

"No. I need you to organize a clean-up crew." I hand over my cell. "Don't tell anyone what's happened until I say. Okay?"

"Okay. What are you going to do?"

"I'm going to find those kids."

I stride across the living room and continue through the house to the front door, my ears flooded with the choking beat of rage and fucking fear.

I don't stop until I'm at the front gate, yelling at the guard to let me out.

As soon as I can slip through the opening metal, I stalk for the motherfucker who was meant to be in charge. I grasp his throat in seconds. Slam my fist into his face.

"Where are they?" I pummel him again. "What the fuck happened to them?"

He stumbles as I hold tight to his neck, blood seeping from a cut on his lip.

"What the hell are you talking about?" He claws at my wrist, shoves at my chest. "Get your fucking hands off me."

I cling tighter, his heartbeat frantic under my fingertips. "Someone has been in my house. The nanny is dead. The kids are missing."

He quits fighting. His face falls. "Nobody has come through these gates except you. I vow it on my life. I've been here the whole time."

"Then whoever is responsible didn't use the fucking gates." I release my hold, shoving him backward. "Call your team and have them properly check the perimeter. Until the culprit is found, this is on your shoulders."

I turn on my heels to run some more, this time to Mavis' house. I slam my fist against the front door. Again and again. Over and over. The outlet doesn't lessen the effects of overwhelming adrenaline.

I'm suffocating here. Drowning in my own mistakes.

"I'm coming," Hunt yells from inside. "Hold on."

I keep knocking until the door flings open.

"What the fuck?" Hunter's hard scowl stares back at me. "Are you trying to wake the whole goddamn neighborhood?"

"Have you seen the kids?" I shove past him, the acrid scent of bleach burning my nostrils.

"No. Why?"

I make for one of the curved staircases bordering both walls in the entry and jump the steps three at a time.

I switch on every light.

Open every door.

Search every fucking room.

When the entire floor turns up empty, I hustle back downstairs finding Hunter still waiting for me in the entry, eyeing me with trepidation.

"It's bad, isn't it?" he asks.

"Yeah." I stop before him, not wanting to break the news when I'm sure this has to be a fucking nightmare I'll soon wake from.

"Tell me and I'll sort it out."

This isn't something he can fix for me. Not this time. No matter how much I'd give to have this all be over.

"It's Stella and Tobias." I lower my voice, unsure of Benji's location. "They're gone. There's no sign of them."

He frowns. "Did the nanny take them somewhere?"

"She's stone-cold, wide-eyed on the bedroom floor, a needle still in her arm."

"Holy shit." He stands motionless. "What about Sarah? Where is she?"

"She's beat up and needs to see a doctor. But right now she's busy making arrangements to get rid of the body."

"Fucking hell." He rakes his hands through his hair. "Tell me what you need me to do. Where do we start? What did the guards say?"

"The guards don't know a damn thing. And neither do I. If Robert is dead, where does it leave the damn kids?"

"He had a man working with him. Young guy. California ID His dead ass is still upstairs. If we follow the trail, he might lead us to someone else."

Footsteps approach from along the hall, and I turn my gaze to find Benji walking toward us with a bloody rag in his hands.

"What's going on?" He glances between us. "Did something else happen?"

I don't have to tell him a damn thing. After his betrayal, I'm not obligated to breathe a fucking word. But this is his daughter. His little girl.

"It's okay." Hunt clears his throat. "Whatever happened, we'll ahh... we'll sort it out. We always do."

"Sort *what* out?" Benji asks. "What's the problem?"

I stare at him. The traitor. The snitch.

Earlier, I wanted him dead.

Now, I'm loath to inflict this punishment on him. The news of Stella's disappearance will be a far more painful torture than anything I could inflict.

"Benji—" I clench my fists, struggling to straddle the line between brother-in-law and betrayee.

"What?" He frowns. "What is it? What's wrong?"

"It's Stella." I shake my head, attempting to dislodge the overwhelming horror. The things that could be happening to her... the things that might happen in the future... "She's missing."

He jerks back. "What do you mean?"

"She's gone. She's not in the house. There was—"

He storms forward, walking around me, heading for the front door.

"Where are you going?" Hunter grabs his arm, pulling him to a stop.

"To Torian's house to show him Stella's fine." He yanks his arm free. "She'd be sleeping in a different room. She bed-hops all the time."

"She's not there." I remain in place as Hunt moves to the door, blocking the exit. "Sarah and I checked. The guards are searching the yard."

Benji's frown deepens. "She's there." He shakes his head, denying the dire possibilities. "Where would she go?"

I hold his stare, my jaw tight, my focus lethal. The beats of silence are painfully informative.

He shakes his head harder as Hunter's expression contorts in discomfort.

"No." Benji backtracks, moving closer to the door. "She'd be asleep somewhere. Hiding. It's probably a big joke to her."

"It's no joke. She was taken."

"No." The rampant back and forth of his head is aggressive. "*No.*" He turns, storming for the door.

Hunter blocks his escape. The two grapple.

"Benji, you're not leaving." I keep my voice level. "We don't have time to waste. Tobias is gone, too. The nanny is dead."

A sound escapes him. A guttural cry more animalistic than human.

He quits fighting and stumbles backward, his face draining of color. "No."

"I believe the kids are still alive. There's evidence they were sedated. But who knows how long that will last."

His chest rises and falls in rapid succession. "Why?" he pleads. "Why would anyone…"

"You tell me." I fight a glare as he hunches over, retching. *He* was the one speaking to a sex trafficker behind my back. *He* was the man who betrayed me to a man capable of something as vile as this. "You need to share every single thing you told Robert. And you need to do it now. Because if I don't find those kids, living with the loss of your daughter is going to be the least of your problems."

7

ANISSA

I remain at the scene, Cole's lingering fury and rejection making it near impossible to leave. If I go home, I'll only work myself into a mental frenzy, questioning my thoughts, my past, my future.

I'll eat my weight in feelings and this body has seen one too many tubs of ice cream lately to justify the additional calories.

So I stay, steering clear of the cops, taking discreet photos from behind their plastic tape barrier, speaking to witnesses who continue to hang around despite the early morning hour.

"Did you see what happened?" I smile at the young blonde cradling a cell in her hands. She looks on edge. Fidgety. Maybe agitated, as her suspicious eyes meet mine.

"It's okay. I'm FBI." I flash her my badge. "You can talk to me. Did you see what happened?"

"I saw the whole thing. And I tried explaining what happened to one of the officers, but he told me to stay here and wait. I even recorded the whole thing on my phone." She sighs, her shoulders slumping. "I'm just so tired. I've got three jobs and I need to be up in a few hours to start my next shift."

"I understand." I step closer. "Why don't you give me a look? I can take your statement."

"Thank you." She focuses on her cell, pressing buttons until a video starts to play. "This is what happened."

The recording is jolted, as if she were running along the sidewalk toward Luca's Suburban which has already been hit in the middle of the intersection. Horns blare. Onlookers speak in the distance. Then there's the unmistakable *pop, pop, pop* of gunfire.

People scream.

The vision lowers, the cracked cement footpath the only sight as a female swears.

"I was hiding," she explains. "Once I heard the gunshots, I dove behind a car parked on the side of the street. I didn't know what else to do."

I nod, my attention glued to the screen.

The camera is raised over the hood of a red truck. Luca's car comes back into focus. I hold my breath as Robert stalks into view, his stride long, his confidence remarkable. He shoots toward something off-screen, making onlookers scream.

"That's when he shot the man in the car behind the Suburban," the woman says. "Shot him dead. Just like that." She clicks her fingers. "I've never seen anything like it in my life."

"I'm sorry you had to witness this." I remain transfixed on the replay as Robert approaches the passenger side of Luca's car, gun raised. He yanks open the door, drags Penny out, and shoves her down the road.

An innocent bystander steps forward, calling for him to stop. But there's no stopping. Robert barely pauses as he raises his weapon and guns the man down.

"It was horrific," the woman whispers. "None of us knew what to do."

"Us?" I don't raise my gaze from her phone.

"There was a group. About five of us. We were all in hiding, not sure if we should risk our lives to help. I feel so guilty."

"There's nothing you could've done."

Robert drags Penny toward a silver sedan parked behind the Suburban and shoves her in the trunk. Then, as easily as if he's heading out for a leisurely Sunday drive, he climbs into the car and leaves the scene. No screech of tires. No frantic escape.

He abducted her effortlessly. Not one hint of doubt.

"As soon as he was gone, we all rushed to help those people. But the man from the sedan was already dead, and the other..." She drags in a ragged breath. "He was so scared."

"It's going to take you some time to come to terms with what you witnessed." I give her a sad smile and fight against the need to get more involved in Cole's drama.

He wouldn't want this recording shared.

And Penny doesn't deserve to be a news headline or a viral sensation.

"But this footage is great." I keep smiling, attempting to exude warmth. "Do you know if anyone else recorded what happened?"

"Not that I know of. I think once the gunshots started, most people were too busy hiding. After the police arrived, everyone crowded me to get a second look."

I nod and pull out my own device, deleting the notices of Easton's missed messages and calls. "I'm going to need you to Bluetooth it to me. Can you do that?"

"Yeah, sure."

I talk her through the transfer and wait patiently for the file to arrive, double-checking it as my stomach churns with foreboding.

I shouldn't be getting involved.

I *shouldn't*. But goddamn it, I can't help myself.

"I'm sorry. I don't think I got your name, ma'am." I inch closer.

"Izzy," she offers. "Isabel Masen."

"Thanks, Isabel." I lower my voice. "Before I let you go, I want to make sure you know the legal risks associated with holding onto recordings of a crime such as this." I'm bullshitting, talking completely out of my ass. All for what? Cole *fucking* Torian. "If someone else gets hold of this—if your phone is stolen or hacked—you could be in a lot of trouble."

"Are you for real?" Her lips part in shock. "I thought I was helping."

"You were. It's the aftermath that gets tricky. You don't want to be responsible for leaking information on an investigation as important as this."

Why am I helping Cole? *Why, Anissa? Why?*

"Can I delete the video?" she begs. "I don't want to be a part of this. I just want to go home."

"Of course you can. I have the footage now. If you delete your copy you won't have to worry about anyone else getting hold of it. And I have your name for future reference. But I'd like to take your cell number, too."

"Okay." She nods and recites the digits as she taps buttons on her screen. "It's gone. Deleted. Do I need to go to the police station to make a statement?"

My stomach dips, the hollow organ seeming to fall to my feet. "No, you're free to go home."

She releases a relieved breath. "Thank you so much."

Sickening guilt works its way through me in an increasing tide. I force myself to breathe normally. I'm going to get fired. Not only that, I could end up behind bars.

The woman pockets her cell, gives me a tired farewell smile, then leaves.

I'm so screwed.

Tampering with witnesses. Destroying evidence. Involving myself in a case that isn't even remotely in my jurisdiction while I'm on leave.

I'm in over my head, trying to convince myself I can't walk away because of my fear for Penny's safety when my reasons for being here are far deeper than that.

I'm protecting Cole. Again.

Risking my career for a criminal.

I stare at my phone, the morning hours growing colder, my breath fogging in the frigid air. I should call Easton. After listening to him spit a quick verbal barrage about Cole's reputation, I could be back on the straight and narrow... but I don't call.

I send him a quick message instead—*I'm climbing into bed. Sorry I didn't text sooner. Night.* Then I get in my car.

I should go home. For the sake of my job and my mental health, I should head directly for my apartment building. But I don't do that either.

I drive to Cole's restaurant. Bright lights continue to illuminate the room as I slowly inch my vehicle forward, yet all the guests are gone. There's only a cluster of waitresses rearranging tables and a lone man with a mop pushing through the kitchen doors.

I park at the curb, the engine still running as self-hatred eats me from the inside out. I need to know if Penny has been found. If she's okay. If she's even still alive. I wonder about Sarah, too. Did she see a doctor? Is she recovering?

And Robert. What about him?

The reasons to call Cole mount on my shoulders.

No, they're excuses. Placations.

Sarah isn't my friend.

Penny is just another victim.

Robert is one of many threats I've earned in my career.

I just want to talk to Cole. For no other reason than to hear his voice.

I cringe through self-loathing as I pull out my cell. I sigh as I dial his number. Then I hold my breath and listen to the phone ring.

He doesn't answer.

After two quick trills his voicemail cuts in, announcing loud and clear he rejected my call.

He's rejecting *me* when only weeks ago he was in front of my building with flowers, demanding my attention.

I throw the phone to the passenger seat and grip the steering wheel.

"This isn't healthy." I exhale long and loud. "It's not normal." I suck a deep breath in. "Go home, Nissa."

I don't know what's worse—talking to myself or using the nickname Cole gave me. But this time, I listen.

I pull into the empty street, cranking the music loud to drown my thoughts, and find my way home on autopilot. I don't pause a second in contemplation once I set foot inside my apartment. I head straight for my medicine cabinet to snatch at the sleeping pills, downing two with a vodka chaser.

The liquid burns. Just like my shame.

I don't trust myself to fall asleep unaided. If left to my own devices, I'll toss and turn, my subconscious feeding me unwanted thoughts of dark eyes and a darker soul.

I don't change. Or shower. I fall face-first into bed and stay there, unmoving, until darkness takes me away.

When I wake, the sun is already creeping through my curtains. It's still early, and the heady lethargy from the pills makes it difficult to get my ass vertical.

I shower. Eat. Tug on my light grey pantsuit and then stare at my phone, willing it to ring. I flick from news station to news station, listening to vague information about the alleged gang-related violence from last night. The footage shown includes a snapshot of Robert and Penny, but neither of their faces are visible.

If authorities had detailed descriptions they would've been shared.

The witness I spoke to might be right. I could have the only video of the crime.

I dial Cole's number, pretending I have an obligation to let him know, when the necessity for contact is far more complicated than that. But the call rings out.

He's cut me off. After claiming he wanted me. When I was meant to be *everything* to him. He severed ties without a backward glance.

I've tried everything apart from exorcism to rid myself of feelings for him, and he flicks off the hinderance like a damn light switch.

Asshole.

Well, good for him. But it's not going to stop me from getting answers on Penny.

I snatch my purse, keys and cell from the counter, ignoring the unanswered messages from Easton, and down my half-filled mug of coffee in one chug before leaving the apartment.

Within a short drive I'm at his front gates with a guard approaching my window.

"Who are you?" He glowers at me with unabashed superiority as I lower the glass.

"A friend of Cole's. I need to speak to him."

He sidles up beside my door and rests a forearm against the roof of my car, making his jacket gape to expose the holstered gun beneath. It's deliberate intimidation. I wouldn't expect anything less from one of Cole's men. "No visitors today. You'll have to come back some other time."

I smile, sweet and pure. "I don't need to see him. I just need to speak to him. Tell him Anissa is here and that I'm not going anywhere until we talk."

"He's not going to give a shit who you are, sweetheart. He's given strict orders not to be disturbed."

My lips tighten, venom entering the upswept curve. "Call him." I pull out my badge, enjoying the tiny flare of surprise in his eyes. "You don't want to be responsible for me returning with a warrant and a full team of agents when all I want to do is chat."

It's a bluff, but given Cole's reputation, even the slightest hint of a warrant should put this guy on edge.

He glares, stepping back to right his jacket with a hard yank of the lapels. "Fine. I'll call him. But it won't mean shit. He'll still say no. They're dealing with a family emergency and want privacy."

"I know all about the emergency. Just make the damn call."

He retreats, unclasping a cell hooked to his belt. He turns away, murmuring words I can't decipher in front of a house that looms tall and menacing in the distance.

I've never been inside the perimeter. Not even a foot. But I've heard stories. I've been told about the wealth on display. The secrets hidden.

There's a whir of metallic sound, then the gates open to expose the path to damnation.

My pulse kicks like an unruly mule.

The guard returns. "Park at the front of the house and ring the bell. Someone will meet you."

Wait. What?

I'm not going in there.

That's not what I want.

"I only need to speak to him." I meet the guy's eyes. "Not enter the property."

"I called," he growls. "I got you an audience. Now hurry up and drive inside, or get the hell out of here."

No. I shake my head. I can already hear the snarled anger from my boss, Taggert, as he lambastes me on why I would even approach the property, let alone slip through the gates.

I've crossed so many lines. All of them dark and dangerous, the distinction between right and wrong clearly defined.

"I swear to God," the guard mutters, "once I close those gates I won't be opening them again. Either get in, or leave."

It's not that easy.

I have legitimate reasons for being here. Penny was abducted. Robert was responsible. Men died. Yet again, there's violence on Portland streets.

I need to be updated on what's happening.

But none of those things will appease my boss when I'm meant to be keeping my distance from Cole.

"*Now,*" the guard snarls.

Goddamnit.

I press my foot on the accelerator, entering uncharted territory.

The landscape before me is pristine. The grass, lush and green. The hedges, trimmed.

The whir of the closing gates brings an icy chill to my arms. The quiet calm of early morning that follows puts me on edge. Every sound is amplified. The crunch of gravel beneath the tires. The sweep of breeze through the trees.

I approach the towering two-story mansion with its perfect white curtains in every window, not a cobweb or tarnish in sight across the entire veneer. I park in front, my discomfort multiplying, the tension inside me wringing tight.

But I need answers.

About Penny. About Robert.

And most of all, about Cole.

I don't let doubt take a stronghold. I turn off the car, get out and stride for the front door, ringing the bell twice in quick succession.

For a while, I don't think he'll answer. I wouldn't be surprised if he let me through the gates just to lock me in his yard until I had to climb my way free.

I press the bell again, this time holding my finger in place.

Trudging footsteps approach from inside, the thuds ricocheting through my chest. I hold my breath as the door is yanked open. But the man who stands before me with a monstrous scowl isn't Cole.

"How the fuck did you get in here?" Hunter barks.

"Cole is expecting me."

He stiffens. Straightens. "Since when?"

"Since now. Are you going to let me in?"

His eyes narrow to lethal slits. "Do you have a warrant?"

I sigh, losing all strength in my posture.

I'm tired. Of the fighting. Of the battle. I haven't felt alive in weeks. There's only the memories of the vicious verbal conflicts with Cole to invigorate me. "I just want to speak to him. I'm not here for drama."

"Let her in." Cole's far-off voice comes from inside the house, his authority brushing over me like a favored blanket. His adamance squeezes my belly.

Hunter doesn't budge. He remains imperial in his defiance.

"You heard him." I step forward, testing the boundaries, strengthening my resolve. "Move out of my way."

He snarls, the dog-like threat entirely fitting for such a pit bull as I squeeze past him, my nose immediately assaulted with the scent of bleach.

The chemical hangs heavily in the air, smothering each breath I take.

"What happened here?" The possibilities fill me with dread. Yet there's a curious niggle of hope, too. A sickening sense of pride at the possibility of Cole having killed Robert.

"Hunter?" I swing back to face him. "What happened?"

"Keep pushing me and you'll experience a reenactment." His poisonous smile is slow to form. The bags under his eyes negate the taunt. He's just as exhausted as I am. "He's in his room." The words grate over thinly veiled hostility. "I suggest you watch your snappy mouth. I don't have the energy to dispose of another body."

Another?

"Robert's dead?" I ask.

He ignores me, marching ahead, passing a staircase that he hikes a thumb toward. "Torian is up there."

The thud of his footsteps continues down the hall, the silence closing in once he turns out of view.

The house becomes eerily quiet. Empty.

I glance around my surroundings—the high ceiling, the artistic photography lining the walls, the light, clean crispness of it all. It's spectacular. I wouldn't expect anything less from Cole.

But it's cold. And not only due to the breeze sweeping my skin from another part of the house.

This place is hollow. Without heart.

I walk to the stairs, the light murmurings of haunted conversation brushing my ears as I climb the first step. The whispers of secrets and scandals are hidden in the unheard words. I grab the banister for grounding. For courage.

I can already sense him. Can instinctively feel Cole's presence wrapping around me. Coiling tight.

My pulse increases as I reach the landing and turn the corner, finding more steps leading to a captivating portrait of a middle-aged woman.

His mother?

Their compelling eyes are the same. The warm skin. The dark hair.

"Cole?" I call his name at the top step, feeling like an interloper.

A shuffle emanates down the short hall to my right. No verbal response. No civil welcome. Just the intimidation of his existence.

I approach the sound, my steps leading me toward the daylight sweeping in through an open doorway. I keep my head high, my shoulders straight, my breathing level, even though all three fight against me.

"Cole?"

Again, no response.

I reach the threshold and pause, my attention skimming over the intimidating king-size bed with its shiny black covers and shifting to the man standing at the open window, his back to me, his attention focused outside.

Air congeals in my lungs, the splinters of unwanted yearning punishing me from the inside out.

He's still in the same suit as last night, the material remaining pristine, his posture oozing power.

"Good morning." I attempt to add authority to my tone. Fortitude. My ears hear it for the weak greeting it is.

He remains immobile. Statuesque.

"Cole?"

He shudders out a breath, the sound foreign for a man with such tenacity. He turns to me, slow, controlled, those dark eyes meeting mine, the indecipherable emotion in them twisting my stomach.

He's almost unrecognizable with the defeat in his features.

A Jekyll to his usual Hyde.

"What happened?" I force myself to remain in place. "Is Robert dead? Have you found Penny?"

He scoffs, his frame jerking slightly before the silence returns. There's nothing but a slight whistle from the breeze.

My unease grows. Bubbling. Spitting. "Answer me. I deserve to know."

The demand is the only leverage I have. I can't throw my badge at him—not when he has enough dirt on me to send me to prison.

"You deserve it?" His voice is a low growl of barely contained anger. "You don't deserve *shit* from me."

The spike of aggression squeezes my ribs.

He's been hostile toward me before. Too many times to count. There's been intimidation and unrest. But this is different. There's no energetic anger in his eyes. No mindless rage.

This is clinical hatred.

I open my mouth to say something... anything... Problem is, I'm isolated from reason. I can't think when he looks at me like that. When *he* looks like that.

His hair is tousled, as if he's raked his hands through it a million times. The bags under his eyes are heavy with fatigue. And those lips, the ones that previously brought me pleasure, are one straight line of disdain.

"Two days ago you knock at my door, demanding to facilitate my safety. Now, I'm what? Your enemy?" I move forward, slow and cautious. "I haven't done anything wrong. I came here because I want information on a man who attacked me. A man who has become a nightmare in my life because of you."

His nostrils flare. His jaw clenches.

The energy of passionate anger builds between us. I'm a slave to the flames. It's always been this way. We burn from the heat of animosity. It fuels us.

"We're not enemies." It's imperative I remind him. If he turns on me, my life is as good as over. But that's not what pains me. It's not what scares me the most.

The reality of how close we are to severing ties, after I've fought so long to do exactly that, is confounding. Soul shaking. I don't want this.

"I think our past proves I'm worthy of inside information." I clear my throat. "I tried—"

"Is that what you really think?" He scoffs. "That you deserve anything from me after you fucked another man?"

I jerk back in shock. In gratification.

This hostility can't all be driven by jealousy. Surely not.

But the thrill of this poisoned treat is something I wish I could sink my teeth into. To taste every morsel of his envy. To gorge on the way he covets me.

"Easton is none of your—"

"He's dead," Cole snaps.

For a moment, I'm not sure who he's talking about—Robert or Anthony. Both possibilities leave me shocked.

"There's no longer a threat toward you." His face turns into an expressionless mask. "And now that you've got the information you came for, leave."

I blink through the mass of unfurling questions. I should do exactly as he's asked. Leave. Never look back. But I can't move. There's no will to walk away—only the determination to stay.

"If he's dead, then what's wrong?" I take another step and another, the exotic scent of his lingering aftershave invading the acrid bleach. "What else happened?"

His face hardens. His upper lip curls. "Get the fuck out." He turns his back to me, returning his attention out the window.

Rejection slaps me cold. I've kissed this man with all the passion I contain. I've taken him inside my body and exhilarated in the resulting pleasure. I've craved him.

Hungered for him.

Pined.

I was stupid to think I could turn those memories to ash. I was even more ignorant to assume I could simply switch off what I once felt. There's no easy withdrawal from this.

He's an addiction like no other, requiring more than a twelve-step program and a lifetime of rehab.

"Please talk to me," I whisper. "What else happened?"

He launches a fist at the wall. The crack of impact startles me. He swings around to storm my way.

There's no time to think. To retreat. He gets in my face, attempting to intimidate, but all I feel is passion. Fire. Flames.

"We're not doing this again." He leans close, eye to eye. Feral. "That was your choice."

His breath brushes my lips, the exquisite tease a shot of ecstasy to my throbbing veins.

"Leave." He holds his voice in check, his gaze steady. Unshakable.

The demand skitters over my flesh. Into my bones.

I breathe deeper. Heavier.

I should do as he says. Common sense squeaks in the back of my mind telling me to listen.

But I don't. I steady my shoulders. Hitch my chin.

His lips curl in a snarl, part rage, part hunger. I can feel him. The vibration. The power.

My palms sweat with the need to reach out. To touch.

He doesn't scare me. Never has. What I fear is this ending. What frightens me the most is being forced to walk away from here and never feel alive again.

I've not been adored like I have been with this man. Even through the lies and deception, my recollections of him always come back to the emotions he inspires. The unwitting sense of belonging. The strange click of a puzzle piece finally fitting in place.

He inches closer, so close I can feel the warmth of his lips, the heat in his eyes.

I could kiss him. I'd barely need to move. All it would take is a slight lean. A mere hitch of my chin. And I want to. *God*, how I want to feel his scorching mouth unravelling me one thread at a time. To taste his aggression. To drown in his possession.

I turn my head instead, denying us both.

His chuckle is a whisper over my cheek. A subtle dose of spite.

I stand rigid, close to breaking point, my insides screaming at me to take, take, take.

He gets closer, his nose nudging my jaw, awakening a flood of tingling goose bumps. The slight connection holds the force of an explosion. It's blinding. Shattering.

Air thickens in my lungs as he nuzzles higher, his mouth moving to my ear.

I stop breathing, waiting for erotic words to soothe my yearning. Waiting for him to say something that will signal my surrender. And it's right there. My submission is his for the taking.

"My little fox," he murmurs, deep and low.

I whimper.

"After everything we've been through, there's only one thing I want to say to you." His admission trickles down my neck, awakening every nerve ending. "Get the fuck out of my house," he growls, "And never come back."

I pull away, embarrassment rendering me speechless.

He truly wants me to leave.

Right... Okay... Fine...

I step back, raising my hands in surrender. "I'm leaving."

"*Now*," he sneers.

"Jesus Christ." I'm already retreating, goddamnit. I'm just too gobsmacked at how the tables have turned to move faster than a snail's pace.

I used to be in his shoes. *I* was the one who despised *him*. At least, that was the role I played.

I backtrack farther, slowly, prepared to pause as soon as he asks me to stop.

But he doesn't.

I reach the threshold without a word. Then I turn and trek to the staircase, then to the lower level.

The silence thickens.

There's so much dense, suffocating silence beneath the pummeling drum of my heart as I drag hospital-grade bleach into my lungs.

Where did Cole kill Robert?

In the kitchen? The hall?

Curiosity takes over my self-pity, and instead of slinking my ass to the front of the house, I stride in the opposite direction, along a vacant hall until I enter an open living area.

Glass doors run along one side of the room, giving sight to the manicured yard and Hunter who stands on the grass, his back to me as he talks on his cell.

"Hello?" a grated female voice asks from somewhere unknown. There's a groan, a shift of movement, then Sarah pokes her head up from a sofa, her frown instantaneously spreading across her bruised face. Her features are more swollen than they were last night, her fierce beauty almost unrecognizable.

"Are you meant to be in here?" She holds my gaze, the questioning expression slowly transforming into a wince before she slumps back out of view. "Don't answer that. I don't give a shit."

"I'm glad you're here." I shoot a cursory glance at Hunter, making sure he hasn't caught sight of me, then continue into the room. "I've been worried about you."

"Sure you have."

I pass a recliner and an elegant glass coffee table to sit on the far armrest of the sofa opposite hers.

It's hard not to stare when her blue eyes are startlingly bright against the backdrop of skin mottled in purples and browns.

"I was concerned." I hold her gaze as she repositions her hands under her head. "Did you see a doctor?"

"I didn't need to. I only had a minor fight with an airbag."

That crash packed far more than an airbag's punch. So much more that I feel sorry for her inability to face it. Nobody should ever have to act this tough after what she endured.

"I don't need your pity," she mutters. "You don't know me."

"You're right. I don't." I break our gaze to search the room, looking for clues to explain the necessity for an oil spill of bleach. But even in here, where the smell is far more potent, I don't see any hint of murder or bloodshed. There's only an abundance of gleaming stainless steel in the kitchen, and immaculate white tiles on the floor. "Can I ask about Penny? Have you found her? Is she okay?"

"She's free from Robert, if that's what you want to know."

Relief eases through my tired muscles. "Unharmed?"

She shrugs. "Not so much. But nothing major either."

I nod, genuinely thankful and also hopeful at the prospect of milking this conversation for all it's worth. "And what about Robert? What happened to him?"

Her lips stretch into a wide grin. "Do you really think I'm going to answer that? Come on, Special Agent. Surely you don't think that low of me."

"I don't think low of you at all. I know you're a strong woman. A smart one, too. I would've thought—"

The slide of a glass door cuts off my words. The accompanying slam makes me flinch.

"What the fuck are you doing in here?" Hunter approaches like a wall of muscle and testosterone that clearly needs to be put on a leash. "Does Cole know where you are?"

I slowly rise from the armrest. "Does it matter? You've got nothing to hide, right?"

He clenches his fists, his teeth gnashing. "Get the fuck out."

"Calm down." Sarah pushes to a seated position. "We were only chatting."

"Like hell. This bitch likes to play the field. First, she's the enemy, then she's an ally. And now what? You're trying to straddle both?" He quirks a condemning brow. "Fuck that. You can move your smug ass out of here or I'll do it for you."

"I'm smug?" I slap a hand to my chest. "Let's get one thing clear: I never willingly crossed sides. That option was forced on me when I was fucking drugged and flown out of the country. I didn't ask to be a part of this."

"Like hell you didn't. You turned Decker into a snitch—"

"Decker was always a snitch," I correct. "I just gave him a megaphone to spill the secrets he'd discovered. That's why you hate me, right? Because I easily turned someone you thought you could trust? Because I outplayed you?"

His eyes flare. His fingers flex then clench tighter. "Keep talking, pig. Keep pushing. See where it gets you."

"Don't threaten me. You might hide behind a macho name and a despicable reputation, but I can pull a trigger just as easily as you can. The only difference is that I rid the earth of people like you, not inspire more."

"Stop it." Sarah raises her voice. "Both of you. You're as bad as each other."

"I'm nothing like him." I hold Hunter's glare, not intimidated by his animosity. Yes, he's a murderer, but he's not indiscriminate. He doesn't kill for fun. He won't touch me.

"Maybe I've been looking at this the wrong way," he drawls. "I think I'm finally coming to understand your obsession with this family, and it has nothing to do with justice."

I cross my arms over my chest. "Please enlighten me."

"You want to be one of us." He grins, his deceivingly handsome face turning sick and twisted. "But you're too much of a chicken shit to take the leap."

"Enough," Cole demands.

My focus snaps across the room as he stalks toward us, his suit jacket discarded, his hair even more disheveled.

"Sarah, are you capable of leaving the room?" His attention doesn't stray from mine, the potency sending a shiver through me. "Apparently, Ms. Fox and I need to have another discussion on why our time together is over."

8

ANISSA

Sarah rises from the sofa, the hint of a grimace squinting her eyes as she finds her feet and heads toward Hunter. "Come on." She grabs the crook of his arm, tugging him into submission.

I watch them leave, my gaze remaining on the hall once Cole and I are alone.

"Why are you still here?" he asks without animosity.

I deny the real reasons. Even to myself. I can't face the shallow truth when everything else should be far more important than my cravings. "I was checking on Sarah."

"You were snooping. You couldn't help yourself. You're back to scavenging for dirt on me."

I snap my gaze to his. "I don't have to scavenge. You sprinkle evidence of your crimes everywhere you go."

He huffs out a half-hearted laugh, but humor evades his features. "Why are you still here, Anissa?"

Because I can't stay away.

Because I need to understand you. And I need you to understand me.

I cross my arms over my chest. "I want to know what's going on. What happened to Robert? What's the story with the bleach? Why are you so…" I look him up and down, cringing at the potent failure ebbing from him. "…different?"

"Gaining any sort of leverage against me won't help take me down. Not unless you're willing to go to hell right along with me. I was smart enough to keep receipts of your crimes in Greece."

Rage chokes me. Shoves the air from my lungs. "You bastard." I glower, hating even more how the smallest spark of appreciation flickers in his tired eyes.

"I'm not attempting to take you anywhere. I just want answers. I want to know if I'm safe. I want specifics on Robert."

"You're safe. I've always made sure of that."

His conviction deflates me. Slightly.

"What?" He quirks a brow. "Did you expect me to forget what happened between us? Did you think I'd feed you to the wolves after I vowed to give you everything?"

I don't respond. The reminder of his softly spoken promises in heated moments renders me speechless.

"I can give you all the answers you want, Nis. Every single one. But the information will drag you back into my world. You won't be strong enough to resist."

"I can resist you just fine." *Liar.*

"I'm not talking about resisting *me.*" He clenches his jaw, as if hating the strength of my rejection. "You'll want to get involved because you're always inclined to help. Even at your own detriment."

I scrutinize him, sensing another trap. "You're baiting me."

"You're the one who wants answers." His lips curve in subdued satisfaction. "If that's changed, you know where the door is."

Self-preservation is a niggling presence on my shoulder, whispering for me to take the opportunity to run. Flee. Never look back.

"Go." He jerks his head toward the front of the house. "Get out of here."

I should.

God, how I know I should. Yet my feet won't move. My legs won't function.

"Tell me," I demand. "I won't get dragged in."

"Have it your way." He steps forward, bridging necessary distance between us.

I tense, my shoulders straight, limbs taut.

He continues into my personal space, predatory in his approach. I hum, my body vibrating like a tuning fork.

"What are you doing?" I raise a hand in warning.

"You expect me to divulge incriminating information without determining if you're wearing a wire?"

Shit.

I should've guessed.

We're back to playing games. The power struggle has returned. The tit for tat.

I clench my teeth, biting back a snappy retort, and force myself to focus. To *win.* He's disheveled for a reason, and I'm not leaving here until I find out why.

"You're not going to argue?" he taunts, the words not packing quite as much punch when his expression remains defeated. "I thought you'd voice a loud protest at the prospect of my hands all over you."

"I know how paranoid you are. You want me to prove I'm not here officially? Then fine." I yank off my jacket, throw it to the recliner, then raise my arms at my sides. "Have at it."

Victory dances in those dark blue eyes. Subtle but strong. "You surprise me, little fox."

"I doubt that's true."

He steps closer, one leg between mine, our thighs grazing, his feet brushing my shoes. "I'm going to touch you now."

I roll my eyes, determined to ignore the rampant beat of my pulse as I focus on keeping my breathing steady.

His palms slide over my hips, making me flinch at the strength in his possession. I'm thrust into the past. Back to a time when I willingly surrendered. When I took him into my body and prayed the bliss would never end.

He ascends, feeling my waist, the outside curve of my throbbing breasts, my arms.

I tingle. Inside and out. Nerves and skin and bone.

With a touch, he undoes me. Enslaves me. The look of ownership he gives only increases my struggle.

"Are you done?" I clear my throat. "I'm not wearing a wire."

He leans in, his mouth to my ear. "Not even close." He sweeps his hands back along the path he's laid, then lower, over my ass, along my thighs.

I hold my breath as he kneels before me, the sight of submission clenching my stomach.

It's just another game. Another tactic to place me in a false sense of security, made even worse when he glances up at me with hunger.

I look away. "How long is this going to take?"

His palms slide down the outside of my leg, around my ankles, to my inner calves. I close my eyes. Swallow. Breathe. I hate that my body wants him. That *I* want him.

He creeps higher, over my knee, along the inside of my thigh.

Each inch of skin blazes. Yearns.

He approaches my crotch and I have to hold my breath to suppress a moan. But he stops an inch from my pussy, his palms splayed on my upper thighs, his thumbs close to my heat.

He doesn't speak. Doesn't move.

For long moments, there's nothing but silence until I'm forced to open my eyes and look down at him. My regret is immediate. Overwhelming. The subdued lust staring back at me makes me want to beg for him to continue.

"After what I've previously done to your body, I never would've imagined you'd hate my touch." His hands fall away. "What changed in our weeks apart?"

I lick the dryness from my lips. "You know what changed."

"I explained myself."

I step back. "You made excuses."

"Bullshit." He lashes out, grasping the back of my legs to keep me in place. "I told you why my father's death had to happen the way it did."

"After promising me there would be no more games. But that's all there is with you. You're still playing me."

His lip curls, his eyes hardening. The punishing grip on my legs vanishes and he pushes to his feet to tower before me. "Give me your cell, then take a seat at the dinner table."

What?

He's not going to deny it?

"Don't make me wait, Anissa." He holds out a hand.

There he goes again with my name. No sentiment. No tease. I've hit a nerve.

"I guess I was right." I pull out my cell and slap it into his hand.

He stalks away, taking my device to the kitchen counter, the power down sound trilling through the room as he yanks open a drawer and pulls out a tiny metal object.

"What are you doing?" I follow after him.

"Taking out the chip." He places the tiny point of metal into the top of my phone, slides out the chip holder and taps it onto the counter. "There. Now I'm satisfied."

At least that makes one of us.

"Take a seat." He indicates the table to his left with an arrogant wave of his arm. "Let's get this over and done with."

"Yes, let's." I lead the way, taking the middle seat while he takes the head. "I'm waiting with bated breath to find out what shit storm you've gotten yourself into this time. Don't keep me in suspense."

He smirks, settling into the old Cole, the one with oozing superiority. "After that pat-down I would've described it as panted breath, but it's your story to tell."

I don't bite. Nope. Not this time.

I'm above this. I have to be.

He sighs into the growing silence. "Fine, Anissa. Let's talk." He leans back in the wooden chair, crossing his arms over his chest. "Robert is dead."

"Please tell me I didn't endure being frisked for a crumb of information you've already given me."

"What I didn't tell you," he grates, "is that before he was taken care of, he'd made plans to have Stella and Tobias abducted."

My world shifts.

It's an unfathomable flip from uncontrolled emotion and anticipation to pure dread. "He planned?"

Now Cole's appearance makes sense. His deathly complexion. The hair-trigger anger.

I sit forward, resting my elbows on the table. "Am I correct in assuming he made an attempt last night?"

His brow furrows, the expression a mix of cringe and devastation.

"Cole?" My heart thunders.

"He didn't merely attempt. He succeeded."

I'm lost for words, caught in a waking nightmare.

"They're gone." He holds my gaze, his brittle voice betraying his pain.

"Where? Has there been a ransom demand?"

"I haven't heard a word. I don't know where they are. Decker is currently attempting to hack one of my neighbor's security tapes for clues, but…" He shrugs. "He's been at it for hours."

"Where were they? Where did this happen?" I fire the questions at him. "What are the authorities doing?"

"It happened here." He glances over his shoulder toward the far hall. "They were abducted from under my roof."

"Please tell me that bleach didn't dispose of critical evidence." I push to my feet. "And where are the cops? They should still be here. They should be setting up phone tracking and scouring the property. They can't—"

"The police won't be involved."

My stomach free falls. My heart follows.

I shake my head, not believing what I'm hearing. "Cole, you need to call the police. You can't seriously think—"

"Don't start," he warns. "The authorities don't mean shit in my world. You already know that."

"But—"

"*Don't.*" He shoves from his chair, the wood clattering on the tile behind him as he jams his hands into his hair. "Even if I wanted to, I fucking couldn't. Robert was killed next door, along with an accomplice Penny slaughtered. And the kids' goddamn nanny was murdered in my own damn house."

I ache for him. For all of them.

He seethes out a long breath, his hand lowering to his side, his stature strengthening before my eyes. "The nanny had a used needle in her arm. The last thing I can handle right now is a drug investigation that will distract my attention from where it needs to be."

I keep shaking my head, struggling to understand how he's coping. How his *sister* must be handling this. "Tell me what else you're doing to get them back. What plans do you have in place? What resources?"

He gives me nothing aside from that fixed stare.

"Cole?" I grab the back of my chair and shove it under the table. "Answer me."

"I thought you could resist." His tone is thick with derision. "Isn't that what you said?"

"Do you want me to admit you were right? Is that what you're waiting for?" I clench my fingers around the top of the chair. "Okay. You were right. I can't walk away. Not from this. Not when those kids are gone and you're refusing help from the authorities."

"Not refusing." He bends over, splaying his hands on the table, attempting to stare me down. "It's not an option."

"Either way, you've limited your resources. So tell me how I can help."

He keeps glaring, his jaw ticking, his knuckles white against the wood. I can't tell if he wants me involved or not. My read on him is hindered by his exhaustion.

"I don't know." He straightens. "I've got no fucking idea."

He turns away and paces to the far end of the table. "We spent the early hours going door to door, waking every neighbor to obtain any security footage they had. Every car that passed along this street was identified and their details forwarded to a contact for investigation."

"A contact?"

"Yes, a fucking contact." He pauses. "It may not be legal, but it ensures I get the information instead of the cops withholding it from me."

"What else?" I start toward him. "What's in motion right now?"

"Apart from me wasting time explaining myself to you, nothing. I have no leads. The man responsible is dead. And there's been no ransom call. I've contacted every one of my father's associates. Hunt's been to all the usual haunts, throwing his weight around, but nobody has heard a damn thing about those kids. There's not one fucking trace."

"And the others? What are they doing?" He has an entire team of people working for him—not just Hunter and Decker.

"The *others* are slightly unreliable at the moment." He grits the admission through a tensed jaw. "I can only count on myself."

"Why?"

"Sarah and Luca are injured. Decker was shot in the leg, but he's doing his best. And Benji is…" He huffs an unforgiving snicker. "He's—"

"I get it. You don't have to explain. He must be beside himself."

"Yeah. Something like that."

I swallow over the dryness in my throat. "Your sister—"

"I don't want to speak about my sister right now. I have to stay focused."

I get that, too. An abduction has to be one of the most traumatic circumstances a parent could endure, let alone knowing the perpetrator was a sex trafficker. "Let me help." I eat up the remaining space between us, stopping in front of him, my fingers itching to soothe the furrow of his brow.

"How?"

The word washes over me.

How.

Yes, exactly how can I help him without committing a crime? How can the benefits of my badge work toward securing those children without making this an official case?

"See?" He raises demeaning brows. "You should've walked away when I told you to."

"No. I can help. I could use the Bureau's resources… I could—"

Fuck.

The burden of loyalty drowns me. The loyalty toward Cole, *not* the FBI.

He scrutinizes me. "Last I heard you weren't back at work."

"I'm not, but…" I pause, attempting to figure out a plan. I could ask Easton. He'd obtain information for me. I'm just not sure if he'd do it without the full story.

"But you'd rely on your boyfriend to get whatever you need. Is that it?" He reads me, plucking my thoughts like painful feathers.

"He's not my boyfriend. But yes, Easton is reliable."

Cole creeps closer, his upper lip twitching as he invades my personal space. "I'll pass."

"You'll pass?" Is he serious? "Two children have been abducted after their nanny was murdered, but you'll pass?"

"I'll pass," he repeats in a sneer, then walks by me, heading toward the kitchen.

"Hold up a minute." I grab his sleeve. "Are you joking?"

He stops. "Do I look like I'm bursting with humor right now?"

No, he looks like a man filled with uncontrollable fear, rage, and jealousy, all of them clouding his judgment.

"I know you can be heartless, Cole. But I assumed that was toward other criminals. Not innocent children."

He yanks his arm away. "I guess you don't know me as well as you thought."

It's true. If he can turn down my offer without a second thought, then yes.

"You're right," I admit. "You've just established I don't know the first damn thing about you."

"You've also earned yourself a one-way ticket out of here." He yanks open the fridge. "Don't let the front door hit you when you leave."

"You're kicking me out?"

"You bet I am. I don't need your narrow-minded ignorance. I've got enough shit to deal with."

9

COLE

SHE WAITS A SECOND, MY MISPLACED ANGER SEEMING TO RENDER HER SPEECHLESS.

This isn't her fault.

None of this has anything to do with her. It's all me. All my failure.

"*Fine.*" She stalks to the counter, snatches up her cell and the discarded SIM, then walks out.

I don't move. Apart from the grinding ache of my tensed jaw, I don't fucking budge until she slams the front door in farewell.

"*Fuck.*"

That woman destroys me. Slays me. Without pause.

And now she's gone.

"It doesn't sound like things ended well." Sarah walks in from the far hall, Hunt following her.

I close my eyes, my hands finding their way back to my hair, my fingers ripping at the strands.

"It's good she's gone," he grunts out. "The stupid bitch shouldn't have come here in the first place."

"Don't start," Sarah warns. "The last thing we need is you running your mouth."

No, the last thing I needed was to push Anissa away. Why couldn't I stop myself?

"What do we do now?" Hunt asks. "I've called everyone I know."

I don't have to look at him to understand what he isn't saying. He made those calls and came up empty-handed. Every stone has been turned.

"Someone is lying." I drop my hands to the kitchen counter. "It's not possible that a plan this big has gone unnoticed."

"I'll pay everyone a personal visit." Hunt pulls his car keys from his pocket. "I'll throw my weight around and see what I can uncover."

"No." Sarah shakes her head. "All you're doing is wasting time. We need Anissa's help."

"Like hell we do." Hunter starts for the front of the house. "She's a fucking viper."

"You're wrong about her." Sarah focuses on me, the bruising under her eyes almost black. "Your sisters continue to blow up my cell, asking for updates. They're petrified, and we're stuck here doing nothing. And things will only get worse once Penny finds out, which you're going to have to deal with any minute now."

"I told Decker to leave her in the dark." I push from the counter. "We've got time."

"Wrong again." She flashes her phone screen at me, showing a string of text messages I can't read from this distance. "Luca has walked out of the hospital. They're all on their way here. And as soon as Penny takes one look at us she's going to know something has happened. If our expressions don't trigger her suspicion, the smell of bleach will."

Fuck.

Fuck.

"We need Anissa," she repeats. "And believe me, I don't like admitting it either, but what other option do we have apart from sitting on our asses waiting for a ransom call? Or worse."

"Don't go there," I warn.

Nobody can fucking go there.

It's bad enough that I lose focus on finding those kids every few minutes and fall into a sinkhole of possible scenarios where their battered bodies turn up in a ditch.

"Cole, we've spoken to everyone we know." Her eyes plead with me. "Benji has been to every transport hub. And your contacts haven't come back to us with even the slightest update."

"They will. We just need to wait."

And wait and fucking wait.

God, I hate this.

I've never hated anything more.

I wish I could throw money at the problem. I'd bleed through my finances to get Tobias and Stella back. If only there was a fucking ransom.

"Anissa has to be able to help." Sarah sighs. "She'd have to have experience in this type of thing. And you've worked with her before, right? She plays both sides."

"Nobody plays both sides." Hunter stalks for the sofa and flops into the far seat. "She's either a turncoat or waiting for an opportunity to take us down."

"She's no threat." I'm not defending her. It's merely the truth.

If Anissa wanted to put me behind bars, she would've attempted it by now. The only risk with her is if she opens her mouth to her piece-of-shit boyfriend.

"Then you have to go after her," Sarah begs. "Think of your niece."

"I can't *stop* thinking of my goddamn niece," I snap.

"Babe, you don't understand how this works." Hunter pats the sofa cushion beside him, wordlessly instructing Sarah to sit. "If Cole's seen aligning with a Fed—"

"Don't even attempt to feed me that bullshit." She cuts him off with a vicious wave of her hand. "Cole has cops in his pocket. He's got other Feds, too. What's the difference?"

"The difference is that she isn't dirty." I scrub a hand over the back of my neck, trying to ease the building tension. "She still believes the legal way is the right way."

"What about Greece?"

"Greece was different." Greece feels like a lifetime ago with the contrast of how things now are between Anissa and I. "She had very few choices while in the islands. And no communication with the outside world. I know her well enough to understand she won't break the law willingly."

Sarah crosses her arms over her chest and straightens to her full height. "Then make her do it unwillingly."

Hunt scoffs.

I don't bother reacting.

Sarah is the most pro-choice woman there is. She wouldn't force an innocent to carry her groceries, let alone be involved in this.

"You know what I mean." She glowers. "Let me convince her."

"It's not about convincing her." I walk around the kitchen counter toward them. "She wants to help—"

"Then why the hell did you let her leave? Go after her."

I didn't *let* her. I *pushed* her. I forced her out of this goddamn house because I can't look at her and not see Easton's hands all over her body. But it's more than that, too. So much fucking more.

I send a warning look to Hunter, wordlessly telling him to pull his woman into line.

He ignores me, sitting forward to rest his elbows on his knees before hanging his head. "We may have limited options, but she's not one of them."

No, we never had any to begin with.

None.

"Please, Cole." Sarah gentles her voice as she pads toward me. "Help me understand why Anissa isn't an option."

"Because she's on leave from the Bureau. There's no way she could gain information for us without causing suspicion."

"But her knowledge alone… Her experience…"

She's right. So goddamn right.

"It all means nothing when she's not one of us," Hunt mutters. "We could never trust her."

Sarah continues to stare at me, her gaze digging under my skin. "You trust her. And you know she can help. So what's really holding you back from running after her?"

Frustration.

Pride.

A whole fucking heap of jealousy.

"She doesn't want to be one of us."

"None of us did," she counters. "Not to begin with. But whatever reason brought us all here also convinced us to stay. So convince her, Cole. Do whatever it takes to bring her to our side."

"*No.* It's a bad idea." Hunt pushes to his feet. "At any given moment she could turn on a dime and make this case official. Then we'd have cops breathing down our necks, digging into shit that will cause a whole lot of complications. I disposed of three fucking bodies this morning, Sarah. Do you want me to go to prison?"

She shakes her head, still staring, still visually decimating me. "If something goes wrong, Torian will buy off the necessary people. He always does."

"That takes time." He reaches her side, pleading his case with a punishing glower in my direction. "Don't listen to her. You've already got men on your lower levels wondering what the hell you're doing being seen with the Fed. Their trust is slipping. Especially when you've made no effort to hide the association. You've got dealers looking over their shoulders—"

"I've got dealers questioning me?" I ask, incredulous. "And this is the first time you've decided to mention it?"

"Excuse me for thinking you didn't need the added drama. I took care of it. I've made it known you were inflicting a little manipulative revenge after she arrested your father. But all my hard work will mean nothing if you keep being seen with her."

The sharp bite of protection sinks its teeth into me.

He's been badmouthing her. Tarnishing her name.

"All your hard work?" I keep my anger disguised, letting the bubble of rage thicken inside me. "Let me make one thing clear—when it comes to Anissa, keep your fucking mouth shut. Don't justify my behavior to anyone. If people question me, *I* will deal with their mutiny. *I'll* be the one to reiterate that my decisions are not up for discussion. And any further doubts will be seen as disobedience and handled accordingly."

His nostrils flare. His eyes narrow.

"Do you hear me?" I snarl.

"Yes, I fucking hear you."

I edge closer, so far in his face I could headbutt some sense into him. "You don't get to speak shit about her. You don't get to decide if she's helpful or not. If she's trustworthy or not. I don't even want to hear you mutter her name in an unwelcoming tone." I grin, the curve of lips threatening. "As far as I'm concerned, you're not entitled to a fucking opinion. What I do with her is none of your business."

He sneers, his gaze silently roaring with animosity.

"Same goes for you." I step back, giving Sarah a direct look of warning before starting for the front door. "Nobody gets to dictate what happens with Anissa."

Nobody but me.

10

ANISSA

I slam Cole's front door behind me and march to my car.

Every step ratchets my emotions up another notch. Anger, fear, and helplessness vibrate inside me. I'm thrumming with energy and exhausted at the same time. Itching to fight but also begging to surrender.

I reach the driver's door, pull it wide, and slump into the seat. But I can't leave.

I *can't*.

I slam my palms against the steering wheel and blink away the traitorous burn in my eyes. I'm not sad. The tear-filled heat is driven by hysteria. Mental pandemonium.

Cole *fucking* Torian is such a stubborn, thoughtless prick. His inability to see past his own pride and allow me to help is not only careless, it's dangerous.

Those kids...

That little girl...

I don't even want to imagine what she's going through or who she's with.

"Goddamn you, Cole." I pummel the steering wheel again.

I should report this regardless of his protests. I should take this into my own hands despite the threat of arrest for residual crimes. I need to put the lives of those children first, even though the thought of betraying Cole makes my throat dry.

All I want to do is help. I could make things easier, not only for those kids, but for *him*. For the man I should be happily distancing myself from.

Yet I still can't start the car.

My body refuses to vacate the premises.

"Come on, Anissa. Move." I force my hand to the ignition as a dark shadow drifts over my window.

My pulse quickens. I tilt my head to face the large frame of my tormentor looming over me from outside the vehicle. He opens my door, one hand remaining on the handle, the other moving to the roof, caging me in.

"What are you still doing here?" His voice is neutral. No accusation. No apology.

I keep clinging to the steering wheel and shift my focus through the windshield to avoid those conquering eyes.

"I shouldn't have told you." The indifference in his tone is far different than how he spoke to me inside. The aggression is gone. Maybe even the animosity, too. "You've got a soft heart. I knew you'd feel obligated to help."

I'm not soft. I'm determined. Righteous.

Those kids need me.

Cole needs me.

"I'll get them back, Nis. I'll stop at nothing."

I can't stand him talking to me like this. I hated his vehemence, yet his kindness is far more lethal to my sanity.

"Or is that the problem?" he asks. "Are you worried about the blood I'll shed?"

"No." The answer comes immediately. Truthfully.

I meet his gaze, letting him know I wouldn't deny him anything in his search for Tobias and Stella. He can maim and mutilate those involved. Murder and massacre.

I guess that's part of the problem. My ethics are scrambled.

They have been since Greece.

That's the real reason I couldn't return to work. Not because I need more time to get my head around what happened. But because I haven't been able to ditch the mentality of a lifelong criminal. I've struggled to convince myself that incarceration is the right punishment for those involved in sex-trafficking and people-smuggling. The animalistic, eye-for-an-eye way of life has grown on me like a fungus and I can't ditch it, no matter what I try.

"The only thing that matters is Stella and Tobias." I swallow over the bitter taste of surrender. "Please let me help."

He releases a tired breath and takes a step back, pivoting away from me. He's quiet for a moment, glancing across the neatly manicured lawn as if searching for guidance.

The new facets I'm seeing in him today have each become more soul-shaking than the next. First fear, then vulnerability and defeat.

Now it's heartache, his harrowing expression making me fragile.

I never knew he had this depth. I'd always hoped, even daydreamed, but never truly believed.

It takes all my restraint not to go to him. To touch. To soothe.

"Your offer is appreciated," he murmurs. "But you have to realize it's unacceptable when on your terms. You'll want to involve the authorities and that isn't an option."

"Then we do it your way." I release the steering wheel, turning my entire body to face him. "Whatever you want, Cole, I'll do it. Just let me be a part of this."

"At the cost of your career?"

I open my mouth to protest, but he's right. The looming threat is real. "I'll be careful... discreet... I can keep a low profile."

"We don't work nine to five. And this isn't a desk job. It's all in or nothing." He swivels back to me, eyes narrowing. "That means being available twenty-four-seven. Everyone else is living under this roof, and I'd expect you to do the same."

My gut flops. Drops. Rolls.

I ignore it and shrug. "Whatever it takes."

There are numerous beats of silence, the gentle quiet thickening around me.

"You'll move in here?" He raises a brow. "Into my house?"

Having him repeat the insanity doesn't help. My stomach does the same acrobatics. Tumbling. Turning.

It's always been a vicious game of push and pull with him. One hand delights in shoving him away while the other itches to drag him forward.

Right now, it's the itch.

I'm sure there's a multitude of psychological reasons for my behavior. But most of all, it's just him.

Just Cole.

Plain and simple.

"Into your house, but *not* into your bed."

"Of course not." The words are snipped. "I wouldn't want to step on your boyfriend's toes."

I have zero intent of informing him of the inaccuracy of his assumption. Absolutely zero.

"*He* can't know anything about this," he continues. "Not a damn thing, Nissa."

I roll my eyes and slide out of the car, having to concentrate on my movements so I don't brush into him as I close the door. "I won't say a word."

"And Easton won't notice when you don't go home?"

"He won't be a problem."

He huffs. "I shouldn't be surprised you've got him bluffed."

I try to ignore the sidestep into a conversation neither of us want to have, but the diversion reminds me of Cole's perfect timing the other night. "Did you lie when you said you didn't bug my apartment?"

"Me? No." He feigns offense. "I'd never stoop that low."

I don't let anger take hold, because that's what he wants. He's baiting me. Taunting. "Have you forgotten I've watched you stoop far lower?"

He stares at me for several heartbeats. His controlled, superior expression doesn't loosen until he sighs, his shoulders relaxing with the movement. "Believe me, little fox, my imagination has punished me enough with thoughts of you and him. Bugging your apartment is a level of hell I never want to reach."

He walks away, his long stride flawless while I'm left cemented in place.

His admission is more bait. This time the delicious kind.

He wants me to believe he's yearning for me. I won't fall for that again.

I lock the car and follow after him to the front of the house where he holds the front door open.

"You're going to need to be patient." His voice is low as I step inside. "My people won't appreciate you being here. It's best to keep your mouth shut as much as possible. Relay any thoughts to me privately."

"I'll be fine."

"You'll be fine?" He closes the door, then turns to face me. "You can handle Hunter's animosity multiplied?"

"Do you even remember what you've put me through?" The question is more of an accusation. He's acting as if he doesn't recollect our past. "Do you even vaguely recall the actions that led to Greece and how you got me there? Of course I can handle your men."

"I remember everything," he states simply, the potency of those three words blissful in their purity, before he distances himself, leading me down the hall to stop at the staircase. "You need to go upstairs for a while. Stay in my room until I come get you."

"Why?"

He keeps his back to me. "Penny will be here soon and she's not aware of what's happened. I hope you understand the need for privacy when I break the news."

More kindness toward others? Really?

This man continues to surprise me.

"It shouldn't take long." He keeps walking, not giving me a backward glance.

I can't help but watch him place distance between us. I wait until he enters the living area and moves out of view before I start on the stairs.

I breathe a little easier at the top step, the light breeze sweeping away the acrid scent of bleach.

I ignore the stare of the woman in the looming picture and make my way to Cole's bedroom, stopping at the threshold once more to take in the sight.

His power oozes from within the large space. It's in the menacing bed with its inky black coverings and shiny red pillowcases. In the dark, polished dresser that lacks any adornment. In the suit jacket neatly placed across the armchair in the corner.

His aura has seeped into the furniture. Into the walls and curtains.

482

The crunch of gravel draws me across the room to the open window. Decker's car slowly makes its way up the drive with Penny behind the wheel and Luca riding shotgun. I withdraw, hiding from view as she parks beside my car, and they all climb out, Decker joining them from the back seat.

They walk quietly to the front door, Decker limping a few steps behind. Once inside, the subtle murmurings of conversation sweep my ears. I can't make out the words. I don't try.

I ignore my need to snoop and give them privacy. A howl of pain rends the air.

Penny knows.

Her suffering finds a home inside my chest. I hurt for her. For those kids. For a family who once seemed deserving of punishment, but this is far too much.

I kick off my shoes and creep down the hall, stopping at the staircase to sit on the top step. I stare at the blank wall in front of me, picturing the confronting scene below like a voyeur on the outer edges of this incredibly emotional moment.

My ass is numb by the time another crunch of gravel travels from the window. Additional people enter the house. The hum of conversation grows, the words still out of reach, but the tones of Cole's sisters' voices are distinguishable.

There are tears. Sobs. Wracking, hiccupping cries.

All of it sinks into me, the torment softening me to a family I've spent so long hardened against.

I use my phone to work on a list of names as they suffer. I jot down the contact details of my informants and the vague recollections of local people who have had links to previous abductions. There aren't many. But it's a start.

By the time I hear footsteps approaching from the hall below, I'm starved for communication.

The crying has petered out to long silences between occasional blown noses.

Cole finally sates my starvation as he comes into view at the lower landing, his look of exhaustion aging his face ten years.

"Are you okay?" I'm the first to break the silence as he remains distanced from me, simply staring with hollow eyes.

"Yeah." One word. A lie.

He's far from okay. I don't even know why I asked, I just… talking is a far better option than fixating on his torment.

He approaches, the slow steps bringing him within touching distance. I stand and move out of the way as he continues past me, down the hall and into his room.

I follow, pulled toward him by an invisible thread to find him discarding his shirt at the foot of the bed. I watch in silence from the door as he lays the material atop the mattress, then starts to unbuckle his belt. I swallow, not looking away as he discards his pants, exposing tanned, muscled legs and black boxer briefs.

The sight drags me into the past. It also seems as if I never left. As if our time apart has merely been a blink of contemplation instead of weeks spent agonizingly alone.

"I need to freshen up." He walks for the closed door a foot next to where I stand. "I won't be long. Once I'm done, I'll escort you to your apartment to get whatever you need."

I nod, ignoring his perfectly muscular chest as he continues out of view, closing the door behind him.

I lean against the threshold as I hear the faucet turn on. There's a slush of water. The sound of him brushing his teeth.

I've listened to all of this before, the menial tasks unlocking warm memories of our time in Greece.

I'd been consumed by him back then. Emboldened. He'd awakened my every nerve. Inspired passion beyond my comprehension.

Everything had felt... right.

The differences in our lives hadn't mattered. The lies and manipulation were forgotten because being with him became a calling.

He felt like my goddamn messiah.

In reality, he was nothing but a magician creating emotional illusions. And shamefully, those tricks would still work on me now.

I already want to go back. To relive the nightmares and injuries just for a taste of passion.

Stockholm.

Goddamn fucking Stockholm.

I don't move when the water shuts off. I remain cocked against the door-frame, staring across his room as he enters, now fully dressed in another pristine suit, his pure perfection sucking up the oxygen and replacing it with smothering humidity.

I push from the frame and glance into what I thought was the bathroom door, finding a huge wardrobe filled with hanging suits, shirts and ties. Shoes are neatly placed in tidy chutes. Jeans are piled on a shelf. The area is bigger than my living room, with an open side door to a tiled area, revealing a seductive two-person shower.

"Do you feel better now?" I return my gaze to him before heated memories burn me.

"I needed to wake myself up. Maybe it would've worked better if you'd joined me in the shower."

I scoff. "I didn't ask to give you ideas."

"Then why did you?" He straightens his lapels, all suave and sophisticated. "Are you starting to care about me again, little fox?"

Despite the taunting question, it's becoming more blatantly obvious I didn't discard any heartfelt feelings toward him in the first place. They're all still here, tinkering inside my chest.

"Don't worry. I won't tell your boyfriend." He winks at me. "This can be our little secret."

I wish I knew the best way to shut down his comments about Easton without exposing the truth. But it's best to keep a slight barrier between us. If I'm not careful, he'll figure out I'm not just here for those kids.

This isn't work to me.

I'm here for him.

"Can you please stop mentioning Easton?" I ask. "Don't talk about him."

"Why?" He flicks out his collar to then smooth it down. "To appease your guilt? To ease your betrayal? Or is it so you can have a break from reality and return to the fantasy life of being with me?"

Yes.

Yes.

Yes.

Each question packs a sickening blow, cutting me at the knees.

"How about this?" He bridges the space between us, his aftershave acting like a drug to my senses. "Admit how you feel about me and I'll forget that piece of shit even exists."

He doesn't reach for me. There are no touching hands or grabby fingers. But I sense them.

Everywhere.

"You're mine, Nissa." There's adamance in his voice. Conviction. "You know this. You *feel* it. Yet you punish me for things I've already explained. You hold me accountable for transgressions that were necessary to ensure our future. And you blame me because it's the only excuse you have to keep me at bay."

His minty breath brushes my lips, sinking into my tongue.

He's right. So right.

And still, I deny him with the shake of my head.

"You'll quit fighting soon enough," he growls. "And when I finally reclaim that sweet pussy of yours it will be worth the wait. But until then, I plan on reminding you of your cheating ways as many times as I goddamn like."

I lower my gaze and bite my lip, holding in a pathetic whimper.

I'm overheating. Sweating.

"You can come downstairs now." He retreats as if immune to the screaming chemistry between us. "Be prepared for a fight and keep your mouth shut."

I blink at the sudden whiplash of topic. "Okay."

He leads the way from the room and I follow a step behind, trailing him down the hall to the staircase.

I'm chilled by the time we reach the lower level. Cole's bedroom is like a sanctuary in comparison to the upcoming firing squad of murmured voices.

He pauses near the opening of the living room, waiting for me to reach his side before we enter the open area together. A united front.

Both of us strip the conversation from the room without a word.

"What is *she* doing here?" Decker pushes from the sofa, his glare more accusatory than his hate-filled tone.

Everyone stares at me. Keira, Penny, and Layla with tear-stained eyes. Hunter, Decker, and Benji with animosity. Luca and Sarah with pity.

"Anissa will be helping us." Cole places a hand at the low of my back, igniting whispers and muttered dissent.

"Help with what?" Keira asks. "What can she do that you haven't already done?"

"Nothing," Hunter answers. "She'll do more harm than good."

"No." I shake my head, directing my answer to Benji and Layla. "I would never risk your daughter's life. I promise I won't interfere."

"Then why be here at all?" Decker growls.

"Yeah, why?" Hunt continues to glare. "You're nothing more than a distraction."

I press my lips tight, keeping my mouth shut because that's what Cole wants.

Whispers of discord arise between them. Layla murmurs to her husband. Penny does the same with Luca. Sarah mouths a harsh warning to Hunter.

"Are you all finished?" Cole adds pressure to my back, encouraging me toward the wolves. "She's here because she has experience on this when we have none."

"She's got no fucking experience when it comes to our people," Decker counters. "The goalposts are different."

"It doesn't matter." Cole drops his hand and moves to the kitchen to open the fridge. "She's here now and she's staying. If any of you have issues, keep them to yourself. I don't have the energy to waste."

Everyone continues to look at me. Hunter and Decker's glares intensify, along with Sarah and Luca's pity.

"How can you help find my baby?" Layla raises from the sofa, slow and fragile. She maneuvers around the coffee table to approach me, her husband soon following. "Are there ways you can search for people on the Bureau's computers? Some sort of facial recognition on public camera or something?"

I glance at Cole, who walks back toward me, a bottle of water in each hand. "She can't help like that, Lay." He reaches my side and hands me a bottle. "Nothing she does can be traced back to the Feds. She's risking her career by being here."

"Then send her home," Hunter mutters.

"What *can* you do?" Benji asks. "I don't understand."

I crack the lid on the water and take a quick sip, needing the liquid to soothe my drying throat. "I've worked on hostage cases before. I know how to negotiate a ransom."

"But there hasn't been a request." Layla's eyes implore me. "There has to be something you can do when we haven't heard from whoever took them."

Her anguish bleeds into me.

486

I don't know what to say. I open my mouth, not even able to form a response.

"There will be a ransom." Cole's hand returns to my back. The subtle unity drags the air from my lungs in a gentle heave. "We have to be patient."

I remain silent, wishing I could reiterate his words of encouragement, but I can't. I won't lie to Layla. Not about her daughter. Not when a sinking part of me is wondering if that little girl is already dead.

"Whoever has them probably didn't anticipate we'd kill Robert." Cole's palm continues to do circle work against the back of my suit jacket. He's providing *me* with comfort. An interloper. An unwanted intruder. "They might be scrambling to find a place to hide."

"And you know Stella," Sarah adds from the sofa. "That feisty little thing would be giving them their money's worth. I'm sure someone will reach out any minute now."

I nod, making myself believe.

I ignore all the statistics on hostage situations that have been drilled into my brain and nod and nod and nod. This isn't a normal abduction. This isn't a criminal against a naive civilian. The rules here are different. The playing field is entirely new.

"A two-person abduction is a major operation." I meet Layla's watery eyes. "Whoever is responsible would want to set themselves up in a stable environment. Especially if they're on their own. They'd want to keep the kids calm."

"Tobias and Stella are probably still passed out," Hunter growls. "Does she even know they were hit with chloroform?"

No, I didn't.

I glance at Cole, witnessing the tick of his jaw before he turns to meet my gaze. "We still have a lot to discuss." His palm stops the circular assault. "I'll fill you in on the way to your apartment."

"You're leaving?" Layla's voice is laced with accusation. "Please, Cole, stay here. What happens if someone calls? What will you do if—"

"We won't be long." His hand sweeps over my wrist, the touch light. "And I need the fresh air. The bleach is giving me a migraine."

He leads me toward the far side of the room, the prying eyes remaining heavy at the back of my neck even once we're striding down an unfamiliar hall.

I can't get rid of the ache Layla's suffering has awakened inside me. The agony chips at my soul. Little by little.

I sniff to beat back the tingle in my nose.

Usually I can detach from a case.

This one seems far too personal. An attack on me and mine, not Cole and his family.

He stops before a door and releases my wrist. "Pull yourself together."

I cringe, hating his ability to see through me. "I'm…" I shake my head, not sure how to finish my response.

Am I sorry? Embarrassed? Weak?

Ding, ding, ding.

All of the above.

I lower my head and suck in a deep breath. Regrouping.

He leans closer. "Fucking pull yourself together, Nis." It's a warning. A vicious growl. "*Now.*"

I don't understand his venom, but I focus on doing what he says. I try to wring myself of emotion. To siphon the weakness.

"Don't fucking break on me." He grips my chin, raising my face so we're eye to eye.

The desperation that stares back at me strips the air from my lungs. That's when I understand he's not demanding—he's begging. Pleading.

"The last thing I can handle is your suffering," he rasps. "Don't do this to me now."

My heart squeezes. Chokes.

I lick my lips to ease the blooming tingle and straighten my shoulders.

I have to be strong for him.

I *will be* strong for him.

"It was a momentary lapse," I whisper. "It won't happen again."

The sorrow staring back at me speaks of disbelief. Of a yearning that could outstrip my own.

"Good." He releases me, but not before his gaze drops to my mouth, lashing my lips with a visual sweep of unadulterated affection.

I want the kiss he promises. I'd almost kill for it.

"Let's go." He reaches behind his back, sweeping open the door to a garage. "We'll take the Porsche."

11

COLE

I fill her in on everything I know as I drive toward her apartment. I tell her about the rag that smelled of chemicals. Of the nanny and her staged overdose, along with the gouge marks in my grass at the side of my property, the divots having come from a fucking ladder still laying in my neighbor's yard.

"What's your assessment of the situation so far?" I stop at a set of traffic lights and glance at her, despising the way her hands are coiled in her lap like she's a meek princess.

She's upset and I fucking hate it.

"I don't know. It's too early to tell."

That's bullshit. She's brilliant. She's logical. She would already have an idea of what could be happening to Stella and Tobias, along with the statistics on successful retrievals.

"Don't fuck with me, Nis." I keep my tone amicable. "You think it's a bad sign they haven't called."

Her silence is loud.

"Tell me." I lower my window, needing fresh air. Needing *anything* to clear my head of the static.

"It's too early to say."

The traffic light flashes green and I turn onto her street. "Do you think I can't handle the answer?"

I pull into a parking space across the road from her building's front door and cut the engine. When I glance at her again, she's still staring out the front of the car.

"Speculation is a minefield. It's better if we focus on facts." She unclasps her belt and opens her door. "Give me ten minutes. I won't take long."

"You're not going alone."

She pauses in her escape, her ass half off the leather seat when she huffs out a defeated breath.

I'm still the enemy to her. Or that's what she wants to believe.

"It's bad enough you brought me here in a shiny dick extension when I shouldn't be seen with you." Her eyes plead for understanding. "You're not escorting me into the building."

She shoves from the car and closes the door.

I do the same. "I won't risk you going in alone."

"I can protect myself," she hisses over the roof of the Porsche. "At least for five damn minutes."

She jogs around the hood and across the street, easing into a long stride along the footpath while I follow at a slower pace.

The distance doesn't feel right. She's too exposed to any asshole with a trigger finger. But I grind my teeth through the paranoia and keep an eye on our surroundings.

I scan the pedestrians along the sidewalk, considering each of them a potential threat to the woman I crave. I even scrutinize the buildings, checking windows for a sniper attack.

Robert has already proven I underestimated what he was capable of. Now I'm left to contemplate what else he could've arranged before his death.

"Anissa," a male shouts nearby.

I fucking know that voice. *Easton.*

The piece of shit approaches from the front of her building with a face full of concern, all anxious and uptight.

At least the fucker is wearing clothes.

She stops before him, ramrod stiff. She doesn't glance over her shoulder at me. She doesn't have to. Easton does it for her.

"What are you doing?" he asks, his voice low. "Why is *he* here?"

I can barely hear him, the low volume spurring me to move faster. Or maybe that's the desire to stake ownership.

She murmurs something quick in reply. A fast snap of frantic words.

"You need to move in with me for a few days." He grabs her arms. "I'll take care of you until you're back on your feet."

Like hell he will. Over my goddamn dead body.

"There's nothing to worry about." She shakes him off. "Trust me. I just have to…"

Her response trails as I reach her side, her pained exhale brushing my ears.

"Easton," I sneer in greeting. "Can I help you?"

He keeps staring at her. "Listen to me—this isn't right. Whatever you're doing is going to get you in trouble."

"I appreciate your support." She gives a fragile smile. "But I'm in control. You don't have to keep checking on me."

"You don't need to come around at all," I growl. "It's best if you leave her alone."

His eyes narrow but he still doesn't acknowledge my existence.

"Anissa..." He moves forward, triggering my rage as he reaches for her again.

"Hands off, asshole." I lunge, grabbing his arm.

He yanks away. "Calm yourself, Torian, before I have you arrested."

The threat is real.

Normally, I wouldn't give a shit. A set of handcuffs and a few hours behind bars while my lawyers ensured any charges were dropped would be worthwhile to draw my gun on this pretty boy and let him know exactly who's in charge. But not today. Not when I could get word on Stella and Tobias at any second.

"It's cute that you think you have any power over me." I smirk. "Naive, but cute. Are there any other delusions we can clear up while I'm here?"

Anissa glares at me.

"Stay away from her." Easton puffs out his chest and gets in my face.

"I did." I keep smirking. "She came to me. It was my gate she was banging on this morning."

"Jesus Christ," Anissa hisses. "You two need to quit it. For starters, I was only at your gate because of the shooting last night. And *you*." She turns her ire to Easton. "Don't babysit me. I'm on leave from work, and what I do in that time is my business."

"You're obsessing over a criminal you haven't been able to put behind bars," he growls. "Let me look after you for a while."

I snicker. This asshole is talking about taking me down like I'm not even here. Like he has a fucking hope in hell.

"I'm looking after her now." I slide an arm around her waist, pulling her into my side. "Don't worry. I'll keep her safe."

She stiffens. Every inch. Every muscle.

"Anissa, this is crazy." Easton's face pinches. "You need to think about what you're doing. Not just with your job, but with me. I thought—"

"You thought wrong." I tighten my hold around her, my jealousy sparking to flame. This asshole has been trying to steal her out from underneath me from the moment we met. But he had his chance. He had all the time they've worked together. Fucking years. He only wants her now because she's mine. "My time with her has proven more productive."

"You've got to be kidding me." She shoves away. "You two can finish this dick-measuring contest without me. I'm not participating."

She turns on her heel and storms for her building, leaving me to seethe at Easton as he watches her walk away.

"You need to leave her alone." He doesn't meet my gaze. "Otherwise, I'll make sure you spend the rest of your life behind bars."

"Is that right?" I huff out a chuckle. "Here I was thinking you should be the one to back off before you go missing."

His attention cuts to me, his fury nothing in comparison to mine. This man has no passion. No backbone. "Are you threatening an FBI agent, Mr. Torian?"

"It sure sounds like it, doesn't it? And if you don't listen, I'll make sure those fragile parents of yours go missing, too."

His eyes flare, the surprise instantaneous before his jaw clenches. "You're blackmailing her as well, aren't you?" He shakes his head, his laugh patronizing. "The righteous Cole Torian is now manipulating classy women for sport. Why is that? Have all your criminal hags grown tired of your games?"

He hits a mark, a fucking brutal target beneath my ribs. Not about the hags, because fuck him, I don't slum when it comes to women. But being unable to get Anissa to engage with me without an underlying threat is a sore spot.

"Manipulation is an art." I keep my voice in check. My smile tight. "What pisses you off more? My ability to easily shape her decisions or the fact you can't?"

His teeth grind. Nostrils flare. "You know what?" He pokes a finger toward my chest. "Fuck you." He steps back. Once. Twice. "She might have fallen victim to your games, but I won't. I'll figure out what's going on, Torian. If I were you, I'd keep my nose squeaky clean."

If I were you, I'd shut my fucking mouth before a gun barrel fills the open space.

I continue smirking as he gives me a wide berth, stalking around me toward the street to climb into a tin-bucket sedan.

He's not what Nissa wants.

He might be the safe option, the *easy* out, but there's no life in that perfectly crafted box.

She needs intensity and adrenaline.

She needs *me*.

I wait until he pulls from the curb and drives away before I start after her, stopping at the security panel to unlock the ground-level doors. I glance around for an approaching resident, find nobody nearby, then pull out my wallet and press the coin pocket against the security pad.

She needs a new building manager. The current father of four took too easily to a three-figure bribe when I demanded an access fob.

The fucker didn't even hesitate when I offered an increased price to obtain a key to her fifth-floor apartment. The only thing keeping him in his job is the fear I witnessed when I assured him he would live to regret betraying her to anyone else.

After a quick elevator ride, I'm standing at her apartment waiting for her anger to greet me after I knock.

She doesn't disappoint, flinging the door wide, her cheeks pink with rage.

"Finished the pissing contest already?" She doesn't wait for a reply before walking off, the door beginning to close in her wake.

I shove my foot inside the threshold and follow her, past the shoebox living area with its tiny kitchen to her darkened bedroom with the closed curtains and messy bed, the sheets twisted, the duvet half on the floor.

Blinding jealousy kicks back in as I picture her disheveling the covers with another man. A split second—that's all it takes for my blood to turn hot and my chest to constrict.

I've got more important things to think about, but her betrayal commands my attention.

"You can't blame me for being territorial." I indicate her bed with a fling of my hand. "Unlike you, I'm not unaffected by our past."

She scoffs, bending over an open suitcase on the floor. She doesn't even meet my gaze before stalking to the closet, her metal coat hangers twanging as she rips out a jacket and several shirts.

"And downstairs wasn't my fault," I add. "He deliberately taunted me with his *move-into-my-place* bullshit."

"No he didn't." She thunders back to the suitcase, dumping the clothes inside. "He's trying to protect me. He thinks you're extorting me."

"He's trying to throw your fucking relationship in my face."

She pauses, hunched toward the ground as she lets out a long breath. She wants to rail on me. To fight.

I want it, too.

Instead, she moves to her bedside table, snapping open drawers to riffle through underwear.

"Admit I'm right." I close in behind her. "He may have you, but he's so fucking insecure he has to shove your affair down my throat."

She straightens. Turns. Glares. "Get out of my way."

"I will once you admit I'm right. Then tell me it doesn't piss you off that he's so fucking weak."

Her face is etched in darkness, but the shadows don't hide her spite.

"I don't know how you can stomach having him in your bed," I sneer. "Let alone your body."

"*Stop.*" She raises a clenched fist that chokes her silken underwear. "You know nothing about me and Easton. All you're doing is proving your jealousy."

"Of course I'm jealous. You're mine. You're meant to be with me."

Her eyes flare in rage. "Don't—"

"Here you go with your feminist bullshit." I cut her off. "You want to call me out on not owning you when you know you've fucking owned me for a lot longer."

I grab her fist, lowering it so I can move closer. "You were my possession in Greece." I hold her noxious gaze. "And I was yours. The only difference is my feelings never changed. I still want you."

Her brows pinch. "No, you want me to lose my job—you made that clear downstairs. You want me scrambling to keep my life together. You want to turn my world upside down, and you have. I still can't pull myself together after what you put me through."

"You forgave me my sins," I reach for her chin, needing to touch her.

She pulls back. "In the heat of the moment, maybe, but not now. You *kidnapped* me, Cole. You *drugged* me. Nobody can simply forgive those things."

"You already did. We both know it's true."

"You're wrong." She walks around me and throws her underwear into the suitcase. "It was Stockholm syndrome."

"Like hell it was. Your fucking shrink has denied that bullshit prognosis repeatedly."

Her eyes snap wide.

"You still have feelings for me, little fox, despite your best efforts to deny them."

"You bribed my psychologist?" Her mouth gapes.

Even in the darkness, I notice her paling skin. She's horrified. But I did what I had to do to get the necessary information. "You'd turned your back on me. I'd been concerned, not to mention agitated. When you refused my calls, I'd been left with no choice."

"I'll have her license revoked." She pants. "I'll..." She stands speechless for long moments, her lips working over silent words before she flees the room.

"The shrink isn't to blame." I follow. "I always get what I want."

"Why am I doing this?" She reaches the far end of her sofa and turns to me. "Why do I keep seeking you out?" She closes her eyes and shakes her head. "The best option was to shut you out of my life."

Her struggle is bittersweet.

The fact I'm still in her head when she's spoken for, and after this time apart, is a soothing balm to my pride.

"I can't do this with you again." Her eyes open, the tired depths blinking back at me. "I'd been ready to move on."

"We never stopped." I continue toward her, despising how she retreats. I don't quit my approach until she's backed against the far wall, her breathing labored, her hands splayed against the plaster. "You might have been with him, but I bet you thought of me."

"Don't." She winces. "My life is here. In the FBI. Doing the *right* thing. I only came to you this morning because—"

"You came because the so-called right thing feels wrong. You hate it there. You can't stand being without me." My pulse chants an erratic beat as I will the declaration to be true.

She loathes being without me. I know she does.

Her wince increases, the furrow of her brow deep. "It's because of Stockho—"

"Bullshit." I step into her, my thighs jolting hers, pressing her harder into the wall. "I bet you can't look me in the eye and honestly tell me you believe your feelings are a mental issue."

494

She turns her cheek, proving my point by glancing away.

I'm so fucking tired. My limbs are drained of strength. But I could stay here forever. I could live in this embodiment of fatigue if it meant I wouldn't be without her.

I breathe her in. The lavender from her perfume dances through my senses, muddling my control.

"It isn't Stockholm, little fox." I lean in, pressing my lips to her neck, the heat of connection scorching.

She shudders. Whimpers.

The sweetest fucking mewl hums in her throat, turning my dick to stone.

"This thing between us is far more powerful than that." I speak against her skin, tasting her salty flesh.

"I don't care how powerful it is," she whispers. "I don't want it."

"At one point, neither did I. But I'm done fighting. This is going to happen."

"Easton—"

"*Fuck* Easton," I snap. "He was a mistake."

"You're wrong. About everything. I was moving on." She shakes her head softly, her jaw brushing my cheek. "And I will again, once those kids are found."

"No you won't. Not with Easton anyway."

She turns her face into me, her gaze questioning, her lips so fucking close. "How can you be sure?"

"Because I'll kill that man before I let him lay another hand on you."

She's not repulsed by my threat. There's no fear or panic or gasp. Only stillness.

"You know I'm not joking, Nis. I'll make sure he permanently keeps his distance."

"You're insane."

I smirk, pressing my chest to hers, her deliciously soft breasts making my dick jolt beyond salvation. Sex is the last thing I should be thinking about. But going through the start of this nightmare alone has only cemented how much I need her.

Every part of her.

"I'm also determined." I sense the heat of her mouth against mine. The delicate sweep of her breath. "I can—and will—slaughter every man who attempts to replace me. For the rest of your life if I have to."

She groans. Softens.

I'd fucking bleed for her. *Die* for her. If only I could have her.

She closes her eyes.

She's succumbing to me.

It's the most immense victory, spurring blood to pump faster through my veins.

I'm about to bridge the distance and claim the prize of her lips when her arms reach between us, her hands splaying on my chest to push me back.

"I'm not like you, Cole. And I don't want to be." Her eyes open and someone different stares back at me. Someone restrained and in control.

Fuck.

"I want to help those kids," she repeats. "But not like this. Either agree to be professional or I'll have to find another way."

12

COLE

I REMAIN CLOSE TO HER FOR LONG MOMENTS, MY FINGERS WRAPPED AROUND THE wrists still shoving against my chest. But she doesn't falter.

If anything, her eyes turned colder.

I'm losing her. All over again.

Without agreeing to her terms of professionalism, I back away, retreating to her room to grab her suitcase. Then I silently walk to the apartment door and wait for her to follow.

We don't speak on the way to the car. She glowers the entire time, climbing into the Porsche to cross her arms over her chest.

"Do you want me to get you something to eat before we return?" I keep my attention on the road, my hands on the wheel. I deny myself the visual and physical connection I crave and stare at the traffic straight ahead.

"No." Her answer is short. Sharp.

"Are you sulking?"

"I'm not goddamn sulking," she mutters. "I'm thinking. I'm trying to do what I'm here for."

"You need to eat. The extra weight looks good on you."

"Oh, wow." Her tone turns incredulous. "You're really going to go there? You must have a huge set of balls to comment on my body."

I hold in a grin. Her anger is like a fucking balm to all my concerns. It's as if I find peace in her volatility.

"Why wouldn't I?" I shoot her a look, my brow raised. "Your body is one of my most favorite things in the world."

She sighs. "You agreed to be professional."

No, she assumed my silence was confirmation.

"How 'bout—" My suggestion is cut off by the vibration of my cell, the ringing connecting with the car Bluetooth to trill through the speakers.

'Unknown number' illuminates across the dashboard screen.

Anissa repositions in her seat, leaning forward. On alert. "Are you going to answer? It could be…"

I connect the call and pray this is the communication we've been waiting for. "Cole Torian."

"Ah, Mr. Torian, I'm glad I reached you."

Apprehension tightens my throat at the unfamiliar accented voice of an older man.

"Who is this?" I drive on autopilot and glance at Anissa as she pulls out her phone and taps buttons to start a recording.

"Excuse me for contacting you out of the blue. My name is Emmanuel Costa. I'm a friend of your father's, although I admit it's been quite some time since we've been in touch."

Foreboding prickles the back of my neck. Any friend of my father's is no friend of mine, but this man's tone holds the quiet calm of a genuine welcome.

"I tried calling him directly," he adds, "but there was no answer. I'm not even sure I have the correct number anymore."

"My father has been hard to contact lately. Is there something I can do for you?"

There's a pause, the quiet deafening.

"No, son, I think it may be the other way around. I'm under the impression I might be able to do something for you."

Anissa's gaze bores into the side of my face as I pull over on the quiet residential street.

"I'm told I may be obtaining something of yours in the near future," he continues.

Darkness edges into the corners of my vision, the build of fury almost blinding. "You're *obtaining* something of mine? I suggest you choose your words wisely before you continue."

"Oh, no, please forgive me." His accent thickens. Italian? "I'm not addressing this correctly. It's not me who arranged these… how should I put this… assets? It's one of my men, who seems to have misjudged a situation and put himself into trouble. Again, I tried to call your father, but when there was no answer, I didn't know who else to reach out to apart from you."

"Cut the shit, Emmanuel. Do you have the kids or not?"

There's another pause, this one siphoning the air from my lungs.

"I don't, no. It's my employee. But I've since instructed him to come directly to me. I assure you they should be arriving safe and sound within the hour. There's no need to worry."

I don't know what to make of this. Is it an olive branch or a Trojan horse?

"Where are you?"

"I've just flown into Sacramento to meet him. He has driven through the night with your two little ones asleep on the back seat. Not a hair on their heads has been touched."

I scoff.

Not a hair has been touched, yet they were sedated. With fucking chloroform. And taken across state lines.

"What do you want?" I cling to the steering wheel, my knuckles white with the tight grip. "Money? Drugs?"

"Son, I don't want anything." He chuckles, the jovial sound a contrast to the sinister darkness surrounding the situation. "Especially not these children when I already have four of my own. I'm merely trying to right a wrong."

I frown. "Are you suggesting I come to Sacramento, and what? Just pick them up?"

"Precisely."

This doesn't add up. Nobody obtains power over me and gives it back willingly. There has to be a catch. A trap.

Anissa's hand slides over my thigh, her face demanding my attention.

She nods at me in encouragement, her eyes filled with confident hope. But she doesn't understand the smoke and mirrors of my world. She's still naive to the complexities.

"Okay." I hold her gaze, needing the strength that comes with her determination. "I'll be there as soon as I can."

"Perfect. I'll text you the address once arrangements have been made."

Anissa smiles, the curve of lips subtle.

This isn't right. The simplicity. The ease. Someone doesn't go to the effort of stealing children from a notorious criminal to then give them back, even if acting under orders from a man who's now dead.

"I want proof of life." My request sounds like a plea. A pathetic show of weakness.

"That won't be a problem. I'll arrange for an image to be sent to you. Safe travels, Mr. Torian, and I'll see you soon."

"Wait," the demand leaves my mouth before I can think things through. But I refuse to spend the next God-knows-how-many hours anticipating an ambush. I need answers. At least a hint as to this man's comprehension of the situation. "I appreciate you not asking a price for the safe return of those kids, but you need to be aware I will require one of my own for the attack against my family. Nobody steals from me and gets away with it."

Anissa's hand tightens on my thigh, the grip a subtle warning.

"I understand." Emmanuel's voice holds regret. "I will make sure my employee is here to explain his decisions once you arrive."

The call disconnects. Anissa's hold gentles. My thoughts explode.

I rerun the entire conversation in my mind. The nuances of tone. The choice of words. I analyse everything, hoping to find a clue to an underlying agenda, and come up with nothing.

"This is good news." Anissa's fingers slide away, the threat of disconnect snapping me back to the present.

"Don't." I grab her hand, refusing to break the contact. She's the only thing grounding me.

She winces, the slight tug of retreat spiking my instability.

"Allow me this one thing, Nis," I growl. "Just this."

Just one hold. One brief grasp of a lifeline to help me concentrate on extraction instead of bloodthirsty revenge.

Her throat works over a heavy swallow. Her lips part.

But she doesn't deny me.

She lets me entwine our fingers as she turns to face the road ahead of us, resting back into the seat.

"What do you want me to do?" she asks. "What travel arrangements need to be—"

"I'll take the jet."

"You don't seem relieved. Do you think this is a setup?"

"Maybe." I clasp the steering wheel and pull back into traffic.

"Why wouldn't he threaten you to begin with?"

"He might be naive enough to think I'll arrive in Sacramento unprepared. Or that I won't dig into his life before arriving." I press buttons on the steering wheel to connect a call to Decker. What I don't do is let go of her hand.

I guide her palm to the gearstick, placing mine on top of it as I ask Deck to make travel arrangements and start digging up dirt on Emmanuel Costa.

"You aren't going to tell him to keep quiet?" she asks after I end the call.

"I don't need to. He knows we'll be home soon, and he'll keep his mouth shut until then." I sense her continued desire to pull her hand away. But she doesn't do it. She humors me with the connection while also refusing to look at me.

"How can you be sure?"

I guess I can't. At one time, I would've sworn my life on the loyalty of my people. Now I don't have that faith.

I think that's why I crave her so much. I can trust her. Rely on her. I've got too much leverage over Anissa for her to betray me. "Decker won't want to upset my sisters without more information."

She nods, falling uncomfortably quiet.

I turn onto my street, then into my drive, and up to the guarded gate before she slinks her hand out from beneath mine.

"What happens now?" She glances across my gardens as we make our way to the back of the house. "Do you want me to come with you to Sacramento?"

Not only do I want it, I expect it. *Demand* it.

"I was under the impression you planned on seeing this through." I pull into the garage and cut the engine. "Are you looking for a way out?"

"No, of course I'm not. I just wasn't sure if you'd want me to assist from here or…" She shrugs. "I'll admit, I didn't anticipate having to get on another jet with you."

I unfasten my belt and push open my door. "Are you worried?" I shove from the Porsche and wait for her to follow, but she doesn't.

After a few moments, I lean back into the car to see her still seated in place.

"Please tell me this isn't another game." Her eyes implore me. "Promise me, Cole. Vow it. Because if this is a trick, I'll…"

I want to catch her fragile threat and throw it back at her.

What would she do?

How would she get back at me?

It's the flimsy shield she holds up against me that stops me from retaliating. She's close to breaking point, and I'm the one who carved the initial fractures.

"I give you my word, little fox." I clutch the top of the doorframe, hating the slight wince crossing her features.

"I want to believe you." She unclasps her belt. "But once bitten and all that."

"Trust me, I feel the same when it comes to you walking out on me." It's a low blow that I punctuate with the close of my door.

Our games might be her trigger but we both participated in those. She attempted to trick me just as much as I did with her.

"Don't hold your breath for an apology." She climbs from the car. "I don't regret the way things ended."

I huff out a laugh and start for the door leading inside. "That's the thing, Nis; nothing ended. It never will."

I don't look back as I enter the house. I force Anissa from my mind with each step toward the chatter in the living room and find everyone still sitting on the sofas, awaiting our return.

The only person who doesn't sit at attention at the sight of me is Decker who keeps his attention on the laptop resting on his thighs, his fingers dancing over the keys.

"Who's Emmanuel Costa?" Keira pushes to her feet. "Does he have anything to do with the abduction?"

I don't acknowledge her, don't even flinch as I approach my other sister, crouching before Layla to meet her watery gaze.

For a second, she takes me in, her eyes searching mine with apprehension. "It's bad, isn't it?" She sucks in a breath. "He's the one who took her, didn't he?"

"I don't know." I clasp her hands as she draws in one weary inhale after another. "I don't think so."

"What is it then? What happened? Who is he?"

"Why are we looking into him?" Benji adds from beside her.

"He called to tell me he knows where the kids are. That they're okay and we can go get them."

Her face alights with hope. Misguided, punishing hope.

"Lay." I squeeze her fingers. "Before you start thanking your lucky stars, I'm not sure how good this news is."

Anissa walks into the room as Layla's hope turns to confusion. "Why?"

"Because it's too easy." I don't want to worry her, yet false expectations are dangerous. "This doesn't feel right. This guy led me to believe this will be an easy resolution. Without a ransom or threats. And maybe that might be the case. But..." I shrug. "You know that's not how these things work."

Her lower lip trembles, the unshed tears building in her eyes.

"Why does his name sound familiar?" Benji asks. "Who is he?"

"A heavyweight in the fashion industry by the looks of it." Decker keeps tapping at his keyboard. "Does the brand Alleya mean anything to you guys?"

"Jesus Christ," Anissa murmurs from the far corner of the room.

"I had one of their handbags a few years ago." Keira pushes to her feet. "Dad gave it to me for my birthday."

"That's the other thing." I cringe. "He's friends with Luther. Or was at one point."

"Tell me what this means." Layla clings tight to my hands. "Why is he involved in any of this?"

"That's what I want to know, too. Robert had to have some sort of familiarity with this guy of Emmanuel's to reach out to him for help. Which means it's likely they know about our father's unsavory business ventures."

Keira shakes her head. "But why would a successful businessman risk any sort of association with our father if he knew?"

"Some of the most high-profile people in the world have maintained relationships with suspected pedophiles well after rumors turned into a conviction," Anissa murmurs. "It's either about power or perverted proclivities."

"Show me a photo," Penny demands. "Let me see who this man is."

I release Layla's hands and raise to my full height to take a look at Decker.

He taps a few more times on his keypad, scrolls, then turns the screen to face us. "I'm not sure how recent this image is. It's on his company website."

The smiling face jogs through my childhood memories. He holds a friendly expression full of laugh lines and kind eyes, his Lego-man hair more grey than black as he sits behind an expensive wooden desk in a tailored suit.

"I've seen him before." Keira points at the laptop. "Back when Mom was alive."

I ignore the thought of my mother, determined not to fall into that well of suffering, and nod. "I remember him, too."

There are no specific instances of familiarity. No recollection of good or bad. But I know him.

"Penny?" I switch my focus to her. "How about you? Have you seen him before?"

Did she see him in Greece while my father held her prisoner?

She shakes her head and lowers her gaze. "No. Not at all."

At least that's a start. Emmanuel may not have any connection to the sex trade at all.

"Please, Cole." Layla inches to the edge of the sofa and reclaims my hand. "We need to get the kids back straight away. Where do we have to go? Where are they?"

"Sacramento," I announce the location quickly, ripping off the Band-Aid.

Someone gasps. Either Sarah or Keira. I don't know. But the sound is far better than the crumpling of Layla's face.

"Sacramento?" she whispers. "Some monster has driven my baby all the way to Sacramento?"

"Yes. But I'm told they're unharmed." The weak platitude leaves a bitter aftertaste on my tongue.

"Emmanuel agreed to send a photo as proof of life," Anissa adds. "That's a good sign."

I nod, thankful for the reminder.

"When?" Hunt leans forward, resting his elbows on his knees. "If he's as innocent as he says, then we should be able to track information from the digital footprint." He looks at Decker for confirmation. "Right?"

"Right." Decker turns the laptop back to face him. "If he's got nothing to hide, then he shouldn't go to the effort of scrubbing the information from the image. And then we can get an exact timestamp of when it was taken along with a GPS location. It's not a lot to go on, but it's better than nothing."

It still feels like nothing to me.

An address won't tell us what kind of man he is.

A timestamp won't prove whether he's abused the children or not.

"What do you think?" Layla turns her attention to Anissa, still standing across the room, doing her best not to intrude. "Did you hear the conversation? What do you think of this man?"

Nissa looks at me, her lips parted as if waiting for permission.

"It's okay." I nod. "Tell her what you think."

She walks closer, swallowing before perching herself on the armrest of Layla's sofa to give her a sad smile. "Yes, I heard the conversation, and I think Cole is right. Even though Emmanuel sounds like a positive influence on the situation, we still haven't received the proof. He hasn't sent the photo yet, and we don't even have his cell number because the connection was private. It's too early to tell what we're up against."

Her agreement stirs something inside me. Not pride. But similar.

It's not often this independent woman agrees with me. It's even less common to have her attempting to soothe one of my family members.

"Do you think they're still alive?" Penny asks her.

"Yes. Although this guy was remorseful for what has happened, he also had an air of confidence. There were no pauses for contemplation or stutters where he may have been lying. He either believes what he's saying or he's done this too many times to feel fear." She meets my gaze. "My guess is the former. Especially with him being the man behind a brand as big as Alleya. I just wouldn't be betting anyone's life on a seamless outcome."

"I'd say the odds are pretty good." Decker turns his laptop to face the room again, displaying a Wikipedia page. "This guy is seriously wealthy. I'm talking balls-deep, filthy-rich territory. Anything he could possibly get out of us would be pocket change to him. Which means this could be exactly what he told you— just an easy handover."

I'm still not convinced. Men who know my father don't do business above board.

"It's possible. I'm just not sure if it's probable." Anissa pushes from the armrest. "We can be hopeful, though, as long as we remain cautious."

The room falls quiet. The mental musings of everyone are loud through the silence while Benji stares at me, questioning. Begging. Fucking pleading for more information.

All I see when I look at him now is a traitor.

A conniving, backstabbing, heartbroken traitor.

He's lucky he's still breathing.

"So, what's the plan?" Hunter stalks for the kitchen. "How many of us are going to Sacramento?"

Layla glances at me in panic. "I want to be there."

"I'm coming, too." Keira's hands drop to her sides.

They both stare at me in anticipation, waiting for me to deny them. "You can both come. But you'll do as I say the entire time. I don't want you anywhere near this guy. You'll have to be satisfied with being in the same city, not the same location."

They nod.

"We're all going," Hunter states from the kitchen, his face in my fridge. "If this is a trap, every one of us needs to have your back."

"I have to be there, too." Penny's eyes plead with me. "I want to be close for Tobias."

"I agree." Luca slides deeper into his seat, his expression lax with exhaustion as he leans against the headrest. "There's no way any of us are staying behind."

That's where he's wrong. Everyone else can tag along, but not him. "You're staying."

He straightens. "Me? Why?"

"From what I'm told, you've got a fucking bleed on the brain. You're not getting in a jet."

"Like hell I'm not."

Penny glances from me to Luca and back again, her mouth opening in panic. "Then we'll drive. It can't be that far. By the time everyone gets to the airport, we could already be well on our way." She pushes to her feet. "We can meet you there."

"It's a fucking long drive. And Luca's in no shape to do it." Hunt snaps the fridge door shut and returns to the group. "From the look of him, he needs about a month's worth of rest and a saline drip. Driving nine hours is the last thing he should be doing."

"I can handle it." Luca scowls. "I've had more sleep in the last twenty-four than any of you."

"Nine hours?" Layla's panic increases. "Won't we already be on our way home with Stella by then?"

Benji grabs her hand and she falls silent with the touch.

"Yes." I keep my tone confident despite the lack of emotion to back it up. "It's a waste of time to drive."

"It's a waste of time sitting here with my thumb up my ass while you guys go without me." Luca pins me with a stare. "I'm driving. You can take Pen in the jet. And if everything is squared away before I arrive, I'll just turn around and come back. As soon as I know the kids are safe, I can find a hotel and rest."

"I'm not letting you drive on your own." Penny pushes to her feet. "I'll help. We can take shifts."

"Says the woman who not only doesn't have a license, but is legally dead as far as the cops are concerned." Luca winces as he moves to stand beside her. "It's not a good idea."

"Do you even have a car?" Decker asks.

"Shit." Luca meets my gaze, his lips kicking in a faint smile. "Can we take the Porsche?"

"Don't push your luck." I jerk my head toward the garage. "Use the Escalade."

He nods and leads Penny to the far hall. "I'll go home first and pack supplies. Keep us posted on any developments."

"Now what?" Keira asks. "What do we do?"

"Get ready to fly," is the only response I have. This is new territory. The fragility of having children targeted doesn't sit well with me. The constant nausea is growing old.

"What do you mean?" Layla stands, Benji following close behind. "What do we need to pack? What should I take?"

I don't know. I have no fucking clue what my sister should bring.

"Pack some things for Stella," Anissa answers for me. "A change of clothes. A hairbrush. Maybe even her pillow or a plush toy so she has something familiar to cuddle on the flight home."

God, she's a fucking angel. A spiteful warrior of an angel, but heaven-sent nonetheless.

"Maybe even some comfort food," she adds. "Bring her favorite packet of crisps or candy. It's usually the little things that help life return to normal."

Layla glances at me for confirmation.

"You need to hurry." I jerk my chin at her. "The jet won't take long to get on the flight schedule. I don't want to be here any longer than necessary."

"What about us?" Hunter grates. "What are we packing for?"

I pause a second, not wanting my sisters to be privy to my thoughts. But it's another Band-Aid that needs to be ripped off. If they're tagging along, I can't hide them behind a shield of pretense forever. I don't have the disposable energy.

I start for the hall leading to my bedroom. "We plan for war and pack accordingly."

13

COLE

It takes two hours to get in the air.

Benji and Layla are seated at the front of the cabin facing Decker and Keira across the small serving table. Hunter and Sarah are in the plush leather seats behind them, while Nissa and I sit toward the back of the jet, side by side along the right wall.

The aircraft has barely leveled out after takeoff when my cell vibrates with a text image from a private number.

I cradle the device in my hand for long moments, staring at Tobias and Stella asleep in what looks to be the back seat of an old sedan.

They seem peaceful. Unharmed. Their faces are free from bruises or scratches. But the fact they've slept through their abduction in the middle of the day speaks highly of the amount of sedatives coursing through their systems.

The children are fine. We have moved them into our home and placed them together in a spare room. They're still resting peacefully. I will contact you again once they wake. Emmanuel.

The message aligns with the old man's MO—kind, placating. Yet no phone number is given. My hands are tied in a one-sided conversation.

More than an hour later, I stare out the window across the cabin of the jet, still seeing nothing but those sleeping faces.

The carelessness toward their lives consumes me.

The danger.

I'm livid at the neglect.

"We'll get them home safely." Nissa fidgets in her chair, playing with the recline. "The continued communication is a good start."

"You don't believe that." I keep my voice low, not wanting anyone to overhear. "You haven't relaxed in the slightest since I received that text."

I didn't show the photo to anyone else. I kept it between us, not wanting to add fuel to the hysteria, and I'll continue to do so for as long as I can.

"That's nothing new. I haven't relaxed since you banged down my apartment door two days ago."

It's another lie. The image put her on edge, and I've been talking myself out of questioning her about it, not wanting to face whatever hint she's picked up on that I missed. But I can't ignore it any longer.

"Tell me what you see." I retrieve my cell from my suit jacket and bring the image back on screen. "What have I missed?"

"Nothing." She doesn't look at the device.

"Nothing?" I hold it higher, breaching her line of sight. "You see nothing?"

She cringes, her brows pulling tight. "Put it away."

"Why? I thought you were meant to be helping."

"I am." She shoots me a glance. "Keeping a level head is imperative. We need to remain positive."

I lean onto our joined armrest and she stiffens. "I'm not positive in the slightest. And it doesn't take a genius to figure you aren't either. I know you, little fox, and there's something in this picture you're not telling me."

Her eyes turn sad as she releases a long breath.

"*Tell me,*" I demand, drawing the attention of Hunter, who glances over the back of his chair toward us.

She waits as he scowls at her, not saying a word until I shoot him a warning glare to mind his own business.

"Come on, Nis." I attempt a softer approach. "What is it? What do you see?"

"I see what Emmanuel wants me to see." Her voice is low, barely audible over the hum of the aircraft. "I see two children peacefully sleeping in the back of an old car. Both, presumably, in the clothes they wore to bed. Both snuggled close in a show of shared affection."

I keep eyeing her, waiting for more. "And?"

"I also see what the picture lacked." She doesn't elaborate—just fucking leaves me hanging.

"It's dangerous to withhold information from me right now." Especially when I trust her judgment and the only thing she's giving me to go on is raised apprehension. "Tell me before I lose my temper."

She glares. "Don't threaten me. I've heard so many from you that they're no longer effective."

"Then maybe I need to graduate to action instead of words."

She holds my stare, one brow raised in a complete lack of fear. She won't bow down to my aggression. Not this time.

Fuck.

"*Please,*" I grind between clenched teeth. "Just fucking tell me."

508

Her expression changes with each of my labored heartbeats. Her eyes lose their hardness. Her mouth gentles. By the time she gives a hard swallow what beams back at me is sickening pity.

Shit.

She didn't withhold information to be a bitch. She was attempting to protect me.

"I see a photo that could've been easily staged." She holds my gaze, barely blinking. "I see subtle smudges of dirt on their pajamas and what looks to be blood on Tobias's toes."

I drag my cell closer, narrowing my attention on what she's pointed out. The blindingly obvious now stares back at me.

"I noticed how both their heads are bowed, supposedly in sleep," she continues. "However, it could be an attempt to hide sightless eyes and gaping mouths. What I see, Cole, is a photo that lacks proof of life. And because it was taken while they were still in that car, even if he didn't delete the image data, the GPS co-ordinates won't lead us to where they are now. Only where they were."

The icy chill of death sinks into me, coating my skin in thickening grime. They can't be dead. If I've contributed to the murder of my niece and half-brother, I'll—

"My observations mean nothing, Cole." Anissa places her hand on my wrist, the warmth breathing the slightest sense of life back into me. "Emmanuel had no obligation to send you anything at all. But he did. That alone is enough to leave me hopeful."

"He could be trying to give me a false sense of security."

She cringes "Yes."

"They could already be dead."

Her brows deepen, her gentle fingers sliding back and forth along my skin. "No more than we thought they could've been before. That photo changed nothing. We're no better or worse than we were. We're just the same." She's silent a moment. A bump of turbulence shuffles us closer together. She opens her mouth to speak again, then stops.

"What?" I frown. "What were you going to say?"

Her hand retreats as she sits taller. "With one phone call, this could all be over. Let me get in contact with the Sacramento—"

"No." I know exactly where this is going—straight into unwanted territory. "Don't bring it up again."

"Please, Cole. If you let me reach out to the local authorities, they could handle this. They're far more equipped—"

"Of course they are. Not only to retrieve the children but to dig deep on why the fuck this happened in the first place." I lock my cell and shove it back into my pocket. "Tell me, Nis, do you have an appropriate story to tell about why Robert would've arranged this? Because I'm sure the asshole who drove those kids away from my house wouldn't take the full blame."

She presses her mouth together in indignation.

"The fun will begin once they tie Robert to my father. Then discover my old man is missing." I don't withhold the antagonism from my voice. "What happens when they dig deep enough to figure out he's dead? Do you have an appropriate story for why you pulled the trigger and didn't report the death?"

She sits back in her seat, turning her focus to the opposite wall of the cabin to cross her arms over her chest.

"It's not such a great idea anymore, is it?" I taunt. "That easy call isn't so easy after all."

Her jaw ticks.

"Believe me, Nissa, if I could get those kids out of there without having to wait, I'd fucking do it. But I'm not risking the freedom of everyone on this jet."

I can't.

It might not be the best call, but it's one I can live with.

Everyone here should be behind bars. Nobody would be spared. Then who would look after Stella and Tobias? They'd be no better than they are now.

She doesn't answer me.

Not while I stare at her, and not after I settle back into my seat and wait out the remaining minutes until we start our descent.

I don't hear anything else from Emmanuel by the time we land. There's no destination point. No cell number. I'm unable to contact him, and he sure as shit doesn't seem in a hurry to contact me again.

"Pretend everything is fine." Anissa tugs on a baseball cap she took from my house as we disembark onto the tarmac of the private airport. "Don't let anyone know you're worried."

I scoff. Not because she's wrong, but because she's homed in on my increased anxiety.

"Easier said than done when we've got nowhere to go. I can't even call this asshole."

"You'll figure something out." She walks ahead, her head hung low as she follows behind the airport staffer who carries the only duffle that doesn't contain anything illegal, along with wheeling Anissa's suitcase.

The pilots will take care of the weapons, either bypassing security or waiting until they can pay someone for the privilege.

It isn't until we're out the other side of the airport, our belongings piled onto a trolley at my side, waiting for our rental cars to pull up, that I notice I have an audience.

Everyone watches me—Hunt, Deck, Sarah, and Benji, waiting for instruction, while my sisters blink at me with silent questions. Anissa stands alone a few feet behind us, remaining an outsider as she keeps her head hung, attempting to shield her face from any cameras.

"We're going to find a hotel." I deliberately keep my attention from Keira and Layla. "We'll freshen up and get something to eat. I want to get a lay of the land first. Sacramento isn't what I'd call an even playing field, and we need to make sure we know what we're up against."

"I don't want to freshen up." Layla glances between me and Benji, as if waiting for support. "I want to see my daughter."

"I agree," Keira adds. "We could spend days trying to get familiar with this city. It's a waste of time."

"I said, we're going to a hotel. Regardless of your protests, I've already told you you're not coming to pick them up, so you'll need somewhere to wait."

There's a beat of tense silence before Anissa steps forward. "I'll book the rooms. Do you have any preferences?"

"I'll do it." Sarah backs away from the huddle, grabbing her cell from her jeans pocket. "I already know the drill."

"I know I didn't protest back home about coming with you to pick them up," Layla starts. "But I want to be there. I'm her mother. I should be the first to comfort her."

Anissa shakes her head. "It's best not to—"

"Stay out of this," Layla snaps, jabbing her finger in Anissa's direction. "I've been patient and haven't questioned your sudden involvement. But don't mistake my silence for friendship. Don't even mistake it for civility. You don't belong here."

I narrow my eyes on my sister. "She's helping us."

"Exactly." Layla returns the accusing stare. "She's a *Fed*, yet she's helping us. How can you trust her?"

Anissa looks at me in confusion. Then dawning shock.

She's finally realizing I kept her secret.

I made no effort to clear up the assumption that I killed my father instead of her. And I've also ensured the news would never be exposed by Penny and Luca, as long as the two of them want to remain breathing.

"Send her home, Cole." Hunter follows after Sarah. "She brings nothing to the team."

A crowd of subtle nodding heads bob before me—Decker, Keira, Benji, and Layla all in agreement.

They don't see what I see.

They don't understand the asset. The impeccable resource.

She's much more than that, too, but they're definitely not going to appreciate the chemistry or history that cements Anissa as part of this team.

I'm about to open my mouth and put them in their places when Anissa squares her shoulders, a mask of no-shits-given settling into place.

"You don't want to send me home." Her voice is authoritative. It's the determined confidence I appreciate more than gold. "From what I can tell, I'm the only one here who has slept in the past twenty-four hours. I'm also the only one who isn't emotionally involved. And this isn't my first rodeo."

Her tone is almost a taunt of superiority. A casual *fuck you* to her haters. "You *need* me. Not just for clarity, but for common sense. You have no contacts here. You've got no connections. I can make things happen if your wrong-side-of-the-tracks agenda doesn't pan out."

She fascinates me with her confident tirade. I'm fucking drained beyond belief, but I'm impressed.

"Anyone require me to reiterate what Anissa put so eloquently?" I glare at everyone in turn. "I'm going to lose my temper real fast if we have to continue going over the reasons for her involvement."

They remain quiet, their protests contained to returned glares.

"I just don't understand why we're waiting," Layla breaks the silence. "Why can't we get them now?"

"Because we're not ready." Anissa steps closer to the road as three Escalades pull up in front of us. "Cole needs to strategize. Contingencies have to be made. So we'll go to a hotel and make a plan. As soon as we're ready, we can move."

I walk for the man getting out of the first car, exchange the necessary pleasantries, and catch the key fob he throws at me.

"Nissa, you're with me." I make eye contact with Decker over the hood. "You, Keira, Benji, and Layla are in the next car. Followed by Sarah and Hunt, who will take the luggage."

I don't wait for another protest as I climb into the Escalade and start the engine. Anissa joins me in seconds, clasping her belt and letting out a sigh.

"You did well." I don't look at her. I place my hands on the steering wheel, denying myself the pleasure of reaching out. "They might not like you, but they respect you."

She huffs out a laugh. "Hunter doesn't respect me. Neither does Decker."

"You have a past with Decker." One I don't care to remember. "And Hunter is beyond loyal to him. They'll never be kind but they're not threatening to kill you."

"At least not to my face."

I grin and start the engine. "True."

"Lucky me."

There's a tap on her window. Sarah's face comes into view. "We're staying at the Saffron Towers in the city." She speaks through the glass. "I booked two rooms to give us a little breathing space. See you there."

She walks away and Anissa lets out another sigh.

"The space is a good idea," I offer, hoping to address whatever added to her discomfort. "It also shows that you've got Sarah on your side."

"She's not on my side. She's just..." She shakes her head.

"What?"

She looks at me, her confidence gradually returning. "Smart. She knows I'm an asset."

"Yeah, well, she's not the only one." I jerk my chin toward the navigation system. "Do me a favor and figure out where we're going."

She does as instructed, leaning forward to tap at the small screen until an automated voice directs me to take the first left up ahead.

"What are we going to do once we get to the hotel?" She settles back into her seat.

"We're going to share the photo of the kids to buy us some time, and if Emmanuel hasn't reached out after that, then we pray."

14

ANISSA

COLE MENTIONS HIS NAME TO THE VALET AND WE'RE IMMEDIATELY TREATED LIKE royalty. Our escort beams a bright smile as he leads us into the hotel foyer while our travel companions are lost somewhere in traffic.

"I'll show you to your room, Mr. Torian. Would you like any bags brought up?"

"No." Cole strides ahead of me, not showing any of the concern I have for the bags of illegal weapons soon to arrive.

I didn't realize the extent of the arsenal we brought along with us until Cole enlightened me on the drive here. Guns, sniper rifles, and ammo are encased in those bags, escorted by Hunter and Sarah. And my FBI allocated weapon is right there with them.

What if they're pulled over? Their car searched?

I'm not sure how these people live with the threat of prison on a daily basis. I've already accumulated enough paranoid arrhythmia to set me on a collision course for heart failure. But Cole lives with this daily. The adrenaline. The naive thrill.

We're led into the elevator. Our escort even handles the button to our floor and we ascend in silence. It isn't until the red neon floor indicator dings our arrival on the penthouse floor that all my accumulated arrhythmia becomes a threatening panic attack.

"The penthouse?" I follow the men into the wide hall, the glistening lights above kissing their features in a gentle way fluorescents never could.

"That's right." The escort stops, turns, and glances between Cole and I. "Isn't this what was requested?"

"Yes." Cole continues forward without pause. "Make sure our companions get a spare key to our room."

"No problem, sir." The young man nods and jogs ahead, beating Cole to the door to open it with an elegant sweep of his arm. "I hope your stay is enjoyable."

I pass both men as Cole arranges a tip. I peek my head into the room along the hall, finding an immaculate bedroom, the massive bed crisp, the furnishings well above my pay grade, and the view... Even from the hall it's nothing but open skyline.

"Come on." Cole walks by me into the open living area.

"The penthouse?" I follow. "We're not staying the night, are we? Why would you need the penthouse?"

I reach the end of the hall, the breath leaving my lungs at the pristine elegance. There are two corner sofas in the middle of the room, facing floor-to-ceiling glass doors leading onto a balcony with more expensive furniture.

There are flower-filled vases, as well as artwork, and a massive television.

The kitchen has appliances I've never even seen before, the sparkling stainless steel gleaming in the sunlight.

"Kick off your shoes and rest for a while." Cole continues to the doorway across the opposite side of the room. "The others will be here soon."

The temptation of taking off these two-inch heels and sinking my toes into the thick carpet is too strong. I slide my shoes against the side of the sofa and groan with the freedom as Cole disappears into unexplored territory.

I don't follow this time. I'm sure the main bedroom is in there and it's not a place I want to be alone with him.

Not when my sympathy for this crime-hardened man is growing.

I need to reassess the walls I've placed between us and make them stronger. Thicker. I have to Great Wall of China this shit and ensure no unwanted emotions breach the perimeter.

I faintly hear the grate of a zipper, which electrocutes my pulse due to the accompanying heated thoughts.

The unmistakable sound of fluid hitting fluid thankfully sucks all the eroticism from my mind.

There's a flush of the toilet, the rush of water from the faucet, then silence.

The quiet stretches long enough to make me curious to investigate, the space between the sofa and the bedroom bridged in creeping footsteps.

I reach the threshold and suck in another breath at the view. This time, the awe is male-inspired. Cole is laid out on the bed, his shoes and suit still on, his hands behind his head.

He's at home amongst the luxury. A perfectly fit piece.

I can't help admiring the sight. The calm amid the storm. The oozing sexuality which needs to be smothered by professionalism.

He lowers his chin to meet my gaze, his eyes tired, yet so fucking captivating.

"You seem nervous, little fox." His tone is smooth, calm, with that infinite cockiness threaded beneath. "Why? Do you fear a carnal repeat of Greece?"

I don't want to humor him, but the innuendo needs to be smacked from his consciousness. "Not at all."

He raises a brow and sits, sliding his feet to the floor. I prepare for him to continue the taunts. Instead, his shoulders slump as his hands fall to the bed coverings. He stares at the carpet, his exhaustion creeping into my chest.

I ache to help him. To make this easier.

No. I need to build walls.

Many, many walls.

"That's probably for the best." He pushes to his feet. "As much as I want to fuck you, I don't think I could bring my A-game right now."

My abdomen squeezes.

Goddamn wrings tight.

It's pathetic.

"A-game?" I drawl as he starts toward me. "I think I've only ever experienced the lackluster version."

A grin is slow to spread his lips. "Is that so?"

Shit. I shouldn't have bitten back.

I swallow, hating myself a little more with each of his predatory steps.

"Don't taunt me, Nis." He stops beside me, his shoulder brushing mine. "I might just be willing to muster enough energy to prove you wrong."

My pulse flutters. A million tiny butterfly wings rapidly bat beneath my ribs.

"You should order room service," he instructs. "When the others arrive, I'm going to need something to keep their mouths occupied."

He continues into the living room as if he didn't just treat me like the hired help.

I don't follow. I remain rooted in place, taking necessary calming breaths.

The others will be here soon.

I don't need to worry about a lengthy isolation with him. With my feelings. With my desires. But the risks claw at me nonetheless.

Seeing him like this is a double-edged sword. The drained, vulnerable Cole is just as alluring as the man who threatens me into a frenzy of lust and carnality.

This man, with his palpable weariness, makes me ache for him because not once has he shown weakness despite his belly being exposed.

He remains a force to be reckoned with. A lethal, conniving soul. And I hate how drawn I am to those parts of him. I'm smothered with attraction even though the facets of his world I despise the most are painted before me in broad strokes.

These feelings aren't normal.

I'm not normal.

"Food, Nissa," he barks behind me, lighting the fuse to my agitation.

I swing around, hands clenched, cheeks flaming. "Who the hell died and made me your bitch?" I raise my voice. "I'm a fucking FBI agent, asshole, not the catering staff."

He smirks as he sits on the sofa, then lays down, mimicking his relaxed position from the bed, only this time his arm moves to cover his eyes. I can still see those lips though, and that conniving son of a bitch maintains the slightest grin.

"You're *a* bitch. *The* bitch. *My* bitch." He crosses his feet at the ankles. "But I wasn't treating you like a servant. I thought you might be hungry, so I disguised my demand for you to eat in a request to order food for everyone. Excuse me for caring."

Well, great. Now I feel like trash.

It doesn't matter that his execution was utter idiocy—his motives were thoughtful.

Through this whole ordeal, he's still taken time to remember *my* needs and *my* sustenance while I stand here struggling to remind myself of the bigger picture through the haze of lust.

"Fine," I mumble. "I'll order the damn food." I glance around the huge space, searching for a phone or menu.

"Kitchen," he drawls, not even raising his arm to look at me.

Damn mind reader.

I pad toward the sparkling stainless steel and round the marble counter, finding the phone beside the fridge and the menu in a drawer. I'm finger sliding through the list of mouthwatering food items when a knock sounds at the door.

"Come in," Cole yells.

The blood drains from my face. I reach for a gun that isn't there. "Are you serious?" I hiss. "That could be anyone."

We're in a foreign city, with foreign threats. This isn't well-known Portland territory.

"Untwist your panties. It's Hunt and the others. They messaged while I was in the bedroom."

The door opens and the familiar mumble of deep voices down the hall has me relaxing my tense muscles.

"You still couldn't have known," I say in defense. "Anyone could walk through that door. So don't do something this reckless again. Not when my safety is in jeopardy."

Hunter and Sarah wheel my suitcase in as I finish my tirade, followed by Decker, Keira, Layla, then Benji, who carries one of the duffels.

"What's going on?" Hunt asks.

Cole shoves to his feet in my periphery, his air of increasing authority building as he approaches. "Bear with me a moment," he growls when he passes them. "Anissa and I need to get one thing straight."

He storms forward, making every inch of me stiffen at his ferocity while our audience watches. Those hard eyes slay me, almost buckle me. He stops in my personal space.

"They followed us to the fucking hotel," he snarls. "They messaged me to say they were here." He leans closer, forcing me to backtrack into the counter.

I should be hating his dominance, despising the demeaning way he talks to me in front of everyone. Instead, my lips tingle, my nipples ache.

I *have to* hate this.

Oh, God, how I have to hate this.

"They even had a fucking key," he enunciates slowly. "Not now, or ever, will I take uneducated guesses. I protect what's mine. I'm not careless with—" He stops, his gaze boring into me, his mouth hinging open a crack.

I hold my breath, struggling to understand what I've done to end the tirade, but then his shoulders lose their stiffness and his face washes clean of the confident aggression.

Have his words come back to bite him? Does he think he's been careless with those children? Does he hold himself responsible?

Yes. I can see it in the slight pinch to his brows. In the uncomfortable scrunch of his nose.

My stomach twists with more unwanted sympathy as eerie silence suffocates the air.

He can't show weakness now. Not in front of his sister, who is resting her daughter's life on his shoulders. Or his men, who need to follow his example.

They're all depending on him to lead them out of this. He has to remain strong.

"I get it. You're the fearless Cole Torian," I seethe back in his face, hoping to resuscitate his conviction. "How could I forget the way you've built an empire on bloodshed and brutality?"

I'm attempting to remind him. Inspire him.

But his stiffness doesn't return. He's still lost in guilt, his gaze unfocused on my cheek.

"Next time, fill me in on what's happening." I inch closer, smothering his personal space, the hair on my arms prickling from the attention of our captivated audience. "I'm not one of your minions who will blindly follow where you lead."

I begin to turn, hoping to end the awkwardness by ordering food, but he grabs the crook of my arm, forcing me back in place, demanding my gaze to his with nothing more than a heated stare.

I shiver. Shudder. Everything inside me quakes under his attention, and I'm sure he feels it.

"Mark my words, little fox." His lips are cruel as his grip tightens. "You *will* follow me blindly. One way or another."

I know I will.

I already do.

He releases my arm and stalks away, shoving past Hunter and Benji to escape into the bedroom, slamming the door behind him.

I don't move. Don't weaken.

I stare at the far wall as Decker mutters something under his breath and limps his way to the sofa. The others begin to follow, allowing me a few moments to close my eyes and slump against the counter to gain composure.

I'm not sure how much longer I can do this.

I'm straddling too many emotions, each one spreading me in a different direction. The calm self-assurance that has accompanied me my entire career is no longer here to depend on. I've got nothing but instability.

"Are you okay?"

Keira's voice snaps me out of my mental shelter.

I straighten and busy myself by reaching for the room service menu. "I'm fine."

"My brother can be pig-headed sometimes."

I huff out a laugh. "Sometimes?" I shoot her a two-second glance. It's a mistake.

Her eyes are kind. Bloodshot and puffy, but gloriously, sympathetically kind.

"There's something between you two, isn't there?" she asks. "Something that makes more sense than the convoluted excuses he's given me about you working together for mutual gain. He doesn't usually lie to me. But I have a feeling he is when it comes to you because he's too tight-lipped."

"I guess it's nice to know something can shut him up."

She gives a sad smile, not buying my attempt at humor. "You know, in my entire life, I've never seen a woman stand up to him like you just did."

I zero in on the menu. The clear-cut words and the crisp white paper. I focus on everything except her admission that's likely to weaken me further. "That's a real shame. Maybe if more women didn't bow down to his smarmy arrogance he wouldn't be such a raging asshole."

"Not only that," she continues, "but I've never seen him walk away from a heated exchange as if he'd lost the fight. And then to hide in his room? That's quite a feat."

My throat tightens. "What can I say? Cole and I have a special sort of toxic relationship only the best of enemies can have."

"Enemies?" I hear the smile in her voice. "Is that really what you are?"

No. "Yes." My response is rapid, and regretted just as quickly. I bit out the lie with too much guilt.

She gives a breathy chuckle, raising the hairs on the back of my neck. I can feel her gaze on me. The narrowing eyes. The scrutiny.

"I know I wanted you to leave earlier, but…" She shrugs in my periphery. "I think that might have been a mistake. Having you here means a lot. We could use someone like you around more often—"

"No." I turn to face her. "Don't even waste your breath. This is a one-time thing. I'm morally obligated to help with those kids. But that's it. Afterwards, I'm done." I snatch the menu from the counter and walk forward to hand it over. "You should order some food. Everyone needs to keep their energy up."

I maneuver around her and take a hard right down the hall, moving away from the quiet conversation to escape into the far bedroom, then farther into the adjoining bathroom.

I wash my face in the basin, over and over again, wishing I could scrub free from reality. But as soon as I turn off the faucet, I hear Cole's voice—the unmistakable growl that collars and enslaves me.

I dry myself with a hand towel and return to the bedroom to sit on the edge of the king-size mattress, listening to him speak. There's no longer any weakness in his tone as he informs them of the photo he received. He's so fucking strong and sure of himself, his authority a commanding force.

He continues talking as someone sobs. He outlines possible strategies for the pick-up of the children. He mentions the names of those who will accompany him, and I'm disappointed to hear I'm not one of them.

Questions are thrown at him. Suggestions are offered. More sobs filter down the hall.

I bow my head, a slave to my unwavering admiration of a criminal, and pull out my cell as a distraction technique.

I do an internet search on Emmanuel Costa, determined to lose myself in the long list of results.

I skim through details of his fashion empire, find out he's a majority shareholder in innumerable well-known companies. He has no fixed address, but owns a rolodex worth of properties around the country and the globe.

Born from poor parents. Father to four children—three boys and a girl. All offspring follow in their papa's footsteps.

I don't find any ties to Sacramento. No real estate ownership or businesses. But all it would take is one text to Easton. One quick question to get him to do a search on the Bureau's database.

I'm tempted.

I clear the browser and open my messages, clicking on his name. I stare for long moments, battling indecision.

Is it worth the risk?

"What are you doing?" Cole asks from the doorway.

"Jesus Christ." The cell fumbles from my hand, falling to the floor. "Did you deliberately sneak up on me?"

"I called your name. Twice." He stalks forward and scoops up my phone, his face hardening as he stares at the screen. "Miss him already? You couldn't even last a few hours?"

I push to my feet and attempt to snatch the device back, only to have it held out of reach. "That's real mature." I try again. "Give it back."

"What did you plan on sending to him?"

"That's none of your business."

He glares. "Like hell it isn't. If you jeopardize Tobias and Stella's safety, I'll ensure you regret it. Or maybe you've already contacted him. Did you send him a message and delete it?

"No." I hold my head high. "I haven't contacted him."

"But you want to." He scrolls through my screen, probably checking past messages that would clearly outline our platonic relationship. "You would've if I hadn't interrupted."

I don't respond. There's no point. He's in a mood I don't want to trifle with.

"What is it about him?" he murmurs. "What could you possibly find attractive in such a pathetic man? I thought you were smarter than that."

I keep my lips shut, not indulging his jealousy spiral.

"Maybe I should keep this." He holds up the phone, taunting me. "Just in case you're tempted to get in contact with him again."

"Just in case I'm tempted?" I raise a brow. "Or just to appease your jealousy?" He needs to get this out of his system. I may have used my partner as a shield, but we can no longer afford the distraction. "Keep the phone if you think it's the only way you can get between me and Easton."

"Oh, I could do a lot of things aside from taking away your phone, Nis. Trust me."

I start toward the hall. "I don't doubt it. But right here, right now, it's your frantic attempt to stop me talking to someone who threatens you." I pause in the doorway and glance at him over my shoulder.

"Do *not* contact him again while you're with me," he warns.

"And if I do?" It's such a stupid question. Taunting. Provoking. I can't help it.

"If you do?" He swings around, storms toward me, not stopping until I'm backed into the wooden threshold. He pins me with his body—no hands, just hips. And eyes. God, those captivating eyes.

He breathes heavily, the rise and fall of his chest brushing against mine.

There are no more taunts left in me. Only heat. Desire.

I ache to drop this charade. I burn with the need to kiss him.

I sink my teeth into my bottom lip to soothe the tingle, only increasing my suffering when his gaze lowers to my mouth.

Memories from Greece haunt me. The flashbacks of pleasure and passion weaken my knees.

"You might be with him, but you still need me." He pockets my cell. "You fucking want me, Nissa."

I close my eyes, hoping he'll bridge the connection and praying he won't. My desire is potent enough to push the air from my lungs, leaving me starved for oxygen.

"You're with him." He leans closer. "But I'm the one who makes you burn."

It's true. Not the being with Easton part, but the burning. The flames lick higher with every passing second. Scorching. Scarring.

My hands find his pecs. I don't know how. I didn't put them there. I couldn't have. Some unknown force has my limbs working without my direction, tangling my fingers in the silken material of his shirt.

"Say it," he growls. "Fucking tell me you want me."

I shake my head.

I won't.

I refuse.

"Have it your way."

His heat vanishes, my arms falling back to my side as he retreats.

I swallow, desperate for the heat to return. The energy. The life. But he doesn't slow his pace.

"Cole." I push from the threshold and grab his arm.

He turns willingly, his menacing frame seeming so much bigger when I'm practically begging for his attention. He glares down at me, nostrils flaring.

I don't fight it any more. I go to him, surrendering, raising onto the tips of my toes to plaster my mouth against his.

I expect a refusal. At least a fight. Instead, his hands claim me. Tight in my hair. Harsh against my hip.

He walks into me, leading me backward, slamming my ass into the wall as his mouth devours mine.

I can't breathe. Can't think.

There's only sensation. Mindless, consuming sensation that starts in my toes and ends at my lips.

The feelings I held for him in Greece come flooding back. Not just the passion, but the connection. The emotion. The unbearable devotion.

My heart yearns for more as he grabs my waist and lifts me, forcing my legs to circle his hips as he grinds me into the wall. The friction is heaven and hell. Relief and increased torture.

One of his hands lowers and he fumbles with something. His belt? His zipper?

I'm about to pull away, panicked at the possibility of him attempting to remove clothes, when he deepens the kiss, making me clutch at his shoulders for support.

I gasp against his mouth. Mewl into the connection.

I claw at his suit. Scratch and tug.

The trap of mindlessness has reeled me in, closing me into its cocoon. I don't care. Not anymore. I just want this. *Only* this.

Someone clears their throat nearby and I gasp, suddenly pushing instead of pulling, shoving instead of yanking.

"I should've brought a hose." Hunter glares at me. "I didn't expect to find you two at it like dogs."

Cole retreats slowly, waiting for me to find my feet. "What do you want?"

"Room service is here. But it looks as though you're already enjoying an unhealthy snack." Hunter continues to visually berate me for long seconds while the scent of deep-fried food fills the space in my lungs where intoxicating after-shave once lived.

"Keep your mouth shut," Cole warns. "We'll be there in a minute."

Hunter scoffs yet follows the command, marching down the hall.

As soon as his back is turned, I quit fighting the need to heave in deep breaths, my cheeks flaming red-hot.

I don't know whether to feel ashamed or relieved over finally giving in.

"You should eat." Cole turns away from me, lowering his attention to my cell now cradled in his hand, his fingers tapping the screen.

"What are you doing?" I step closer, attempting to see, but he hands over the phone, giving me a clear view of the new message he sent to Easton.

A fucking video.

"What have you done?" I snatch the device and play the recording, feeling all the euphoric goodness slide from my soul one slow inch at a time.

"I'm claiming what's mine." He walks away as I watch myself on the screen, my lips plastered to Cole's, my hands clutching his shoulders.

He recorded us.

He fucking recorded us and sent it to Easton.

"You son of a bitch." I storm after him. My chest tightens with the betrayal. My heart beats in a rigorous frenzy at the thought of the repercussions. "Why the hell would you do that?"

"I already told you." He keeps walking, his stride confident, his shoulders strong and sure. "Now he knows the truth."

"The truth?" I scream. "No, this doesn't show the truth. It doesn't tell him how much of a fucking thoughtless, psychopathic idiot you are."

I throw my cell at him, my rage increasing when he easily leans out of the projectile's path. The phone ricochets off the wall, clapping to the tile floor.

"You're a fucking asshole," I choke out.

He inclines his head. "Yes. But you already knew that before you threw yourself at me."

I gape, stuck for words, filled with shame.

He continues into the living room, the attention of everyone falling on us as I follow close behind.

I want to strangle him. To fucking slaughter.

But he isn't wrong.

I threw myself at him. *I* latched on to his shoulders like a monkey starved of affection.

"You're a sick son of a bitch." My words are barely audible. "You deliberately—"

"Stop it." Layla raises her voice. "Both of you, just *stop*." Tears streak her cheeks as she glances between us, wide-eyed. "Stella is missing and you two are wasting time arguing. Where is my daughter, Cole? Why can't you put as much energy into finding her as you do fighting this woman?"

Benji wraps a hand around her waist. "It's okay. He's—"

"*No*, it's *not* okay." She steps out of reach. "None of this is okay. Not that those innocent children are missing. Or that we're in this godforsaken city waiting to hear from a man we know nothing about. And it sure as hell isn't okay that we've got a Fed here watching our every move. I don't even know what I can and can't say, because I'm waiting for her to arrest me."

"She's not going to arrest you." Cole strolls for the mass of food on the coffee table and picks up a chip from a pile of nachos. "Sit down. Eat. Try to relax."

"Don't dictate to me. Don't for one second think I don't hold you accountable. *You* made us attend that function at the restaurant. *You* gave Robert the opportunity to attack." She jabs a finger in his direction as everyone remains quiet. "*You* promised all of us we would be safe."

He eats the chip, dusts his hands, and takes her vehemence without a flinch.

I just wish I couldn't sense his underlying torment.

"Are you finished?" His face remains impassive, his tone perfectly balanced.

"You know what? Anissa's right." She flicks a glance my way before returning her attention to him. "You're a fucking ass—"

"Yes, I'm a fucking asshole. I'm fucking responsible. The fate of those kids rests on my fucking shoulders." There's no waver in his voice, only an increase in volume that vibrates into my chest. "I fucking know all that, Layla. But have you ever wondered if this would've happened if you hadn't sold me out to Robert?"

"She did what?" Keira gasps.

I have no idea what he's talking about. And the only response comes from a subtle vibration of a silenced cell.

"I'll let your sister fill you in." Cole starts toward me, reaching into his pants pocket to pull out his phone. "Emmanuel," he says in greeting. "Where the fuck are you?"

15

COLE

I SHUT MYSELF INTO THE MAIN BATHROOM, CLENCHING THE CELL IN MY FIST.

"I'm in Sacramento, son. Have you arrived yet?"

"I arrived a fucking hour ago. I've been waiting for your call. I don't have your damn number."

"Ahh, yes. I forgot my details are blocked. Sorry. Technology isn't my friend."

Bullshit. Fucking bullshit.

"Where are you? Where are the kids?" I pace, not appreciating his chilled tone. He's too relaxed to be concerned for their safety. He's too fucking smug.

I don't trust this piece of shit. Not in the slightest.

"They are here with me. Safe and well. To tell you the truth, my wife has become quite smitten. It's been a long time since young ones were under our roof. She's enjoying this immensely."

"Where are they?" I repeat.

"As I said, they are safe. But still very tired. It's best if they remain with us for the night. That way, I get to indulge my wife's maternal instincts. She was a nurse, you see, and she's making sure they're under constant observation due to the sedatives. You should enjoy your time in Sacramento while you wait."

And there it is—the thinly disguised threat.

The extended hostage situation.

The thickening of his plan.

I pace faster. Harder. I gnash my teeth and pray I have the patience to kill this motherfucker slowly. "As you can imagine," I grate, "my family are beside themselves with worry."

"I understand." His accent thickens "But there is no need. My wife assures me the children are perfectly healthy. They have been laughing and playing.

Their smiles are bright when they're with us. We may not be blood, but my friendship with your father ensures we are family."

I press my closed fist against my forehead, pushing harder and harder. "Emmanuel, I insist—"

"Insisting will not help me against my wife's wrath if I return these precious gifts from God too soon." He chuckles. "Trust me, they are in good hands. They are happy. Tomorrow morning we will meet, and they will tell you all about the lovely time they had. Until then, enjoy yourself, Mr. Torian."

"No. This isn't—"

The call disconnects. The hold on my anger goes with it.

I roar, slamming my fist into the tiled wall.

He's starting a fucking war. In unfamiliar territory. I have no leverage here. No assets.

"Cole?" Anissa's voice carries from outside the bathroom. "What is it? What happened?"

I close my eyes and pinch the bridge of my nose. I need to think. I need to figure out how the fuck to get a hold of this asshole.

My cell vibrates. A text message illuminates the screen. A cell number.

What the hell is Emmanuel playing at?

I click the details as the door opens, and connect a call.

Nissa stares at me, one gentle brow raised in question while I plaster the phone to my ear and listen to the monotonous ring.

"Mr. Torian," the fucker answers. "Did you forget something?"

Jesus *fucking* Christ. He's entirely cavalier.

"Listen to me, you son of a bitch." I have to expel all my breath and drag it back in to stop myself from detonating. "I want those kids returned to me. *Now.* Not tomorrow. Not after your wife plays Mary fucking Poppins. *Now.* Tell me where they are."

There's a pause. A frantic beat of silence before his kind tone rockets my rage. "Mr. Torian, your lack of patience is quite disconcerting after I've gone out of my way to help you. But I understand your anxiety. I will send you some more pictures of them to ease your concerns."

Fuck him.

Fuck this pathetic game.

"I don't care about pictures or your fucking wife. If you don't tell me where you are, I'll—"

"You'll what?" Steel enters his tone. "Please, do not mistake my kindness for weakness, child. I do not take well to threats."

There's a pause. One that I can't fill.

I have no power. No fucking move to make.

"I am a man of my word," he continues. "You will see these children tomorrow. But not a moment before. Now please do not call again unless it is urgent. It is not healthy for me to become agitated by such unnecessary concerns."

The line disconnects.

My vision darkens. I raise my arm to throw the phone.

"Cole, don't." Nissa runs at me, grabbing my hand to pry the cell from my fingers. "You need it."

What I need are answers. What I need are those fucking kids.

My breathing quickens. Mindlessness takes over. I can't think clearly through the rapid-fire thoughts screaming in my ears.

My fingers itch to squeeze around that bastard's throat. My arms throb with the need to hear bones crack. I want blood.

"What happened?" Anissa pockets the cell and stares at me in concern.

No, it's pity.

"Nothing." I walk around her and stalk from the bathroom. Every goddamn step toward the living room is a struggle while she remains hot on my heels. What's worse is Layla's face when I enter the room.

She rushes for me. "What did he say? Where do we go to get them?"

I ignore her, meeting Sarah and Keira's gaze over her shoulder. "All the women, out."

"What?" Layla stops before me and grabs my upper arms. "No. I'm not going anywhere."

I sidestep and pin Sarah with a scowl. "Where's the other room you booked?"

"The next level down..." Her voice is hesitant.

"Then get going. Hunt can update you later."

"No." Layla follows after me, still clinging to my arms. "You need to tell me what's going on. Are they okay? Oh, God, did he hurt them?"

"They're both fine." I refuse to meet her gaze. The guilt is suffocating. "Now go."

"No," she screams in my face, slapping a hand across my cheek.

I take the impact without a flinch. I prefer the sting to the ache in my chest.

"Fuck." Benji runs for her as she continues her assault.

Sarah and Keira, too.

They grab her arms as she thrashes and kicks, cursing my name and vowing to never forgive me.

I don't back down. Don't even falter. I lock all the punishing shit inside. Keep it buried deep as I clench every muscle in my body.

"Make sure she's sedated until morning," I direct to Hunter, who remains unmoved on the sofa, throwing a French fry in his mouth as if the suffering of my family is just another fucking Friday on his work calendar.

I wish I was as immune as him. As capable of shutting off emotion.

"No." Layla bucks in Benji's hold. "You can't do this."

"Go." I jerk my chin at Hunter, then turn my attention to Decker, then Benji. "Make sure they're all calm before coming back. The last thing I need is a scene."

They nod, Hunter and Decker stalking toward my sisters like enforcers, wordlessly demanding obedience.

I don't hear a protest from Keira. I feel it instead. Her judgmental gaze bores into the side of my head, slicing deep as she's ushered toward the hall in my periphery.

Layla doesn't need to tell me she will never forgive me for this. I knew she wouldn't as soon as I found Stella's empty bed. This situation has fractured our foundations. Permanently. There's no recovering from the damage that's already been done.

"I hate you, Cole," Layla screams down the hall. "Let me see my daughter."

The door clicks shut moments later. The muffled sounds of my sister's wails haunt me until she leaves the penthouse floor.

I close my eyes against the deafening silence. I breathe deep of the stillness that feels sinister instead of welcoming.

The gentle pad of footsteps approaches. I stiffen farther at the potential of another bitch slap.

"What about me?" Anissa asks softly. "Do you want me to leave?"

I scoff.

I don't get her. I fucking don't.

She wants me, then she doesn't.

She needs me, then shoves me away.

One minute, she hates me. The next, she's all over me just like on our last night in Greece.

I can't figure her out. I doubt I ever will. I think that's half of the appeal.

"Do whatever you like." I open my eyes and scan the room until I find liquor bottles perched on a golden cart near the television. Then it's full steam ahead until the scotch is in my hand, a glass in my fist, and the burning liquid is flowing down my throat.

"Is that a good idea?" She comes up beside me, wreaking havoc with my nerve endings.

"Don't mother me." I pour another finger and throw it back.

"You're exhausted. You're panicked." She reaches for my arm and grips my suit. "Alcohol isn't the answer."

"Then what is?" I snap. "What the fuck is the answer, Nis? Because I'm clueless here."

She takes my fury with the raise of her chin. So confident. So composed.

She's a force I want to lose myself in.

Drown in.

"What happened?" Her hand falls to her side. "What did he say?"

I huff a sarcastic laugh. "That him and his wife are having such a lovely time with my niece and brother that they're going to keep them a little while longer." I fling my arms wide in frustration. "Ain't that fucking nice."

"What do you mean? Is he refusing to release them? Did he threaten you?"

"He's not doing shit. Not threatening, but certainly not playing by the fucking rules. He's messing with me. Pushing. Just wait until I get the chance to push back."

There's a buzz of a cell. *My* cell. Coming from her pants pocket.

She pulls out the device, then meets my gaze. "Can I?"

"By all means." I reach out, unlocking the screen with my fingerprint. She can't fuck up this situation any more than I already have.

I refill my glass as she focuses on the screen.

"I don't understand his strategy." She raises the cell to me, showing a picture of Stella and Tobias in a fancy kitchen, the counter smothered in flour, their hands and faces marred with white smudges as a grey-haired woman grins behind them.

The kids wear new clothes. Fresh. Brand name. Expensive.

But it's their faces that speak the truth.

Even though they smile, there's no joy in their eyes. They know they're being held prisoner. They understand the seriousness of the situation and are playing along.

I look away, my throat tightening. My eyes burn.

I'm going to cause unfathomable bloodshed. I'm going to maim and torture and slaughter. I'll kill every son of a bitch Emmanuel knows.

I slam my glass down on the cart and grab the scotch, drinking heavily from the bottle in the hopes it will dilute the venom in my veins.

"Please stop," Anissa begs. "Please, Cole. I need you to help me with this. I need you to make me understand."

I guzzle the burning liquid until it runs down my chin, the alcohol dripping onto my shirt. My shoes. The carpet.

"Cole." My name is a warning this time. "You're better than this."

I almost choke over her lie and lower the bottle to turn to her. "Am I? Am I fucking better, Nis?"

She snaps rigid at my harsh tone.

Fuck.

I throw the scotch. It smashes against the far wall. Glass scatters, the destruction giving me no satisfaction. "Layla's right. *I* did this. *I'm* responsible."

I stalk toward Anissa, getting in her face. There's no point putting off the inevitable. She needs to commit to hating me. I want her to despise me as much as I despise myself. To loathe me. To fucking run.

"I'm the reason they were taken. I'm the one who has to live with the guilt of the nightmares they'll endure until the day they die." I let out a bark of laughter. "And that's if they live at all. Who knows what this sick fuck is capable of?"

She reaches for me. "It's not your fault."

"Fuck off." I back away. "You know it is. It's just more ammunition for you to pile against me."

"No. You're not responsible, Cole. You didn't do this. You would never willingly place those kids in danger."

"But I did." I swing around to the alcohol cart and reach for the gin.

"No more alcohol." She grabs my wrist, holding tight. "Put it down."

"I'm not done."

"Yes, you are." She shoves me sideways, catching me off guard, and places herself between me and the liquor. "You've had enough."

"And you've got a death wish." I bridge the space between us, the heat returning to her eyes as she raises her chin. "Move."

"No." She shuffles her feet apart, taking a fighting stance. "Get a glass of water instead."

"I don't want water." I step toward her.

"Back off." She raises her hands and aims them at my chest.

I snatch her wrist, but she does the same, snapping her palm around my forearm, then lunging in a flurry of movement. She twists my arm behind my back and shoves me face-first into the wall.

My cheek slams hard into the plaster, the pain holding no comparison to the agonizing punch to my pride.

All I can do is laugh.

I laugh because a woman has dared to manhandle me this way.

I laugh because the one person I want by my side is the same person who can easily defeat me.

But most of all, I laugh because despite it all, I wouldn't want anyone else here to witness me at my lowest. Nobody but her. A fucking Fed.

"You need to calm down." Her voice is soothing near my ear as she gentles her grip, no longer threatening to tear muscle.

She's all warmth and stability. Perfection and excellence. Even now, when I'm drowning in defeat, I want her. *Need* her.

I crave the goodness to wash all the suffering away.

"No more drinking," she continues. "No more games. You have to sit down and tell me what happened on that phone call. And while we're working on a plan, we're also going to figure out when you can get some sleep. Your mind has to rest."

My mind and my soul.

I'm so sick of this life. Of the betrayal. The sabotage. I'm ready to burn the world to the ground, along with everyone in it.

Except her.

I'd keep Anissa around, if only to listen to her tell me how much of an asshole I am.

"Are you listening?" Her voice is low. Too fucking gentle and caring for the hard-ass bitch I know.

"Yeah." I shove backward, catching her unaware, and duck to spin out of the twist to my arm. Then I'm all over her, foot to foot, my hand claiming her throat.

She gasps, her eyes widening, her fingers moving to my threatening hold.

I've done this before, felt her delicate neck in my grip. In Greece. In passion.

This moment isn't overly different. Her eyes blaze with heat. Her lips part in shock, but also in that sweet, submissive seduction.

Her lack of fight is all I need to tell me she wants this as much as I do.

She craves my control. The mastery—even though it's now clear I'm a master of nothing and no one.

She aches for me to fuck her. Practically screams it through the silence.

My dick throbs, already agonizingly hard.

It wouldn't take much. A yank of a zipper. A tear of her underwear. I'd sink deep before she could form a protest. But we both know she wouldn't anyway.

Those eyes don't lie. Maybe to others. Never to me.

This woman is mine. She has been from the moment I laid eyes on her. And I'd thought I'd been enough. I'd mistakenly thought my concept of right and wrong was better than hers.

Now, my well-defined superiority is crashing around me.

"It's normal to be emotional," she whispers. "But you have to move past it. Push it aside. We need to think strategically. And I can't do that until you tell me what happened."

She's still thinking of those kids. With my hand around her throat and my restraint threadbare, she remains focused on the children I put at risk.

"Stop torturing yourself." Her fingers slide from my hand, her palms moving to cup my face. "Jesus, Cole, I can't stand to see you this way."

This way. This weak.

I walk into her, leading her backward to the elegant dining table, not stopping until her butt bumps into the wood.

"Tell me what you see." I snarl an inch from her lips, inhaling her heat. "Tell me all the shitty things you feel when you look at me."

She sighs, her shoulders slumping. "It's not like that. We just…" She shakes her head despite the restriction of my hand. "We're enemies." The frantic lick of her lips tells a different story.

Her body and mind don't match up. Her morals may dictate that we're adversaries, yet the way she physically responds to me is entirely different. Always has been.

I keep my attention on her mouth. "We didn't leave Greece as enemies."

"Like hell we didn't. We arrived as enemies and left the same way." Color floods her cheeks. "The middle may have contained some shady decisions and a wealth of regret, but that's to be expected through all the adrenaline."

"Shady decisions and regret?" I meet her gaze, stroking my index finger along the sensitive column of her neck. "Is that all you remember about us fucking?"

She breaks eye contact.

"Tell me." I tighten my grip. "I want to know exactly what you think when you recall me being inside you."

She shudders and the fragile tremble rocks right through me.

"We were made to fuck." I lean closer, brushing my stubbled cheek over her perfectly smooth one, my lips near her ear. "Admit no other man has moved you like I have."

"You're looking for a distraction, Cole. That's all this is. You need an outlet." She pulls back an inch and meets my gaze. "You don't want to think about what's really happening."

No, I need her.

I've never been more reliant on someone in my entire life.

This is about us. About forming an unbreakable alliance that will help bring my family back together. It's about the future and a shaky past. It's about strength and power and pride.

I brush my lips over her cheek. "I'll tell you all about that phone call once you admit you want to be with me."

She straightens, her chin jutting higher.

"Tell me I haunt your dreams." Like she haunts mine. "Tell me how no other man compares." Like no woman ever could. "Tell me how you want to commit to me even though our lives are worlds apart."

She stiffens and I pull back to see her glaring in fury.

It's not the reaction I expected. But I've never been able to predict this woman perfectly every time. It's one of her many highlights.

"What exactly did my shrink tell you?" She grates through clenched teeth. "How much do you know?"

I smirk, rerunning those questions in my mind to hear her truth.

I haunt her dreams.

No other man compares.

She wants to commit to me.

That shrink had given me very little information. There wasn't much other than a contempt-filled explanation that Nissa continued to beg for a Stockholm diagnosis to excuse her lingering feelings for me.

"Your secrets are safe, little fox." I part her thighs with a shove of my knee and sink between her legs. "I'm not the bastard you think I am."

"Yes, you are." It's a weak protest. Feeble at best.

I reach between us with my free hand, finding the waistband of her pants to release the button with a flick of my fingers.

"Cole," she pleads. "Don't."

This time there's strength in her voice. Panic. She nudges forward, probably attempting to free herself, but all it does is bring her closer. Hip to hip. Chest to chest.

Her pulse beats harder beneath my fingers. Her breathing increases. And those breasts. *Fuck*. With each pant they brush against me, turning my already hard dick to stone.

"You want me," I whisper.

"That doesn't make it right." She swallows, her throat working overtime beneath my palm. "None of this is right."

"We've discussed right and wrong in the past." I hold her gaze. "And I've convinced you your perception was misguided before. This is just another example."

She blinks back at me, shaking her head. "I can't want this. You just sent a goddamn video of us to my partner."

"But you *do* want it." I lower her zipper, the slow grate of friction loud between us.

She mewls. Whimpers.

I slide my hand beneath the elastic of her panties, expecting her to protest as I delve deeper, but there's nothing.

No demand.

No threat.

Only the frantic grip of her fingers clinging to the arm at her throat as if she's battling the desire to beg for more.

She's done fighting me and the realization is invigorating. Soul cleansing.

I glide my hand lower, past her mound, to her opening and groan at the slickness awaiting me. She's wet as fuck, her greedy pussy clenching as my fingers part her folds.

"Oh, God." The words are a barely audible prayer as she closes her eyes and clings tighter to my wrist. "We can't do this."

"Yes, we can." I tease her entrance, stroking back and forth.

She shakes her head. "We shouldn't."

"This is fate." I inch my fingers inside her, slowly delving as deep as the restriction of her pants will allow.

"I've tried so hard not to want this," she whispers. "It's not right, Cole."

"It's right for us." I stroke her, making her hips roll. "Perfection isn't meant to be easy."

"Perfection?" She grinds her hips, her nails digging deep into my wrist. "How can you think that?"

"Because it's what you are. It's what *we* are."

She pants. Clings. Shudders.

I press my thumb to her clit and the resulting gasp is heaven to my ears. I'd give anything to fuck her right now. To have my cock inspire those gasps. But I don't deserve it. Not yet.

"Cole," she whispers. "I don't want to do this."

My chest squeezes with the kick to my ego. Deep down I know she's only protesting to save face once all this is said and done. It's a defense mechanism. A shield.

She needs to think this is my fault. My doing. That she had no choice.

I won't allow it.

"Then push me away, Nissa." I place my nose an inch from hers, staring her down. "Stop grinding against my fingers and walk."

Her teeth sink into her lower lip. Her brows furrow. Her eyes plead.

"Or simply enjoy what's meant to be." I inch closer, hovering my lips a breath from hers. "Take what I willingly give."

Her gasps increase. The buck of her hips, too. She grinds against my fingers, driving me to madness with her desire, when a heavy knock sounds at the door.

Fuck.

"Oh, shit." She scrambles like a feral cat.

"Stop," I growl. "We're not done."

"No." She tries to pry my fingers from her neck. "There's someone at the door."

"They can wait. We're not finished here until you come."

She shakes her head rapidly. "I can't."

"You fucking can. And you will." I back her harder against the table, clench my grip tighter around her throat, and work those digits in her pussy like we're seconds from death. "You're going to fucking come, Nis. No woman of mine is left wanting."

I plaster my lips to hers, tasting her, devouring her. She moans, melting her tongue against mine.

The knock sounds again, but we don't stop. I deepen the kiss. Press harder against her clit. Her pussy drenches my palm while her core clamps tighter around me as Hunter yells for me to, "Open the fucking door."

"Come," I demand in her mouth. "Fucking come, little fox, or I'll let them in here and they can watch."

"I can't." She shakes her head.

"You know I'm not bluffing."

Of course I am.

I would never allow another man to see her like this.

Her pleasure is mine. I own these gasps.

But my men have a key. If they grow concerned about my lack of response, they'll quit waiting for permission to enter and simply storm in.

"Fucking come." I reclaim her mouth, squeeze her neck, making her struggle for air.

She trembles. Scratches.

The knocking continues. My cell vibrates in my pocket.

This time, Decker yells, "What the hell is going on, Cole?"

Nissa's trembling intensifies. She shudders. Claws at my wrists.

"Cole," she pleads. "Please, Cole."

"Tell me what you need."

She responds by releasing my arms to circle her hands around my neck, dragging me closer. She hypnotizes me with her frantic kiss. Tortures me with her demand for nearness.

Then soothes me with the release.

She comes undone in my hands, whispering my name, holding me so fucking tight I never want her to let go.

She's the most beautiful thing I've ever seen. Ever felt. Always wanted.

I love her.

That's all there is now—my obsessive worship and the inability to walk away.

Her arms fall from around my neck, her shoulders relaxing. Her eyes slowly blink open, her breathing remaining a frantic mess.

I release her throat and hope to escape to the kitchen before her remorse hits. But I'm not fast enough. My fingers are sliding from her pussy as regret stares back at me.

"Don't look at me like that." I pull a handkerchief from my pocket and wipe my hand. "The time for second-guessing is over. We're done fighting this. You hear me?"

16

ANISSA

I'M STILL IN A MINDLESS TRANCE OF REFLECTION AND SELF-LOATHING, LEANED against the dining room table, when Cole opens the penthouse door.

It isn't until Hunter stalks into the living room, his gaze narrowing on me in a new level of heightened spite, that I realize how I must look.

Disheveled. In a post-orgasm haze.

Shit.

I shove to my feet, my head high as I walk toward him and the banked up wall of men behind him to maneuver through the crowd and into the hall. I scoop my discarded cell from the tile floor, thankful I didn't break it in my fit of rage, and shut myself into the main bathroom to stare at my blissed-out reflection in the mirror.

My cheeks are pink, my lips bright red. And the marks on my neck from Cole's restricting grip stand out like a brutal reminder of my flaws.

I touch the flaming skin, still feeling him there, his hand around my throat, the threatening yet erotic grip inundating me with adrenaline.

There's something sick about how much I enjoyed the menace of that hold. Something twisted and unhinged about the undeniable thrill. It's made all the worse when the man inspiring the nirvana is entirely capable of strangulation.

I don't doubt he could kill me.

Maybe that's the appeal. The danger. The thin line between life and death.

Not only do I see flashbacks of what just happened, I feel them. Cole's touch remains tangible, raising goose bumps, stealing breath.

I use the facilities, my cheeks flaming hotter at the slickness drenched between my thighs. I need a change of underwear.

I need a goddamn lobotomy.

Even with the self-loathing and shame, there's still a tingle of exhilaration emanating through my chest. It's a silent demand for more. A hunger that can't be sated by a lone orgasm or stifled by remorse.

How can that even happen after everything Cole's done? Why do I still feel this way when moments earlier he'd humiliated me and risked my career by sending Easton that video?

I should hate Cole.

I *need* to hate him. Yet, I fucking don't. There's only an agonizing ache where anger should be as I unlock my cell and stare at the blank home screen.

The radio silence from Easton says it all. I can't even imagine what he's thinking right now. I don't want to.

I navigate to my text messages, then Easton's folder. I prepare to watch the video again but pause at the tiny red icon beside the message.

Error. Message not sent. Turn on cell data.

I stare in amazement.

The message didn't go through. Cole turned off my data?

He took the video. Prepared a message. But deliberately made sure it wouldn't send.

Why? To trigger my fear? To assert his authority?

Regardless of the reasons, I'm thankful. Almost overwhelmed with relief at Cole's exposed decency.

I delete the evidence capable of ruining my life and ignore the shake of my hands as I turn the data back on.

Notifications of missed calls blink onto the screen. A text from Easton, too.

I'm worried about you. We need to talk. Please call me.

My heart pangs. I can clearly visualize his concern. His face would be somber. His eyes gentle. But I don't crave his sweetness. Not his affection or his attention.

All for one reason—he's not Cole.

Sorry about earlier. I text back. *I'm working on something important. I promise I'll fill you in once this is over. I'm fine. Trust me.*

My moral compass is so far out of whack I don't even feel guilty with the lie that's barely veiled by the truth as I place my cell back in my pocket.

I lean against the basin and stare at myself in the mirror, finger-combing my hair until the freshly fucked look leaves my features. It isn't until I'm completely devoid of adrenaline, lust, and anticipation that I cautiously leave the bathroom, remaining out of sight in the hall to listen to the conversation in the living room.

Cole speaks with authority as he asks for an update on his sister's well-being.

There's a murmur of reply about crying and sedatives. It isn't until Cole cuts back into the conversation, relaying information pertaining to his latest phone conversation with Emmanuel, that I enter the opening of the hall, not caring that I'm in view of Hunter's evil stare.

"He's refusing to let us see them until tomorrow." Cole removes his suit jacket and drapes it over the armrest of a sofa. "He's holding them hostage yet somehow thinks he can downplay the act of war behind false promises and insane excuses."

"What excuses?" Decker asks. "What reason could he possibly have for keeping them from us?"

"Some bullshit about his wife being smitten with the kids and wanting to spend more time with them."

"They could already be dead." Hunter begins to pace beside the wall of glass leading to the balcony, his face stone cold. "He's buying time."

"Jesus." Benji leans forward in his seat at the dining table, elbows on the wood, hands raked into his hair.

He's seated in the same place I'd been earlier, with Cole's hand in my underwear. Panting. Gasping. Now the position is filled with such sickening mourning I can barely stand my own degradation.

"They're not dead. I have a photo." Cole reaches into his pants pocket, coming up empty. "My cell…" His attention raises, his eyes finding mine. "You have my phone."

I nod, approaching him to hold out the device.

He's in business mode now. Stern. Sterile.

There's none of the dominant heat in his expression from before, and there shouldn't be. I shouldn't even be looking for it. I don't know why my head is still back there. Lathered in seduction.

I'm broken.

He takes the cell, navigates to his gallery, then shows the screen to Benji. "They at least made it to Emmanuel like he promised."

I start toward Benji as he pushes from the table, his steps frantic as he snatches the device to stare at it cradled in his hands.

"She looks scared." He shoots a glance at Cole. "She's fucking petrified."

I pause a few feet away, not wanting to encroach on the private moment, while also itching to catch sight of the evidence. "Can I see?"

Benji continues to focus on the image, his eyes hollow, his suffering soul deep.

"Please?" I hold out a hand. "Just a quick look."

Hunter huffs at my request. Decker scoffs. But Benji reluctantly hands the device over and returns his attention to Cole. "What do we do?"

The men continue their conversation as I scrutinize the digital image.

The setting would seem wholesome to the ignorant eye. Even loving. Two young children with a doting elderly woman. Benji is right, though. Stella's eyes are haunted, while Tobias seems almost angry beneath his fake smile.

Their innocent faces are enough to siphon any lingering desire from my veins and put me back on track.

I scan every pixel of the photograph, painstakingly noting the finer details. "This image is important." I raise my voice above their chatter and meet Cole's gaze. "Have you checked for the GPS details embedded in the file?"

"There's not much point," Decker replies. "The last pic didn't have any. He knows how to delete the information."

I hand Cole's phone back to him, our fingers slightly brushing. "We still need to check. And regardless of the outcome, there's a wealth of information in this picture. We might be able to pinpoint the skyline in the background. The children have been cleaned up, too. They've been given new clothes. They're even wearing T-shirts that expose their forearms, showing no signs of bruising or abuse."

"You think they're okay?" Benji asks.

"I think they're being taken care of," I correct him. "Stella's eyes aren't red, so she hasn't been crying. Yes, she's scared. But that's only natural. The kitchen is clean apart from the flour, which alludes to a healthy environment. The woman with them is showing her face, which means she doesn't see this as incriminating evidence."

"Are you saying that they might actually be keeping the kids from us because they seriously want to play happy families?" Hunter scrunches his nose in disgust. "That's insane."

"It's a possibility."

"I don't give a shit about possibilities. I just want Stella and Tobias back home." Cole taps on his phone and seconds later, a chorus of vibrations hum through the room. "I just sent you all a copy of the image. Study it. Dissect it. I don't care what it takes. We're going to work over every last detail until we find them."

The room falls silent, everyone focusing on their cells, staring blankly or tapping at the screen.

"I'm going to go back downstairs and get my laptop." Decker hobbles to his feet. "I won't take long."

We work autonomously for hours. Hunter spends his time on the balcony, speaking on his phone. Decker is constantly focused on his computer, with Benji acting like an eager assistant at his side. Cole makes calls, asking for favors from undisclosed people while demanding compliance from others.

I try to keep busy, too, but it's hard. All the resources I've come to depend on in situations like this aren't available. Normally, I could obtain warrants for phone records or credit card statements. I could order cell traces and hopefully get a tower ping or two to narrow down a location.

Instead, I spend the entire afternoon familiarizing myself with the Costa family, delving through their company's social media to fixate on the few personal posts about Emmanuel and his children.

They seem close.

A regular hard-working family.

Their involvement in this hostage situation doesn't make sense. It's careless when they're such high-profile people.

The sun has begun to set when Hunter comes back inside. "Costa flew into the same private airport we did." He slumps onto the sofa and places his cell on the coffee table. "And it wasn't only him and his psycho wife. Two of their three sons were on the flight, along with three of their security detail."

"Reconfirming their preparation for battle," Decker mutters. "I've come close to figuring out their location from the skyline in the image." He turns the laptop screen to face Cole and I on the opposite sofa. "They're somewhere in this area." He shows a map with a highlighted circle encapsulating more than a handful of blocks. "Or they were earlier. But it doesn't mean shit when each of these city blocks would house God knows how many people."

"Can you narrow it down?" Cole massages the back of his neck. "He'd be staying somewhere expensive. Cut out all the noise and focus on penthouse suites or pricey short-stay apartments."

"To what fucking end, though?" Hunter asks. "We might narrow that list to fifty places but then what? We go searching one by one? That'll take all week, when this asshole is meant to be handing them over tomorrow anyway."

"As tough as it's going to be, I think we need to wait this out." Decker closes his laptop and places it on the sofa beside him. "The ball is in Costa's court. There's nothing we can do."

I don't voice my agreement, but it's there, burning a hole in my chest.

"We're dealing with kids now," he continues. "Even if we did know the location, we couldn't storm in there. I won't be a part of a risky operation where one stray bullet will take a child's life. I say we call it a night. Try to get some sleep. We'll reassess in the morning."

"We can't just do nothing." Benji glances between Hunter and Cole, his eyes widened with panic.

The heartbeats of silence press in like a closing vault.

Nobody has the correct answer because there isn't one.

The only choices now are to keep digging with no certainty that information will even help once we find it. Or rest and recuperate so we're ready when Emmanuel makes arrangements in the morning. *If* he makes arrangements.

Cole lets out a long huff of breath, his torment sinking under my skin. He doesn't want to say it. He doesn't want to do nothing while Stella and Tobias are suffering. But he needs sleep. They all do.

"Decker's right." I stare at Cole as his gaze raises to mine, the pain of his defeat hitting me full force. "We're better off getting some rest. You're going to need it to think clearly tomorrow."

"No." Benji pushes to his feet, shaking his head. "*No*. We can't quit."

"We're not quitting, man," Decker soothes. "I promise. We're only waiting."

"And while we're waiting, can you imagine what's happening to my daughter? She's with a man aligned with sex traffickers. They could be—" He shakes his head, wincing.

"I'll call him again." Cole stands and pulls out his cell. "I'll ask for more proof of their safety."

"Ask for a video," Hunter interjects. "Demand to speak to Stella."

"Don't demand." I approach Cole. "You need to keep a level head. Don't give him a reason to hang up on—"

"Shut the fuck up." Hunter scowls his hatred at me. "We don't need your input."

"I want to speak to her." Benji strides around the sofa, approaching. "Let me talk to my daughter." He reaches for the cell.

Cole broadens his shoulders and straightens to his full height. He transforms from tired and lethargic to territorial and lethal in the blink of an eye. "Get out of my face before I give you what you deserve. I don't care about your wants or needs. My only concern is for those kids."

His vehemence is beyond scathing. It's downright cruel.

"Cole..." His name is whispered from my lips. It's pulled from me in sympathy for a man who is clearly hurting. But I get no response.

The call is made as Cole moves to the main bedroom.

Benji follows.

"Don't step foot in that room," Hunter threatens. "You've pushed your luck too far. There's no more lenience now."

I don't understand why they're hating on Benji. They're treating him like an enemy, not a distraught father.

I glance to Decker for understanding, then Hunter. Both of them scowl at me in return, leveling me with the same contempt. "What's going on?" I ask.

"Mind your own business." Hunter shoves from the sofa and stalks to the kitchen as Cole starts talking in the bedroom.

I switch my attention to the conversation, moving to the doorway alongside Benji to watch Cole pace before the wall of windows.

"I'm being patient," he mutters. "But I need more proof that those kids are okay. I want video or—"

He quits speaking. Stops moving.

"Yes." His chin hikes. "I understand."

He turns toward us and raises a hand, one finger pointed in warning before he lowers the cell and taps the screen. He places the call on speaker, the rustle of unknown sounds rumbling from the phone.

"Uncle Cole?"

The young girl's voice devastates my composure, dragging all the air from my lungs.

"Stella?" Benji gasps.

I grab his arm, taking the curl of Cole's lip as a sign that the rule of necessary distance hasn't changed.

"Be patient," I whisper. "Let him handle this."

"It's me, princess." Cole keeps his tone level. "How are you?"

"I want to go home. Where are you? Where's my mom? Are you coming to get us?"

"We'll be there in the morning. I promise. Are you okay?"

"Yes." One word. No conviction.

It's hard to tell if she's being coerced.

"I don't know what happened." She lowers her voice. "We woke up here and we don't know these people. They say they're friends with Grandpa, but I've never seen them before. Did something happen to Mom and Dad? Is that why we're here?"

Benji jostles his arm, attempting to loosen my grip.

"Please, Benji." I cling to him. "Let Cole handle this."

"Your mom and dad are fine, Stella." Cole remains incredibly strong, not showing an ounce of panic or heartache. He knows exactly how to speak to her fear to strengthen her. "You'll see them tomorrow."

"What about Penny and Uncle Luca? Tobias is worried. Emmanuel said there was an issue last night and that's why he's looking after us, but he won't say what happened. Why haven't you come to get us?"

Benji's face crumples. He grabs my wrist, clinging to me like I'm clinging to him.

"There was an issue." Cole rakes a hand through his hair. "But it's been taken care of. Everyone is okay. There's nothing for you to worry about."

"Then why haven't you come?"

"We are coming, sweetheart. We'll be there tomorrow. Is Emmanuel looking after you? Do you feel safe?"

There's a pause. A frantic heartbeat where my fear overrides comprehension.

"Yes." She stalls again. "Mrs. Costa has been watching movies with us all afternoon. We've eaten cakes and pastries and ice cream. We had pizza for dinner."

Cole's gaze meets mine. His eyes are questioning. Hopefully pleading.

He wants to know if I believe her. If I'm hearing anything he's not. And I honestly can't tell.

I'm too invested now. Emotion has taken over my intelligence.

I shake my head and shrug, mouthing, "*I don't know.*"

"Is anyone else with you?" he asks. "Other men, or—"

A rustle emanates from the speaker.

"I think that's enough for tonight," Emmanuel's voice cuts in. "The children are tired and need to get ready for bed. I will contact you in the morning to make arrangements. Good night, Mr. Torian."

"Wait." Benji runs for Cole. "I'm here, baby. You're daddy's here."

There's no answer.

No response.

No noise at all.

"He disconnected the call." Cole's jaw ticks as he pockets the cell, his attention focused over my shoulder. "What are your thoughts?"

I turn, finding Hunter and Decker standing a few feet behind me, their faces solemn.

"She didn't seem under duress." Decker limps closer. "And I don't think a kid that age would follow a script if she feared for her life."

"She's our little ball-busting princess," Hunter adds. "She would've screamed the house down at the first sound of your voice if they were hurting her."

"Unless she's already been beaten into submission," Benji snaps. "How can you give up on her so easily?"

"We're not giving up on anyone." Hunter speaks through clenched teeth. "And before you go blaming anything else on us, you might want to take the time to remember why she was taken in the first place."

"You know why she was taken?" I glance at Cole. "Why haven't I been told? That information could be—"

"We're calling it a night." He speaks over me. "I trust that Stella and Tobias are okay for now. Hire another suite. Eat and get some rest. Tomorrow is going to be another long day."

"Fuck you." Benji continues toward the hall. "Fuck you all for giving up on my daughter." He yanks the front door wide and slams it on his way out.

"Is someone going to tell me what's happening?" I glance from one man to the next, taking in their stubborn resolve to shut me out.

"Go after him." Cole jerks his chin at Hunter. "Make sure he doesn't cause any trouble."

"What about me?" Decker asks as Hunter stalks for the door. "What do you want me to do?"

"Update the women. Keep them calm. Make sure they have dinner and an early night."

"Can I opt for being shot in the leg again instead? Don't get me wrong, I can handle Keira, but Layla? And Sarah? Those two aren't going to appreciate sitting on their hands for another fourteen hours. They'll tear me to fucking pieces."

"Do you want me to speak to them?" I ask.

Decker ignores me apart from the upturn of his nose.

"No, he can deal." Cole makes his way out of the bedroom, passing me to stand near his younger sister's partner. "Tell everyone to keep their cells close by. I'll let you know if I hear anything else."

Decker gives me a scorn-filled look before he nods and hobbles toward the hall, closing the penthouse door behind him.

Then it's just the two of us.

Cole and I.

Alone.

Again.

17

ANISSA

C<small>OLE STROLLS ACROSS THE LIVING AREA TO STAND BEFORE THE FLOOR-TO-CEILING</small> glass, staring down at the city below.

He doesn't break the eerie quiet and neither do I. There's nothing but hollow isolation until my stomach rumbles, demanding sustenance loud enough to wake the dead.

I'm not hungry, but I need to eat. My energy reserves are low. I even struggle to drag my feet to the kitchen to mumble a random selection from the room service menu to the operator.

Cole is still at the wall of glass after I hang up. His silence is in stark contrast to the storm raging through his tight posture and I can't help wishing I could do something to gentle the turmoil.

"I hope you don't mind me ordering you dinner." I walk around the kitchen counter to lean against the armrest of a sofa. "I thought taking a wild guess at what you might eat would be better than asking you to make menial decisions."

"I appreciate it."

I hear the truth in his words. The utter fatigue.

"I should head out and get something to wear tomorrow," he murmurs. "I have no clothes. I didn't plan on staying overnight."

"Is that something the concierge could organize?"

He shrugs, not meeting my gaze.

My hunger pangs turn into cramps, my insides twisting and squeezing in empathetic meltdown. "What are your sizes? I'll get the hotel staff to arrange something."

He relays measurements I note down in my cell, then I turn my back as I reclaim the penthouse phone. I can't look at him anymore. Not when all I want to do is comfort him.

I've witnessed male suffering before. But never like this. Not with a man who prides himself on strength of character and sterility of emotion.

I distract myself with the concierge, asking about dry-cleaning timelines and personal shopper availability. This time when I hang up, I swing around to find an empty room. There's no image of sorrowful mourning at the window. There's not even a glimpse of the crime lord who's battling against a devastating downfall.

"Cole?"

"In here."

I follow his voice toward the bedroom. "The concierge said he would send someone to arrange a selection of suits for you to wear tomorrow." I enter the doorway, finding him at the side of the bed, unbuttoning his shirt and throwing it on the mattress.

My heart quickens without my consent. My stomach twists. I force myself to look away, focusing on the closed curtains across the room. "He also mentioned you can have your current suit dry-cleaned within the hour, so I asked for him to send someone up to retrieve it."

"Thanks."

There's a clink of a belt. A grate of a zipper.

My quickening heart and twisting stomach increase, my insides somersaulting like an Olympic gymnast despite my exhaustion.

"I didn't even think about dry-cleaning," he mutters. "I can hardly think at all."

"That's why you need sleep."

"The sun has barely set."

"But it's currently setting the day *after* you last slept." I chance a glance in his direction, and there he stands, gloriously naked except for his boxer briefs, his chest a masterpiece of tanned, defined muscles as he pulls on a hotel robe.

He cinches it tight around his waist and grabs the discarded clothes from the bed. "I'll leave these at the door." He starts toward me, the approaching proximity causing arrhythmia.

"Here." I hold out my hands. "Let me do it."

He pauses before me, meeting my gaze. I'm sure there's skepticism hidden in those dark blue depths, resentment at my coddling, too. But he doesn't voice a protest. Only stares, melting me into a puddle.

"Go to bed." I reach for the clothes. "I'm going to stay awake for a while and do more research."

"You need the rest as much as I do." He keeps his folded suit tight within his strong hands and continues into the living room, his retreating footsteps carrying down the hall until the penthouse door opens and closes.

I have a few moments to breathe freely before his dominating presence returns.

"The food shouldn't take long." He strides back into the room, still a sight to behold even in a plush white bathrobe. "I'm going to take a shower."

He continues into the bathroom, not closing the door.

I remain nailed in place as the sound of rushing water seduces my ears.

I don't know if he's attempting to entice me, or if he's so entirely bone-weary he doesn't have the strength to close the barrier between us. It has to be option one. It always is.

I become entranced by the melodic flow of water, the gentle sound soothing parts of me hardened from the last twenty-four hours. I've showered with him before. I know what it feels like to be surrounded by warmth. And hunger. I remember how powerless I was to resist Cole when the world had faded from view and it was only the two of us.

My stomach hurts with the memory. With the lost affection.

I'd thought he was falling in love with me. I truly had.

The worst part was those feelings had been reciprocated.

I had loved a *criminal*.

A *murderer*.

And now those feelings are clawing their way back from the depths of my despair.

"No," I whisper to the empty room. "Not again."

I drag my feet to the living room to sit on the sofa. He's so quiet it's unnerving.

He remains in the shower long after our food is delivered and I've eaten my burger and fries. He stays in there while I fight against concern for his welfare. To the point where I'm almost ready to check on him. Then the water finally turns off.

"Your dinner is out here." I raise my voice to carry through the rooms. "Hurry, while it's still warm."

"I'm not hungry."

"You need to eat." I grab a plate filled with fries, steak and salad, along with a set of cutlery, and return to the main bedroom only to pause at the threshold.

He stands at the bed, a towel wrapped around his hips, his chiseled chest on full display as he ruffles his damp hair.

He's gorgeous. Purely divine. So incredibly tempting it pains me to keep my distance.

I wish I understood the effect he has on me.

I should be daunted by the ease with which he displays himself. He doesn't care that he's naked beneath that towel. The bigger problem is—I don't either.

It feels natural to be here like this. But it's not. I just don't get why panic isn't setting in.

"Here." I pad forward, placing the plate and cutlery on the end of the bed before backing away. "Eat."

"I've lived a long time without a mother, Nis. You don't need to baby me."

"Even someone as ruthless as you needs to be taken care of every once in a while."

He quirks a brow. "And you're the person for the job?"

"I'm the only one here."

He inclines his head. "Be careful, Nis. You might start to expose feelings for me other than lust."

I don't let the strike penetrate. It hits hard though, the efficient barb making me wince.

"Just eat," I beg. "Neither one of us has the patience to argue."

He surprises me by doing exactly as I ask, stepping forward the few feet to grab some fries. Everything about him is smooth. His chest. His composure. The way he continues to lazily eat, his gaze raking me the entire time.

"What happened between you and Benji?" I rest my shoulder against the doorjamb. "What's with the hostility?"

"It's family business. You don't need to concern yourself with the details."

"It must be something big for you to be angry at him during what has to be the most excruciating time of his life."

He grabs a piece of cucumber and throws it into his mouth, chewing with casual arrogance.

The shower must have pepped him up. He's got energy back in those eyes. Lethal efficiency.

"Is it that you don't trust me with the information?" I ask. "You don't want me to know?"

"You don't need to know."

"But I'd like to."

He gives a snake of a grin. "There's many things I'd like from you, too. Will I get those in return?"

Heat skitters along my skin, the flashover wild and intense. I picture what he wants as payment. I *feel* it. Lucky for me I have just enough strength to look away from his demanding gaze in the hopes of severing his train of thought.

He sighs in response. "Benji is a snitch. He's been ratting on me to my father for God knows how long at my sister's request."

"Layla betrayed you?" The question leaves my lips in a rapid evacuation of breath. "Why?"

"Money. Security. Intimidation. Who the fuck cares? There's no excusable reason to make their actions acceptable."

Holy Jesus.

This isn't good. Not for Cole's reputation or his stronghold in Portland.

"Don't look so worried, little fox. I'll sort it out."

"How?" I push from the doorframe. "How can you sort something like that?"

"You don't want to know." He holds my gaze, the slightest conniving smile tilting his lips. He's alluding to violence. To torture. Possibly death. But the thirst for bloodshed doesn't reach his eyes. All I see is hardship in the ocean-blue depths.

He wouldn't kill Benji, would he?

"What about my phone?" The question rushes from my lips in an attempt to change the subject. "You deliberately turned off my data before sending that video to Easton. Why?"

He resumes ruffling his hair, scattering water droplets over his bare shoulders. "Because I knew I would get the desired effect without having to risk your reputation."

There's another twist to my heart. A cautionary tweak. "And what was the desired effect?"

"Does it really matter?" He starts toward me, his relaxed stride seeming predatory. "You already judged me for my actions."

"Why, Cole?"

He stops before me, the scent of soap filtering into my lungs as he reaches out to run gentle fingers along my jaw.

My nerves tingle in response. My throat dries.

I should run. I should scream. I should do anything other than stand here basking in his touch, but I don't.

"Your initial response wasn't to blame me for manipulating you. Or to rail on me for playing games. You didn't even claim some pathetic mental excuse for your enjoyment of that kiss. Instead, you got angry because I exposed the truth."

I close my eyes, hating his accuracy.

"You threw your phone at me because you could no longer hide behind lies." His fingers grip my chin, lifting my face upward. "But I'm not entirely heartless, Nis. Not when it comes to you. If you want to keep your job I would never take it away."

I squeeze my eyes tighter, wishing the darkness could shut out my growing need. "Not heartless, yet you still threatened my shrink."

"I was concerned for your well-being. I won't apologize for that." The pad of his thumb brushes my lower lip, back and forth, stimulating every nerve in my body. "But I admit taking you to Greece wasn't one of my finest moments. I did things I regret. And I needed to make sure my actions didn't have a lasting effect on you."

They did.

They always will.

I open my eyes and immediately regret the decision when I'm ensnared by the intensity peering back at me. His fierce scrutiny. His inviting mouth.

"You suffer because of me." He continues to rub his thumb over my lip. "I don't like it."

"Be careful, Cole. If you keep talking like this you might expose a soft side." I throw his own taunt back at him. We're all about games and ridicule. Even now. It's all I've got to shield myself.

"I'm more concerned with how hard you make me." His mouth kicks in a faint smile.

Goddamnit.

My pussy clenches at the thought of his arousal. My nipples bead.

I'm a vibrating mess of building adrenaline and humming endorphins as his fingers tease along my jaw to my cheek, gently guiding stray strands of hair behind my ear.

"I asked you to be my queen once. I wanted you to stand by my side. That hasn't changed."

I shake my head. "I'm a Fed. You're a murderer."

"Yes, I'm a murderer. But so are you. You killed my father and didn't report it. You remained silent while Luca and I disposed of bodies. You're a criminal, too, Nis."

"Don't." I pull back. "Please don't throw my mistakes in my face. I know exactly what I've done."

"It wasn't a mistake. You rid the world of a man underserving of life. You saved tortured women. You ensured no more would be targeted by him. How can you still not see that?"

"Because I didn't do it the right way."

"The *right* way?" His jaw ticks, nostrils flare. "What was wrong about it?"

I don't answer. There's no point. He'll only twist my words and use them against me.

He'll break me down with his infallible logic.

"Please don't," I beg.

He holds me captive beneath those hard eyes for long moments, my pulse pounding in my throat. "Have it your way then."

He turns and makes for the bathroom, momentarily disappearing inside before returning without the towel as he thrusts his arms into the robe.

I get an eyeful of his perfect body. Head to toe. Nothing left unseen. Especially not the hardened length of his cock.

The display is deliberate. A calculated reminder of how easily he can make me burn.

"It's my dad." I finally answer his question, needing the necessary distraction. "You told me in Greece that he turned bad because of me."

He frowns, cinching the robe's belt around his waist. "That's not what I said."

"You told me he sought out your father to help protect me and my mother. You said he had no choice but to hire a hitman. And he lost everything because of it." I clasp my hands in front of me, tangling my fingers tight. "He made shady decisions to keep me safe. He threw away all he had. All so I could have this life. This career."

"So you plan to live the life he couldn't? You're giving up on your own freedom for him?"

Hearing my feelings spoken so simply makes them seem naive. Wrong.

"Doing the right thing isn't giving up on my freedom. I made the choice to distance myself from you because I cherish his sacrifice."

"My family *helped* yours. Yet you make it sound like we did the opposite." He huffs out a laugh. "You treat me as if I'm the scum of the Earth, but when the rest of the world failed your father, he turned to us. And we saved him. We saved *you*. And still you punish me for it."

I wince.

"The thing is, you don't know the half of it," he growls. "You've only heard the start of your father's story. He's not—"

"*No.* Please." I hold up a hand for him to stop. "Don't manipulate the memories I have of him. They're all I've got left."

He drags his gaze away, returning his attention to the food on the bed, claiming another piece of cucumber. "I wouldn't dream of it."

His cell vibrates on the bedside table beside his gun. He moves to snatch up the device, his expression remaining unchanged as he reads the screen.

"What is it?" I start toward him, stopping at his side to read the message from Luca.

We've arrived. Hunt filled me in on what's happening. We're booking another room. Call if you need anything.

"He made good time." I step back, removing myself from Cole's personal space.

"I'm surprised they made it at all." He begins typing a reply. "After what they've both been through in the last twenty-four hours, I've been waiting to hear news of a car accident."

He's been worried.

Why am I surprised?

He continues to tap, tap, tap on the screen, then returns the cell to the bedside table and runs his hands through his hair in a slow glide of tired frustration.

"You've handled this situation well." My comfort is barely audible. It's as if saying it too loud will mean I've finally switched sides, when I've already done far worse.

"Have I?" Sad eyes meet mine. Sad, defeated eyes.

My walls fall. Crumbling. Brick by brick, they succumb to his vulnerability.

What makes it worse is that I'm sure he's never shown this side of himself to anyone else before. Just me.

I'm the only one he's let in.

"You've done everything you can. There's nothing left to do but wait."

A knock sounds from the front of the suite, the interruption filling me with trepidation.

"Don't worry." Cole grabs his gun from the bedside table and some cash from his wallet. "It should be the dry-cleaning."

I follow him to the living room and watch, on alert, as he opens the door, reclaims his clothes, and tips the hotel staff.

It's then that I realize there are no more scheduled interruptions coming to save me.

He needs rest and I'm going to remain awake, stewing on all the bad decisions I've made.

Cole and I always seem to move in circles. Around and around. Never getting anywhere. Never learning from our mistakes.

It's such a demeaning routine, but the worst part is how right it feels.

The closeness. The exposed vulnerabilities. Even the passion... It seems like I've been pulled toward this by fate.

He pads back into the living room, the crinkle of plastic the only sound as he continues into the bedroom and out of sight.

"Can you come in here for a minute?" he asks moments later.

I'm loath to walk back in there.

Well, my mind is. My heart and nerve endings are the opposite as I enter the doorway.

"I'm going to sleep." He grabs the plate of food from the mattress and places it on the armchair in the corner. "Which side of the bed do you prefer?"

I huff out a half-hearted chuckle. "Nice try."

"The left side it is." He makes his way to the right and pulls back the covers. "It's time you got some rest, too."

He's right. I'm dead tired. But Goldilocks is *not* suited for this bed.

"I'll sleep in the spare room."

"No, you won't." There's no authority in his tone. No demand. Just pure, one hundred percent expectation.

"Good night, Cole." I back away, my heart thudding when he turns to me with narrowed eyes.

"I currently don't have the energy to chase you and haul you over my shoulder, but I assure you, I'll find it."

A chill skitters down my spine—a short, sharp thrill that leaves a hollow aftertaste. "You're only doing this for a distraction." I shake my head, correcting myself. "No, you consider me a challenge, don't you? That's why this time between us is never-ending. It's a cat and mouse game neither of us can win."

"You're no challenge, Nis. I had you in Greece. You threw yourself on me earlier in the hall. And you came on my fingers at the dining table. What part of that do you think was challenging for me?"

Shame heats my cheeks. Building disgust.

His face softens and it seems as though pity now stares back at me. "You stopped being a challenge and a game a long time ago."

The humiliation multiplies. Suffocates.

"What we have is far more complex than that." He drops the corner of the bedcovers and faces me. "You've become everything to me."

I haven't believed it before—his words of devotion, his continued commitment. Yet now it sinks in, warming the edges of my frigid insecurities. I'm a slave to his admission. A captive.

"We're made for each other. But you already know that." He discards the robe and slides onto the mattress, gloriously naked. "Now get in bed. I won't sleep unless I know you're safe at my side."

18

COLE

I EXPECT HER TO CONTINUE PROTESTING.

I'm more intrigued than relieved when she doesn't, instead turning on her heel after announcing she's going to get a change of clothes.

She returns moments later to enter the bathroom and close the door with a definitive click of the lock. She showers, the water's spray tempting me to break the barrier between us, but I force myself to remain in bed.

I don't even protest when she reenters the room covered neck to foot in soft-pink winter pajamas.

"Don't say a word." She turns off the light and rounds the bed to climb in the opposite side. "I'm doing this for safety's sake."

Sure she is.

If this is an attempt to throw me off my game by surrendering without a fight, it won't work. I'll take being near her any way I can.

She lays down as far away from me as humanly possible, then turns her back. The snub is an annoyance I don't have the energy to rally against.

I'm fucking dead inside. I need her warmth. But I'm done pushing. At least for now. Instead, I stare at the ceiling and watch the city lights peeking through the curtains as I brainstorm strategies for tomorrow.

I need to find leverage. Blackmail. I have to figure out a way to extort Emmanuel into giving those kids back without placing them in harm's way. Maybe his own children are the answer. But once I have Stella and Tobias safe in my care, I'll burn Costa's world to the ground.

I'll plant evidence. Pay law enforcement. Bribe city officials.

I'll do whatever the fuck it takes to rattle his cage. Then I'll level up to violence.

Revenge will be slow. Sweet.

It isn't long before I reach for my phone to message Hunt with tactical ideas. I tap out my anger against the glowing screen and hit send.

"What are you doing?" Nissa rolls toward me.

"Getting organized for the morning." I place the cell back on the bedside table and return to the previously broadcasted blank ceiling show.

"Why don't you reconsider letting me make a call or two? I could—"

"Don't waste your breath," I warn. "I'm not going to change my mind."

She sighs. "Then I really don't understand why I'm here. My hands are tied. I'm not helping."

"You're helping just fine."

"How?" She pushes onto her elbow, peering down at me. "What have I contributed apart from a few comments on the photos you received?"

I've asked myself the same question on repeat, and the answer has always remained the same. "You're here for me. For no other reason than to keep me grounded. I won't fail in front of you. You keep me in check."

She doesn't reply. She doesn't even move.

"Does that annoy you?" I direct the question toward the ceiling. "Do you hate knowing you're here for my benefit and nothing else?"

"It's more complicated than hatred," she whispers. "It always is with you. I just wish I would've realized sooner so I didn't mistakenly think I could've actually helped those kids."

"You're helping. Just not in the ways you planned."

She gives a breathy scoff. "Sorry, how silly of me to forget it's always your way or the highway."

"That's not the case."

"Yet here I am, in your bed, after you demanded I sleep here."

I clench my teeth, hating the way she cheapens her submission. "I didn't hear one fucking protest."

"Why bother when you always get what you want?"

"If I always got what I wanted, I would've fucked you four times by now. Once in my room this morning. Then when you plastered yourself against me in the bathroom. And again when you ground yourself into my fingers until you fucking orgasmed."

She sits up, her breathing increasing.

If I always got what I wanted, she never would've walked away from me after returning to Portland. Nothing would've stood between us. Not her morals. Not my family. And certainly not her fucking career.

"That was three, not four." She glowers down at me.

I release an anger-filled laugh. "Don't play coy, Nis. You know the fourth is right now. I'd fuck you within an inch of your life if I thought you'd consent."

"I wasn't being coy. I pointed it out because you didn't make sense. You never do. It's all smoke and mirrors. I don't understand you."

"That's another lie. You know me. You understand my motivations. You even agree with a lot of them—"

"No."

"*Yes*. You're fucking strong. You've never succumbed to my manipulations, as you like to call them. Or been tricked. Or unwillingly persuaded. You've *given* yourself to me, over and over again, because what I represent is familiar to the parts of yourself you try to hide. You like to think you've been fighting me this whole time. But the truth is, you've been fighting how much this feels like home. You've been battling your natural instincts. You've waged war with who you're meant to be."

"*No*." She slides from the bed and starts for the door. "Believe what you want but that's not true."

"Is that why you're running?" I drawl. "Because I'm wrong?"

She pauses at the threshold, back straight, shoulders stiff.

"Tell me, Nis, if I haven't got you pegged, why are you fleeing? Why not stay and prove me wrong?"

"Because there's no proving anything with you." She turns toward me. "You're always right."

I sit up. "If that were the case, you never would've returned from Greece to fuck another man, because I sure as shit didn't see that coming."

She winces.

"I wouldn't have ever expected you to move on with someone who's my complete opposite," I snarl. "Someone who isn't worthy of you. Someone who could never give you what you want."

"Don't talk about Easton."

"Why not?" I throw back the covers and slide from the bed. "Does the reality of your pathetic sex life upset you?"

"I never fucked him," she snaps.

My heart skips a beat. "No? You're telling me he practically lived in your apartment, but never had the balls to make a move?" I storm toward her, needing to see her lying eyes up close and personal.

"You said it yourself." She hikes her chin. "He's the exact opposite of you. He's a gentleman."

"So you *made love*? You didn't fuck?" My disappointment is stifling. I get in her face, wanting to taste her, to fucking claim her. My cock thickens with the need, painfully engorged. "I bet it was mediocre after what we shared."

She sucks in a breath, her shoulders hiking farther.

"If you would've come back to me I would've fucked you until your bones ached." I wrap an arm around her waist and haul her into me, pressing my dick into her abdomen. "If I always got my fucking way, little fox, you wouldn't have risen from your back since the night you returned."

"Because this is only about sex for you." She doesn't fight my hold. Not aggressively. Her only show of resistance is the way she leans away. "You claim I'm everything. But it's purely lust. You need to get laid more often."

My smirk increases. "Trust me, my sex life before you was envious."

I've bedded women who wanted nothing more than to earn my favor through my dick. By gold-diggers who thought they could win a lifetime worth of paid bills and extravagances if only they fucked me good enough.

And none compare to her.

"You're toxic." She looks me in the eye. "One hundred percent pure poison."

Slowly, I raise my arm, teasing my fingers up her neck to grab her hair in a tight fist. I drag her forward, her lips almost against mine. "And you're a bitch. Which makes us a perfect match."

She shudders.

Her enjoyment is always evident whenever I touch her. Rough or gentle. Harsh or soft. She loves it all.

"Now, tell me you want me." I nip at her lips, breathing her fractured inhales. "Tell me you want to be fucked."

She shakes her head.

"Do you think I won't slide my fingers back into your panties to feel the evidence of what you're denying?" I run my other hand down the curve of her waist, then along the elastic band of her pajamas. "Come back to me."

"No." She grips my wrist. "Not like this."

"Then how?"

She continues shaking her head, her brows pinching. "I don't know."

"Yeah, you do." I creep my hand lower, forcing myself into her panties. "You know exactly what you want. All you need to do is ask."

"Stop. This isn't what I want." Her nails dig into my skin and she pushes me backward. My fingers reluctantly leave her.

Fuck.

I could've sworn she was malleable tonight. I would've bet my life she'd be a willing participant.

I huff out a laugh. I guess I don't know her like I thought.

"I don't want this." She keeps shaking her head at me. "I can't live like this."

"I've made you feel good before—"

"That's not what I'm talking about." Her expression turns pained, her bleak eyes all the more tortured in the dim light. "I can't live with lies and threats. Yes, the adrenaline is euphoric. And the sex was incredible. But everything else is…" She throws her arms up at her sides. "The fighting. The bickering. The constant cat and mouse game—"

"You enjoy that as much as I do."

"That doesn't mean it's healthy… And then there's my job."

Fuck this. I turn away, my cock's eagerness vanishing at the mention of her career.

She thinks she loves the Bureau. So why hasn't she gone back? Why has she remained on leave since we were together?

Denial, that's why.

"We can't exist, Cole. I enjoy my job too much."

I grind my teeth, clench my fists.

"That's all there is to it," she adds as if her words are a royal flush to win this argument.

"Your job is bullshit," I mutter under my breath. I seethe the words. "Your *job* is nothing but a scam. We've gone over how you're a puppet for the hierarchy which manipulates the constitution for its own gain." I swing around to face her. "You're not saving the world one criminal at a time. You're a meaningless soldier helping more powerful criminals."

"I don't expect you to understand."

"You don't expect *me* to understand?" Holy shit, she's fucking demeaning me? "If you had any idea of the corruption in your office alone you'd realize your badge is worthless. Everyone can be bought."

"Not me."

"Not you?" I snicker. "How about Greece? How about when I offered you the chance to take down a criminal, illegally, and you took it?"

Her eyes narrow. "That's different."

"How is it any different than if I'd paid you? You went against the law to obtain an illegal outcome."

She stands her ground, her ferocity building.

"And I could help you do it over and over again. If justice is your calling, *true* justice, then work with me. Work without confinement under my protection."

"No."

"Why? Give me one reason."

"They're my family."

"Like hell they are." I get in her face. "They treat you like shit. They ostracized you because of your father. Apart from Easton, whose only goal is to remain between your thighs, not one of them cares about you."

Her expression crumples.

"I'm the family you're meant to have. I'm the home you need to seek comfort in."

She stares at me for long moments, blinks those thick lashes. "Comfort? Is that what you think I get from Hunter's animosity? And what about Decker's seething hatred? Every single one of your *family* despises me."

I guide my hand around her waist and she trembles beneath my hold. "They're scared of you." I lean close, grazing my cheek over hers to whisper in her ear. "You're fucking fierce. They know you're a force to be reckoned with. What you see as animosity and hatred I know to be respect."

She shakes her head.

"It's true." I breathe her in, the scent of soap and sweet shampoo sinking deep into my lungs. "If you'd told them you were mine, they'd welcome you."

"You're a liar." She tilts her face away. But all it does is give me better access to her neck.

"You're my queen." I speak against her carotid, the pebble of goose bumps rising against my lips. "We're your family."

This is me begging. Pleading.

I don't do that for anyone.

Anyone but her.

I'll swallow all my pride for this woman. I'll get on my knees. Grovel. Slit my wrists at the shrine of her existence if it means seating her in the rightful place by my side.

I scrape my teeth along her neck. Kiss her jaw. Palm her face.

"It's not right." She keeps shaking her head. "*This* isn't right."

"Maybe not." I drag my lips along her skin. I nip and suck, drawing gasps from her throat, trembles from her body. "But then why does it feel so good?"

19

ANISSA

He's wrong. This doesn't feel good. It goes beyond that. Over and above.

When I'm with him, our bodies close, it seems the rest of the world exists only for us to be together. The perfection of his touch makes it hard to imagine being like this is anything other than heaven-sent.

But the devil was sent to tempt weak souls and I've proven to be the most feeble.

I place my hands on his shoulders and add pressure, hoping he'll back away. He doesn't.

My lack of adamance seems to spur him to grab me tighter, stronger, his other arm snaking around my waist to hold me against his chest.

I whimper, wanting this and hating it, too. "I'm not like you," I whisper.

I wish I could live on sensation alone, not giving thought to morality. But once the pleasure fades and the panted breaths subside, I'll be left to wallow in self-loathing. It happens every time.

"I agree, to an extent." He brushes my lips with his fingers, the soft scrape of sensation grazing against aching nerves. "You're far better than I deserve. You're the light to my darkness."

"I don't want you to be dark."

He slides a fingertip into my mouth, only slightly, teasing the tip of my tongue. "Yes, you do."

I shudder. Tremble.

That finger in my mouth... his hard cock against my abdomen... the unrelenting strength of his chest against my breasts.

I close my eyes as his finger retreats, his mouth taking its place. He commands me with a punishing kiss, stealing my breath and my common sense.

Everything is his for the taking, including my body, which he leans down to scoop into his arms. He carries me back to the bed. Morality becomes the tiniest voice in my head, the words of warning no longer heard over the screaming desire.

He sits me on the mattress and grabs my ankles, swinging me around to face him towering above me. He stands entirely naked, remarkably hard, without one hint of insecurity. Not that I'd expect anything other than arrogant confidence from him. Not when he's carved from stone. Every muscle etched. Every limb strong.

He leans in to steal another kiss, his lips manipulating mine in a flawless dance of victory and possession. It's pure bliss. Torture, too.

Adamant hands grab my waistband, those fierce fingers gripping my pants and underwear to strip them from my body.

I should protest. I should open my goddamn mouth and stop this. But even the contemplation is laughable.

I'm lost to him. I always have been.

My surrender has never been more apparent than it is now as he holds my gaze despite my partial nudity.

"We're meant to be together." He spreads my legs apart, places a knee between my thighs, and forces me to lie down with the sheer intimidation of his approaching body. "I can't live without you."

Rough hands find my hips, skimming upward, dragging my top along with them. He exposes every inch to his hungry eyes, his adoration speaking silently in his tight expression.

I love the way he looks at me. I always have. As if he's starved and I'm his sole sustenance. But his attention only remains on my body momentarily before those eyes are back on mine.

He tugs my top over my chest, my neck, my head. In brief moments, I'm completely bare before him. At his mercy. My breathing hard to control.

"You don't know how many sleepless nights I've spent remembering your beauty." He hovers above me, one hand stabilizing his weight while the other relearns my curves. "You'll always be the most beautiful thing I've ever seen."

My heart weakens. Crumples.

He strokes the outer curve of my breast, then underneath, and over my stomach. He holds my gaze, his focus wild and intense.

"There will never be another woman for me," he vows. "There hasn't been since the moment we met."

I hear an unspoken admonishment in his admission. Or maybe it's just guilt that has me thinking he's silently accusing me of a lack of reciprocation because of Easton. The anguish lashes me regardless.

I didn't betray him.

Not the way he thinks.

But I'm compelled to seek his forgiveness.

I wrap my hand around his neck and drag his mouth back to mine. I give him my apology through the connection of eager lips. Beg for absolution in that kiss.

He matches my passion, resting his weight into me, the adamant length of his cock pressing hard into my pubic bone.

We act like teenagers. Making out. Engaging in heavy petting. Gasping for panted breaths.

He grinds his erection against me, his hand still roaming my skin, his fingers digging into my ass.

I moan, cupping his cheeks, forcing the kiss so much deeper. I can't get enough.

I claw at his hair. His shoulders. I wrap my legs around his waist and squeeze tight enough that the groan emanating in his chest rumbles through my ribs.

"You're mine, Nissa." He speaks into my mouth. "Always mine."

He reaches between us to grab his cock. It's all the prelude I get before he shoves inside me, the delicious severity making my back arch off the bed.

He thrusts hard. Over and over. Not once stopping his assault on my mouth.

It's too much. The pleasure. The consumption.

He touches every part of me. My heart. My soul.

This is why I couldn't forget him. This, right here, is why I can't move on.

This man, with his overwhelming power and undermining determination, treats me like a goddess. Like his next breath depends on my existence.

He's rabid for me, and the potency of his hunger is contagious.

"Please, don't stop." I kiss him over and over, luxuriating in his groans, demanding more of his severity.

I pulse my hips in time with his, squeezing my legs harder around him.

When he pulls back, claiming a nipple with his scorching mouth, I hiss through the burst of tingles. They're everywhere, the sensation awakening all my nerve endings.

He pays both breasts homage, licking, sucking, never stopping his thrusting assault on my pussy.

I'm a writhing, mindless mess by the time he grabs my waist and moves off the bed, his cock still inside me as he guides my ass to rest at the edge of the mattress.

"This time, I'm taking you fast and hard." His fingers dig into the flesh of my ass. "Next time, you'll be savored."

Next time.

The thought of a reoccurrence brings hope and fear. I can't commit to more. I can't even commit to a single sensible thought around him.

"Yes, you heard me." He reads my mind, his gaze narrowing. "*Next time,* you'll be savored. And the time after that. And the time after that, too."

He grips my knees, holding them at his sides as he slams into me.

Hard.

Vicious.

I claw at the bedding, needing something to cling to while he groans with the repeated impact, his eyes rolling.

Pleasure is everywhere. In my aching breasts. Tingling down my neck. No place pulsing harder than my pussy.

"I need more," I beg.

More words. More touch. More possession.

"And you'll get it," he promises. "You'll get everything you want."

I believe him. Right here, with my body at his mercy and my soul within his grasp, I unequivocally believe him.

He splays a hand over my abdomen, his thumb sliding to my clit. I gasp with the wave of bliss, my core clenching, my muscles tensing. I could come already. My mind was well within orgasm territory before he laid a hand on me. Now my body has caught up, the eager need for release growing into an obsession.

I rock into each of his thrusts and squeeze my core every time his cock slides home. I shake my head, overwhelmed, out of breath. "*Cole.*"

He doesn't quit devouring me with his gaze, wordlessly complimenting me with the hunger in his eyes.

He makes me feel adored. Cherished. I never have to question my worth when we're together this way because he stares at me like I'm his entire world.

His universe.

With the next retreat of his cock, he moves his thumb lower, sliding it inside me as he thrusts home. The delicious stretch of my core pulls a gasp from my throat. The friction of his palm against my clit brings mindlessness.

I pant. Whimper.

He doesn't stop fucking me. His rhythm only increases—harder, faster—as his thumb remains hooked inside me.

"Give me what I want," he demands. "Come on my dick."

I couldn't deny him even if I wanted to. I unravel, my neck and back arching, my core spasming with each thrust.

I don't cry his name, even though I want to. I keep the pleas locked inside as wave upon wave of pleasure wracks me. It's all I can do not to blurt my unwanted feelings as he releases inside me, his animalistic display far more erotic than I remember.

I wanted this.

I needed it.

But regret inevitably hits me before the pleasure truly subsides. He's thrusting with the last of his release when I reach rock bottom.

I'm pulled in different directions, my body begging to relax into satiation while my mind admonishes my stupidity.

"Eventually, you will stop second-guessing yourself." He steps back, leaving me cold, and makes for the bathroom to return with a damp cloth. "When you quit fighting this and realize it's fate, you'll be much happier."

"Is that what you've done? Do you simply ignore the fact we're enemies?"

He stares down at me, his eyes gentle despite his hardened face. "You're no enemy of mine. Even if you wanted to be."

His sincerity tears strips from me. Layer upon layer of hardened skin.

I ignore the offered cloth and scoot from the bed to escape into the bathroom. I lock myself inside and use the facilities. I wash my face. Scrub my hands. Glare at myself in the mirror.

"Quit fighting, Nis," he calls from the bedroom. "I won't let you shut me out again."

I clutch the counter, feeling compelled to comply.

I want to stop fighting. I want it more than anything.

It seems as though the last few years of my life have been one unending battle. First, I waged war against those who tarnished my father's name. Then I fought with my hatred toward Cole. And now, I combat my yearning for the same man.

I don't want to struggle anymore. But what's the alternative?

I grab a towel from a nearby rack and secure it around my breasts, as if the plush material can shield me against more foolish decisions, then leave the bathroom.

The bedroom is now in shadow, the soft glow from the living room seeping in from the partially opened door.

Cole is back in bed, the sheet covering him to the waist, one arm resting behind his head. "We'll make it work."

"How?" I remain a foot from the bathroom. "My conflicts aren't something that can be wished away. My career is—"

"I'll figure it out."

"You can't."

"Nissa, let me deal with one problem at a time." His voice is tired. "Let me get the kids back, then I'll convince you."

Guilt assails me at the reminder of why I'm here. But I can't help wanting him to convince me. More than anything, I want to stay in this bubble of passion and possession.

I've spent too long surrounded by people in a big city while remaining entirely alone. Even with Easton practically living in my apartment, I felt completely detached from the human race. But it's different when I'm with Cole. Our arguments are adrenaline-filled challenges. He wakes me up to the reality of the world. He teaches me—

"Get back in bed." He rolls away from me, toward the middle of the mattress, and pats my pillow. "And take off that goddamn towel."

I smother a half-hearted smile, vowing to never admit how much I love it when he slips into bouts of dictatorship. Especially when the directives are for my benefit.

I pad around the bed, meeting his gaze before I drop the towel to my feet.

His eyes don't stray from mine. He doesn't take the opportunity to visually ravage my nudity, and it's more than slightly disappointing.

"You don't care too much about looking at me anymore, do you?" I climb onto the mattress, fighting insecurity, and pull the sheet up to my shoulders.

"Why do you say that?" He reaches out, locking an arm around my waist to haul me closer.

Because since I put on the tiny bit of extra weight he so kindly pointed out this morning, he doesn't seem to want to do anything other than hold my gaze while I'm still entirely starved of the sight of his body. I could stare at the contours and sinew forever and never grow tired.

"It's just an observation, Cole."

He remains quiet for a while, his eyes holding mine, his fingertips lazily circling my back.

"I never stopped watching you in Greece," he murmurs. "I ate up every moment with you naked beside me. I watched you while you slept. I learned every curve. I even have the security footage from your room when we first arrived."

I tense, not appreciating the reminder of my invaded privacy. The hit to my pride is made all the worse when a subtle smirk curves his lips.

"Good night." I shuffle backward, moving away from his touch.

"You're not going to let me finish?"

"Nope." I roll over, turning my back to him. I need rest. It's not in my best interests to let him stir up my anger before I try to fall asleep.

He huffs out a breath. "The reason I hold your gaze is because I've never forgotten the beauty of your body, but what I struggle to recall are the memories of you looking at me in return."

My pulse increases, the gentle thump building into a tremendous boom.

"I crave the truth in your eyes, little fox. I need to see those feelings you work so hard to hide because they're what keep me fighting for you. They're the only things that help convince me you can't be entirely in love with that piece of shit who spends all his time in your apartment."

My heart squeezes, my lies gouging at me with sharp claws.

"I'm not in love with him," I admit.

He doesn't respond. The only shift in the room is the anticipation thickening the air.

"I haven't slept with Easton. I've kissed him once. And that was at the exact moment you knocked on my door the other night." I place my hands under the pillow at my cheek and tangle my fingers together. "There's never been anything substantial between us. Not even a proper date."

I wait for the gloating to start. But the boasting and bragging I expect doesn't happen.

Instead, there's a subtle shift in the bed before Cole's arm glides possessively around my waist.

"Don't." I scoot toward the edge of the mattress, needing space to come to terms with my admission. My feelings. I can't avoid them any longer.

There's no Stockholm to excuse how much I want to be with him. There's no manipulation or intimidation. Just misguided, unavoidable love. It feels like home here with him, and I don't know how to make it stop.

"Don't deny me." His arm turns to stone, imprisoning me as he closes in tight against my back. His mouth finds my shoulder, his warm lips brushing my neck. "Not when this is the best news I've heard in weeks."

"I don't want to talk about it anymore."

"Then we won't. But I *will* hold you. It's all I ask."

I shouldn't allow myself the affection. It's one thing to fuck in the heat of uncontrollable lust. It's quite another to succumb to tenderness. And that's exactly what it feels like when his lips continue to pepper kisses along my shoulder blade—pure loving tenderness.

His soft side slays me. Enslaves.

"Get some rest, my little fox," he murmurs against my skin. "I'm going to need your strength tomorrow."

I close my eyes, aching for a myriad of reasons. The danger upon us. The emotional exhaustion. The inevitable goodbye.

This will all come crashing down.

"Good night." I attempt to clear my mind, forcing unwanted thoughts away. I pretend this thing between us is normal. Natural. We're not complete opposites. Or enemies. We're everyday smitten schmucks who have white-picket-fence and two-point-five-kids potential.

His arm grows heavier, his breathing deepening into something resembling slumber. I will myself to do the same. To be at peace.

It takes forever to get to sleep, and when morning comes a few seconds pass before I register the lack of muscled warmth surrounding me.

Cole isn't in bed. He's not even in the room.

"Where are you?" I sit and throw back the covers, sliding from the mattress.

"Out here." His voice carries from the living area, behind the now closed bedroom door.

What also carries are other voices. Hunter's. Decker's. Layla's.

Shit.

I rush to tug on my pajamas and stumble to the door, pulling it open a crack to see everyone scattered around the living room. Keira, Benji, and Sarah are on the sofas. Luca and Layla drink from mugs in the kitchen. Decker and Hunter give me scathing scowls from Cole's side, while Penny smiles with gentle warmth as she picks up a piece of bacon from a large serving tray.

Goddamnit. How the hell did I sleep through this?

"Have you heard anything yet?" I pull the door open a fraction wider and rake a hand through my tangled hair.

"Not yet." Cole meets my gaze. "But one of my assets from the bank has some potential leads on where they could be."

"Why didn't you wake me?" I regret the question as soon as it comes out. I regret it even more when the knowing stares of everyone in the room weigh down on me. "Don't answer that. I'm going to get dressed."

Their murmured conversation rekindles as I retreat into the bedroom, closing the door behind me, and hustle into the bathroom. I take a quick shower and brush my teeth.

I'm barely dressed and frantically combing my hair when Cole opens the bathroom door.

"I'm leaving," he states simply. "I should be back with the kids soon."

He speaks as if he's picking them up from school or band practice, not from the clutches of a man who could potentially kill them all.

"You heard from Emmanuel?" My hands fall to my sides, my heart dropping along with them.

He pulls his cell from the pocket of his suit jacket and passes it over, showing a text message with an address.

"I want to come with you." I rush to place my brush on the counter and straighten my blouse. "I'll keep watch from nearby."

"No, you need to stay here." He steps closer, reclaiming his phone. "Look after my sisters."

"But it could be a setup. I should—"

"I know." He stands tall. Strong. Not an ounce of fear in sight. "But my hands are tied regardless. If we have to shoot our way out of this, we will, which is just another reason why I want you to stay here. If this turns south, I know you'll get my sisters home."

My stomach sinks, and not only from the responsibility he lays at my feet. This feels like goodbye.

"Cole—"

"We'll be fine. I thought about this all night and Emmanuel can't be stupid enough to risk a legitimate empire to start a war with me. The handover will be smooth."

He doesn't believe that. I know he doesn't.

No sane person would keep those kids like Costa has.

"Look after my sisters." He leans closer, pausing when he's a breath away from my mouth, as if waiting for me to back away.

I don't. I can't.

I bridge the space between us, placing my lips against his, and wither into the kiss. I don't want to be scared for him. I don't even want to care if he lives or dies. But I've never been more fearful for someone's death than I am right now.

I can't lose him.

"It'll be okay." He pulls away, turning to walk for the door before I can meet his gaze. "I'll see you soon."

20

COLE

Hunter and Benji climb into the Escalade with me, while the injured party of Decker and Luca ride in another vehicle behind us. It only takes a few short minutes to get to the apartment building where Emmanuel told us to meet.

I park in the one available space nearby and climb out, straightening the lapels of my suit as I stalk across the road toward the front doors of the towering construction.

My plan is fluid, the myriad of multiplying strategies dissected with my men this morning while Anissa remained asleep.

All that matters is getting those kids out.

"Decker and Luca are going to try to get on the rooftop across the street like you asked." Hunter keeps pace at my side. "Let's hope they can get eyes on us once we figure out what floor we're on."

Benji jogs to catch up. "Let's hope we're not in there long enough for them to bother."

I ignore the chitchat. I don't need the distraction.

"What happens if they're hurt?" Benji asks. "What if they're not there at all?"

I reach the glass doors at the front of the building and pull one open, letting them precede me. "They'll be there."

"But if he's done something to them—"

"The kids will be fine." I won't be able to control my rage if they're not. I'm at risk of putting all our lives on the line if Emmanuel has hurt them. "We're getting them back and taking them home. End of story."

I follow them inside, my focus switching to Hunt as we continue toward the sign pointing us to the elevators around a corner. "Are you ready?"

He nods. "Always. This isn't going to be a problem."

I don't know if he's faking the bravado, but I appreciate it. I need all the confident positivity I can get because the farther we walk through the lobby, the more this feels like a trap.

Nobody is around. Not a single soul.

I'm already antsy to draw my gun. I'll be a fucking hair-trigger away from a bloodbath by the time I face Emmanuel.

We turn the corner and find a hulking man standing in the middle of the elevator bay, the three gleaming doors positioned to his right.

He uncrosses his arms from his chest and stares past Hunter and Benji to look me up and down. "Are you Mr. Torian?"

"Yes. And you are?"

"I'm the one escorting you today. The others will need to remain in the lobby."

My plan takes its first hit. I'd hoped I wouldn't have to do this on my own. No backup. No fucking shield for those kids. But this isn't unexpected.

"Like hell," Hunter growls. "He's not going anywhere alone."

"Then he doesn't go at all." The guard shrugs. "Your choice."

Hunt reaches behind his back, preparing to retrieve his gun. "What's to stop us relieving you of your duties and going floor to floor until we find them?"

"Probably the infallible level of security." The guy smirks. "I'm merely the gatekeeper."

"You fucking son of a bitch." Benji rushes for him.

I lunge, grabbing my brother-in-law by the arm to haul him back to my side. The guard doesn't flinch. There's no fear or concern. Whatever he means by infallible security, it's enough to make him confident of his protection while in front of three men salivating for revenge.

"This is the father of the little girl." I pat Benji on the chest in a subtle warning to remain calm. "Surely he's allowed to accompany me for the sake of his daughter's comfort."

"She's comfortable enough. All you're doing is wasting time. Nobody else will accompany us. Take it or leave it."

Benji bristles. "What the fuck does that mean? If we refuse, what happens to my daughter?"

"Those decisions are above my pay grade." He steps toward the bank of elevators, hovering his finger above the call button. "Are we going up or not?"

Hunter mutters a string of unintelligible garble under his breath as he retreats, then says, "Cole, I need to speak to you."

I contemplate escaping into the elevator before he can outline more issues to compact my already heavily stacked deck. Panic isn't something I need right now.

"Give me five seconds." He continues backward.

I follow, keeping my attention on the guard. "Call the elevator. I'll return in a minute."

Benji remains at my side as we meet around the corner, Hunter immediately reaching into my suit jacket to retrieve my phone.

"What are you doing?" I scowl.

"Calling myself," he murmurs, holding the device up to my face to unlock the recognition software. He taps through screens until a vibration sounds in his pants. "I'm not going to bother talking you out of this. I already know you've made up your mind. But at least this way I can hear what's going on." He keeps his voice low, barely above a whisper as he pulls out his device and answers the call. "We'll start scouring floors. If there's all this security that asshole spoke about, it won't be hard to determine where you are."

I agree. But starting a search isn't an option. Not when Benji is fidgeting like a crack addict. He's not in his right mind. I never should've brought him along.

"I want you to remain down here." I reach into my pants pocket, pulling out the car fob. "Better yet, wait in the Escalade. I can't risk this being fucked up by someone acting on emotion."

"No." Benji gives a frantic shake of his head. "I won't fuck—

"Go to the car." I shove the fob at Hunter's chest. "Keep him under control, and link Luca, Deck, and Anissa into the phone call."

"Anissa?" he snarls.

"You heard me. If this is a trap, I need her to be aware so she can get my sisters to safety."

His eyes harden with disapproval. I don't give a shit.

I'm so fucking impatient to have this over and done with. "Go." I jerk my chin toward the doors. "Be ready for when I return with those kids."

I don't wait for compliance. I turn on my heels and walk around the corner, coming face-to-face with the guard who shoves his finger against the elevator call button, the doors gliding open instantly.

I lead the way into the enclosed space and clear my head of toxic pessimism.

I'm going to get those fucking kids. It'll be a cakewalk. No dramatics. No foul play.

The guard follows, pressing the button to close the doors once he's inside. "I'm going to need you to surrender any weapons you might have." He holds out a hand. "And before you think about keeping any hidden, I'll be patting you down to make sure you comply."

I grind my teeth and retrieve my gun to slap it into his palm. "I expect to get that back."

"What else have you got?"

"Nothing." I spread my arms wide and glower as he frisks me.

"You're a smart man." He says once he's done. "Mr. Costa will appreciate that." He turns to the doors, using a security panel to tap in a pin code before pressing the button to the penthouse.

The restrictive coffin glides into movement, the smooth ascent raising the hair on the back of my neck. My only saving grace is the cell in my pocket giving me some sense of backup. But that's a mirage at best. Nobody can help me here. The success or failure of retrieving these kids is on my shoulders.

After the elevator stops, the doors open into an expansive sunlit entertaining area.

"Walk toward the kitchen," the guard instructs. "Once you reach the dining area, continue down the hall to the first door on your left. You'll find Mr. Costa in the study. I'll have your gun waiting for you on ground level."

I step out onto the marble tile. "Why am I not surprised he's in the penthouse?" I say for Hunter's benefit.

There's no reply apart from the gentle glide of closing steel as the elevator leaves, taking the guard with it.

This place is wide open space. The living room before me with its modular sofa and towering artistic paintings transitions into the dining area up ahead, with the kitchen beside it on the left. Closest to me is a staircase with a glass balustrade leading to a hall on the upper level.

But there's no fucking security.

There isn't a soul in sight as I continue forward, scanning nearby rooftops, hoping a familiar rifle scope is tracking my movements. There's no sound either. No voices of children or of men—only the slow thud of my footfalls.

I reach the kitchen, eying the darkened hall up ahead with the soft glow of artificial light coming from the open office doorway. I stop, waiting for a hint of the approaching trap to shut in around me, and hear the low murmur of muffled conversation in the distance.

I don't doubt it's Costa, but when there's no evidence those kids are even here I'm loath to move further. I'm lacking alternatives though.

I have to keep walking.

I follow my instructions to the start of the hall, the foreign conversation growing louder. I keep my head high, letting anyone watching via hidden surveillance know that I'm not fucking daunted in the slightest when I reach the office threshold and scowl as I look inside.

"Mr. Torian." Costa sits behind a grand oak desk in a cream woolen sweater, smiling enough to make deep wrinkles around his eyes.

Two men—his sons—flank him in black suits, their posture stiff, faces blank. Even if I hadn't done my research, it wouldn't be hard to recognize the resemblance in the chiseled jawlines and tightly pressed lips.

"It's good to see you again." The old man beams. "You were a child the last time I laid eyes on you."

I keep my mouth shut, unable to reciprocate the civility, and focus my attention on a younger man seated on what looks to be a dining chair at the left side of the desk, facing me.

There's no natural light in here. The curtains are drawn. But I can clearly see the fear emanating from the guy as his leg jolts a frantic rhythm. This fucker has *guilt* written all over his pockmarked face.

"Let me introduce you." Costa reclaims my attention, sliding backward in his plush office chair to pivot to the left, waving a hand at the raven-haired man behind him. "This is my oldest boy, Salvatore."

He swings in the other direction, indicating the son with lighter features, dark blond hair. "And Remy."

Both men are roughly my age, the spite in their eyes matching my own. They're battle ready. I may not be able to glimpse a weapon but I'm sure they're locked and loaded under their designer suit jackets.

"Enough with the pleasantries." I return my stare to Emmanuel. "Where are my niece and brother?"

"Your brother?" He raises a brow. "Interesting. I wasn't aware your father had another child."

"Where are they?" I add vehemence to my tone.

"There's no need to rush. We have a lot to discuss." He indicates one of the leather chairs in front of the desk. "Sit. Please. These unfortunate circumstances could work out to be an exciting opportunity for us all."

My palms heat, the building sweat the first sign of my waning restraint. "I have no time for exciting opportunities. My sister is beside herself with worry. And those kids must be—"

"Those kids have had a wonderful time. And I told you there was nothing to concern yourself with. We're all family here. Now sit."

Burning animosity claims me. Heat lashes my neck. Cheeks. Throat.

"Sit." His smile fades, his psychotic jubilation simmering. "While I have you here, I want to discuss some business I had with your father."

"I'm not discussing anything until I see those kids." I stride forward, grabbing the top of the chair he's trying so hard to get me into, the leather squeaking beneath my harsh grip. "Not a damn fucking thing, old man."

He sighs. "As you wish." He glances over his shoulder to Remy. "Take him to see the children. Make it quick."

The son jerks his chin in acknowledgement and strides around the desk to the office door. I stalk after him, following back down the hall, past the kitchen.

"Wait here." He continues up the stairs to walk from view.

The eerie silence returns, the open and close of a door in the distance the only sound. None of this makes sense. Costa is far too calm and collected. There's no malice. And the fatherly act grates on my nerves.

The door opens again bringing numerous sets of footfalls. Heavy ones.

A hulking guard comes into view at the top landing. Another passes, descending to the bottom of the stairs. Then Remy escorts an older lady, two surprised kiddie faces peeking out from around her waist.

She must be Emmanuel's crazy-ass wife.

"Uncle Cole?" Stella's eyes widen before she rushes down the steps.

My relief is suffocating. I grin at her, dropping to a knee as she runs into my arms.

"I was so worried." Her arms squeeze around my neck, tight enough to stifle circulation.

"I know, princess." I return the hug, resting my head against hers. "But everything is all right. You're safe."

She clings tighter, refusing to let go.

"Did anyone hurt you?" I whisper in her ear. "Are you okay?"

"I have a big bruise on my stomach." She leans back, meeting my gaze. "And my head is sore."

My veins surge with the searing need for retaliation.

"That didn't happen on our watch." Remy makes his way down the stairs, passing the guard. "They've been looked after since arriving here."

Stella nods, but the confirmation doesn't lessen my struggle. That fucker in the office hurt her. *Bruised* her. What else did he do while she was unconscious?

"I understand what you're thinking," the older woman adds from the upper level. "And I assure you there's nothing to worry about. I would stake my life on it."

How the fuck would she know? She better not have examined my niece.

"Don't worry, Uncle Cole." Stella cups my cheeks. "My stomach hurts a little, but I'm okay."

She calms me the slightest bit, only enough to stop me seeing red.

"And how about Tobias?" I guide Stella to my side and reach for my half-brother who slowly walks toward us. "Are you okay?"

"I'm good." His gaze seeks Remy's, as if in approval.

The man doesn't react.

Pressure builds inside my skull. Someone has to pay for what's been done. Someone here, within these walls. "Do you have any bruises?"

Tobias shrugs. Once. Succinct. "Mine aren't as bad as Stella's."

"And Emmanuel has taken good care of you?"

They both nod, not needing encouragement from the man's son to make their decision. Not that the lack of prodding makes their response genuine. It merely means it's possible they were trained prior to my arrival.

"It's time for us to get back to the office," Remy instructs. "We've got a lot to discuss. Tobias why don't you take Stella back upstairs to play for a while?"

Both children look at me with widening eyes. It isn't fear exactly. There's surprise. Followed by heartfelt disappointment.

"I want to go home." Stella grabs my hand, entwining her small fingers with mine. "They've been nice, but I don't want to stay any longer."

I raise my gaze to Emmanuel's son. "You heard her. It's time to go."

The guy smiles, the curve of his lips contrasting with his harsh eyes. "I insist." He slides a hand beneath his jacket, making a barely subtle move for his gun.

The guards do the same.

Fucking pricks.

At least they're not obvious enough to upset the children.

"Fine. I'll give you a few minutes." I untangle my fingers from Stella's.

"Wait." Tobias dives for me, wrapping his arms around my neck to snuggle close in an unexpected show of affection. He's not a clingy kid. He's barely touched me since I found out about his existence in Greece, so having him bury his face in my neck is a fucking shock.

"They're not good people," he murmurs in my ear. "They didn't hurt us, but they're not good people."

I stiffen and force myself to wrap my arms around his shoulders, the reciprocated affection the only acknowledgement I can give as the adults scrutinize us. "I miss you, too, kiddo."

"Come on now." Remy jerks his chin toward the stairs. "Go back to your room and play for a while."

"It's okay, children." The older woman coos from above. "We can start another game of Candyland."

Stella remains hesitant while Tobias releases me, slowly inching backward.

"Go." I nod. "Don't worry."

I battle an invisible army as they reluctantly walk side by side to the guard at the bottom of the stairs. I'm thrumming with the need to act. To fucking slaughter. The compulsion for revenge makes goose bumps break out along my arms. But I keep myself in check and push to my feet, not saying a word as they climb the steps to meet the woman at the top.

"My father isn't a patient man," Remy warns.

A plethora of my own subtle threats bite at the tip of my tongue, demanding to be heard. I swallow their bitter taste and glare before making my way back through the living room, down the hall, to the office, finding Emmanuel in the same place behind the desk. Salvatore has remained at his side, the jittery fucker still anxiously pulsing his foot against the floor.

"I told you they would be well looked after." Emmanuel's face lights with sickening enthusiasm. "They have been a delight for me and my wife to spend time with. We're yet to be blessed with grandchildren. So our hearts have been warmed by this act of fate."

I breathe through my temper. I clench my teeth against the possessive violence inside me.

Emmanuel is fucking insane if he isn't unsettled by the current situation. He has no clue what I'm capable of. Or if he does, he's too maniacal to care.

Either way, he'll soon learn.

"Is this the man responsible?" I glower at the young guy who repositions himself in the wooden chair. "Did you steal them from my home?"

He doesn't respond as I stalk forward, sidestepping the leather seats to stop before him. "Are you the one who bruised their skin?"

His mouth opens, closes, opens again. He's a pathetic gaping fish, gulping for air.

"Yes," Emmanuel answers. "This is Jordan. I assure you he's remorseful for his actions. And accepts whatever punishment necessary."

Whatever punishment? I scoff.

No, he would never accept if he knew what was going through my head. Instead, he'd run, and so he should.

"How did you do it?" I snarl, discreetly scanning my surroundings. I take in any potential weapon within reach, every glint of metal, every sharp, pointed object.

He shakes his head. "I just did what Robert told me to do. We timed your guards. We knew when we could slip in and out unnoticed. It wasn't hard."

His confession is a lethal hit to my pride.

He stole from me. Easily. Without concern.

"And their bruises? If the crime against me wasn't hard, then I assume hurting those kids was intentional."

He glances to Emmanuel.

"Look at me, asshole." I grab his chin, wrenching his attention back to mine. *"Why* were they hurt?"

"I-I dropped the girl while trying to climb over your wall." He frantically shakes his head. "It was an accident. I never meant to—"

"It wasn't an accident to abduct them. So what did Robert plan to do with them?"

He keeps shaking his head. "I don't know. I swear I have no idea."

"Were you aware he was a rapist? A human trafficker?" I get closer, right in his face as I dig my fingertips into his jaw. "Did you even spare a single thought to what could've been done to them?"

There's no response.

"You stole from me," I grit through clenched teeth. "You handed over two of the most valued people in my life to a man capable of unfathomable atrocities, and you don't even have the balls to answer me?"

The whites of his eyes increase. His shaking doubles.

"Did you kill their nanny?"

"No." He reaches for the edge of the desk, clinging tight. "I didn't kill her. I just injected her with some—"

I lunge for the metal letter opener partially hidden under the stack of papers on Emmanuel's desk, twisting it in my palm before stabbing it into the top of his hand, straight through to the wood beneath.

Jordan yells, the sound vibrating off the walls before I slam my palm over his mouth.

I press harder and harder, until his suffering is nothing more than smothered whimpers. "You killed her. She was barely an adult herself and you gave her a lethal dose."

Moisture fills his eyes as he frantically attempts to dislodge the weapon pinning him.

"You're struggling." I narrow my gaze. "Let me help."

He stops. I'm not sure why. Maybe he senses my delight at his suffering and the barely leashed hunger for more.

The best part is that Emmanuel doesn't say a word. He doesn't attempt to stop me. For all the wrongs he's done, the silence from him and his sons is a start toward atonement.

"Please," Jordan begs under my palm. "I'm sorry."

I nod, removing my grip from his mouth. "I'm sure you are. Did you even know who you were messing with when you agreed to work with Robert?"

"No. I just thought you were some rich business guy. I thought—"

I tug the letter opener from its pinned place in the desk, releasing his blood-covered hand.

"Shh." I place a finger to my lips as he whimpers. "You wouldn't want to scare those children again. They've been through enough."

The first tear falls down his cheek while he sniffs back the dribble from his nose. "I'm sorry, man. You've gotta believe me."

"Don't worry. I do." I wipe the carnage from the letter opener onto his pants, and he tenses. "You made a mistake you'll never repeat."

He nods. "I promise I won't. I'll never do anything to you. I'll never even—"

"I know you won't." I keep holding his gaze, devouring his fear, letting it sink deep into my chest to soothe my anger. "I'm going to make sure of it."

I launch the letter opener at his temple.

His eyes widen. His mouth drops.

My pulse thunders as I pierce the metal blade through skin, then bone.

He shudders, then slackens, his entire body turning limp. Dead.

For a few heartbeats, there's nothing but deafening silence. Pure, euphoric revenge. Until the *drip, drip, drip* of his blood begins to pool on the carpet.

Still, there's no response from anyone in the room as I jiggle the weapon free and wipe my fingerprints from the shiny metal with the handkerchief in my pocket.

"I hope you don't mind me borrowing your letter opener." I meet Emmanuel's gaze as I return the weapon to its original place on the desk. I'd wanted to see fear reflected in his features. At the least, I expected trepidation. But he lacks emotion. All of them do.

"That was unfortunate," he murmurs. "I would've appreciated if his mistake wasn't punished with something as barbaric as death, but I understand the reputation you must need to uphold."

Unfortunate?

He's not intimidated by me at all. Or at the very least, he's fucking good at not showing it.

"Boys, drag Jordan into the bathroom. He's an unnecessary distraction, and I don't want the blood to settle into the carpet."

His sons round the table, undeterred as they grab the chair and carry the body from the room, smearing a trail of carnage along the way.

"That's better." Emmanuel holds my attention through the removal. "Now, we can finally talk."

"What's to talk about?" I try not to scramble even though my options are narrowing.

"Our future." He smiles, mischief lighting his eyes. "And the things we can achieve if we work together. Would you like a coffee or maybe some tea? We might be here a while."

After what I just did, I'm surprised this fucker is offering me a beverage. He knows I don't want anything other than those kids. At a close second, I want this psychopath to drop the joker grin and level with me.

"Please take a seat, Cole. This is important. I wouldn't hold you up if it wasn't."

I stroll to the front of the chair, sit, and lean back to cross my feet at the ankles, ignoring the deep red staining the carpet in my periphery. "Start talking."

He claps his hands together in delight. "Now, as I've mentioned numerous times, your father and I were once close friends."

"Drifting apart from him is common. He hasn't kept in touch with many people since moving to Greece. Myself included."

"That's what I'm told." He nods. "Among other things…"

He's alluding to insight. To secrets.

I don't bite. Not even a fucking nibble.

"When we were close," he continues, "we had many plans to align our families. Combining my legitimate empire with your…" He frowns as if attempting to find the right word.

"Lucrative one?" I drawl.

He chuckles. "*Criminal* was the description I was looking for. We discussed in detail how my reputable imports were a great way for your family to smuggle product into the country—either what you already specialize in, or something more diverse. And the strength of my distribution channels has only increased with my business's success."

"I have no problems with my distribution, Costa. And no interest in aligning with anyone I don't trust. So unless you have something else to offer, I'm going to have to politely decline and be on my way."

"You have no problems now. But who's to say things won't change?" His smile fades with his rising brows. "Especially if you're using the same strategies as your father. He always tended to be generous with sharing information when he had a few too many drinks."

Is he threatening to shut me down? To rat me out?

I bark a laugh. "What do you want?"

"A partnership." Those white veneers flash at me again, bright and fucking sickening. "I want in on your little slice of heaven and to expand the playing field beyond your wildest dreams."

No.

This guy wouldn't know the first thing about the drug trade. And expansion isn't for chumps like him. It takes a lot of balls to claim someone else's territory, and when this guy has come to me for help instead of trying to take for himself, it's clear he doesn't have a decent set.

"I want what your father promised me." His tone loses any hint of civility as he opens a desk drawer, retrieves a sheet of tattered paper, and slides it toward me. "And this is what I'll get."

I take the scuffed offering to read my father's handwriting, my jaw tightening with each new line of text.

"Luther promised you an arranged marriage with one of my sisters?" I place the informal signed contract down on the desk and eye the letter opener within reach. "And you think that's going to happen? We're not living in the eighteenth century."

"I'm afraid I'm at a point where I must insist."

His sons return to the room, hands clean, faces impassive as they reclaim their soldier positions behind a man who's soon to die.

"Marriage is the best option to ensure an unbreakable agreement." That indulgent fucking smile doesn't fade. "We are both going to make more money than we ever dreamed possible. And generations to come will praise us for it."

"Thanks for the generous offer." I push to my feet. "But I'm not interested."

Maybe if he'd come to me a year ago. Before my father's degradation was exposed. Before those fucking kids were stolen. Before Anissa became everything.

"Well, you should be." His tone deepens, losing the edge of delirious kindness. "You seem to be in over your head, Cole."

He stands, leaning forward to rest his knuckles on the desk. "There are rumors your father is dead. Killed by his own son, no less. I'm sure it would be harmful if that information were to begin circulating. Especially with the loyalty Luther demanded. It wouldn't just be those children you'd need to worry about. It would be your sisters. Your men. Your entire empire."

I clench my teeth, the pain radiating into my skull. "Is that a threat? Because I take just as kindly to those as I do to theft."

"Of course not." He skirts the desk to walk toward me and rests his ass against the closest edge. "I'm merely pointing out that you may have taken a path you need help to retreat from. I'm that help, son."

I have no response. Not unless it involves snatching that fucking letter opener and slamming it into his throat. But I wouldn't get close before his sons filled me with bullets.

"Layla is already married." I force a placating smile. "And Keira is committed to one of my men. So, unfortunately, your sons will have to find their own unwilling brides."

"How about you?" Salvatore speaks for the first time, his voice graveled. "From what we're told you're still unattached."

I sneer at him. "You want to marry me, asshole?"

Remy grins, the curve of lips quickly disappearing into a tight line.

"He's referring to a match with my daughter," Emmanuel clarifies. "Abri would be well suited to a man like you."

My fingers itch to claim a gun I don't have. To pull a trigger that's nowhere in reach. "Again, that's a generous offer. But an arranged marriage isn't something I'm interested in. And I'm sure your daughter would feel the same. Now, if you'll bring the children back downstairs, we'll be leaving."

Silence reigns as the three men stare at me. The sons with eagle eyes. Their father with demented optimism.

"I understand where you're coming from." He remains perched on the desk, crossing his feet at the ankles. "However, I think your father would be disappointed in me if I didn't push for this opportunity. So I'm going to insist you take a night or two to think it over. Speak to your family. Contemplate the success. I'll continue to look after the children until you've had a chance to consider this more thoroughly."

21

ANISSA

Penny covers her mouth with a shaking hand as she stares at my cell sitting on the coffee table, the muffled conversation from the four-way phone call filtering through the speaker.

Keira is pale beside her.

Layla quit reacting a long time ago. She's now catatonic. Apart from the relieved cry she released at the sound of her daughter's voice, she's sat in shock, the only sign of life coming from her blinking eyes and trembling fingers.

At first, I hadn't known why Hunter called me. There was no greeting. Only silence. Then Cole's voice filtered through, announcing something about a 'penthouse'.

For long minutes, we've sat listening to his exchange with Emmanuel. We heard Stella's excitement. Vaguely made out a murmur from Tobias. Through it all, I've battled not to excuse myself to the bedroom to secretly call for backup. Well, I *had*, until Cole's conversation with Jordan.

Now it's too late.

The person who drove the kids to Sacramento is dead and the man I slept with last night is responsible. There's no requesting FBI support for that. There's no longer a claim to innocence in this situation.

"He's trying to force an arranged marriage?" Keira asks. "How is this even a thing?"

Layla closes her eyes. "How can you be surprised with everything else our father has done?"

She's right. This isn't as shocking as it should be.

It's sickening, though, the sinking sensation leaving me cold.

Only yesterday I'd convinced myself there might be a way to further indulge in my feelings for Cole. To somehow make it work between us. This is a slap in the face to those ignorant wishes. A shaking of my reality to show just how different our lives are. This archaic, arranged marriage only cements the extremes.

"What are we going to do?" Sarah stares at me, waiting for an answer.

"Let me listen."

The call has gone quiet, the conversation seeming to vanish mid-threat.

"Why aren't they talking?" Keira reaches for the phone. "What happened?"

I claim the cell and raise it to my ear.

There's nothing. No sound. No hint of static.

I unlock the screen and my heart drops. "The call ended. Either Cole disconnected or Hunter kicked us from the conversation."

"Why would that happen?" Penny stumbles to her feet. "What could possibly be worse than what we already heard?"

"He would've accepted the arranged marriage," Layla whispers. "He would've given his word to get my daughter out but wouldn't have wanted anyone to overhear him bowing under pressure."

Bile screams up my throat.

This wasn't meant to happen.

"Everything will be all right." Sarah reaches for Penny, dragging her back down to the sofa. "Cole needed to say whatever necessary to bring those kids home. But we'll fix it afterward."

Keira shakes her head. "If he commits, then he won't back out. He doesn't give his word without meaning it. Not even to his enemies. He either plans to marry this woman or has every intention of killing her to nullify the agreement."

"No," I blurt. "He could've lied."

They all look at me. The sisters with pity. Penny and Sarah with confusion.

"He plays games and manipulates the truth. He won't go through with it. Once he has Stella and Tobias, he'll pretend none of this happened."

"Maybe he's done that to you." Keira cringes. "And I apologize on his behalf, but this is business. In your world, there are contracts and legal documents to outline agreements. Here, Cole's word is his bond. He won't go back on it. Otherwise he'll never be trusted again."

My heart twists.

He'd given *me* his word. He'd promised to make us work. To figure out how we could indulge in this crazy compulsion between us.

I guess I should count myself lucky the universe is acting as my handbrake when I can't keep my grip on the wheel.

"Try not to panic." Sarah gives me a pointed look. "The kids are what matter right now."

Keira wrings her hands in front of her as she stares at the carpet. "Aligning ourselves with this family after what they've done is a horrible idea. Betraying them could be even worse."

My stomach churns. "I have to use the bathroom." I escape into the main bedroom, closing the door behind me to focus on not losing my shit.

I need space. Air. Clarity would help, too.

This is what I should've wanted all along. Having a valid reason to distance myself from the temptation of Cole has been a huge issue for me. *No*, not a *valid* reason. I had a million of those all along. But this would act as an immovable stop sign between us.

A definitive brick wall.

So why does it feel like Armageddon is approaching? Why does this growing ache inside my chest resemble heartbreak? For *him*. For what he's going through.

I breathe through the searing burn in my lungs and shake off the instability. I need to forge ahead. Focus on Stella and Tobias. It's not the time to wallow.

"They're on their way back," Sarah calls out moments later. "They should be here in five."

I scramble for the doorknob and launch out of the bedroom. "All of them? Are they okay?"

Sarah raises her cell, showing me the tiny text on screen. "That's all I know— *We're on our way back. Should be there in five.*"

Layla remains catatonic on the sofa, slowly rocking back and forth.

Keira continues to wring her hands, squeezing her fingers.

Penny bites hard into her lower lip, staring into space.

I'm not helping here. Why am I not helping?

"The kids are coming home, ladies. This is good news." I force positivity into my voice and walk to the closest sofa. "We need to get our things and prepare to leave as soon as possible. We're going home."

Nobody moves. Not even Sarah.

I crouch before Layla, placing my palms on her knees. "Stella's on her way."

She stares at me. Stares right through me.

"The weapons and tactical equipment are the only things that need to be packed," Sarah murmurs from the sofa behind me. "And I'm not putting my fingerprints on those. It's best if we wait here."

"I don't want to go anywhere either." Keira stands, hugging her arms around her waist. "Let's just wait."

I rub Layla's knees, waiting for a response that doesn't come.

She's deathly quiet, yet those eyes scream with foreboding.

"It's okay. They'll be here soon." I don't know what else to say to break the building silence. There's no encouraging chatter. Not even nervous tears. The room is still and unsettling as I sit on the carpet, one palm remaining on Layla's leg.

I sink into the uncomfortable void, consumed with selfish thoughts of Cole when Sarah pushes to her feet.

"They're here." She starts for the hall. "Hunt texted that they're just about to get in the elevator from the underground parking lot."

My heart races, the arduous pace disrupting my stomach to the point of nausea as she walks from view, the swish of the penthouse door opening moments later.

I can already picture the reunion. The gasps of relief. The happy tears. The hugs and kisses... Then Cole.

I imagine meeting his eyes again and how I'll react. How *he'll* react. Will he care about my response to an upcoming marriage? Will he arrogantly expect me to be his mistress? Will my obsession for him have me stooping that low?

It takes an eternity for the elevator to *ding* in the distance. A lifetime of suffering before we all stand. Layla pushes to her feet before me to rush to the start of the hall. Keira follows close behind. Penny only takes a few steps and I remain in place, unmoving.

I don't hear the patter of kiddie steps over the thud of heavier feet. The *thump, thump, thump* is dooming as Cole strides into the open area, his expression stony. Hunter and Benji follow in single file.

"Where are they?" Layla shoves between them to clear her view down the hall. "Where's Stella?"

Nobody replies.

My throat constricts.

Their faces say it all, especially Benji's, with his nostrils flaring and eyes watering.

"Where are they?" she repeats. Louder. Frantic.

"They're still with Costa." I barely recognize Cole's voice. It doesn't hold a hint of his usual confidence.

"You left them there?" Keira rushes forward.

"You left Stella with those monsters?" Layla shrieks. "How could you?" She lunges for her brother, striking out, pummeling his chest with closed fists. "*How could you?*" she screams. "You heartless piece of shit."

Nobody attempts to stop her. Not even Cole. He stares straight ahead as she assaults him, his shoulders stiff, his chin high.

"I fucking hate you." Her voice wavers with the punches. "I'll never forgive you."

"That's enough." Hunter moves between them, grabbing Layla's wrists. "He had no choice."

"He had every choice in the world. How could he leave them?"

I don't take my eyes off Cole. I keep watching his masked pain, breathing in his resilient suffering, feeling helpless to do anything but stare.

"Layla, you need to calm down." Keira walks up behind her sister, placing gentle hands on the thrashing woman's shoulders. "We have to figure out what comes next."

"I know what comes next," she wails. "Somebody has to go in and get my daughter. Someone who isn't willing to turn their back on my innocent baby girl."

She jerks free and lashes another strike at Cole, the meaty slap clapping across his face. Benji steps forward, trapping her arms to her sides with a bear hug before walking her backward.

"We'll figure this out." He keeps moving, forcing her to retreat as she cries in protest. "We're going to get her back."

She crumples, her knees buckling. Benji lets her drop to the floor, her sobs building for unending minutes while the rest of us remain silent. It takes forever for the tears to fade into hiccups, the sniffles transforming to ragged breaths as she curls into a ball to bury her face into her knees.

Nobody says a word.

There's no clarification. No strategy talk. No plan. Everyone appears transfixed with grief.

"What happened?" I break the awkward quiet, willing Cole to look at me.

He doesn't answer. He barely bats an eye as he walks for the bedroom, ignoring me to close the door.

I start after him.

"Don't," Hunter warns. "Give him space."

I want to argue. To fight to be with Cole. But that's selfish. My response is all about me, not him.

"Where are the others?" I ask. "Where's Decker and Luca?"

"Watching Costa's apartment from a nearby rooftop." Hunter glares at me, maintaining his hatred. "We're going to need these rooms for a while longer. Sarah, can you—"

"I'll call reception." She nods and strides for the kitchen to snatch up the penthouse phone, asking to extend our reservation.

After she hangs up, the thickening tension builds around us. The unsettling awkwardness is stifling. I want to go after Cole. To comfort him. To ask questions. But I won't add to his burden.

"Do you know what happened?" I ask Benji. "What was agreed upon?"

"Nothing was agreed upon," Hunter replies. "Torian isn't committing to anything. Not yet."

"They want in on the drug trade—that much is clear," Benji adds. "Torian's buying himself time to figure out why they're taking this strategy."

"Buying himself time? My daughter is still in there. In the same place a man was just murdered by her uncle." Layla pushes to her feet. "She's gone through hell and Cole left her there. Left his only niece." She wipes the tears from her face with her forearm and sniffs. "I think we all know the reason he paused." Her gaze turns to me, accusing and spiteful. "He didn't agree to marriage because of you. You're what's stopping me from getting my daughter back."

I frown. "No."

Cole wouldn't do that. Not for me. Not at the cost of Tobias and Stella's suffering.

"Calm down," Hunter warns. "There was no choice but to leave them. He's not going to give his word on a threatening agreement that could kill us all in the long run."

"He's right." Keira's forehead wrinkles. "But I think Layla is, too. Cole has never walked away before. Not from something like this. He would've stayed and negotiated."

I keep shaking my head. "This has nothing to do with me."

I'm ignored.

"I swear it doesn't," I add steel to my tone. "There's no way Cole would walk out on those kids for me."

They have to believe it's the truth.

I have to believe.

Because otherwise I'll fracture.

Nobody has ever risked anything for me. Nobody but my parents, and now they're gone. I've made a life on my own. I'm independent. Isolated.

For Cole to even contemplate our relationship through any of this would be... I don't know. Overwhelming... Confusing... Crazy.

A cell rings and Penny is the only one to break the statuesque stance to drag her phone from her pocket.

There are murmured affirmations. Nods of agreement. Then a soft farewell before she disconnects. "Luca and Decker are asking for food supplies." She starts for the hall. "I'll be back later. Please keep me informed."

"Wait, I'll come with you." Keira hustles to catch up with her, both of them leaving without another word.

It returns to the bitter quiet of grief, the occasional sniffle or hiccupped breath from Layla the only thing to temporarily disrupt the hollowness. And there's so damn much of it. A wealth of unanswered questions to leave me empty. A heart full of speculation I need to fill.

"Did Cole say anything else?" I look to the men for answers. "What did you discuss in the car?"

"Look, there's nothing that can be done," Hunter sneers. "Nothing by *you* anyway. Stay out of it."

Benji moves behind his wife, clasping her shoulders. "Let's go back to our room. You should take a Valium to help settle—"

"Go to hell." She wrenches away from him. "I'm not taking another goddamn Valium just so you can shut me up. You might not care that it's our daughter who's been left in there, but I do."

Benji's face falls. "I care."

"Then show it," she demands. "Get her back."

His pain morphs to shame, then animosity. He clenches his fists, his cheeks turning red. "I'm going to our room."

"Of course you are. Leave, just when your daughter needs you the most."

"*Layla*," Sarah snaps. "Stop it. There's nothing he can do."

Benji stalks for the hall. The penthouse door slams seconds later.

"I won't stop fighting for Stella." Layla climbs to her feet. "You can all stand here and pretend to care, but it's not your child who was abandoned by her own uncle." She storms after her husband, but it's the far bedroom door that smacks shut, the force rattling the windows.

"I don't know what to do," Sarah admits. "I feel helpless."

"It's up to Torian." Hunter slumps onto the sofa, his heavy frame dwarfing the furniture. "It's his choice whether to negotiate with these fuckers, bringing them into our lives long-term. Or to risk the safety of those kids by attempting to retrieve them with force."

"What about the man Cole killed?" I ask. "Is he just going to leave him in their hands?"

Hunter kicks his boots onto the coffee table, crossing his feet at the ankles. "Who the fuck knows?"

The master bedroom door opens and Cole steps out in a new suit, his hair damp, his arms full of clothes. He strides for Hunter, handing over the bundle of material. "I need these incinerated. Make sure nothing is left behind."

His expression is devoid of emotion. Not one hint into his psyche.

Hunter inclines his head. "I'll get it done."

The exchange is sterile. Entirely bleak. It tears me apart.

"Are you okay?" I ask.

Cole doesn't look at me. Doesn't even acknowledge my existence. "I'm taking a walk."

I start after him. "I'll come with you."

"No," he grates over his shoulder. "Stay here."

I don't know what hurts more—the dismissal or the distance he's placed between us.

I'm tempted to defy him. To follow. To insert myself into his bubble of animosity until he lets down his guard. But that's all for my benefit. To make *me* feel better. To ease *my* suffering.

I can't make this harder on him.

Instead, I let him go, my heart breaking as he walks away.

22

COLE

I CIRCLE THE BLOCK BUT THE FRIGID AIR DOES NOTHING TO DISLODGE THE GUILT choking my clarity.

Layla's right. I chose to walk out on those kids. I left them behind.

I could've given my word and figured out a way to break it later.

I should've agreed to marriage. To a lifelong commitment. Anything and everything to get Stella and Tobias back.

Instead, I got caught up obsessing about my reputation if I gave in to Costa. I fought against pride, disgust, and fucking rage. I struggled to come to terms with not only a conversation that was out of my control, but the potential future where my family would be the weakest link.

And I thought about *her*. Anissa. The woman I wouldn't disrespect by claiming as my mistress if I became entangled in a mess that could drag me to hell.

I contemplated her too fucking much when I should've said whatever was necessary to secure those kids.

That option is gone now.

I abandoned them and have to live with the guilt. I also have to figure out what the fuck to do next when every possible option isn't an option at all.

There's no easy way out. No cheat sheet.

I stop in the middle of the sidewalk and rake my hands through my hair, pulling at the strands. My limbs thrum with the need to retaliate. To fucking kill.

If given the chance, I'd wipe that faux smile from Emmanuel's face with a slap of his son's dismembered hand. But while those children are in his possession, I'm powerless.

I call Decker for an update, and find out Stella and Tobias are clearly visible in the living room watching television with Emmanuel's wife.

They're safe. Calm.

"He's still taking care of them," Decker assures me. "I know it felt like shit to walk away, but it was the right decision."

I disconnect the call, not wanting his goddamn approval.

I didn't make the right decision, because there wasn't one. There still isn't.

"Fuck this shit." I keep walking, circling the block—once, twice—until I find myself back in front of the hotel doors, the window to the bar a temptation I can't ignore.

I stalk my ass inside and seat myself at the back of the room, the lone staff member behind the bar eying me with unease.

She wipes her hands on her apron and makes her way toward me, her steps cautious before she stops a few feet away. "Excuse me, sir. The bar doesn't open until noon."

"Make an exception." I grab my wallet and retrieve a wad of cash, sliding it toward her. "I need a drink. Scotch. Heavy handed."

I keep my attention on the cash, not wanting her to see the devil in my eyes.

"I, umm…" She clears her throat. "I really shouldn't. I'd have to check with the manager."

"Not even for a penthouse guest?" I rest into my seat, leaving the offer on the table. "I'm sure staff of this fine establishment are told to give their highest-paying customers the best service."

She straightens. "Umm. Yes, sir, of course. I'll be right back with your drink."

"Bring the bottle. Top shelf."

She turns on her heel and hustles away, returning with my prize and a glass with ice. I stare past her to the world outside as she pours a finger, wishing I had something stronger to ease the rage. To fucking eviscerate it. But there's no escaping this.

"Can I get you anything else, sir?"

"Privacy," I grate. "I don't want to be disturbed."

She nods, retreating. "I'll be setting up the bar if you need me. The doors will open in less than an hour."

I clasp the glass, tilting it in acknowledgement before throwing back the contents. I don't question the stupidity of lowering my IQ. The liquor is a necessity. If I don't dull the sharp edges of my self-loathing none of us will make it through the day.

We're all fucked if I can't get my shit together.

My cell vibrates in my pocket before I can pour another. *Anissa.* I know it's her before I pull out the phone and read the screen.

The device flashes as it pulses in my palm, over and over, the disturbance ratcheting up my discontent. I barely blink as I will the call to end, too fucking pathetic to reject it. I can't sever anything with this woman. Never could.

The buzzing stops, bringing a surge of isolation with it.

I drop the device onto the table and drink some more, searching for clarity or maybe oblivion.

She's helped to create such a fucked up mess. All it took was one glance. A superior smirk at my uncle's funeral. A few taunting words.

Since then I've savored angering her, disgusting her. I've even lavished the struggle to turn her hatred into affection.

It was meant to be fun.

A challenge.

It never was. There's always been more—the compulsion driven by a chemical attraction I can't deny.

No female has ever distracted me the way she does. No man, woman, or child has choked me of common sense like my little fox.

My cell vibrates again, her name mocking me.

I grasp the device, itching to throw it. Like always, I succumb to the addiction and swipe the screen, listening in silence.

"Cole? Where are you?"

I close my eyes. Clench my teeth.

"Cole?" she pleads. "You're worrying the hell out of me. Tell me where you are."

I know her fears. I always have. She may be concerned for my safety, but I'd bet my life she's more worried about her freedom. Her future.

This has gone far beyond abduction.

It's blackmail now.

Extortion.

Murder.

I never should've dragged her into this.

"Listen to me," she demands. "I'm calling Easton. I can't keep quiet any longer. You need help—"

"Like hell you will." I slap my hand on the table at the whiplash of that asshole's face in my mind. "You call him and I'll make sure he's dead before he can organize any so-called help."

"Then tell me where you are."

I stiffen. Straighten.

She deliberately triggered me.

Fucking Nissa.

I scoff out a sickening laugh and pour another finger of scotch.

"Cole, please. Let me come to you so we can talk."

I clench the glass in my fist. I do the same with the cell as I attempt to withstand her allure. Effortlessly, she does a number on my pathetic weakness, calling to my obsession with her endearing voice.

"Hotel bar. Come alone." I disconnect the call and slide the cell back onto the table.

I should send her home.

Everyone else needs to be here—my sisters, Luca, Penny, Decker. They all have an emotional tie to this situation. Everyone except Anissa. She's an unnecessary risk. And becoming an even bigger crutch.

The weight of her impediment only becomes more evident when she strides into the bar, her eyes frantically seeking mine, her beauty flawless as she wordlessly strips me of strength.

Worry settles into her features as she stops at the seat across from me, eying the scotch glass. The bottle. My face.

"Tell me what happened." She pulls out the chair and sits before me.

I don't respond. Not in words. I merely stare at her, sipping my scotch, willing her to walk away.

"Cole?" She raises a brow. "Talk."

"Why? So you have more information to give your boyfriend?" I tilt my glass at her in sarcastic praise. "Nice move with threatening to call him. I should've guessed he'd be the first person you thought of when I failed."

"You didn't fail." She cringes. "And it wasn't a threat. I don't know what to do. Easton is the only person I could possibly turn to. I have no family. No friends. I'm alone here. I want to help and I have nobody else to rely on. But I didn't call him. I blocked his number yesterday because I felt guilty whenever he messaged me."

"Let me be clear." I place the glass on the table and lean close, glaring. "Involving him will never help me. Not even if I'm on death's doorstep. Do you understand?"

"I understand your stubbornness," she counters. "I understand your wounded pride."

I flash my teeth in a snarl. "Go back to the room, Anissa. I can't focus with you here."

"I'm not going anywhere. Not until you tell me what happened."

"You heard," I grate. "You were on the damn call."

"No, I heard *parts*. Snippets at best. One minute, Emmanuel was discussing an arranged marriage. The next, there was nothing. I don't know what happened after that. I don't know why you left or what agreement you made."

I swirl the remaining liquid in my glass. "Does it matter?"

Her eyes soften into a look of sympathy. Pathetic pity. "Of course it does. I'm worried about those kids." Her tongue snakes out to moisten her taut lower lip. "And I'm worried about you. Are you considering marrying this woman?"

"I have little choice." I hold her gaze, attempting to decipher her thoughts over the prospect of my pending nuptials. "Right now, Costa has all the power. I can't wait around while he's got Stella and Tobias."

She swallows, her nose crinkling.

She's hurting.

I'm hurting her.

"It would be temporary." I want to reach out. To touch the pain away. "If I take that option, I'd marry her until I was in a position to get rid of her without leaving my hands dirty."

She winces, shaking her head. "Wouldn't Costa assume as much? Why would he risk his daughter?"

"My guess is that he either thinks I'm not capable of killing a woman, or that he can convince me of the benefits of the marriage before she's dead."

She keeps shaking her head. Keeps denying what has to happen if I take that route. "Would you at least meet her first? To see who she is? What she's like?"

"This is a business decision. Not a love match. Looks and personality don't matter."

Her wince deepens, her unease multiplying.

"You don't agree with what has to be done?" I ask. "Do you have a better idea?"

"It's not that I don't agree. I just don't understand. If this was the only choice, why didn't you commit straight away and bring those kids home?"

She's fishing for answers I don't want to give. Admitting my exposure is loathsome. Fucking deplorable. But maybe that's what needs to be brought to light to help cement my way forward.

"Only one thing stopped me from giving in to Costa on the spot," I admit.

She sucks in a breath as if sensing the severity of my approaching truth. "What was it?"

I throw back the remainder of scotch, needing the burn to lessen the instinct to keep my mouth shut. "You, little fox. You're the only thing."

It wasn't the freedom of those children I thought about when the arranged marriage was put on the table. It wasn't my sister's pain or Benji's struggle.

My mind had focused on Anissa. The fucking Fed. The woman who has brought me to my knees without even knowing it.

I've convinced myself the kids were relatively safe under the watchful eye of the old woman. I've told myself that buying time to strategize was the only option.

But there was little strategy in my delay.

It all came down to selfishness.

I hesitated because I didn't want to give Nissa up.

If it wasn't for my narcissism, those kids could already be free.

Stella would be in Layla's arms. Tobias would be snuggled close with Penny. The jet would be in the air, taking us home, and I'd be making wedding plans with a woman I'd soon dispose of.

But at least the children would be safe.

"Say something," I demand.

For numerous pained heartbeats Anissa stares right through me, blinking her wild eyes. "What do you want me to say?"

I scoff. "I dunno. Maybe something to address the fact I risked everything for you. For *us*." I slam my glass down on the table. "I should've agreed to marriage as soon as it was mentioned and worried about figuring out a way to gain the upper hand over Emmanuel later. But what I couldn't do is spit in the face of what we have without speaking to you first."

"You shouldn't have." She shudders. Cringes. Shakes her head some more. "Why would you do that? I don't understand why I was a part of your process at all. It's too much."

"Is it? Have I got us so completely wrong that I'm imagining shit that doesn't even exist between us?"

"It existed." She looks at me with despair. "But it shouldn't have. This is getting too complicated."

"So that's your decision? You're telling me to marry her?"

"No." She balks. "I'm not telling you to do anything. It's not my choice to make."

"That's exactly what this is," I add spite to my tone. "I'm letting you know right now, my decision to marry this woman rests firmly on your shoulders."

"No." She glares and pushes to her feet.

I do the same, grabbing her wrist to drag her back down and hold her across the table. "You're meant to be at my side," I snarl. "It's where you belong."

"I don't know where I belong." Her voice cracks. "But I'm certain it's meant to be in a far simpler life than this."

There's a plea in her words. An unspoken cry for help.

It fucking kills me.

"I'm drowning, Cole. I don't know how to help you."

"Then go." I release her. "I'll book you a flight and arrange a car. I'll have the concierge send your belongings back tomorrow. You don't even need to go upstairs to pack."

She continues to glare, yet there's no venom in her focus. The viciousness is smothered under a far heavier emotion. She wants to admit her desire to stay. She needs to, if only she wasn't more stubborn than I am.

"Leave, Anissa." I jerk my head toward the lobby. "Go and don't look back. I won't stop you. I won't seek you out again either. If you want this to be done, it's done."

The admission burns holes in my throat. But it's the truth. If she walks, I'll give my promise to be married, and retrieve those kids. I'll figure out how to break ties with Costa later, while siphoning revenge along the way.

She pushes to her feet, this time slower, her weary caution staring down at me. "You need to do whatever it takes to get Stella and Tobias back. You never should've hesitated for me."

"Wouldn't you have done the same?"

She flinches, her chin hitching slightly before she glances away, denying the truth.

She doesn't need to admit it out loud. I already know. Her initial reaction would've revolved around me, just like mine did for her. It's the settled dust that causes the problems. The callousness of the decision.

"We're meant to be together," I growl. "I've been committed to you since the day we met. But now it's your turn to decide. You can't sit on the fence anymore. Do you pick me or your unhappy life?"

"That's unfair." She crosses her arms over her chest, building a barrier between us. "You can't make me decide your future."

"You were my only future until today. So quit thinking of life as unfair and just. Good and bad. Moral and corrupt. Say you'll be my wife and I'll do anything to make that happen. I'll tell Costa his daughter isn't an option because I've vowed myself to you."

She sucks in a breath, the shock fading under a quickly descending frown. "Stop it."

"Why? Because you're scared?"

"Of course I'm scared. My chest physically hurts due to my fear for you and those kids, but I also don't want to spend a lifetime in prison."

"Instead you'd prefer to spend the rest of your life in misery? Wasting every day wondering what it would've been like to be happy with me? Prison is a minimal risk, Nissa. I'd always protect you. You'd have the world at your feet if you were with me. I could give you the opportunity to set up foundations. Charities. I'd give you all the money you'd need—"

"I don't want your money," she snaps.

"Then what do you want?" I shove the scotch bottle and glass to the side, leaving nothing between us. "Why are you still here? Why haven't you thrown my marriage proposal back in my face and stormed out?"

"That was a proposal?" Her mouth gapes. "You're serious?"

"Marry me." I say it louder, strengthening the words. "Commit to me and be my wife. Show my family I haven't made the wrong choice in hesitating with those kids, because you make me stronger. You make me fucking unstoppable."

She winces, those beautiful hazel eyes pinching as she swipes her tongue frantically over her lower lip. When she glances over her shoulder to the lobby, I'm in trouble.

Her doubts are winning the fight.

"You've never felt at home in the FBI, Nis. They're not your family."

Her fingers twitch at her side, her gaze once again returning to the lobby.

She's going to run.

"I'm sorry," she murmurs. "I can—"

"I know more about your father," I cut her off, using the low blow as a leash to keep her with me. "I know so much more than you'd want to believe."

Her face pales, the color draining to reveal the starkness of the heartache I'm causing.

"You wanted him to be moralistic and pure. To be an agent who everyone looked up to, but—"

"*Don't.*" This time her plea is pained, torn from the depths of her soul. "Don't start the games again. Don't say something you can't take back."

"He's exactly who you're meant to be. He makes his own rules. Follows his own path. He's on my side now."

The color continues to fade from her features. "I don't believe you. You're only saying this because you know things are—"

"You're right. I'm telling you because I know you're going to run." I push to my feet. "Because like I said, I can't follow this time. And even if this shitstorm could work out, I have pride, little fox. I won't chase you again."

She squares her shoulders. "Where is he?"

"Chicago. Working for an associate of mine. Slowly paying off the debt he owes my family."

Her lips press tight, her stubborn disbelief creeping in as she says, "He wouldn't have stayed away."

"Are you sure? Do you really think he could've faced returning to you?" I make my way around the table. "He threw away the career you idolize. He turned to criminals for help. And he left you alone while you grieved your mother's death."

She retreats a step. "You're doing this to hurt me."

"Maybe." I take caution in my approach. "Maybe I'm doing it in retaliation for you wanting to walk away from me again. Or maybe I'm trying to make you fucking realize this is where you're meant to be."

"You're lying. He wouldn't have abandoned me."

"Who says he did? Haven't you ever wondered why you have such remarkable rent control? Not one damn change in your payments in how many years?"

She straightens, her face betraying her shattering emotions. She glances toward the bar, her arms finding their way around her chest again, her sniffle an agonizing grate against my ears as she blinks through rapidly building tears.

"Why didn't you tell me?" she whispers. "Were you waiting for a time to use this as ammunition?"

"It wasn't my plan to keep the information from you. But laying his secrets bare in Greece was too soon. You wouldn't have believed me. And after we returned, you made it your mission to build distance between us."

I hate her suffering.

When we're fighting and spiteful, it's different. I usually thrive on her venom. Not when she's like this, though. Not when her pain is palpable and her devastation is threatening to break free.

Her lips part, then close again. She struggles to remain composed as she keeps eying the escape.

I grab her arm, ignoring how she stiffens as I drag her into me. "I was going to tell you. You need to believe that."

"I don't know what to believe. My entire reality is changing. Nothing is what it's supposed to be. Not my memories of my father. Not my feelings toward you. I can't make sense of any of it."

I hold her through the arduous heartbeats, her palms resting gently against my chest. I've always loved her strength. Her tenacity. But this—the lost, vulnerable side of her—is what breaks down my walls to leave me a chained slave at the altar of her existence.

She owns me.

She always will.

"Be my wife," I whisper. "Give me a reason to take a different path with Costa."

She doesn't move, doesn't even say a word as I struggle through her silence.

"My life will be yours." I rake a hand through her hair, placing my lips to her forehead. "You'll be happy with me."

She sucks in a shuddering breath and holds it tight. She doesn't return my hug. Doesn't reciprocate the affection at all, except for the subtle lowering of her head to my shoulder.

I could hold her like this forever. My possession. My treasure.

Before I can get enough, she steps back, sniffing away her emotions to stand tall. "I appreciate you telling me about my father. Although, I'm sure you could've found a way to do it sooner."

She looks anywhere but my eyes—at the bar, the lobby, my fucking suit.

She's about to leave.

"I, umm." She frowns, the words seeming to be agonizing. "I need to go. Like you said—I'm a distraction. And that's not helping get those kids back."

"So you're telling me to marry her?"

Her nose crinkles as she nods. "If that's what you think needs to be done… If that's how your world works…" She shrugs. "I don't know. I'm out of my league here. This is all beyond my comprehension."

"It's not my usual wheelhouse either, little fox."

Her lips curve in a pained smile. It's only brief. The slightest glimpse of heartfelt beauty before it slips beneath her suffering. "I really need to go." She jerks her head toward the lobby, killing me slowly. "I'm not going to waste any more of your time."

"Nissa." Her name is a warning. A brutal fucking plea.

She can't walk out on me again.

She has to know I won't chase her a second time.

"Leaving is the right thing to do." Her face crumples. "But I want you to know I wouldn't go back and change anything. Not even what happened in Greece. Luther needed to be taken down and I'm glad I was there to do it. Everything worked out the way it was meant to."

Even us?

Even the sweat and seduction? The addiction and compulsion?

I want to ask, but my pride won't allow it.

I'm done. Fucking shattered.

"Go get those kids." She retreats. "Do whatever needs to be done."

I want this conversation to stop. I fucking need it to, if only severing her words didn't mean cutting short the last moments we have left.

"Goodbye, Cole." She scrunches her nose and swallows hard. "Stay safe."

23

COLE

She leaves me standing there, her head hung as she walks through the lobby to the city street, disappearing into foot traffic.

I don't follow.

Some sick, sorry part of me thinks she'll come back. That she can't possibly leave me again. But deep down, I know that's not my Nissa.

When times get tough my woman clings to stability, and obviously, I don't make the cut.

"Can I get you anything else, sir?" the bartender asks from behind me.

"No." I pull out my wallet and throw more cash on the table. I have to get away from here.

I reach the penthouse, finding the kitchen and living room empty. Everyone's gone. Even my sisters. There's no note on the counter. No sign of life... apart from a faint rustle coming from the main bedroom.

"Hunt?" I palm my gun and aim it at the open door.

"Yeah. In here."

I stash my weapon and stalk to the threshold, finding him standing near the bed. "What are you doing?"

He shrugs. "I just got back from grabbing something to eat."

I scrutinize the room. The bed is still unmade. The bathroom door is wide. Everything seems normal except for Nissa's suitcase that was neatly packed on the floor the last time I checked and is now a pile of tangled clothes.

My pulse quickens, the heavier beat inspired by a protective nature I need to ditch.

"I came in here looking for you," he adds.

"Did you think you were going to find me in Nissa's suitcase?" I can't keep the aggression from my tone. "Why were you touching her things?"

He grins. "It's my job to make sure you're safe. I bet you wouldn't have checked to make sure she didn't stash anything suspicious."

He's right. I didn't.

I trust her. Even despite the threats to involve Easton.

"Leave her shit alone. She's not your concern." I check the safety on my gun, then lob it toward him. "Give this a once-over to make sure the guard didn't tamper with it. When you're done, relieve Luca from his watching post. I need him back here digging up information."

"Benji's already on his way to them now."

"Jesus Christ. Why the fuck would you think that's a good idea?"

He waves me away as he releases the magazine and drops it to the bed. "He wanted to see his daughter. And from what you've told me, it won't be a major issue if the sight of her gets the better of him. If he jumps off the roof and plummets to his death, it saves you from doing it, right?"

He keeps dismantling my gun, feigning disinterest even though I know that fucker is starving for a nibble of insight.

"Benji's a problem I don't want to think about right now." I discard my jacket and walk forward to throw it against the bed coverings. I can't get Nissa out of my head. Even with her gone and the ties severed, she's still the air I breathe. "Instead, we should start planning my buck's party."

"Yeah?" He starts inspecting each piece of my gun, not showing any shock. "You're going to cave to Costa? You don't want to go in there guns blazing?"

"I'm not placing those kids in the line of fire. It was bad enough leaving them behind."

"You had to stall. The old man is testing you. He's trying to figure out what you're made of."

I scoff. "I thought so, too. I anticipated him backing off once I killed the fucker who drove Stella and Tobias from Portland. But then he doubled down."

"He's a prick, that's for sure." Hunt starts clasping my gun back together. "There aren't many men who would witness murder, then immediately offer their daughter's hand in marriage. This girl of his must be nasty."

I don't give a fuck what she is. All that matters is that she's not Nissa. And I'll make sure she knows it, too.

"It might not work out too bad, though," he continues. "If you marry this bitch, then slowly knock them off one by one, starting with the father, you could end up owning a fashion label. Wouldn't that be ironic?"

"Ironic?" I grate. "How?"

"Because you're the least fucking fashionable guy I know." He shoves the magazine back into the gun and grins. "You've got one look and it's been done to death, my friend."

He's attempting humor. He might even be aiming to raise my sour mood. But

597

he only has the opposite effect. Trying to make light of this situation when Nissa is already on her way home is eating me alive.

He sighs and lobs the weapon my way. "Where's the Fed? Who's keeping an eye on her?"

"She's gone." I return the gun to the back of my waistband.

"Gone where? To get her hair done? To paint her nails?"

I glare, despising the constant ridicule of a woman undeserving of his spite. "She's on her way home. She won't be back."

His grin increases. "Good riddance."

I clench my fingers, biting back the need to lash out. He's testing me. He wants to know where my head's at, and I don't want anyone aware of my lacking mental state.

"Go relieve Benji of his position. I don't want him watching those kids. I can't trust him to keep his head."

He watches me release the buttons on my sleeve cuffs. I need more room to breathe. These clothes are fucking choking me.

"Yeah, I can do that. But what do you have planned? What's your next move?"

"I'll let you know when I figure it out." I sit on the mattress and kick off my shoes. I need a shower. A cold one. To wash Anissa from my life.

"She messed with you, didn't she?"

I don't react to Hunt's question as I unclasp my belt and slide it from my pants.

"How the fuck did she get under your skin?"

I push to my feet. "I've asked you to do something."

"Damn. When you said she was gone, I assumed you kicked her to the curb, but you didn't, did you? She walked." He huffs out a laugh. "What the fuck have you become?"

"Leave," I warn. "*Now.*"

"What are you going to do?" He straightens his shoulders. "You've gone soft, Torian. The man I originally came to work with would've thrived on Costa's proposal. You would've taken it as the perfect opportunity to infiltrate his business and pull it apart from the inside out. Especially after he dared to involve children in the games of men. But I'm beginning to think you're doing it as an easy out. You won't attack because you've become a pussy, and you're caving to him for the same fucking reason."

I glare, my anger fighting to break free.

"Holy shit." He laughs. "I'm right."

"No, you're not fucking right," I lie. "Kids are involved. I won't risk—"

"Fuck the kids. Don't let them be a weakness. Tobias has gone through heavier shit than this. The boy is Satan's fucking prodigy, for Christ's sake. And Stella isn't your responsibility. None of this is. Layla knew what world she was bringing her daughter into. She fucking knew. Yet she was the one who went behind your back. She risked that little girl when she started talking to Robert. This is on her head, not yours."

"You're a heartless son of a bitch, Hunt."

He inclines his head. "And you used to be, too. It's how we've survived this long. But the future is fucking grim if you're negotiating with assholes for the wrong reasons. If you cave because you think they're in control, then I'm out. I'm done. I won't work for someone with no backbone."

I gnash my teeth. I fucking thrum with volatility.

"You know it all started to go downhill when you set your sights on that bitch," he continues. "You got drawn in by a Fed and you couldn't even see that she was taking you down."

I grin. It's all I can do to stop myself from killing him. "You don't know the first damn thing about her."

"You might be right, but I know the exact effect she has on you." He looks me up and down, his nose scrunched in disdain. "She made you sloppy. You're not focused."

"Without her, I never would've taken down my father. She's far more valuable than you give her credit for."

"I'm aware of her value," he grates. "I always have been. Having a Fed in your pocket is far better than having one on the loose, but she wasn't in your pocket. She was riding your damn cock while she held the fucking reins."

My pulse pounds in my ears. My eyes burn with hatred. "Relieve Benji before you get yourself in trouble."

"I don't give a shit about trouble. I'm not leaving until you shake her off. The Fed's gone. Get over it."

I suck in a slow breath, willing the rage to subside without success. "You've always had a problem saying her name. Why is that?" I cock a brow. "Could it be because you're threatened by her? Maybe even a little jealous?"

"Jesus. You're losing your fucking mind."

"No, I don't think so. Not on this. You know she belongs here. You could see it just as well as I could, and that worried you."

"Of course it fucking worried me," he snaps. "She's the enemy and you gave her the keys to the kingdom."

She deserved them. Those keys were hers.

"Torian, listen to me." He moves closer, grabbing my shoulders with force, digging his fingers into muscle. "I wasn't threatened by *her*. I was threatened by what she could do to *you*. To our whole fucking set up. And I was right. You missed things you never would've missed before. You didn't even notice the betrayal from your sister and Benji because you were too head-fucked."

I launch a fist, striking a warning punch to his gut.

He takes the hit with a puff of air.

"You're wrong." I shove him backward. "My failings are mine and mine alone. She hasn't fucking weakened me. *Life* has done that." I shove him again.

"Finding out the degree of my family's filth has caused this. Burying my fucking uncle. Discovering what was done to Keira. Not to mention Decker's betrayal, and yours, for that matter. Then there was Greece. Now this." I stalk forward and shove him again. "That fucking *Fed* is the only reason I'm still standing. She's the strength that got me to this point. She's the only goddamn thing that kept me going."

"She was a distraction."

"No," I snarl. "She was my peace. My fucking redemption. And you owed her respect, not animosity."

His chin hikes, his hands fisted at his sides.

"I would've made her mine." I hold his gaze, letting him know the brutal truth. "She would've helped right this fucking shitshow. She would've had authority over you. Over everything. And I would've trusted her with it."

His jaw ticks. "Then you're a fool."

Maybe. But I would've done it without regret.

Nissa was a risk I couldn't back away from. Even now, I regret vowing not to chase her. I need her here. I crave the adrenaline-filled clarity she provides.

"Look…" Hunt huffs out a breath. "I get the infatuation. Seriously, I understand how messed up that shit is after meeting Sarah. But her leaving is the best thing—"

A knock at the door cuts him short.

He raises a brow, silently asking if I'm expecting visitors.

It could be anyone—my heartbroken sisters, any of my men, or goddamn housekeeping for all I know.

The knock sounds again, this time louder.

"I guess I'm answering that." Hunt stalks from the room, retrieving his gun from the back of his pants.

I follow into the living area as the knock comes again, and again.

"I'm coming," Hunt yells. He reaches the door, places his barrel against the wood and checks the peephole. "Jesus *fucking* Christ."

The hair on my nape prickles as I start toward him, my hand on my weapon. "Who is it?"

He snarls, "Trouble."

24

ANISSA

I SIT MY ASS IN THE GUTTER BETWEEN TWO PARKED CARS, HIDING FROM PEOPLE passing by the front of the hotel.

Marriage.

Cole proposed marriage. Not just from left field, but from outer fucking space.

There's no way it would work. Not in a million years.

So why does it feel like I've made a mistake? Why is it so hard to now be separated from him?

My insides churn with abandonment, as if he's the guilty party who left me, instead of the other way around. This is exactly what it felt like when I turned my back on him after Greece. Only this time, it's stronger. The invisible hands wrapped around my throat are tighter.

I pull out my phone, needing to find grounding in the one person I can rely on, and ignore the guilt as I unblock Easton's number.

He'll know how to right this train wreck. He'll give me a dose of that Cole-is-a-maniacal-psychopath speech and I'll be pulled back from the brink of disaster. It's my trembling heart that makes it hard, even now, to defy Cole.

Message after message downloads to my cell, all the vibrating notifications coming from Easton. There are phone calls. Texts. Emails.

The guilt thickens over blocking him in the first place, followed by more shame over the barrage of unanswered communication. But I'd wanted the barrier. It felt right to be with Cole without distraction. At least until now.

I dial Easton's number and don't have a chance to back out before the line connects.

"Where the hell are you?" he demands in greeting. "I've been worried sick."

Despite his anger, it's good to hear his voice. "I needed to get away." I bend my knees, dragging them to my chest. "But I'm fine. There's nothing to worry about."

"Why do I find that hard to believe?"

"No, truly. I'm okay." I nod, attempting to convince myself of the lie. "Things just got a little hectic with my shrink, and us, and..."

"And Torian," he finishes for me.

I don't verbalize my agreement. We both know I don't have to.

"Take all the time you need, Fox—just quit ignoring me. I was about to file a missing person's report."

"I'm glad you didn't." I rub the heel of my palm over my sternum, attempting to dislodge the ache beneath it. I want to tell him everything. About Cole. And Emmanuel. Even the increase in my psychosis. But I can't get those words out yet. I need to fill the void with something else.

"I'm sorry." My voice cracks. "I shouldn't have kissed you the other night."

There's a beat of silence. The slightest pause that pummels me with remorse.

"Don't worry about it," he murmurs. "It was nice."

He nailed it. Out of every possible description, he picked the perfect one to explain our brief press of lips.

It was agreeable. Friendly. And in complete contrast to the sheer force of nature that happens when my mouth is on Cole's.

"Look, I know things are complicated with us working together," he continues. "But sometimes it's okay to do the wrong thing when it feels right. We're not always meant to follow the rules. We're born with instincts for a reason. That, by far, should be the ultimate measure of what's right and wrong."

I squeeze my eyes closed, hating that he's putting voice to what I've been trying to deny with Cole. The instinct to be with a man I'd usually despise goes far beyond anything I've ever experienced. I'm drawn to him. Even now, I want to run back to his side.

"I've hidden feelings for you for a long time, Anissa. We'll figure this out. There's no rush."

I shield my face with a hand, so fucking ashamed to have led Easton to this point when I'm in a completely different mental space to him.

The last twenty-four hours have solidified that there can never be a future between us. Maybe even between me and any other man. I'm lost to the hunger of Cole. Trapped in this thrilling desperation. I may have left him, but there's no returning to normal life after what we shared.

"I'm sorry but you misunderstood." I swallow over my agonizingly parched throat. "I don't feel the same way."

His silence is deafening. A car horn blares in the distance. The brakes of a bus hiss nearby.

"I wish I did," I murmur. "I wanted to feel the same. I pushed and pushed in an attempt to create those emotions because you're everything that's right in this world. But…" I shake my head, unable to explain. Or maybe I'm just scared to admit that even though something good was wrapped in a bow and placed before me like a prize, I decided to throw it away.

"It's him, isn't it?" He sighs. "What I feel for you, you somehow feel for him."

I'd love to be able to agree, but his statement holds no accuracy. There's nothing nice between Cole and I. There's fire and passion and flame. There's battle and so much bloody war, and beneath it all, there's a devastatingly sweet rebirth that captures my breath and infuses me with unbelievable strength.

"Are you with him now?" he asks.

"No." It's not a lie. I'm not with Cole. Not anymore. Even though my heart still is.

"But you want to be." He announces my weakness with bitter simplicity. "Is that why you're calling? Because you want me to make you feel better about throwing your life away?"

That hadn't been my intent at all. But maybe I'd been kidding myself.

I bury my head in my hand. "What sort of person does it make me if I say yes?"

"I guess it makes you more brutally honest than I anticipated."

I crinkle my nose to fight the burn. "My father works for him," I admit. "Or for someone aligned with the family. All this time, I thought he was one of the good guys. I pictured him as this unflinching voice of integrity and honor. Now I've found out he's…"

"He's what?"

"I don't know." I shrug to myself. "Like Cole. Like the person I feel drawn to become."

"You're not a bad person, Anissa. I don't know what happened to make you think you've got anything in common with those people, but it's not true. You're one of the good guys. You're one of the fucking best."

His words don't hit their mark. I'm not persuaded by his beliefs this time. And I'm unsure if I still want to be.

Being *good* doesn't hold the warm fuzzies it once did. There's no comfort.

"You're wrong." My conviction builds. "I've done things that go against everything I signed up for with the Bureau. I've committed crimes and—"

"Fox, this isn't a conversation to have over the phone. Why don't you come to my place? We can talk this out face-to-face."

No, I don't think I can.

Conviction is gaining the better of me. It's intensifying. Strengthening. The pull toward what I want is outweighing what I'd once thought was right.

"I'm like him, Easton. I'm exactly like Cole. And all the illegal things I've done lately don't come with remorse. If anything, I'm proud." I want to tell him about Luther. That a monstrous sex trafficker is now unable to hurt more women because of my actions. I've done bad things for good reasons and I'm okay with that. I'm emboldened. "I did something you would never forgive me for. It wasn't by the book and I don't regret—"

"Anissa, I'm hanging up. This line isn't secure."

"No, wait. I just need..." God, I don't know what I need. Approval, maybe. Acceptance? Closure?

Cole is an adamant vision in my mind. His hold on my heart is strengthening the more I fight it.

He's everything. And I don't think I can live through more weeks fighting where I'm drawn to. I can't let him go again.

"You've decided to be with him." The words seem to fall easily from his lips when I'm still trying to deny them.

I've relied on Easton to remind me of Cole's abhorrence. I've used him as a shield against my cravings when I never truly believed the negativity he spoon-fed me. I even had to self-diagnose a mental illness in an effort to protect myself. Yet, it's now clear Cole is a calling.

He's my path.

"Yes," I admit. "I have."

Easton's ragged exhale carries down the line, his pained emotion coming with it. "Do you realize you're going to lose everything? Your job. Your friends. Your life."

"Yes." And still I can't walk away. From Cole. From this compulsion that's worked its way into the marrow of my bones.

"That means me, too," he adds. "I can't stick by you through this. I won't watch you ruin your life."

My self-loathing builds. I hate even more that the decision to go after Cole still feels right. It's all there is. Conviction and growing determination.

"I'm sorry." I squeeze the cell tighter. "I wish I could explain—"

"Don't. I'd never understand anyway." There's no bite to his words. Only resignation. "But if you ever need a way out, I'll still be here. You'll always know where to find me, even if you can't find yourself."

I want to tell him I'm found. That after so long running, I'm right where I need to be. No longer a special agent of the FBI. Not the isolated woman who couldn't find her place in the world.

I'm Anissa Fox. Current lover to an underworld mastermind. Future queen to a lawless empire. And devoted slave to a man I never imagined I could admire.

As long as I'm not too late to claim what's mine.

25

COLE

"She's gone, is she?" Hunt shoots me a glare and yanks the door wider. "Doesn't look gone to me."

I stand tall as Anissa walks into the penthouse, keeping her distance from Hunt to continue along the hall toward me.

"Come back for your things?" I keep my tone level, not buying into the optimistic throb in my gut. "I told you I'd have them sent to you."

She stops at the entry to the open living area and glances over her shoulder, eying Hunt before shaking her head. "No."

"I swear to God," he growls. "You two are the stupidest fucks I know."

I scowl at him. "Go get Benji."

"Do you want me to tell the others what's happening?" He pastes on a malicious smile. "I'm happy to break the news of your agreement to the arranged marriage."

Anissa stands straighter, her chin inching higher.

I flex my fingers. "I suggest you keep your mouth shut."

"Well, I'd suggest you keep your dick in your pants, but we both know that ain't gonna happen."

He storms out, slamming the door behind him, the vibrations momentarily ringing through the penthouse until the noise fades into uncomfortable quiet.

The distant sound of city traffic is the only reminder of the outside world. But I don't break the silence. Not for a long time. I lean against the wall, pretending I'm okay with the suspense, as she rounds the sofa to stop at the glass doors and stares across the Sacramento skyline.

She doesn't talk. She merely stands there with her back to me, chin high, shoulders straight, posture perfect.

"What are you doing here, Nis?"

Her head bows momentarily before returning to the confident angle. "I came back."

"I can see that. What I want to know is why?" I should kick the superior undertone from my voice. I really fucking should. But superiority is all I have until she retrieves the knife she embedded between my ribs.

"I thought you'd already be halfway to the airport by now." I push from the wall. "Do you need me to arrange a car?"

"No."

She's fucking killing me with this subdued bullshit. I want to shake the answers from her. And maybe I will. I can't handle this twenty-question routine.

"Nis, I don't have time for whatever the hell this is. What do you want from me?"

She turns my way with stark eyes, her fragility clearly visible in those hazel-green depths. "I called Easton."

Motherfucker.

The rage is instantaneous. The heat suffusing my face becomes a fucking furnace.

"Don't look at me like that." Her expression hardens. "I didn't do it to upset you."

"Give me your phone." I stalk toward her, thrusting out a hand. She's played this card before. I need to make sure she's not bluffing again. "*Now.*"

She raises her brows as she pulls the device from her pants pocket with a faint sniff. "Are you going to break it?"

Not as much as I'm going to break him. "Unlock it."

She does that too, her stare turning haughty as I scroll through her recent calls, finding the truth about her deception.

"Fucking hell." I lob the device at the sofa. "What did you tell him?"

She holds my gaze, her jaw tight.

"What the fuck did you tell him, Anissa?" I close in on her, almost nose to nose, making it impossible for her to escape my fury.

She crosses her arms over her chest and raises her chin, attempting to stare me down. "I said goodbye."

Shock hits me. Confusion, too.

The silence returns, but this time it's loud. The absence of sound deafens me. The beat of my pulse thunders.

"He doesn't know where I am," she murmurs. "But he knows I'm choosing you—your life, your world."

This is a trick. A game.

She's telling me exactly what I want to hear, and I'm not sure why.

"Now it's your turn to say something." Her teeth dig into her lower lip. "What are you thinking?"

"I want to know what you're playing at."

She winces. "I'm not playing. I told him how I feel about you."

"And how is that?" I growl, biting back the tension growing in my gut.

She breaks eye contact to stare at the sofa. "You already know."

"I certainly thought I did back in Greece. Then again after last night. But you've walked away from me twice now. I'd be a fool to give you the opportunity to do it a third time."

"No, you'd be a fool for not realizing I wasn't walking from you, but instead attempting to hide from what I didn't want to accept." Her gaze raises to mine. "Fear drove me away. Nothing else. I understand that now."

I want to gorge on her words. To dive into them with unwavering faith. If only it were that easy. "What changed?"

"The thought of losing you outweighs the fear." Her arms fall to her sides as her chin regains the slightest hitch of determination. "I can't see you with someone else."

That's good to know. But still, I won't sink my teeth into the prize standing before me. Not when I'm sure it's a mirage.

She sighs. "You're not going to make this easy on me, are you?"

"It wasn't easy watching you walk away."

"I'm sorry, okay? You say things that scare the hell out of me. Marriage, for starters. Then the constant talk of ownership."

"That's this life, Nis. It's how I live. If I don't own every single aspect of my existence, I'm as good as dead. I need to own every move I make, every thought, every action, and every damn woman I stake a claim to, otherwise my enemies target the weakness, just like they did with those kids."

She hikes her chin. "I won't be owned, Cole."

"Why not? You've owned every damn inch of me for too fucking long. Is it really that demeaning to return the favor?"

Her eyes flare before she quickly hides the shock. "I don't own you."

"Yes, you do."

"Well, I don't want to. I need something less sterile." Her throat works over a heavy swallow. "I want to know there's more than just heated games between us. Ownership means nothing to me when it's your heart I want." Her cheeks darken as if she's embarrassed by her admission. Such pink, beautiful cheeks that emphasize the intensity in her gaze.

I prowl closer, her request a lead weight in my throat. "You want love."

She shifts her focus over my shoulder, denying me eye contact.

"You can't admit it?" My palms sweat, demanding touch. "Why is that?"

"Is that emotion even possible for you?" Her attention snaps back to mine in accusation. "Do you even know what love is?"

I take her savage blows without retaliation. "Yes, I know." I reach out, brushing my hand over her neck.

She flinches, attempting to back away only to be captured in my grip, my fingers tight around her throat.

I get in her face, demanding her attention, her heated breath brushing my lips. "I fell in love with you that night under the tree in Greece. With your makeshift shiv and your desperation to stab me. And I've loved you in every moment since."

Her pulse quickens beneath my touch, her inhales increasing.

"There's nobody else, little fox. There never will be."

Her throat convulses under my palm, her gaze growing with determination.

"You *will* marry me." My murmured demand snaps her rigid. "Maybe not this week or the next. But you will be my wife." I lean closer, unable to resist the need to taste her as I press my mouth to her jaw. "And you will be happy. I vow this to you."

She shudders, closing her eyes. "I think I fell in love with you before Greece. Back in that café, when you manipulated me with so much ease and confidence before Luther's escape from custody that it was impossible not to appreciate your brilliance."

I grin, falling victim to her admission. Her truth warms me in a way I've never experienced. It brings weakness yet so much fucking fortitude.

There's no going back from this.

No walking away.

No goodbyes.

"Tell me you're mine." I kiss her chin, her cheek, the corner of her mouth. "I need to hear you say it."

She whimpers. "I don't know—"

I slam my lips against hers, still holding her neck tight. I punish her with my tongue, dragging her body into mine with the tight wrap of my arm. When I ease back, she gasps for air, clinging to my shirt.

"Cole, I—"

"Tell me," I demand. "Convince me you're done walking away."

She shakes her head. "What about the children? And this woman you're meant to marry? What about Hunter and your sisters?"

"Leave that shit to me." I'll figure a way to right this train wreck. What I need is to know she'll be waiting for me at the end.

"I don't want to lie to you." She inches back. "I'm in love, Cole. I'm just not sure how this can work."

"*Trust* me," I growl. "Forget Costa. Forget Hunter and anything else outside this room. And tell me, right now, that I'm what you want. That *this*—" I point between us. "—is how you want to live your life."

She licks her lips, her brows pinched.

I'm waiting for her to attempt to look at the door, and holy fuck, I'll hold her head in place if I have to. She wants this. I need her to have the conviction to own it.

She swallows, holding my gaze, her eyes glassy with vulnerability. "This is what I want."

Relief is an overwhelming bitch.

I plaster my mouth to hers, sinking my fingers into the flesh of her hip. I devour her, stealing her breath and losing my own.

She mewls against my lips, her hands clutching tight against my shirt. She's fucking everything. My guidance. My meaning. She's going to pull me out of the shitshow that has become my life and help right the downfall, but more than that—she's going to be there. Beside me. Always.

Forever mine.

"God, I want you." She grabs my waistband, unclasps my belt. "I need you."

I'm rock hard before she's yanking at my zipper. I'm fumbling to catch my gun, my dick fucking throbbing by the time she grabs at my boxer briefs.

"Wait." I snatch her wrist in warning. "This time you're meant to be savored."

She shakes her head, her eyes wild with lust. "Call me impatient."

I snicker as I release her arm to place my gun on the sofa. "You need to be taught some restraint."

"To hell with restraint." She kicks off her shoes and steps closer, placing her hands around my neck. "We have the rest of our lives to savor. I want what comes naturally."

A growl of appreciation vibrates in my chest. "Natural means rough." I grasp her hips, yanking her into me. "Natural means we get our fill, fast and intense."

She tilts her pelvis, grinding against my dick, making us both moan.

"That's what I want." She reaches between us, unbuttons my shirt, exposes my chest. "I can't do slow right now."

I swoop forward and pick her up, one arm cradling her back, the other behind her knees, and carry her to the bedroom. I sit her on the mattress as she scrambles to pull out her gun, shoving it toward the top of the bed.

She reefs off her suit jacket. Discards her holster. Undoes her pants.

"Stop." I kick off my shoes. "You're unwrapping my present without permission."

"This isn't your birthday. We don't have time to mess around with packaging."

I grin, unwilling to further my protest as she fumbles to release her blouse buttons, then leans forward to shove down my open pants and boxer briefs, exposing my dick.

She grasps my length in her hands, squeezing the hardness. Tempting fate.

"Wait," I growl.

Her eagerness is killing me, especially when I'm being denied the full sight of her.

I grab her panties, forcing her to let go of me as I yank them off. Her socks, too. "Spread those gorgeous legs."

She rests back on her elbows, splayed before me like an artist's inspiration. I want to remember this until the day I die—the burn in my chest, the hunger in my veins.

Her knees part slightly as a faint grin teases her lips.

"I said, spread 'em." I grasp her knees, forcing them wide, making her gasp.

This sight is even better, her pussy lips parted, her arousal glistening.

I should do as I promised and savor her. I should dive between those legs and eat my fill. I could do a million things to ensure she's aware of my unwavering commitment, but my vow to go slow means nothing when pitted against what she wants from me.

"There's no going back." I place my palms on her thighs, sliding them upward. "This is your life now."

She blinks those dark lashes my way, a lock of hair hanging low to seductively cover one eye. "I know."

She's utter brilliance.

My complete downfall.

"Forever, Nis. Not just until the next hurdle or you grow tired of me." I swoop over her, climbing onto the bed from between her thighs. My chest brushes her stomach along the way, my mouth latching on to one nipple to suck and tease as I reclaim her throat in my grip.

"I won't grow tired."

I pay those breasts homage, kissing one, then the other, until my dick can't take it any longer. I move higher, trekking my lips over her sternum. Shoulder. Jaw.

"No other man will experience this again," I whisper in her ear, settling my hips into hers. "No other man will even dare to touch you."

"That works both ways." She grasps my shoulders, digging her nails into my skin. "Now stop attempting to scare me off and fuck me."

"My pleasure." I grasp my dick, take a second to reposition myself, then give her what she wants, thrusting hard inside her, all the way to the hilt.

Her tight pussy fits me like a glove. The ultimate vice.

Her mewl of rapture only affirms the perfection.

I fuck her rough. Savage thrusts. Slamming home. Over and over, the brutal repetition burning my muscles with fatigue.

I keep my hand tight around her throat, the high tilt of her neck making it obvious she wants more as my other hand digs into the soft flesh of her hip.

I squeeze. Claiming her. Owning her.

Her breaths become fractured—broken and manic. So fucking delectable.

She digs her claws into my wrist, her gaze holding mine as she whispers, "I own you."

I grin. "Yes, you own me."

I fuck her harder, wanting to temper her sass and increase it all at the same time. But she feels so fucking good, those legs around my hips holding tight.

"Oh, fuck." She tilts her head back, closing her eyes, and shudders.

She's fucking coming.

Already. Without me.

I grind harder, thrust deeper.

I pound into her until she screams, the sound echoing off the walls and into my chest.

Her orgasm is the greatest show I've had the pleasure of witnessing. Her euphoria. Her peace. Those nails dig deeper into my wrist.

Her core pulses around me, the agonizing shudders making it almost impossible not to follow along with her. But this isn't over. Not yet. Not even when her body becomes soft beneath mine, her bliss turning into relaxation.

"You done?" I drawl.

She smiles, her eyes still closed. "Like you wouldn't believe."

I can definitely believe it. I'll never forget it either—the moment when she truly succumbed to me will forever be a treasured memory.

I lean closer, my stubble grazing her cheek as I growl in her ear. "Don't for one second think this is anywhere near over, little fox."

She chuckles. "I wouldn't dream of it."

I release her neck, trailing kisses where my fingers have heated her skin until her breathing levels. I want her to start all over again. From beginning to end.

I grind slowly, coaxing her into a moan, but instead of enjoying my gentle lethargy, she places her hands on my chest and pushes me backward.

"Off," she demands. "Get off the bed."

I frown. "We're not done."

"I know." She pushes again, and this time I oblige despite the vacuum of bliss that's sucked from my senses when my cock leaves her pussy.

I raise to my knees between her thighs, then climb off the mattress. I stand before her, tall, proud, with my fucking cock bobbing like a buoy in troubled waters.

But she won't leave me unsatisfied. I know she won't. It's not her style.

My fear is that she'll give more than what I deserve. Too much pleasure. A dose of something beyond lust to make me fall deeper into this mind-fuck of slavery.

"Step back." She slowly rises, creeping from the bed, as I do her bidding.

She holds my gaze as she stands before me, chin high, eyes glazed, cheeks flushed. Then she descends, falling to her knees to deliver my wildest fantasies.

"I want to taste you," is all she says before her unfathomably brilliant mouth engulfs my cock, her lips sliding halfway down my shaft with exquisite suction.

I groan, clenching every fucking muscle imaginable as she tongues my length.

It's beyond words—the lust, the waning restraint.

I could come with one stroke, but I force myself to prolong this, to take her offering as the gift it is and treasure it.

I slide my fingers through her hair, unable to stop myself from squeezing tight as she sucks harder.

"*Fuck.*" My pulse becomes a pounding beat in my ears. There's so much pressure. Beneath my ribs. In my temples. No place more adamant than my fucking balls.

Her tongue works overtime along the underside of my shaft. I can't help directing her, my hands almost balled into fists in her hair as I force her back and forth, back and forth.

She groans with my force, the vibration adding a new layer to my torment.

"You're going to make me come," I speak through clenched teeth.

She nods, taking me all the way to the back of her throat, her eyes rolling as she retreats and starts all over again. Her hands slide to my ass, her nails digging deep.

I groan, my orgasm building beyond my control.

"Keep sucking like that and this will be over real soon."

Those pretty eyes meet mine, her mouth stretched over my dick, the glistening juices of her arousal and saliva coating her lips.

She bobs faster, keeping the attention at the sensitive head of my cock, knowing exactly what I need. Those nails dig deeper. Those lips suck harder. She moans again, and I'm almost done for.

"Don't stop," I growl. "Keep sucking until I come down the back of your throat. Then swallow everything I give you."

I pull at her hair, thrusting my hips into her mouth, inspiring more of her moans.

But it's her nod that sends me over the edge. The sweet acquiescence that draws the orgasm out of me and makes me buck uncontrollably.

She doesn't stop. There's not even a pause as my cum releases down the back of her throat, those eyes forever holding mine.

"Jesus," I groan. "*Fuck.*"

The euphoria continues, the drawn-out bliss on a whole new level until the last of my seed escapes.

She may not be convinced about marrying me, but that right there was a commitment pledged by both of us.

There's nobody else now.

Just the two of us. All I have to do is keep her safe in my fucked up world.

She releases my length with a loud pop, then swallows in a show of erotic simplicity, her tongue confidently swiping her glistening lips.

"That was perfect." I grip her chin to drag her to her feet, placing my mouth on hers. "*You're* fucking perfect."

"That's because I now own every part of you." She pulls back with a smirk and walks for the bathroom. "And those were some of my favorite inches."

"Feel free to pay homage whenever you like, little fox. Those inches are yours to command."

She chuckles and closes the door behind her.

It takes a split second for the high to fade. As soon as she's out of sight, the darkness of reality creeps in to steal the warmth.

I can't mess around anymore. I can't lose myself in distraction or put off the upcoming war with Emmanuel. I have to get us all home. I've finally got what I've craved for too long—and I won't let anyone fuck with it.

I've pulled my clothes back on and I'm buttoning my shirt by the time she returns to the bedroom, still gloriously naked with a subtle afterglow.

The space around us isn't the same though.

I see her differently, too.

She'll have a bigger target on her back now. One unlike anything I'm accustomed to. Law enforcement will see her as a traitor. Those I work with may never fully accept her despite my threats for them to comply.

The road forward won't be easy for either of us.

"Are you okay?" She moves in behind me as I fix the last button on my shirt, and wraps her arms around my waist.

"Yeah. You?" I turn to face her subtle wince.

"The after-sex vibe with us is never kind." She keeps her arms locked around me, her fingers working intricate patterns on the low of my back.

"We haven't had the best start. But things will change once we return to Portland."

"What's going to happen in between now and then?"

"I don't know. I still have no clue what Costa's capable of." I press my lips to her forehead, picturing that asshole's smirking face. "I anticipate having to negotiate with him for a long time. But we'll eventually come to some sort of agreement."

"What if you don't?"

"Every man can be bought. One way or another. I just have to find the right price."

Her arms fall to her sides as she leans back to meet my gaze. "Do you truly believe that?"

"In ten years, I haven't been proven wrong. But the right price might not necessarily be money. Getting out of this could mean getting my hands on what he values most." I glide my fingers through the silken strands of her hair. "That could mean his sons. Or his wife."

"What would you do to them?"

"Whatever necessary."

I brace for her flinch of disgust. It never comes.

Instead, she holds my gaze with steadfast assurance. "Do whatever it takes. This has gone on long enough."

The hardened pressure of pride strips me of my defenses. I'm so fucking besotted, and even though I know it's a deficiency, I can't help wanting more of her.

"I will." I drag her back to me with a gentle grip around her neck. "And no matter what carnage I create, you'll be waiting for me once it's all over."

She nods. "No matter what."

This thing between us doesn't make sense. There's no rhyme or reason. It's mindless obsession and uncontrollable fascination. But it's here to stay.

Nobody will take her from me.

"Get dressed—" My cell vibrates in my pants, the buzz bringing unwelcome dread as I pull the device from my pocket to stare at the screen.

"Who is it?" Nissa grabs her clothes from the floor to pile them on the bed.

"Layla."

The endorphin binge is well and truly over. I swipe to connect the call and raise the cell to my ear. "Where are you?"

"Our hotel suite." Her voice is brittle, the tone doing a number on my guilt. "Please, tell me you've figured out how to get my little girl back."

26

ANISSA

Cole tells his sister to meet us in the penthouse in half an hour then disconnects the call.

"She's coming up here?" I keep my gaze on him.

"They all are." His posture tightens as he taps at his cell screen and walks for the door. "Get dressed and meet me in the living room."

I make quick work of my underwear, blouse, and jacket, then shimmy into my pants. I'm striding from the bedroom, finger-combing my hair when I find him in the kitchen, his back to me as he stands in front of the coffee machine watching dark liquid gurgle and spit into two mugs.

"How was Layla?" I cock my hip against the counter, giving him space.

"Predictably upset." He grabs the filled mugs and approaches, placing one in front of me. "There's no escaping her suffering until I can get Stella back."

He's different now. Hardened. Focused.

"I know she's hurting, but it's unfair for her to blame you for this."

"Blame keeps her occupied." He sips his coffee, not holding my gaze. "It's a better alternative to letting her mind run wild with thoughts of what her daughter could be going through."

"But it upsets you, right?" I cock my head, forcing myself into his line of sight. "You seem different after the phone call. Are you worried about facing her again?"

He huffs out a breathy laugh. "No."

"Then what is it?"

He eyes me over the rim of his mug and leisurely takes another sip, as if waiting for me to figure out the answer.

"Cole?" I raise a brow.

He places the mug on the counter, giving me his attention. "I'm worried about you."

"Me? Why?"

"Nobody will appreciate this new turn of events between us." A subtle grin tilts his lips. "Vowing my life to a Fed isn't a typical day at the office."

"Wait." I bristle at the declaration, my mug clattering to the counter, coffee sloshing over the rim. "You're going to tell them?"

"Layla may have stopped screaming at me but she's going to expect answers. They all need to know."

My heart grows claws, the sharp tips digging into tender tissue.

"This isn't the right time." I'm still treading water with my own feelings. I need to get used to this reality first.

"No, it's not. But it's necessary. They already know you slept in my bed last night." Those deep blue eyes hold mine as if trying to give me strength. "They're fully aware something has been going on between us. It's time they learned to trust you."

I shake my head. They can't trust me. Not yet.

God, I don't even trust myself right now.

"They're going to attempt to tear you limb from limb," he continues. "If not physically, then mentally."

"Jesus Christ." I release the air in my lungs with a heavy heave. "You didn't want to break that to me a little more gently?"

"There's no time for gentle. They'll be here soon."

My throat threatens to close.

They're going to kill me.

"You'll be fine." He takes another sip, those eyes still intently coaxing me to be stronger.

"Fine?" No, not fine. Anything but fine. "Hunt wanted me dead *before* we started sleeping together. Finding out we've committed to some sort of permanence will... I don't know. It's just not the right time. Can't you let me get used to us first?"

"For starters, there's not *some sort* of permanence. This is infinite, little fox." He places his mug on the counter and bridges the space between us. "I also know you're going to take your sweet-ass time getting used to this, and I have no plan to coddle you with postponements."

"Well, I hope your impatience is worth my death."

His grin returns. "Hunter is protective. He knows you're a threat and not because of your badge. He was well aware of your hold on me before I was. Same goes for Luca, although, unlike Hunt, he's slightly conflicted about hurting women."

"Slightly?" I roll my eyes. "Your gushing words of comfort fill me with confidence."

He chuckles, soft and breathy. "You can handle it."

"You're joking, right? We haven't even touched base on Decker, who I dragged to hell and back to get information on you and your family. Which is why Keira will never trust me." I swallow to ease the ache in my throat. "It's too soon, Cole."

"It's no longer up for discussion." He wraps a hand around my wrist and pulls me in for a hug. His lips find my temple, his gentle warmth enveloping me. "You can be quite endearing when you're vulnerable. It's not my favorite facet of you, but it's growing on me."

"This isn't funny." I lean back to meet his gaze. "What are you going to say exactly?"

"I don't have a script, little fox." He glides strong fingers through my hair, teasing my scalp. "But they'll be told you're here to stay. And that they now have to answer to you."

My heart lurches. "Again. That's not funny."

"As far as I'm concerned, you're an extension of me. They will answer to both of us."

He's sincere. Batshit, loco serious.

"You'd be throwing me to the dogs." I step back, demanding space.

"I'm placing you on your throne."

Hell no.

Luca doesn't approve of me. Decker despises me. Hunter wants to slay me alive. And I have no clue what the women in Cole's life are capable of.

"Nobody is ready for this." The weak defense is murmured from my lips.

He reaches out, his hands sliding up my forearms, over my shoulders to my neck. His fingers work their magic at the base of my skull. Teasing. Coaxing. "Holding off will only delay the confrontation."

"I'm good with a delay."

He grins, half-hearted and incredibly sly at the same time. "You can handle this. The faster we put this behind us, the sooner we can focus on the bigger picture."

The bigger picture.

I slump my shoulders, my perspective finally settling on what matters most— Stella and Tobias. The only thing that matters is those kids.

"Okay?" He leans in, placing his forehead to mine.

My stomach lurches. I'm not merely drowning in the deep end. The water here is one unending rip filled with bloodthirsty sharks and pummeling waves.

"Okay." I suck in a breath. "But I came to Sacramento in an attempt to make things easier, and it seems I've done the opposite."

He huffs out a laugh. "You never make things easier, yet I keep coming back—"

A knock raps at the door, flooding me with panic. "I thought you said we had half an hour."

He gives me a quick kiss and starts for the hall. "It sounds like the attack dogs came early."

He's such a masochist, deriving pleasure from my suffering. Yet in the same heartbeat, I know he's taunting me out of a desire to create strength.

I'm about to be attacked. My choices. My loyalty. My life. He needs me to be resilient.

I square my shoulders at the sound of the door opening, bracing for the upcoming onslaught.

But it's not his sisters' voices I hear. It's men, their grumbled undertones unfamiliar.

No, not entirely foreign—just initially indistinguishable. The longer they mumble, the more I remember.

I dash for the hall, finding Cole at the door, his profile a tight line of hostility.

"Our father wants to see you," the unseen man says. "Now."

I don't stop running, not until Cole raises a hand at me in warning, his gaze snapping to mine.

"Stay there." There's no fear in his eyes, only angered determination before he returns his attention back to the men. "Where are we going?"

"You'll see."

The response sickens me. If Emmanuel's sons had to dispose of one body today, there's nothing to stop them from getting rid of two.

"Don't go." I creep forward, my throat drying when the men come into sight.

They're both tall, broad, lethal, their hard stares and tight lips exuding malice.

"You know the drill," the blond with the beard says. "No weapons."

Cole reaches behind his waist, flipping the back of his suit jacket to retrieve his gun.

"No." I grab for his arm, but he counters by snatching my wrist to guide the weapon into my palm.

"It's okay." His features don't soften as he meets my gaze. "I'll call you when I can."

"No, you won't," the taller man mutters. "Leave your cell behind, too. We don't want any distractions."

My panic increases, hollowing my stomach. They want Cole entirely vulnerable, with no ability to escape.

"Look after this." He retrieves his cell from his jacket pocket, holding it out to me.

I'm too numb to take it. Too busy scrambling for a way to stall while his gun remains a heavy weight in my hand.

"Please listen to me." Cole's team is meant to be here soon. Any minute now there could be a wall of backup to stop this from happening. All I need to do is buy time. "You're meant to be meeting your sisters. Don't leave until they show up."

Cole slides his cell into my pocket and leans close, kissing my cheek, using his proximity to murmur in my ear, "The password is your birthday. Call Hunter."

I shake my head and whisper, "If you go with them, you might not come back."

"And if I don't, then the same can be said for those kids."

Every organ in my body twists, demanding action.

I can't let him go. He can't stay either.

I have to find a middle ground and I don't know how. I just need a little more time to figure this out.

"Let me go with you." I step away from Cole, pushing in front of him to block the doorway as I face Emmanuel's sons. "He's not leaving on his own."

"Nissa," Cole warns.

"Stop wasting our time." The blond stares over my shoulder. "We're not taking anyone except you."

Strong hands fall on my hips, the pressure building to move me out of the way.

"No." I raise the gun in both hands, mindless of what else to do. "He's not going anywhere. Not like this."

The men don't move. Don't even flinch.

They remain standing there as if I don't exist, their attention focused on Cole.

"We retrieved those children for you," the guy with the dark stubble says. "We cleaned up the mess you left behind in the penthouse. And our father has even offered you an opportunity most people would sell their soul for. Yet this is how we're repaid?"

A hard body settles in behind me. "Lower the gun, little fox," The growled demand brushes the back of my neck, making me shiver. "Trust that I'll sort this out."

I ignore him, switching my aim from one brother to the next. I can't trust anyone when there's no humanity to be seen in the men before me. "You're going to bring those kids here and end this."

"Get your bitch under control," the blond snaps.

"Anissa, lower my gun," Cole sneers this time, his arm wrapping around my stomach. "Because if he calls you a bitch again, I'm going to have to kill him."

I need more time. Just a few more minutes. I don't know how to win in their world. I haven't learned the ropes. The only thing I'm familiar with is intimidation and threats. Whoever calls chicken is the loser, right?

"Now, Nissa." Cole's hold tightens. "Before they lose patience."

The darker-haired man reaches into his suit jacket, completely undaunted by my threat. Is he going for a gun?

Shit. He probably knows I won't shoot, and I have no doubt he will.

"Okay." *Fuck.* I raise my hands in surrender and stumble as Cole pulls me back into the penthouse.

"Behave." His hand sweeps over my wrist, giving a gentle squeeze. "Get in contact with the others. Make sure nobody meddles. *Including you.* I'll return with those kids soon. Be ready to leave."

I'm scraped hollow as he turns his attention to the threat and walks directly toward it. Fearless.

My insides scream at me to do something. Anything. But I'm clueless when my only experience involves avenues Cole would despise me for taking.

I can't alert the authorities.

I can't make threats revolving around the law.

The three of them walk to the elevator, the two men flanking Cole as he presses the call button and waits for the doors to open.

I'm a trembling mess of internal suffering by the time they step inside the small space and swing around to face me with matching expressions of cold calculation.

I hold my breath, holstering the gun in my waistband while the doors close. As soon as they're gone I run after them, diving deep into my pocket to snatch Cole's phone. I press the button to call for another elevator, then unlock the cell by entering my birthday.

My pulse is erratic as I scroll through the contact list to find Hunter's name and connect the call, the *ding* of the elevator's arrival filling me with temporary relief.

I dash inside, slamming my hand against the lobby button as the line connects.

"Yeah?" Hunt says in greeting.

"It's Anissa." The elevator jolts into movement, slowly descending. "Emmanuel's sons showed up and took Cole."

"Wh—you—Torian." His gruff words are cut short, the garble undecipherable.

Shit. "I can't hear you. I'm in the elevator. They made him leave his gun and phone behind."

"Get—there—wait."

Goddamnit.

I hang up and stare at the descending numbers on the indicator screen, silently begging them to move faster. Once I stop at ground level, I reef the doors open and run barefoot to the front of the building, rushing to the city street, spinning in a full circle in the middle of the sidewalk.

Cole's nowhere in sight. Not in the passing cars. Not walking nearby.

They can't have disappeared. I wasn't far behind them.

The cell vibrates in my hand, Hunter's name appearing on the screen.

"Cole's gone," I answer in a rush. "They took him."

"Yeah, I got that part. You don't know where they're going?"

"No." I rake a hand through my hair, my toes throbbing from the frozen cement. "They didn't say."

"Well, I've got eyes on the kids. They haven't moved. My guess is they're bringing him here. So you can tap out." His voice fills with annoyance. Disdain. "Mind your own business, and leave Cole to me."

27

COLE

I'M TAKEN TO THE HOTEL'S UNDERGROUND PARKING LOT WHERE A BLACK SEDAN IDLES a few feet outside the elevator, the windows tinted.

"Do you plan on telling me where we're going?" I stop a few feet from the vehicle, not overly enthusiastic about being at their mercy.

"It's a surprise." Salvatore opens the back door. "Get in."

His audacity is becoming more than a thorn in my side.

He's nobody.

Nothing.

Yet he dares to throw his weight around, and his brother is stupid enough to call my woman a bitch.

I'd slit their throats right here if they didn't have me by the balls. Instead, I calmly step forward, biding my time until I can gain the upper hand as I take a look inside.

Emmanuel sits on the far back seat, his wrinkled face smiling up at me. "Let's go for a drive."

I fucking hate this guy. I'm unsure if I've hated anyone else more. But strangely enough, I have an unwanted appreciation for his unprecedented level of cockiness.

"Are you going to be more hospitable about where we're going?" I place a hand on the roof, another on the open door and check the interior. There's no sign of Stella or Tobias. No blatant show of weaponry either.

"I have something you need to see. Call it an incentive." He pauses, holding up a finger as if to warn me from taking his words as a taunt. "A gift," he clarifies. "All I want to do is show it to you."

He can call it a gift, a bribe, or a fucking curse for all I care. In the end, it will only ever be a delay in getting those kids.

I slide in, sticking to my side of the car as the door is slammed behind me.

"Your seat belt, please." Emmanuel watches me patiently. "It's going to be quite a drive."

I keep my mouth shut and fasten the belt as Salvatore climbs in behind the steering wheel while Remy takes shotgun.

"Good." Emmanuel nods in appreciation. "Let's go."

We exit the underground parking lot to stop out the front of the hotel and wait for passing traffic. That's when I see her. Barefoot. Her face pale with panic.

Nissa stares at the car, her focus on Salvatore, her hand sliding beneath her jacket.

"Is she going to be a problem?" Emmanuel asks.

I try to ignore my anger at him recognizing her even though he wasn't upstairs, but my aggression is unescapable. It consumes me, increasing my need to protect her.

"She pulled a fucking gun on us," Remy grates as we accelerate onto the road. "She's lucky to still be breathing."

The hair rises on the back of my neck, the distinct prickle crawling its way down my spine. Nissa runs after us, her hand still inside her jacket, her hair flipping around her face.

"She isn't a problem." I feign disinterest, unwilling to reveal her true value just yet. "What's this *gift* you have for me?" I turn to meet Emmanuel's kind, lying eyes as Nissa haunts my periphery. "Has your wife grown tired of the kids already?"

"On the contrary. She's become quite attached."

I stiffen.

"There's no need to fear, Mr. Torian. I assure you, they're in good hands and will be returned to you as soon as our business dealings are taken care of."

"Where are they?"

We turn a corner, and I fight to ignore relief when Anissa disappears from view.

"Where you left them. But it's come to my attention that we're running out of time. I heard news of a scene between you and that woman at the hotel bar, and I must admit I was a little disappointed when rumors of your FBI fling proved true."

"Disappointed?" I scoff. "I thought a man of your underhanded capabilities would understand the benefit of having an agent in their pocket."

He raises a brow. "Is she in your pocket, though, or in your bed? I heard whispers of a marriage proposal and wanted to make sure you were still considering my generous offer."

"Have you been spying on me, Costa?" This asshole is more thorough than I anticipated. "All this strategy and foresight is leading me to believe you were in on Robert's abduction plan from the beginning."

"I give my word that I wasn't. Like I told you, my involvement started once I heard Jordan had the children in his possession. I've helped you ever since."

I scoff a laugh.

Maybe he believes he helped. Maybe he's so fucked up that he's convinced his actions are benign instead of an act of hostility.

"What about the proposal?" he asks. "Is what I heard true?"

We drive onto the I-5 heading away from the hustle of the compacted city streets.

"It's true." I meet his gaze. "I'm sorry to inform you I won't be aligning our families through marriage. But I'm sure we can come to some other kind of arrangement."

Disappointment enters his features. Calculated, fraudulent disappointment.

He nods and tangles his fingers in his lap. "That's okay. I'm not giving up."

Of course he isn't. He doesn't plan to stop until he has me nailed to a wall.

"I've made up my mind, Costa. Whatever you plan to threaten me with won't work."

He clucks his tongue. "I've never threatened you. And I don't plan to start. What I offer is enlightenment. I want to show you the alternate options to marrying a Fed who will only threaten your empire."

"Why don't you just tell me what—"

He holds up a hand. "Please. Give me this last opportunity to prove myself. I've lived long enough to make many mistakes. All I'm doing is trying to stop you from making one yourself."

"I can handle my own problems."

He inclines his head. "I admire your confidence, son. But marriage isn't just a personal commitment. Not for men like us. You're balancing the success of your entire empire on this woman. And I assure you the lust won't last. You might be having fun now, but soon it will wear off."

Bullshit.

I know things with Anissa will be challenging. But my want for her goes beyond lust. It always has.

"How many long-term relationships have you had?" he asks without curiosity, because I swear he's already aware. This asshole has dug deep enough into my past to understand my previous lack of interest in commitment. "Have you shared your house before? Your belongings? Your trust? What will you do if she betrays you? What will happen if after you commit to her in the eyes of the Lord, things don't work? Will she walk away with a lifetime's worth of your secrets? Or will you be able to silence her?"

Silence? No, he means kill, and for once, the imagery of that act leaves me cold.

623

"Weren't you the one trying to tempt me into marrying your daughter?" I scowl. "You're not doing a good job selling commitment."

"That's the thing, son. My daughter is malleable. You can shape Abri however you like. If you want a doting wife, she can be that for you. If you prefer a business partner, she's smart enough to hold her own. And if you desire no strings, she can stand by your side in name alone, turning a blind eye to a long line of mistresses." He sighs and relaxes back into his seat. "What I'm trying to say is that a marriage to someone in law enforcement will forever be a noose around your neck, waiting for you to slip. Yet the alternate option of my Abri will bring nothing but ease and prosperity."

"And if things don't work out with her?" I drawl. "Does she walk away with a lifetime of my secrets, or do I get to *silence* her?"

"You will never need to worry about that. As I will be as heavily invested in a successful marriage as you, I'll make it my duty to ensure my daughter is everything you need her to be."

This fucker is proving to be more like my father with every word. Maybe more misogynistic and cruel.

"Trust me, Cole. You don't want to align yourself with a woman for anything other than financial gain."

I hadn't planned to marry at all. Until Anissa.

There'd been no concept of commitment. No desire to slice myself open and share my secrets with anyone until my little fox came along.

Now, life is different.

"I appreciate your concern. Unfortunately, it won't change my mind." I stare out the side window as we drive farther away from the city. "How long until we reach our destination?"

"A while." Salvatore grunts. "We're heading out of Sacramento."

I'm getting farther and farther away from those kids. From civilization and witnesses.

"I understand you're not convinced." Emmanuel leans closer and lowers his voice. "I was young and hopeful once. But tell me, how can this woman possibly improve your future? What will she bring to your family other than risk?"

I don't owe him answers. I shouldn't even acknowledge his question. Yet his scrutiny eats at me, coarsely grating away layers of protective coating to expose flaws in my future.

"Perspective," I say on instinct. "Insight. Strength. New blood."

Anissa isn't a prop or a fling. She's the outsider who will fortify my empire.

"And you've weighed this perspective and insight above the threat she will pose when everyone who has ever worked with your family begins to question your sanity? What do your men think of her? What about your suppliers? Your informants?"

His biting inquisition isn't new. I've been through all this on my own. I've weighed the options. And every time I convince myself Anissa is worth the risk.

Emmanuel heaves an exhale, as if hating to be the bearer of bad news. "The cartel won't be pleased—"

"Enough," I growl. "I'm done talking about her."

He sucks in a long breath and slowly nods. "I understand."

The ride becomes silent as we coast for miles. The further we go, the less traffic follows. Away from the city, past the outer suburbs, until there are few cars on the road and even fewer houses in sight.

They want desolation, and we're close to getting it.

This ride could be my last.

This old fuck, with his disturbing smirk and lack of self-preservation, might be making a move to wipe me out now rumors of my father's death have started to circulate.

And why wouldn't he? I have no successor. My sisters are neither capable nor inclined. Decker lacks the ingrained brutality. Luca hasn't been around long enough. Benji is a fucking traitor. And although Hunter knows every aspect of my business and could handle taking over, he wouldn't want the responsibility or the leadership.

Tobias is the only replacement who can rule my family, and he's not even within a few years of being able to grasp the helm.

Salvatore takes an exit off the I-5, taking us over a bridge to cross a river. My prospects are even worse out here. Houses are separated by numerous acres. We pass a vineyard as the sun lowers toward the horizon and I'm sure the approaching darkness is all a part of their plan.

"It's not much farther." Emmanuel stares down the middle of the car, focusing out the front windshield.

We follow alongside a wire fence for mile after mile of farmland before the road curves wide, taking us in a new direction.

"Here." Emmanuel points up ahead. "We've arrived."

We approach a dense barrier of trees on the left, bordered by a white ranch fence, the billowing scrub blocking the view of what I presume is a house yard. I remain quiet as we pull into the property, passing open metal gates and the thick tree line into an expansive manicured garden.

This place is its own oasis shielded from the rest of civilization.

The trees block out the world, enclosing us amongst the dense lawn, sculpted rose bushes, and, from what I can see, an impressive farmhouse up ahead.

"Is this place one of yours?" I ask.

"No. Just a rental in a perfect location. I want you to have privacy while you reconsider your future with Ms. Fox."

I stiffen at her name.

His insight into Anissa is no longer a revelation—it only makes the dust settle on the level of exposure I've placed upon her. The risks will increase once the world learns of her value to me. But I've known that all along. It's the distance currently between us that makes the reminder fucking brutal.

"My gift." Costa juts his chin at the lavish house as the car pulls up a few yards from the wraparound porch. "Have an open mind."

I drag my gaze along the pristinely painted exterior, the orange glow of the late afternoon sun gleaming off the windows. For a second I think he's offering to buy me the property, until I see the woman leaning against the porch railing near the front doors.

Slim, blonde, and cover-model pretty, she's a vision of perfectly choreographed temptation that fills me with adrenaline. "Your daughter, I presume?"

"She's beautiful, isn't she?" He releases his seat belt and opens his door. "Come meet her."

"This is a waste of time, old man."

He slides out to peer down at me. "Maybe. But humor me. Spend some time with her before you make a rash decision." He closes the door on the conversation, leaving Salvatore to glare at me through the rearview mirror.

"We'll be watching," he warns. "Don't do anything stupid."

I laugh. Can he sense my sudden thrill?

This woman is exactly what I've been looking for—their fucking soft underbelly.

I get out, the smirk still haunting my mouth as I leisurely stroll after Emmanuel and climb the three stairs to the front porch.

The woman eyes my approach, her appraisal sly as she seductively bites her lower lip.

"Cole, I'd like you to meet Abri." Costa greets his daughter with a kiss on the temple, then retreats. "Abri, this is the man I've been telling you all about."

I don't take my gaze off her, scrutinizing every detail from the deep blue eyes that sparkle with mischief to the way her fingers loosely tangle in front of her, showing no hint of apprehension.

She's beyond visually appealing, with high cheekbones and enough subtle makeup to accentuate her beauty. And even though she's covered from shoulder to foot in her designer sheer blouse, peach blazer, and tight white pants, it's clear she's sporting an astronomical body.

She's a viper.

I may have been born to rule and lead, but this woman was a strategically raised Trojan horse who only has one aim in mind—temptation.

"Cole." She says my name like a lover's call, the syllable whispering past my ears as she saunters forward in ankle boots to offer her hand. "I've been told a lot about you."

"I promise it was all lies." I play the game, sweeping my palm over hers for a quick shake, the connection increasing my thrill.

"I assure you, every word was kind." She chuckles.

"Like I said, all lies."

Her laughter continues, bubbling like a gentle brook. "Let's take a walk."

My pulse quickens as I remain in place, anticipating discouragement from

Costa that never comes. He doesn't voice disapproval of me being alone with his daughter. He doesn't even drop the faux friendly expression.

"That's a great idea. Just don't go too far." He claps me on the shoulder and strides away, his polished shoes thudding along the porch. "Take this seriously, son. I assure you my Abri is a far better option for your future."

Leaving me alone with this woman, even though unarmed, is senseless. He's banking her safety on my reputation for not involving women in the games of men. But that moral high ground is no longer on the table.

"You seem worried." Abri inches closer as her brothers leave the car, their stares fixed on us. "Don't you want to be alone with me?"

I meet her gaze, searching for sincerity, and grin when I don't see any. "I'm not the one who should be worried."

She rolls her pretty eyes and passes me to descend the stairs. "I'm far too prepared to be worried."

Meaning?

Maybe she has a weapon. Or more eyes are watching from the overbearing tree line, even though the sedan is the only car out here.

Neither would matter, though, if I wanted her dead.

Problem is, she only holds value as a hostage. Breath needs to remain in her lungs.

"Where are we going?" I stroll after her, catching up on the pebbled drive to head in the opposite direction to the men in her family.

"Anywhere." She shrugs. "I don't care, as long as we can talk."

So she plans to lure me into marriage through conversation and the gentle sway of her lush hips? This bitch gets ten points for optimism.

"What do you want to talk about, snowflake?" I hold the aggression from my tone.

Fuck this beating-around-the-bush bullshit. I need to get back to Anissa. She's exposed without me. And the thought of Stella and Tobias approaching another night without their family is gnawing at my impatience.

Abri shoots me a grin. "We need to talk about us, of course. *You* mainly. Tell me about yourself."

"You want menial chitchat?" I shoot a glance over my shoulder. Her brothers still eyeball me.

"It's not menial anything. We'd be creating a foundation that will hopefully start a very beneficial future for all of us. You're a highly successful businessman, Cole. But your wealth can't be anywhere near the level of my father's. Aren't you excited at the prospect of unimaginable success?"

"I'm satisfied with where I'm at."

"Liar." She snickers. "Men like you are never satisfied. I bet you thrive on new opportunities. You're just daunted by how different my father's offer is from what you're used to."

"And you appreciate the prospect of marrying someone you don't know?"

She pauses, her smile remaining in place as she focuses aimlessly across the yard. "Let's just say you're a far better prospect than I anticipated."

"That doesn't answer my question. If you want to talk, then tell me how a pretty girl like you would ever agree to an arranged marriage."

She stops and turns to face me, her expression remaining bright as she raises a brow in condescension. "For starters, I'm no girl, tough guy. And agreeing to marry you didn't take much convincing. I do what needs to be done for the success of my family."

I'm not buying it. Not unless she's clueless.

"Do you know who I am, Abri?" I stare into those sky-blue eyes. "Do you have any idea what being with me would entail? It would be a loveless marriage completely devoid of emotional connection. Surely you want more than that."

Her sly smile widens, exposing a dimple in her left cheek. "I'd never set my sights on something so pathetically whimsical as love. I know it doesn't exist. Neither does God, for that matter. Both were created to appease the masses." She pivots on her heel and continues forward. "What I *do* know is that you're a piece of the puzzle that will help bring diversity to my family's wealth. And I can do the same for you."

"You didn't answer my question." I grab the crook of her arm, making her stop. "Do you have any idea who I am?"

She snaps rigid.

In the distance, a throat clears in subtle warning.

I grind my teeth, struggling not to tighten my fingers as her haughty gaze lowers to my grip.

"Sorry. I thought you were being rhetorical." Her menial expression remains in place as she yanks her arm away. "But my answer is yes. I know who you are. Somewhat." She shrugs again. "I don't have specifics. I don't need them. I'm well aware your business dealings are more aligned with my mother's side of the family, and that doesn't faze me."

Her mother's side of the family? Who the fuck is her mother?

"See?" She beams at me. "This is why we need to talk. Clearly you're at a disadvantage with information. Let me enlighten you." She keeps walking, reaching the end of the house to lead the way around the side.

She doesn't give a shit that she's now out of sight from her protectors. She gives no fucks at all because she knows I'm currently a sucker waiting to be ass fucked by her father. But that won't last forever.

"Cole?" She pauses a few yards around the corner. "Come on. This is good news."

Like fuck it is.

I've been blindsided again, and the worst part is knowing that seemingly kind old woman looking after Stella and Tobias may have blood like mine running through her veins. She might not have a loving heart or gentle intentions. She could be just another fucking Trojan horse.

I glance over my shoulder again, glaring at Salvatore and Remy who stand at the front porch steps before I stalk after Abri, my palms itching to squeeze the life from Costa's only daughter.

I scrutinize the tree line to our left as I catch up to her. Someone has to be hiding in the scrub. Someone with a rifle scope to stop me from giving this family what they deserve.

"My mother has a large extended family." She holds my focus as she speaks. "She's a Cappelletti."

The name hits like a physical blow.

Italian fucking mafia.

I let out a long, slow breath, refusing to let shock grip me by the balls, and focus straight ahead. The tall trees stop at the edge of the side boundary to give sight to the leveled paddock of dry grass and dirt behind the house yard. "This obviously isn't public knowledge."

Decker and Luca would've found the information otherwise.

"My father went to great lengths to cover up the connection before they were married. He previously wanted nothing to do with their reputation. Our legitimate businesses would've suffered—"

"Previously? What about now?"

She's quiet for a moment, nothing but the building chorus of cicadas calling to the approaching night.

"Abri?" There's a warning in my tone. "You wanted to talk, so fucking talk."

She sweeps her arm out to snap a rose from a nearby bush. "Yes, previously. Don't ask me why he's had the sudden change of heart. I'm not privy to his reasons. All I know is that he's now eager to diversify, and sees you as the golden goose."

Not a force to be reckoned with. Not a threat to his future or an upcoming menace to his existence. A fucking golden goose.

"You have no idea what you're getting yourself into," I seethe. "If I were you, I'd reassess your willingness to help your family with anything that involves mine."

She leads me to the back fence, placing her booted foot on the bottom rung of the white horizontal railing as she picks petals from the rose and throws them one by one to the ground.

"Why?" she asks simply. "I don't understand your refusal to contemplate the possibilities. You don't even know what my father has planned."

I grasp the fence tight enough to make my fingers ache, my anger volatile beneath the surface as she rambles on about our future and unfathomable potential for too fucking long.

She has no clue of my desire to choke her.

To make her fucking scream.

I want her entire family's blood spilled at my feet, their pleas for mercy tattooing my memory.

"Cole?" Her attention bores into the side of my face. "Are you listening?"

"No. I'm not fucking listening. What I'm doing is waiting for you to drop this act." I push from the fence. "Up until now I've kindly ignored your father's attempts to start a war, but that window is closing." I turn toward the house, still trying to see the audience I know hovers nearby.

"Look, I know you're reluctant to be here." She throws the flower stem to the grass. "But you also need to understand that my father went to a lot of trouble renting this house and flying me here to meet you. He's gone to great lengths to welcome you into—"

"He's gone to great lengths to test my patience."

She sighs. "Please, Cole, you need to loosen up. Neither one of us will be allowed to leave until we've given this partnership ample consideration. So relax, and stop thinking you can rush this." She raises her brows, waiting for a response I'm not restrained enough to give. "Why don't we go inside and have a drink? It might help take the edge off."

I don't want a fucking drink. Or to waste ample time, considering this bogus bullshit.

What I need is a new plan to get those kids, the intricacies seeming all the harder to finesse now that they're being held by a woman with mafia ties.

"Come on." She sidles up to me, running her fingers along the sleeve of my jacket as she continues toward the back of the house. "One drink. That's all I ask."

"Then what?" I growl.

"Well, if you hear me out and finally realize this opportunity is too good to pass up, my father will call in the helicopter. We could be married in Vegas by the end of the night. And those kids would be right by your side."

Laughter festers in my throat, the slightest hint of mania edging its way into my psyche. "And when I don't?"

She keeps walking for the house. "That isn't for me to decide."

I don't follow. Instead, I clench my hands, struggling to hide my instability.

The Cappellettis aren't people who mess around. They're big fish in a pond I don't want my family dragged into. It doesn't matter that they're based on the other side of the country. This shit is too close to home.

"Come on, Cole." This time Abri's voice holds sympathy. The slightest edge of compassion. "Let alcohol take the edge off your concerns. You'll see sense afterward."

She doesn't wait for a response as she weaves around the rose bushes and steps onto the porch, heading toward French doors with the glass windows illuminated by the warm light inside. She pulls both handles wide, disappearing into the house, leaving me with the cicadas and whoever lurks close by.

Maybe it's just her brothers.

Maybe the whole East Coast mafia are watching.

Either way, I'm running low on options for a resolution. At least ones that don't involve high risk. Or marriage.

"*Fuck.*" I run a hand through my hair, digging my nails into my scalp.

Hunt was right.

Before Nissa, I would've handled this situation differently.

I would've jumped at the marriage opportunity, either eager to be aligned with another like-minded family, diving in headfirst, palms itching for action, or salivating at the prospect of taking them down from the inside out for daring to intimidate me.

This inaction is a deficiency I can no longer allow.

I need to make a decision and stick with it.

No path is without risk or suffering. No choice is devoid of pain. But I have to make one, and fast.

I follow after her, my determination reaffirmed, my focus steady. I step onto the porch, my pulse thundering as I stop at the open doors to an expansive living room, the ceilings high, the thick draped curtains open, the furnishings expensive.

"I've heard scotch is your drink of choice." She stands before a freestanding alcohol gurney beside one of the brown leather sofas, her long hair draped over her shoulder as she holds up a bottle of Macallan single malt. "Would you like me to pour you a glass?"

"No."

She shrugs. "Have it your way."

She ditches the scotch and claims a bottle of champagne from an ice bucket, taking a few seconds to struggle with the cork before pouring herself a glass. "This was meant to be reserved for good news, but I'm confident I'm only jumping the gun a little."

I ignore her and scope the room, searching for make-shift weapons. There are no knick-knacks that could be used to bludgeon. No vases or sculptures able to be smashed. There's nothing but books and furniture… unless I take into account the champagne bottle in her hand and the Macallan within her reach.

"Looking for something in particular?" Her faux curiosity pisses me off. "My brothers swept the house clean earlier. They took out anything sharp and pointy."

I lean against the doorjamb, crossing my arms over my chest. "And you're not daunted by the need for that preparation?"

She shoves the champagne bottle back into the ice, the crunch and swish momentarily drowning out the internal whispers of vengeance before she saunters to the sofa to take a seat. "You don't seem like an animal."

Her assessment is inaccurate. I'm nothing if not entirely feral right now.

"Come sit with me." She crosses her legs and pats the space beside her. "I've already told you we won't be able to leave until my father is satisfied."

Yes, I heard her the first time, but now I home in on her words.

We won't be allowed to leave.

Not just me. Both of us.

"Suit yourself." She gives a wicked grin. "I don't mind admiring you from afar."

"Admiring? Is that how you're going to play this?"

"What other way is there? You're a handsome man, Cole, and although I know no marriage of convenience can start perfectly, you'll come to learn I'm quite a catch." She tweaks that grin up a notch, her dimple resurfacing. "I have many talents I'm sure you'll enjoy."

"You're quite the generous offer."

Her expression doesn't falter. "But you're hung up on someone else."

"I am." I cross my arms over my chest as she sips the champagne, her tongue sneaking out to swipe her glossy lips.

"If the woman is your reason for denying me, I can assure you she's the wrong choice." She places the flute on the coffee table and slowly glides to her feet. She's lithe as she saunters toward me with a complete lack of self-preservation. "A man like you can't be naive to the risks involved in pairing with a Fed. How do you know she won't double-cross you?"

"She's aware of what happens to those who mess with me." There's a harshness to my tone I can't suppress.

"Careful, big guy." Her brows rise as she sidles closer, sliding her palms over my biceps. "A lady might consider that a threat."

"Maybe a lady should." I remain still while she dares to skirt those hands higher, up to my shoulders, around my neck. "You wouldn't last a week under my roof."

"I don't know about that." She laughs, the husky sound brushing my ears like a lover's touch. "Your devilishness only makes me eager for more."

She's definitely beautiful. Flawless, even. Given normal circumstances I'd fuck the spark from those dazzling eyes. But right now, all I want to do is suffocate it.

"Your delicious dominance doesn't frighten me." She lowers her voice to a teasing whisper. "I don't scare easily." Her fingernails tease my nape, sending a rush of sensation down my spine.

"You're making a mistake with the Fed." She leans closer. "Women love a bad boy. But only temporarily. The timeline is even shorter for someone with a strict moral compass, and I'm assuming that's what this woman has." Her eyes fill with lust, whether it's fake or not, I'm unsure. "You're a phase, Cole. Her interest in you won't last. Eventually, she'll humiliate you."

She nips at my triggers. Her teeth dig deep into insecurities I never wanted exposed.

"I know women like her," Abri continues, her voice soft. "Strong, forthright women. Even if she did stick around, your lifestyle would change her."

The clarity of her insight slices deep.

That's what I've been worried about. That Anissa, with her unshakable determination and infallible fortitude, would weaken in my world.

I don't want that for her.

"She'll become someone else," Abri whispers. "Someone you're not infatuated with. You know she will."

"So marrying you is the best option?"

"Marrying me is the only option. I'm the perfect replacement—easy on the eye, yet strong, smart, and determined. I'm everything you need, with the bonus of financial security instead of ruin. And strings that never need to be attached."

She's a choice of convenience and prosperity in comparison to the path with Anissa, which is riddled with landmines.

"Let me show you one of the benefits of having my company." She slides a hand down my arm and grabs my wrist to lead me to the sofa. "And as soon as you realize being together is the best option, we can tell my father and have the kids brought out here to celebrate."

28

ANISSA

It's been hours without word from Cole and no movement from the children as I sit in the Escalade parked across the road from Emmanuel's building.

Normally, I'd keep myself busy through a case by chasing leads. I'd run Costa's license plates and track them through traffic surveillance. I'd have the option to call local law enforcement for assistance. I'd even go through the process of watching credit card transactions in the hopes of pinpointing Emmanuel's location.

But I chose to be here as part of Cole's team—his partner—and legitimate, legal means are only used if they're discreet and without trace, which is something I can't provide.

I've done my best to ensure all our bases are covered though.

Penny is in the hotel lobby if Cole returns.

Keira and Layla remain in the penthouse suite in case his arrival bypasses the front doors.

Luca and Decker are situated on different rooftops, giving us numerous angles of sight on the children, while Sarah and Benji are in another car at the back of Emmanuel's building, watching the exit to the parking lot.

If anything happens, we'll know.

But nothing has happened. Not since Cole was taken.

It's been radio silence, and the quiet is killing me.

"Would you quit jolting your fucking leg," Hunter snarls from the driver's seat. "You're pissing me off."

I plant my foot and glare straight ahead.

Why I got paired with this asshole is beyond me. He's made it damn clear he would love to see me disemboweled and rotting in a shallow grave.

"You should go wait with Sarah and Benji," I snap. "I'm sure you'd prefer their company."

"No shit. I'm only here to keep an eye on you." He white-knuckles the steering wheel. "I'm playing goddamn babysitter because I don't trust you."

He's itching for a fight, and I'm beyond tempted to give it to him. But the distraction won't help Cole. At this point, I'm not sure if anything will.

"You'd make my job a lot fucking easier if you'd just leave." Hunt looks at me, his angry stare haunting my peripheral vision. "I bet you've been tempted to call in the license plates on the black sedan. Or to cave to your impatience by contacting the cops."

"It's not impatience. It's concern. I'm worried about him."

"And you think that makes you special? We're all fucking worried, but the rest of us know to trust his ability to handle the situation if he specifically said not to meddle." He lowers his window, letting the chilled air sweep in. "No matter how bad Torian wants to believe you can be one of us, you never will be. You're too much of a high and mighty bitch to change your ways."

I drag in a long breath to keep myself composed. "There's no going back. I've made my choice. So get used to me being here."

"I've got no plans to get used to anything where you're concerned. You'll be gone soon enough."

"Not if I get rid of you first."

He laughs. "You think that's possible?"

"I don't know." I look him in the eye. "But I'd sure enjoy trying."

He stares daggers at me. "I suggest you mind your manners."

"And I suggest you focus on why we're here and quit being distracted. It's unprofessional."

His nostrils flare. "Fucking bitch," he mutters under his breath, then turns his attention out the windshield.

More time passes as Cole's phone remains silent in my hand. I grow nauseous. Anxious. Angry. Anything would be better than sitting here doing nothing, because the sound of Hunter's barely audible breathing is enough to make me homicidal.

"We've got movement." Luca's voice carries through the car speakers. "Get ready."

Hunter reaches for his cell propped against the vehicle's display screen and turns the call off mute. "What's happening?"

"The woman and the two guards are escorting the kids into the elevator," Decker announces through the four-way conversation. "It looks like everyone is leaving."

I sit forward, scrutinizing the street. There are no lingering cars at the front of Emmanuel's building. "They're either leaving on foot or not coming out this way."

Nobody acknowledges me. Not even with a scoff of dismissal.

"I'm coming down," Luca says. "There's no point keeping two of us in the sky if they're on the move."

Cole's phone vibrates in my hand, ratcheting my pulse. I rush to unlock the screen and open the awaiting text from Costa.

"What is it?" Hunt asks.

I click the notification, find a video recording, and immediately press play.

The first sight of Cole makes my eyes burn with overwhelming relief.

He's alive. Uninjured.

It's the passing seconds of what appears to be a surveillance feed that suck the gratitude from my system.

I watch as a beautiful woman straddles his lap on a sofa, her blouse loose, maybe even gaping at the front. I can't tell from the angle of the camera. His hands are on her thighs though, his gaze intent on her face.

"I said, what the fuck are you looking at?" Hunter leans forward, muting his cell again before snatching Cole's phone from my grip. His expression doesn't change as he replays the video while I struggle not to vomit. "This must be Costa's daughter." He pivots the screen in my direction and raises a taunting brow. "They look cozy, don't they?"

Bile climbs my throat as I glare.

"Your man didn't stay loyal for long." He lobs the device back at me and I fumble to catch it in my lap. "Are you ready to walk yet? If I were you, I'd take off and never look back."

I clench the cell in my fist. "You'd love that, wouldn't you?" My voice cracks with bitterness. "I bet all your dreams would come true if I scrambled out of here with my tail between my legs."

"If the collar fits, why not run with it?"

My hatred of this man knows no bounds. I want to shove my gun down his throat. To claw at his eyes and slap that superiority from his arrogant face.

"I'm not going any-fucking-where." I pivot in my seat, turning my whole body to him. "Not now. Not because of this. That video means nothing. I know Cole. I trust him."

"You don't know shit. You've got no fucking clue what he's like."

He pokes at my insecurities.

No, he punches them, beating me into a submissive state where I question my choices all over again.

"We've got eyes on them." Sarah's voice breaks through my turmoil. "It looks like those guards are driving a black Lincoln from the parking lot. They're pulling onto the side street."

Hunter remains focused on me, cocking his head in question. "This is your last chance to bail."

I should. For self-preservation's sake. For sanity and safety, too. But I won't give up on Cole. Not this easily.

I pull on my seat belt and find the black Lincoln waiting at the traffic lights up ahead.

"I see it." I jerk my head toward the intersection. "Hurry up and follow."

He doesn't comply. He keeps sitting there, staring at me. "Stop fighting this and fucking go. You know this bullshit between the two of you won't last."

"*Drive,*" I snap, unleashing my anger and animosity, even my fear.

Again, the car doesn't move.

My pulse quickens with the closing window of opportunity to tail the Lincoln. We can't lose them. We can't miss the only chance to find Cole.

"I said fucking drive, you arrogant prick." I snatch the gun from inside my jacket and slam the barrel against his forehead. "*Now.*"

There's a beat of volcanic animosity where I question who the hell I've become, my pulse ratcheting higher, my heart thundering. Threatening him like this goes against everything I used to stand for. It's careless and impulsive. And feels so fucking right I can't quit.

"Where are you guys?" Sarah asks. "Does anyone else have eyes on them?"

Hunter smirks, the curve of lips more of a sneer.

"So help me God, motherfucker, if you don't hurry up and follow I'll pull the trigger and dump your ass in the street. There's no way I'm losing that car."

He keeps the grin in place as he rolls his eyes, then without a word, he starts the ignition, my gun still digging into his head as he cuts into traffic.

"Hunt, where are you?" Sarah's' frantic voice adds to my building adrenaline. "What's going on?"

He bats away my arm and unmutes the call. "I'm following. We'll be a few cars behind the Lincoln."

"What was with the radio silence?" Benji interrupts.

"We've had contact from Costa." Hunt indicates into the middle lane, remaining a few vehicles behind our target. "He sent a video of Torian."

"What video?" Decker demands. "Is he still breathing?"

"He's breathing just fine." Hunter shoots me a grin. "Isn't he, Miss Piggy?"

I clench my teeth and shove my gun back into its holster before I'm more tempted to squeeze the trigger.

"The footage showed Torian with a woman. I assume it's Costa's hot-as-fuck daughter. And the two seem to be getting along well, if her position over his dick is anything to go by."

"A sex tape?" Sarah scoffs. "Are you serious?"

"Not a sex tape." Hunt takes a left, following the Lincoln down a busy street compacted with traffic. "Just the prelude."

"Fuck you," I mutter under my breath. He's only saying this to destroy me. To cut and slice at what I have with Cole. "I'm not leaving, no matter how hard you push."

"We'll see."

"We can figure out motives later." Luca talks over our mutterings. "For now, keep an eye on those kids and give me directions. I've only just made it to my rental."

Sarah relays the information from her position somewhere behind us, while I force myself to remain focused on things that don't whip up volatile emotion.

"We're moving onto the I-5." Hunter pulls onto the exit, remaining out of sight behind other vehicles as daylight fades to black.

The cover of darkness will work in our favor, as long as we don't lose the Lincoln.

And if we do… My throat squeezes, the dryness of apprehension taking over my mouth.

I can't handle the unknown. My fear over what happens next is blinding. Suffocating. It doesn't help that riding alongside Hunter is a task drowning in complete sterility.

We don't communicate through the passing miles. Not apart from the telepathic messages of hatred I send his way.

He's entirely cold to my existence. An invisible barrier has been built between us.

As the minutes drag by, I unlock Cole's phone and replay the video. I watch it over and over, reading expressions and body language. I scrutinize Cole's fingers on the woman's thigh and his intent focus on her face so close to his.

Their physical contact turns my veins to ash, my thoughts to suffering. I press play so many times I memorize the footage from start to finish, the valves in my heart seeming to rip apart from one another to create a chasm of carnage.

"Quit looking at it." Hunt reaches out to mute his cell. "You're eating out of their fucking hands. Buying into their stupid game."

I can't stop. All I want is one hint to ease my suffering. Just one little clue to tell me Cole hasn't succumbed to Emmanuel's plan. I keep watching. One more time. Then two.

"Fucking stop," he grates. "They sent it to make you jealous, and it's working."

"How do you know?"

"Why else would they send it? Do you think Torian asked for a souvenir?" He rests one arm against the car door, chilled as fuck in the middle of a wildfire. "My guess is he declined the arranged marriage. And they're attempting the soft-cock option of getting rid of you."

I replay the footage again. The hands. The proximity.

"If it were me—" Hunt indicates into the second lane, passing another vehicle. "—I would've taken pleasure in putting a bullet through your brain. But women usually cut and run when they see their man fucking around with someone else. So I guess whatever works…"

I wince, even though the slightest sense of hope warms me. "You think this is staged?"

"Not staged. But not a true indication of what's going down." He doesn't look at me. There's no emotion to his words either. He's still calm. Cool. Arctic. Yet his insight could almost be considered an act of kindness. *Almost*. If I wasn't fully aware of his raging asshole status.

"Why are you telling me this?" I attempt to read his caged expression through the soft glow of the dashboard lights and come up with nothing.

"The shooting you part or…?"

"No," I grate. "Why did you say he must've declined the arranged marriage? Why be nice enough to tell me the one thing I want to hear when you've made it clear how you feel about me?"

His jaw ticks, his fingers tightening on the steering wheel.

"Hunter? Why say anything at all?"

"It's my job," he snarls. "I do what's in his best interests."

"But you didn't when the video first arrived."

"Yes, I did."

I don't understand. "How?"

"Jesus *fucking* Christ," he mutters under his breath. "I didn't think you would stick around. I thought you'd walk."

"So you taunted me about the recording to speed up the process?"

He keeps staring straight ahead. "I should've tried harder."

"And now you suddenly think it's in his best interest to have me here?"

"Hell no. I still want you to fuck off. The only difference now is that I don't think you will."

He's right.

I won't.

At least not unless I'm forced out by an arranged marriage.

I want to explore what life could be like in the grey, where things aren't clear-cut and right or wrong. I want to hold on to the strength and confidence he's stoked inside me. I want to delve deeper beneath his vicious love.

"That video means nothing," Hunter mutters. "There's nobody more loyal than Torian, not only to his men, but also his women. He'd never stoop low enough to cheat on you. He's more likely to kill you than ever go behind your back to fuck someone else."

I huff out a breath, strangely comforted.

"What I'm saying," he continues, "is that there's a story behind that video and it's got nothing to do with him wanting her to ride his dick and everything to do with strategy."

"And you're telling me because I stuck around," I repeat, needing validation.

"I'm telling you because you're his now, which means you're also mine to inform and protect, no matter how much I fucking hate the prospect."

I want to scoff. To laugh in the face of his admission. But there's something in his words that brings me more comfort than I care to admit. In his own fucked up way, Hunter has made me feel at home in this foreign world.

"*Shit.*" He slaps a meaty finger against his cell. "We're heading off the I-5. Nobody follow. We don't want to make this obvious."

I lock Cole's phone and shove it into the glove compartment, sitting forward in my seat as Hunter waits for the Lincoln to take the exit and drive from view before he cuts his headlights and continues with the pursuit.

We're out in the middle of nowhere, surrounded by darkness. There's no glow from nearby houses. No sign of life.

"This doesn't look good." I take off my jacket and drape it over the illuminated dash screen, blanketing us in shadow. "Why would Costa want the kids out here?"

"Your guess is as good as mine." He eases off the accelerator as the road straightens, the red tail lights of the Lincoln now tiny dots in the distance.

We struggle to keep up through the limited vision, crossing a bridge we almost miss, only to have our target disappear.

"We lost them." My chest squeezes with impatience. "Where did they go?"

"We didn't lose shit. The road curves up ahead. So pipe down and let me do what I do."

We drive with nothing but the full moon to cast the slightest glimmer over the asphalt.

I fidget, my leg returning to the constant jostle. "Whatever you do, don't touch the brakes. They'll see our lights."

"Are you fucking serious right now?" He shoots me a glare. "You're really going to give me pointers?"

I ignore his ego and the constant churn of nausea in my belly. We can't have much farther to go. This has to end soon.

"Sarah, kill your headlights and follow." Hunt raises his voice and jerks his head at me. "Send her our GPS location."

I do his bidding, using his cell to text the information.

"I'm on my way," she responds. "Luca is riding with us now. We'll catch up soon."

When I raise my vision from his phone, the Lincoln seems so far away. The tail lights are barely a blip in the distance. "We're losing them. You need to catch up."

"I know what I'm doing." He waits until the red glow disappears, then presses his foot down. For long minutes, we drive like this. Slow, then fast. Following lights, then seeing nothing but darkness, until we reach a sweeping curve that sends us in a different direction.

"Where the fuck are they going?" Hunter grates. "This could be a goddamn trap."

We round the bend and he leans forward at the sight of an illuminated entrance to a property roughly half a mile away.

There's no Lincoln in sight. No sign of another car at all. Only a wall of trees stretching along the property's border, the towering barrier stretching into the night.

"Look." I point to a speck of red through the dense foliage. "A tail light."

He jerks his chin in acknowledgement. "And house lights."

I see them, the slithers of orange slipping through the thick trunks.

"Sarah, we're stopping." Hunter quietens his voice. "I'm going to hang up and send through our final location but make sure you lay low. There's nothing out here. Any noise will draw attention." He pulls off the road, inching the vehicle slowly through long grass before cutting the engine. "I'll have earpieces and extra ammo waiting for you. Let me know when you arrive."

"We will."

He grabs the phone, disconnects, and taps his screen a few times before shoving it into his pocket. "This is it, boss bitch." He reaches into the back seat to retrieve a duffle. "Are you going to do me a solid and stay in the car?"

My adrenaline and apprehension surge, flooding me, the energy buzzing through my veins. "You know the answer to that."

Hunter reefs open the duffle and pulls out a hard plastic case to reveal earpieces hidden inside. Six different sets. All encased in foam padding. "I know what I want your answer to be." He settles back in his seat to look at me. "Whatever is happening in there isn't going to be pretty. And it sure as shit won't be legal."

"I've made my decision." My chest tightens. Restricts. I made the choice back in Greece. My future was always going to revolve around Cole. "I'm all in. He means too much to me."

Hunter sighs and lobs an earpiece in my direction. "Then keep your fucking head in the game and make sure your heart stays out of it."

29

COLE

"I THINK IT'S TIME FOR THAT DRINK." I SPREAD MY ARMS ALONG THE BACK OF THE sofa, allowing my gaze free rein to stalk Abri's body as she straddles my hips like a stripper itching for a generous tip.

"Okay." She slides off me, clearly doing her best to provide as much friction as possible before she walks to the alcohol cart. "See? I'm not too proud to do your bidding."

"I can definitely see that."

I've given her what she wanted.

Time. Attention. Indulgence.

I've listened to her husky promises of a bright future. I held my disinterest at bay as she removed her blazer and undid the top button of her blouse, attempting to seduce me with the barest hint of cleavage.

I even ate up my rage and frustration, humoring her enthusiasm while I gained insight.

Now, I'm done playing with my food.

"Tell me, Abri, why did you say earlier that we wouldn't be able to leave unless your father was satisfied with the time we spent here?"

She frowns and grabs the bottle of Macallan. "Because he wants to make sure you think this through properly."

"You said 'we,' though. Not just me. But both of us." I scrutinize her, noting the slightest twang of tension entering her shoulders.

"We're both involved." She pours my liquor, then dumps the bottle back onto the cart. "I thought that would be obvious."

I incline my head. "It's the way you said it. It made me think you're not such a willing participant in this after all."

She chuckles, the jovial show unconvincing. "I'm willing." She pastes on a smile and saunters back to me, handing over the scotch before reclaiming her seat on my dick, her hands finding my shoulders.

"Well, unfortunately, my feelings haven't changed. I won't be humoring you or your father any longer."

She reaches for me, raking her fingers through the hair at my nape. "He'll be disappointed. Why don't we sleep on it?"

"I'll pass." It's my turn to laugh, the low snicker encouraging her genuine smile to return. "You also said you know who I am. What information did your father give you? How deep did Daddy dig into my life?"

"I was smart enough to do my own research."

I latch on to more clues, eating up her crumbs as she continues her seduction.

"Your own? Interesting." I swirl the liquor in the glass, my arms remaining outstretched over the back of the sofa. "Doesn't your father keep you well informed?"

"On the things that matter, yes. Of course he does."

"Good." I nod, doing my best to resist the numbing bliss of the alcohol. I've used the sedative trick too many times to fall for it myself. "That means you'll be able to alleviate my concerns about what happened with the body this morning. What did your brothers do with the guy executed in the penthouse?"

Her expression pauses. Confusion sets in.

"Where did they dump him? And the blood…" I lower my free hand, placing it on her hip. "Did they get it out of the office carpet? I've got a man who knows a trick or two about cleaning up a scene."

She breaks eye contact to reach for her champagne flute on the corner table. "I'm sure everything was handled properly." She raises the glass to her lips, gently sipping, pretending she's okay with the information she clearly hadn't been privy to.

"Yeah." I swirl a lone fingertip in a slow pattern along her leg. "I'm sure you're right."

Her sickeningly sweet smile is no longer fixed on me when she places the flute back onto the table. She's let down her mask enough to show I rattled her.

"How do your brothers usually handle clean-up?" I tilt my head, attempting to regain eye contact. "Are they the type to dump a body in a river? Or do they prefer the 'dismember and dissolve' trick?"

She doesn't look at me as she huffs in humorous disbelief. "I'm not sure."

"So you're not informed on those type of things?" I keep trailing a swirling pattern with my fingertip, lazily taunting. "What about information about the people your father does business with? Are you aware that my family isn't new to yours?"

"Yes." She raises her chin slightly, emboldened by her insight. "Your father and uncle attended some of our house parties when I was little. They were both ladies' men, if I recall. Always surrounded by a swarm of beautiful women."

"Slaves," I correct. "Beautiful women, yes. But slaves who had no choice in the company they kept."

Those lashes continue to bat. Her chin remains high.

For brief seconds, she stares at me in silence before she says, "I know what you're trying to do and it won't work."

"What am I trying to do, snowflake?" I swirl my scotch and slide my other hand higher, over her hip, her waist, all the way up to her shoulder. "Other than continue the discussion you've forced upon me."

"You're attempting to frighten me. Even after I've made it clear I don't scare easily."

I guide my palm to her neck, a move once reserved for Anissa, but this has nothing to do with pleasure and everything to do with destruction.

"I'm beginning to see that. It's admirable." I tighten my hold, firm and fucking direct. "Especially if you're undeterred by the knowledge of your family's association with sex trafficking. Or that the hand gripping your vulnerable throat is the same one that stabbed a letter opener through a man's temple mere hours ago."

She purses her lips. "You're lying."

"If you think so, why not ask your father?" I keep adding pressure against her neck, tighter and tighter until she begins lifting her chin from the restriction.

"Careful," she warns. "They're watching."

I keep my hand in place, undaunted.

"Cameras." She hikes her brows with confidence. "Two of them. On opposite sides of the room."

"You think cameras will save you?" A slow grin spreads across my lips. "You have my brother and niece." I keep my voice low as I dig my fingertips into her delicate skin. "You're holding children hostage from a man who's spent his life perfecting the art of revenge. Do you really think I'll spare voyeurs a second thought if I decide I want you dead?"

Her throat works over a heavy swallow, her pulse increasing beneath my fingers.

"What's wrong?" I lean closer, grazing the stubble of my cheek against hers as I murmur in her ear. "You seem unsettled."

She doesn't answer. Not in words. Her continued rigidity is enough of a response.

"You don't want to marry me, Abri. You don't want to live with a man who is currently eager to see you suffer."

Her breathing deepens—long, measured inhales followed by heaving exhales.

"So tell me how I get out of this." I nuzzle her jaw. "Tell me how to wake your father up to the slaughter he's approaching."

She swallows again, remaining quiet.

"I'm convinced you're a smart woman. But you'll be a dead one if you continue to play his games." I claw my fingers, digging nails into flesh.

644

"I don't know."

"Sure you do." I lean back. "Are there any other men on the property? Any guards? Or security?"

She doesn't respond.

I squeeze tighter. "Abri?"

"No." She chokes in a strangled breath. "Nobody else is here."

"No fucking snipers? Don't you have another brother somewhere?"

"He's not here." She licks her lips in a frantic rush. "Nobody else is, either. It's just us."

I can't figure out if she's telling the truth. She seems panicked enough not to lie, but that could be an act, too. "What does your father have planned if I deny him?"

"I don't know."

"I'm losing patience," I growl. "That doesn't work in your favor."

She lowers her attention to stare at my chest. "I swear—"

"Look me in the fucking eye when you talk to me." I release her neck and grasp her chin, demanding compliance. "Give me the respect I deserve."

Her attention gradually raises to mine, the sparkling blue gleaming back at me with vehemence.

"Dear ol' dad hasn't come to save you yet. Why is that?"

Her nostrils flare, her jaw ticking.

I've hit a nerve.

This is what I've been digging for. The anger. The bitter truth in her emotions.

"Tell me, Abri, if he's watching, why hasn't he run to your rescue?"

She struggles over her answer, her lips tight before she admits, "He can't hear what you're saying. He can only watch. He probably thinks your attention is a good sign."

"You don't think your discomfort is obvious?"

She glares her hatred, but it doesn't seem aimed at me. My guess is that her animosity is toward the man leaving her in danger.

"He doesn't give a shit about me," she grates through clenched teeth. "He never has. I'm an asset to him and nothing else."

Perfect. So fucking perfect. "Then why maintain this charade?"

She plasters her mouth shut, holding her answer hostage.

"Come on now. Why are you shy all of a sudden?" I dig my fingers harder into her chin, making her grimace. "Tell me why you're playing along."

"You're a way out." She unsuccessfully attempts to tug her head away.

"Of what?"

"This hell." Strength enters her tone. "He controls everything I do. Who I speak to. When I work. My goddamn money. He acts as if he's doing me a favor by choreographing my life, but all I am is a commodity in some sick game."

She's convincing, yet she's also a manipulative actress.

"And your brothers?"

"They're biding their time until they can take over the family estate."

I release her, allowing her to inch back a little. "Then tell me what he's attempting to achieve with this marriage and I'll help you."

She blinks as if startled by my offer. "I have no idea."

"Yeah, you do. Maybe not directly, but you would've heard something. You'd have a fucking clue."

"I'd only be guessing."

"Then fucking guess."

Her mouth opens, her lips working over silent contemplation. "It has to have something to do with my uncles. My dad could be trying to prove a point."

I tense at the Cappelletti reminder. I don't want those fuckers anywhere near this. "What point?"

"I don't know. They always ridicule our side of the family—our business. They think my father is weak. Maybe this has something to do with him showing them he's more than a fashion label."

I'm not buying it. There has to be another reason. "What would your father do if you were under threat?"

Her eyes flare, the whites blazing as she pulls away from my grip on her chin. "I have no idea."

"Yes, you do. Tell me what he'd do if I held you hostage."

"You don't have a weapon."

"Anything can be a weapon when you have a thirst for blood." I grab her around the back of the neck and pull her toward me. "What would he do, Abri? Would he care enough about your safety to negotiate the release of those kids? Or would he cut and run from his so-called asset?"

There's a faint crunch of noise outside. The cacophony of cicadas is replaced by the disturbance of pebbles. A car approaches.

"Someone else has arrived." I narrow my gaze. "Who?"

"It has to be my mother with the kids. As far as I know, she's the only other person here in Sacramento."

Apart from those fucking guards.

"Why would she come out here?" I flick my gaze to the open doors leading to the porch before returning my glare to Abri. "What's going on?"

"My father must think I've either convinced you or he's given up waiting." She shakes her head. "He said I'd have a few hours. After that…"

"After that, what?" I grab her throat again, my impatience about to detonate.

"I don't know." Her expression transforms to a plea. "I swear."

"Then tell me what he'd do if you were under threat." I jolt her with a quick shove of my hand. "*Now*, Abri."

She whimpers, clutching her hands onto mine to fight against my grip. "If I'm right about my mother being here, he'd do everything he could to protect me. He wouldn't be careless with my life in front of her."

Good. That gives me options. Not many, but enough.

I smash my scotch glass against the side table, sending liquid and shards scattering, the sound loud in the silent house.

"Oh, God." She screams and attempts to scramble off my lap. "Stop. *Please.*"

I hold tight, demanding her compliance. "Calm down."

She claws at my wrist, scratching and shoving. "What are you doing?"

"I'm finishing this. I just have to spill a little blood first."

30

COLE

CLARET OOZES BETWEEN MY FINGERS CLAMPED AGAINST ABRI'S NECK AS I STAND, dragging us both to our feet.

She releases another bone-chilling scream, her heart and soul belting out with the piercing decibels.

"Be quiet, snowflake." I drag her backward into me, holding her against my chest. I feel her terror in her trembling limbs. Despite her tough act, she's petrified. "Don't struggle or this will all be for nothing."

Footsteps thunder toward us from the porch. A door squeaks somewhere inside the house. Her brothers clamber through the French door entry, guns drawn moments before her father fills the archway from the hall.

All three of them stop in rage-induced panic.

"How valuable is she to you?" I jab a shard of glass toward the exposed side of her throat. "Lower your weapons or I slice the other side, too."

Emmanuel takes a cautious step forward, raising his hands.

"Stop." I use his daughter as a shield and dig the shard into her skin, making her whimper. "My hand around her throat is the only thing keeping her from bleeding out." I relax my grip, proving my point by allowing the carnage to freely flow down her neck, soaking her blouse.

This time she sobs, her fingers clinging to my wrist. "Please don't let me die."

"Everyone relax." Emmanuel takes another step. "I think we can all agree this has gone too far."

"Too far?" I ask. "You've held me to a disadvantage from the beginning. I've merely leveled the playing field."

"I'll fucking kill you." Salvatore keeps his gun trained on me. "If anything happens to her, I'll make you suffer."

"I don't doubt it for a second. But can you achieve greatness before your sister dies of blood loss? Because if it were me, I'd be setting my sights on getting her out of here as soon as possible."

"Salvo, please." Abri's breathing becomes labored. "Do what he says. Call in the helicopter. I need a hospital."

"It's done," Emmanuel growls at me. "I'd already organized our departure. There was no need for this."

"There was always a need." I smirk, giving him a healthy dose of flipped history. "You step on my toes and I cut off your feet. You threaten my family and I destroy yours."

"Enough." He stands taller. "You're making a big mistake."

"I don't think so. Tell your boys to drop the weapons."

His jaw ticks as the faint *whoop, whoop* of a chopper approaches in the distance. He wasn't lying. At least, not about his departure. I'm well aware he didn't say shit about whether or not he planned to take the children with him.

"I'm lowering my gun." Remy leans over, placing the Glock on the floor. His brother reluctantly copies. "Just stay calm."

"Where's my niece and brother?" I glance between them, waiting for someone to offer an answer they all seem reluctant to give. "You brought them here, right? You were going to take this excursion to the next level by flying them out of Sacramento."

"No. This was over." Emmanuel shakes his head, showing minimal sympathy for his daughter. He doesn't look at her, not her neck or the threatening glass. He's more fixated on leveling me with spite. "I never threatened you, son."

I ignore him and jerk my chin at Remy. "Kick the guns my way. One of you is going to want to get a first-aid kit. The other can retrieve the kids and bring them to me."

"No," Emmanuel repeats.

"Please, Dad." Abri shudders against me. "Do what he says."

"Let her go first,' he demands. "Let her come to me."

I dig the pointy tip of the broken glass into her throat, making her squeal. "I'm afraid your time to manipulate and make demands is finished." I turn my attention to Salvatore. "Do as I asked before I lose my temper."

The noise from the chopper increases as everyone remains in place.

They don't listen.

Don't move.

I drag the glass down Abri's neck, lightly, but enough to draw blood.

"You fucking prick." Remy starts for the porch, doing my bidding.

But Salvatore still doesn't move. "There's no fucking first-aid kit here, you piece of shit. We removed anything with scissors or sharp blades before you arrived."

"That's too bad." I shrug. "You might want to take off that shirt then so she's got something to stem the blood."

His lip curls in a sneer as he shucks his suit jacket to the floor, then starts on the buttons of his white shirt. "If she so much as loses consciousness, I swear to God—"

"You'll do what?" I rage. "Endanger my family? You'll take our children hostage? This is the result of your actions. However this ends is your doing, not mine."

He yanks off the shirt, his muscles tense, waiting for a chance to strike. He juggles the material in his hands, finding a sleeve, then proceeds to rip it off. "Help her secure this around her neck. Make sure it's tight." He throws the makeshift bandage to his sister, his eyes leveled on her in concern. "Are you okay?"

"Please just do what he says," Abri pleads. "Bring the kids in here."

"He will *not* bring those kids." Emmanuel storms for the French doors now rattling from the whip of outside air. "One of the guards will hand them over at the back of the house yard once my family is already safely in the helicopter."

"No, *Remy* will hand them over," I clarify. "Your two for my two, old man."

His shoulders straighten in response but he doesn't say a word before escaping onto the porch. He doesn't even give a heartfelt farewell to his petrified daughter as he steps into the thrashing air to walk out of view.

Abri wasn't lying about him after all.

"Let me help you bandage her throat." Salvatore steps forward.

"Get out of here." I yank her farther into me. "Make sure your father doesn't try any shady shit. I'll be holding you responsible if he does."

He stares at his sister. At the blood dripping from my fingers.

"Hurry." Abri clings to the hand at her throat as if struggling to remain upright. "I don't want to die here."

His nostrils flare. His father might not care about her, but he does.

"She'll be fine," I drawl. "As long as none of you try anything stupid."

"Give your word that you won't do anything else to hurt her." His glare cuts to me. "That once the helicopter leaves the ground, this all ends. No repercussions. No more acts of vengeance."

No. I won't.

"Fucking give your word, Torian." He clenches his fists. "My father will kill those kids—"

"No." Abri struggles. "He wouldn't."

"He's lost his fucking mind." He raises his hands to his head, shoving them through his hair. "You know he doesn't give a shit about you. He's only complying because our mother is here. He won't risk her life. Nobody else matters to him." His arms drop to his sides, his surrender on display as he meets my gaze again, this time without hostility. "Give your word and I'll make sure to keep him under control."

I don't have to give him a damn thing. Not promises. Not protection. Nothing other than pain and suffering.

But those kids are out there somewhere. In the dark. Scared and vulnerable. They don't deserve to be tortured by another second of delay.

"You have my word."

His shoulders straighten in response.

"I said, you have my fucking word. Now *go*." I jerk my chin at the French doors. "Before your sister runs out of time."

A second of contemplation passes before he nods. "I'll get everyone in the helicopter."

"We'll be right behind you." I increase the wattage of my smirk. "Won't we, snowflake?"

She shudders out a breath and trembles in my hold.

She's the perfect victim. Her vulnerability is flawless.

"I'm holding you accountable, Torian." Salvatore trudges to the door. "Don't fuck this up." He disappears outside, his footsteps thundering back down the porch, the sound quickly fading under the mass of swirling air.

I wait one second. Two. Then release her throat and turn her toward me. "Give me the shirtsleeve."

"Are you crazy?" She grabs my wrist, flipping over my hand to inspect the deep gash along my palm. "You're the one who needs a bandage."

"Stop fucking around." I ignore the biting sting of the open wound and focus on her neck. "I need to cut you so they don't think you were in on this."

"No." She retreats, running her fingers over the slight scratch on the other side of her throat. "You've already done enough of that. I'll make up a story later."

"Get over here. Have you forgotten the cameras? And what motherfucking story are you going to make up?" I start after her, the shard of glass ready in my hand. "I won't cut deep. Only enough for them to think you believed you were dying."

"Seriously. *No*. Just help me with this." She raises Salvatore's shirtsleeve and begins wrapping it around her neck. "I'll keep the bandage on until I get to a hospital. If I have to cut myself then I will. There's no way my dad is out there watching the security feed right now. He's furious. He probably can't even see straight."

"You better be right, otherwise you're on your own after this."

We made a deal.

She'd play along with my slice-and-dice act if I vowed to get her away from her family when she decided it was time. But that agreement only holds up if this goes off without a hitch.

"Don't worry; he bought it." She inches back toward me and raises her head to allow me access to secure the material around her throat.

"Maybe he did. But we need to finish this before any of them start to question why you're still conscious." I place my sliced palm against the spot where her cut carotid is meant to be, letting the blood oozing from my wound seep into the material. "Don't fuck this up."

I spin her, reversing her into my chest to drag her toward the porch. I pick up the guns along the way, shoving one into the back of my waistband, out of her reach. The other takes the place of the jagged glass to point against her cheek.

"Do everything I say." I grasp her throat with my bloodied hand. "One wrong move and you'll regret it."

She nods as I lead her outside, the air whipping around us.

Immediately, I feel eyes on me. I don't see them through the darkness. But they're there. Watching. Waiting.

"Where are they?" I scan the shadows, unwilling to expose my back until I can see my enemy. The chopper whoops close by, the floodlights from beneath the metal bird illuminating part of the open field up ahead.

"There's my mother." Abri tilts her chin a smidge. "At the back of the house yard."

I squint, scanning the night to find the silhouette of the woman being escorted through the wooden slats of the fence with what looks to be the two guards from the penthouse.

"I told you my father is taking you seriously." Abri's voice is barely loud enough for me to hear. "This is working."

Not good enough though. I want eyes on everyone before I step away from the house. One bullet to the back of the head is all that's needed to take me out.

"Find your father," I grate in her ear. "We don't move until we see him."

Her head pivots, scoping the yard, while I do the same.

There's not enough light. Too much noise.

"Over there." Abri shrugs her right shoulder.

I follow her line of sight, finding Emmanuel on the pebbled path, Salvatore at his side, both hustling toward the helicopter. "I don't see the kids."

Where is my fucking niece and brother?

"We're running out of time, snowflake. And if this doesn't work, nobody is going to like what I do next."

She stands taller, her posture rigid despite our agreement. "Give Remy a few more seconds. He won't hurt them, I promise. He'd never harm a child. And he'd never risk my life either."

My adrenaline kicks up a notch. My paranoia, too.

I need to come up with another plan.

Fast.

"Look," she blurts. "There they are."

Remy walks out from beside the house, the kids in front of him, his grip on their shoulders one of casual intimidation.

"You better hope you're right about him." I snarl, despising his audacity to touch them, and take the first step away from the house. "Otherwise my hand won't be the only thing that's left bleeding."

31

ANISSA

Dɪʀᴛ sᴄʀᴀᴛᴄʜᴇs ᴍʏ ᴇʏᴇs ᴀs Hᴜɴᴛᴇʀ ᴀɴᴅ I ʟᴀʏ ᴏɴ ᴛʜᴇ ᴍᴏɪsᴛ ɢʀᴀss, ᴛʜᴇ ᴄʜᴏᴘᴘᴇʀ's blades whipping dust and mulch around our faces.

We've stuck to the shadows, slowly creeping past the tree line and farther into the house yard as Cole stands on the porch with the woman, one bloodied hand around her throat, the other holding a gun to her head.

"They're leading Stella and Tobias toward the helicopter." Benji's voice carries through my earpiece, his tone frantic. "I won't let them take her again."

"Stay out of sight," Hunter warns. "We don't know what's going on yet."

That's not true.

We know Cole has taken a woman hostage. He's hurt her, the carnage from her neck soaking into her white blouse, the liquid staining his hand.

I should feel sympathy. Even compassion.

I don't.

I can't muster anything with this gnawing hunger to get the kids and Cole to safety eating away at my soul.

"We're not going to let anyone take them away from here." I have no basis for my assurance. Not when the Costa's bearded son is marching the children toward the fence leading to the open field. All I know is that I'll risk my life before I let Emmanuel succeed.

"You can't expect me to wait, Hunt," Benji growls. "Make a move before I do it myself."

"I swear to God, if you don't fucking stick to the shadows I'm going to have an even bigger issue with you than I already do." Hunter crawls farther along the grass, keeping in line with Cole.

I glance behind me, toward the house and into the darkness, trying to find the rest of our team among the trees.

Hunter and I took the far side of the property. Sarah, Luca, and Benji took the opposite. They're meant to be mimicking our position, staying in line with Cole, waiting for any sign that he's lost control of the situation.

"We need to wait." I keep my voice low. "We don't want to scare anyone into making a rash decision. Cole included."

I keep slithering along the grass as our target walks the woman through the garden and around some bushes, approaching the wooden fence. The kids climb through a few feet ahead, the man guiding them closer and closer to the helicopter.

"Still feel loyal to him with what he's doing to that woman?" Hunter asks beside me.

"Yes." I don't hesitate.

She's one of them—the enemy.

If anything, Cole is teaching her a valuable lesson about straddling the laps of men who are spoken for.

"Maybe we're wearing off on you after all." He raises into a crouch, retrieves his gun, and starts moving forward again.

"Wait." I hustle to keep up. "What are you doing?"

"We need to—"

"Benji, pull back." Sarah's concern cuts into my ear. "They're going to see you."

I swivel, panicked, and scan the other side of the yard.

"You better fucking listen to her." Hunter's voice is lethal. "You're walking a knife's edge as it is."

"That's my daughter," Benji pleads. "What the fuck would you do in my position?"

"Listen," Luca cuts in. "I'd fucking listen. Now get your ass back here."

The bearded blond leads the kids away from the fence, as Cole and the woman climb through the railings. They're too close to the helicopter. I can already picture Costa's son hauling their little bodies under his arms to run them toward his family.

"*Stop.*" Cole's shout is heard over the constant whip of air. "Stay there."

The blond shakes his head, relaying something indecipherable in return. He indicates for his sister to move forward with a wave of his hand.

They're doing an exchange.

"This isn't going to work." Benji's voice is brutal. "As soon as he lets her go, he's dead."

Tobias and Stella's faces are pale against the floodlights, their eyes wide with panic.

"He's got a plan. He knows what he's doing. Just look at him." I keep crawling as I focus on Cole. He stands tall, confident, unshakable. He isn't cowering. The gun in his hand doesn't tremble. He believes he has this under control, and we need to trust him.

"Fucking hell." Hunter points across the yard, his finger leading to Benji who steps from the shadows in his tailored suit to stand in plain sight, his gun raised.

My stomach nosedives. "If they see him…"

I can't finish the sentence; the fear is too much.

"Get back," I snarl the demand, my vehemence explosive. "Before I take you down myself."

Cole keeps the woman tight against his chest, the guards, the sons, and Costa all watching him as Benji continues to inch forward.

It's only a matter of time before he's seen.

I huddle next to Hunter. "We need to get closer." I raise into a crouch and pull out my gun. "Once they notice—"

"Benji *no*," Sarah's shout rings through my earpiece.

"Fuck." Hunter takes off in a run.

I do the same, not understanding what's happening or where I'm going until I see Benji sprinting through the garden, his gun bobbing in front of him, his focus on his daughter.

I witness the moment the guards notice. I see them aim their weapons as the older son shoves his father into the helicopter.

"*Benji*," Luca yells. "*Stop*."

Shots are fired. Stella screams. Men shout.

Hysteria descends as Hunter drops to his knees in front of me, raining bullets at the helicopter.

"Take cover." He grabs for me as I pass.

I don't listen. I don't stop.

I slap away his hand and push my legs as fast as they'll carry me, diving between the fence railings while the bearded man sprints for his family.

"*Get down*," Cole roars at the children, still standing tall, his gun blasting at the enemy as he pushes the woman free.

There's so much noise. Destruction bombards my ears, filling me with terror.

A guttural shout breaks through the commotion. A guard falls to his knees, clutching his thigh.

I anticipate the pain of that shot. I imagine the impact of a life-threatening bullet as my legs burn from exertion. Still, I don't stop. I'm the closest protection the children have and I won't let them down. Not even when Stella and Tobias turn to me in fear, Cole's niece taking a backward step at my approach.

I barrel into them, arms outstretched, slamming us all to the ground.

"Don't move." I stay on top of them as Stella gasps for air and tries to scream. I use my body as a shield in the dry grass, cradling their heads with my hands. "Stay down."

So many shouts break through the night. Demands. Threats.

The whip of the chopper increases, the swish of blades kicking up dirt and twigs. I squeeze my eyes shut as I drag the kids farther into me, covering them the best I can as more gunfire rains down around us.

A tornado of movement swirls above my head, the brightness from the flood-lights dimming behind my eyelids.

"You're okay." I talk to the children, rambling nonsense. "This will all be over soon."

Footsteps thunder toward us. A heavy weight slams into my back.

"I've got you."

It's him. *Cole.*

He helps to shield the children as the noise above us lessens, the whoosh of air fading with each heartbeat until the storm of sound is almost gone.

I could cry with relief, the burn of threatening tears taking over my closed eyes... until the pungent smell of blood fills my lungs, the scent stealing my hope to leave me cold.

32

COLE

"*Daddy.*" Stella scrambles out from beneath us and runs for her father.

"Toby?" Luca yells. "Where are you?"

"He's here." Nissa shifts, giving the boy freedom to rush to his feet.

I don't move. I barely budge an inch from my resting place against her back while the commotion of a heartfelt reunion sounds behind us.

I need a moment. Just one. To breathe her in and remember she's mine.

"Is everyone accounted for?" Hunt shouts. "Torian, where the fuck are you?"

"I'm here."

Anissa wiggles, attempting to free herself.

"Don't move." I speak against her neck, drawing the scent of her deep into my lungs. I'm owed one fucking second of calm before I have to concentrate on getting everyone out of here. "Tell me you're okay."

She stills, relaxing. "I'm fine."

"Good." I shift to the side and help her turn to face me, those emotional eyes staring back at me through the night. "That didn't go down how I'd expected."

"I know." She cringes. "I'm sorry. Benji wouldn't listen."

I ignore the anger over my brother-in-law's actions, not wanting anything other than my little fox claiming my attention through the adrenaline detox.

"I smell blood." Her tongue anxiously slides out to swipe her lower lip. "Are you hurt?"

"My palm is going to need a few stitches."

"Why?" She grabs for my wrist, turning over my hand to inspect the injury. "Jesus Christ, what happened?"

"I told Costa I'd sliced his daughter's neck. It had to look real."

"So you stabbed yourself?" she asks. "Next time draw the enemy's blood, not your own."

"I'll make sure to do that." I grin and lean in, pressing my forehead to hers. "How'd you find me?"

"We followed the scent of your dumbass decisions. Didn't you ever learn not to get into a car with strangers?"

I snicker, plastering my mouth to hers. I part her lips with my tongue, delving deep, drowning in her. All it takes is a taste and I'm grounded.

"Let's get out of here." Sarah claps her hands nearby. "If a helicopter and gunfire don't draw the cops, I don't know what will."

I'm not ready. Not even close.

I keep my lips smashed to Nissa's, needing her, craving her.

"Come on, Torian." Hunt approaches, his boots crunching in the grass. "We've gotta move."

"He's right." Anissa breaks the kiss, placing her hands on my chest to push me back. "I can't be here if police arrive." She climbs to her feet and waits for me to follow. "We've got two cars parked at the front of the property."

"We're going to need to clean up inside first. My blood is on the floor."

"Where?" Hunt walks backward toward the house, reaching into his pants pocket.

"Through the French doors. Maybe on the porch."

"Leave it with me. You guys get out of here." He lobs a car fob through the darkness at Nissa. "Take the kids and Benji. We'll follow a few minutes behind."

"Are you sure?" she asks.

He turns his back, striding hard. "Get the fuck out of here."

"Come on." I grab her hand and lead her toward Benji and Luca who are huddled with the kids on the pebbled path. "Let's go." I raise my voice, drawing their attention. "Benji, you and the kids are coming with us. Everyone else can get a ride in the second car."

"Sure thing." Luca grabs Toby's shoulders. "It's all over now, little man. Penny's waiting for you back in the city. We won't be far behind you."

I slow my steps at the sight of my half-brother. The poor kid is going to have a lot of unpacking to do once we get home. His mental suitcases were already stuffed with trauma before he arrived in Portland; now he's got this shit to deal with, too.

"Hey." I stop before him, looking down at the resilient jut of his chin. "How are you holding up?"

He nods. There's no reassuring expression or search for comfort—just wide eyes and thin lips.

"Are you ready to get back to Penny?"

Another nod. No emotion. No warmth.

"Come on." Anissa places a hand on his shoulder, leading him along the path.

I lag a step behind, giving him space. In the coming days, I'll need to make decisions about his future—who he'll live with, what school he'll go to, what role he'll play within the family.

If he doesn't already despise me, I'm sure he will by then. But right now, I have enough of that toxicity focused toward Benji to drown out the static of what's to come.

We pass the house, then the front porch, with Stella and her father dragging their feet behind us. Every scrape of his shoes against the stones grates on my nerves, building my resentment.

I'd had the situation with Costa under control. I'd been fucking heartbeats from getting Stella and Tobias free without a goddamn bullet exchange, until he fucked it up.

Now he has even more to answer for.

Nissa leads the way out the front gates and along the road, the distance growing between us and the huddled father and daughter duo trailing behind. When she reaches the Escalade, she helps Tobias into the back seat, closing the door behind him before meeting up with me at the front of the car.

"I can already tell you're pissed at Benji. But go easy on him. He was worried for his daughter."

"Don't soften for him, little fox." I glide stray strands of hair behind her ear, smudging blood near her temple. "He caused this. Not only tonight, but the entire situation. If it wasn't for—"

"I know." She steps into me. Foot to foot. Hands to my chest. "I really do. Just let it go for now. Let him be with Stella without having to worry about what lies ahead. If not for him, do it for her. She needs her father's comfort after everything that's happened."

She's right. But it doesn't lessen my animosity.

Benji needs to be dealt with. There's no escaping punishment. Whatever that is, I still haven't determined.

"Please, Cole." She twists her fingers in my shirt. "Let them have a few days."

"Yeah. Okay." I hold out my good hand. "Give me the keys."

"I'm driving." She turns for the car, striding away like a confident warrior. "You have to bandage yourself up."

"When did you turn into an overlord?"

She laughs. "When you left me alone with your thugs."

"I guess I need to do that more often in the future." I head toward the passenger side, ignoring the humorous glare she gives me.

"Don't even joke about it. Hunter and I almost killed each other."

"But you didn't, which is better than ninety percent of the people he works with." I open my door and slide in, Nissa doing the same on the driver's side.

She starts the engine once Stella and Benji round the hood, the headlights illuminating Sarah, Hunt, and Luca casually jogging toward us in the distance.

It's all done. Over. Yet there's no sense of relief when the damage has already been inflicted.

"That was quick." She waits for the father-daughter duo to climb inside, then puts the car into gear.

"Hunt knows what he's doing." I turn, meeting my niece's gaze as she crawls into the middle seat and clasps her belt. "Ready to go, little one?"

She nuzzles into Benji's side and nods.

"How about you, Toby?" I switch my focus to the boy who stares out the window, not meeting my gaze.

"Yeah," he mutters.

The poor kid deserves a lot better than what I've given him.

"Time to go home." Nissa pulls onto the road, doing a U-turn to drive back toward the city.

We sit in silence, rounding the wide corners as we skirt the darkened farmland.

I glance at my niece and Benji every now and then, needing the sight of their bond to soften my thoughts for his future.

They're arm in arm, huddled close. Stella blinks back at me each time, but Benji is lost in the moment, his eyes closed, his face hard with emotion as he clings to his little girl.

He may not be a loyal soldier, but I'll admit he's a good father. A doting dad.

That's the only thing working in his favor.

"Where's Mom?" Stella murmurs.

"She's waiting for you." Benji's voice is roughened. Emotional. And so it should be.

We wouldn't have a building vendetta against Costa if it wasn't for him. There'd be no mental scars for Stella. No death of her babysitter. No bullshit to cover up with Robert.

I turn back toward the road, my thoughts of punishment building.

I'd worked out a plan with Abri—one where I'd promised no retaliation toward her father. One where I could be left in peace to enjoy Anissa. Now all the future holds is vengeance for the motherfuckers who dared to fire their weapons in the presence of children.

"Why didn't she come to get me?" Stella asks.

"We weren't sure…" Benji grunts, the sound born from pain.

Nissa shoots me a glance, frowning in question as the hair on the back of my nape rises.

"She's waiting in the hotel." Benji's words are forced. Labored. "You'll see her soon."

I peer at him over my shoulder, his eyes opening to meet mine. Even in the dim light, the grip of agony lancing his features is clear. "What happened to you?"

"It's a scratch." He winces. "I'll be fine."

"Are you hurt?" Stella raises her frantic gaze to her father, sitting up straight. "Daddy, you're wet." She pulls her arm away from his waist to inspect her sleeve. "Uncle Cole..." The terror in her voice cuts through me. "He's bleeding."

"What's going on?" Nissa glances from me to the road and back again.

"Slow down." I reach for the roof, flicking on the interior light, then hold in a curse.

A sheen of liquid is cast over the lower left side of his suit jacket, the shirt beneath drenched in blood, his face now a sickening shade of grey.

"Pull over." I release my belt as the car brakes. I'm shoving open my door and jumping out before we come to a stop. I skirt the hood, anger and dread thrumming through me.

Anissa is right behind me, cutting the engine to climb out, the beam of Hunt's approaching headlights blinding me as I pull open Benji's door.

"I'm okay," he rasps. "You need to get Stella back to her mother."

My niece sobs, her hands covered in dark crimson as she clutches her father's fingers. "What's happening?" she pleads. "Is he dying?"

"He'll be fine." I flick back Benji's jacket and raise the sodden material of his shirt, exposing something far more sinister than a scratch.

He's got two fucking bullet wounds to the abdomen, the holes purging blood.

Nissa draws in a breath behind me. "He needs a hospital."

It's too late for that.

We're in the middle of nowhere. We'd never make it in time, and the condemned look in Benji's eyes says he knows it.

"Cole." Nissa grabs my arm. "You need to get back in the car."

"No." Benji winces and leans down to kiss Stella's forehead. "This is payment for my mistakes. Please just let me be with my daughter."

Jesus. *Fuck.* Bile stirs in my gut as my pulse thunders. The trauma only increases when Hunt's car pulls up beside us, the windows lowered.

Benji was always meant to pay for his mistakes with his life. But not like this. Not in front of his daughter. Not in a way that would devastate my niece beyond repair.

Hell, I might've even weakened and let him run, as long as he ghosted for the rest of his snake-ish existence. He could've started a new life far away from here. Now that option has been taken away from us all.

"What's going on?" Luca asks from the back seat.

I meet his gaze, relaying the seriousness of the situation without saying a word.

He frowns, scrambling to unclasp his belt, then flings open his door. Hunt and Sarah follow.

"Uncle Cole, do something," Stella pleads. "Help him."

Her agony pierces me deep, destroying the hardened parts of me as Luca bumps Anissa out of the way to reach my side.

"There's nothing to be done." Benji cups Stella's face in shaky hands, her wide eyes filled with despair as her father strokes her cheeks with his thumbs.

"You're going to be okay. I promise. I'm not going anywhere. I'll always be with you."

"No," she sobs. "You're hurt. You need help."

"I love you, baby girl."

"No, Daddy. Please." Her voice trembles. "Tell Uncle Cole to take you to the hospital."

Luca freezes beside me, staring down at his brother, taking a split second of contemplation before he shucks his jacket in a rush and lunges into the car. "We need to stem the bleeding." He grabs Stella's hands. "Hold this, sweetheart. Push as hard as you can."

She wails, the tears beginning to fall as Luca glances over his shoulder at me. "Get back in the car. We need to leave. *Now.*"

I don't move. Don't answer.

Nothing I say will help the information sink in until he's ready to understand it.

"Did you hear me?" He straightens and swings around to face me. "Get in the fucking car, Torian."

I remain in place, hating his suffering, but unwilling to humor his attempts to save an unsalvageable life.

Hunt comes up behind him, placing strong hands on his shoulders. "You know he's not going to make it back to the city, bro."

"Don't fucking give up on him." Luca glares at me in accusation. "Get in the fucking car."

I step back, lowering my voice so Stella can't hear. "You have a decision to make—fight the inevitable and tarnish his final moments, or leave him in peace to be with his daughter."

"No." His face crumples as he violently swings his shoulders, dislodging Hunt's hold. "Get the fuck off me."

"Luca, please." Sarah inches toward him, her hands held up in surrender, her eyes glistening with building tears. "I know you're hurting. But Stella needs you to be strong. They both do."

"No." He makes toward the car again and Hunt grabs him, hauling him backward, battling the thrashing and jerking. "*No.*"

"Stop fighting it." Benji croaks from inside the Escalade. "I need you to be strong."

Luca slumps. Surrenders. Stumbles, almost falling to his knees.

I clench my jaw as he suffers before me, the grief already stealing his breath.

"I'll get Tobias out of the car," Anissa whispers. "He shouldn't be left in there."

She hustles to the other side of the vehicle to help my brother out, then guides him across the road, leading him into the solitude of darkness, murmuring words of comfort.

I love her more than I ever have in this moment.

Her level head. Her compassion.

"I can't just stand here." Luca shoves his fingers into his hair, choking on breath. "What the fuck do I do?"

"Give them space." Hunt walks him toward Anissa and Tobias. "It's out of our hands now."

"I'll stay with Stella." Sarah creeps closer to the open door, inching herself inside to offer comfort.

I don't feel my feet as I follow Luca's reluctant steps. I don't feel anything.

I'm numb to the world. Hollowed by this vicious poetic justice. But the crunch of my shoes against the asphalt isn't enough to drown out Benji's voice.

"Tell your momma I love her, okay?"

"No," Stella pleads. "Daddy, no."

Giving her these moments alone with him might be a mistake. The trauma could be too deep to surface from. But I can't strip her of these last memories.

I would've killed to be by my mother's side when she died. To make the promise that her legacy would live on. To hold her one last time.

"*Daddy?*" My niece's cry cuts through the night, her pain scarring me as Luca forges back toward the car.

"Nothing can be done." Hunt grabs him. "Let him go."

"No." Luca reignites his fight, striking a punch to Hunt's ribs, scrambling to break free. "*No.*" His demands turn into guttural pleas. "Don't you fucking die on me, brother."

"I love you, baby girl." There's no strength left in Benji's quiet voice. No life. "Never forget how special you are."

Anissa comes to my side, Tobias peering up at me with anguish.

The silence that follows is deafening.

The five of us stand at the edge of the road, the grim reaper at our backs, the ghosts of our sins fast approaching.

Sarah's cries drift softly from the car. Luca's breathing becomes harder. I reach for Nissa, dragging her against me, Tobias following along with her to stand at my feet, his head resting into my stomach.

I squeeze his arm, not giving a shit about the pain in my palm or my blood staining his clothes. "I've got you."

My promise is all I have to give.

I can't fix this mess. I can't stop the misery.

All I can do is vow retribution and make sure the punishment goes above and beyond the crime.

"*No,*" Stella's wail carries through the night. "No, Daddy, please don't go."

33

ANISSA

THE FUNERAL WAS LOW-KEY. CLOSE FAMILY. NO OUTSIDERS.

Stella cried rivers, the wetness on her cheeks dripping down to leave damp patches at the top of her floral dress while Layla remained quiet at her side, her face an emotionless mask.

Luca took a different approach. His anger shrouded the room, his glare baring down on the coffin as it lowered into the ground. With every breath, he silently promised vengeance and all of us agree that time will come. Maybe not in the coming days. But eventually. Once we've pulled ourselves together.

None of us have been the same since Sacramento.

Not Hunt and Decker, who were left in charge of driving Benji's body home and paying off medical officials to hide his cause of death. Not Layla, who blames herself for what happened to her husband. Not Stella, who is plagued by ongoing nightmares. Or Cole, who acts as if he's immune to their suffering even when I know it's killing him to remain emotionless.

Not even me, because I can't ditch the rage that's made its home under my skin. It keeps me up at night, the anger making me toss and turn until Cole wraps his arms around me, his proximity the only thing capable of lulling me to sleep.

"How's he holding up?" Hunter comes to stand beside me in the kitchen, mimicking my position leaned against the counter, his focus straight ahead on Cole and the others in the living room. "Does he need anything?"

"He's doing okay." I shrug. "I think everyone is dealing the best they can."

"Yeah." He pauses a moment before turning to me. "I'm going to have to deal some more bad news, though."

I stiffen and tilt my head to look at him. "What is it?"

"I'm getting Sarah out of here for a while." He meets my gaze with indifference. There's still no love lost between us, but since returning to Portland, the animosity has taken a back seat. "We're eloping. With all the shit that's gone down, she needs something good in her life. It's time to make her mine."

"That's far from bad news."

"Maybe." He shrugs. "I know Torian needs me here. But she needs me more."

"I don't think you have to worry. Cole would appreciate what you're doing. You should tell him."

His brows pull tight. "Nah. I'll leave that to you. You'll know when the timing is right better than I will."

My brow quirks before I can stop it. He wants *me* to do something for *him*… because I'd be a *better* option?

"Don't look at me like that. We won't be gone long. A week. Or two. If that's suitable."

"You're asking me?" I fight not to give him a side-eye of disbelief. Who the hell is this man and what did he do with the dumpster fire of a thug I previously knew?

"Yeah." His frown deepens. "Is that a problem?"

"No. I think you should take all the time you need." I swallow over the awkward lump in my throat. "I'll let him know. When do you plan on leaving?"

"Now. I'm not going to say goodbye. But I want you to make sure you don't make a move on Costa until I get back."

"I can't promise that. Cole deserves closure, and I won't stand in his way."

He scoffs, a saccharine grin quirking the corner of his lips. "Look at you being a heartless bitch all in the name of revenge."

"And look at you, giving up the opportunity for vengeance because you're pussy whipped."

He snickers, sly and half-hearted. "Touché." He walks from the kitchen, giving a subtle jerk of his head to Sarah who strides forward to take his hand.

They disappear down the hall, nobody else noticing their departure as the murmured conversations continue around the room. Cole chats with Decker and Keira. Luca and Penny snuggle on the opposite sofa. Tobias and Stella play a subdued board game on the dining table, while Layla stands at the glass doors, alone, blankly staring into the backyard.

I want to go to her, offering my millionth condolence. Instead, I stack dirty plates in the dishwasher and busy myself wiping the counter.

I'm not a part of the inner circle yet and I get it. No matter how many promises Cole makes or the devoted level of his attention, the others aren't used to having me here.

It's going to take time to build on the smidge of trust I've earned.

"Anissa?" Penny walks into the kitchen, her hands clasped in front of her.

"Hey." I smile. "How are you?"

"Good." She sucks in a fortifying breath and lowers her voice. "I realize this is a day of mourning and I'm truly hurting for Luca's loss, but I didn't know Benji so the devastation is kept at a distance, if that makes sense."

"I understand."

Her eyes drift to her partner still on the sofa, the adoration in her expression clear. "My life is incredibly different now. I'm starting to finally find my feet. He's such a good man. Even with everything he's going through, he always puts me first."

"I'm glad to hear it."

She nods. "I knew you would be. That's why I wanted to thank you for all you've done. Both in Greece and back here in Portland. You changed my life, and I'll be forever grateful."

My heart pangs at her sincerity. "You don't need to thank me."

"Yes, I do." She unclasps her hands to place a palm over her heart. "I'm so unbelievably grateful for every morning that I wake up with Luca. He's…" She releases a heavy breath. "He's my happiness. He's everything. And I never would've met him if all our paths didn't converge."

My eyes tingle. "You need to stop before you make me cry."

She laughs. "I wouldn't want that. Not in a room full of these guys. I know you need to stay tough, and I've definitely got your back."

I keep the humor in my voice despite the reminder of the potential snake pit I now live in. "You make it sound like I shouldn't walk around without a bodyguard."

"No, not at all. I don't think anyone would be stupid enough to even risk offending you with the level of devotion Cole has shown toward his queen." She snickers. "But in all honesty, Sarah and I think incredibly highly of you. Apparently, Hunter does, too."

"Hunter?" I scoff.

"No, seriously, he does. Sarah said he spent most of the drive home from Sacramento berating my brother on how he now needs to treat you with respect. He instigated some sort of no tolerance policy on giving you a hard time."

Hunter wouldn't have instigated it. Those directives would've come from Cole. But I appreciate knowing the big, bad wolf is willing to throw his weight around for me.

"I bet Decker didn't take the news kindly." I act blasé, pretending I'm not impatiently waiting for a response. "I did some pretty shitty things to him when we first met."

"Don't worry. I heard that, too. But you did them because you were trying to take down Luther, which, in my book, gave you grounds to do absolutely anything in the name of success." She shrugs. "Sebastian will come around soon enough. I'm sure, deep down, he appreciates what you did."

"Deep, deep, *deep* down." Maybe buried under layer upon hardened layer of macho aggression and thick hostility.

She smiles again. "You're meant to be here. Just like I am. Despite how different this is from the future we envisaged for ourselves."

I don't voice my agreement. I keep my thoughts to myself in the hopes of preventing the tightening in my throat from exposing how emotional I am about being here.

It feels right to spend time under Cole's roof. In his bed. Held in his arms.

Even with their world hitting rock bottom and the depth of misery suffocating us, this place has become my new home.

Each day I learn more and more about the way Cole lives. His agenda. His thought process. And for every one of those days, my understanding of him grows.

I've been exposed to the corruption that I've always been blind to. I'm discovering the false reality I once existed in, which makes the way these people live not only justifiable but logical.

"You soften his ragged edges." Penny inches forward, grasping my wrist for a light squeeze. "He's a harsh man, but so uniquely honest and clear-cut that it's hard not to appreciate him. I'm glad the two of you found each other."

My eyes burn hotter, the heat filtering to my cheeks. "Thank you."

"*Hey.*" Cole's shout steals my attention, his pointed frown fixing on me. "What are you two talking about that's made you upset?"

"Oh, boy," Penny mutters under her breath. "Please don't let him kill me."

I chuckle and sniff back the emotion tingling in my nose. "We're just chatting."

"Well, come chat over here. No woman of mine is going to look unsettled unless I'm the one unsettling her." He pats his lap with a wink.

I roll my eyes, my heart fluttering as I walk toward him. Then I tingle with warmth as he grabs my arm and drags me to sit on his thighs.

"You okay?" he murmurs against my neck, his delicate lips in contrast to the possessive hand on my hip. "Need me to destroy someone for bothering you?"

I glide my fingers over his, entwining our hands. "You're not funny."

"Sure I am." He kisses my nape, increasing the flutters and tingles. "Decker just admitted I'm hilarious."

"What's that?" Decker interrupts. "Are you talking about me?"

"Yes." His hold tightens on my hip. "I was just about to tell Nis how we were discussing leaving the past in the past."

Decker's eyes harden. The tight set of his jaw does, too.

It's now obvious what past they're referring to—my history with Decker. Specifically the sex and manipulation to make him my informant.

Tension settles around us. Quiet falls.

I shift uncomfortably. "Maybe this is a discussion for another—"

"No." Cole's hold strengthens, the hand on my hip becoming possessive, his fingers tangling tighter. "From this moment on, no grudges will be held between those in this room. The time for spite and animosity is over. Are we all clear?"

"I think that's a good idea." Keira meets my gaze. "You're welcome here and you always will be, especially when you keep my brother in line."

I smile at her, but it's forced. I can't hold the kind expression when Decker continues to scowl.

"I agree." Luca's eyes hold a sense of pleading sincerity as he looks at me. "I'd be thankful if the messed up shit I contributed to in Greece was left behind us."

"It's already forgotten." There's a slight falsity to my admission. I don't think I'm capable of fully forgetting the role he played during my abduction. However, the way he selflessly saved Penny, and the way he's conducted himself toward her ever since, is enough evidence to prove to me that he's an incredible man.

"What about you, Decker?" Cole prods. "Do you have something to say?"

The guy flares his nostrils and takes a few moments to mask his intolerance. "I'm more than happy to forget everything to do with this woman. I—"

"Watch your tone." Cole's fingers grip tighter around mine.

"More importantly," Penny adds, "watch your goddamn disrespect toward someone who helped rescue me. You, of all people, should be thankful—"

"It's complicated," he grates.

"It's only as complicated as you want to make it." Keira nestles into him. "You slept together. She played you. Move on. Lots of other people have been forgiven for a whole lot worse."

"She's not wrong." Luca leans back into the sofa, crossing his legs at the ankles. "And all this drama has me well and truly cooked. I'm over it. Can't we have some peace for once?"

Decker sucks in a long breath and lets it out on a huff. "Fine. I accept that she was a contributing factor toward getting Penny back. And yes, she risked her life for those kids in Sacramento, too. She's an asset. Not to mention some sort of balm against you being such an asshole." He jerks his chin at Cole. "I'll try my best to treat her with respect from now on, if she can do the same."

"I respect you." I admire him, too. He's yet another great man who risked everything for someone he loved. "And I know me being here doesn't feel right. It's going to take a while for this to be normal."

"It'll take no time at all. It's a cakewalk in comparison to the shit we usually do." Luca pushes from the sofa to walk toward Penny. "We're going to head home."

"Us, too." Keira stands, dragging Decker with her as she looks at her brother. "Are you going to be okay with Layla and the kids?"

"They're fine." Cole drags me back into his chest. "I'm going to take them out for ice cream later. They all need some fresh air."

They leave after subdued farewells to the children and Layla, the house descending into quiet calm.

"Hunt and Sarah didn't say goodbye." Cole's breath brushes my neck. "Did my two favorite people get into another fight?"

"No. We're fine." I drag my feet onto the sofa and turn into him, meeting his gaze. "Hunter actually asked me to tell you something."

He frowns. "I'm listening."

"He's heading out of town for a while. Eloping."

His brows rise in casual surprise.

"You're not angry I didn't stop him, are you?"

He glides a stray strand of hair behind my ear. "No. If anything, I'm envious."

"That he told me?"

"No, that he gets to marry his woman. Somehow I don't think you're ready to walk down the aisle."

"Not ready in the slightest. And yet again, you're not funny, Cole."

"This time I agree." He holds my gaze. "Because I wasn't joking. I'm prepared to make this official whenever you are."

"You're incorrigible."

"I'm determined." He kisses below my ear. My jaw. "And impatient. There's no changing my mind on this. When you know, you know."

I push back against his chest, getting a better look at him as he stares at me without an ounce of sarcasm.

"You're seriously ready to marry me?" I shake my head. "How...?"

"There's nobody else for me, Nis. There never will be."

Emotion drowns me in a wave, squeezing my chest, clogging my throat.

"Does your silence count as a yes?" He drags me back against him, one hand gently wrapping around my neck. "If so, I could have us on a jet to Vegas in less than thirty."

"It wasn't an affirmation." I melt into him, smiling.

"But it wasn't a no."

"Cole," I warn. "This isn't the time to talk about this." It's not even close to the time to think about making a time to talk about this.

"Agree to marry me then." He kisses my jaw. My ear. "Be my fiancé."

I fight not to moan against the pleasure of his lips, my heart searing and sizzling like a firework waiting to explode. "Your family is in mourning."

"Exactly. They need some happiness in their lives. You'd be cruel to deny them."

I chuckle, the sound morphing into a groan when his teeth dig into my neck.

"Commit to marrying me," he growls. "Agree to be my wife. My queen."

"I can't."

He continues torturing my neck, kissing and nipping and teasing. "Then say yes to saying yes in the future."

"I don't even know what that means."

He releases my throat and leans to the side to retrieve something from his pocket.

No, not something. *Everything.* A small velvet jewelry box that sits on the palm of his hand right in front of me. He opens it, shocking me with a dazzling diamond ring.

I'm momentarily lost for words. For breath. Then the questions start to pummel my mind, scratching and clawing for answers. "How long have you had this?"

"Since we got back from Greece." He rests his stubbled cheek against mine, both of us staring at his offering. "There's never been any doubt."

"Cole..." It's too much, too soon.

I'm crazy for this man, and he knows it. I ended my lease to move in with him. I quit my job. But this...

"Say yes to saying yes," he repeats. "Agree to accept my proposal when I ask."

My head says no. Nope. No way.

But my heart. Oh, *God*, my heart flutters and thunders *yes, yes, yes*.

"Nissa?" His fingers glide over my chin, tilting my face to meet his. "Say yes."

"Okay." My voice cracks with the onslaught of adrenaline. "I say yes to saying yes when you ask."

"Promise?" He brushes his lips against mine, teasing me with a kiss.

"Yes," I whisper. Melting. "I promise."

"Good." He gives me another chaste kiss then grabs my hips, shifting me off his lap.

I'm underwhelmed with the whiplash of his departure. That is, until he drops to one knee in front of me, still holding the ring box open. "Marry me, little fox."

I frantically shake my head, my gaze finding Layla at the glass doors as she watches us with a sad yet encouraging smile. "You said when you ask in the *future*."

"This is the future. The conversation we just had is already in the past."

I glare at him even though I want to tackle him to the floor and smother him in kisses. "You tricked me."

"I did." He smirks. "And after everything we've been through, you still fell for it. So make good on your promise and commit to being my wife because you're all I'll ever want."

There's more to come from these characters. Layla's tale of revenge comes next in Seeking Vengeance.

ALSO BY EDEN SUMMERS

HUNTING WORLD

Hunter

Decker

Torian

Savior

Luca

Cole

Seeking Vengeance

RECKLESS BEAT

Blind Attraction

Passionate Addiction

Reckless Weekend

Undesired Lust

Sultry Groove

Reckless Rendezvous

Undeniable Temptation

Reckless Encore

THE VAULT

A Shot of Sin

Union of Sin

Brutal Sin

More information on these and more titles can be found at www.edensummers.com or your online book retailer.

ABOUT THE AUTHOR

Eden Summers is a bestselling author of contemporary romance with a side of sizzle and sarcasm.

She lives in Australia with a young family who are well aware she's circling the drain of insanity.
Eden can't resist alpha dominance, dark features and sarcasm in her fictional heroes and loves a strong heroine who knows when to bite her tongue but also serves retribution with a feminine smile on her face.

If you'd like access to exclusive information and giveaways, join Eden Summers' newsletter via the link on her website - www.edensummers.com

For more information:
www.edensummers.com
eden@edensummers.com

11468000R00403